HOPE

Also by Mary Ryan

Into the West
Mask of the Night
Shadows from the Fire
Summer's End
The Seduction of Mrs Caine
The Promise
The Song of the Tide
Whispers in the Wind
Glenallen

HOPE

Mary Ryan

HEADLINE

First published in 2001 by
HEADLINE BOOK PUBLISHING

10 9 8 7 6 5 4 3 2 1

HOPE is a work of fiction based on, and inspired by,
the lives of Thomas Francis Walsh and his family.

British Library Cataloguing in Publication Data

Ryan, Mary, 1945–
Hope
1. Gold mines and mining – United States – Fiction 2. Irish –
United States – Fiction
I. Title
823.9'14[F]

ISBN 0 7472 6910 X (hardback)
ISBN 0 7472 6928 9 (trade paperback)

Typeset by Avon Dataset Ltd, Bidford-on-Avon, Warks

Printed and bound in Great Britain by
Mackays of Chatham plc, Chatham, Kent

HEADLINE BOOK PUBLISHING
A division of Hodder Headline
338 Euston Road
London NW1 3BH

www.headline.co.uk
www.hodderheadline.com

To the memory of Thomas F. Walsh and
Evalyn Walsh McLean.

And to Seán with love and gratitude.

Acknowledgements

I am indebted to many sources for the help and information without which I could not possibly have written this book.

I would like to express my gratitude to:

The National Library of Ireland;

The Library of Congress, Washington DC;

Denver Public Library;

Ouray County Museum;

Littleton Historical Museum;

Ratmoko Ratmansunu ('Kiko') of the Embassy of Indonesia, 2020 Massachusetts Ave NW, Washington DC, who was outstandingly kind in showing me around the mansion that was once the Walsh home in Washington, and furnishing extremely helpful contacts and materials.

Adrian O'Brien of the Embassy of Ireland, Washington DC, who orchestrated my crucial contact with Mr Ratmansunu.

Hugh Walsh of Lisronagh, Co. Tipperary; Larry O'Gorman of Lisronagh, Joe O'Gorman of Ballylanigan, Co. Tipperary, Sean O'Gorman of Kilvemnon, Co. Tipperary, Michael O'Brien of Clonmel, who so kindly and generously gave me of their time.

Ann Connell Hoffman of the Ouray County Museum, Colorado who furnished invaluable information.

Doris Gregory whose wonderful books on Ouray and its mines were such a cornucopia.

Carl Miller of the National Mining Museum, Leadville, Colorado, who furnished newspaper material dating from Tom Walsh's days in Leadville.

Carol Ann Rapp of St Louis, Missouri, for furnishing photocopies of, and allowing me access to, private papers.

Joseph Gregory of Nashville, great-great-grandson of Thomas Walsh who furnished the photographs used on the cover, and elsewhere in this book.

John McLean, grandson of Evalyn Walsh McLean, who had lunch with me in Paris and reminisced about his grandmother.

Bertram Lippincott III of the Newport Historical Society, Newport, Rhode Island who helped with microfiche access to old newspapers.

Kathleen M. O'Brien of Worcestor, Massachusets and John Stewart of Denver for helpful information.

My friend Minou Parente, author of the French poem and the philosophical reflection in French in chapters nineteen and twenty who kindly gave me permission to use them for the purposes of the novel.

My cousin Gerard Mulhearn of Belfast who furnished me with a copy of a letter Tom wrote to my great-grandfather John Healy.

Michael who, with Seán, drove me the length of Colorado and helped with the research.

Johnny who printed up the MS as often as required as it went through its various drafts.

Seán for his tireless and unstinting help.

I am particularly indebted to Evalyn's own book FATHER STRUCK IT RICH for many of the details of her own and her family's life.

Last, but by no means least, I am indebted to Headline's wonderful editorial support – Jane Morpeth and Shona Walley, and copy editor Yvonne Holland.

You've got the wind, and ships; your dream's come true.
Was it the way you thought your dream would be?
The story books would paint that ocean blue;
each mile for you was stitched in salt at sea.
. . . the world you stumbled on you hardly knew
a random clash of hemispheres undressed
each member of the then known world, but you
saw glimpses of God-promised lands.
Did you foresee how crassly rich this earth
would prove in sprouting seed and forcing birth
from powder spores secreted in your hands?
Whatever motives we ascribe to you
another world replaces one we knew.

from *Discovering Columbus*
by Mark Patrick Hederman

Book I

Tom

'. . . He was a man of extraordinary fine parts, generous to a fault, warm-hearted, chivalrous and genial – a typical Western American gentleman.'

(From the entry on Thomas Francis Walsh in the *National Encyclopaedia of American Biography*.)

Chapter One

Carraig Mór, Clonmel, Ireland, 1856

The boy was freckled, red-haired. The henhouse, where he stood in bare feet, was full of the smell of feathers and the low clucking of the hens. He emerged into the overcast day, walked through the pools of rainwater to clean his feet, passed the struggling fuchsia his mother had planted by the wall, and came through the open half-door of his whitewashed home. Clutched against his chest were four warm eggs. He put them on the deal table, one by one with care; looked anxiously at his mother who was hanging clothes on a line before the hearth. The room smelled of wet wool.

'Four!' Margaret exclaimed. 'Was that all?'

'That's all I could find, *a Mhamai*,' Tom said. 'The brown hen is missing again.'

'That good-for-nothing, broody bird!'

Margaret pushed back the tendrils which the steam from the wet clothes had coaxed from her combs. She was thirty-seven, with red-gold hair, pale skin and dark blue eyes. She straightened, arched with a small groan, put her hand to the small of her back. The boy wondered for a moment why his mother had got so fat in her tummy.

'I'll put her in the pot,' Margaret added dangerously, 'if she doesn't mend her ways!'

Tom thought of the mad hen, plucked and defeated, simmering in the black *pota mór* that hung from the crane above the fire. The indignity of it displaced his hunger.

'But she can't help it,' he whispered. 'She *needs* to make her nest . . .'

Margaret picked up the eggs and put them into an earthenware bowl on the dresser. They would be sold in a day or two, along with any others laid in the meantime. Every egg was precious – represented another farthing of the rent – and the antics of the runaway hen were a serious problem. But when she turned, her six-year-old's stricken face made her smile.

'Seeing you're such a good counsellor, sure maybe we'll commute the sentence . . .' She laughed and his heart lifted.

Behind her the turf fire settled. Tom took sods from the creel, leaned into the fireplace where the black crane stretched its row of pot hooks, and placed the sods on the hot embers. Despite his care, the yellow ash puffed from the fire, quickly followed by aromatic smoke that rose visibly up to the mantelshelf where Margaret had arranged her three precious plates with painted roses – the last of a set once owned by her grandmother. It was on this shelf that his father's pipe, the long clay *dúidín*, rested beside the fiddle that his father would play of an evening, closing his eyes and losing himself in the music.

Above the mantelshelf was a smoke-stained *Crois Naomh Bríd* – St Bridget's cross – plaited in reeds, and above that a clothesline hung from rafters through which the thatch was visible.

Tom turned to find his mother's tender eyes on him.

'Thank you, *a stóirín*,' she said softly. 'You are a good boy!' She sat down on the settle with one of the tired sighs that came from her of late.

Tom stood uncertainly, bare feet on the flagged floor and whispered, 'Will you be all right . . .?'

He knew from the careful way his father would not allow her to lift any weight, the way he constantly urged her to rest, that they should mind her. But this had made Tom secretly afraid that something was wrong. She was his world; he loved her with an intense and focused love. Recently, unable to sleep, he had crept to the door of the room he shared with Michael and Maria and covertly watched his parents as they sat by the hearth. He'd been afraid of the thump he would receive if he woke his eldest sibling, but seeing his parents had made him feel warm and safe.

His father had been emptying his pipe into the ashes of the fire, tapping the bowl to dislodge the dottle before putting the pipe back on the mantelshelf. He'd bent down to his wife. Tom had seen his mother hold out to him the pillowcase to which she was stitching the strip of white lace she had been making for over a year.

Her words were said in a low half-jesting voice: 'That's for my laying-out . . . if God takes me!'

Seán had shaken his head, whispering in Irish: 'My heart's love, don't talk like that.' He'd kissed her brow, before going into their bedroom on the other side of the kitchen. Margaret, left alone by the hearth, had put in a final stitch, bitten the thread and surveyed her handiwork. Then she'd put it away, kneeled awkwardly on the floor and raised her eyes to St Bridget's Cross. Her prayer had been softly spoken, a mixture of Irish and English.

'*A Thiarna*, keep my family in Thy holy care. Guide and protect them . . . Give me a healthy child . . . And spare me this time also if it is Thy holy will . . .'

4

The words, with their dimly perceived meaning, had gone round in Tom's head ever since.

'Sure why wouldn't I be all right?' Margaret asked now. Her voice was tinged with amusement, but her eyes as she regarded her son were full of tenderness.

'Because . . .' Tom shrugged, unable to tell her because he did not know himself. His eyes travelled to her stomach and widened, for he was suddenly sure that it had moved.

Margaret following his rounded gaze, laughed, put out her arms and said, 'Come here.'

Tom laid his head against his mother's breast, heard the soft thud of her heart.

'Now,' she said, raising his head and looking into his face, 'you know that soon we are going to get a new baby?'

He nodded. The children knew there would soon be an addition to their number and looked forward to it. Babies were brought by fairies, although Michael, who was eleven, had professed doubts.

'Where is it going to come from, *a Mhamai*?' Tom asked now, filling the silence left by his mother's attempt to find the right words.

Margaret, with a careful glance over her shoulder to the open door, put his hand against her belly and said with the air of a conspirator, 'What do you feel?' and her stomach suddenly lurched alarmingly behind her apron, as though possessed of a life of its own. She laughed at his startled cry.

'That's only the baby, *a stór*. That's where they stay, grand and snug, until it's time to be born.'

Tom's mouth fell open.

'It's having the life of Riley,' Margaret added, her eyes full of laughter at the expression on her son's face, 'waiting until it can come out and take a good look at the lot of us!'

'But when will . . .?'

'Soon, I think, *a leanbh*. And then you'll have a new brother or sister!'

'Was I . . .?' Tom whispered, as the ramifications of what she had told him began to sink in.

'Of course you were, *a pheata dílis*. And it was warm and happy you were under my heart!' Then she added, 'Don't be talking about this to anyone else. It's our secret!'

When Tom nodded with adult gravity, she put her hands on his shoulders, looked into his eyes and whispered: 'You will make me proud yet, I'm thinking . . .?'

Tom grinned sheepishly.

'Tell me now that you will!'

'Och, I'll try,' Tom said, shifting his weight from one foot to the other, uncomfortable with maternal earnestness.

His mother laughed and patted his cheek. 'Away with you to the high field and help your father. And, for the love of God, find that *óinseach* of a hen.'

On his way to the high field Tom wondered how the new baby would get out, imagined a little door in his mother's belly. He tried to remember being in her tummy, but was distracted by the rainbow that arched above the fields, touching the ground in the Farrellys' meadow. He knew that where it touched the earth the fairies had left a pot of gold. He jumped over the wall and ran towards this spot, but like every other time he had tried it, the rainbow dissolved and moved away.

Tom found the hen near the high field where she had made a nest under a hedge not far from the river. She gave long unhappy clucks, spreading her wings above the nest. He shouted to his father, whose wiry form he could see on the rise above him. With him were the other children, Michael and five-year-old Maria. They were picking stones from the potato field, a necessary precursor to the new planting.

'*A Dhaidí, a Dhaidí!*' Tom shouted to make himself heard above the song of the river that rushed by him to the fields below.

They came at his call, his siblings with laughter and exclamation. His father pursed his mouth wryly, reaching for the broody hen who was still brazenly squatting.

'So, madam, you're up to your old tricks!'

The hen squawked.

'She ought to sit in Parliament!' Seán added, picking her up and removing the three eggs from the warm nest. He put them into his pocket. 'She'd make as much sense as any of them! She'd be a voice for Ireland, anyway!'

Bunched under her owner's arm, the bird bobbed her red comb unhappily and looked around wildly.

'Where's that?' Tom demanded. 'Parliament?'

'It's in London, you little eejit,' Michael said, turning to his younger brother with scorn. 'It's in England, where they make laws.' His face suddenly darkened. 'The Master told us in school! They make laws for *us* in England.' And then he added under his breath, 'That's why we are paying rent for land that was always ours!'

'Did the Master tell you that too?' his father demanded.

'No. Josie Farrelly did.' Michael looked at his father sullenly, as though challenging him to deny it. 'Is it true, Father, that there were laws against Catholics that let English *Protastuní* take their land? Without paying anything for it?'

Seán understood his child's fury.

' 'Tis true. But 'twas done long ago,' he replied without conviction.

Only eight years ago, at a time when famine had stalked the land, he had stood with a small crowd outside the limestone courthouse in Clonmel while the 'Young Ireland' leaders had been condemned to be hanged, drawn and quartered. Only eight years ago he had seen the 17th Hussars with cannon, cavalry and infantry, and the Scots Greys, on fine horses and in scarlet cloaks, escorting the weekly barges of meat and wheat down the Suir from Clonmel, bound for Waterford and shipment to England.

But since the Famine, the country seemed quelled; a million people were dead, another million had emigrated; the country was dotted with deserted villages and overlain by a pall of sorrow. The Tenant League, an organisation that sought fair rents and a better deal for tenants, was moribund.

'It's not that long ago!' Michael cried. 'Josie's grandfather tells stories of when things were different, when the Walshes owned all the land around here . . .'

Seán thought of the documents he had once seen in his own grand-father's hands, papers dating from the preceding century that spoke of forfeiture – of tracts of Walsh property that were handed over to foreigners. He knew that during the time of the Penal Laws, when Catholics had been forced to give up their lands, it had been common to lease the lands of the forfeiting owners back to them as tenants. Anyone who rebelled risked arrest, imprisonment, transportation or hanging. Now, young as the boy was, he felt afraid for his son.

'Well, whenever those things were done,' he said, 'there's no point in bothering your head about them now. The old days are over.'

'How can they be "over", Father, when they haven't given us back the land?'

Seán looked at his eldest child, already on the verge of manhood; saw he had begun to challenge him. Soon it would be a clash of wills and, in the ordained way of things, the old way must lose.

'Because Might is right, my boy, at least until a new order moves the world! Learn that and keep yourself out of trouble.'

Michael regarded his father with scorn. 'Are you afraid of them, Father?'

Tom jumped out of the way as his father took Michael by the ear.

'Listen to me now. Seven years ago I saw plenty of people around here who tried to eat grass. I saw them dead on the roadside with green on their mouths. And I swore that the most important thing in this country is that hunger like that never comes back. You, Mammie and me were lucky to live through it!'

Michael replied stubbornly, 'Josie says there was plenty of food in Ireland, Father; that it was just the potatoes that failed. He says the harvest was sent to England every year – *all* the wheat, *all* the meat . . .' Tears started in his eyes. '*Why* didn't they care, Father? Why did they take our food and let us die?'

Seán dared not allow himself to be drawn into this bitter topic. He looked up at the massing grey clouds and held out his hand for the first drops.

'Go home, let ye now, or ye'll be drowned,' he said sternly to indicate the subject was closed.

'Tommy,' he shouted, raising his voice at his younger son, who had listened in silence to most of the exchange before slipping away to the river, where he was about to tread the rocks above the waterfall. 'Tommy, come back here.'

But Tommy was too busy daring himself to cross the rocks of An Cailleach. An Cailleach, meaning 'the witch' or 'hag' in Irish, was a deep ravine where the small river ran from the hill to gurgle between two great rocks on its way to the farm below. These rocks were stepping stones for the wary, but only when the river was not in spate. He had concocted a private fantasy. In his mind he was crossing the falls of Niagara. He had learned about the great waterfall in school.

But he lost his footing. One misplaced step and he fell, turning his ankle and wetting himself thoroughly before clinging to a branch overhanging the river's edge. He screamed.

His father dropped the hen – who immediately ran back to her nest – and hauled his son from the water.

'You're a bold pup,' he said, smacking Tom's face. He scooped the pieces of shell and yolk from his pocket, 'And you've made me break the eggs.'

Tom shivered, relieved at being out of the river, in pain from his wrenched ankle, wretched about the loss of the eggs, deflated that his imaginary feat had found him wanting. He tried to stand, but his injury cried out.

Then they heard the cry that came all the way up the meadow. It was his mother, and she was calling his name. He turned to see her hurrying uphill, heard her breath catch with effort.

'What's after happening?' she gasped, looking from one of her family to the other. 'I was out in the yard . . . Was that *you* I heard, Tommy?'

'He's grand, he's grand. For the love of God, woman, will you go easy. Rushing up here in your condition . . .'

Maria went flying towards her. 'Mam, Mam, it's Tommy, it's Tommy . . . He was on the river and he's hurted his foot.'

Margaret crossed the potato field to him. Tom saw her anxious, loving face, loved the sway of her movements, the mane of her hair coming loose from the combs and picked up by the breeze.

Below her was the sweep of the valley, Kilduncan House, the landlord's home, hidden among its trees, and nearer, their own whitewashed, thatched cabin, and the *botharín* that led through their farm to the road. The farm was twenty acres, yielding enough potatoes to feed them, and barely enough produce to pay the rent. Rents in Ireland were high – double the rate prevailing in England. The people had no option but to pay. Industry had been suppressed to obviate competition with British industry, and without land one died. So everything except potatoes was sold, and every penny put into the tin box under his father's bed against the gale days when Steven Lurgan, Lord Kilduncan's despised steward, would sit in the big house at the end of the beech avenue, and take in the rents. His master lived in London, and let his steward milk his Irish estates.

'What did you do to yourself, Tommy?' Margaret now said, looking down at her younger son who sat on the ground, clasping his ankle.

'*Tá sé maith go leor,*' the boy's father said. 'He'll be grand. He's just sprained his ankle. I told him not to go to An Cailleach, but nothing would do him but to go jumping off the big rock. It's the strap he'll feel on his backside when I get him home.'

'*A Mhamaí!*' the boy cried, turning to his mother.

'He'll feel nothing of the sort, Seán Walsh,' Margaret said, still panting, 'for he can't help the spirit that's in him!' She bent and put out her arms. Tom reached up, clung to her neck and she staggered for a moment under his weight.

'You can't carry him, Margaret,' Seán said in a flat voice of alarm, 'so don't attempt it!'

Margaret could not refuse her child's outstretched arms. But she cried out under his weight, and sank down with him to the damp ground. The pain was such that the boy in her arms could almost hear it.

'Mammie!' he cried in alarm, pulling back to look at her. 'Mammie . . .'

Seán whispered anxiously, 'What is it? *Cad tá ort?*'

Although they brought their children up to speak English, Seán and Margaret used Irish when they wanted to converse in private. The old language was under siege, beaten out of the children at school, but they knew it better than they pretended, whispered it when the grown-ups were not around.

'I'm all right!' She spoke in English and forced a smile, but Tommy heard the sibilant intake of her breath. 'I'm grand. Just let me sit here for a moment. Show me that ankle of yours, Tommy.'

She touched the bare foot and leg gently, pressed and released it while the boy grimaced. But he suddenly knew from the way her mouth tightened and her eyes closed that, whatever was wrong with his ankle, something worse was wrong with his mother.

'It's not broken anyway,' she continued in the same unnaturally even voice. 'But it's swelling already and you won't be able to walk on it for a week. You should do what your father tells you and not be such a disobedient boy!' She paused, dragged her breath through her teeth.

9

She looked up at her husband, who was regarding her anxiously; said abruptly, 'Take him home, Seán.'

Tom saw that his father's eyes were full of fear.

'I'll help you first, Margaret.'

'You can come back for me when you've brought the children home! It's better that way.' And then she dropped her voice and said in Irish the words that Tom would carry to his grave: '*Táim ag cur fulla.*' He knew what they meant – 'I'm bleeding' – and he looked fearfully for blood, but there was none.

His father's face was white. 'I'll send Michael for Mrs Hegarty,' he said.

'Do, *a ghrá.*' Margaret touched his sleeve and looked up at him. 'I'm all right. It's just started a bit early, that's all!'

She looked at Tommy, who was sobbing and biting his lip. 'Go on now. Daddy will come back for me. I'm grand.'

Maria clung to her mother's skirts and screamed, 'No, no, *NO* . . .' when her father tried to disengage her; but eventually she obeyed, looking back at her mother and sobbing brokenly.

'Will you stop that,' her father said crossly. 'Your mother will be all right.'

Tom, from his father's arms, watched his mother for as long as he could, and waved at her over his father's shoulder. She did not wave back, but lay down flat, as though she wanted to talk to the sky.

Seán put Tom to bed, brought his other children to the Farrellys, and went back to the high field for his wife. Tom hobbled to the door of the room he shared with his siblings and watched through a chink as his parents came into the kitchen, his father carrying his mother whose black skirt seemed to be wet – from the field, he presumed until he saw that his father's shirtsleeves were smeared with blood. He stifled a cry and waited, his heart sounding like one of the drums he had seen the red-coated soldiers beating one day in Clonmel.

He saw Mrs Hegarty come; she spoke briefly to his father, threw off her black shawl and hurried into the bedroom on the other side of the kitchen. Then the door was shut. Tom waited. He saw his father strip off his bloodied shirt, don another one, which he took from the line by the fire, then sit by the hearth, his head in his hands. The firelight danced across the whitewashed kitchen walls, glanced on the old churn in the corner, on the dresser with its few dishes and enamelled tin plates, on the black-painted settle and the *súgán* chair by the hearth. His father rose suddenly and Tommy limped back to bed and pretended to be asleep. His parent's form darkened the doorway.

'Can't be that much wrong with him . . .' his father muttered in Irish.

Seán returned to the kitchen, and resumed his vigil by the fire. The night deepened. Tom dozed, but woke at the sounds from his mother's room, Mrs Hegarty's soothing voice, then terrible groans. He returned to his vantage point by the crack in the door, saw the midwife come out, pour hot water from the old black kettle into a basin. The candlelight from the room threw shadows for a moment; then she was gone and his mother's door was shut.

After a while came the thin wail of a baby. Tom saw his father jump to his feet. Mrs Hegarty reappeared in the kitchen and they conferred in whispers. She was shaking her head.

When his father went into the room where his mother lay, Tom hobbled across the kitchen to the open door of his parents' room. He was unprepared for the sight before him.

'A Mhamaí!' he whispered, holding on to the door jamb, stunned by the stench of blood and the saturated crimson of his parents' bed. In the small wooden cradle, wrapped in a towel, was a tiny baby, red face screwed up. But Tom was consumed with something other than this miracle. He watched as his father pressed his mother's hands to his face and said into her ear, in Irish, the Act of Contrition.

The midwife kneeled. Tom saw his father gather his wife into his arms and kiss her lips. He heard his own violent sob above the wail of the newborn and hobbled towards his mother's bed, ignoring the fire in his ankle. His father turned, rose to his feet. His face, haggard and white, glowered and he pulled his son from the room.

'Stay out, you *amadán* . . . You've done enough mischief.'

He shut the door in the boy's face. Tom shivered, crushed by guilt, tasting tears and mucus. 'A Mhamaí!' he cried hysterically, beating at the bedroom door.

In a moment Mrs Hegarty came into the kitchen and took him in her arms.

'You have a baby sister! She's beautiful . . .'

Tom cared nothing for baby sisters at that moment. He flailed at the midwife. He knew she was trying to distract him and this made him more frightened than ever.

'I want to see Mammie.' His teeth were chattering. 'I want to see Mammie. What's wrong with her? Why is she bleeding . . .? It's my fault; it's my fault . . .'

The midwife held him tightly to her. 'It isn't your fault, little heart. It's God's will. You can see her in the morning. She's . . . gone to sleep now.'

She wrapped him in a blanket and bandaged his ankle.

In the morning Margaret was covered with her one good bedspread she kept in the chest by the window; they had covered her pillow with the pillowcase edged with her own lace; it was faintly scented with lavender.

Tom stood with his father and siblings by her bed. He reached for her hands where they were joined on her breast, found them stiff and cold. His father said she was gone away, that only her body was there now, and he glared at Tom as he said this. Michael's face was white; the tears poured silently down his cheeks and trickled into his mouth.

Maria suddenly sobbed, 'I saw it . . . I *saw* it . . . while we were up at An Cailleach . . .'

'Stop it,' Seán told his daughter. 'Stop that nonsense now!' Tommy smelled the whiskey on his father's breath, and saw the red rims to his eyes.

Later that day the neighbours came. The men doffed their caps; the women kneeled by the bed and keened.

'What's her name – the new baby?' Tom heard one of them ask Mrs Hegarty. She was rocking the infant in the kitchen.

'Margaret,' the midwife said. 'She'll be named for her mother.'

But Tommy evinced no interest. He hardly looked at the new baby; he did not grieve or weep. When the neighbours tried to comfort him he looked at them as from a great distance, and made no reply. And when he finally slept they found it difficult to rouse him.

They waked Margaret for two days, never allowing her to lie alone in an empty room. And then they buried her and for two days and nights her grave was constantly attended.

Three weeks later, Michael suddenly demanded at supper, looking at his father in accusation, 'Why is there no cross on Mammie's grave? I went to the graveyard after school, and still there is no cross.'

His father did not reply for a moment. Then he said in a low abrupt voice, turning his head away as though he could not look his son in the eye, 'I'm no mason, and we've no money.'

Michael took up a sod from the creel and flung it across the room where it hit the wall and broke.

'You work, *a Dhaidí*,' he screamed, while the tears started in his eyes, 'all day, every day. I work before I go to school and when I come from school. Maria works: she picks stones until her back is broke. Tommy works. But still we do not have enough to put a cross on Mammie's grave! And I know why,' he added on a high note of rage and grief. 'Because the Sasanaigh have taken everything from us and turned us into slaves!'

'Enough of that!' his father said. 'What happened in this country wasn't done by the English. 'Twas done by the Government. Governments don't care two straws for anyone, and that includes their own, which you'd realise if you knew a bit of English history.'

'All I know is my mother has only an old heap of stones!' Michael continued, and burst into a storm of tears.

'She needs no cross,' his father said sternly. 'She has a cairn. Long ago we buried our queens this way. And it is a queen's grave.'

*   *   *

'Tommy won't talk and he's eating nothing,' Seán told Father Doyle, the parish priest, on one of his calls to the bereaved family. 'He won't look at the baby, but he wakes us more than she does at night, crying in his sleep. In school he just sits there. The Master is worried about him.' He lowered his voice. 'He says the boy thinks it was because of him . . .'

The old priest glanced sharply at his parishioner and asked softly, 'Why should he think that?'

'Because he *is* to blame,' Seán said bitterly. 'Nothing would do the little pup but to damn her . . . and the woman near her time. If I could but have that day back,' he added with a moan, staring defiantly at the priest out of red-rimmed eyes, 'the devil could have my soul and welcome . . .'

The priest lowered his head, looking up at Seán from under his bushy grey eyebrows.

'Hear me now,' he said sternly. 'Your son is six years old, a small child breaking under the weight of his collapsed world. Do you want his mind to go? Would you lose him to a darkness from which he could never be rescued?'

Seán put his head in his hands.

'And leave the devil out of it, Seán Walsh . . . because he's one gentleman who's all ears.'

Children's voices could be heard in the distance. The priest waited, heard the sough of the wind, the sigh of the fire as burning sods collapsed into embers. Seán straightened, wiping his face with his forearm. Michael appeared in the doorway, his school books in his hands. He greeted Father Doyle respectfully in Irish

'*Dia dhuit, a Athair!*' – God 'with you, Father!

'Where is your brother?' the priest asked.

'Tommy's coming. Maria keeps trying to make him talk, but he doesn't seem to hear her!'

Father Doyle watched Tom as he came into the kitchen, saw the glazed suffering in his small face, saw his eyes rest for a moment on his father.

'Will you come for a walk with me, Tommy?' Father Doyle asked.

The boy made no response, so the priest took him by the hand, left the warm kitchen and walked around the farm, talking gently all the time. He led the boy to the high field. The daffodils were opening their yellow trumpets in the ravine at An Cailleach. The child stared at the waterfall and began to tremble.

'You must miss your mother very much, Tommy?' the priest said softly. 'But what happened was a terrible accident.'

The boy suddenly wailed, a cry that shivered across the field and down the glen. The kind old priest held him; his eyes were full of tears. 'She is a terrible loss, but she is safe in Heaven, still loving and watching you. And

13

Tommy,' he added firmly, turning up the boy's face and looking into his eyes, 'it was not your fault.'

'A Mhamai . . .!' Tom screamed. 'A Mhamai, a Mhamai . . .' He threw himself into the old priest's arms, howling his loss.

When they went back to the house, Tom looked into the cradle, and, while Father Doyle spoke to his father, he put his finger into the baby's hand. Michael, doing homework at the table, saw his brother's signs of recent grief.

'Are you all right, Tommy?' he asked softly.

Tom came to him, saw the sums in rows down the page and, peeping out from under the copybook, what looked like a poem. Michael looked furtively over his shoulder and handed the piece of paper to him.

Tommy registered the first lines:

Oh Ireland, do thou lift up thy head
Thy day also shall come . . .

'It's St Malachy's prophesy,' Michael whispered fiercely. 'It's about Ireland . . . Someday . . .'

As the light faded, Tom slipped away to the graveyard beside the little church. Normally he would have been frightened to have come here on his own, his mind full of the dreadful knowledge of what lay under the earth, but today he walked heedlessly, hardly aware of the creaking trees, or the whistle of the wind. He went straight to the mound of new stones.

'A Mhamai,' he whispered.

He crouched beside her grave, repeating her name. After a little while he felt warmth inside him, her love filling him. It was as though he were with her after school, drinking a cup of new buttermilk and laughing by the fire.

'I promise you, a Mhamai . . .' he whispered, putting his face against the stones and remembering what she had asked of him on the last day of her life.

Sometimes, during the succeeding years, Tommy would surreptitiously take out the pillowcase with the lace edging and hold it to his face.

One day, some five years after his mother's death, his father found him in his room, saw the pillowcase in his hands.

'What are you doing with that, sir?'

'Just remembering.'

'Memory is all very well,' Seán said, 'but your business now is to build a future.' He paused, put a hand briefly on Tom's head. 'If your mother were here . . .'

Tom looked at his grey-haired father, at the pouches under his eyes, and the tired stoop to his shoulders. He felt the touch of his hand as a benison and a forgiveness.

'I know, Father,' he replied in a low voice.

That evening, Michael, now a strapping sixteen, came into the kitchen, took off his boots inside the door and went to stand by the hearth. The steam rose from his saturated clothes. The rain came down the chimney and hissed as it died in the fire.

' 'Tis one fierce day,' he said. He turned to his father. 'We'll have to manure the field if we're to have any wheat this year!'

'Divil a market there is for wheat now,' Seán said. 'There's so much coming from America there's no price at all. And,' he added sourly, 'Lurgan will raise the rent again.'

'Get out of those wet things,' ten-year-old Maria said hurriedly to her brother, 'before you catch your death.'

It was Maria who ran the house now; but her schooling had suffered as the mantle of surrogate mother had descended on her. Denied a normal childhood, she had turned inwards, looking at things from a perspective peculiar to herself. She loved to gaze into the fire; her father called it daydreaming, but her siblings knew she was trying to see things hidden in the hot swirl of the flames. Tom taught her the lessons he received at school, gave her his school reader, was pleased when she learned to read almost as quickly as he had. The Master dropped by sometimes with a book or two, and muttered to her father that it was a shame such a bright mind was going to waste.

'She's a girl,' her father always said. 'Sure what use is education to her?'

The family sat down to a dinner of potatoes and a jug of buttermilk. Seán, in a morose mood, said grace, then addressed Michael as he helped himself to the food. 'Did you finish ploughing the high field?'

'I did. But I'm mortal tired of trying to do anything with this place. There's no point in staying here. No matter how hard you work it's all for nothing!'

'I've told you before and I'll tell you again – things in this country will change in God's good time.'

'Maybe. But it won't be *my* time, Father! And my time is all I've got.'

In the ensuing silence Maria looked anxiously from her father to her brother. Tom kept his eyes on his plate. He was thinking of school that day and the praise he had received for his English composition and the homework he still had to do after supper. He was tired. Since coming home that afternoon he had stacked turf, dug potatoes, and helped block a gap in the hedge where the Farrellys' donkey had broken into the meadow. Seamus Farrelly, his schoolmate and friend, had helped by stacking branches fallen from a nearby ash during the February storm. Then Tom had milked the new cow, a Friesian, his father's pride and joy.

Seated beside Tommy at the table was little five-year-old Margaret, whom they called Peggie. The adored baby of the family, she was still so small that only her face – large blue eyes; auburn corkscrew curls cascading down her back – and her shoulders were visible above the table top. Tom sensed her dismay at the family tension; saw her push away her plate.

'Eat your dinner, miss,' Seán commanded.

The child's eyes filled with tears. Reluctantly, she drew back the plate and took another spoonful. Tom smiled at his little sister encouragingly.

When Peggie refused to eat any more, sitting there stubbornly and sniffling, her father said crossly, 'Peggie, go to bed.'

'But I don't wanna . . .'

Maria, who had polished off her dinner, slipped from her seat. 'I'll put her to bed. Come on, Peggie; I've a great story entirely for you tonight . . .'

The child went with her sister.

After a while Maria returned, took the empty plates from the table and put them in the old enamelled basin, glancing nervously at her father and elder brother, whose differences were becoming a feature of every evening. She sat on the stool by the hearth. Tom saw how she had combed her hair, pinning it behind her ears. It shone in the firelight. He was proud of the small, three-legged stool that he had made for her during the winter; it meant she could sit close to the fire. She took hot water from the black skillet, poured it on the plates and began to wash them.

Tom got up, sought his precious copybook and pencil, reseated himself at the table and began to do the sums he had been given for homework.

Seán sighed. He looked through the small square window, to the hedge of fuchsia that Margaret had planted not long before her death, to the *botharín* that led down to the main road, now grey in the dying light.

He went to his bedroom, returning with a dog-eared volume which he proceeded to open, and sat down with it on the settle. Leafing through the pages he found the poem he wanted to read that evening: Thomas Gray's 'Elegy Written in a Country Churchyard'.

He read it aloud, verse after verse, his voice caressing its cadence. And then he took his fiddle from the shelf and played one of his favourite pieces, 'An Cualainn'. The children listened to its haunting strains as they worked: Maria dried the dishes, put them away, tidied the table; Tom continued his homework; Michael sat at the table, quelled for the moment by the verse and the music. Little Peggie crept to the bedroom door to listen, her thumb in her mouth.

When Seán was finished he put away the fiddle; sat for a while looking into the fire before lifting his pipe from its place on the mantelshelf. Michael took this as his cue and rose from his seat.

But his father wanted to talk to him. 'I met Denis Farrelly earlier,' he offered. He used a paper taper to light his pipe, bending towards the fire and pulling on the pipe with small sucking sounds. 'His cow had a bull calf there yesterday.'

Michael sat down again, but he looked at his father with an expression bordering on contempt.

'Did he also tell you, Father, that Josie is going to America? He's off from Queenstown in three weeks.'

He turned to his siblings, widened his eyes and rolled his voice in mockery. 'He's going away . . . on a great ship across the big Atlantical say!'

'He told me,' Seán said dismissively. 'Far away hills are green!'

'He's enlisting in the Union army! They've sent him his ticket.'

'Is that a fact?'

'And I'm going too,' Michael announced defiantly. 'Just as soon as I can.'

Seán looked thunderous. 'You'll join no foreign army. It's not lucky to disobey your father. If your brother had obeyed me five years ago . . .' He glanced at Tom, saw how he started and was silent.

'It's America or join the Brotherhood,' Michael said. He was referring to the new organisation discussed in whispers at firesides throughout the country. It was called the Fenians, also known as the Irish Republican Brotherhood.

His father said nothing for a moment, but his eyes flashed under his grey eyebrows and his mouth tightened.

'You'll end up transported to Australia or hanged.'

'Look, Father, I can transport myself – but to the other side of the Atlantic. America is a great new country and needs strong men.' He stared hard at his father, then glanced at Maria. 'Maria can come with me! And Tommy too if he wants.'

'No they cannot, sir,' cried his father, rising from his seat. 'They're children. And I need a son for the land.'

'We haven't got any land, Father,' Michael said, dropping his voice as though aware that he was going too far. 'Can't you see that? If it's land you want you'll have to find it somewhere else! We may have been lords here once, but Kilduncan has it all now! And Tommy,' he added, 'is no farmer. Look at him, sitting there and working out his arithmetic! Look at how he's doing in school, the way he reads and writes. He's not a farmer; he's a scholar and that's the truth of it!'

'I'll get land,' Tommy said quietly, glancing up from his copybook. 'I'll get all the land the Walshes owned once and I'll give it to Daddie!'

Michael laughed derisively. 'Will you now? And what would you be thinking of using in the way of money?'

'You shouldn't laugh at Tommy,' Maria said slowly. She was staring into the fire, rapt and still at what she saw in the flames, the dishcloth limp in

17

her hand. Her voice was a monotone. 'When he grows up he's going to . . .' She started, turned abruptly to look at her brother, and cried out, 'A Dhia . . .' adding in English after she caught her father's eye, 'I've just had a terrible queer feeling.'

Michael took his cap from the peg. He gave a derisive laugh. 'It's no use calling on God, Maria, when you are about to give us the benefit of your forecasts. *Queer* is right!' He reached for his cap. 'I'm going over to the Farrellys, Father.'

'Don't be drinking any of that *poitín* of theirs,' his father warned. He was referring to the illegally distilled spirit made from potatoes. 'It's enough to blind a body . . .'

When the door was shut Tom turned to his elder sister, who was regarding him quizzically.

'What is it you think I'll do that's so queer, Maria?' he whispered. He knew that Maria, however much his father and brother tried to silence her, sometimes knew things the rest of them did not.

She shook her head as she looked at her eleven-year-old brother, said in a low voice, putting her hand to her head and looking back at the fire, 'I'm trying to feel it again . . . It was as though . . . you would become . . . one of the *High Kings* . . .'

'I've warned you before about this oul' nonsense,' their father said testily. 'You know what Father Doyle says about telling fortunes and trying to see the future, miss. You'll have to stop this carry-on. It isn't right!' He pulled angrily on his pipe.

Maria took some mending out of a box in the corner of the kitchen, brought it to her stool, sat down and threaded her needle by the light of the fire.

'I *would* like to go to America too, Father,' Tom said diffidently after a few minutes, when he estimated that his father had relaxed sufficiently for the subject to be raised again. 'I'd earn money there to buy our land back.'

But Seán only turned on his son with haunted eyes. 'Is it leave Carraig Mór? Leave Ireland? Don't talk *ráiméis* and don't mind that brother of yours. If it's money you want there are trades. You're good with your hands; you could earn a living that way and it wouldn't stop you farming as well.'

'What kind of trades, Father?'

'Well, you could be a mason, or a smith . . .'

'I'd prefer to make things with wood, Father.'

His father thought for a minute, puffing the long, clay pipe and the pungent aroma of tobacco filled the room.

'Donald Grubb, one of the Quaker millwrights below at Clonmel, might take you on as apprentice,' he said eventually. 'How would you feel about that? There'd be a fee for his trouble, but sure we'd manage it somehow. You'd learn a good trade. And you'd never be without a bit in your mouth as long as the country needed mills or carpenters.'

Tom thought about this. Suddenly he saw himself building something as big as a watermill, imagined a millrace pushing a great wheel, the work of his hands. If he was able to do that surely he would be able to go to America? His face brightened.

'That would be grand, Father.'

Tom finished his long division, opened his headline copybook and copied out in careful copperplate the verse required by the Board of Education:

> I thank the goodness and the grace
> That on my birth have smiled
> And made me in these Christian days
> A happy English child.

But half of his mind was on other things.

I will go to America, he told himself. I'll go someday.

As soon as he left school at twelve, Tom was bound to Donald Grubb as apprentice. He said goodbye to his family and his friend Seamus Farrelly, and went away to the town of Clonmel.

The smell of sawdust became his home. He slept in the mill in a settle bed that Mr Grubb reminded him with a grin would also serve as a coffin if he put a hand wrong; he had his meals with his master's family. Donald showed him the secrets of wood – of oak for serious constructions such as mill wheels, ash and beech for carts, pine for plain tables and furniture, hickory for tool handles and carriage wheels. He learned the use of planes and chisels, hammers and screwdrivers, the coping saw that cut curves, the radial saw that made crosscuts.

Donald showed him how to measure with the folding wood rule – 'measure twice, cut once' – how to use steam to bend to any shape. Sometimes he was desolate for the kitchen of his home and his siblings, for his father's face. But he knew he had no option but to be strong. He was twelve years old; his childhood was over.

He persevered. He read on Sundays – the Bible, the works of William Shakespeare, all the newspapers, pamphlets, periodicals he found in the Grubb household. His master approved.

' 'Tis good to read,' he said. 'Keeps your mind alive! Just so long as you don't start dreaming about any of the scandal you might come across in those newspapers . . .'

Tom nodded. He had his sights on other things. He loved what he was learning. He loved the feel of wood.

'There's nobility in wood,' Donald Grubb said. 'It lives and talks to you. It commands respect. Don't ever waste it.'

Seán had aged. He had lost most of his teeth. The farm was poor as ever; it had taken the strain of paying the premium for Tom's indentures, and lacked his labour. Maria became a young woman and little Peggie grew slowly into beauty.

Bitter unrest simmered in the countryside. Michael became unnaturally quiet, slipping out at night and returning in the dawn. His father had lost his authority and could not command his fiery son. In 1867 came the Fenian Rising. It was a gentlemanly affair, led by intellectuals. A few police barracks were captured before the rebellion was crushed. Michael, after days of furtive behaviour, suddenly disappeared, leaving a note to say he had gone to join the Union army in America.

Tom, working in bare feet on Donald Grubb's mill, treading the woodshavings, smelling the rich scent of freshly sawn timber, watched the seasons change and the years hound each other. He waited for adulthood with patience and single-minded determination, entering young manhood with one purpose – America.

As he approached the end of his indentures, he told his master of his dreams.

'There's a man in Boston I know of,' Donald said, 'a Mr Vandermeer who has a sawmill and a building business. My cousin used to work for him and says he's always on the lookout for skilled carpenters. Why don't you write to him? I'll give you a testimonial that'll put hairs on your chest.'

Tom wrote in the fine copperplate hand he had perfected at school.

Dear Sir,
I am about to complete my indentures with Mr Donald Grubb, millwright of Clonmel. I am a competent carpenter, and enclose a testimonial from Mr Grubb so confirming. I intend to emigrate, am seeking a position and would be glad to hear from you if you have any employment I might take up.
    I have the honour to be, sir, your most obedient servant,
    Thomas Francis Walsh

He reread with pleasure and embarrassment the testimonial he had received from Mr Grubb, before folding it and enclosing it with his missive. The reference said:

Dear Mr Vandermeer,
Thomas Francis Walsh has been my apprentice for the past seven years and has faithfully carried out his duties. He is now an accomplished craftsman and one of the finest young men I know, sober, industrious and of sterling character. I recommend him without hesitation.

But the weeks went by and no reply came from America. Dreams, Tom mused, are long thoughts.

On a visit home during the last month of his apprenticeship, Tom found his father tucked up in bed.

'It's just a cold,' the old man said. 'Your sisters have me bullied into staying in, and poor Seamie Farrelly bullied into doing most of the work. I'll be grand in a day or two. Now tell me about yourself.'

'I'm nearly finished at Grubb's, Father.'

'The years run around,' the old man said croakily. 'I suppose you'll want to be off to foreign parts like your brother!'

Tom regarded his parent's haggard face. Duty, like a demon from hell, presented itself. How could he go when he was clearly wanted here?

'No, Father,' he said slowly, although his heart was sinking. 'I'll stay with you.'

'Go if you must,' his father said sadly, coughing. 'I've been thinking about it. It's your life. I've had mine and I've no right to keep you.'

Peggie came in from the kitchen.

'Poor Daddie,' she said, leaning over to stroke his lined face. 'You'll always have me.'

Her father patted her hand. 'You're only thirteen, *a stór*. You'll take wing too.'

Peggie began to straighten the bed, humming in her lilting voice and breaking into song as she unfolded a blanket from the chest by the window.

Tom listened. For some reason the delicacy of his young sister as she crossed the room to his father, moved and saddened him.

He said abruptly, 'You need me here. I tell you, Father, I *will* stay.'

'Will you? Maria has a letter that I think will change your mind.'

Maria, who had been milking, came through the half-door into the kitchen with a pail of warm, frothing milk. She put it on the table, washed her hands and came to the open bedroom door. Behind her was Finn, the mongrel pup that Seamus Farrelly had given her, his tongue lolling happily.

'Show your brother the letter,' her father commanded.

'What letter is that?' she asked innocently.

'Show it to him, girl.'

She made much of putting her hand into her pocket. 'I don't know where I put it . . . Oh *a Dhia*, where is it?' She glanced archly at her brother. 'Ah, here it is!'

She handed Tom an envelope with American stamps, and went back to the kitchen. Tom glanced at his father, opened the envelope, drew out the letter. Thirty dollars fell out on to the bed.

The missive, in Michael's writing, said:

It's the best I can do, but it will pay your fares. They're sending us west to fight the Indians. Write to me care of the regiment and let me know what you decide.

Tom avoided his father's eyes. He followed Maria into the kitchen. It smelled of the fresh milk that she was straining through muslin into a bowl. She looked up at him, bright-eyed.

'Will you go?'

Tom was full of excited speculation. 'I would like to, Maria,' he said after a moment.

She dropped her voice, 'If you go, Tommy, I'll go with you.'

Peggie had come into the room behind her and overheard. The song died on her lips. Her face was troubled and her eyes were full of tears.

A week later came the reply from Mr Vandermeer. He had a position to offer Tom; the pay would be three dollars per week and lodgings would be provided. There would be a probation period of six months. But he needed to be assured that if his probation period was found satisfactory Tom would stay for two years.

Tom showed the letter to his father.

'Three dollars a week and your lodging!' he exclaimed sadly. 'There's nothing here that will give you that! I've begun to think that Michael was right. By the time things change in Ireland we will all be dead! Go, and good luck to you.'

Tom wrote to Mr Vandermeer to say he would come. But he had a sister, he said, who was a great housekeeper. Did Mr Vandermeer know of any position she might apply for? One way or another he knew that everything had changed for ever. He was nineteen, a young man hungry to live.

Chapter Two

The train from Cork to Queenstown was full, third-class compartments crammed so tightly the windows misted. The track was crossing water, had almost reached Great Island. Someone reached for the leather strap and let down the pane. At once came the blustering sea breeze and the acrid smoke blown back from the engine. The tide was ebbing, and along the railway embankment brown seaweed glistened in the spring sunlight. The rhythm of the wheels on the rail now seemed to promise the new horizons awaiting the emigrants. In a sense they were already at sea. Eyes, still red from last night's farewells, brightened with excitement. But Tom and Maria sat immobile, thinking only of the morning's leave-taking and the fathomless future.

They had said goodbye at daybreak. Half blinded by tears, they had seen their father's grey head bow before his children as he struggled for control. Peggie put porridge on the table in silence, but no one could eat.

Maria wiped her eyes and leaned into the hearth to put new sods on the embers. I will never do this again, she thought, never again in this house . . .

Everyone was exhausted; the preceding evening the neighbours had come to say farewell, and they had stayed talking around the fire well into the night.

'I'll come back, Father,' Tom said in a hoarse voice, breaking the silence. 'I'll buy Kilduncan's mansion for you and a thousand acres of land to go with it.' And then, thinking of the small cairn in the churchyard, he added: 'And I will put the finest headstone money can buy on Mother's grave.'

His father raised his head and looked at his son. 'Sure what would I do with Kilduncan's oul' house? And if you do come back it'll be long years from now and I'll be lying beside your poor mother, pushing up the daisies.'

There was a short bark from Finn, who was lying at the open door, followed by the sound of a cart. It was Seamus Farrelly, come to take them to the railway station in Clonmel. He waited in the yard, discreetly looking away to the fields.

'There's Seamus!' Seán said gruffly, looking from one of his children to another. 'Let us kneel down now and pray.'

They kneeled and, in a tight, aching voice, the old man asked God's blessing on his children who were going away for ever.

Maria and Peggie burst into heartbroken sobs.

'I'll be back, Father,' Tom vowed again in a low voice as he rose to his feet. 'It is not for ever.'

'That's as may be,' the old man said without much conviction. He gestured to Maria. 'Well, look after your sister, anyway.'

Maria was clutching Peggie as though she could not bear to let her go. It was Peggie who drew back. She turned salt-stung eyes on her brother and put her arms out to him for a last embrace.

'Write to me,' she said, clinging to him. 'Tell me everything about your life. And sure maybe you *will* come back sometime.' Then she smiled through her tears, reached up on tiptoe and whispered in her brother's ear: 'Will you send me some ribbons when you get to America? Just to let me know that you are safe?'

Tom looked at his pretty thirteen-year-old sister and laughed in spite of himself.

'I surely will,' he said, tweaking her unruly auburn curls.

The countryside, Tom thought, as he carried the wooden trunk to the cart, had never looked so fine. The sun was just up; a white mist hovered over the fields and clothed the first ascent of Slievenamon.

'Seamie,' he said, putting a hand on his old friend's shoulder, 'you must be tired out. You were here until nearly cockcrow.'

Seamus shook his head. 'It's not the lack of sleep! It's the taking you away . . .'

'Will you have a bite of breakfast, Seamie?' Peggie called from the door.

Seamus regarded her tenderly. 'No, thank you, Peggie. I'm grand.'

Finn sat outside the door with his head on his paws. Maria fondled his head for a moment, looked into his adoring eyes, climbed into the cart, and Tom sprang up beside Seamus on the driving seat. Seán and Peggie walked to the gate; waited as horse and cart rumbled out of the yard and down the boreen. Finn trotted behind for a little way, before turning back.

The emigrants waved until Peggie and their father were hidden by the hedgerows; but even then they knew they would still be standing at the gate, listening for the last sounds of the wheels on the stony road.

The station at Queenstown was built at the water's edge. It was made of red brick, had a glass and wrought-iron roof and an air of bustle. The train hissed as it broke steam. The place was full of smoke, the rumbling of trolleys, porters' whistles, and the voices of the newly arrived asking directions to the shipping agent's office. Names were passed around – of the best lodging houses in which to spend their last night in Ireland; of the best shops for purchasing eating utensils and other necessaries for the voyage.

Tom found the Walsh trunk, hoisted it on his shoulders and pushed his way through the throng. Then he and Maria walked out of the station and up the hill to the town. The wind blew Maria's hood down and her hair into her eyes.

'Isn't that thing heavy?' she asked, clutching her hood at her throat so that it secured her heavy brown hair.

Tom laughed. 'Now, Maria, you know perfectly well there's nothing much in it!'

Queenstown was filled with the voice of the sea and the harsh cry of the gulls. The town rose above the visitors as they approached from the station: Victorian houses in tiers above the harbour, and rising above them the walls of the new cathedral that was under construction.

Tom and Maria joined the queue at the shipping agent's office. Eventually, their tickets were inspected and retained. They handed over their trunk; it would be put on board for them. There followed a cursory medical examination. Then all they had to do was find themselves accommodation for the night. Their ship, the SS *Samaria*, would arrive tomorrow.

The next morning they rose early and joined the eager crowd in the harbour who were awaiting the shipping agent. The port was full of tall ships, dipping and rising in the gentle swell; voices of sailors, hawkers and passengers rose on the salty air; a lone piper started up a lament on the uilleann pipes. Word went around that the SS *Samaria* had arrived, that she was anchored off Roches Point. A tender would take her passengers to her. People stood on tiptoe to look to the distant mouth of the bay.

Tom was aware of the smell of the sea and the screeching of the sea birds. He occupied himself by watching the huge canvas mailbags being delivered to the quay, and loaded on to one of the tenders that plied the harbour. Then he turned his attention to the ships, studying their lines and the complexity of their rigging with intent curiosity. The SS *Samaria*, he knew, was equipped with sails as well as steam.

There was a sense of unreality about this hour before embarkation. Years before, Tom had decided that all the anger in the world was futile; that success was the reward of inexorable patience. But his mind was feverish now. Doubt had replaced euphoria; fear nagged at him. What if he were being presumptuous? What if he failed, if Vandermeer didn't want him after all, or found his skills old-fashioned? What if he couldn't send money home? What if he and Maria went hungry in a foreign land? He thought of his father, left behind in Carraig Mór with Peggie. How must it feel to know you had little prospect of ever seeing your children again?

It had been bad enough after Michael's precipitous departure. There had been an initial relief: at least he was safe from arrest and imprisonment, or worse. But then had come the realisation that Michael's energy and fire were also gone from their lives. His father never took down his fiddle now; he had taken to sitting morosely by the fire.

'I'll stay at home, Father,' Tom had repeated just the week before his departure, 'if that's what you would really like me to do.'

But Seán had changed. Life had broken him and he saw no reason why it should be permitted to do the same to his children. He shook his head.

'You'd never rest easy here. Your brother was right: the young should not be sacrificed to the old. I can manage this place myself. Seamus Farrelly will help when I need it.'

This was true enough. They were no longer growing crops such as wheat and barley to pay the rent – the British market was glutted with cheap imports – but there was still a market for mutton and beef. So sheep now grazed the former wheatfield of the Walsh farm.

Tom tried to read the future in the wild sky over Cork harbour. So much depended on him that success was not an option. But he knew he was nineteen, knowing nothing of the world, his assumptions predicated on a narrow experience. He had nothing to assure the future except his courage. He gritted his teeth against the nagging fear. *I will. I will, I will . . .*

He turned and walked back along the harbour to where Maria was waiting. She was talking to another woman, her cloak flapping in the sea breeze despite her attempts to draw it tightly around her. He watched her for a moment, saw the dull flush in her face, then asked gently in her ear, 'How are you, little sister? You look tired.'

She gave a nervous laugh. 'I'm just frightened. I didn't sleep much last night. Right now I think I'd rather wait here for ever and watch the goings-on than take that ship.'

She gestured to the woman beside her, 'This is Mrs Teresa Blake. Her husband is the gentleman over there in the black coat.'

Tom followed the direction of her gaze and saw a middle-aged man, hands clasped behind his back, standing at the edge of the quay and staring into the water. He had his hat in his hand; his coat bulged in the wind, but he seemed oblivious to his surroundings. Maria dropped her voice and added in tones of respect, 'He's a *teacher*. They'll be travelling with us.'

Tom took Mrs Blake's outstretched hand, noting the large green eyes in the pinched face.

'Pleased to meet you, ma'am.'

When her husband turned his head in their direction their new acquaintance called out, 'Denis, here are two young people who are travelling on the *Samaria.*'

Denis approached. He was fortyish, with shoulders a little stooped, reminding Tom for a moment of his father. He had grey hair, with a snowy wing at his right temple, and whiskers, still russet, covering most of his cheeks. The corners of his white wing collar set off an open and authoritarian face. He smiled as he was introduced, and Tom noted, as they shook hands, that his were the hands of a gentleman.

'Where are you from, Mr Blake?' Tom asked.

'Crosshaven.'

'But why are you going to America,' Maria demanded diffidently, 'when you're a teacher?'

She reddened at the look Tom gave her. His standards for everything – for himself, for his work, for social conduct – were high. She wanted to make him proud of her. She was aware of how tall he stood, his blue eyes intent, and the red of his hair bright in the sunshine.

'I *was* a teacher until I taught my pupils some Irish history!' Denis replied, untroubled by her curiosity. 'But I have no future as a teacher here now!'

'Why not?'

'Because our history is outlawed, young lady, like our language. Didn't you know that? Didn't it ever strike you as strange when you were at school that not one single lesson was ever taught about your country's past?'

Maria flushed, a crimson that stained her face to her hairline. She was ashamed of having had such a truncated schooling and envied anyone in possession of an education. But, before she could murmur a response, Teresa said in a raised and bitter voice that filled her face with fire and momentarily silenced the crowd around her: 'Sure wouldn't it be grand and convenient if the *whole lot of us* left the country – or, better still, if we *died*!'

Tom, watching the life flood her green eyes, realised that once this woman had been beautiful, no doubt the proud boast of her countryside, and he knew, as he glanced at Denis, that in her husband's eyes she still was.

Denis put a hand on her arm. 'Whisht, Teresa, love. Don't be upsetting yourself . . .'

'My wife isn't herself,' he said to Tom a few minutes later. 'We lost our only child last year and she's still in a bad way over it. All we have left is her parents . . . But we couldn't take them on this journey, even if they would have come.' He glanced tenderly at his spouse. 'I'm hoping the Californian climate will put the roses back in her cheeks.'

'Have you family there?' Tom asked.

'A cousin of mine runs a boarding house in San Francisco. She and her husband went out there in '49.' He gave a low chuckle. 'They went after the gold, God help them!'

'Did they find any?'

The man laughed. 'Och, not an ounce.' His eyes met Tom's with sly humour. ' 'Tis much easier sought than found!'

Teresa whispered to Maria, as though ashamed of her outburst, 'I'm sorry. I'm that tired and contrary I hardly know what I'm doing.'

'Sure why wouldn't you be?' Maria replied. ' 'Tis mortal far to be going. But when we get there, sure we'll wonder why we were ever afraid.' Maria wondered at her own words. She had only said them to console someone, but it occurred to her suddenly that if you believed in something maybe it happened. 'Remember that however hard it is . . . saying goodbye . . . there'll be a grand new place to live in America.'

But she did not really believe her own counsel. America was a place she had never seen. It might as well be on the moon, and her heart felt hot at the strangeness of it. And soon it would be too late for any change in plan. At this moment they could still return to Carraig Mór, live out their lives where they were born, like the girl from Clonmel who had recently caused a certain amount of hilarity. She had gone to Liverpool to embark for New York, but when her ship had arrived off Roches Point, en route for the New World, the sight of the Irish coast had changed her mind, and she had insisted on coming ashore. Her family, who had wept at her departure, and indebted themselves to provide her with a ticket, were bewildered when she arrived back on the doorstep.

But a glance at her brother's face assured Maria that they would not be following her example.

She heard Mr Blake ask Tom, 'Have you a trade, young man? America is a great place for a man who can use his hands.'

'I'm a millwright.'

Maria intervened proudly: 'Tom can build anything.'

'Well, in that case you'll have no bother at all finding work. They're crying out for builders over there. You know their houses are all made of wood!'

Maria remembered what Michael had said in one of his letters: 'The houses are made of wood, and the roofs of shingles, and divil a thatch from here to eternity!'

'Tom has a job waiting for him,' she said. 'There's people called Vandermeer expecting us in Boston. Mr Vandermeer owns a building business and Tom is to work for him. I'm to be their parlourmaid . . .' She looked at her audience uncertainly. 'What exactly does a parlourmaid do, Mrs Blake?'

'Sure they'll show you. Serve at table and dust the place. That sort of thing.'

The government emigration agent arrived, consulted with his clerk, took his fob watch from his waistcoat pocket and glanced at it. He was a portly man with a brown moustache that stuck out along his upper lip like a brush. When he mounted his platform a hush descended; every face looked up expectantly. He cleared his throat, held up his list and began calling out names at the top of his voice.

'. . . Liam McCarthy, Seamus and Anne O'Shea, Cornelius and Mrs O'Callagan, Denis and Mrs Blake . . .'

Tom saw his new friends prepare to make their way forward for their boarding passes. The agent's sonorous voice droned on; he had almost finished his list before he said the words the intently listening duo from Carraig Mór had been waiting for: '. . . Thomas and Maria Walsh . . .'

Maria clapped her hands to her mouth. Her heart was filled with panic. She saw that Tom's face was intense and that his eyes had darkened until they were almost violet. He put a hand on her arm.

'It will be all right, Maria, I promise you.'

The panic ebbed and she laughed.

Later, on board, the smoke from the funnels staining the sky, they watched the land slip by as the ship sailed along the south coast of Ireland to the Atlantic. In the distance they saw the Old Head of Kinsale, Seven Heads, Clear Island, Mizen Head, places known by repute, and now as dear as though always familiar. They were the last glimpses of home.

The wind stiffened as the ship slipped into the ocean. Tom stood beside his sister in silence as the Irish coastline disappeared below the horizon.

'I wonder – will we ever see it again?' she whispered. 'Our Ireland?'

'I'll come back, anyway! There's a few promises I have to keep . . .'

Maria turned to her brother and shook her head. 'I know the promises you mean,' she whispered. 'But there's a long road ahead of you, Tom Walsh! For I think Daddy will be long gone, and Lord Kilduncan too, before you ever set foot again in Ireland.'

'Why do you say that, miss? Isn't there ships going over and back almost every day of the week?'

His eyes were narrowed, as though trying to glimpse the mysteries of the future, but in reality he was afraid of the swelling that was closing his throat. Maria gripped her hood around her face, let her cloak billow into the wind, and listened to the growling, ever repeating, swish of the sea.

'Because it won't be as easy as you think, Tom Walsh, that's why. But maybe you'll do strange things in America!'

Tom glanced down at her and broke the tension with a chuckle. 'Maybe I will! Maybe the great thing about life is its total uncertainty!' Then he added, 'Sure you can always look into the fire again, like you did long ago.'

Maria frowned. 'Father Doyle told me to stop. You can do it yourself!'

Tom gave a teasing laugh. 'I wouldn't know how . . .'

She held his eyes and said in a slow deliberate voice, 'Hold out your hands.'

Tom extended his right hand.

'Both of them. Cup them together.'

He obeyed, raising his eyebrows, smiling. Maria put her two small hands into his open ones as though depositing something into their care.

'I give my gift to you.'

She closed her hands over his, pressing them together. Tom would have laughed out loud but that his sister's face was serious.

That night, lying on his bunk in the men's dormitory, Tom dreamed of a winding road among snow-capped mountains. It was bitterly cold. In the cry of the wind he distinguished a refrain, repeated over and over. With a start he identified it: *Ór*.

He woke to the pitching of the ship, the howl of the wind, and the snores of his compatriots. He was half frozen; his blanket had slipped to the floor and he retrieved it. '*Ór*,' he whispered sleepily under his breath, and repeated it in English: 'Gold . . .'

Once out to sea, the hell began. The wind screamed like a million banshees bunched together in a bag; the ship rolled. Timbers groaned, people kept to their bunks, were seasick. Provisions brought from home – brown bread, salt bacon, cheese – succumbed in a matter of days to thick green mould. After a week everything was damp and rimed with salt. Nothing could be dried. The stench was overwhelming. Tom was sick but, to his surprise, Maria was a better sailor.

'Just go along with it,' she told him as he staggered to find his bunk. 'Let it take you. If you try to fight it you're done for!'

But this same advice did nothing for Teresa Blake, who lay on her bunk as day followed day. She could keep nothing in her stomach and now refused to eat either the rations provided by the ship or the titbits her husband, and others of the passengers, pressed on her.

'I'll be grand when we get to land,' she told Maria.

Denis spent much of the time trying to write. He had a box with him, in which he kept pen, ink and paper, and would often reach for it, saying with a wry grin, 'I'm keeping an account of this journey, for if there's one thing certain in this life it's that I'll never do it again!' But the rough weather made writing impossible, and eventually the box was locked and put away under the bunk.

Maria watched over Mrs Blake.

'You have to eat something,' she said. 'Teresa, you'll lose your strength if you don't!'

'Ah, sure I'm fine,' the woman said, accepting the cup of water Maria handed her. 'How much further is America?'

'Another week.'

'We've already been at sea for almost two!'

The wind quietened after a few days. The hardier passengers went up on the third-class deck to take the air, among them Tom and Denis.

When they returned to the crowded salon someone demanded with a laugh: 'Mr Blake, is there e'er a sign of Americay yet? Or is it around in circles we're going?'

Denis replied, 'There's nothing to see except the waves. For all we know we could still be off Mizen Head!'

'I could swim home so,' someone offered in lugubrious tones. 'I forgot me teeth!'

'Ah, don't do that, Pat!' came the response to general laughter. 'Sure you'd only dazzle us with your beauty!'

Tom looked around. The passengers were playing cards, or talking, divided into roughly ethnic groups, and sounding like the Tower of Babel: Irish, English, German voices. In a corner a group was watching the fiddler Johnny Gallagher tune his instrument with a staccato *plink, plunk* of strings.

'Give us an oul' reel, Johnny, before the wind gets goin' again . . .?'

A space was cleared, benches pushed back. 'I'll give ye "The Walls of Limerick"!' Johnny cried, and in a moment the cleared floor was alive with dance. The young people moved forwards and backwards in the age-old precision steps, faster and faster, and every girl linked her arm to her partner so that they whirled and retreated. Tom and Maria joined in, laughing while Denis Blake looked on. Maria left the dance and pulled him by the hand.

'Come on, Mr Blake, it'll do you good.'

Denis was soon breathless. He had not danced a reel for years, not since the early days of his marriage when he had put his hands on his young wife's waist and she had laughed into his eyes.

'Do you think I could see Teresa for a moment?' he asked Maria when, pink and panting, she retired from the fray. 'Now might be a good time . . .'

Maria led him to the women's dormitory, put her head in, and saw that it was empty except for Teresa, who lay awake in the dim yellow light of a solitary lantern. She was passing rosary beads through her hands. The music could be heard here too, but overlain by the straining, heaving sound of the ship.

Teresa's face lit up at the sight of her husband.

'I was just thinking how grand it is to hear the music,' she said with a smile. 'I made me think of the old days . . . But I'm beginning to wonder if America really exists at all! I suppose this is how St Brendan felt when he crossed the ocean in his little boat!'

Denis reached for her hand. 'How are you at all, *a stór*?' He moistened a handkerchief from her small container of water and tenderly wiped her brow. 'Are you feeling any better?'

She smiled at him. 'Ah, that's nice, Denis, thank you. Sure I'll be better soon.'

The wind freshened; the dance ended; the passengers ate their frugal suppers, then drifted away to their bunks.

Denis and Tom looked at each other. The former was wearing his reading spectacles and had a book in his hands; the latter, with pencil and paper, was drawing the outlines of a tool that could be used to groove timber. The ship lurched suddenly, and his pencil scrawled across the paper.

Denis put his book down. 'It's the devil's business, trying to read in this commotion . . .'

He looked expectantly at Maria as she returned from a visit to the women's dormitory.

'Teresa is sleeping now,' she said.

She sat beside Tom, took from a bag under the bench a shirt and needle and thread.

'Aren't you the right *amadán* to tear your good shirt,' she said crossly, surveying the rent in the sleeve.

She began to sew, trying to overhear the men's conversation. But the sea was heavy and her back hurt from the wooden seat against which she was thrown every time the vessel rolled. She pricked her finger and threw down the shirt with an exclamation, sucking the small wound.

'I've put blood on your new shirt!'

'Sure it won't do it one bit of harm,' Tom said, inspecting the small crimson drop. 'It'll give it a bit of colour!' He took her hand, examined the finger. 'Are you badly damaged?'

'I'll live!'

He turned back to Denis and resumed their conversation.

'And how will you get to California? Is there a railroad?'

'There's one just about completed, but I think it will be very costly. It's cheaper to go by covered wagon, but it's a long trek that takes months.'

'Mr Blake,' Maria said archly, 'I hope you're not putting notions into Tom's head?'

He turned to smile at her. 'Isn't he young and strong, Maria? He would do well out West. Land is still there for the taking.'

When it became clear the men were mutually engrossed and that sewing was increasingly hazardous, Maria said good night and went back to the dormitory. Teresa woke and Maria put her arm around her.

'Keep thinking,' she said to the sick woman, 'about where you're going, the sky and the warmth and the valleys. Imagine yourself there in the pure air, with a grand place to live. Don't be thinking at all about this oul' bucket.'

Teresa nodded. 'Girleen, I know where I'm going,' she said after a moment.

Next morning Maria woke early. She heard the snores of the other women and listened for Teresa's breathing, but she could not distinguish it.

'Teresa,' she whispered, 'are you all right?'

There was no response. Maria slipped from her bunk and went to her.

The woman was lying stiffly. Her eyes were open, her hands across her breast. Maria touched her. She was cold. She's been dead for hours, Maria thought, the tears starting in her eyes. She died without as much as a whimper!

She pulled on her dress and went to find Mr Blake.

Denis came through the small crowd of women that were now surrounding Teresa's body. He bent over his wife, whispered her name. The arms with which he gathered up the corpse trembled. '*A mhuirnín dílis . . .*' he whispered. 'My dear and only love, you promised you'd outlive me.'

'It's God's will,' one of the women said gently. 'He knows best.'

'*Knows best?*' Denis spat the words and turned to look at the speaker with wild eyes. 'Will you answer me this – where is this God? Why has He forsaken us? A Christian people for one and a half thousand years – what have we done that we should know only famine, exile and death?'

The woman made the sign of the Cross.

'There is no God!' Denis cried, and his despair filled the regions below deck, momentarily drowning the noise of the elements.

Teresa Blake was buried at sea that evening during a lull in the wind, but the rain still beat on the slippery deck. A priest recited Prayers for the Dead, and led the mourners in the Five Sorrowful Mysteries of the Rosary. Denis leaned on a capstan as though in a trance. When the words, 'We now commit her body to the deep', were spoken and the body was slipped into the sea, he suddenly retched, but as there was nothing in his stomach all he produced was green bile. As though on cue, the wind began to rise again.

A sailor approached Tom with a tot of rum. 'Give him this,' he said. 'Get him below now as we're in for another squall.'

Below decks Denis waved away the rum. Tom sat beside his friend and waited for him to talk, but the hours went by and the older man remained monosyllabic, responding in starts to attempts to comfort him.

Next morning, when Tom saw that Denis's bunk was empty, he got up and went to look for him. In the salon a group of men sat playing cards. One of them cursed when the sudden sideways lurch of the ship sent the cards flying to the floor.

'Have you seen Mr Blake?' Tom asked.

'He went up on deck about twenty minutes ago,' one card-player replied. Another, stooping to pick up the cards, added, 'He hadn't a word out of him. Poor oul' divil looked a bit drawn . . .'

Tom thrust his way up the ship's ladder. The wind knocked the breath from him; but the deck was empty in the grey dawn.

It was much later that Tom found the note that Denis had left under his pillow. It was folded over a small, iron key.

Dear Tom and Maria,

It has been a pleasure knowing you both. I am very grateful for your company and for Maria's kindness to Teresa, which has helped make this terrible journey bearable. I don't know where tired souls go, but wherever it is I'm going to follow her there. I have no heart left in me, so judge me gently.

My box is yours now, and everything that's in it. I hope it will help you both. If there is anything you want from our trunk it's yours also.

God bless you and keep you.

Denis Blake

Tom took Denis's writing box from under the bunk and opened it. Beneath a small sheaf of paper he found a pocketbook. When he opened it he exclaimed aloud.

'What is it?' Maria asked.

Tom counted the wad of money into his sister's lap.

'A Dhia,' she cried, 'two hundred dollars! And to think they were travelling steerage . . .'

'It was probably all they had,' Tom said. 'They would have wanted to conserve it.' He looked at his sister. 'We'll have to send it back to the old people they left behind.'

'But, Tom, he said it was for us! And we don't know where to find their people.'

'The parish priest at Crosshaven will know.' He looked at his sister's wistful face, trying to contain his anger and grief. 'Maria, we have to do what is right. We cannot take this money; there'd be no luck in it. God knows how their old people are at this very moment; God knows how they will be when they get the terrible news. While we are young and strong, and have our lives ahead of us.'

Maria bit her lip. She wanted to say, 'Strong? You should see yourself. You're getting thin as a herring with the bones standing out of your shoulders.' But all she said was, 'All right.'

Later, after the inquiry about the missing passenger, and the conclusion that he was lost overboard, Tom gave the box into the custody of the captain, who undertook to return it to Crosshaven with notification of the two deaths.

A week later Tom and Maria Walsh took their first steps on to the wooden pier of Castle Garden. Situated at the edge of Manhattan Battery, it was the first immigrant receiving station and boasted an information centre, a labour exchange and a money exchange.

The two young people stood for a moment and gazed around them at the bustling landing depot that was full of the rumble of porters' trolleys and the buzz of hundreds of voices. There were hordes, it seemed, of tired people with wooden boxes and bedrolls.

Maria touched her brother's arm.

'We have come to a different world,' she said in a tight, awed voice, indicating the forest of shipping masts and the paddle steamers in the harbour. 'Did you ever in your born days see the like of it?'

Tom drank in the strangeness, the masts of hundreds of ships, the steamers, the sonorous boom of shipping horns, the hoists and cranes, the sense of limitless wealth beyond anything he had imagined. Into these considerations there suddenly intruded the memory of a small whitewashed cabin and a lonely boreen. He thought of a forsaken, ageing man and a young girl. He thought of a lonely grave under a pile of stone.

When he did not reply his sister asked him gently: 'What are you thinking of?'

'Ah, I was just wondering,' he said shakily, indicating the miles of sheds and warehouses, 'if there was any place at all I could find some ribbons for Peggie's hair!'

By the time they came to Boston they were so tired they felt they were dreaming on their feet. The journey from New York had taken the last of their resources and they had not eaten for more than a day. They left their trunk at the depot and walked. Hunger gnawed at them and every stable they passed seemed to invite them to lie on its straw and sleep. Everything was strange – streets full of well-dressed people; ladies in hooped dresses; omnibuses; carriages; stores full of every kind of merchandise. It was like stepping between the pages of a storybook.

They found the home of Mr and Mrs Carl Vandermeer, an imposing, red-brick house with a flight of steps to the front door. An aproned woman was cleaning the basement windows. They stood uncertainly at the steps.

'Mrs Vandermeer?' Tom said uncertainly.

The woman turned, stared up at the two famished-looking young people in tired clothes, the youth with his red hair, the girl in the dark blue cloak with the strange frilled hood.

'Mrs Vandermeer is not at home.'

'And Mr Vandermeer?' Tom asked.

'He's at the sawmill.'

'Where is the sawmill, ma'am?'

The woman put down her cleaning rag. 'What's it to you?'

Maria said desperately, 'I've come about the parlourmaid's position . . .'

'It's taken. Our new girl will be with us any day.'

Maria's eyes filled with tears. She would have turned away, but she felt suddenly weak and sank down on the steps.

'Perhaps we should introduce ourselves, ma'am?' Tom said quietly. 'Our name is Walsh. I am a carpenter and am to work for Mr Vandermeer. This is my sister, Maria. We're just come from Ireland.'

Years afterwards Maria would recall the hot bath, the new uniform, the small, spotless bedroom with its patchwork quilt which was to be hers. She would recall how Mrs Clarkson, the housekeeper, had suddenly become an angel, so that by the time Mrs Vandermeer returned Maria was as neat as could be, with her newly washed hair coiffed under a cap, and her starched white apron crisp over a black dress. She had also eaten the first omelette of her life.

'Two eggs!' she exclaimed in awe as she watched the housekeeper prepare it. 'For one person! Sure 'twould be pure sin.'

'Don't talk nonsense, girl. You have to eat to live.'

Later she was introduced to her employer, a stern-looking matron in a black dress with lace at her throat.

'What a pretty young woman you are,' she said. 'But you're very thin; are you quite healthy?'

'I am, ma'am. It's just the journey . . .'

'Of course. Your duties will start tomorrow. Take the rest of the day off and rest. Tomorrow Mrs Clarkson will show you everything.'

Tom started in the sawmills. He was at home as soon as he smelled the heavy resinous dust and felt the saw bite under his hand. He noted the scale of things with interest, the abundance of the tools, the great band saw, tensioned by two pulleys, with its large flexible steel blade in the form of a loop. It cut logs into boards as though they had been made of butter.

He was lodging in a boarding house nearby that had been built by his employer to house his workers.

Mr Vandermeer was a balding middle-aged man with a Puritan work ethic and an honest mind. He watched his latest employee closely for the first few days. But he saw, as the time passed, that the youth was capable of intense concentration and that his skills were excellent. He also noted that other young workers began to look up to Tom, that he possessed some kind of innate authority. Foreman material maybe, his employer thought.

Maria, meanwhile, was becoming a parlourmaid, and exclaimed privately at the wonders of silver and lace.

'You must set the cutlery like so,' Mrs Clarkson told her. 'When people are dining they start from the outside. Isn't it the same in Ireland?'

'In Ireland,' Maria replied, 'sure we don't worry too much about it. We just do our best to stay alive.'

Within a year Tom had been promoted. But as time went on his sister realised he was increasingly restless.

'What is it, Tom?' she asked him one Sunday afternoon as they strolled together down Beacon Hill and admired the beautiful Georgian houses of Boston's patriarchs. She considered his brooding face. 'What's eating you? Every time there is a letter from home you get like this. Father and Peggie are both well . . .'

There was a stone bench on the Common. She sat down, drew the letter from her pocket, and read aloud from it.

'Father and I are in the best of good health, so don't be worrying your head about us. Thank you for the money, but don't be sending so much. You need it yourselves . . .'

'I want to send them some real money, Maria. I mean enough to buy a really fine place.'

Maria looked at her brother with a great deal of love. 'You've only been here ten months. You've saved sixty dollars. Is it pure daft you are?'

After a while she added, 'Do you still want to go West?'

'Yes.'

Maria shook her head. 'But you're doing fine here; Mr Vandermeer has made you a foreman. And you agreed to stay for two years.'

'I'll honour my agreement. But then, Maria, I'm going West.'

'Where exactly do you want to go?'

'To the territory of Colorado.'

'I suppose you think you'll find gold or something!' she said bitterly. 'I may never see you again.'

'Maria, half the world is rushing to Colorado. There is a new railroad being built there; they need men with skills. And I have skills. Come out with me.'

'I don't want to die at the end of an Indian tomahawk!'

Tom threw his head back and laughed. 'Oh, ye of little faith! Tell me, what has happened to the excellent forecasting you used to do on my account – the great wonders you said I would achieve in America? Or have you changed your mind?'

Maria shrugged as though the subject embarrassed her. 'I never used the word *great*,' she muttered, as Tom watched her affectionately. 'I only ever said it would be something very strange. And I am afraid of what that thing might be, Tom, if you want to know the truth. Because I think that everything comes with a price tag attached to it.'

'Oh, let it,' Tom said expansively. 'I don't mind paying a fair price for anything.' After a moment's silence he added, 'There's something I have to do, something I have to find.'

Maria regarded him doubtfully. He laughed at her expression and added, 'The problem is – I don't know what it is or where I'm supposed to find it!'

But Maria changed her mind about leaving. The lure of the West affected her too; above all she did not want to stay behind when her brother was gone. It took them longer than anticipated to prepare for their journey, but when Tom took his leave of the Vandermeers she went with him.

It was March 1872. They had been almost three years in America.

Chapter Three

Tom took out the sheet of writing paper he had folded in his pocket. He said to himself as he moistened his pencil: 'I suppose the strangest thing about the plains is the limitless sky. How do I describe it?'

He wanted to respond to the latest letter from home now that he had a chance. He read it for the tenth time.

Dear Tom and Maria,

Thank you for writing again so soon, and for the money. Daddy and I are both well. I was able to get him a new coat in Clonmel. We've had the thatch done too, so we were grand and snug for the winter.

I'm worried about you going on that long journey to Colorado. People have been telling us terrible things – about how fierce the Indians are and how you have to hold on to the top of your head in case they make off with it! I hope that's not true, for as you know well there's some in this parish would tell you anything.

Seamus Farrelly is a great tower of strength. If there's a thing needs doing he has it done before either Father or myself can turn around. He cleared the ditches in the old meadow, and now the spot where it used to flood is grand and dry. He was great with the lambing.

We've had thirty lambs, and the old wheatfield is full of their bleating. One of them was so poorly when it was born that it couldn't feed, so I took it into the kitchen and gave it a little bed by the fire, and fed it from a bottle. It's grand now, but the poor little creature thinks I'm its mother and follows me around – just like the old nursery rhyme. Seamie Farrelly thinks it's all very funny and calls it 'Bealín Bocht', but my lamb doesn't take one bit of heed of his insults.

Daddy says to look after yourselves. Write as often as you can. I want to hear everything about the journey, but don't be sending money all the time. You need it for yourselves and your new life.

Your loving sister, Peggie

PS, I did as you asked and approached Neddie Nolan, the mason, about the price of a headstone for Mother's grave. He said 'twould depend on what we wanted. A fine Celtic Cross in limestone, with an inscription, is the most expensive – about £5. It includes the cost of putting stone edging to the grave.

Tom folded the letter and put it away in his pocket, then began his letter home: 'Dearest Father and Peggie, I'm here in the middle of America.'

He was dissatisfied with this start. He loved, when writing home, to describe things with something of their atmosphere, and now the words were sluggish.

He sighed, looked up at the sunset, smelled the woodsmoke from the camp stoves and fires. He was tired and dusty after a long day, but replete from his dinner of beans and potatoes. He was due to come on guard duty at sundown. He was already three hundred miles into his journey West. They had passed Fort Kearny, had rested about two miles from the fort in a place where grass, wood and water had been plentiful. Here they had attended to resetting the wagon tires and whatever other repairs were called for.

Because he had been hired to help drive the wagons, the trip for both Tom and Maria had cost only a hundred dollars; in addition there had been the price of a new horse, a set of tools and some spares, a saddle, a tent and a new rifle – his prized lever-action Spencer with which he was now something of a marksman.

They had made the long journey from Boston to St Louis, Missouri, where the journey West had begun, mostly by rail, and had seen for themselves the great confluence of the Missouri and Mississippi rivers, the riverboats moored side by side almost as far as the eye could see, and crates, barrels and boxes stacked along the levee. They had travelled up the Missouri to Independence. The wide streets of this city, like those of St Louis, were filled with emigrants and their covered wagons, soldiers and adventurers bound for the West. Merchants sold flour, cured bacon, wagons, tents, canvas, guns, horses, and everything necessary for the journey.

Tom had signed the rules of the company with which they travelled: no swearing, no drinking, and the Sabbath must be observed.

' 'Tis little enough to expect!' Maria had exclaimed, prepared to append her signature but then found that hers was unnecessary. Only the men need sign.

There must be women somewhere able to swear and drink with the best of them! she'd thought, but she'd let it pass. It was, after all, a kind of compliment.

There were twenty families travelling West on this wagon train, as well

40

as four single men and a few hired hands, such as the scout Ted Lafferty, who had made the journey many times. Maria helped with the children, and gave lessons to the little ones, using slates to write the alphabet.

They had missed the preceding wagon train – with which they had originally arranged to travel – and had had to wait in Independence for a week while they negotiated their trip with the next one. But the time had passed pleasantly, everyone giving them advice about the journey, about the plains and the Rocky Mountains, until they dreamed only of the trip ahead.

Now they were well into their marathon and already the white bonnets of the wagons had turned a dull grey from the dust of the plains. These wagons were now corralled for the evening to form a protective circle around the tents, with the tongue of each securing the wagon in front. It was within this circle that the families slept in their tents at night. The men took turns standing guard; two of them were on duty at all times, alert for Indians or wolves.

Tom loved the great wagons, and he loved their name – prairie schooners – and would roll it privately on his tongue. He thought their construction a marvel. Empty, each of them weighed 1,300 pounds, was approximately ten feet long, four feet wide and two feet deep. The cover was a double thickness of white canvas, tied down and overlapped in the back, supported by five bows of white oak, which had been soaked until pliable and then bent to fit. The hardwood wheels were of two different sizes, fifty inches diameter in the back and forty-four in the front; they were bound in iron, and their hubs screwed into iron skein axles. There was a wooden brake block controlled by a lever to the right of the driver's seat.

The wagon 'box' – the part of the wagon where people and goods were carried – was made of hardwood too, and caulked so that it could be used as a boat. It was bevelled outwards at the sides to keep out water in the event of a river crossing.

Now Tom leaned back against the spokes of a wheel, moistened his pencil again.

Don't imagine for a moment, *he wrote*, that this is hardship; 'tis grand beyond belief – the world around us as God made it – oceans of tall blue-stemmed grass, a great sky that is mostly blue, but sometimes it clouds over and then you'd think the whole world was under a blanket. Our worst problem is the dust, for it rises in clouds when the train is moving, and everyone behind the lead wagon has to keep their mouths shut (an awful effect on conversation, Peggie, but I can tell you that the women make up for it in the evenings when we camp! Maria is not famous for her silence here either; you can hear her laughter from one end of the camp to the other).

41

On the move the train is a sight to behold, thirty white-topped wagons moving one behind each other across six hundred miles of the flattest land you can imagine. We have had no trouble so far, except for a few broken axles and a cracked wheel which I was able to mend. One of our people is sick with dysentery, but will recover, I think, for he has a devoted wife who never leaves his side.

But why is it that, although I do appreciate the wonder of this empty place, I cannot help longing for sight of something resembling a hill?

He laughed to himself when he thought of his sister. He could almost hear her say: 'Lord God Almighty, the place is flat as a tombstone for six hundred miles!'

Maria, *he continued,* says she wonders if we'll ever get a place fit to live in. I suspect she's sorry she didn't stay in Boston with the Vandermeers. I suppose she's told you that she lived in a grand house with polished floors of the finest wood and had her own room and plenty of free time and served coffee from a silver pot? Now she's travelling with one of the families here, and finds the lurching of the wagons is not to her liking. But she denies she's gotten used to luxury and claims she's not one bit afraid of the Indians. In fact, although there are Cheyenne to the north and Pawnee to the south, we now see little of them. Sometimes they sit at bridges and look for a toll and sometimes they visit us when we camp, dressed in breechclouts and carrying their bows and arrows, but so far I have detected no hostility.

We're in far more danger, I think, from the unexpected rattlesnakes – which are rare on this route, but none the less virulent, as a young member of our company discovered recently. The boy – James Bryant – was bitten on the arm by a rattler that had crept under one of the wagons during the night. Our scout, Mr Lafferty, saved his life by tying a ligature above the affected flesh and sucking the poison from the wound. (He spat it out, Peggie!) The flesh around the wound had already turned black, but the boy will live.

I wish I could send you more money with this letter, but I won't be earning any more for some time, although they say there's gold and silver jumping out of the ground at you in Colorado; thousands of people have flocked there, at any rate, hoping to strike it rich, but I'm not such an *amadán* to pin my hopes on something so dependent on chance. I'm going there to build the new railroad.

Something moved on the horizon. Tom had his hand on his rifle immediately. What was it – buffalo, antelope, wolf? Or human? It disappeared from sight, and he stood to watch for a moment, putting into his pocket his unfinished missive, aware of the smells around him – axle grease, the linseed oil used to weatherproof canvas, drifts of woodsmoke. Voices, laughter, came on the light breeze; a child cried suddenly and was comforted. A dog yelped. Beyond the camp were the horses; on arrival the teams had been released from shafts and tethers to graze, but were now tied to long lariat ropes, attached to picket pins driven into the ground. They were still grazing peacefully, flicking their tails and tearing mouthfuls from the prairie.

He skinned his eyes until the distance became only a shimmer of approaching night. Nothing stirred except the wind in the long grass.

Wilhelm Schmidt, known as Willie, who would be sharing the first watch with him, came walking round the wagons. He was a little older than Tom, two years in America, and now going out West to farm in California.

'Well, Tom, looks like we'll have another quiet night.'

Tom nodded. 'Maybe. I thought just this moment I saw something on the horizon. But it's gone.'

Willie squinted into the distance. 'I see nothing. But if there's Indians out there the horses will tell us quicker than the dogs!'

They both glanced at the horses, but the animals were grazing quietly and did not evince any interest in the darkening landscape.

The two men walked around the camp's periphery, and joined the other men and the leader of the train, Captain Hartigan, for the evening's meeting. The latter had a map out on a table, beside a lantern. In the yellow light the scout, Ted Lafferty, dressed in fringed buckskin, and sporting a grizzled moustache, pointed out the road ahead with a stubby finger.

'Quicksands!' he exclaimed, bringing his index finger down on a spot on the map. 'You see here, where the river bends? Anyone who doesn't keep to the road, who thinks he can ford the river, will go right into them.'

The captain nodded. He turned to Tom. 'Tom, will you take the Warners' wagon tomorrow? Frank is still poorly and I don't want his wife driving that team.'

Tom nodded. 'Sure.'

'We'll strike camp at first light,' Captain Hartigan continued. 'Ted here says that the train in front of ours is just one day's travel away now. They were delayed at Fort Kearny. If we hurry we should be able to catch up with them tomorrow. The more of us travel together the better for everyone!'

The men checked their horses, saw that their tethers were secure; if they were stolen or wandered off, the wagon train would be stranded, sitting ducks for mischance or hostile Indians.

Sounds in the camp gradually died; a woman's scolding voice rose and fell; someone hummed a lullaby. After a while everything was still.

Tom spent his time on watch imagining the wild West. There would be vast mountains in Colorado and terrible winters. But forests abounded and wood was free – you could log what you needed; building lots cost little or nothing, and cabins could be built for a small outlay. With his tools he had also brought a substantial supply of nails. By the time the snow came, if everything went to plan, he and Maria would have a home of their own.

When he was relieved by the next watch, Tom lay on his bed roll under one of the supply wagons, his saddle under his head, and drifted to sleep immediately. But after a while he woke, muttering, from a dream; in it he had seen his father's haggard face and the whitewashed cabin that had been his home, heard the sound of a battering ram against the wall. Peggie, a child in the dream, pale and thin, lisped that she wanted some ribbons for her hair. He heard the hoarse breathing of the horses, and their shuffling and the tearing sounds of their now desultory grazing. The sense of the limitless space around him, the lingering taste of the dream, in which things were far from the snug contentment Peggie had represented in her letter, made him feel as though he were drowning. He needed to think, to be on his own. He got up, reached for his Spencer, and walked out into the night.

When he was about a mile from camp he lay down on his back in the long grass, hidden from everything except the sky. The same stars, he thought, looking at the canopy overhead – Orion, the Plough; the same stars that looked down on Carraig Mór! Except it would be day there now. What kind of a day?

He rose restlessly, moved further on. The grass was high, behind him and before him and around him, a giant meadow that went on for ever. Walking through it was a strange experience; it was as though the earth were trying to envelop him.

But it was good to exercise. After weeks spent in the saddle or on the driving seat, his body cried out for normal activity, and this was the nearest he had come to it for some time, this walk through the harsh grass sea of the prairie.

The glow of dawn and the small wind that moved the grasses reminded him that day was breaking. He was about to turn back when an unexpected whiff came to him on the breeze, one he knew well: the pungent scent of tobacco. Then he saw, against the lightening sky, the small curl of smoke rising from the grass some twenty yards away. He clenched his rifle and approached it cautiously.

It was an Indian. Tom, crawling on his stomach, stifled his surprise. The man was wearing the white buckskin dress of a Sioux chief. He had made a private space for himself where he now sat cross-legged on a blanket. He

44

wore beaded moccasins, and braids of grey hair hung over his shoulder. He was smoking a pipe, but was otherwise immobile. His eyes were closed.

Tom watched him for a moment and eased his grip on his rifle. There was nothing threatening about this person. The Sioux in general were regarded as being a nation friendly to the whites. The man opened his eyes, stared at the spot behind which Tom lay in the grass, and spoke softly, as though he had not only seen him but had been expecting him.

'White man sit? Talk.'

Tom started. Feeling foolish, he came from hiding and moved into the flattened circle. He was aware of his vulnerability, for if this Indian were here how many more of them might not be hidden around him, watching his every move? But he felt no alarm, put his rifle down and sat, as invited, on the blanket.

The Sioux looked at him. He was about sixty, with deep-set eyes in a face that was dark and pitted as a walnut. He extended the pipe to Tom.

'You smoke?'

Tom took the pipe, inhaled, coughed until the tears started in his eyes. He handed the pipe back. 'Thank you.'

The Indian took a pull from the returned pipe, but otherwise remained immobile. Then he said without raising his voice, 'Why have you come?'

Tom was stumped. The last thing he expected in this lost place was interrogation. But he answered truthfully.

'Like everyone else, I have come from a country far away to make my fortune, to have a home, own some land . . .'

'The land is our mother. How can you own your mother? All you do is put fence around her to keep her other children away.'

Tom did not know what to say, but courtesy insisted that he say something.

'I was poor in my country. And this country is great and empty.'

'Poor!' the Indian exclaimed. 'I am as "poor" as you were in your country, but I am rich.' He pointed to the east. 'See, the sun rises.' He pointed to the clouds coming from the west. 'The sky gives rain. The Great Spirit smiles upon the earth.'

'That is true,' Tom said, 'but the sun and the rain will not feed or house a family.'

The old man replied, 'My people have no houses.' He gestured to the north. 'They have no food. This place not so empty once; full of buffalo. My people make long journey here, but now buffalo few. Instead your people, like a river, cross the land.'

Tom was silent. There was no answer to this and he had to get back to the wagons which would soon be on the move. He searched in his pocket for some small offering, found a piece of jerky wrapped in wax paper and his penknife.

'I must go,' he said, holding out the jerky and the knife in his palm. 'Will you accept these small gifts from me?'

The Indian took them gravely, bit on the jerky and pronounced it good, turned the penknife over, opened the blade. 'Thank you.' He reached inside his buckskin tunic and produced a circle of feathers and small bones. He held it out to Tom, who took it, turning it over in wonder.

'What is it?' Tom asked with a smile

The Indian did not smile back. 'Dreamcatcher. Good fortune.'

Tom thanked him and rose to his feet.

'You think you have for ever, young white man,' the old man murmured softly, 'but your days too will be spilled like grains of sand.' He dropped his voice and added almost in a whisper, 'Go slowly on your journey.'

When he was some yards away Tom glanced back, but already it was impossible to pinpoint the Indian's location. He could no longer see or smell the tobacco smoke. But a sense of unease lingered, as though he had met a ghost and had not known it.

He hurried now, hearing the welcome sounds of the awakening camp, the chirping voices of children and the deeper tones of the adults. He smelled coffee, and the mouth-watering scent of freshly baked biscuits. The wagons seemed fragile in that vast landscape, rose-tinted in the first rays of the sun.

'Ah, there you are, Tom,' Maria said. 'I saw your bed was empty and I was worried for a minute!' She was giving breakfast to the Connor children and proffered him a cup. Tom accepted coffee and biscuits spread with molasses.

Ted Lafferty appeared on horseback. He had ridden a little way down the trail, and now spoke to the men who gathered around him.

'If we go easy we'll have no problems. Remember, we take no chances – when the river curves, follow the bank. Don't assume because it's shallow that it's safe!'

'A bite of breakfast, Ted?' Mrs Connor called.

'Why, thank you, ma'am.'

The scout dismounted and tethered his horse to the wagon tongue. Mrs Connor handed him biscuits on one of her china plates, of which she was inordinately proud. Everyone else had left such nicety behind them. She had also had the foresight to bring a small stove, which saved her back-breaking fatigue.

'Help yourself to molasses.'

Maria passed him the jar and the scout glanced keenly at her. She blushed under his gaze.

'I met an Indian out there,' Tom said, oblivious to the sudden *frisson* in the air, 'a Sioux chief by the look of him. He was just sitting there on his blanket, smoking.' He watched covertly for Lafferty's reaction, hiding his need for reassurance.

Ted said from a full mouth, 'They do that when they want to parley!'

'He said his people are waiting for the buffalo.'

'I wish them luck. There used to be millions of those beasts; they used to come within fifteen miles of the trail every year . . . now they're rare as trees.'

He finished his meal, stood up and thanked his hostess.

Maria turned her blue eyes on him and said, 'We're very grateful to you, Mr Lafferty, for looking after us so well.'

The scout shuffled his feet and muttered awkwardly, 'Shucks, ma'am, it ain't nothin' . . .'

There were shouts and whinnies as the horses were harnessed, and the wagons rumbled back on to the trail. Soon they were again a convoy heading west.

In the driving seat of the Warners' wagon Tom concentrated on the trail and on the team under the reins. Frank, lying inside the wagon, commented caustically on being laid low with what he called 'this damn fool plague'. Frank's wife, Julia, kept an eye on her husband and their teenage daughter, Sarah, who rode alongside.

But although Tom entered into occasional badinage with the Warners he could not shrug off the lingering unease. He kept hearing the Sioux's words as he had bid him goodbye: *Go slowly on your journey.*

'Why do I keep feeling,' he muttered, 'that the man was trying to warn me?'

When the convoy stopped to eat and rest through the midday heat, he sought out Captain Hartigan and told him of his early morning encounter.

'I'm a bit concerned about what he said. I can't get it out of my head. Was he speaking in riddles or was it a warning?'

The captain frowned. 'Of what? If they give us trouble we are in far greater danger if we travel slowly. The sooner we catch up with the train in front of us, the stronger we are. That's why I want us to curtail our midday break and move on.'

Tom watched him mount his horse and chivy people to get going again. Captain Hartigan considered himself an expert on Indians. But still Tom was no easier in his mind.

The wagons travelled on the north side of the Platte, which was high with melted snows. When they came to the river bend the lead wagon, following Captain Hartigan, turned right to follow the curve of the river. This was the spot of which Ted Lafferty had warned the evening before. The river was spread out here and seemed to be shallower; the temptation was clearly to attempt fording it at this point and so cut out unnecessary miles.

Frank Warner, who had been watching the route through an aperture in the canvas, now called out in a quavering voice, 'Tom, why are we turning right? Straight on, man; we can ford the river easily.'

Tom turned in the driver's seat. 'We were advised to follow the route around the river bend. Mr Lafferty says there are quicksands.'

Frank muttered something about Lafferty being fond of the sound of his own voice. He crawled to the driver's seat and told Tom to give him the reins. Tom saw that the man was feverish; his skin had an unhealthy yellow cast to it and his eyes glittered.

'Frank, dear,' Julia said behind him, 'you should stay in bed. Leave the driving to Tom.'

'Give me the reins, son,' Frank ordered. 'I know what I'm doing.'

'That sandbar looks suspect, Mr Warner. I think Mr Lafferty was right,' Tom said stubbornly. But when Frank repeated angrily, 'I know what I'm about, young man. This is my wagon!' Tom obeyed, handed over the reins and jumped from the driving seat to the ground.

Fourteen-year-old Sarah, who was riding alongside, said loudly, with a sideways look at Tom, 'Daddy's right! That sandbar looks fine,' and as though to prove her mettle and impress him she spurred her horse into the river.

The Platte at this point was more than three hundred feet wide. The young girl moved quickly on her mount until she had almost reached the sandbar. But then she paused, looking back over her shoulder uncertainly as her pony began to flounder. She screamed as she was thrown from its back, but her cry was abruptly truncated; she had disappeared into the water. In a moment she reappeared, but it was immediately evident that she was in serious difficulty. Her father, with a curse, whipped the team and rushed the wagon into the river after his child.

'Sarah!' he shouted. 'Sarah . . .!'

There was a chorus of voices shouting 'Whoa'; all the wagons behind came to a halt.

Tom ran for a rope, threw one end of it to Jim Tanner, a young farmer from Missouri, and shouted, 'Secure it.' Then, lashing the other end around himself, he jumped into the river. For the first fifty yards the water was thick with the mud churned by the Warner wagon and the frightened horses. Keeping clear of the floundering team, he neared Sarah. The river was shallow here, and by now he felt the bottom soft under his own feet. But even as he grabbed the girl's outstretched arm, his legs sank into the thick mud and sand. He called to the terrified Sarah, 'Don't move.' He tightened his grip on her wrist and shouted back to the men on the riverbank at the top of his lungs, 'Pull!'

The rope around his waist tightened and in the same moment he dragged Sarah to him, wrapping her in his arms.

'Hold on now,' he said into her ear. 'We'll be grand in a minute.'

Frank Warner was shouting encouragement; he had eyes solely for the rescue of his only child. But he himself and his wagon were in dire straits; his team was struggling in the quicksand, and Julia sat behind him, her hands over her mouth. Swimmers, however, were approaching through the water, carrying ropes. Meanwhile, on land, horses were being prepared to pull the wagon and its team out of their difficulty.

Tom reached the riverbank with a great appreciation of the sweetness of life. Maria was waiting; she kissed her brother with tears in her eyes and then made a show of brushing off the mud – 'Will you look what you've done to me!' She wrapped a blanket around a weeping Sarah. The young girl sobbed and thanked her rescuers and looked desperately back into the river where her parents and their wagon were being slowly dragged to firm ground, and where her pony, Beauty, was still struggling.

When the wagon was on firm ground once more Frank was abrupt in his apologies.

'I'm an old fool,' he said, as he expressed his gratitude to all and sundry. 'An old sick man.'

'Just you go back to that bed, Frank, and stay there until Julia says you can get up.'

There was laughter, more from relief than anything else. But Sarah wept inconsolably. It had not been possible to rescue her pony, which had simply disappeared from view in the murky water.

The wagons that had gone on ahead had turned back to help. Captain Hartigan, looking more than a little angry, surveyed the scene. The day was advanced; the men who had taken part in the rescue were tired. The dark clouds that had begun to gather in the morning now covered the sky.

'It's going to rain,' the captain said. 'Best make camp and start out fresh in the morning. We'll still catch the other train. But it will probably take us an extra day or two now.'

Tents were rapidly put up; Sarah emerged from her parents' wagon in a fresh dress, chastened and contrite.

'It was my fault, Captain Hartigan,' she said. 'I didn't know . . .'

'It was your damn father's fault,' the captain muttered. 'But it's done now and we'll make the best of it. We could all do with a respite, anyway.'

There was a flash of lightning, an ominous rumble, and then hail came in sudden sheets. The women ran for shelter and secured the canvas tent flaps. The men ran to tether any loose horses. Tom, in dry clothes that Maria had brought him, sat with Willie in the back of a supply vehicle and listened to the rain drumming off the canvas. He put a finger to their roof and, even through the double thickness of the canvas, the water ran icily down along his forearm. He pulled back with a smothered exclamation.

49

'Why don't you come to California?' Willie said. 'The climate would suit you. Colorado is a cold place in winter.'

'You have your brother's farm to go to, Willie. I have to make my way!'

They ate biscuits and drank water. Then both young men donned India rubber coats, took their rifles and went out for their stint of guard duty, pulling their widebrimmed hats down against the deluge. Some of the tents were already flattened, and their owners, soaked to the skin, were piling into every available wagon space.

Tom could not slough off the sense of menace. He looked around him at what he could see of the prairie, darkened in the downpour. Away to the east and to the west ran the trail, deeply rutted. The horizon had vanished.

But the morning dawned bright and the air was sweet. Everyone exclaimed with pleasure at being able to have a hot meal again; the camp was quickly fragrant with the odour of freshly made pancakes and biscuits. The horses were none the worse for the storm and submitted patiently to the halters.

The going was slow because the ground was now soft and muddy, but there was little dust and spirits were high that the convoy was on the move again. Ted Lafferty left them after breakfast and disappeared down the trail. He returned towards late morning and rode, grim-faced, along each of the wagons, signalling to the drivers to stop.

'What is it?' Captain Hartigan demanded. But Ted, with a small shake of his head, indicated that this was too grave a matter for open disclosure.

The wagons stopped. The men conferred in whispers.

'A Dhia,' Maria said under her breath, as she tried to stop the Connor children from jumping down. 'What is it at all? 'Tis surely something terrible.'

Ted Lafferty told the men to corral the wagons and arm their weapons. He told them what he had found. The wagon train ahead of them was just over the horizon, but it was not a sight fit for Christian eyes.

Tom, with some of the other men, accompanied the scout. As they moved away from their wagons they saw, in the distance, the white bonnets of the preceding wagon train, standing still and silent on the prairie. As they approached Tom knew, at last, the source of his foreboding.

The fifteen wagons were corralled as they had been when the Indians had come on them; but the horses were gone. Some of the wagons were burned out. Others sat there, strangely innocent, with the bloodied corpses scattered around, some scalped, some fire-blackened. A dog cried piteously over the remains of a family, a father, mother and two children.

The men dismounted and removed their hats.

'It must have happened early this morning,' Ted Lafferty said. He walked among the dead, treading warily, his left hand holding his soft felt hat, his right hand clenched on his revolver, his knuckles white. Someone shot at the red-muzzled coyotes that skulked among the wagons.

'No shooting,' the captain said. 'We don't want to advertise our presence.' He looked drawn, bent over the body of a young boy. 'The corpses are fresh. The murdering savages will pay for this.'

Someone muttered, 'We'll get us up a posse . . .' But Captain Hartigan was silent, his face pale.

Eventually he said, 'We'll form no posse. Our first duty is to our women and children. We can't abandon them. We must leave it to the army to go after the murderers.' He examined an arrow imbedded in one of the wagons. 'Pawnee,' he said. In the trampled ground were hundreds of hoof marks. 'The irony of it, Tom! If we'd made better progress yesterday we would be lying here now!'

The rest of the morning was spent in digging graves, covering them with stones to protect them from wolves, and setting up makeshift crosses on the prairie. Tom, with the other sharpshooters, kept a lookout. But all was still. The flat grassland swept out to infinity.

High overhead, rising and falling, they saw the buzzards, hundreds of them, watching.

When the men returned to camp they told their women the dreadful truth, speaking in hushed tones so that the children might not hear.

'I knew from Mr Lafferty's face that it was a catastrophe,' Maria told Tom when he gently broke the news to her. 'But what will happen now? Are we to be next? Should we go back?'

'We have no choice but to keep on, Maria, to the end of the trail.'

He went to the supply wagon, took a revolver from his pack – a Colt 1851 Navy – and a box of bullets. He handed the gun to her, his face grim.

'Keep this by you. Be ready to use it if you must.'

Maria stared at the weapon with chagrin. 'I don't know how to use it.'

'I'll show you . . .'

She watched him carefully. He opened the gun, showed her the six empty chambers, filled five of them with bullets, leaving the top one empty.

'Unless you're going to fire, never close the gun on a chambered round.'

Then he emptied the gun, and had her load it under his supervision. He stood behind her then, holding her hands with the gun and made her cock the hammer. He told her how to assume a stance and stiffen her arms.

'Aim at that stone over there and squeeze the trigger.'

Maria squeezed the trigger and missed. She realised that if Tom had not been holding her hands, she would have broken her nose. The recoil of the weapon was shocking.

'You'll have to practise, Maria. Forget any notion of firing it with one hand. Only a very strong person can do that and still be an accurate shot. Above all, keep the gun clean. If there's dirt in the barrel it could explode and take your hand off!'

Ted Lafferty, riding by, reined in his horse and said to Tom, 'Haven't you a rifle to give her?'

'No . . .'

Ted leaned over and said to Maria. 'You'll need a holster for that, Miss Walsh. It makes it more accessible – if you have to use it. I'll get her one,' he said to Tom. 'We are arming the women!'

When he was gone Maria looked in terror across the empty land. '*A Dhia*,' she whispered, 'we have come all this way for this . . .'

Chapter Four

Maria wore her new revolver in the holster Ted Lafferty had given her, and counted the days until they would be in Colorado. But the great flat sweep of the prairie went on and on as though God had never made a hill. Every dawn brought the same start to the day, quick breakfast and departure, with wagons creaking, horses unwilling, men tired, women walking silently, children increasingly fractious. Everyone felt exposed and vulnerable; the train could be seen for miles and no one knew what eyes examined them.

Maria kept herself alert, scanning the horizon often, examining anything that seemed to stir in the immensity of the plain. She looked after Tom, cooking what could still be salvaged from their store and wondering what would happen if they didn't soon get to Denver.

'It's a bit like the Atlantic,' she told herself. 'You can't see the other side, and you wonder if you've moved at all.'

Eventually the wagon train arrived at North Platte. Here the river forked, one part continuing westwards, the other veering to the southwest. The latter was the route that the Warners and some ten other families would take to Denver, so here they said goodbye to their friends.

Tom grasped Willie's hand.

'Goodbye, Willie. The best of good luck to you in California.'

'We'll meet again, I think,' Willie said, regarding Tom gravely from his china-blue eyes. 'Although it is a big country I think our paths will cross . . . If ever you come to California I will be glad to see you.'

Maria said goodbye to the children she would probably never see again, who wept when they realised that they were being deprived of their teacher and sometime storyteller. She said goodbye to the strong women she had known as friends, to the men who had kept the wagon train safe, and to Willie, who kissed her hand with a Continental flourish. And then the tired vehicles, less than half the original wagon train, laboured on behind the gaunt horses, up the South Platte to Colorado.

*　*　*

Far in the distance the mountains came into view, rising slowly from the flat land. Maria, pointing to the snowy crests in the distance, exclaimed in delight to Ted Lafferty, who came riding alongside.

'Mr Lafferty, are those the Rocky Mountains?'

She saw the sweat-stained red bandanna around his neck, his reddish brown moustache, and the tired way he sat slumped in the heavy saddle.

He turned to look down at her for a moment before answering calmly, 'They sure are, ma'am.'

His eyes lingered on her, as though she presented a sight far more interesting than the distant peaks.

'I never saw mountains like that in all my life!'

Ted whistled. 'That's one heck of a long time!' he said, laughing suddenly, looking at her from the corner of his eye and shaking his head. 'Ain't it, Tom?'

But Tom was hardly listening. He breathed in deeply, exhaling in secret relief. The sight before him was surreal; he had invested so much hope and expectation in it that it was almost a dream. We have crossed the Great American Prairie, he thought. The fabled place is now before us, the Promised Land. And then he thought – *almost* crossed it. There's still a way to go, and only God knows what hazards.

He was sitting in the driving seat of the Warner supply wagon and Maria was walking beside him. The canvas wagon bonnet was now a dirty grey and the horses were thin and tired, their ribs showing through their dull, dusty coats. Everyone's clothes were the worse for wear and grime.

Ted Lafferty's black slouch hat was greasy at the brim, and covered at the crown with a fine layer of grey dust, but under it his eyes twinkled as they had not during the long journey. He patted his horse's neck. All along the wagon train, above the slow rumble of the wheels, came a murmur that would lift the heart. Suddenly, after days of weary plodding and exhausted silence, there was laughter. The horses pricked up their ears and seemed to gladden their steps.

The land began to rise. The road became a cliff trail and, looking down, the travellers could see the waters of the river as it sparkled in the sun.

'Look,' Tom said later that day, pointing into the canyon. 'I think that's Lafferty. What's he doing down there?'

'Keep your eyes on the road, Tom **Walsh**,' Maria replied tartly. 'We don't want to end up down there too.' She picked out the tiny figure walking his horse through the canyon; let her eyes linger. Even at this distance she could sense his alertness, his awareness of every nuance of the territory through which he rode. There was something good about Mr Lafferty, she thought. Wherever he was there was safety and strength. He was kind too. But she chafed at the heavy leather holster he had given her; it was around her waist with its complement of bullets. The revolver was loaded, except for the chamber on which the hammer rested. She had greased the holster with axle grease, as advised, to prevent the gun from rusting, and now in a moment of irritation put her hand to the buckle and pulled on the belt.

Tom hardly glanced at her, but he said, 'Leave it on, Maria.'

'But it's awful. It's ruining my dress. It's awkward. And I'm not going to need it!'

'You don't know whether you will or not. And if it's visible it's a deterrent.'

I hadn't thought of that, she acknowledged privately. Is this what life will be like for us in the West? Will I have to go around armed all the time – as a deterrent?

The precipitous path gentled and soon the wagon train was down by the river again. In a grassy place identified by their scout, where wild flowers grew in abundance along the bank, the caravan halted. The children called to each other, jumped from the wagons with cries of delight; the men slid from their horses, groaned as they got themselves upright after so many hours in the saddle, rubbing their behinds and stretching their legs. Everyone brought their water carriers to the river to be filled. The horses were released from the shafts and they rushed, nudging and nipping each other, to the water's edge where they stretched their necks and drank with long, sucking noises. Then some of them rolled in the shallows, throwing up thousands of droplets to dazzle in the sunlight; others rolled on the ground. When they rose they tossed their manes, whinnied and began to graze.

'I thought the horses were tired out,' Maria said. 'And will you look at them!'

'They untire themselves quick enough when there's a bit of refreshment in it!' Tom replied with a grin. 'Rather like people!'

Upstream, the children paddled in the crystal water.

'I wish we could stay here for a few days,' Maria said to Tom. 'It's a grand spot and we all need a rest! You could do a bit of hunting with that fancy rifle of yours, get us some fresh meat!'

'Is that a complaint, miss?'

Maria eyes darkened. She shook her head.

'Sure what is there to complain of? Haven't we the best of everything? Salt bacon, ham, beans, rice, coffee? Better than a lot of people ever get to eat and drink . . .'

Tom knew from the cast of his sister's face that her thoughts were far away.

How are they now? he wondered. Father and Peggie? So far away that the distance seemed incalculable; so far away that they seemed like the inhabitants of a strange story. Yet he could remember his old home as though he had left it yesterday – the scent of turf smoke; Sliabh na mBan – the Women's Mountain – looming against the sky; the valley below with its little school and small church. And the graveyard with its quiet pile of stones.

Maria glanced at him, looked away. 'All the same,' she added, pursing her lips, 'a bit of fresh food would be grand.'

Tom did not reply. Emotion had ambushed him and he needed to be on his own. His sister had just given him a perfect excuse. He reached for his rifle, found the oily rag he used to clean it.

Mrs Warner called to Maria, and she went to help with the children, who were returning shivering from their bathe in the river. When she turned round there was no sign of her brother.

The wagons were now corralled into a circle and the women were busy preparing the evening meal. Maria used the last of the wheat flour and the best of the remaining potatoes to make potato cakes, cooking them on a hot griddle over the campfire. The smell was wonderful. The children came clamouring for them and she handed them out as fast as they were cooked, crisped golden brown. She kept a few aside for Tom. But where was he? Night was not far off and he had not returned. She knew she had upset him earlier by reminding him of Ireland.

As the shadows lengthened, ululations began – the howling of wolves. The sound crept stealthily across the plain, a primeval voice in the wilderness. Listening to them, Maria felt an aching loneliness, as though she had been dead for a hundred years and something had disturbed her grave.

'Have you seen Tom?' she asked nervously of anyone who chanced her way.

'Last time I seen him was when we halted . . .'

'I saw Tom Walsh riding out to the prairie about four hours ago,' someone else said.

'Which way did he go?'

The woman pointed. 'Over there, across the river.'

Maria walked through the camp, thinking to find Ted Lafferty and share her misgivings with him. But the scout was nowhere to be seen either.

'Where's Mr Lafferty?' she asked Mrs Warner.

'Lord, Maria, you never know where Ted is. He goes and comes. Probably won't be back here till tomorrow mornin'.' And then she asked, 'You worried about something?'

'I think Tom is gone hunting. But I expected him back before now!'

Frank Warner came along. He was recovered, thin after his illness, but in good spirits, a man who compared his lot against what it might have been. He was chewing a wad of tobacco. 'No need to worry your sweet little head about *him*, Maria. He's a fine shot.'

Maria nodded. She knew that since the rescue from the quicksand Frank had a very high opinion of Tom. She told herself she was being foolish, but the misgiving would not go away. The more she dwelt on it the more it became a certainty: Tom was out there somewhere, in danger, alone in this savage land.

Eventually she could stand it no longer and, creeping underneath one of the wagons, she left the camp, though she knew this was dangerous. She looked at the ground; hoof prints and footprints were jumbled together in the trampled earth. She walked to the river. It was wide and sandy and shallow. Away to the east the sky was darkening. Soon the moon would rise above the prairie.

I wish I was wearing boots and breeches, she thought irritably. I would be able to cross this river. Then she thought, I should have bought my own pony. I had enough saved. But she knew it would have been an extravagance she could not really have afforded.

She walked up the riverbank, and when she looked back found that she had put a distance between herself and the camp. But she heard the reassuring voices on the evening breeze, and smelled the scents of cooking.

In the distance were the snow-tipped mountains. Nothing stirred. There were a few clouds high up, already darkening with the approaching night.

Something moved beside her so suddenly that she jumped. It was about six feet away, slithering towards her through the long-stemmed grass. Before she could think, the hated revolver was out of its holster, the chamber moved, the hammer cocked. She held it with both hands as Tom had shown her. The gun's report seemed to echo off the sky; it filled her ears with its sound and her nose with its smell. A small cloud of black smoke hung in the air.

The slithering thing convulsed three feet from her. She saw the reptilian head, the darting black, forked tongue, the bluish green of its upper body, the yellow of its underside. She knew that she had just shot at a snake and missed. The creature reared its head above the grass, arched, hissed. Suddenly, casually, Death was there, looking at her in the failing light. With a surge of cold detachment that would later astonish her, she raised her revolver again. 'Don't close your eyes when you fire,' Tom had said. She held them open, aimed at the creature's head as it reared, pulled the trigger. The snake leaped into the air, and collapsed thrashing at her feet. She stood over it, saw quite calmly that she had blown its head off, but that its convulsing body still lived. Only then did the scream come, high-pitched, frightful to her own ears as though it belonged to someone else.

She heard Ted Lafferty calling, 'Maria! Maria!' He was fording the river, his horse splashing through the shallows. Other people were approaching from the camp. Ted reached her first, took the smoking revolver from her hand as she threw herself into his arms.

'It's all right . . .' he said. 'It's all right, Maria. You did well.'

She could hardly see his face; but his voice was a husky whisper, and the arms that held her seemed strangely glad of the contact, for they were in no hurry to release her. Maria was ashamed of shaking, but being in his arms felt like heaven. She didn't mind the smell of his sweat, or the rasp of his beard, or the tobacco on his breath, or how his clothes, wet from the river, soaked through her own. He released her as the others arrived. They looked down at the headless serpent and murmured, grinning, to each other in the maddening way of men.

Then came another horseman, galloping furiously. Even from a distance Maria knew it was Tom and tried to straighten the damp dress that clung to her legs, glad of the falling night; he would not be able to see her burning face.

Her brother reined in his frothing mount and jumped to the ground, looking from his sister to the dead snake, to the small knot of men. She registered, as she often did when she saw him in unusual circumstances, how clean cut he was, how decisive, how he was as poised as the older men.

'I'm all right, Tom.'

Tom took Maria by the arm, looked into her face and then suddenly hugged her to him until she thought her ribs would crack.

'Thank God,' he whispered. 'For a moment—'

'She's fine!' Ted said, blowing casually at the muzzle of the still-smoking Colt.

Tom pushed at the corpse of the snake with the toe of his boot. He bent to examine it. 'Seems dead enough, anyway,' he muttered. 'That was some shot, Mr Lafferty!' He looked at his sister and added: 'When I got back to camp, they said you'd gone for a walk, Maria.' His voice was suddenly stern. 'Didn't I tell you not to stir out of the camp on your own?'

'Oh, let me be,' Maria said angrily. 'You disappear for hours and I'm supposed to be inspired where you are. And I'm sick to death of being told what to do. I'm not a child. I've spent weeks and weeks on this endless prairie, and every single day I've been told what to do and when to do it!'

'And *I* didn't kill that there snake,' Ted interjected laconically. 'Your sister did!'

Tom's expression faltered. He took the proffered revolver from Lafferty. 'So my lessons didn't fall on deaf ears after all!' he said uncomfortably, glancing at his sister with a reluctant grin. 'I knew you'd make a good shot . . .'

58

'No you didn't. You were only too ready to think me incompetent!'

Tom gestured to the corralled wagons and said, still grinning, 'Maria, you indicated earlier you would like some fresh meat. There's an antelope back there that wants cooking. If we don't hurry it'll be all gone . . .'

He lifted her to the saddle, mounted behind her and turned towards the camp.

Ted Lafferty smiled into his moustache. He picked up the dead snake and flourished it after the departing pair. 'You can cook this too, ma'am,' he called. 'The Indians say it's mighty good to eat!'

Maria gave a screech, and the men laughed good-naturedly as they followed, ribbing Lafferty quietly about maidens in distress in general and this one in particular.

Tom had been right about the antelope. It was in great demand. The travellers skinned it, seasoned it with flour, covered it with mud and roasted it. When it was cooked they broke the mud off; underneath, the flesh was daintily cooked. Tom divided it among the weakest in the community – a fillet for Mrs Stonebridge, who was recovering from a miscarriage; other portions for the children. He put a piece on Maria's plate.

'That's for you, miss, to restore your nerves.'

'There's nothing wrong with my nerves!' she replied tartly.

'A bite of venison, Ted?' Tom called suddenly to Ted Lafferty.

'Don't mind if I do . . .'

Maria moved to make him welcome at the fire, more acutely aware than ever that the wagons enclosing them gave the illusion of safety. She saw the firelight on tired faces, the sleepy children nestling in their mothers' arms. Tom was joking with Frank Warner; their laughter flowed easily. Maria threw back her head and saw the stars twinkling far above. And then, glancing to one side, she saw that Ted Lafferty was looking at her. His eyes, deep-set, bloodshot in the flickering firelight, were inscrutable.

'Thank you for coming to the rescue, Mr Lafferty,' she whispered, leaning towards him.

'But I didn't rescue you, ma'am. You dealt with the situation very well yourself.'

'I feel a bit foolish to have caused such a stir. Sometimes I can't help wondering if I should have come out West at all.'

'Why is that, ma'am?'

'I don't think I'm cut out for it. It's just awful having to be on the lookout all the time for snakes and Indians!'

Lafferty laughed. 'But there are cities in the West where you won't give those things a thought. Denver, for example. No snakes, and few Indians, although some of the poor critters pitch their tents near the city.'

'You feel sorry for the Indians, Mr Lafferty?'

'Yes, ma'am.'

'Even after what you saw on the trail? The scalped bodies . . .?'

'It was the white man who taught the Indians how to scalp,' he replied grimly. 'There used to be a bounty for redskin scalps.'

Maria put her hand to her mouth. '*A Dhia*,' she whispered.

'What does that mean?' he asked diffidently. 'You so often say it.'

'It means "O God". It's Irish.'

'Well, God didn't help them. It was one betrayal after the other . . .'

The fires, already augmented with dried dung, were burning low and would not be replenished. The women had left the fireside and were putting the children to bed.

Maria expected the scout to move away, but when he did not she ventured after a moment, 'Is Denver like Boston?'

'Pretty much.'

'Then I'll stay in Denver if I can. But Tom wants to work on the railroad and I'm afraid it will be terribly hard and dangerous.'

She glanced at her brother, who was now talking to Captain Hartigan.

Ted regarded him for a moment and then turned to look at her from under grizzled, tangled eyebrows.

'Your brother will do jess fine, ma'am. There's a stamp on him . . . I've seen it in men before . . . something that's born in them! You can see for yourself how much everyone respects him.' After a moment he whispered, '*You* sure did well earlier, Miss Walsh. That was a good shot!'

She saw the way his grey eyes dwelled on her, registered with shock the hunger in them. The sudden sense of radical contact this brought with it made her feel as though she were alone with him, as though they filled up the world. Part of her wanted to respond; part of her wanted to flee. But she refused cowardice, held his gaze shyly, reached out and touched his calloused hand.

'*Maria*, Ted. And thank you.'

He glanced around, said hesitantly, 'Miss Wa— Maria, I will be gone before dawn. I need to stretch my legs before I hit the saddle again. Would you take a turn with me around the wagons?'

Maria felt her face burn in the darkness. She whispered, 'I'll follow you.'

Ted got up and left the fire. Maria excused herself a few moments later and found him in the shadows.

'Maria,' he said, 'I'm just an old scout . . .'

'You're not *old*, Ted.'

She put up her hand and tentatively touched his face. He turned to her in the gloom; she could smell his tobacco breath, the scent of his sweat, the leather of his buckskins. He took her hand; his own was warm and calloused. When his arms enclosed her, when his lips took hers, she felt no alarm; it was like going home. All the worry, all the tension of the long trek left her.

60

Long before dawn the whole camp was stirring and, after a hasty breakfast and the filling of every available water carrier to the brim, they set off again. It was surreal trekking through first light, seeing their moving shadows as the sun rose behind them, the bonnets of the leading wagons, and the mounted men, silhouetted against the sky. Tom drove the heaviest-laden supply wagon, and Maria walked beside him, but he did not tease her now.

'What would have happened if I had missed that snake a second time?' she asked him softly during the course of the morning, raising the subject casually. She had barely slept the night before; her head had been full of Ted Lafferty and the kisses that still burned her lips. But when she had finally succumbed to sleep it was the snake fangs that had filled her dreams.

Tom gave a reluctant grin. 'Nothing much. That poor snake was just a blue racer. It wasn't poisonous! So all your heroics were superfluous!'

Maria laughed out loud in spite of herself, flushing at the memory of her 'heroics'. She thought of Ted, of his compliments on her bravery, and then of his lips, and his arms and the delicious, miraculous sense of visibility and homecoming. He had known the snake was not dangerous and had not told her, presumably to allow her to retain her sense of personal daring.

After a few moments she said quietly, 'Tom, was Mr Lafferty ever married?'

'I don't know. He strikes me as a confirmed bachelor. He's shy with women!'

'What age do you think he is?'

'Could be forty. Hard to say. His kind of life weathers people very quickly.'

'I . . . like him, Tom.'

Her brother turned to stare at her. 'Do you now? Women always fall in love with their rescuers. But he's far too old for you, Maria. You're looking for a father. You'll soon forget him when we get to Denver!'

I won't, Maria thought crossly. I will never forget him.

The grassland petered out. Here and there lay the skulls of big-horned sheep, sinister with their twisted horns and their eyeless sockets. Some were on stakes.

'Killed by wolves,' Tom said.

'Wolves didn't put them on sticks!'

He looked at her, grinned. 'I suppose not . . .'

Maria glanced around anxiously, but there was no sign of any Indians, hostile or otherwise.

The road seemed to go on to the edge of the world, and beyond it were the tantalising snow peaks of the Rockies, no closer apparently, despite all the progress.

It was hot and the children were fractious and quarrelsome. When they stopped for a hasty lunch Maria took four of them into one of the wagons and entertained them with stories from Irish mythology.

The children listened, their eyes wide and their mouths open.

Tom heard his sister's soft, flat voice and the old stories, told around many a winter fireside of his childhood and, despite himself, his throat tightened. He remembered how his father would take down the fiddle and play a lament, so haunting that the hair would rise on the back of his neck and all the company would close their eyes in either grief or rapture. But rather like the characters in her stories, all of it – Father, Peggie, the Farrellys, the Comeragh Mountains, the whitewashed house, the lonely boreen – today seemed, like one of the old stories, lost and dreamlike, something he suspected he would never see again. And then he thought of the cairn on a lonely grave, and he looked out through a private mist at the wild, foreign land.

That night they rested by a spring, a place in a small valley used by successive wagon trains, where every one that passed cut down some trees for the ring of campfires that enclosed the campsite.

The horses were watered, rubbed down, allowed to eat. As they munched Tom ran his hand along the legs of his team, and along their backs and flanks, grieving privately for their poor condition and their patient stoicism. The men conferred, the map was studied, Ted Lafferty pointing with a stubby finger at the road ahead.

They rested for two days, during which Maria looked around covertly for Ted, but there was no sign of him. The fires were fed all night, and threw long shadows over the valley floor.

When the wagon train moved again, men, women and children followed along the road in virtual silence, the hoarse breathing of the horses, the clop-clop of hoofs on the rocks and muted footfalls, the children's voices, drowned in the noise of the river. As the day wore on the children were fed on the march with biscuits, dried fruit, water. The men took turns at guard duty. And in this way they came at last to the outskirts of Denver.

Ted Lafferty came to say goodbye, choosing a moment when Tom was unhitching a team from one of the wagons. He took off his hat.

'Miss Walsh . . . Maria . . .'

'Ted . . .'

His eyes held hers. He spoke awkwardly. 'It's sure been a pleasure . . . I hope that we'll meet again.'

'Yes,' Maria whispered, hating the sinking feeling in her stomach. 'I hope so too.'

'Right now I have to git up to Fort Laramie – but when I am next in Denver – should be around September sometime – I'd be mighty pleased if I could call on you . . .?'

'I'd like that, Ted. But I don't know where I'll be.'

'Oh, I'll find you, Maria,' he said with a smile. 'There ain't no doubt about that!'

Chapter Five

Building bridges for the Colorado Central Railroad was not for the weak or the work-shy. Tom presented himself to Mr Posthorn, one of the engineers, who immediately took him on as foreman. His job was to oversee the cutting of timber, the ascertaining of its quality and strength, the laying of ballast, the bedding of the sleepers.

He soon found he was putting in shifts of ten to twelve hours, six or seven days a week. The winter of 1872 demonstrated Nature's sovereignty in this empty land – blizzards, snowdrifts, sub-zero temperatures and tool metals so cold they took the skin from the hands. But the work went on – the rock blasting, the song of sledgehammers filling the ravines and echoing in the eardrums even after the working day was over.

Gradually the great wooden bridges rose across the chasms among the Table Mountains and the first ravines of the Rockies.

> Washington Avenue,
> Golden,
> Colorado
> 3 April 1873

Dearest Father and Peggie,

I know Maria has written to tell you of our safe arrival in this territory. I am now helping to build bridges for a railroad company called the Colorado Central Railroad. This is not just any old railway, for it has to cross mountains, and span gorges the like of which you won't find in Ireland, or anywhere else in Europe, except perhaps Switzerland. It is a three-foot narrow-gauge line, a continuation of a broad-gauge track that runs between Denver and Golden.

I cannot describe the fever in this land, of building and expansion, attempting mastery over some of the roughest terrain on earth, which can only presently be accessed by hazardous wagon roads. But even in this perilous place there are mountain cities (a town with more than 2,000 people is called a 'city' here) with grand names like Black Hawk and Forks Creek. Everywhere you can see evidence of 'placer' diggings (they pronounce it 'plasser'), where the rivers have been panned for gold, dug and washed over until there can be nothing left of that precious metal in the rivers. I've made a couple of 'sluice boxes', and clever contraptions they are – designed so that the gravel shovelled into them is washed by the river, and any gold particles or nuggets are left behind.

The railway follows the course of the streams; they have created natural avenues of access for the cutting and blasting and bridging that is necessary. Sometimes it seems that the whole world rings with the effort; you should hear the never-ending racket of the stone breakers, the reverberation of hammers on iron, the shouts of the gangers, the ear-splitting explosion of the dynamite.

The slopes and sides of the mountains are clothed with trees – pine and cedar and spruce, up as far as the timberline, beyond which only a few stragglers grow. The smell of them is powerful. There are quaking aspens with their shivering leaves as round as gold dollars and just as yellow in the autumn, and small purple flowers called columbines.

High over the mountains we sometimes see eagles watching us, hovering with great spans of wings; they must be wondering what the devil is going on in this land that has known no change since time began. And there are marmots (big, fat, furry rodents, Peggie) that sit up to look at you from a distance, and queer little characters called chipmunks or ground squirrels, just like baby squirrels except that they're grey and white, unlike our native red squirrel. They're very tame and will eat out of your hand. And then there are bears, Peggie, but you don't let them eat out of your hand at all!

There is a great blessing in being allowed to put one's energy into great projects, and to see those projects take shape before your eyes. And there is great pleasure, privilege even, in being involved in building a nation.

There are plenty of our fellow countrymen here, labouring in groups, and alongside them are hundreds of Chinese who are fine workers, but who don't speak much English. So there is a Chinese agent, who is the link between the gangers and the men.

The Chinese wear wide hats, and pigtails down their backs and they have the queerest singsong voices you ever heard. But they probably think we're a queer lot too, and sure maybe they're right!

I worry a bit about the quality of the wood; it's too fresh and may warp, but the railroad can't wait until it's seasoned, so the ballast it's bedded in has to be very thick, which entails much labour.

Maria is snug in Denver; she's doing a bit of housekeeping for a Mrs Cramer, and I have lodgings in Golden, which is about fifteen miles away from her. My window looks out on Castle Rock, a knob-like formation known as a 'butte', which is formed by the weathering of the rock.

The city is in a basin surrounded by mountains. Colorado is a great red land, not a bit like our green island, but magnificent. The bedrock is a grandly coloured sandstone, rust red and salmon pink. With the evening sun on it you'd think it was on fire.

I have written to Michael; he is still in Arizona but thinks he may be coming northwards later in the year.

Please go ahead, Peggie, with the cross for Mother's grave – make sure it's a fine Celtic cross and have it inscribed as you decide yourself. I'm sending you ten dollars now and I'll send you some more again soon.

God bless you,

Your fond son and brother,

Tom

Tom was not entirely right about Maria. She *was* in Denver, but not as snug as he liked to think. She had been taken on as replacement housekeeper for a Mrs Eliza Cramer, the wife of a bank manager called Arthur Cramer, laid low after the stillbirth of her first child. The previous housekeeper had left suddenly, and the only other servant was a skinny little cook with a pock-marked face, called Nora Mulcahy.

Nora was Irish too. She came from north Mayo, and had been in America three years. She was timid, secretive, sure that the world was a place of frightful dangers, ready to do anything to hold on to her job. Sometimes she spoke of her old home in a place Maria had never heard of called Baile Crua.

'It means "Hard Town" . . .' Maria mused.

'Sure I know. 'Twas well named . . .'

With the mistress of the house sick there was no social activity, no dinner parties such as Maria had known in Boston, no soirées. A fat, middle-aged nurse by the name of Miss Euphemia Evans looked after the invalid; the doctor visited daily. Over the big clapboard house there hung a pall of gloom, so that even the light seemed reluctant to penetrate through the heavy lace curtains. Every once in a while some quiet visitors, relatives and close friends came to see the patient and then departed.

Through her bedroom window Maria saw the fine city of Denver, red brick, stone, and beyond it the white peaks of Mt Harvard and Mt

Princeton. The sight of the latter brought back the memory of the first ecstatic moment when they had risen from the horizon and gladdened the hearts of the emigrants. But what Maria did not like to admit was that she actually found herself missing the wagon train: the danger, the evenings around the campfires, the camaraderie and shared peril. Neither did she like to admit how much she missed one member of that community. Ted Lafferty had gone on to Oregon, and although he said he would call on her when he came to Denver in September, that month had come and gone and brought no word from him.

He has forgotten, she told herself. But still she lived over and over the feel of his arms, the moist, hungry, pressure of his mouth, and the sense of being visible and cherished. She thought of what Tom had said – that she was looking for a father.

It's not true, she asserted to herself – who'd want kisses like that from a father? I know Ted's twenty years older than me, but it's him I want.

She glanced around her tiny bedroom. It had a narrow iron bed, a small wardrobe, a chest of drawers with a basin and ewer. The walls were covered with pretty wallpaper depicting small blue and white flowers. The attic window had a white cotton curtain keeping out the night.

She looked at herself in her washstand mirror. In the lamplight her skin bloomed and her eyes were full of softness. She compared herself suddenly with the weak and sallow woman in the master bedroom below her, who was being cared for by a nurse.

'She looked like this once,' she whispered to herself, thinking of the wedding portrait she dusted in the library, 'healthy and well. *A Dhia*, what happens at all to women? Is it that marriage is the most dangerous place for us in the world?'

She thought of the poor woman's husband, Mr Arthur Cramer, who had taken to ringing for her when he was alone in his library, with puzzling requests for her to dust a bookcase already dusted that morning, or attend to the fire when it was still blazing, and she would comply and turn to find his eyes on her, his mouth beneath his moustache curved in a faint smile. She would lower her eyes and leave the room, but then he would ring again and she would have to perform some other small task, such as pouring his brandy.

She blew out the lamp and got into bed. But just as she was drifting to sleep she heard the scratching at her door, and instantly was wide awake, listening, waiting for the sound to repeat itself.

What or who was it? It had to be Nora, who had the adjoining box-room.

'Nora – is that you?'

She got out of bed, opened the door a crack. In the landing, holding a lamp, was Mr Cramer. He was wearing his satin-trimmed dressing gown;

his face was so close that she could smell his breath. It stank of garlic and other unpleasant things. She recoiled and drew back.

'Ah, Maria . . . would you get me a drink of milk? My dyspepsia is troubling me . . .'

'I'll get you some from the kitchen, sir,' she replied after a moment's hesitation, 'if you will wait just a moment.'

Mother of God! she thought to herself. Is it pure helpless he is? The kitchen is much nearer his room that it is mine!

But she took her woollen dressing gown from the peg behind the door, donned it, tied the belt and emerged on to the landing to find her employer waiting for her.

'Oh, thank you, Maria . . . How nice you look in your night attire.'

She pulled the dressing gown tightly around her and went downstairs without replying, rushed to the pantry and returned with the full glass just as her employer's step followed across the hall. The last thing she wanted was to find herself alone with him in the kitchen while the house slept.

She held out the glass of milk.

'Put it by my bed, Maria.'

She hurried up the stairs ahead of him, uncomfortably aware that he followed a few steps behind.

'Don't rush,' he said softly. 'There's no hurry. You'll only spill the milk.'

But Maria hurried all the more.

Mr Cramer slept alone in the room adjoining that of his wife, a chamber with heavy mahogany furniture and a brass bed. Maria deposited the glass of milk on the nightstand, but as she turned she found the door blocked by her employer, who stood watching her, his eyes dilated and his mouth slack. Maria felt her heart miss a beat; but behind it came a surge of angry contempt.

She strode towards the door before he could close it.

'Good night, sir,' she said loudly in her crispest voice, in which all trace of fear had been suppressed. 'I hope the milk will ease your trouble!'

Arthur Cramer started, glancing sideways at the connecting door to his wife's chamber.

'Good night, Maria,' he replied. His face registered an angry frustration that had nothing to do with lack of sleep. He stood aside to let her pass.

'I'm going to Durango tomorrow morning,' he said in a masterful voice. 'Please prepare my breakfast for six o'clock.'

'I'll tell Nora . . .'

'No, Maria. I want *you* to prepare it – ham and eggs and hash browns.'

She ran up the stairs to the next floor, found her room and put her chair against the door.

Next morning Maria made sure that Nora was with her in the kitchen as she prepared breakfast for Mr Cramer. The little maid had grumbled at being got up so early, and then had come sleepily downstairs.

'That's my job,' she said when she saw Maria at the stove. 'What did you get me up for if you're doing it yourself?'

'Christ, Nora, he told me to do it myself.'

'Why?'

Maria put a finger to her lips as Mr Cramer came into the room. He started when he saw Nora.

'You're up early, Nora! Maria kindly offered to get my breakfast today.'

'I'm just seeing to the fires, sir!' Nora replied in the soft, servile voice she affected when he was around.

'I'll be ready to serve in a moment, Mr Cramer,' Maria said in a tone that was very crisp by contrast.

'*Sir*, Maria. You will call me sir, if you please!'

Nora raised her eyes to heaven as their employer removed himself to the dining room. 'Right ould bollocks,' she whispered with a glance at Maria. But the latter looked grim; she put his breakfast on a tray and followed him.

As Maria brought in Mr Cramer's breakfast he said suddenly in a low voice, giving her a small indulgent smile: 'You're a good girl – getting up in the middle of the night like that to look after me . . .'

His tone invited complicity, a smile, a glance, a shy demurral. But Maria did not reply. She disliked his eyes on her; she could not wait for him to eat his breakfast and leave the house.

'I have to be away for a week, Maria,' he said as she bent to collect the plates, and for a moment his hand strayed to her buttock in an almost accidental caress.

When Mr Cramer finally left, Maria was in a panic. Was this going to happen again? Had he really intended to touch her? And the night before – had it been a calculated attempt on her virtue or an isolated episode, where all he had wanted was some milk for his indigestion? She put the dishes into the sink and Nora began to wash them.

'I suppose himself wasn't bothering you last night?' the latter said in an innocent tone of voice when the door had closed behind their employer.

'He wanted me to get him some milk for his indigestion.' Maria looked up to see Nora's sceptical eyes. 'That's what he said,' she continued. 'I got it for him and left it on his nightstand. And then he said he wanted me to cook his breakfast for him in the morning. But I got you up because I didn't want to be alone with him.'

Nora threw a surreptitious look over her shoulder. The kitchen door was shut, but Nora went to it quickly, opened it, looked out, shut it again.

'You can't be too sure that Evans one isn't listening . . . Look, Maria, that fella'll be up to you again. Why do you think poor Molly Dunne left? She was half damned by him following her around . . . And when he finally cornered her one night, oul' nurse Evans saw them and the missus threw her out. She didn't want to hear Molly's side of the story. Oh, he'd be after me too, only I look like something the divil designed!'

'I keep my door locked,' Maira said in dismay. 'Last night I even put the chair against it.'

'Sure, but he'll always need something! And then you'll have to unlock it to look after him! That's what you're paid for.'

Maria thought about this. 'He's gone to Durango today – for a whole week. That'll give us a rest from the sight of him.'

Should she tell Tom, enlist his help in moving to another place? Would he think she was imagining things? Then she thought – I should be able to look after myself. But eventually she wrote, asking if she could visit Tom on Sunday. This would be an opportunity to mention her worries. His reply came by return, telling her to take the train, that he would meet her at Golden.

On the following Sunday, her day off, Maria took the train to Golden. It was a fine spring day. The train slid out of the Union depot with a warning jangle and a sonorous hoot, passed manufacturing establishments as far as the bridge to the Platte River where it gathered speed.

Maria marvelled at the ease of rail travel, comparing it favourably to the exhausting trek she had experienced across the prairie. The track began to climb; they passed Argo, with its smelting works, and on to Summit from where, looking back, she could see Denver lying among its trees, with its churches, private residences and commercial buildings.

To the south were the mountains – the Plum Creek Divide – with Pikes Peak putting up its head behind them.

The Platte River valley, the sweeping plains, bounded on the west by the mountains – the beauty of everything made Maria feel that she had been too long immured in domesticity. How wonderful to be a man like Ted Lafferty and spend one's life out of doors. The longing for him rose unbidden from every nerve in her being.

The train descended to cross the bridge at Clear Creek, then Ralston Creek, moved on to the outposts of the Rockies, passing the remains of the old mining town of Arapahoe.

The track now followed the chasm cut by the Clear Creek River through the Table Mountains, the flat-topped sentinels of the Rockies, and pulled into Golden, fifteen miles from Denver.

Tom was waiting for her. As soon as Maria saw him she knew she could not burden him with her problems. He looked tired to death. But for a young man who was not long into his twenties he seemed mature beyond his years, his body filled out and muscular, his red moustache pronounced on his upper lip. The hands with which he grasped hers were lean and calloused.

'They're working you too hard!' she whispered. 'Twelve-hour shifts are too long.'

'Nonsense, Maria. It's the way I want it.'

'But you're educated compared to many people working on the railroad; there are easier jobs.'

'But not so well paid. I have things to do, miss, and do them I will!'

'Anyone would think you were expecting some kind of magic.'

'Not magic, Maria. Just fair play.' He lowered his voice. 'At home there was nothing. Here there is hope. Insofar as I can determine the future I have willed for something with all my soul.'

'For what?'

'For riches beyond measure,' Tom replied in a low intense voice, looking her in the eye as though daring her to laugh. 'For the chance to set up Father and Peggie; for the chance of going home, buying that white mansion of Kilduncan's and his stolen land, and giving some respite to our people. The railroad is a start. When I lie awake thinking about it at night something strange happens . . .' He stopped as though he had disclosed too much.

'What happens when you lie awake at night?' Maria whispered after a moment.

'Ah, Maria, you will laugh.'

She shook her head.

'It comes to me in the darkness,' he said softly, 'that there is some extraordinary chance coming my way, for which I have to remain awake.'

He looked at her sideways, but Maria's face was closed and grave.

Is this the result of the stupid forecasting I used to do? she wondered. She had tried to 'feel' the drift of the future since coming to Denver, but her talent seemed to have deserted her, as though she really had given it to her brother that day on the SS *Samaria* as the last sight of Ireland had disappeared below the horizon.

Tom took his sister around Golden, along the covered boardwalks of Washington Avenue, and down the road that rambled between fields and orchards to Lena Creek. They had lunch, and later he showed her from a distance the lines running north to Longmonth and west to Black Hawk.

'There will be a rail network here to beat the band – all the way to Georgetown and Silver Plume, and northwards to a junction with Union Pacific. It's a three-foot narrow gauge because of the climb . . . and that means an extra rail . . .'

Maria sighed, but she tried to share his enthusiasm.

'It sounds great . . .' After a moment she added, 'Tom . . .'

He waited, raised his eyebrows. She saw again the tired cast to his face and the glaze in his eyes.

'Yes?' When she didn't reply he looked at her doubtfully. 'Is everything all right, Maria?'

'Sure.'

She couldn't tell him; it seemed petty here in this wild, male world of new railroads and high mountain walls. Instead she added as casually as she could, 'Have you heard any word of Ted Lafferty?'

Tom shot her a keen glance. 'Funny you should say that. I was just going to tell you that he was here during the week. He said he might drop in to see you in Denver!'

Maria felt as thought her heart would take flight. 'Did he say when?'

Tom shook his head. 'No. But he told me a bit about himself. Seems he was married sixteen years ago – in 'Frisco!'

Maria felt the disappointment, the sinking of her heart.

'But his wife died,' Tom continued. 'She was killed in an accident on a trip to see her mother back east. It was after that that Ted became a scout.'

'Has he children?'

'No. Leastways he didn't mention any.' He glanced at her. 'So he's free, Maria, if that's what you wanted to know.'

Maria kept her face deadpan, but she flushed. 'I was just curious.'

'Yes,' he said softly, looking down at her with a smile. 'The heart's an inquisitive oul' timepiece, isn't it?'

He saw her to the train and into her seat, kissed her cheek. If you don't tell him about Mr Cramer now, Maria told herself, you've lost the opportunity.

'Look after yourself,' Tom said.

'Tom . . .' But she couldn't say it. Even to speak of such things was to somehow smear herself.

Tom looked at her quizzically, but when she just opened and closed her mouth he sighed and said, 'Maria, Lafferty is a sound man. But what kind of a life would a woman have with him? He'd always be away, a scout for this wagon train or that wagon train . . . Is that what you want?'

Maria made no reply, except to shrug as though the matter didn't concern her one way or the other.

Tom moved to alight before the train pulled out, then waved to her from outside.

'In the name of God,' Maria whispered, angry with herself, as the train gathered speed and she had time to consider her day, 'what is it with men that you have to spell everything out to them? And why am I such a half eejit? Tom *would* have understood.' And then she heard his voice in her head: '*Ted was married . . . but his wife died.*' God help him to have lost her . . .

She looked out the window at the evening panorama, the city of Denver coming into view. But what it means, she told herself, with a tight feeling around her heart, is that he *is* free!

She went back to the Cramer household, letting herself in the backdoor, taking off her hat and coat.

'Did you have a nice day, Maria?' Nora asked her. She was up to her elbows in hot soapy water.

'Yes, very nice. What are you doing?'

'Washin' the silver.'

Nora removed from the suds a silver teapot and Maria took a clean dishcloth from the line and began to dry it, noting with approval how the silver shone as the tarnish came off on to the cloth.

'How is Mrs Cramer today?'

'Still poorly. She doesn't eat enough for a bird.' Nora lowered her voice. 'If you ask me, it isn't that she can't get better, it's that she won't!' She threw a sly look at Maria. 'But himself was asking for you. He's back!'

'Holy God,' Maria said in dismay. 'I thought we had until tomorrow. He said he'd be away a week.'

'He came back at midday . . . and oh, before I forget to tell you,' Nora added slyly, 'someone else was looking for you too.'

'Who?'

'A man I've never seen before. He had a greying kind of a moustache . . . wearing buckskins he was . . . He left something for you!'

Maria paled, then blushed. Nora dried her hands and went to a cupboard from which she removed a small parcel, tied around with a string.

Maria took the parcel, noted her name printed on it – 'Miss Maria Walsh' – turned it to one side and carefully untied the string. Inside was a strange object; when she took it out she saw that it was a belt – made of blue and yellow snakeskin. Pinned to it was a note, the writing square and unpractised. It said:

My dear Maria,
I thought you might like to have this – all good hunters are entitled to their trophies. Ted.

And I had to miss him, she thought, the tears starting in her eyes. I haven't seen him for a whole year. He was here, and I had to miss him!

'Did he say he'd come back, Nora?'

'No. He asked for you and when I said you weren't here he just asked me to give you this.' She looked at the belt curiously and then at Maria, and added: 'Who is he?'

'Oh, just someone I met on the wagon train.'

The library bell jangled. Nora threw Maria a commiserating look.

'Will you answer it, Nora? Tell him I'm not back yet . . .'

Nora's eyes were suddenly wide with fear. 'I can't tell him a lie. You know what he's like.'

Maria donned her white apron, strode to the library, crossing the polished hall, catching a reflection in the oval mirror above the hall table of a grim young woman in a white apron. She knocked and entered. The room smelled of polish and cigar smoke. Her employer was sitting in his leather armchair by the fire.

'Ah, there you are, Maria. Did you have a nice day?'

'Yes, thank you, sir.'

'Meet your young man?'

'He's my brother, sir. He's working on the railroad.'

He looked at her appraisingly. 'Is that so? You should invite him to visit.'

'Thank you, sir.'

She waited. There was silence except for the settling of the fire. 'Will I build up the fire, sir?'

'Oh, yes, of course. Thank you, Maria.'

She bent down for the shovel and the tongs, feeling his eyes on her. 'Will that be all, sir?'

There was renewed silence. Then Arthur Cramer said, 'There was a man here today looking for you . . . rough-and-ready sort of fellow. You seem to have quite a complement of male admirers.'

Maria flushed. 'Indeed I do not, sir!'

Her employer put down his glass, rose from his seat and approached her. There was a hot look to his eyes, and the familiar slack smile to his mouth.

'I am a lonely man. My wife is not . . . Will you give me a kiss, Maria?'

'No, sir.'

He leaned towards her suddenly and wrapped his arms around her. Maria felt his moustache against her face, the smell of alcohol on his breath, the tightening of his arms so that her breast was crushed against him. It was sickening and insulting, completely different to the only other experience of its kind she had known. She twisted her head to evade his mouth, and levered her elbow into his stomach.

Tom did his sums. After his latest pay packet he had saved $670. He set aside $50 to send to Ireland.

He thought back on the day before; Maria had looked well, if a little subdued. Maybe she was bored after the excitement of the plains. And, of course, a house with a sick woman couldn't be much fun.

He knew she had been right when she said there were easier jobs than his. But it wasn't ease he was after. It was success.

'As soon as I've saved some more money,' he told himself, 'I'll go to Denver and start my own business!'

In his mind's eye he saw Kilduncan House. It would be a fitting home for his father and Peggie. He saw the grand new gravestone on his mother's grave. He saw the future, a fine place he would build for everyone he loved.

Maria knew that she would have to find another position. There was no point in pretending otherwise. She had managed to extricate herself last time – levering herself from Mr Cramer's arms – but knew that if she didn't go at once the situation would repeat itself and she would end up branded in some horrible way. So on the morning following her encounter with him she went to see his wife in her sickroom.

Every time Maria saw this woman she was always struck by her air of defeat. She was in her mid-thirties, thin and pale, still grieving for the dead baby. She was propped up on several snow-white, frilled pillows, staring out the window at the blue Denver sky.

'Ah, Maria, there you are. My husband tells me you are running the house like clockwork,' she smiled. 'I don't know what we'd do without you.'

Maria gulped. She looked into the hollow hazel eyes that were smudged with shadows.

'Thank you, ma'am. I was just . . . wondering . . .'

Maria glanced at the nurse who was sitting beside the fire with her knitting, her round, curious eyes fixed on her.

'Wondering what, Maria?'

'. . . If you had any orders for dinner this evening.'

'Well, my husband will be dining out as usual,' the woman replied in apparent puzzlement, 'and I will have a little soup again.' Then she frowned and demanded, 'Is something wrong? You look troubled.'

'Nothing, ma'am . . .'

She went downstairs, cursing herself. 'Oh, you eejit, why didn't you say you were leaving? Why didn't you ask for a character?'

That night Mr Cramer did not return until ten, and then the library bell rang. Maria, alone in the kitchen, felt her heart miss a beat, and wished that Nora had not gone up to bed. She debated furiously what she should do, and then decided to ignore the bell. It rang again, this time imperiously.

I'll slip upstairs, she thought, and lock my door. I can always say I was in bed asleep and didn't hear him. And I'll leave in the morning; I'll go to Tom in Golden.

But as she gently opened the kitchen door she saw Mr Cramer approaching along the hall.

'Didn't you hear the bell, Maria?' he asked in a soft, insinuating voice.

'Yes, sir. I was just going to . . .'

He came up against her and backed her into the kitchen. 'Then why didn't you answer it promptly?' His hand strayed to the buttons on her bosom. 'This button is loose. You should attend to it. I do insist on neatness, Maria,' he added, not unkindly, looking down at her, 'neatness and obedience.' His hand rested on her breast and the smile she had begun to dread formed on his lips. 'Neatness and obedience . . .' he repeated, 'in all things!'

For a moment she wanted to run, but a haughty defiance surfaced from deep in her soul. She thrust his hand away.

'Do you indeed, sir?' she answered just as softly. 'Perhaps it is what has your wife sick and your house silent. Perhaps what you should insist on instead is decency and an upright life!'

He started and the smile died on his lips. 'How dare you, you little Irish trollop?'

Maria stood her ground. 'If you touch me again, sir,' she said on a rising tide of outrage, 'I will scream the house down. I am certainly Irish, and prouder of it than I can say, but I am no trollop. And I cannot stay in a house with a man the like of you!'

The slap connected with her cheek, a short sharp rebuke that stung to the bone, and shocked her to the point of tears.

'Then leave my house at once, you impertinent hussy.'

He took her by the arm, propelled her to the back door and thrust her out into the night. She heard the small thud of the bolt as it slid home.

Merciful God, she thought, shivering in the cool night air. She looked up at the top of the house to Nora's window. She took up a few pebbles and aimed them, wondering if there was any point in trying to rouse someone with a mouse for a soul.

The curtain stirred and Nora's pale, scared face appeared for a moment at the window. She looked down at Maria; then she shrank into her shoulders and raised her hands in a gesture of hopelessness.

Maria picked her way around the side of the house in the darkness, and down the street. She would go to the Marmions; she knew their house-keeper, Jane, who would surely help her.

On the dark, dusty road a carriage passed her, then stopped. The window was let down and a young man's face looked out at her.

'Hello, darlin',' the slurred voice said. 'How much do you charge?'

Laughter erupted from his companions.

'You're making a mistake,' Maria said, as the import of what he had said came home to her, shocking her to the core. She walked on, aware that she should not have spoken, that by so doing she had unwittingly licensed presumption. The carriage moved to keep pace with her.

'You're in a great hurry,' the voice said. 'Why not let us bring you to your destination? We'd be only too delighted, wouldn't we, boys?'

This was greeted by a chorus of guffaws and ribald comment.

Maria did not reply. She was now very frightened. There was no one else within sight; the houses were set back from the road, and there was no other traffic or pedestrians.

Her tormentor opened the door of the carriage, stepped down, walked behind her and touched her on the shoulder with his cane.

Maria turned on him furiously. 'Leave me alone!' But she hated the fear she knew was in her eyes.

The young man looked up and down the street, but there was only the carriage with its smirking driver and its complement of young men, their heads sticking out of the window, urging on their friend. She saw her pursuer's face, his dilated eyes, realised that he did not really see her, that to him she represented only illicit opportunity, the thrill of plunder and the opportunity to swagger in his friends' esteem.

The Marmions' house was still some distance away. She began to run.

He thrust out his cane. She fell heavily, hurting her wrist and grazing her face. In a moment the young man was standing over her.

'Right little firebrand . . .'

There was a chorus of encouragement from the carriage. As she saw his hand move to his flies a voice in Maria's head said: I will not suffer this, endure this, no matter what. She thought longingly of the Colt she had worn on the long trek West and the hated holster Ted Lafferty had given her. If only she had it now. She had once killed a snake with it; a harmless creature apparently, unlike the one who now loomed over her, urged on by his friends. She did the only thing she could, something she knew would reach any ears that were open. She screamed.

Sometime during the following afternoon someone cried out in horror. Tom heard it from almost half a mile away, and felt the hairs rise at the back of his neck. He had been checking the sleepers that were to be laid the following day, but he shoved the list he was making into his pocket, and ran towards the sound. The men around put down their sledgehammers; a crowd converged on the spot where half a Chinaman slumped in death, still staring at the truncated mess that had been the rest of him.

'Caught in the winch,' someone said.

The body had been cut clean in half by the steel rope of the winch. The word ran back along the lines of men. One by one the Irish workmen made the sign of the cross.

The ganger came up, looked down at the remains, paled.

'Bloody Chinks, that hawser will have to be checked for damage . . .'

He looked around. 'What are you all standing there for? Take him away.'

And to Tom. 'Walsh, will you see to it? The rest of you get on with the work. You can't tell these Chinks anything.'

Tom nodded to the Chinese agent who spoke rapidly.

Immediately four Chinese workmen came forward and moved the remains to the tents.

Tom walked back to his position further down the track. Cut in half! he thought and suddenly, overwhelmed by nausea, bent over and retched.

A man's life has to be worth more than this, he told himself, wiping his mouth. There has to be a point to being alive. Am I a half *amadán* to be working here at all?

Alastair Sutherland, another foreman and one of his friends, came along. Alastair was from Manchester, and kept talking about the chances of another gold boom. 'We might hit it right where we're building the railroad,' he was fond of saying. But at this moment he looked green.

'Disgusting,' he groaned. 'Poor little bastard! I'm getting out of this, Tom. You should too . . .'

When Tom returned to his lodgings that evening he realised at once that something strange had happened. The wooden trunk he and Maria had brought from Ireland was in the hallway; he heard her voice through the door of the sitting room, sounding small and diffident as she responded to Mrs Stornheim, the landlady.

He hung his cap and coat in the hall and entered the room.

'What are you doing here, Maria?'

The face his sister turned to him was covered with bruises and grazes to cheek and chin. She lowered her gaze and burst into tears.

'Poor child was nearly . . . last night,' the landlady said in a low voice, raising her eyebrows expressively and shaking her head. 'You left her in a nice pickle – with that awful Mr Cramer! And he threw her out on the side of the road!'

Tom crossed the room. 'What has happened to you?' he demanded gently, but his voice was dangerous. 'Tell me . . .' He gestured to her face. 'Did Cramer do that to you?'

Maria sobbed her response. 'No. It . . . was on the road last night . . . A man tripped me – he got out of his carriage . . . He wanted to . . . He was with his friends . . .'

'In the name of God,' Tom demanded, holding her and staring into her face, 'what are you talking about? What were you doing out on the road at night?'

'I'm trying to tell you!' Maria cried. 'Will you listen?'

Tom sat opposite her, still holding her hands. He looked grimmer and grimmer as she told the story.

'And this Mr Cramer actually struck you?' he demanded when she was finished.

She nodded, bursting into fresh tears.

Tom rocked her. 'You're safe now,' he said. 'Don't cry!'

'Please don't do anything foolish, Tom,' she said as she dried her eyes. 'It was probably my fault . . . I was very rude to him . . . Look, I'm fine now . . .' And she tried to smile, but only winced.

Mrs Stornheim shot Tom an anxious look. 'She'll be fine,' she said in a placating voice. 'It was a fright more than anything else.'

'Oh, it was much more than that,' Tom said softly, his face grim. 'Cramer used his position to abuse my sister, and put her in the way of danger.'

'I'll get over it,' Maria said, looking at him with some anxiety. 'I'll just have to get another job. But if you do anything to Mr Cramer, Tom Walsh, you'll end up in jail. And I'll never be able to get another position. As it is . . . it will be difficult enough . . . I have no reference,' her voice fractured, 'and now where am I going to stay?'

'Don't you take on like that, young lady,' Mrs Stornheim said. 'I've a spare room you can have – it's beside your brother's and big enough for a small bed. And I've a job for you too if you want it. I need someone to help me run this place. Wages won't be great, but you'll be with your brother, and I can't help feeling that's the best place for you just now!'

Tom went to bed that night wondering why nothing was working out according to plan. He dwelled on Maria with increasing apprehension, wondering why he had not foreseen problems. Young emigrant women perforce took up positions without knowing much of their employers. He should not have cajoled her into coming West. And now she would be waiting at table in a mining camp boarding house. Was this what he had brought her to, with all his promises? His beautiful, ladylike sister?

He reviewed his own situation – three years in America, a few hundred dollars saved. Enough for a start maybe. But first he knew there was something he had to do. There was a visit to be paid to one Arthur Cramer.

On the other side of the wooden partition, Maria lay awake, sick with relief at being safe, her head full of the events of the night before. She still heard the high-pitched sound of her own screams, saw the lights that had come on in the houses, heard the barking dogs, the rattle of her tormentor's carriage as it sped away, the kind arm of Mrs Marmion, who had brought her indoors and sent word to the sheriff.

The deputy sheriff had accompanied her to the Cramers', overseen the removal of her trunk, and the payment of her overdue wages.

Mr Cramer had appeared in his dressing gown. She could still hear his voice, full of silky innuendo. 'I had to turn her out, officer. Look,' he had added, holding up his gold fob watch, 'I found my belongings in her room.'

The deputy sheriff shot her a doubtful look.

'That's a lie,' she cried. 'And he knows it is!'

'Are you charging the young woman with theft, sir?'

Maria listened to the exchange with consternation. To be accused of theft, however unjustly, was to her mind a permanent blemish.

'The girl probably didn't know what she was doing,' Arthur Cramer said. 'You know what these poor creatures are like . . .'

That was too much for Maria. She turned to the deputy and said scornfully, 'When I refused this man's advances, he slapped my face and put me out. Surely to God you only have to look at him, at the two shifty eyes of him, and the mean little mouth of him, to see how he is lying!'

'I seem to recall there was another young woman who left your employ in similarly hurried circumstances not so long ago, sir,' the deputy sheriff said.

It was then that Mr Cramer had allowed Maria to put her things into her trunk, while the lawman looked on.

But Maria had told Tom none of this. She smarted from the memory of it; but she was afraid of what she had seen in her brother's eyes. I should have kept my mouth shut, she told herself. You know perfectly well you can't tell men anything. She fingered the scratches on her face, now covered in small scabs, winced when she moved her wrist.

They cremated the Chinaman in a clearing at the side of the track. His compatriots had prepared a pyre from logs felled for the railroad. The victim's corpse lay on it, dressed in a long silk robe, looking oddly composed. In death he seemed whole again. When the flames took hold the Chinese workers chanted strange prayers and burned incense sticks. The wood spluttered, the smell of pine and woodsmoke filled the chasm, drifted into the trees. As he watched, Tom saw the robe burning from the body, the two halves of which could be seen blackening in the inferno.

Afterwards he offered his sympathy to Dr Chen Mung, a cousin of the deceased, who was employed by the railroad to look after the Chinese workmen.

'I'm very sorry, Dr Chen. Your cousin was a good man and the accident should not have happened. Did he have a wife?'

The man bowed. 'He was saving for marriage. Bride waiting in China.'

'So he had not been long in America?'

'Two years. In China my cousin was civil servant. But he want freedom. Money very good on railroad, but many times I tell him go home.'

'Why?'

'I cast the sticks, but *I Ching* not good.'

Tom frowned. 'What do you mean?'

'*I Ching* tell future – very old Chinese wisdom. In English it called Book of Change.'

When Tom looked blank he added slowly, as though searching for the right words, 'It understand . . . how all life is transition . . .'

That much is true, Tom said to himself. Life is a book, where one chapter must succeed another if there is to be a story. But sometimes it gets stuck in the one episode, and grinds on.

As though he had devined Tom's thought Dr Chen continued with a bow, '*I Ching* tell future for you, honoured sir, if you wish?' and he took from his pocket an ivory container full of small ivory sticks and held them out to Tom.

Tom was curious. He thought how Father Doyle would have said he was damned if he went along with this, how the priest had warned Maria on more than one occasion about the spiritual dangers inherent in fortune-telling. But damning people was a great way to keep them in line. Why not? he thought.

Dr Chen bowed, took a square of silk from his pocket and spread it on the ground. Tom took the proffered bundle of small ivory sticks.

'First you ask question – what you want to know. Then throw sticks on cloth.'

Tom, feeling a little foolish, murmured the question that formed itself immediately: 'Will the future be worth the work?' He threw the sticks.

Dr Chen took some time examining the way the sticks had fallen. He seemed almost perplexed; turned to glance at Tom and then back to the configuration before him. Then he shook his head, gathered them up and put them away.

'So what is my fortune?' Tom demanded, trying not to smile.

The Chinaman glanced at him strangely and looked away.

'*I Ching* not work well today . . . Sometime it make mistake . . .' He bowed and moved away.

Tom sighed inwardly, reminded himself he had more to do than involve himself in nonsense. One of the things he had to do was pay a visit to Denver.

It was Sunday. The road was almost empty. Tom opened the gate to the large clapboard house and, barely glancing at the garden behind its wicket fence, approached the hall door. A little pockmarked housemaid answered; looked up at him nervously.

'Are you Nora?' he asked.

She nodded. 'I know who you are,' she whispered. 'You're Maria's brother?'

'I've called to see Mr Cramer.'

Nora looked over her shoulder into hall and lowered her voice. 'Is Maria all right?'

'She's fine.'

'You'd better come round to the back.'

'I'm quite comfortable with the front.'

She cast another nervous glance over her shoulder. 'I don't think he'll see you . . .'

Tom excused himself, stepped past her into the hall, walked to the door at which the maid cast her frightened glances, and flung it open.

'Oh please . . .' came Nora's timid voice behind him, but Tom had already stepped into the room and closed the door behind him.

Arthur Cramer started to his feet as the tall, red-haired stranger came into his library, filling the room with his size and his strength.

'Let me introduce myself,' Tom said quietly. 'My name is Walsh.'

But already his ire was dissipating. He saw immediately that the man before him was a paper tiger. It was there in every line of his self-important face, his stiff white collar, his prissy mouth; Tom had met them before, insignificant men who lived through tyranny.

'Well, Mr Cramer,' he said, striding across the room and staring the man in the face, his chin jutting, 'what have you to say for yourself? You insulted and struck my young sister, exposed her to danger and affront!'

'How dare you force your way in here—'

'Maybe you thought she was fair game because she's a woman,' Tom continued in the same quiet voice. 'I've come to give you the chance of trying out your tricks on me instead.'

Arthur Cramer reached swiftly for a desk drawer. Tom knocked his hand away.

'What are you waiting for, Mr Cramer?' he asked softly. 'Why don't you strike and insult *me*?'

Cramer backed away. 'It was all a misunderstanding. There's no need for this . . . My wife is ill . . .' He gestured to the small safe on the opposite side of the room. 'There's money . . .'

Tom grunted his contempt, pressing Cramer into the chair by the desk.

'Some people have standards, Mr Cramer. You will write an apology to my sister.' He tensed the muscles of his shoulders and leaned forward, handing Arthur Cramer a pen.

The man took it, looked angrily at Tom. 'What do you want me to say?'

'*Dear Miss Walsh,*' Tom dictated.

Arthur Cramer nervously wrote it down, then looked up at Tom with resentful eyes.

'*I wish to offer you my heartfelt apology for the manner in which I have treated you,*' Tom continued.

'I can't write this—'

'I think you can, Mr Cramer.'

Their eyes met again. Arthur Cramer looked back at the page.

'*Your conduct and service has at all times been exemplary,*' Tom continued. '*Unfortunately, I am a natural bully, who likes to pick on people over whom I have a little power.*'

A blob of ink snaked off the pen and on to the paper. Arthur Cramer blotted it automatically, and put down his pen.

'This is preposterous!' he said.

'I don't think it is,' Tom said, staring at him fixedly. 'In the circumstances I don't think it is at all! *I beg to remain your most contrite servant,*' he continued. 'Now, if you would be so good as to sign it and address an envelope . . .'

Cramer obeyed reluctantly, writing the address as Tom spoke it and directing a glance at a drawer beside his right hand.

'Thank you.'

Tom put the envelope in his pocket. Then, intercepting the sudden move that Maria's former employer made in the direction of a desk drawer, Tom flipped it open, drew out a revolver, removed the chamber, emptied the bullets, and put the chamber into his pocket.

'With your permission I'll leave this in your hallway,' he said. 'A coward's bullet in my back is as lethal as any.'

Arthur Cramer was white with rage.

'You'll regret this, Walsh.'

'I don't think so,' Tom replied. He left the room and quietly shut the door behind him.

The little maid came hovering, looking at him anxiously. Tom tossed the revolver chamber to her and let himself out.

Two days later Mrs Stornheim called, 'Letter for you, Maria.'

Maria opened the stiff, white envelope and gasped as she read.

'Imagine Mr Cramer writing me an apology,' she said to herself in utter perplexity as she perused the missive. 'Maybe he has a conscience after all . . . And will you look how he speaks about himself . . .'

'He can't have been that bad,' she said to Tom that evening. 'He had the grace to write me a very full apology.'

Tom drank his coffee and made noncommittal noises.

The time passed. Tom was promoted. The railway moved westwards to Black Hawk and north to Floyd Hill. Half the men were in love with Maria. Tom saw the burgeoning jealousy among them of anyone to whom she spoke for more than a few minutes. He watched her to see if she were interested in any of the railway men, but she went about her work quietly, and seemed oblivious of the *frisson* her presence caused. Not surprising, Tom thought, as he looked around him. This bunch are not exactly the answer to a maiden's prayer!

He saw that she read a good deal, and he tried to procure as many books for her as possible. He had no way of knowing that every night she went to sleep thinking of one person, murmuring his name: Ted Lafferty, a man old enough to be her father.

Tom went to sleep weighing up how much longer he should continue working for the railroad, calculating the capital he would need to set up in Denver, dreaming of the construction business he would one day own.

In August 1874 something happened that was to change for ever the course of Tom's life, and the lives of his family and friends. He received a letter from Michael with startling news.

> The regiment is now stationed in Dakota Territory under Lieutenant-General George Custer. We've been here for the past couple of months, setting up a new military post. Some experienced miners came with us and they have found gold. They say the creeks are yellow with it. The news will be out in no time, so if you want to get rich now's your opportunity. It may never come again.

The letter was dated 15 July, but by the time it arrived the rumour was already sweeping though the railroad men like a fever.

Tom showed the letter to Alastair Sutherland.

'What did I tell you, Tom? I'm going; I've handed in my notice.'

'But it's in the Sioux reservation!' Tom said. 'Isn't that land protected by the Treaty of Fort Laramie?'

Alastair shrugged.

'The injuns won't be allowed to interfere with progress. They won't mine the gold themselves. The Government needs it. And I, for one, intend to go.'

As the rumours intensified the report of Custer himself confirmed the presence of quantities of gold in the rivers. Hundreds of men joined Alastair Sutherland in throwing down their tools, collecting their wages and leaving for the Black Hills.

Tom thought of the years ahead. He thought of this opportunity opening before him; of Maria waitressing in a boarding house; of the great adventure, the success, he intended to make of his life. And he thought of a promise he had made many years ago.

He handed in his notice and went back to Mrs Stornheim's to tell Maria he was leaving for the Black Hills.

'You don't believe you'll find gold in Dakota Territory, do you?' she demanded. 'You're not so foolish?'

'Maria, it isn't gold I'm after. Half the world is going to the Black Hills. Half the world has to be housed! I'm going back to doing what I know best. We'll have to move you to some decent position in Denver before I go. I'd like you to come, but the journey is dangerous – another long trek by covered wagon – and the life there will be very rough.'

Maria imagined being separated from her brother while she pursued a life in service to some other Arthur Cramer.

'Let me come too.'

'It will be by far the roughest place you've been.'

'But I'll be with you!'

'The conditions will be terrible – no proper accommodation until I can get a cabin built . . . And the Indians are angry; I can't say I blame them.'

'I don't care; I'm not as much a softie as you think! I'm coming too.'

Chapter Six

Deadwood Gulch, South Dakota, was a narrow valley covered with tents. Some tents were small one-man affairs, others were large enough to provide living space for several people. The gulch echoed with the rattle of sluice boxes and the voices of men; some of them stood to the waist in icy water, giving vent to oaths or exclamations as the streams yielded up their gold. In the evenings they played cards or dice in tents set aside for gambling. Sometimes they brawled. Sometimes the report of gunfire reverberated in the hills. The claims divided the land – strips of ground stretching from one rim of the gulch to the other. Extending three hundred feet along a stream, they were the location for sluice boxes and 'rockers' – the smaller boxes used to separate the gold, where the gravel and sediment of the creek was washed by the prospectors.

Tom knew he had come to the right place. Not only were log cabins urgently needed against the approach of winter, but so were the wooden sluice boxes that permitted the work of placer mining to proceed.

'We'll have to get a sawmill going here,' he told Maria. 'But in the meantime I'll have to make do.'

She was the only woman in the place and was still astonished by the strange experience she had had in venturing forth from their tent that first morning, when every single man in the gulch had stood up to stare at her. Some of them had come down from the hills, she heard later, just to see her, the 'petticoated astonishment' that had come into their midst.

There were thousands of trees around Deadwood but little flat land except along Whitewood Creek. Tom quickly acquired a building lot and began construction. He did not lack help. The men came in droves; they wanted to build a proper cabin for the lady, they said, and they looked at her sideways as though she were something from a fairy tale.

'Haven't seen a lady for nigh on two years, ma'am,' one of them said to her, removing his hat awkwardly as though he were in church.

The logs were cut from the forest with saws, and stacked on the building lot; they gave up their heady perfume to the crisp air.

'I'll have a home for us soon, miss,' Tom told Maria, 'and after that I've got more work lined up than I can cope with.' He looked at her carefully; asked in a gentle voice: 'Are you content to stay?'

Maria nodded. Privately she wanted to go back East; but what was there for her except loneliness? Besides, she wanted to look after Tom, whom she suspected would work himself to death. And getting back East now would be like getting to the moon.

When they had been in Deadwood for little more than a fortnight a soldier rode into the encampment on a big bay horse, dressed in the blue uniform of the Union army.

Maria started when the open tent entrance was blocked by a military man. At first she did not know him. The light was behind him and for a second she thought it was Ted Lafferty, and her heart missed a beat. Then she saw her elder brother's bemused and oddly vulnerable face, older, weathered. The boy who had left them was now a man, full-shouldered, moustached. Instantly she was back at home in the kitchen at Carraig Mór with the scent of burning turf, and the sound of the cow lowing to be milked, the rain hissing behind her in the fire, and her father arguing with the fieriest of his children. A sob wrenched itself from her throat and she flung herself at her brother who caught her in a bear hug.

'Micheál, is tusa an fear laidir anois . . .' she cried when she drew back to look at him. She had thought she had forgotten Irish, but it surfaced of its own volition to tell him how fine he looked, how different, with his whiskers, and his grown-upness.

'Nílim,' he said, disclaiming admiration. 'My God, Maria, how strange to find you in this godforsaken place. You bring the whole of Clonmel with you, as though there were ghosts in every hair on your head! I thought you would have married a merchant prince by now out East . . . but here you are in this mud bath!'

She noticed the smell that clung to him: yesternight's spirits, sweat, horse, dubbin and leather. The whites of his eyes were smudged with small red veins, and the hands that held her own were rough and thickly calloused.

'Where have you come from?'

'Custer – fifty miles over a dog of a road.'

'How long can you stay? Tom is over at our building lot near the creek. He's going to build us a cabin!'

'I can stay one night. But he shouldn't have brought you here. It's no place for a decent woman!'

'I'm very well treated,' she replied stiffly. 'My decency is in no way compromised, I assure you.'

'But wouldn't you be better off in Boston, or in Denver where you were?'

That was Michael all over, she thought, ready to run everyone's lives for them. It came with a sense of shock that time had not softened him, nor distance, nor even seeing each other after so long a separation.

'I *wanted* to come,' she replied shortly. 'And no, I wouldn't be better off where I was! You know nothing of what I had to put up with in Denver and you needn't assume that decency is the preserve of so-called gentility. I am protected here in a queer kind of way; Tom has many friends, and if anyone bothered me—'

Michael sighed. 'I know,' he said caustically. 'All these saints around you would spring to the rescue.'

She would have made a sarcastic retort, but remembered that he had come on a long and treacherous journey just to see them.

'Are you hungry?' she asked. 'Will you have something to eat?'

'I'd rather find Tom. We can eat later.'

He went outside to where his horse waited patiently, took a parcel from his saddlebag and threw it to her.

'A few little dainties. Thought you might do with them . . .'

He was gone in a moment. Maria opened the package. There was flour and rice, and a packet of cocoa, something she had seen only in the Vandermeer house in Boston. There were also several tins of condensed milk and some precious coffee.

Later that evening, after a supper of boiled bacon and potatoes, the three siblings sat together on the groundsheet in the tent and talked of old times. Michael produced a bottle of bourbon from his saddlebags and poured his brother a tot. After a while he became garrulous.

'You're a driven man, Tom – Boston, Golden, now Deadwood Gulch! Are you here for the gold?'

'I'm not going to gamble on that aspiration,' Tom replied. 'Technically this is Sioux land and prospecting is still illegal. I know the Government is turning a blind eye, but if I can't do it decently I won't do it at all. Besides, as there is huge demand for builders, I have more work lined up than I can cope with.'

Michael lit his pipe, filling the tent with pungent smoke. Maria opened the flap to admit some air. It was raining; the air was damp and sweet with the smell of the firs. She heard the wind in the trees and the voices behind her, Tipperary accents in this distant land.

'How often do you hear from home?'

'I'm not much of a letter writer as you know,' Michael said, 'but I get the odd letter from Peggie. She says everything's grand. You know she's getting married?'

'I didn't!'

'There's probably a letter waiting for you in Golden.'

'But she's only eighteen!'

'It's old enough.'

'Who is she marrying?' Maria demanded. 'Do we know him?'

'It's some peeler or other, a man by the name of Healy. They're going to live in Cork!'

Maria shook her head. 'A policeman! And Father will be left alone.'

'Oh, she puts a good complexion on it all; says that Seamus Farrelly will look out for him. Seamie was always a very decent man . . . Now that we're so far away,' Michael added, 'and our noses are no longer stuck in it, doesn't it seem a queer bloody way to live out your days, half starved and destroyed in your own country by impertinent gobshites, and bearing it with such cursed fortitude?'

'Perhaps the Government never meant to make it so terrible . . .' Maria whispered.

'An accident, you mean, Maria? Like when they used to cut the hands off our pipers, hang our harpists?'

'You sound like a man who'd like to go back,' Tom said softly. 'You know things are changing? There's secret ballot now; and a new party that's looking for Home Rule.'

Michael tamped down his pipe. 'Fat chance of that! Aye . . . I'd like to go back and start a revolution, a real one this time. The French were able to do it right, so why couldn't we?'

'With this difference – the French army were themselves revolutionary, whereas the army is Ireland is an army of occupation . . .'

'Arragh, go on with you. Many of the soldiers are as Irish as the next! But I may as well face reality,' he added, 'I'll never get home. Our pay is poor; and the West has got into my bones.' He looked up, and added with a half-laugh, 'It suits me – a wild life for a wild man . . .'

He turned to his sister and said in a slurred voice, 'You've little to say for yourself, Maria. Is it that you're worn out listening to our *ráiméis*, or that you're not entirely enchanted with your new surroundings?' He addressed his brother. 'Was it out of your head you were to bring her to a place like this – with the Indians in scalping mood and the whole place liable to find itself in a fight to the death . . .?'

Tom looked stricken.

'I suppose you're relying on the army to protect you?' Michael added, and Maria saw Tom's face stiffen.

'You always had a wasp for a tongue when you had a sup too much,' she said. 'I came with Tom because I didn't want to stay back without him. And right now, as there isn't a gentle word out of you, I'm going to bed.'

'Ah, sure don't heed me,' Michael said. 'You needn't worry your head. The Sioux will cede this territory anyway. What else can they do? They're outgunned and outnumbered. The army will be sending troops here in the spring to keep an eye on you all.'

Maria went to the small section of the tent that was screened off by a sheet of canvas and lay down on the bedroll.

She was frightened by what Michael had said. She heard her brothers' voices, lowered now, Tom's increasingly nostalgic, Michael's increasingly slurred as he recited one poem after another, some in Irish, some in English. When they came to Gray's 'Elegy' they recited the verses in turn, their voices tense with emotion. As she drifted towards sleep the words engulfed her like a tide bringing her home:

'But Knowledge to their eyes her ample page
Rich with the spoils of time did ne'er unroll;
Chill Penury repress'd their noble rage,
And froze the genial current of the soul.'

When she got up in the morning, her elder brother was gone.

Ten days later Tom and Maria received the long-awaited letter from Peggie.

I have a bit of news that will interest you. Your little sister is engaged to be married – someone you don't know. His name is John Healy and he is a constable in the RIC! He's from Cork, but was stationed here when I first met him. Father likes him, probably because he talks to him a good deal about the way things are in the country.

He looks very handsome in uniform and teases me that I just fell in love with what he calls his 'green working suit'. We're saving up to get married but it'll be a long engagement, I'm thinking. I'll be moving down to Cork with him, for he's stationed there.

Father is just after coming in from the milking. He says to send you all his love. As you know, the neighbours here are the best, but I feel sorry that I will be leaving Father. He will be all alone.

Do you remember the ribbons you sent me after you went away? I never wore them; I still have them. But I'll wear them on my wedding day and think of you.

Maria read the letter and wept from homesickness.

Maria admitted to herself that she hated Deadwood. She hated its mud street, the stagnant pools left by the rain, the smells, the absence of the comforts of life. It was impossible to go anywhere without struggling through mire and being eyed by hundreds of men. But as the time passed she couldn't help being caught up in its air of feverish expectancy.

The population was expanding by the day – with Irish, English, Chinese, Scots, Slovenians, Italians, Swedes, Danes, Germans and almost every other nationality under the sun. But there were few other women.

She was accosted only once – when a drunk pulled her into a tent. She screamed and Tom came running. The man fell like a stone when Tom's fist connected with his face.

She clapped her hand over her mouth as she surveyed the man's apparently lifeless form, and cried, 'He's dead! Oh holy God, Tom, you've killed him!'

'Well, if he is, he's the first corpse I've seen breathing,' Tom said drily, looking down at his handiwork.

He turned to the small crowd that had gathered, said in a voice so quiet that all hushed to listen, 'Let this be clear – I'll deal with any man who bothers my sister through the sights of my rifle. I'll shoot first and ask questions afterwards.'

Seán Clarke, who had recently found a considerable quantity of gold, shouted, 'Ye needn't bother yer barney, Tom. That lassie's our good luck and we'll skin anyone who lays a finger on her!'

Maria was becoming accustomed to the gauche gallantry with which she was treated by most of the miners.

But as the autumn wore on and the mud dirt floor beneath the tent became a slippery nightmare, she longingly remembered the houses she had known in Boston and in Denver, the polished floors and the fine rugs. And then she thought of Mr Arthur Cramer, and shivered. Here, in this outpost of the world, among these rough men, she felt oddly safe.

But I don't want to spend my life chasing safety, she thought. I wish I could wear breeches and a shirt and high boots like the men.

With the rumours of Indian attack, Tom had restored her revolver to her and sometimes she spent hours at a time practising her aim. She became adept at shooting tin cans. Tom watched her progress with approval, but warned her not to stray into the woods. But Maria did not always obey him. She loved the smell of pine, the sharp, heady freshness that sang its way up her nose and cleared a path to her brain. She would finger the leather of the holster fondly. Once it had been in Ted Lafferty's hands.

Her heart lifted in spite of herself as the cabin that Tom was building rapidly took shape.

As there was no band saw here, Tom and his helpers went about splitting logs with axes. He marked the dimensions out on the plot of ground, cleared and levelled it, put down a rudimentary stone foundation – a single line of unmortared stones – and then set about putting up the cabin. It was going to be a much bigger cabin than any of the others around, and this was for a reason.

Tom was going into business. He wanted a small shop, a kitchen-cum-parlour with a fireplace, and two small bedrooms. Maria heard him discussing the plans with the men who were helping him, and whom in turn he was to help – heard him speak of 'chinking' and 'corner notching'.

'Steeple notching,' he told the pipe-smoking men who were considering the options, 'is probably the fastest and the best for the corners of a log cabin – makes for a very stable structure that will last. Look, you shape a ridge on the top of a log and a groove on its underside like this – so that ridge and groove meet.'

The strange house grew, with tightly knit split-log walls and a tamped dirt floor.

'Now don't be worrying about the floor,' Tom told Maria. 'As soon as we have a sawmill here I'll put a floor in that will gladden your heart.'

You'd think we were getting married, Maria thought ruefully, instead of being brother and sister. And then a loneliness filled her, and into her mind came the sight of certain eyes smiling above a greying moustache. Even if he returns to Denver, I won't be there, she thought, and Ted won't know where to find me. Life is so unfair.

The cabin was rough on the outer walls, but the interior walls were almost smooth, and any gaps between the logs were filled with pale plaster-like chinking.

'A bit of fancy wallpaper and you'd think you were back with the Vandermeers,' Tom said with a twinkle. 'But you'll have to wait for it . . . I don't think it features as top of the list on most supply wagons . . . and I'd glaze the windows too if there was any glass to be had hereabouts.'

Instead the windows were 'glazed' with oiled canvas, and Tom made strange shutters to close them off from the elements. At the gable end of the kitchen parlour was a large fireplace, a chimney built of mud and stones. For a chimneypot Tom used an empty whiskey barrel, and sat it outside atop the flue, just above the level of the roof.

'What it lacks in aesthetics it compensates for in practicality, wouldn't you say, Maria?'

His sister suppressed her laughter. The thing looked ridiculous, but everyone else was full of admiration for it.

'That's a grand sort of a chimney entirely,' Tadg Casey, one of the Irish contingent, said. 'Is it trying to tantalise us you are, Tom, or dropping some class of a hint?'

Laughter. 'Tadg, you *amadán*, when it comes to whiskey since when did you need hints?'

There were good-natured chuckles.

The final work was to cover the wooden roof with sods.

'A variation on the thatch, Maria. It doesn't look great but it will keep us snug, providing the rain doesn't come down in sheets. And in spring it will probably sprout wild flowers!'

'Flowers on the roof? Is it mad you are?'

Tom laughed. 'Sure why not?'

'*A Dhia*,' Maria said, 'what would they say at home?'

'They'd say we were using our heads!'

Shortly before the house was finished someone arrived in Deadwood that Tom had not expected to see again. Willie Schmidt, his old friend from the wagon train, stood at their tent opening one evening. Maria, who was about to throw out a basin of dishwater, stared at the newcomer, then shrieked with delight.

'Are my two eyes deceiving me,' she demanded, 'or is it yourself, Willie Schmidt? I thought you had gone to California!'

Tom arrived back to find the friend he thought he had lost being entertained by his sister.

'I told you we'd meet again!' Willie said laconically, as Tom shook his hand, clapped him on the back, invited him to stay to supper.

'So what has brought you here, Willie? Or is that a silly question?'

'I am here to make my fortune!'

'So California didn't do it?'

'Farming is only worthwhile when it is your own place . . . My brother got married, and I must make my own life.'

'You should have come earlier. Winter is almost on us!'

When they had eaten he brought his friend to see the new log cabin that was now almost finished.

'You must stay with us, Willie, until your own cabin is built.'

Before the first frost Tom and Maria and Willie moved in. They threw a small party for their new friends. Maria cooked a stew with the elk meat that Tom had brought home from a hunting foray. She used pine nuts to flavour it and served it with potatoes she had roasted in the ashes; she and Tom had brought a supply with them from Golden, now stored in the root cellar built underneath the floor. Logs crackled in the new hearth; the firelight lit up tired faces and worn hands, cheered the small room with its newly made table and stools.

Some of the men had already found quantities of precious ore on their claims – gold dust washed clean by the rivers; they kept it in 'pokes', sewn inside their shirts. Willie stared when they spilled it out on the table; he couldn't quite believe his eyes. He had purchased a claim from a man who had become too ill to mine, but as yet it had yielded little.

'How pure it comes from the water!' he exclaimed. 'So different from hard rock mining.'

'It won't last, the river gold,' Tom said. 'You know that, Willie.'

'Nah, but it will last long enough to make our fortunes,' one of the men said with a laugh. 'And then we go home.'

They spoke of their families back home in Ireland, or England, or Germany, in Iowa and Missouri and Montana and Wyoming, of their hopes and dreams. They spoke of the Indian threat with lowered voices. A supply train had been burned out, its drivers scalped.

'The army are sending reinforcements in the spring,' Tom said.

Maria looked troubled.

'Can you blame the Indians,' she said when the visitors had gone and Tom and Willie were still seated by the fire, too tired to find their beds. 'This is their land, and we have come uninvited . . . A bit like what happened in Ireland!'

'I know,' Willie replied. 'But is it right that vast areas should lie fallow, that nothing should be mined or exploited, or built, that wealth should be left hidden in the earth? That is the Indian way, Maria . . . They leave the earth as they find it. They may even be right, but the world cannot progress if everyone does the same. I think the Government would honour the treaty if the Sioux were prepared to mine the gold. It doesn't much care, after all, who mines it so long as it is mined!'

'Are you trying to persuade that fellow beside you to change his mind?' Maria asked with a sly look at her brother.

'As long as prospecting is illegal,' Tom said, 'even if only technically so, I'll have nothing to do with it. The only thing I'll take from this place is some hard-earned profit from my trade. Even though the Government is turning a blind eye, I won't prospect, or stake a claim. And after we've left here, Maria, the cabin can be dismantled or left to rot, and so there'd be little to show for our having passed this way.'

'Deadwood is here to stay, Tom,' Willie said quietly. 'It's fairly obvious; the region is full of ore.'

And we're here now, Maria thought, and I might as well make the best of it.

The following day she tore up one of her petticoats and made frilly curtains from it, '. . . to give the place some class of an atmosphere,' she explained when Tom said there was no need for curtains as no one could see through the 'windows'.

'Atmosphere is right!' Tom said, laughing heartily when she told him the source of her material. 'But maybe you shouldn't disclose where you got these curtains to our prospector friends . . .'

Maria blushed. 'Men!' she muttered darkly.

* * *

94

Willie and Tom cobbled together another small cabin and Willie moved in. Maria missed the additional company in the evening, especially as Willie was not above helping with the cooking. She loved his stories of his home town of Leipzig where his fiancée, Gretchen, whom he had not seen for years, was still patiently waiting for his summons.

'Poor girl, she waits – months, years, and still she is faithful . . .'

Rather like me, Maria thought. But what am I waiting for?

Being a housewife in a new mining town was the next best thing to being a miracle worker. Almost nothing was available: candles had to be made out of tallow; ash pit soap had to be made; sewing in poor light was a nightmare.

Maria got her hands on a laundry kettle, and every Monday she lugged water from the stream and boil-washed everything that needed washing.

When the wash was done there was the rinsing. There was no mangle and the wringing had to be done by hand – Tom's woollen long johns and canvas overalls were the worst – and then the sodden load was half dragged by her to the line set up in the 'yard', where it was hung up to dry. When the cold weather set in the wash froze solid.

She refused to be defeated. She covered the dirt floor with burlap, stitched her brother's shirts and turned the cuffs, darned his precious socks, made undergarments from flour sacks, lined the mantelshelf with old newspaper.

Tom was partial to coffee, and when a sack came in on a supply wagon Maria made sure to secure a quota. She had to roast the beans, then grind them by hand, but it was worth it. The smell, the taste, was wonderful.

Tom made sure she was well supplied with firewood and, in the evening, when he was out in other tents or cabins, she would sit alone by her blazing fire and reread by its light the books she had brought from Denver. But, as the year drifted into winter, the loneliness closed in on her.

The snow descended on Deadwood, falling softly. It blanketed the woods and the streams, covered the new log cabins and the tents, the firs and the pines.

Two days before Christmas Willie brought over a wild turkey he had shot in the woods. And something else – a small fir tree in a pot.

'For the love of God, Willie, what are you bringing a tree into the house for?'

'It is Christmas, *Liebchen*. You must have a tree!'

Maria watched as Willie installed the tree in the corner of the room, and decorated it with baubles on which the firelight flickered. She had seen something of the kind in Boston at Christmas, through the lighted windows of some of the houses. But the Vandermeers themselves had eschewed such frippery as godless.

'Where did you get those things, Willie?'

'I made them from tin cans,' he said diffidently. 'See, Maria, here is the Angel Gabriel.'

'He has little wings!' Maria exclaimed. 'Willie you're an artist!'

He grinned, delighted at her enthusiasm.

The Walshes invited their new friends to share Christmas Day. Alastair Sutherland, Tom's old mate from Golden, came down from his claim in the hills, glad to sit by the roaring fire and tell them of his tribulations. His mine had a small vein that kept appearing and disappearing.

'I'll stick it for another year,' he told Tom ruefully, 'then I'm selling up! I don't want to end up half demented like my neighbour – poor old bloke called Jones who's got a claim a few miles away . . . He thinks it's worth a million, but all he's got to show is a nugget from the river!'

Rueful laughter filled the cabin.

'The millions are hard come by,' Seán Clarke said as he poured tots of the *poitín* he had brought with him. His voice was thin with Limerick mockery. 'But the gold is under our feet all right . . . if it would only tell us where.'

'I know the man you mean,' Tom said suddenly to Alastair. 'The Jones fellow . . . He asked me for advice not long after we came here. Needed beams for a new drift tunnel.'

'He'll kill himself,' Alastair said grimly. 'He's not strong enough for single jacking.'

There was silence. They were all only too familiar with 'single jacking' – the work of a lone miner, who would hammer a drill into the rock wall and then insert dynamite.

Maria broke the moment of introspection by pointing out the wonders of Willie's festive tree and his little home-made angels.

'Do you always do this at home, Willie?' Tom asked him.

'Of course. But we put tiny candles on the tree, and when they are lit it is like magic.' He turned to Maria. 'What do you do in Ireland?'

'We put a candle in the window to light the Christ Child, and to remember loved ones far away!' she replied. Nostalgia overwhelmed her and, to her consternation, her eyes filled.

Willie suddenly excused himself and went out, admitting into the warm room the icy, resinous tang of the forest. They heard his boots crunching the snow as he made his way to his cabin. He returned in a moment with a real, wax candle. It could not be put in the window, because the 'window' was made of canvas, so Maria put it in a jar the middle of the dinner table and, as Tom said grace, she added a private prayer for Peggie and her father, and for Michael. It was such a pity he couldn't be with them for Christmas. But perhaps he would come again in the spring, with the army.

The turkey made a fine meal, and the leftovers lasted for days, as did the flavour of companionship and human solidarity.

* * *

All through the cruel winter months, when the weather made building impossible, Tom worked at making tables and stools, and other domestic necessaries, in the stable he had erected behind his cabin. One of the mining hopefuls, Joe Cunningham, a carpenter who hailed originally from Lancashire, came to help. He was a small, wiry man who never tired of complimenting Maria – 'What's a beautiful girl like you doing in a midden like this . . .?'

Tessa, his wife, had come to join him on the last supply train before winter. She and Maria were so glad of the sight of each other that they became instant friends. The two women would spend the long evenings together sewing by the hearth, while the men sawed and hammered in the stable. Tessa told stories of the Lancashire cotton mills where she had worked as a girl.

'I used to think we had it rough. But at least we weren't frozen solid, and gaped at like zoo animals. Did you ever see anything like the way the men stop and stare at us? Just thank the Lord there'll be more women coming in the spring!' And she reeled off the names of several men whose wives were due to arrive on the next wagon train.

But, instead of the wives, a troupe of prostitutes arrived and with them a madam. They were accommodated in hastily erected shelters called 'cribs' at the outskirts of the settlement.

'Come by special wagon train, if you please,' Tessa hissed when she came to tell Maria the news, 'as though they were a pack of princesses instead of a bunch of tarts. We'll have to run them out of town!'

'Will you have sense,' Maria said laughing, hoping Tom didn't come in and ask about the joke. 'You'd have to run the men out first!' She glanced at her new friend and said primly: 'But Tom wouldn't go anywhere near women like that!'

'It isn't Tom I'm worried about,' Tessa replied with an edge to her voice. 'It's the other beauty . . .'

Indian harassment went on sporadically over the winter. Tom kept his rifle by him at all times. Maria took to wearing the hated holster whenever she went out.

When spring came, it brought the expected soldiers to Deadwood, but Michael was not among them. His regiment had been sent south.

The soldiers pitched tents at the edge of the settlement, where the black streams were emerging from their winter blanket and where the rattle of the sluice boxes was unending in the icy thaw.

As Willie had predicted, Deadwood prospered. As the spring of 1875 advanced its population swelled to many thousands. Camps sprang up everywhere and the new 'city' became the centre of their commercial life.

Tom was rushed off his feet. The muddy thoroughfare where he had built his cabin began to fill with one-storey houses, most of them with false fronts to impart an air of elegance. As the only flat place in the gulch, Main Street was long and coveted. It paralleled Whitewood Creek, which served as a sewer, but the latter's evil smell was cloaked by the scent of fresh pine that filled the air as the new buildings went up. Water was available from the numerous springs in the hillside and was piped to the new buildings and businesses.

Tom and Maria saw little of Willie now. He was spending most of his time at his claim.

As the year wore on Tom had a share in the new sawmill that commenced operations in the spring of 1876, and he orchestrated the delivery of supplies and materials. The town now had breweries, bakeries, newspapers, hotels. The gold meant that the town's bustle never stopped, day or night. The mail came on the stage coach. It arrived to much 'yipping' and churned up the muddy street. Guards sat on top with buffalo guns.

As spring became summer two newcomers set everyone talking. One was a man called William Hickock, better known as Wild Bill, and the other was a young woman. As soon as Maria saw her sauntering along in buckskin trousers and jacket, with a vest and a slouch hat, and carrying her rifle over her shoulder, she knew she would never see the world in quite the same way again.

'Who on earth is that woman?' she demanded of Tom. 'She's wearing men's clothes, and goes around with the soldiers and with that man Wild Bill!'

'She's the pony express rider between here and Custer; she's spent years as one of General Custer's scouts. They call her Calamity Jane!'

'What kind of a name is that?'

'Her real name is Martha Cannery. She joined Custer when she was eighteen, went with his regiment on the Arizona Indian Campaign. They say she's one of the most fearless riders and the best shot in the West!'

'How does she do it – dress like a man, live like a man ... among men ...?'

Tom laughed drily. 'Nobody gives that girl trouble!'

A few days later, as Maria went down the new Main Street, now littered with wood shavings and chunks of timber, Calamity Jane, in high boots and breeches, approached along the muddy thoroughfare.

Maria stared. Here was a woman who took respect and freedom as her due. She longed to talk to her, but stood aside shyly to let her pass.

'After you, ma'am,' Calamity Jane said politely. 'You'll ruin your dresses in this kind of country,' she added, as Maria lifted her hems to step across the mud.

Tom came up behind his sister and tipped the brim of his hat.

'I've been hearin' all about you,' the pony express rider said to him laconically. 'You're Tommy Walsh, ain't you?' She added with an expectant ring to her voice: 'They say you're the best shot hereabouts.'

'That report is greatly exaggerated, ma'am,' Tom replied hastily. Maria had to prevent herself from laughing out loud. Her brother was evidently in no hurry to enter into a contest of skill with Calamity Jane.

With the advent of the sawmill the face of Deadwood changed. Lumber was available now. Frame cabins began to replace log cabins. Stores and saloons made their appearance alongside banks and lawyers' offices. Wives were joining their men, and with them came a semblance of civilisation. An air of quasi-respectability began to permeate the strange town that had mushroomed over a winter.

Tom replaced their sod roof with shingles and put in a sound plank floor. Maria smoothed the planks with sand from the stream in which she detected specks of gold.

Tom stared at the specks, then laughed.

'Our floor is paved with gold, Maria. Tell them that in your next letter home!'

'I wonder if Peggie's hair is still the same colour,' Maria mused aloud. 'You remember the gold sparks in it—' She stopped abruptly when she saw the vulnerability in her brother's face.

One day in April, as Tom was about to close his shop for lunch, a man stumbled in. It was the prospector Jones whom Alastair Sutherland had referred to at Christmas as half demented. The man was gaunt, ragged and dirty, with long matted hair and beard; the smoke of his campfire had browned his skin and hands until he resembled a slab of bacon. Tom vetted him quickly for liquor, but he was completely sober.

Poor fellow, he thought. Every time I see him he looks worse than the time before. Alastair was right: the hills *are* killing him.

'I haven't seen you around of late, Mr Jones!' he said kindly. 'What can I do for you?'

Maria's voice came from the kitchen: 'Tom Walsh . . . will you come in for your dinner for the love of God before it's stone cold?' The scent of ham and baked potatoes came through the open door.

Tom looked wryly at his customer. 'Will you join us, Mr Jones?'

'No, thankee . . . very kind . . . I've a bit of business to put your way. I'll come back later.'

But Tom saw how the smell of food had set the poor man to swallowing.

He remembered the tired, sick taste of hunger, how it could float you away between this world and the next.

'We'd be mightly glad of some company, my sister and I,' he persisted. 'And I'd be happy to discuss your order over the meal.'

The customer was persuaded. Tom ushered him into the warm kitchen. A boiled ham sat on a plate in the middle of the table, beside a bowl of potatoes and one of chopped cabbage.

Maria turned from the range and started when she saw the stranger.

'This is Mr Jones, Maria. Mr Jones, this is my sister.'

'You betcha,' the man said awkwardly, as Maria extended her hand. 'I 'pologise, ma'am, for my appearance. They call me Smoky Jones.' He laughed, showing blackened teeth. 'Ain't that a good name for an old fellow from the hills?'

'You're very welcome, Mr Jones.'

She set another place at the table and the three sat down to their meal.

Maria was annoyed at Tom for inviting this filthy individual into their home, but as the meal progressed she became impressed at the calibre of the human being behind the matted exterior. For one thing, he was sober. For another he had manners, rough-hewn perhaps, but manners all the same.

'Some more potatoes, Mr Smoky?' She reddened. 'I mean, Mr Jones.'

He roared with laughter. 'That's all right, ma'am, and I don't mind if I do.' He began to talk of his claim in the hills. 'I ain't placer mining at the moment, though I thought I'd give it a go, as it might give me something to pay my expenses; and there's a stream up by my claim that's as likely as not. That's why I want you to make me a sluice box, Tom. But placer mining is too time-consuming for me; my real faith is in my hard rock mine. I've been single-jacking there all winter and I jess know there's more gold in that mine than ever was found in this territory!'

Tom and Maria listened patiently. Prospectors are like fishermen, Tom thought. They always *know* there's treasure in some dark pool; and they can always tell you about the ones that got away.

Smoky Jones took some rock samples out of his pocket, put them on the table. They looked unremarkable, except that there were small threads of black running through the rock.

'That's gold . . .'

Tom concealed his scepticism. He knew that gold only shone when it was pure, such as the samples found in rivers, where the water had already separated it from other material. But there was no lustre at all in the selection on the table, nothing to warrant a second glance.

And then Smoky Jones put a small gold nugget on the cloth.

'My good luck charm,' he said, looking from one of them to the other with a grin. 'Found it in the river, up there in the cold hills. It's just a small sample of what's waiting inside the rock. My real problem, Tom, is I ain't got the capital to develop my mine. I'm looking for a partner. They say you're doing well and you have a reputation as a man to be trusted. If you can bring the capital I'd give you a half-share and we could work it together. You're a strong young man, and good company too!' The crow's-feet crinkled at the edge of Smoky's sunken eyes. 'I know we'd make a go of it!'

Tom frowned. In this part of the world it did not do to dismiss anything out of hand. Negotiations were now under way with the Indians and prospecting would probably soon be completely legal. If there was even a modest lode in Smoky's claim it could well be worth a fortune. On the other hand, the man was clearly an eccentric, possibly more dreamer than anything else.

'Let me think about it.'

'You do that, Tom.'

When Smoky Jones was gone Maria looked at her brother. 'Well – what's the verdict?'

'Oh, he's in earnest all right, Maria! But this is a man who lives with loneliness, hunger and cold. How much of his certainty is dictated by them?'

Next day Tom went to see some experienced miners, men who had made the journey with him and Maria from Golden, men who had been to the far reaches of Colorado in search of gold and knew a thing or two about mineral-bearing rock formations. They were unanimous.

'Old Smoky Jones?' they cried. 'Oh, he's been in the hills for the past two years or thereabouts . . . But it's all slate formation up there, Tom. Maybe he's found a little gold; it's hard not to stumble on some hereabouts. But it's a freak. You'd be a damn fool if you put good money into his claim!'

Tom came home and told Maria the consensus.

'Well, they should know, I suppose,' she said. 'But all the same . . .'

'All the same what?'

'There was something weird about him coming here. I got a queer feeling when he put that nugget down on the table!'

Tom looked at her doubtfully.

'Why don't you get some proper sampling done before you decide?' she pressed on. 'Have the assayers test them?'

Tom thought for a moment. 'It would entail a long, time-consuming journey into the hills . . .' he said slowly. 'Comprehensive assaying could be an expensive exercise for nothing, just when I'm getting a good profit going for us. And the experts *were* categorical that it was a slate formation with little likelihood of gold.' After a moment he added, half to himself,

'And I am rushed off my feet. Should I stop for several weeks to look into this thing, lose business momentum – as likely as not for nothing?'

'I don't know!'

'On balance, Maria, I have to be practical. The man is obviously stressed and desperate. And I can't afford whimsy, however tempting.'

When Smoky Jones returned to town two weeks later Tom told him regretfully that he had to decline his offer.

'Pity,' Smoky said resignedly. 'I'd sooner it was you than anyone else.'

In September the Sioux, as Michael had predicted, ceded the Black Hills to the Government, and entered into a new treaty. It was no longer illegal to prospect in this territory. But before that something happened that shocked even the hard-bitten community in Deadwood Gulch.

Wild Bill Hickock, while sitting at a gambling table in the Bell Union saloon, was shot in the back of the head. The murderer – one Jack McCall – was arrested by Calamity Jane and locked in a cabin, but escaped, to be caught later at Fagan's Ranch at Horse Creek.

The trouble with mining camps, Tom thought, is that there is only *ad hoc* law. And the situation will probably get worse before it gets better. And this is where I have brought Maria!

We'll get out of here, he thought, as soon as I have a tidy sum.

It was strange, Tom thought, to find oneself prosperous. He was examining his ledgers. He had taught Maria the rudiments of double-entry book-keeping, but once every month he set aside an evening for going over the books with her.

'Eight thousand dollars,' she said to him proudly towards the end of 1876. 'That's your profit for the year.'

'*Our* profit, Maria. I could not have done it without you.'

He turned to look into her eyes. 'I want you to know that. This is not an easy place for a woman, but you have given me a home, looked after the shop, cooked the meals, washed and cleaned, done the books. Half of this money is really yours. I am going to open a bank account for you in your own name, although I can't lodge what you are entitled to just yet.'

'That's all right. I'm not looking for anything!'

'That doesn't mean you're not entitled to it!'

Maria asked him the question she longed to put to him: 'What can we send home? Peggie could do with something now that she's getting married. And Father is not able to farm any more!'

Tom looked troubled. 'I've already sent some money to Peggie, and a few dollars to Father. At the moment we can't send much more. You see, all this profit is earmarked.' He glanced at her to assess her reaction. 'It's not for me, Maria, it's for Father and Peggie, and you! I've bought into a claim – one that looks likely. I know it's a risk . . . but not, I think, a big one.'

'But Tom, the placer mines are giving out. There's less and less gold in the streams.'

'Credit me with some sense,' he replied testily. 'It's a hard rock mine I've put my money into.'

'Whose?'

'Whose do you think?'

Maria immediately thought of Willie, who had visited recently, and had spent much of the time in Tom's workshop, the two men talking in low voices.

'Not Willie's?'

He nodded. 'I'm going to start double-jacking with him next week.'

Maria paled. She knew that double-jacking was the method by which one miner would slam home the sledgehammer while the other held the drill in position.

'You could get yourself killed!'

'Willie's safe enough with a sledgehammer,' Tom said. 'And I am too, miss!'

'I thought you said you would never mine here.'

'It's no longer illegal, Maria, not since the Sioux Treaty. You know that. And recently I have realised that if anything is to fall from the Tree of Life I have to shake it. It's not enough to sit at its foot and hope!'

'What about your business?'

He looked at her apologetically. 'I'm selling it. I've made my mind up. I've already had an offer.'

'And if you don't make a strike, what will we do then?' she demanded after a moment.

'Maria, we'll move on.'

'And if you do make a strike?'

'Move on also. There are things I must accomplish that I'll never be able to do here. And then Father and Peggie – and you – will have everything.'

Why is Tom so restless, so driven? Maria asked herself. And what about me? What must I accomplish, or am I doomed to follow my brother around like a stray cat? Where am *I* going? I want a life of my own.

Where are you, Ted Lafferty, and why have you forgotten me?

Almost a year to the hour when he had first entertained Smoky Jones, Tom was stopped on his way home from the mine by Alastair Sutherland. Alastair had sold his claim, and was about to go back East. He seemed strangely troubled and excited.

'Tom, have you heard the news?'

'What news?'

'You know the mine poor old Jones has been working on for the past few years?'

'Sure. He sold it!'

'Yeah, same time as I did. But the mining engineers have been up there all month. Seems the assay results are extraordinary.'

'. . . It's only a slate formation . . .'

Alastair shook his head. 'They're saying it's the biggest gold find ever made in this territory, or maybe anywhere in the world. They're saying it's huge, Tom – one of the biggest *ever*.' He paused, added with a grunt, 'Poor old Jones. He's gone to California, but he's bound to hear all about it!'

Tom felt as though he had been kicked in the stomach. A cold sweat broke out on him. He mopped his brow, noting as from a distance the black blasting powder that came away on his handkerchief.

'You all right, Tom?'

'Just a mite tired . . .'

Later he said bitterly, as he regarded his sister's dismayed face: 'I lost it, Maria. I was offered it on a plate, but I wasn't awake. I *knew* it was coming; I felt it for months, for years. But when it stared me in the face . . . Oh God, how could I have been such a fool? How can you ever forgive me?'

'Have you checked out this story, Tom? It mightn't be as good as has been rumoured. Stories grow in the telling.'

'I've talked to the assayers. Fifty thousand dollars worth of gold in every ton of ore!' He put his head in his hands.

'So if you had taken up Mr Jones's offer you would now be very rich?' she whispered.

'Rich? Maria, we would at this moment be richer than the President, or the Vandermeers, or any of those people we saw back East with their fine houses and carriages; richer than any English duke or American industrialist, or all the millionaires you have ever heard of put together. No matter how hard we tried, we could not possibly spend our wealth during our lifetime! Maria, this mine is being touted as the biggest gold find in world history! It would have made us some of the richest people on earth!'

Maria was white. 'And he came to *you*!' she whispered. 'He sat at this table and offered you *half*. We could have had everything . . . we could have bought a mansion back East, we could have bought Kilduncan's place and thousands of acres for Father . . .'

'Don't, Maria! Don't reproach me. You cannot do it any better than I'm doing it myself.'

Tom changed after that. He became quiet; he spent a great deal of his time at the mine. He read every book he could find on the subject of minerals and metals. He invited successful prospectors back for meals, and listened carefully to everything they said. He wrote up notes at night.

'You're burning the candle at both ends,' his sister told him.

'Maybe. But it's still burning, Maria. I just want to be sure of one thing: that the next time *I* will know fortune when it stares me in the face; *I* will be the one with the knowledge; I don't ever want to rely on so-called experts again!'

Next time? Maria echoed privately. Is he mad entirely that he can even imagine a chance like that will *ever* come again?

But Tom's candle was not burning as brightly as he thought. He returned home one day looking yellow.

'My God,' Maria said, putting her hand to his forehead, 'what's wrong with you? You're burning up!'

He staggered to his bed, and when she came to bring him his supper he was delirious. In the lamplight she saw the sickly cast to his skin, and, when he looked at her, the pale gold in the whites of his eyes.

The doctor listened through his stethoscope to the patient's heart and lungs, pulled down his lower lids and examined his eyes.

'It's a form of hepatitis. Give him plenty of water, fresh fruit if you can get it – there's some wild raspberries came into town today. No fats.'

'Is this serious?'

'Potentially. It may recur, affect the whole of his life.'

'Will he pull through?' She said this slowly and fearfully, and her eyes filled with tears.

The doctor pursed his mouth. 'Well, ma'am, he's got two things going for him. He's got youth on his side,' he smiled gently at her, 'and he's got you!'

After that Tom lost track of time. Sometimes he surfaced to find himself slick with sweat, saw Maria sitting by the bed, would try to talk. But the dream world would claim him again – his father and mother, young and laughing by the hearth in Carraig Mór; Peggie walking along a Boston street with velvet ribbons in her hair . . .

Willie came to see him, sat by his bedside and tried to tell him some good news. A lode had been found, just where they were last double-jacking. How extensive it was he didn't yet know, but he was having it assessed.

He turned blue eyes on Maria. 'I've a feeling it will surprise us!'

Tom seemed to listen. He rambled about rock formations until Willie left.

Maria bathed her brother's forehead, sponged him with warm water. Tessa came to help for short periods to let her get a little rest. But Maria discouraged her, afraid of this sickness, especially now that Tessa was pregnant.

Early one morning Maria woke with a start from her doze at her brother's bedside and knew at once that something had changed. She examined her patient anxiously, put her hand to his forehead and neck. Tom was cooler; his breathing was normal and he had slipped into a quiet sleep.

'The fever's broken,' she whispered. She kneeled on the floor and put her face in her hands.

'Thank you, God,' she whispered. 'Thank you.'

That evening, when he was able to sit up and take some nourishment Tom seemed bemused by his thin and exhausted state.

'How long have I been like this.'

'You've been sick for ten days.'

He looked alarmed and astonished, and tried to get out of bed.

'I have to get back to work, Maria. I've lost enough time!'

'You'll ruin your lungs. What good is gold if you destroy your health? But there's something I have to tell you. Willie came today while you were asleep.'

Tom slumped back on the pillows. His eyes darkened anxiously. 'And . . .?'

Maria gave a joyful laugh. 'Good news, Tom. The payload is worthwhile.'

Willie visited again the following evening and confirmed the news in person. The two men spoke in low tones together for more than an hour.

When their visitor was gone, Tom said to Maria, 'I'm selling out to Willie. There will be enough money to set us up. We can move on.'

'To where?'

'To a place called Leadville in Colorado. There's a fortune to be made there.'

'But, Tom, Leadville is silver and lead, isn't it? And millions of people?'

Tom grinned. 'Twenty thousand is more like. What do you say, Maria? With the sale of my interest in the mine, we'll have in the region of eighty thousand dollars all told. That'll be enough to give us a good start in the greatest mining boom town of the West.'

'It's a huge sum of money! We could go back East. We could go home . . .'

Tom looked solemn. 'I know. But I am convinced there are greater things ahead . . . my second chance!' He smiled at her suddenly. 'Say yes, Maria. We're on our way to a real fortune!'

Maria shook her head. 'How can you talk like this when you have at last come into some considerable money, and when you have just returned from death's door? It's tempting Fate.'

Tom took a long drink from the glass of water beside his bed.

'Oh, I'll tempt it,' he muttered, half to himself. 'I'll tempt it till it gives in . . .'

Is it illness or the Smoky Jones business that has made a hole in your brain, Tom Walsh? Maria wondered anxiously. And where will it lead us now?

A month later Willie came to say goodbye.

'I will miss you both,' he told them. Turning to Maria, he added, 'And you especially, *Liebchen*. What will Deadwood do without you?'

'Charm will get you everywhere, Willie,' Maria replied with a chuckle, retrieving the hand Willie raised to his lips. 'No wonder Gretchen is still waiting.'

You lucky girl, she thought. Your waiting is over. He will surely send for you now!

Chapter Seven

The Grand Hotel,
Chestnut Street,
Leadville, Colorado
2 May 1877

Dearest Peggie,

First of all congratulations on your marriage. I hope your husband deserves you and that you will both be very happy.

I'm writing to you from a place called Leadville in the territory of Colorado. It's very high up in the world, about 10,200 feet – as high as the clouds – and all around it are mountains and mines and heaps of 'tailings' from the drifts (that's a mine tunnel with one opening) that have been burrowed into the mountains.

The town itself is more elegant than you might expect, some good buildings and passable sidewalks, and there are thousands of people living here. But the streets are streams of mud from the constant activity, great teams of up to eight horses hauling ore from the mines to the smelters, and hard-worked hauliers of wood who are responsible for freighting most of our building materials.

Everyone is working like beavers. There are miners, looking for silver and lead and anything else that will bring them money. Some have made massive fortunes – like Mr Horace Tabor, who was a storekeeper here once but who now is called the Silver King.

In addition to miners there are carpenters and builders and assayers (people whose job it is to determine the level of precious metal in rock samples), storekeepers, a bank, attorneys, women and children.

There's a newspaper and all the trappings of modernity, and it comes as a shock to remember that the only roads to this town lead over high passes that are open but part of the year. In winter, the temperature here falls to forty below (that means forty degrees below the point at which water freezes! Can you imagine that,

Peggie? The river at An Cailleach would be solid!).

All around us we have the Rocky Mountains, sweeps of trees – pine, fir and spruce – and below the town is beautiful Turquoise Lake. The air is full of the sounds of horses, and hammers, and smells from the smelters, and woodsmoke. Outside the town you smell pine everywhere. It is strange, to live up here on the roof of the world, and to find oneself surrounded by so many people, with the sense that all of us have been thrust out into the wilderness to build a civilisation.

Now, about myself! I have a stake in three mines hereabouts and my partner – Geoff Diamond (isn't that a grand name for a pro-spector?) – and I had a bit of luck with a silver mine. I've also put money into the purchase of a hotel. So now I'm a hotelier! But I confess I'm bitten by the mining bug fair and square. It's hard to avoid hereabouts, for all the talk is about the latest piece of mining luck. I'm making a great study of geology and minerals every chance I get, and of the different ways gold and other metals manifest themselves. (Gold doesn't always gleam, for example. Sometimes it disguises itself. In fact the stuff that does glitter is often what they call 'fool's gold', not the real thing at all, but only copper pyrites.) And when I make it big I'll come back and give you and Father everything you can dream of.

Your loving brother,
Tom
PS, $50 enclosed.

'Fortune is an odd beast,' Tom said to Jerry Daly, one of his partners, one spring day in 1879. 'It has made me a prospector, a miner and a hotelier. Ten years ago I had five dollars in my pocket and a steerage ticket to New York. I suppose I should settle down and be glad of what Fate has been given me.'

'You mean get married?'

Tom nodded. 'Why not? But I have no one in mind, Jerry,' he added with a laugh, 'so you can take that look off your face!'

They were sitting in the office of the Grand Hotel, formerly called the City Hotel, in Leadville. Tom had bought into it with the money he had brought from Deadwood, enlarged and renamed it. Upstairs were Tom and Maria's suite of rooms. A young clerk by the name of Frank Jenkins was behind the desk and a party of tired prospectors with unkempt whiskers were signing the register.

This town was bigger than Deadwood, and of longer standing. Gold had been found here in '53, and after that silver and lead. There were now tens of thousands of people. Accommodation was at a premium, which was why Tom had purchased a one-third share in the hotel; but he had also invested in mining – buying a share in a claim called the General Shields and also in some promising properties in the 'Frying Pan' district around Leadville.

'If you were to settle down,' Jerry said, 'with whom would it be?'

'Ah, Jerry . . . The trouble is that among all the striving humanity in this town there are so few marriageable young women.'

'What has put marriage into your head?'

'I don't know. Maybe because Maria was talking to me about our sister back home in Ireland. She's a mother already, has a baby girl . . .'

'Are you sure there are no marriageable young women in Leadville?' Jerry said softly, indicating, through the glass panels of the office door, a mother and daughter crossing the foyer. The mother was in her fifties; the girl about twenty-three, tall and striking. They had about them an aura of distressed gentility.

Tom sat up straight to watch them.

The mother spoke to the clerk; he checked his book and shook his head. They heard his voice through the open office door.

'No, ma'am. I'm sorry, but there's nothing in the book.'

'But we *sent* our reservations . . .' the woman replied. 'Will you check again? The name is Reed –' she spelled it out – 'R-E-E-D.'

Tom got to his feet, went out to the desk, smiled at the woman.

'What seems to be the trouble?'

'This lady says she made reservations – but they're not in the book and we're full.'

Tom looked at the girl. She had the shy demeanour of a fawn at bay, hazel eyes, dark hair, a proud cast to the mouth.

'It doesn't matter, Mother,' she said in a low, urgent voice. 'There must be other hotels.'

'I'm afraid you'll find the same story obtains everywhere, ma'am,' Tom said quietly. 'There is no accommodation to be had at the moment in Leadville. But the situation is not desperate. We do have one room available, but there is only one bed. We can install another, but it will take a short while. Meanwhile, perhaps you would like some refreshment, Mrs Reed . . . Miss Reed?'

The woman looked relieved. The girl heaved a small sigh and looked down at her creased and dusty clothes.

'We've just come off the stage coach,' she confided to Tom with a shy smile. 'We're from Alabama. I'm a schoolteacher and I've got a position here.'

'You're very welcome, ma'am,' Tom said. There was enchantment in the musical southern accent, the clear, diffident gaze and the flush that suddenly stained her cheeks.

110

The clerk was agitated. 'But, Mr Walsh—'

'What is it, Frank?'

'The room . . . what room are you talking about?'

'Number five, Frank. Get it prepared and put in a second bed.'

The clerk's mouth dropped open. He said in a whisper: 'But that's your—'

'Exactly. See to it, please.'

Upstairs Maria looked out on Chestnut Street, which was lined with tall telegraph poles. She was standing on the balustraded balcony outside her window, thinking of the news from home. Peggie was now a mother and living in Boherbue! That would be about sixty miles from Clonmel, she thought. Too far away to see her father every week; but near enough to see him sometimes. She wondered about the old man, now alone. In her mind's eye she saw the small whitewashed house, the hedge of fuchsia, the hens in the yard, the valley filled with the dancing rain.

The wooden sidewalk below was hidden from view by the overhang of the balcony; the main street was muddy and full of traffic – men on horseback, mules, a team struggling through the mire with a heavy load on its way to one of the smelters. Across the street was the small brick building known as the Miner's Exchange Bank, and beside it the Tontine Restaurant, reputed to be the only real restaurant in the West. Nearby were several important establishments – the Vienna Laundry, Mr Mater's grocery shop, and the leading hardware and miners' supply store in the city owned by Messrs Manville and McCarthy.

Down the street were gambling houses – in one of which George Connors, the first marshal, had been killed only the year before by a policeman ironically named Bloodworth. A few doors above the hotel was the Pioneer saloon, where miners spent their earnings on card games and liquor, and from whose doorway sounds of an argument could now be heard.

Leadville was much more of a city than Deadwood. It had already enjoyed two decades of prosperity. It had three stage lines and was expanding rapidly; new buildings were going up. The air smelled of horse manure, woodsmoke, smelter fumes, and money.

There was a knock on her door. Maria went back into her room and opened it. It was Sally, one of the chamber maids.

'Mr Walsh says his room is to be made over for two guests, ma'am. Will I lock the door to the sitting room, or let them have the use of it?'

She was referring to the private sitting room positioned between Tom and Maria's respective bedrooms, with connecting doors.

'Who are these people, Sally?'

'Two ladies, ma'am. A mother and daughter.'

111

'When you say "ladies", Sally, do you *mean* ladies?'

'Oh yes, ma'am. No doubt about that at all. I seen them myself.'

'Then by all means let them use it,' Maria said with a smile. 'I'll just remove my sewing. How long are they staying?'

'Just for a couple of weeks, ma'am, I think. The young lady is a teacher, just starting here. She and her mother are waiting for a cottage on Spruce Street to be ready for them.'

When Sally had gone Maria tidied herself and went downstairs to see what was going on. When she and Tom were seated at their table in the dining room two strange ladies appeared and stood hesitantly in the doorway. Instantly he rose, introducing the newcomers to Maria, and invited them to join their table. Miss Reed looked at him shyly, ate her soup daintily and talked of Alabama and how hot it was there. Tom listened. When he looked at her there was a soft sheen to his eyes that told Maria everything. Love, she thought sadly, is the most maverick and unpredictable of diseases. Why has it never come again for me? Am I to be an old maid?

Caroline Reed, for all her soft and gentle looks, was no pushover. She found Leadville awful, with its mud and cold, but not quite as appalling as she had expected. The hotel was tolerable. The proprietor was quiet-spoken; he had an Irish brogue, blue eyes, red hair. There was about him a great strength, as though he had been hewn from living rock. She had felt the chemistry as soon as he had spoken to her.

She had dreaded coming to this mining town, but her mother had pointed out that she had little option. There was a teaching position available here; there were rich men and few respectable single women. She needed to marry money.

'But I don't want to marry a rough, ignorant miner, Mother.'

'Nobody, Carrie, is suggesting you should. Plenty of men who are neither rough nor ignorant live and work in mining towns. Everyone, from the lowest to the highest, has gone west. We can always leave if the place is intolerable. But the pay they offer is good . . .'

Now, entering this hotel dining room, and finding herself invited to the proprietor's table, Carrie experienced a stab of surprised elation.

'We don't lack for entertainments in Leadville,' Maria said as the main course was served. 'Our Ladies Relief Society, for example, will shortly put on an amateur family entertainment in the Academy of Music under the auspices of the Knights of Robert Emmet.'

Carrie was listening. Academy of Music? You'd think the place was Paris, she thought. But it proved it was not such a backwater as she had expected.

She creased her brow and asked her host, 'Robert Emmet? Who is he?'

'He was an Irish Patriot who was executed about eighty years ago,' Tom said. 'There is quite an Irish contingent here. Most of them are congregated along Sixth Street; they are called the Sixth Street Irish.'

'Would you like to take part in this, Miss Reed?' Maria asked. 'It's a literary and musical evening?'

'My daughter has a lovely singing voice,' Mrs Reed said, 'and she is an excellent pianist. She also plays the organ.'

The young woman reddened. 'I'm not as talented as my mother would have you believe, but I would be glad to take part.'

'That's grand,' Maria said. 'We'll arrange it so.'

Tom, who until that moment had had no intention of attending the soirée, added enthusiastically, 'We'll look forward to it all the more, Miss Reed.'

A fortnight later Tom and Maria sat through a literary and musical entertainment, with several tableaux vivants, such as 'The Warrior Seeing a Child at Play Kneels Repentant', and 'The Peri Admitted into Paradise by Presenting the Penitent Tear'.

Tom gritted his teeth, and waited. He knew the *pièce de résistance* would shortly appear.

Carrie came on stage. Willowy, blushing, graceful, she bowed to the audience, sat at the piano and began to sing one of Tom Moore's lovely songs.

> 'Believe me, if all those endearing young charms
> Which I gaze on so fondly today
> Were to fade by tomorrow, and fleet in my arms,
> Like fairy gifts fading away.'

The audience sat, spellbound by simplicity, the quality of the singing, the sure touch on the piano, the innocent grace of the young woman as her voice soared and fell and her fingers tripped along the keys. They applauded rapturously. Maria, glancing at her brother, who sat beside her in evening dress complete with diamond shirt stud, saw how he clapped, saw his delighted face. She had to admit that Miss Reed's voice was superb, and that she looked beautiful.

When the entertainment was over Tom was quickly on his feet and approached the new diva, offered his arm.

'May I take you into supper, Miss Reed?'

'Thank you, Mr Walsh.'

'I very much enjoyed your contribution. I am particularly fond of Tom Moore's melodies!'

'Yes,' she said, glancing at him with a shy smile, 'your sister told me.'

'Did she now . . .? But you sang it beautifully, and played so well.'

Later, in the ladies' room, Maria, arranging her hair behind one of the silk screens, overheard Mrs Reed whisper to her daughter, 'What did you think of Mr Walsh?'

'He is very kind, I think.'

'A handsome *single* man too,' her mother said. 'And rich it would seem.' She raised her eyebrows. 'Partner in a thriving hotel and the owner of several mining interests from what I hear . . .'

'Mother, I don't care whether he is rich or not,' Carrie said abruptly. 'I just happen to like him. I find him charming, and *real*. He makes all the other men seem like paper cutouts.'

Good for you, girl, Maria thought, as Mrs Reed replied to her daughter. That is just what I wanted to hear. She rose and approached the two ladies from behind the screen, enjoying Mrs Reed's consternation.

'Miss Walsh . . .!' that lady said, her voice petering out in some confusion, 'I didn't know you were there . . .'

Next day the *Leadville Chronicle* waxed lyrical.

Seldom has such an array of amateur talent possessed the varied attractions that charm the eye, please the ear, furnish food for the understanding. . . . The best amateur talent of the city took part in the exercises. Miss Reed, but recently arrived in our city, a lady whose musical culture is of the highest order, played her own accompaniment upon the piano.

Maria read the article aloud to Tom over the breakfast table and noticed how his attention was focused on every word.

'It was a grand evening, wasn't it, Tom?'

He nodded.

'Miss Reed has a lovely voice, don't you agree?'

'She has indeed.' He leaned towards his sister and announced evenly: 'I have decided, Maria, that she is the girl I am going to marry!'

He saw her pupils widen, and then she laughed.

'I don't think anyone could accuse you of indecision, Tom Walsh. But wouldn't it be a good idea to ask her first?'

'Oh, I'll attend to all the niceties. And, of course, she may not have me. But you approve?'

'Completely! And I am quite certain that she will have you!'

'Are you indeed. How so?'

Maria tapped the side of her nose. 'Little bird told me . . .'

I hope everything works out for Tom, she thought as she studied her brother's beaming face. But why do I feel so bereft?

Tom said, 'What is it, Maria? What is troubling you?'

114

'Oh, nothing. It's seems very selfish of me . . . I know you will marry lovely Carrie Reed, and have a real life, Tom. But I will be an old maid!'

'Fiddlesticks, Maria. Half the men in Leadville would have you tomorrow! You know that.'

'But I don't want them.'

'Is there someone you do want?' her brother asked gently after a moment.

'You will scoff and tell me I'm childish or something. But the only man I want is someone who has forgotten me . . .'

'Ted Lafferty?'

She nodded and her eyes filled with tears.

'He hasn't forgotten you, Maria.'

'How do you know?'

He laughed and tapped the side of his nose. 'Little bird told me.'

During the course of the morning Maria heard from a customer that a number of new constables had been recruited, and would go forward for election. Most were already well regarded; one was a newcomer, just arrived in town but known by repute.

Maria mentioned this to Tom at lunchtime and wondered why he was smiling to himself.

'This is a very good thing, Maria. We *need* more law enforcement officers.'

'We certainly do. Every time I look down Chestnut I hear the racket in the saloons.'

'One of the recruits will join us at table this evening.'

'Do we need that?' Maria said, surprised.

'He's new in town. It would be polite.'

That evening, as she joined Tom in the dining room, Maria came face to face with a tall, raw-boned man. He was dressed in a suit and seemed quite different from the buckskin-clad man she had thought never to see again. Her heart jumped and she blushed to her hairline.

'Teddy Lafferty!' she stammered. 'I thought you had gone back East!'

'You sure move around a lot, Maria,' he said, his eyes lighting up and his whole face suddenly animated. 'If it weren't for your brother's fame in these parts I doubt I'd have managed to find you!'

Maria contained the heat in her heart, smiled with as much urbanity as she could summon and introduced Ted to the Reeds.

Later she and Ted took a walk together to see the new buildings going up on Harrison Avenue. Ted reached for her hand and held it as though he were afraid she might fly away. He told her of his efforts to locate her; he had returned to Denver to find she had moved, that Tom had left Golden, some said to go to the Black Hills. In Deadwood he had been told they had gone to Leadville.

115

'And you followed me . . . you were really looking. I thought,' she burst into tears, 'that you had forgotten me!'

In a moment Ted had her in his arms. Then he went down on his knees in the middle of the darkened sidewalk and asked her to marry him.

The Grand Hotel,
Chestnut Street,
Leadville, Colorado,
12 June 1879

Dear Peggie,

I haven't heard from you for an age and hope everything is all right and that you are thriving in your new life. I hope the bronchitis you suffered over winter got better quickly.

I am writing to give you some interesting news – I've met the grandest girl. Her name is Carrie Reed and she is a teacher. She walked straight into the hotel one day, just as I was wondering if I was going to be a bachelor for the rest of my days! She has the loveliest singing voice. We are to be married in October. Enclosed is a small picture of her.

Maria, I know, has written to tell you of her own plans. She is engaged to a man called Ted Lafferty – a famous scout whom she met on the wagon train. He is about to settle in Leadville, and has been elected one of its newest constables.

I wish you could be with us for our weddings. It's hard to believe that on those big days in our lives you and Father will be four thousand miles away, in dear old Ireland. All the Irish here talk a good deal about how things are at home and the efforts being made by the new Land League and Mr Parnell. It will be a great thing if Justice triumphs and the Irish land system is changed at last.

Please write and let us know how you are.

God bless you.

Your loving brother,

Tom.

PS, $50 dollars enclosed for the baby. I have written separately to Father to tell him my news.

Tom went to Spruce Street to see Carrie. Even before he opened the gate of the small clapboard house he heard the music, ripples of it along piano keys, followed by laughter. Music and girlish giggles, Tom thought, grand sounds altogether.

He found that the door behind the fly screen was ajar, but he knocked all the same, called out, 'Miss Reed?' in a teasing voice, removed his hat and stood for a moment in the polished hall. The parlour door opened and Carrie stood there. She *was* just like a fawn, he thought, struck again by her grace and diffidence. Her brown hair was swept up, her figure was wonderful. That he should have had the luck to find such a creature in this far-flung corner of the world!

Carrie put a finger to her lips, put a hand on his arm and drew him into the parlour.

'These are some of my pupils. They have come to wish us happiness. Girls, this is Mr Walsh, my fiancé.' The girls giggled.

'Look at the lovely quilt they have made for us!' Carrie continued, and she took from a chest a folded patchwork quilt and opened it out.

Tom examined it. The squares were each different, but the colours blended and the design overall was harmonious.

'It's very fine,' he said gravely, noting how Carrie's colour had risen. She blushed for anything and nothing. He turned back to the assembled company. 'It must have taken a long time to make.'

'A year,' the child at the piano said. 'We were going to give it to Miss Reed for Christmas, but then decided it would be a good wedding present. We all made it together.'

She was about twelve, Tom estimated. In a few years' time she herself would be snapped up by some ardent beau.

'Will you play something for us?' Tom asked her, and in a moment the notes of Strauss's 'Blue Danube' filled the room.

Tom bowed to his fiancée. 'Miss Reed, will you do me the honour . . .' and in a moment he had her in his arms and was whirling around the parlour in a waltz, to the giggles of the girls, who suddenly began to clap. When at last the waltz ended, the children left. As the young pianist shyly took her leave, Carrie called her back.

'Wait a minute, Mary.' Carrie went into the kitchen and returned with a jar of cookies. She handed them to the girl. 'I nearly forgot. Will you share these with the others? I made them for the class.'

'Why thank you, ma'am,' Mary said, and went away smiling.

When the child was gone Tom pulled Carrie on to his knee.

'You are as kind, my southern belle, as you are beautiful!'

He kissed her lips, nuzzled into her neck, felt the warm rise and fall of her bosom, and the wild rush of desire. Carrie, flushed and laughing, put her hands on his shoulders and pushed him back.

'Mother will be in shortly. But I have something to say to you, Tom Walsh,' she added, suddenly serious.

Tom waited, but Carrie blushed and hesitated. 'What do you have to say to me, Carrie?'

She stood up, looking him in the eye. 'I love you, Tom Walsh. I want to tell you that I will love you always, come hell or high water!' She drew back and continued, still holding his eyes with her own, 'You see, despite being poor, I *do* have something to offer you – complete devotion, and a certain resilience. They may yet prove useful in the business of life.'

She blushed brighter. Locks of chestnut hair, loosened by their embrace, fell on her neck. She went to the mirror above the mantle to fix them; her reflection glanced at him from the glass.

'Carrie, you have consented to give me yourself,' Tom said gravely, much moved. 'You cannot give me a greater gift!'

Why did I never see the steel in her? he thought, enchanted. She is not a fawn; she is a swan, faithful to death and fierce for her own. I am so happy now that nothing will ever make me unhappy again. I have strength and fortune, love, family and home.

In the fall of 1879 a miscellany of unusual events occurred in Leadville. The first stage coach hold-up took place; there was a fire in Harrison Avenue that destroyed several businesses; the telephone company employees strung wires from the new exchange to yet more business houses; lawlessness gained in momentum and the constables had their work cut out for them; the Wolfe Tone and Highland Guards prepared for possible action as a result of the Thornburgh and Meeker Indian massacres. But most important of all for two young people was a small ceremony that was heralded by the *Leadville Chronicle*.

WEDDING BELLS

Their peals will be loud and clear on the occasion of the marriage of Mr Walsh, one of the Grand Hotel proprietors, to Miss Carrie B. Reed. The wedding takes place one week from next Tuesday evening. Miss Reed is the talented organist at the Spruce Street Methodist Church.

The Walsh-Reed wedding is to be a strictly private and unostentatious affair. The friends of both bride and groom are so numerous that to invite them all would quite call together the entire town. That none may have occasion to be blighted it has been wisely concluded to issue no invitations whatever.

A week later, in the parlour of his bride's home, Tom listened to the words he was impatient to hear: 'Wilt thou have this man to be thy wedded husband . . .?'

She was all his – this vision in her dress of silk brocade trimmed with lace and her head wreathed in orange blossoms.

Tom saw Maria standing with Ted Lafferty, tears in her eyes. Arabella

118

Reed, the bride's mother, wept openly with joy. Judge Murphy was officiating and Father Robinson gave a blessing. Then the wedding party entered the waiting carriages for the short drive to the Grand Hotel, where a corp of waiters stood by to serve the wedding feast. A buttonhole bouquet nestled in each of the table napkins and the bill of fare comprised raw and stewed oysters, brook trout, roast beef, turkey salad, chicken salad, venison with redcurrant jelly, tongue with calf's-foot jelly, Malaga grapes, apples, pears, cream cake, nuts, raisins, champagne, tea or coffee.

Afterwards Maria could remember every moment of the ceremony and the supper after it.

Afterwards Carrie remembered only her husband's eyes when he said, 'I will.'

It was 7 October 1879.

Chapter Eight

Almost ten years had flown since that October wedding. It was now April 1888. Tom was in the parlour of Arabella Reed's house in Denver where the first light of morning was creeping into the room. Upstairs the doctor was delivering his third child. He had paced the floor during a sleepless night, thinking only of Carrie, listening to the sounds of her travail. He prayed that Carrie would come through it safely, as she had on the last occasion, nearly two years earlier, when Evalyn, his daughter, had been born.

His thoughts wandered restlessly – to Maria and her marriage to Ted Lafferty some months after his and Carrie's; to her son, Paul, who was now seven; to little Evalyn asleep upstairs, oblivous to the momentous event taking place a few rooms away.

Outside on Vine Street a carriage clattered by. The street was waking; there was the sound of doors shutting and footsteps on the sidewalk. Tom pushed back his chair and went to the window, pulled back the brown velvet drapes. The day had broken; the April morning was fresh. He blew out the lamp that had kept him company during his vigil, and walked around the room, glancing at the watercolours favoured by his mother-in-law, at engravings in heavy frames, at the buttoned chaise longue in black leather with its colourful throw.

He opened the door, listening carefully to what was happening on the floor above. The doctor had been up there for hours. He heard movement, muted voices, an anguished cry from Carrie that froze his blood. He wanted to mount the stairs, enter the room; he wanted to mop Carrie's brow and hold her hand, but he knew that his modest wife did not want him there while giving birth, and that Arabella would banish him from the room. Lizzie, the shy maid, came from the kitchen with a pot of coffee and some toast on a tray. Her eyes were still gluey from sleep.

'I'm sure you could do with some coffee, Mr Walsh. Would you like breakfast?'

'No thanks, Lizzie.' He lowered his voice. 'Do you know how things are upstairs?'

She shook her head. 'I don't, sir. But I'm sure everything will be all right . . .'

Tom helped himself to coffee. His eyes felt as though they had been rolled in sand. All night long he had listened to the groans from his wife's room, and all a haggard Arabella Reed, whenever she came down, had been able to tell him with a worried frown, was that things were taking their time. 'This baby,' she said, 'is in no hurry to be born.'

If Carrie survives – if they both survive and are well – I'll really settle down, he promised the Unseen Presence. I'll stop this endless searching. I owe it to them . . .

And as he waited, this prompted a review of the past nine years, almost half his adult life.

He was thirty-eight now, a shrewd, strong man, with lines deeply etched around his eyes. The red-gold in his hair had faded. He had a reputation for straight dealing. Whenever he permitted himself a personal stocktaking he looked back on a full life – the growing up in Ireland, the crossing of the Atlantic, his time in Boston, the wagon train across the prairie, his work with the railroad, the years in Deadwood, Leadville and marriage, the silver mines in which he had invested, the real estate he had bought in Denver, the birth of his daughter Evalyn, the comfort he now enjoyed.

But he knew it was tenuous; there were rumblings of recession in the mining world. The price of silver was not what it had been. Many mines were exhausted. But he was still filled with frustrated energy. He was driven by demons he could not exorcise and that had become stronger over the years. They always told him that just over the next hill, in the next gully, in the next abandoned mine, he would redeem his mistake. Just a mile further on was El Dorado.

And as the time rolled by, Tom often promised himself: next year I'll make a visit to Ireland – I'll make a point of it. Carrie and Maria will come with me. But the years had passed and still the time was never right, although by railroad, the journey East would have been easy by comparison with the long trek West. There was always something that required doing, that required his presence, that required whatever assets he had at his command. And that something was always to do with mines and the secrets hidden in the earth. He had ruefully followed the fortunes of a certain gold mine in South Dakota, discovered by one Smoky Jones. Now called The Homestake Mine, it was pouring forth riches seemingly without end, possibly the biggest gold strike in history. His common sense told him not to expect anything like that again. But his guilt at what he had turned down drove him on. He felt he had to make it up to his family; he had to redeem the chances they would all have had. And his instinct whispered: Keep going; there's something waiting . . .

As the years had passed, Ireland had become dreamlike, a land from another dimension, wrapped in nostalgia. Letters were sparse. Peggie, the erstwhile inveterate letter writer, did not take pen to paper so often now. She was the mother of three children and wrote at Christmas, as did Tom's father, greeting him in his stiff unpractised hand. Always the letters were optimistic: things were better in Ireland they said. Don't worry about us.

But the news he gleaned from newspaper articles and from the Leadville Irish, was not so cheerful. They told him that the old country was in the throes of another famine, not as bad as the last, but terrible in the west where the people had borrowed to buy food, only to be driven off their land when they couldn't pay their rents. The whole country was seething with unrest, with incipient violence and with demands for justice; the new Land League was talking of tenant ownership – the land of Ireland for the people of Ireland.

'There's many say they'll die for it, Tom,' his Leadville friends told him grimly. 'History will repeat itself again.'

Tom's heart felt sore; a *mélange* of homesickness and anxiety.

'Poor little Ireland,' he said to Carrie one day not long after their marriage, shaking his head grimly, 'to have on her doorstep, as her implacable foe, the greatest power the world has ever seen!'

'But Peggie and her family are all right, Tom. She would let you know if they, or your father, were in any difficulty, wouldn't she?'

'I suppose so . . .' But he wondered. After all, she never wrote of the troubles in the country so maybe her letters were all rose-tinted.

That night he had a strange experience. He woke and wondered: where am I? The ceiling of his Leadville bedroom bewildered him; he looked for the rafters and the thatch, and did not find them. For a split second he was a being without memory. And then it came back: he was not Tom Walsh of Carraig Mór, County Tipperary, Ireland; he was Thomas F. Walsh of Leadville, Colorado, USA, stakeholder in several mines, American citizen, inveterate prospector.

Mining had become ingrained in him, a necessity, almost an instinct. Eighteen months after his marriage, tired of being a hotelier, excited by what the mines around Leadville were producing, he had become impatient and dissatisfied. There was some great property waiting in the hills for him, he told Carrie, if he could only find it. He broached the subject in their sitting room where Carrie was embroidering the corners of a tablecloth.

'You're doing very well as it is, Tom, you have several irons in the fire.'

122

'But I want to *devote* my time to mining, Carrie. I was never really cut out to be a hotel owner. Can you bear it if we sell up, if we move to the hills?'

'We *are* in the hills – Leadville qualifies, I believe, at almost ten and a half thousand feet!' she replied with one of her quiet sighs. He knew by now that Carrie never confronted him with what she wanted, contenting herself with hints. He looked at her, elegant and beautiful as she bent her head over her embroidery. The tiny needle flew deftly in and out, pulling the shining thread.

'This is satin stitch,' she said, holding her work up to the light. He saw the sheen from the petals worked into the cloth.

'It's lovely, darling. Carrie, the fact is I need the money from the sale of the hotel to invest in mining properties. But if you *really* object to this course, say so. I want to make you happy, and it would be very selfish for me to insist on something that would make you miserable.'

Carrie looked at him quizzically and then back at her work.

Tom found it an ongoing miracle that this beautiful woman loved him. Once he had asked her why.

She had replied with one of her arch smiles: 'Well, Tom, I suppose you think it's your muscles, or your good looks, or maybe your humour, or even your kindness, that makes me so adore you?' She shook her head. 'It is none of these. It is quite simply because the world is a vibrant, exciting place when you are near, and an anxious, doubtful place when you are not.'

Now she added, plying the needle unfalteringly, 'If you are restless and unhappy I cannot be happy either. If you want to sell this hotel then sell it you must!'

Tom was so surprised that his jaw dropped. He sat beside her and kissed her hand.

'Did ever a man have such a wife! But the life will not be easy. Ask Maria. She went through it after a fashion in Deadwood. But this time, there'd only be the two of us. We'd be quite alone. Of course we would leave for the winter, go to Denver to your mother's . . .'

'Actually, Tom, I find the prospect of being *toute seule* with you rather interesting,' she said in her low-pitched, southern lilt and raised her dark eyebrows, her mouth curving in a mischievous half-smile.

'Do you now, you minx?'

And so it was settled. Tom Walsh took a chance. He sold out the Grand Hotel and went into the hills east of Leadville with his bride, to Sowbelly Gulch where he had a stake in several claims, among them the Griffin and the St Kevin's.

'What a terrible name, Tom! "Sowbelly Gulch!" It's so coarse. Can't we change it?'

'To what my love?'

'How about . . . the St Kevin's Mining District?'

Tom laughed. 'Shades of old Ireland? Why not indeed?'

They lived in a log cabin. But this cabin was different from the one in Deadwood; it lacked for no modern comfort that could be dragged up from Leadville. There was a stove, windows with gingham curtains, a beeswaxed floor, a big brass bed and the patchwork quilt Carrie's pupils had given them as a wedding gift.

Carrie kept geraniums in a window box and mourned that their flowering was so short. For a young married pair the log cabin in the hills was paradise. Carrie was happy, and when she sang her lovely voice filled the cabin and spilled out to the lonely reaches of the mountains. In the evenings she entertained her husband on the banjo by the fire. Tom offered to have her piano dragged up from Leadville, but she said he would do nothing of the sort: 'A piano dragged all the way up here – are you mad?'

But gradually the isolation began to gnaw at the young woman. For Tom's sake, she hid her loneliness. He would return in the evenings to a warm and tidy home, to a beautiful wife, a hot meal, a loving bed.

But although Carrie never complained Tom did recognise that she was much too alone. He brought her to visit other families living within ten miles. The nearest were the Fahys, about three miles away. Tom had known Des Fahy during his days in the Black Hills. He lived with his wife, Kate. Kate, who had come all the way from the East End of London to find her fortune in the New World, had taken to the wilds of Colorado as though born to it. She made wonderful bread; her herbal remedies for headache and other ills were well regarded among the small, scattered community living high above the world. Her two sons, the children of her first marriage, had decamped to California, but Des was a prospector to the bone, refusing to leave the wilderness, wintering in Leadville with its blanket of snow.

'We're going down to Denver for the winter,' Carrie told Kate. 'Mother has a house there now.' She laughed and added, 'I'll be able to wear some of my nice gowns again!'

'Good for you,' Kate said. 'And I hope you wear your toes out dancing!'

Tom bought Carrie a pony and she and Kate established a rapport, taking the stony path in the wilderness to see each other, or, when the weather was mild, visiting the other women living within a wider radius, or making the journey down to Leadville together to do some shopping.

Leadville was a substantial city now. It had thirty thousand inhabitants, many fine buildings along Harrison Avenue, and an opera house built by Horace Tabor, the 'Silver King'.

★   ★   ★

124

One evening in May 1881 Tom returned home to find his wife full of suppressed excitement. She put his supper down before him, picked at her own, glanced at him occasionally and smiled to herself.

'Well, what is it, Carrie?' he asked after a moment, bending towards his wife and looking with smiling quizzicality into her eyes. 'What's the story that you can't wait to tell me?'

Carrie laughed. 'My face gives everything away! Maybe I should have told you earlier, but I was afraid you would have shelved your plans. And I had to be absolutely sure.'

She got up, came behind him, put her arms around his neck, and whispered in his ear: 'We're going to have a baby!'

For a moment Tom was speechless. He turned to stare at his wife, who hunched laughingly into her shoulders like a schoolgirl.

'Aren't you pleased, Tom?'

That this gift of all gifts should be given him! Words from a hymn long forgotten surfaced as he struggled for composure: *What shall I render unto the Lord for all the things that He has rendered unto me?*

He stood up, picked up his wife, and lifted her into the air. 'You wonderful, wonderful girl!'

'Put me down, you bad boy . . .' Tom returned her gently to terra firma. 'That is the best news that anyone has ever given me,' he said into her hair. 'When is the baby due?'

'October.'

Tom's face registered shock. He leaned back on his heels. 'So soon! You don't show it! I thought you were just putting on a little weight. Oh, Carrie, you should have told me before now.'

Carrie tried and failed to look contrite. 'I'll show it soon enough,' she said ruefully. 'I've had to let out my waistbands!'

'You can't stay here,' Tom continued in an alarmed, no-nonsense tone after a moment. 'You'll have to go to your mother in Denver. I'll see you as often as I can.'

'And how often would that be?' Carrie cried. 'Denver is eighty miles away! This is exactly what I was afraid you would say,' she added, 'one of the reasons I didn't tell you sooner. I'm not leaving you here and going down to Denver to fret over you every day. Don't ask that of me, Tom. I couldn't bear it. I will go – when it's nearer the time. Pregnancy is a perfectly natural state, after all,' she added in a pragmatic tone, 'so there's no need for fuss or bother . . .'

That evening Tom began a cradle; he fashioned it lovingly from seasoned timber.

Three months later, in mid-August, on one of his prospecting trips into the Frying Pan district, Tom stopped at an abandoned claim. He dismounted, inspected the old mine shaft and dump, and with some disappointment found them to be of decomposed granite, absolutely barren. He was tired, sat on an outcrop and lit his pipe, hearing with pleasure the sound of the mountain streams, the sigh of the wind and the small tearing sounds as his horse cropped the grass.

As he smoked, he looked at the derelict log cabin that had once housed the prospectors who had worked here. It was little more than a roof held up by poles. The low sun touched quartz particles among the debris piled on the roof. Tom went into the cabin, saw that the earthen floor had in it several chunks of exposed rock. He broke off sections with his pick, examined them with astonishment; it was quartz, silver-bearing in what looked like good concentrations. He realised at once that the former owners had obliviously built their house on the apex of the vein, and had then sunk their shaft in barren granite some fifty feet away. He filled his saddlebags with samples.

Silver was a money-spinner, literally and figuratively. Every time he took a coin from his pocket he thought of the effort that had gone into finding the ore to make it in the first place. But as long as the Denver Mint gobbled it up, everyone in Leadville, everyone involved in mining in Colorado, would do nicely.

When he came home he said to Carrie: 'I've some interesting samples from an old mine I found today.'

But Carrie did not seem to share his enthusiasm; she just turned away, half wearily, half in disgust it seemed to Tom. Was she ill? he wondered in alarm. Now seven months pregnant, she was still postponing her removal to Denver – had told him that very morning that there was plenty of time – 'In another week or two . . .'

'Are you all right, Carrie?' he now asked her anxiously.

'I have neuralgia,' she said crossly. 'I've had it for most of the day. I get it a good deal these times; I think it's the altitude.'

'My poor darling. Come on, I'll tuck you up in bed.'

Carrie went to bed. Tom sat beside her, bathed her forehead with a cool, damp cloth, and crooned a lullaby from long ago, one his mother had sung:

> 'Seoinseó í ló ló,
> Seoinseó is tú mo leanbh . . .'

tasting the Irish on his tongue with wonder that it was still there, rooted deep inside him, alive and unforgotten, as though it had a place of its own that could never be colonised. He was pleased to see that the tension left Carrie and that she soon slept.

He sat by the fire, thinking of how he would bring his new samples to the assayers in the morning. He could not help the optimism; he knew from looking at the quartz that it was silver-rich. He would just have to locate the former owners, give them their price; or if it was a tax title pay the outstanding taxes. He was full of the joy of life. Soon he would have a son and he would be able to give him everything. And someday, maybe sooner than later, he would find the big one, the mine that would answer his dream, restore to his family all that could have been theirs if he had only been awake . . .

In the morning Carrie said she was fine. But Tom noticed that she was pale; she had dark circles around her eyes and she ate little of the breakfast he brought to her on a tray.

'Please eat something, my darling.'

She nibbled at the toast he had spent some time making before the fire.

'This is pure carbon!' she said querulously, and pushed it away.

It was so unlike her to make any kind of complaint that Tom was startled. He looked at the blackened edges of the toast and conceded that it might be construed as a trifle overdone.

'I'll make you some more.'

'No. I don't want any.'

'Would you like me to stay at home?'

He said this gently. Both of them knew it was important to get the samples assayed with as much speed as possible. There was always the risk that another prospector would find the abandoned claim, see its potential and beat them to the prize.

Carrie was lying back on the pillows; her hair, unplaited, lay loosely about her head and he gathered it into his hands. For a moment something flared in her dark eyes.

Then she said plaintively, 'I can see you're just rarin' to get down to Leadville to the assay office. Go on, Tom; I'll be fine!'

Tom kissed her tenderly and said goodbye. 'I'll be back as soon as I can, Carrie. Mind yourself and stay in bed. I'll call in on Kate and ask her to keep an eye on you.'

He bridled his horse, loaded the heavy saddlebags, jumped into the saddle. Tom kept the horse to a walk, aware of the load, the animal's harsh breathing, the clink and small shifting of the rock samples, the clunk of the iron-shod hoofs on the trail, the swish of the wind in the trees. He did not take the most direct route down the mountain, but instead guided the horse the three miles to the Fahy cabin.

Des was outside in breeches and suspenders, splitting logs for firewood. He put down the axe, mopped his brow with his sleeve, shouting a greeting as Tom approached from the trees. Kate, greying hair in a bun, wearing a blue apron made of the jeaning many of the miners wore, came to the open door to see who had come by.

'Ah, Tom,' she said, 'you're like a stranger. Come on in for some hot coffee.'

Tom shook his head. 'Thanks, Kate, but I'm headed for Leadville with some samples.'

'How is Carrie?'

'A bit tired. I left her in bed. She's still refusing to go to Denver.'

Kate frowned. 'She's a stubborn gel.' She lowered her voice and muttered, 'Tom, you should make her go. She doesn't know what's ahead of her.'

Tom looked so stricken that she added, 'I've Des's lunch box to do and then I'll ride over. I could do with a good long natter anyway.'

Des laughed as he split another log down the middle. 'Women!' he said. 'If that new-fangled telephone ever gets up here there'll be no work done from mornin' till night.'

Tom went down to Leadville, easier in his mind now that he knew someone would be keeping an eye on Carrie. As always, he was acutely aware of his surroundings. He noticed how blue the Colorado spruce was, how green the quivering aspen leaves, and how the wilderness gloried in the summer sun although the great behemoths, Mount Elbert and Mount Harvard were hoary at their peaks. In a distant clearing above the timber line some marmots straightened to look at him. Nearby, chipmunks left the forest floor and scampered up the trees. A brown eagle hopped and swooped against a slope in the distance, and then took wing.

In Leadville Tom left the samples with the assay office, dropped in on the Grand Hotel, and talked to a few of his friends – 'Stay for lunch, Tom. There's a nice bit of lamb today . . .'

Tom was ravenous after his ride through the hills, but he declined. 'I told my wife I would be home as quickly as I could.'

The chef fixed him a hasty packed lunch; then Tom set out for the cabin in the hills. He urged his horse up the long inclines, hearing the rattle of the stones as they slid down behind him, aware of the how the breeze had become chill. He was looking forward to seeing Carrie, to their long night together in each other's arms, to feeling his unborn kick against him.

When he got to the cabin the light was already failing, but the window was lit and the house looked cheery. It was only when Tom dismounted and saw Kate Fahy in the open doorway, sleeves rolled up, that he realised everything was not as it should be. There was a determined, businesslike cast to his neighbour's face.

Tom's heart stood still.

'What is it Kate?'

'The baby's on the way,' she whispered urgently. 'I'm no midwife, but I'll do the best I can.'

'But Carrie's only—'

He heard a hoarse cry from his wife and rushed into the bedroom where

128

Carrie, pale, sweat streaming, arched and groaned in their dishevelled bed.

'I'm going back to Leadville to get a doctor,' he told her. But the labouring woman put out her hand.

'Please don't leave me, Tom. I'm so frightened.'

Tom suppressed the panic. An old memory surfaced, like a waiting foe.

'I have to get the doctor, darling. I'll be back soon. Everything will be all right, my sweetheart,' he added, trying to keep his voice steady. Then he rushed from the cabin, turned his horse around, and hastened down the darkening trail to the twinkling lights of Leadville.

By the time he had found Doc Moran, organised a fresh horse, and they had set out, the night had advanced. Occasionally the horses stumbled in the darkness; their riders pulled on the reins to drag up their heads. The doctor asked a little too casually at one point if there were any bears around and Tom said he had seen none recently.

'There's no point in worrying yourself sick, Tom,' the doctor said suddenly. 'Carrie is young and strong. It's the baby I fear for. At seven months, and a first birth, at this altitude . . .'

Tom found that he was trembling by the time they approached his cabin. What news was there for him behind that lamplit window with the pink gingham curtains she had made with such care? Life or death?

He rushed to his wife's bedside. Carrie looked at him as though she didn't know him; she cried out, her face twisted, her lips drawn back. The doctor put his black bag on the table, spoke to her in soothing professional tones, told Tom he would be better off somewhere else. Tom went outside to see to the horses, his ears full of the strangled sounds behind him. He retched.

The baby was stillborn. The doctor came to tell Tom, whispering the terrible news.

'Carrie will be all right. I'm so sorry, Tom. I couldn't save the baby.'

Carrie cried and wailed brokenly when the dead baby was put into her arms – a little girl, tiny, exquisite, slick with blood and water, accusing in her perfect silence. Tom wanted to go outside and bang his head against a tree. My fault, he told himself, remembering another birth long ago. I should have made her go to Denver! My stupid, criminal fault!

He rocked his wife, wiped her tears, soothed her until the combination of exhaustion and the sedative the doctor had administered took effect, and she became limp in his arms. For a moment he thought with heart-stopping terror that she too had died, but then he realised she was only asleep, her hair damp, her body crumpled. He covered her carefully, wiping his eyes with the sheet.

When the doctor had left Tom went out into the night and buried the firstborn he would never know.

'May Almighty God,' he whispered, paraphrasing an old Irish prayer as he tamped down the Colorado earth on the tiny grave, 'hold you for ever, my little daughter, in the hollow of His hand.'

The assay report on the abandoned claim reached Tom a week later. The results ran at a hundred ounces of silver per ton. It was a valuable find and would once have been a cause for rejoicing, but now there was a pall of grief over everything.

At least he comforted himself, Carrie had emerged alive from childbirth. But the loss of the baby had affected both of them deeply. She was very quiet now; her forays into song had been silenced. Tom wondered privately if he had any right to make love to her ever again.

But even after her trauma Carrie had refused to go to her parent's house in Denver. 'I couldn't bear the journey; I don't want to go.'

Instead her mother had come and nursed her heartbroken daughter in the hills.

'It's not right to have a delicate young girl up here!' she said to Tom. 'At this altitude it's hard enough for an able-bodied man to put one foot in front of the other. You're wearing out your own life and health; but for a woman to be expected to give birth up here is preposterous. It's a terrible strain on her heart.'

'I don't expect her to give birth up here, Mrs Reed,' Tom said. 'In fact I spent the last twelve weeks trying to persuade her to go to Denver! I suppose I should have insisted, but she has a mind of her own!'

'I know that Tom,' Arabella conceded ruefully. '*I* reared her!'

Carrie had changed. She took to reading her Bible a good deal, discussed chapters from the Holy Writ, and when her husband took her in his arms her response was muted.

Four years later Carrie had become pregnant again. It happened while they were wintering in Denver, but this time she needed no admonishments to stay with her mother. Tom had returned alone to the mountains, came down to Denver as often as possible. Evalyn was born on 1 August, 1886, yelling her lungs out at life.

'*The mother of the living!*' Tom said to Carrie, endorsing her choice of name. 'A strong name.'

'You're thinking of Eve, darling,' Carrie replied in a serious tone. 'Remember Eve was tempted, and succumbed.'

Carrie's religious leanings were more pronounced than ever. Tom sighed inwardly. He was a God-fearing man, but he had long ago left behind him adherence to any particular dogma.

'It wasn't a very sensible stricture, not to eat the few miserable apples!' he muttered. 'But either way,' he added with a laugh as he looked down at his new daughter, and the baby's roars explored new decibels, 'I don't see this young lady going in overmuch for any kind of servility!'

'Are you saying that the Lord's command should not have been obeyed, Tom Walsh?'

'No, Carrie,' Tom said hastily.

And now, here in her mother's house in Denver, Carrie was in labour again with their third child. Although he had not expressed it to her or anyone else, he hoped this time that she would give him a son.

Tom's reverie was broken by the bewildered, anguished cry from upstairs, the cry of the newborn. He jumped, upsetting his coffee cup, threw open the door and bounded upstairs, taking the steps two at a time. The doctor came into the landing. He was smiling.

'A fine boy, Mr Walsh; seven pounds, two ounces. Congratulations.'

'And my wife?'

'What she needs now is a nice long sleep. It wasn't an easy birth, but she'll be fine!'

'I'm not as young as I used to be!' Carrie said to Tom with a tired smile a few minutes later. 'I'm glad I don't have to do this every day!'

The room was filled with morning, and Carrie's hair, although her mother had newly brushed it, was lank with sweat. Lying in her arms was a small sleeping bundle. The room smelled of blood and instantly Tom was hit by a *mélange* of memory. But Carrie seemed all right – certainly exhausted, trembling a little, but far from death's door. He exhaled a slow, thankful breath. Arabella Reed, a grandmother for a second time, was all smiles, although her face was white and her eyes bloodshot from lack of sleep.

'Congratulations, Tom. I'll leave you young people in peace!'

She left the room quietly, directing a fond smile back at the tableau – mother and newborn infant, father bending over them – as she closed the door.

Tom kissed his wife's forehead and kneeled by her bed.

'My wonderful darling,' he whispered from a full heart. He pulled down a corner of the towel that cocooned the baby, stared at the tiny, sleeping face. 'And who have we here?'

'A little person who is anxious to meet you,' Carrie whispered. 'He's not looking his best just yet, but as he's had a rough journey he hopes you'll excuse his appearance!'

Tom looked at the red face, the small fists, the minuscule clenched toes, the clot of blood in his hair.

'He's the image of his mother,' he whispered, placing his hand over the little foot that fitted so neatly into his palm.

'I hope not, Tom,' Carrie exclaimed with an exhausted laugh. 'No, he looks like you,' and she put the baby into his arms.

From outside the door came the sounds of a newly awakened Evalyn. Mrs Reed knocked and put her head around the door.

'I spoke too soon. There's a young lady here who's just got up and who knows in her bones that something's happened!'

'Let her come in, Mother, of course.'

Evalyn, nearly two years old, plump and dark-haired, shot into the room like a bullet. She stared at the new bundle in her father's arms. Her mouth opened and her eyes rounded.

'Look who's come to live with us?' her mother said, taking the baby back from Tom. 'Come here, darling, and kiss your new brother.'

Evalyn came to the bed and regarded the new baby with suspicion. She put out her hand but was restrained before she could get a grip on him.

'That's enough now,' her grandmother chuckled. 'We don't want him throttled.'

Evalyn struggled in her grandmother's arms, stared at her new sibling as though hypnotised. Then, turning to her father for clarification, she pulled fiercely on his sleeve and pointed at the newcomer.

'It's your little brother,' he whispered into her ear. 'You'll have to mind him, you know, because you're his big, sensible sister.' He turned back to Carrie. 'Have you decided on his name?'

They had discussed this two weeks ago, but without coming to a firm decision.

'Vinson,' Carrie said. 'It's derived from the Latin verb *vincere*, to conquer. What do you think?'

'It's a wonderful name!' Tom said.

On a sign from Carrie, Mrs Reed took the sleeping baby and put him into the little wooden cradle that Tom had made for the first of his children. Tom rocked it, put a hand on his son's tiny head in loving benediction.

Evalyn suddenly sat on the floor and began to wail. Mrs Reed scooped the child up.

'She's just looking for notice,' she said. 'Her monopoly is gone and her nose is a bit out of joint . . .' To the child she added, 'Your mother's tired. Let her sleep now,' and she took a wailing Evalyn from the room.

Tom stayed until Carrie was asleep. He stood for a few moments looking down at her. Then he leaned over the cradle where his newborn son slept. He put his finger against the baby's hand, felt the sudden fierce grip of the tiny fingers. 'My son!' he whispered. 'I have a son!'

He stayed for a while, then he gently detatched his finger from the baby's grip, kissed his wife's forehead and left the room. There was work to be done. His mind reverted to the business problems he was facing. The price of silver was fluctuating; his mining interests were producing less. He would think carefully of the new smelting process; it might be just the thing to make his fortune in the face of the downturn in silver. The future for everyone he loved depended on him.

When Tom and Carrie returned to Leadville, Maria and Ted called to see the new baby. With them came their seven-year-old son, Paul.

Maria had hardly aged, except that the heavy auburn hair was now streaked with grey. She, Ted and Paul were living in a clapboard house in Sixth Street, bought with the money Tom had made over to his sister on her marriage.

Maria had continued to do the books for the Grand Hotel after her marriage. Ted was now an established Leadville constable. His was the job of bringing discipline to the lawless, getting up posses, calming tempers before they got out of hand. He tracked outlaws with the acumen of an Indian, bringing to his current employment all the insights and decisiveness that had made him such a famous scout. But it was a dangerous job and Tom saw the frown lines that appeared in his sister's forehead whenever she spoke of it.

'Maybe I'll become a miner instead,' Ted would say with a twinkle when his wife complained about his work, and Maria would answer that the only job more dangerous than the one he was doing was blasting rock underground.

'The mines always take the lungs,' she said, 'and without them you can't do anything!'

'Well, it's true that I find breathing quite useful!' Ted would concede, 'and I've every intention of doing it for a long time yet.'

Now the two of them bent over the latest Walsh child and wished the parents joy. Paul gazed at the baby.

'Dat's my brudder!' Evalyn informed him.

'He's very small!' Paul replied scornfully, but after a moment he glanced at his mother and asked softly, 'Mother, can I have a brother too?'

'I don't know, darling. It's God who decides these things . . .'

Later, after Ted had been called out to a fracas in Chestnut Street and Carrie had gone to nurse the baby, Tom asked his sister: 'How are things in the Grand Hotel?'

Maria did not reply for a moment. Then she said, 'Can I talk to you fairly and squarely, Tom?'

'Of course . . .'

He expected some confidence of her own, but she said, 'It's a good thing that you invested in real estate in Denver. You should unload your mining properties around here. Leadville is not what it used to be and I doubt it will ever be again!'

Tom prevaricated. 'My interests are doing all right, Maria . . .'

She shook her head. 'For how long? You know perfectly well the silver market is saturated. And the values in most of the mines are decreasing. I can see the result in the business we do at the hotel. Trade is falling off; the bar is no longer filled in the evenings; the numbers eating lunch and dinner have gone down. Sometimes, rooms are vacant for days, even weeks, on end.'

Tom listened. He knew there was a downturn, but he had already made plans to circumscribe it.

'I worry about you, Tom,' his sister went on. 'I think you're after the impossible – year after year, month after month you're in the hills killing yourself. Why can't you recognise that you have enough? I don't know how Carrie stands it, being left so much alone, particularly with children to think of.'

'Maria, I'm thirty-eight years old . . . Would you put me out to grass? You were full of some notion once,' he added in a teasing voice, 'that I would do strange things in America!'

'And so you have. You're a success!'

Tom was unimpressed. 'Success is relative. There's nothing even re-motely "strange" about anything I've done, except of course that I managed to pass up the greatest opportunity any man was ever offered . . .'

Maria looked at him in the old way of hers, jutting out her chin and narrowing her eyes. 'Are you still sore about that?'

'Was that it, Maria? What you used to go on about? What you forecast for me in the old days when you were still a witch?'

'For a big strong man you have a great dollop of superstition in you. Witch, indeed! Why can't you be content to be like everyone else?'

'I can't!'

'Why not?'

Tom sighed. 'I don't know why not.'

'I suspect you're up to something new, Tom.'

'Well, Mrs Lafferty,' he said, 'if you want to know what I'm up to, I'll tell you. There's a new smelting process called the Austin process. It extracts good values from low-grade ores. Just the thing, Maria, for mines that are close to exhaustion! I'm thinking of going into partnership with the man who has the franchise for the West.'

'You're wasting your money!' Maria said abruptly. 'If you ask me, you will lose everything!'

Chapter Nine

The Colorado franchise for the Austin pyritic method of smelting was owned by David S. Wegg, and Tom went into business with him in 1891 with a substantial investment that represented most of his assets.

This precipitated the erection of smelters at Kokomo and Silverton, as well as a new one at Leadville. To facilitate the establishment and running of the smelters the family moved, from cabin to cabin, from hotel to hotel, before settling in 1892 in a clapboard house in the tiny new town of Ouray, in an enclosed mountain valley of San Juan County, about thirty miles from Silverton, and two hundred miles from Leadville. With them was their Scottish maid Annie MacDonald, who was devoted to the children.

Ouray was exquisite. Hidden in a valley at seven thousand seven hundred feet, it was almost surrounded by a semicircle of folded mountain the townspeople called the Amphitheatre. Behind this rose Mount Hayden and Mount Abrams, snow-crested for most of the year. The sides of the mountains were clothed with firs, but the valley floor had been cleared to make way for the settlement. As no natural means of access to Ouray from the south existed, a road to nearby Silverton had been gouged from the mountain wall above a gorge of breathtaking proportions. It was a toll road built by a man named Otto Mears and they called it the Million Dollar Highway.

The town was now seventeen years old and boasted over two and a half thousand souls, enough to designate itself a city. It had a school, at least ten saloons, a sawmill, a bank, a hospital, an opera house, a courtroom, six brothels, two hotels – the elegant and expensive Beaumont and the inexpensive Western – two assay offices, two haulage businesses, two newspapers and five doctors. It had natural hot springs and electric lighting.

Above the town, hidden in the hills, were a number of successful silver mines. Many of the miners lived in the boarding houses at the mines, or in the town. The railroad had arrived in 1887, and opened the town to the outside world.

'It's like something from a picture postcard of Switzerland,' Carrie said. 'What do you think you'll find in a place this lovely?'

'Beauty is not a negative yardstick, my darling . . .' Of late an edge had come to Carrie's voice, an anxiety that hovered around the children and around Tom, and that was almost claustrophobic in its intensity.

They were in their parlour on a Sunday afternoon. The room was furnished with a chaise longue, several fine prints, a large rug, some easy chairs, a piano and a coffee table. Outside the first snow lay thick on the roofs, on the firs, on the rock striations of the Amphitheatre. The children were playing on the floor, Annie was busy in the kitchen and the terrier, Dandy, was asleep by the stove. Carrie was intermittenly fingering notes on her piano, and leafing through a new music book. She liked to play for the family in the evening, sing hymns, or songs. Tom would join in with his rich baritone; Evalyn would screech her few notes, and little Vinson would lisp his personal interpretation, making everyone laugh.

Tom leaned over, lifted Carrie from the piano stool and put her on his lap. It was something he had not done for years. He wanted to hold her as though they were still newlyweds in the mountains, rich with their first love; he wanted to reassure her. The children were delighted. Evalyn decided she would join them and clambered on to her mother's knee, and little Vinson, laughing, climbed on top of her.

'The Walsh layers!' Tom exclaimed, feigning suffocation. 'First Vinson brings the considerable weight of his years, then Evalyn, who weighs about a ton, then my beloved wife . . .' he caught the dangerous glint in Carrie's eye as she turned her head to look at him, and continued hurriedly, 'who is as light as thistledown. I suppose we'd have Dandy on top of us if—'

'Dandy!' Vinson shouted.

The dog stuck up his ears, ran to the armchair and tried to leap on top of the laughing Vinson.

'Are ye all mad?' Annie demanded, coming into the room with a tea tray.

'Get down out of that!' she told Dandy, 'before I get the broom to ye. Do ye think ye're human?'

'Dan-di, Dan-di,' Vinson screamed, clutching the dog by the ears.

'And you, young rascals,' Annie said firmly, 'it's time for your nap!'

'No!' Evalyn and Vinson howled in unison. Carrie put her children on the ground, got off her husband's knee and settled her dress with the primness that had in recent years become her hallmark.

'You go for your nap now, Evalyn,' she said in a no-nonsense voice. 'When I've had my tea I'm going too.'

'What about Vinson?' Evalyn protested hotly.

'Vinson also.'

Tom put his hand on his little son's head. The child smiled up at him.

Evalyn stared at her father and brother, felt the intimacy, the special bond between them.

'Father will have a nap too,' Tom said with a twinkle. 'So everyone in the house will be napping and there will be no excuse for any undue activity!'

Carrie caught his eye and suddenly blushed. Annie smiled to herself as she left the room with the children.

In their bedroom a little later, Tom embraced his wife as he began to unlace her. He had never become used to the wonder of her, not in thirteen years of marriage, nor would he, he thought, in a hundred years. He saw her familiar curves, smelled the tantalising scent of her cool, white, powdered skin. This feminine country was his very own; it had known no man but him and never would.

'This damn corset of yours!' he whispered as he struggled with the laces, 'I've a good mind to throw it out the window!'

Carrie tried to look reproachful, but had to put her hand to her mouth to contain her mirth. 'If you do that, Tom Walsh, you will have disgraced me. How could I hold my head up in Ouray when half the town would be talking about the stays my husband threw out the window?'

'The other women would be jealous,' Tom retorted in a sly tone, 'and would look on you with new eyes!'

'That much at least is true!' she said with a reluctant shriek of laughter.

'I love to hear you laugh like that,' Tom whispered. 'I would love to hear it much more.' He nuzzled against her neck . . .

'Sanctifying grace,' he whispered a little later, lying back on the pillow beside her, his eyes tender.

Carrie smiled. 'Sweetheart, sanctifying grace comes from Heaven.'

'Agreed,' Tom replied, 'though I might not concur with orthodox notions as to where Heaven is to be found!'

'You're incorrigible, Tom Walsh,' his wife said, reprovingly. 'You should show more respect for God!'

'Ah, we get along well enough,' Tom replied, 'God and myself. Although in the old days in Ireland I wondered about him.'

Carrie felt the dismay. The one topic of conversation she tried to steer away from was anything to do with Ireland. It brought back the subject of his mother, and things at which she could hardly guess. She remembered only too well the time Evalyn had demanded, 'Father, tell me about Ireland!'

Tom had been evasive.

'You should tell her about her grandparents, at least,' Carrie had whispered to him reproachfully, but Evalyn's acute ears had heard her.

'What was she like,' the child had demanded eagerly, 'my Irish grannie?'

'She had red hair.'

'Like you, Father?'

He'd smiled. 'Like me when I was young.'

'Your moustache is still red.'

Tom had sighed. 'Some of it, Evalyn!'

'And bits of your hair,' she'd added generously. 'Was my grannie beautiful?'

'Very.'

'Is she dead?' The child had asked this in a low voice, looking at her father from rounded eyes.

Tom had nodded. 'She died a long time ago,' he'd said evenly.

'And my grandfather?'

'He is very old now. But he liked to read poetry aloud when I was a child; and he used to play the fiddle. Neighbours would come to listen.'

'Not the piano, like Mother?'

'No, Evalyn. There was no piano.'

'Will I ever see him?'

'No, child,' Tom had whispered. 'I do not believe so.'

Carrie had glanced at him and said swiftly, 'Don't be bothering your father now, Evalyn. Can't you see he's tired?'

There had also been the time she had held up a lace collar for his approval in a shop in Denver.

'Look, Tom, real Irish lace!'

His face had suddenly saddened, and when they had got home he had been taciturn and abrupt.

'What is it, Tom? Please tell me. Did I do something wrong?'

'Oh, Carrie,' he'd said, his voice unsteady, 'I'm sorry . . . It's just that my mother had a pillowcase with lace edging she made herself, her poor little treasure. Someday, I will stand again by her grave, tell her about my life, about you and the children . . . But I want to tell her that I have succeeded. That her son has triumphed in the great world she never knew.'

Is that what's driving you, Tom Walsh? Carrie had wondered, pondering for a moment the kind of woman who could inspire such devotion thirty-six years after her death.

'Vinson loves school,' she said now to change the subject, sitting on the edge of the bed and getting Tom to lace her up again. 'I worried about sending him so young, but he's coming on very well – not like Evalyn who doesn't want to do a tap of work. She keeps looking for notice. Mrs Hurlburt is in despair over her.'

Tom smiled behind his moustache, and gave the laces a few firm tugs as directed.

'I don't know how women breathe in these contraptions,' he said teasingly. 'Now that they've won the right to vote in Colorado, wouldn't you think they'd show some sense?' He glanced at Carrie, saw she was ready to take issue. 'Evalyn is a lazy minx,' he added, evading her tart response, 'but she has a good heart!'

The price of silver was still dropping. But Tom, spurred by an instinct backed by personal study of the terrain, was acquiring defunct claims in the Imogene Basin above the town, and employing men to sink the shafts and blast the tunnels that would, he hoped, find new ores. Carrie, beside herself with anxiety, looked on in astonishment.

'Why do you put what's left of your money into those old claims?' she exclaimed in an uncharacteristic outburst one day. 'We could have bought a house in the East; you could have retired with the money you have wasted on them!'

She had neuralgia and migraine on a frequent basis now, and was often irritable. And although Tom suspected all of this was anxiety-based, he could not stop. He needed good fluxing materials for the smelters; if he found them in reasonable quantities he would have snatched success from an increasingly depressing situation. If they contained enough traces of gold to pay for their transport, he would regard himself as blessed. If something more significant turned up, something hidden since the dawn of creation and waiting for him through the millennia, he would regard himself as vindicated at last.

'Tom, if there was anything left in them it would have been found long since!'

Tom shook his head. 'Not true, Carrie. People give up. Life demands persistence, patience, endurance. It demands the capacity to overcome obstacles and continue on. Not everyone has that.'

'And where do I feature in all this? You're never at home. All I have is Evalyn and Vinson. Their conversational skills, while interesting, are not unlimited, and Annie has more to do than keep me company. Isn't your marriage important?'

Tom heard the desperation sharpening his wife's voice. He put his arms around her, pulled her close to his chest, and said into her hair: 'Bear with me, darling. I know it's lonely for you, but I'll be home as often as I can! I'll make it up to you! I promise I will.'

She glanced up at him.

'There is so much locked up in you, so much passion. I want it, and yet you give it to those . . . hills!'

Tom laughed. 'But I do give it to you. Everything I plan and do is for you, my family! Someday, Carrie, I am going to make you all very rich.'

'Rich!' Carrie exclaimed. 'You've been talking like this for years! You're in your forties. If you were going to find something extraordinary, you would have found it by now! We were rich in Leadville,' she added a little bitterly. 'You were a rich man when I married you, and it's all gone!'

'I am absolutely convinced,' Tom said quietly, 'that there is plenty of gold in the mountains around us.'

Carrie shook her head impatiently. 'And I will tell you what I am convinced of. I am afraid that this absolute conviction of yours, Tom Walsh, will beggar us.'

She left the room. He sat alone and looked out the window at the snowy Amphitheatre. Recently some of his old mining friends had voiced similiar comment.

'Have you taken leave of your senses, Tom? There is no significant gold in the San Juans! You're wasting your money. And as for fluxing materials, will you find them in sufficient quantities to repay your transportation?'

Tom sighed. 'Maybe they're right,' he whispered aloud. 'After all, Carrie spoke the truth. My best years are already gone.'

But still, the next time he saw Andy Richardson, the old prospector who knew the mountains around Ouray better than anyone, he asked him to do some more sampling for him. Andy had a cabin high in the hills and had, years before, named the Imogene Basin for his wife.

'Someday,' the latter was fond of saying, 'someday, Tom, something will give!'

Something did! In 1893 came the bombshell that had seemed to hover in the wind for so long. The Government repealed the Sherman Act that required the Treasury to purchase a specified amount of silver each month. Silver was 'de-monetised'. It would no longer be used to make the coins that jingled in everyone's pocket. Silver mines closed overnight in Colorado; the smelter Tom managed at Silverton limped along, but the one at Kokomo had to close. Ouray went into recession. Businesses closed; the town could no longer afford electric lighting for the streets, or to water them to keep down the dust. In order to pay his miners, Tom quickly mortgaged the last of his assets in Denver. The choice before him was now stark: he had to acknowledge that either he gave up mining or bankruptcy was staring him in the face.

He was not alone in his troubles. Hundreds of banks closed, many railroads went into bankruptcy, insolvency and unemployment overtook a multitude. People he had known – like the multimillionaire Horace Tabor in Leadville – were reduced to penury. Maria wrote that lawlessness had returned to Leadville. Many newly destitute miners there were solving their problems in an age-old manner. She was worried about Ted and wished he could retire, and she fretted that Paul was growing up with incipient violence all around him.

'He'll be thirteen on his next birthday. He'll grow into manhood thinking this is the way men act,' she wrote.

'She sounds frightened!' Carrie said when she read the letter, adding with a sigh, 'I'm glad we're living in Ouray!'

A knock came to the door that evening and Annie, who had been putting the children to bed, ran downstairs to answer it. Evalyn peeped over the banister; saw it was the boy from the Beaumont with a telegram.

Annie took it from him and brought it straight to Tom and Carrie in the parlour. Tom ripped open the envelope. The telegram was from Leadville and said simply:

TED KILLED STOP PAUL MISSING
MARIA

Chapter Ten

'I have to go to her at once!'

Carrie nodded and Tom rushed to the Beaumont Hotel to wire his reply to his sister.

Carrie went upstairs to pack a bag for her husband. She felt sick. It was as though everything was going wrong, as though life itself was off course, like a derailed train blundering towards a precipice. Poor, poor Maria, she thought. What on earth had happened?

'What is wrong, Mother?' Evalyn whispered, creeping into her mother's room in her nightdress. 'What was that message?'

Carrie sat her little daughter down on her bed.

'Oh, Evalyn, it's from your Aunt Maria.'

'Is she coming on a visit?' Evalyn demanded, her face lighting up. 'Uncle Ted too and Paul?' But her voice petered away as she regarded her mother's face.

'No, darling. You see . . . your uncle has had some kind of accident. I'm afraid he's . . . dead.'

Evalyn looked blank. She could not imagine a world where all the players in her private universe were no longer part of it. Uncle Ted had always been fascinating. She had never tired hearing him tell the story of how her father and Maria had crossed the prairie on the wagon train for which he was the scout, and how he had scoured the West looking for Maria afterwards. She loved her aunt and her cousin. He was five years older than her, almost grown up.

'What happened?'

'We don't know yet, darling. Your father is going to Leadville.'

'Poor Paul,' Evalyn wailed, bursting into tears.

'Sshh,' Carrie said. 'Your brother will hear you. I don't want you to upset him!'

I shouldn't have told the child, she thought with a sigh. And I certainly won't tell her that Paul is missing.

'Not a word to Vinson about this,' Carrie warned. 'Let him sleep now.'

142

Tom returned from sending off the wire. The next train out of Ouray was at first light.

'I'm taking the early train tomorrow,' he said to Carrie.

'I'll follow the day after,' she said sighing. 'Maria can do with all the support she can get.'

Evalyn could not sleep. She crept out of bed and went to stand on the landing, then pushed open Vinson's door a crack, and looked in on him. She longed to talk about the catastrophe that had set her head reeling and turned her world upside down. But her brother was fast asleep, sucking on his lower lip the way he still did sometimes. She tiptoed downstairs; she knew Annie was in the kitchen.

The maid was ironing linen, but Evalyn saw that her face was shining with tears. She crept to her and wrapped her arms around her waist.

'Oh, Annie . . .'

Annie kissed and rocked her. 'We will know more tomorrow. Your father is going to Leadville. Go back to bed now like a good wee bairn.'

But, although Evalyn obeyed, she could not sleep. She heard her mother come up to bed; she heard Annie go to her room. From downstairs she heard Dandy whining. Maybe dogs knew, she thought. Maybe they just knew when things had gone wrong. Then she heard him scratch at the back door.

He wants to go out, she said to herself, but Father doesn't hear him. He's probably too upset.

She went downstairs, creeping past the parlour to the kitchen. She opened the back door. An eager Dandy shot out across the yard to the stable. Evalyn hesitated, shivering, wondering what had so riveted his attention. Then she threw on Annie's old coat that hung on the hook by the door, slipped into her galoshes and followed. She saw a furtive figure in the shadows of the stable. Her pony, Dewdrop, whinnied, and Nig, her father's horse, shifted his iron-shod feet. She stifled the scream that formed in her throat. From the darkness came her cousin's shaky voice:

'Evalyn . . .?'

Tom found the backdoor open, and the cold night wind blowing through the house. He crossed the yard to the suspiciously open door of the stable. Above the sound of the horses' snorting and shifting, he heard a whisper.

'Who's there?' he demanded sternly. 'Is that you, Evalyn?'

'Yes, Father,' came his daughter's voice. 'Paul is here. I think there is something wrong with him.'

Tom ran to where the bales of straw were stored, found his twelve-year-old nephew sitting rigid. When he spoke to him the boy was monosyllabic, so he picked him up and carried him into the house. Evalyn followed in silence.

'Go to bed, Daughter,' Tom whispered when they were in the warmth of the parlour. 'I'll deal with this.'

Evalyn looked sympathetically at Paul. She tried to catch his eye, but he looked at her as though she didn't exist. She left the room in tears and went upstairs. His father is dead, she told herself. If my father died I would run away too. But these thoughts brought such anguish that she had to banish them.

Tom wrapped the boy in a blanket, put him in an armchair by the fire, heated some soup and brought it to him.

'You must eat, Paul.'

The boy hardly seemed to hear, but he took a few spoonfuls of the hot liquid.

'What happened?' Tom demanded gently. 'I got a telegram from your mother.'

'It was my fault . . .' the ashen-faced child said over and over. 'It was my fault . . . my fault . . .'

Next morning, on the train that took him on the first part of his journey to Leadville, Tom went over the events of the night. He had got the story from Paul, who was now sleeping on the parlour sofa with the help of a sedative administered by Dr Rowan.

Paul had described to him how the family had been at supper in Leadville when a knocking had come to the door – a frightened messenger looking for his father. A fight had broken out over a poker game at the Horseshoe Saloon in Harrison Avenue.

'Father got up, put on his boots. Then he got his holster.'

Tom could imagine the scene – Maria suddenly pale, Ted buckling on his holster with practised speed.

'Mother asked him not to go, but Dad said she was not to worry. As soon as he was gone she went upstairs. I followed her up. She was kneeling praying by their bed, with her old Rosary in her hands . . .' The boy's voice had faltered. 'She said Daddy was too old for it,' he had sobbed brokenly. 'She said that if anything happened to him . . .' The child had heaved and choked on his grief. Tom had put his arms around him, held him in a silent bear hug while he tried in vain to blink back his own tears.

'I thought I could help Dad,' Paul had continued after a moment, 'so I sneaked a Colt out of the box he kept under the stairs and I ran after him . . .'

The boy had stopped, stared at the fire, then convulsively put his head in his hands.

It had taken Tom all his diplomacy to elicit the rest of the story. Ted

Lafferty had been facing down the drunken gunman when Paul had entered the Horseshoe Saloon. Ted had turned, shouted at his son to get out. Paul, recounting it, had begun to weep again in jerky spasms. He'd told how the gunman had used the interruption, the break in Ted's concentration, to shoot him dead. The crazed boy had then tried to shoot the murderer, who had only laughed as he'd kicked the gun from his hand and told him to go home to his mother.

'But you didn't?' Tom had prompted, wiping the boy's tears. 'You didn't go home?'

Paul had shaken his head.

'I couldn't . . . I wanted to die. You were the only person I could think of. I ran to the depot and hid on a goods train that was just leaving. Uncle, you have to help Mother . . .'

'We will both see her tomorrow,' Tom had said gently, wiping the boy's face with his handkerchief.

'I can't go back,' Paul had cried, breaking from his uncle's arms and staring at him accusingly. 'Mother hates me now.'

'If you do not go home, Paul, what will you do? You can't stay here!'

'You could get me a job in the mines.'

'Paul, *grown men* are out of work in the mines these days. You know that!'

'I'll go to Denver! I'll get work in a bar!'

'I see. You'll do anything to help your own pain; you'll leave your mother to cope alone?'

The boy had shaken his head, and wept in small, exhausted sobs.

'I think I know what you will do,' Tom had said, turning the child's face up to him and looking into his eyes. 'You will return home. You will attend your father's funeral and you will look after your mother! You will deal with this disaster like the man you are, and tonight you will learn there is only one way around trouble and pain, Paul, and that is straight through it.'

Carrie's step had then been heard on the stairs. She'd entered the room in her dressing gown, looking alarmed. She'd started when she saw Paul. Her eyes had moved from him to Tom's grim face, then she'd gone straight to the boy, holding out her arms.

'Look after him,' Tom had said. 'I'm going back to the Beaumont to telegraph Maria that he is safe. And I'll ask Doc Rowan to look in.'

He'd put his hand on Paul's head. 'You must never run away,' he'd said in a low voice. 'And someday, you will realise that it was *not* your fault!'

'I just want my daddy,' the child had wailed against Carrie's shoulder, like someone from whom all understanding had fled.

*   *   *

Carrie followed Tom to Leadville, bringing Paul with her. Maria received her son with restrained love, said not a word to him about his actions on the night of Ted's death. She refused Tom and Carrie's offer of hospitality in Ouray. She did not want to stir from Leadville, she said. She wanted to continue living in the house where she had been so happy.

'I'll go on doing the books at the Grand . . . I keep getting this feeling that Ted is near, and that all I have to do is reach out and somehow I'll break through whatever barrier is keeping us apart.'

Carrie picked a moment before departure to talk to her sister-in-law about Paul.

'He must not go through life thinking he is responsible.'

'I have talked to him,' Maria replied in a whisper. 'I have told him his father would not blame him. But Paul has changed. I can feel it. He is no longer a child!' She added in a shaking voice, 'Carrie, my whole world is gone!'

Tears started in Carrie's eyes. She put out her arms. In her embrace she felt Maria tremble, heard her sudden, wrenching sobs.

'You are exhausted,' she whispered when Maria drew back to dab at her eyes with a sodden handkerchief.

'I am just so frightened, Carrie. What will become of my son – to grow up without his father?'

'Paul has Ted's strength,' Carrie told her after a moment. 'Only last night Tom said he was made of the same stuff. And you know as well as I, Maria, that character decides the future!'

Tom wrote to Peggie to tell her what had happened. He received a letter from her shortly after. Carrie watched his face as he read it. More bad news! she thought. This is surely our testing time, the winter of our discontent! Tom passed the letter to her without a word.

Boherbue,
Co. Cork
15 February 1894

Dear Tom,

I'm sorry to send you bad news, but Father is dead. He died last Sunday. It happened in the haggard – some kind of seizure of the heart. Seamus Farrelly found him in the evening. He was still warm, but beyond help. The whole parish came to the wake and we buried him on Wednesday. I never missed you and Maria as much as I did that day.

I comfort myself that we saw him for Christmas. The children, of course, were thoroughly spoiled by him; he had presents for them all.

I did up the house with holly, and cooked a goose, and we laughed and cried over the old days. Seamus Farrelly came around, and I saw the Donnellys and the Murtaghs. I think they have forgiven me for marrying a peeler! Poor Father looked so lonely, standing by the gate when we were leaving until we could see him no more, with his hand raised in farewell.

I know it's a long time since I wrote. I seem to be busy all the time and so is John. With the unrest in the country I never stop worrying about him. I often wonder what you look like now, whether you have any grey hairs! I still remember you as you were the day you left.

Do you ever see poor Michael at all? Maria never mentions him now in her letters.

Lord Kilduncan is dead, but his nephew has inherited and has a new steward. Steven Lurgan is dead also; he died of pneumonia in his bed; he must have had as many lives as a cat.

Since Parnell died there's been a new Land Act which provides more money than any previous act for the buying by tenants of their land. Father would have borrowed, only he said there was no point as the family was flown.

I am afraid that now we are gone the land will forget us, although our people must have been on it since Time was born. For some reason I keep thinking of the daffodils up by An Cailleach in the spring.

I am afraid that I will never see you again.

God bless you and yours.

Your loving sister, Peggie

'She doesn't know about Ted,' Carrie said when she had read the letter.

'By now she does!' Tom looked at the postmark. 'Our letters have crossed in the post.' Next morning he sat at his desk and replied to his sister.

My darling Peggie,

I am so sorry about Father and keep thinking of how I meant to return to see you all. Since I got your letter all sorts of things have haunted me, especially that old lament, 'An Cualainn', that he used to play in the winter evenings. Do you remember? I woke up today with its searing sadness going through my head. By now you will have received my letter with the tragic news about Maria's husband. He was a fine man, a great loss.

Things are not so good here at the moment; the bottom has fallen out of silver. But I have various irons in the fire and will soldier on.

Other than neuralgia and migranes, which are probably due to the altitude, Carrie is fine. The children are grand. Michael has left the army and is living in on his pension in Denver. I try to help keep him going. I'm enclosing $5 and wish it could be a lot more. But my ship will come in and when it does the first thing I'll do is go to Ireland and bring the family.

Of course you will see me again.

My best regards to your husband John and your children.

Your loving brother,

Tom

But Peggie never replied to this letter.

Tom was aware that his health was increasingly precarious. He fought the weakening of his body, dreaded the jaundice that had blighted him intermittently since his days in Deadwood. Once he would have travelled East for rest cures; but he could not afford that luxury now.

I have to keep going, he told himself. Carrie watched him anxiously, looked after him to the point of fussing.

When another letter arrived from Ireland in the fall she handled it gingerly, apprehensive about its contents.

Tom scanned the envelope.

'A strange hand . . .' he murmured.

As soon as he opened the letter faded velvet ribbons fell out on to the table. A shiver climbed his spine.

Boherbue,
Co. Cork
30 September 1894

Dear Mr Walsh,

You will have heard of me through Peggie's letters. I am sorry to tell you that she passed away on the 26th of the month, a victim of the consumption that has this country damned.

She was sick for almost two years. For a while there was hope, as there seemed to be a remission, but it was short-lived. In the last few months she insisted on removing herself to the shed at the end of the garden, where we put in a bed for her, and where the childern came to look at her through the window. That was very hard. They cried for her and she for them, but of course she could not hold them, although it broke her heart.

She often talked of you and America. She said before she died to send you the ribbons she kept in a box down the years. I suppose you will understand. She said all her love for you was in them.

She is buried in Boherbue.

I hope you and your family are well. Give my compliments to your wife.

I am sorry to be the bearer of such sad tidings.

I remain sincerely yours,

John Healy

Carrie glanced in perplexity the old crimson ribbons on the table.

'The saddest words in the English language,' Tom said in a low voice, picking them up and running his finger along the faded pile, 'are "Too Late".' He put them down, looked out the window at tranquil beauty of Ouray, the mountains that kept so many secrets. Into his mind came the memory of a tearful teenage girl and her whispered request on that last morning.

'What is it about time?' he demanded hoarsely. 'It rings no alarms to mark its slippage, lulls you into false complacencies. Poor little Peggie! No wonder she stopped writing. How long did she suffer without a word to the brother who did so little to help her?'

'You did what you could, Tom,' Carrie cried. 'I never knew anyone to remember his people so much. You are not single-handedly responsible for the happiness of everyone.'

'I should have made her come out here, to the dry air of the Rockies.'

'You asked her often enough. You can't run people's lives for them!'

Where, Tom wondered, can I hide from my shame? My little sister, ravaged with consumption, died in a shed. At any point along the years I could have changed her life immeasurably. A fraction of the money that I put into mining . . . But, of course, I was waiting for the big one . . .

Maybe it was a mirage luring the fool on; maybe it will never come. And I have invested my all in it, my assets, my stock of life!

He went to the window. The morning light seemed to speak. It shone on the glorious white Amphitheatre. It said: Too late, too late, too late, reminding him of the lines from Shakespeare learned long ago: 'When sorrows come, they come not single spies, but in battalions.'

He looked at Carrie and she said in tones of alarm: 'Don't stare at me like that, Tom!'

'I'm sorry, Carrie. I think I have ruined everything for you!' He sat down, put his head in his hands.

'You're not well, Tom,' Carrie whispered. 'You're not well at all . . .'

I know I'm not well, Tom told himself with desperation. But that isn't the point. My arrogant optimism has destroyed everything for the people I love.

He thought frantically of Andy Richardson, who was doing sampling

149

for him in the mountains. If only he had some good news . . .

'I'm going to see Andy tomorrow,' he told Carrie.

'Tom, the snow is thick . . .'

'No matter. I'll take the sled.'

'But that road, at this time of year! I beg of you, please don't take the risk!'

'I know the road well, Carrie. I'll be fine.'

He slept badly that night; his dreams were full of Peggie and his father.

In the morning, Evalyn, to whom he had promised a trip on the sled, begged him to take her with him.

'I have no school today, Father. Mrs Hurlburt is ill.'

'Well, I don't know, Evalyn. Perhaps another time.'

'But you promised! You can't break your promise.' Evalyn knew that this would work. Her father was fanatical about keeping his word. 'Please, Father!'

Tom looked at Carrie.

'It gets dark so early and I'll be worried sick!' Carrie said, and she turned to her daughter and added crossly, 'You can't have everything you want, you know, young lady. No one does!' She put her hand to her forehead as she did when a migraine threatened.

Evalyn's eyes filled. Tom put his finger under her chin and lifted her face, wiped away her tears.

'Carrie,' he murmured, turning back to his wife, 'it's a sunny day; we'll be back before nightfall!'

'It gets dark early. I still don't think you should bring Evalyn!'

'But I want to go,' the eight-year-old said petulantly. 'And Father *promised*.'

Carrie sighed and clicked her tongue.

'It would give you a bit of peace, Carrie,' Tom whispered. 'You could rest.'

'Well . . . if you're absolutely sure . . .'

'Goody!' Evalyn cried, clapping her hands and dancing around the room.

'I'd like to come too, Father,' six-year-old Vinson said quietly.

'Only room for one in the sled, young man,' Tom said gently. 'Next time, maybe. I need a man in charge here while I'm away.' He raised his eyebrows at Carrie who turned to Evalyn.

'You see,' she said to her daughter, 'how your brother accepts what we tell him. He doesn't start screaming to get his way.'

Evalyn stuck her tongue out at Vinson, and then felt sorry, for he just looked at her reproachfully and turned away.

Tom put his hand on Vinson's head. He saw Evalyn watching him, with that strange wistful expression she used whenever her brother had his father's attention.

Evalyn was taken in hand by her mother, dressed in her warmest clothes,

150

a woollen dress with red flannel underdrawers, a fur hood, and fur-lined mittens and boots.

'Be careful, Evalyn,' Carrie said. 'Do everything your father tells you. The mountains are more dangerous than they appear, particularly at this time of year. Make your father come back early, before the light is gone.'

When Evalyn was presented to Tom she was trussed up like a prize turkey. Tom, dressed in a warm, fur-lined coat, heavy woollen trousers and fur-lined boots, wrapped the long scarf Carrie had knitted for him around his neck and kissed her. 'I'll be careful, Carrie, don't worry. We'll be back in good time for supper.'

'*Please* don't be late, Tom. You know how I fret.' Tom went out to harness the pony to the sled, and Evalyn ran joyously across the yard, her small feet leaving tracks in the fresh snow.

The road was snowbound, but the pony was sprightly and apparently indifferent to the cold. Evalyn, glad to be out of doors and going on an adventure, was seated by her father in the sled and covered in a smelly bearskin. The sun shone. The snow threw back the light and they had to squint. It filled Evalyn with euphoria, this winter wonderland of snowy peaks, where the only sound was the scrape of the sled and the hoarse, rhythmic breathing of the pony. She began to sing a ditty they had been taught in school, but her father told her quietly to stop. 'We don't want to give an avalanche any excuse, do we, Evalyn?'

'I'm sorry,' she whispered. 'I didn't think. But I love the mountains. You do too, Father, don't you?'

'I do, darling.' He added wistfully, 'I was born in the shadow of the Comeraghs, mountains you will probably never see. And all mountains are the Comeraghs to me. I see them with the sun on them or covered by the clouds every time I look up here at the Rockies! I cannot go back to them, so I turn these here mountains into home!'

Evalyn could think of nothing to say to this strange avowal, uncharacteristic of her father and smacking of dimly perceived vulnerability. She thought of the conversation with one of his mining friends she had recently overheard. It had had to do with his changing the names of some old claims he had bought.

'Is that why you have changed the names of two of the mines, Father, to "Old Ireland" and "Tipperary"?'

Tom laughed in spite of himself. 'You don't miss much, young lady, do you?'

After a while, when the narrow, dangerous road gave on to a wooded spot overlooking Canyon Creek, Tom reined in the pony, looked around at the majestic winterscape and asked his daughter what she saw.

'I see the mountains all around us. I see the clouds. I see the pines. Over there on the ground I see lumps and stuff, covered by the snow . . .'

'That's the dump of an old mine,' Tom said. 'In fact, it's an abandoned zinc and silver mine I bought recently, with a few other old claims hereabouts.'

'But what do you want them for, Father?' Evalyn asked, parroting what she had often heard her mother say. 'Anything good will be gone from them!'

Tom shook his head. 'Not so, Evalyn, not so. You are assuming that people are thorough and patient and wise. They are not! They are impatient and greedy, and they make exactly the same assumption you have just made yourself. You must look with more than your eyes, Evalyn. You must look with your mind. You must look underneath what is visible, *feel* beneath what is visible. Sight is not limited to the eyes. So, tell me, Daughter,' he demanded, 'what do you see when you look with your mind?'

Evalyn shrugged, glanced at her father, squinting against the brilliant reflected sunlight. 'Nothing. Just snow.'

He laughed, flicked the reins and the pony began to walk again.

After a while Evalyn said, 'That was a queer-looking crag back there, wasn't it, Father?'

'What crag was that?'

'It was just behind you when you stopped that time.'

'You often see strange rock formations up here,' her father said. 'Once I saw one that looked just like an Indian, complete with headdress.'

'This one looked a bit like a knuckle,' Evalyn said, half to herself, 'a knuckle pointing at the sky!'

Tom was preoccupied, half listening, looking out for the cabin of his friend and assistant, Andy Richardson.

After travelling for more than two hours Tom stopped at a cabin they came upon suddenly in a sheltered place. Set into the side of the mountain wall and built of logs, now half-covered in snow, it had a welcoming smoking chimney, and a stack of chopped wood under a tarpaulin. Father and daughter alighted from the sled, tethered the pony in the wooden shelter, gave the hungry animal a nosebag and covered him with the bearskin.

Andy, whom Evalyn knew well – bearded, kindly, lonely, with red flannel underwear showing under his woollen shirt – drew them into his untidy home, which had a strange dusty smell, a dirty wooden floor and a heap of gunny sacks in a corner, bursting with rock samples. But a pot-bellied stove radiated heat and comfort, and the door was quickly shut behind them against the bitter wind. Andy threw some wood into the stove, stirred the contents of pot and offered it to them.

'What's that?' Evalyn demanded suspiciously.

'Venison ragout, ma'am,' he replied with robust laughter. 'French recipe. Ain't nothin' here but the best!'

Evalyn, who loved food, tucked in and soon polished off her lunch. When she was finished she went to sit by the window. Andy gave her a couple of books with coloured plates to look at, but the books were for grown-ups and didn't interest her. She spent the time gazing out of the window, making up stories, and ignoring the discussion underway by the two men; it was mining business and very boring.

When it began to snow she amused herself by forcing her eyes to follow the path of individual flakes to the ground, imagining them as fairies, dancing to their own secret music. Soon they were dancing in her brain: the whole world beyond was dim and mysterious with whirling white. As the light began to fade, she remembered her promise to her mother.

'Father,' she said suddenly, 'won't Mother be worried if we are back late?'

The two men stopped their intense discussion. Andy lit an oil lamp; Tom went to the window, took out the silver fob watch he always wore.

'It's later than I thought and coming down heavy,' he said. 'We'd better be getting back.'

Andy followed him to the window. 'It's in for the evening now, Mr Walsh! Best stay the night!'

Tom shook his head. 'I promised my wife I'd be home for supper. She'll be worried. She's too much alone as it is.'

'Well, you know best, but it ain't gettin' any lighter, an' you could lose your way in weather like this!'

Tom shook his head. 'I know this part of the world like the back of my hand! I know it better than you do, Andy!'

Andy looked at him sideways and said quietly, 'No one knows these mountains better than I do, Mr Walsh. I was the first white man to set foot in them!'

'Well, *almost* as well as you do, Andy,' Tom conceded with a smile.

He took his leave. Evalyn said goodbye, thanked her host politely for the meal, and followed her father outside to where the pony was patiently waiting under the bearskin. Tom removed it from the animal's back, wrapped Evalyn in it and sat her in the sled, loaded up some gunny sacks and then, with a wave, they were on their way. The smell of the bearskin didn't bother Evalyn so much now; she was just glad of its warmth. She looked back until the yellow light from the cabin window was lost and then there was only a merciless, grey whiteness.

After a while, its endless swirling and whirling made her think she had gone blind. She didn't think the snowflakes were fairies now; even when she shut her eyes they were there, thick and whirling. And then came the ghostly blue darkness where every sound was muffled; she knew it was still snowing, but there was no light to see by. Her father joked for a while, but soon he too became silent and then all that was left in the world was the rasping breath of the pony and the laboured sounds as it tried to pick its feet out of the drifts. The cold seemed to suck the blood from Evalyn; even the bearskin could no longer keep it out. It was like a greedy force against which she was powerless. She tried to adjust her muffler, but found that her hands would not move. Then she realised that she was like glass: if she moved at all she would break.

'I'm so cold, Father,' she whimpered through chattering teeth, startled by a sudden pricking at the base of her neck and the subliminal certainty that she was facing cataclysm. Tom took so long to reply that she wondered if he had heard.

'Father . . .'

'Courage!' he said then, in a strange cracked voice. 'We'll be home soon!'

In fact, Tom was aghast with horror and fear. He had already lost the strength from his massive arms, which felt as immobile as blocks of ice. In a world where a blizzard raged and he could see nothing, where his little daughter whimpered of the cold and the temperatures had plummeted a long way below zero, he was lost.

He tried to speak again and his voice, coming from a mouth rimed with ice, sounded more like a croak than speech. But Evalyn did not respond. She had already lost consciousness. Even as Tom wondered if their bodies would ever be found, he registered with a sudden start what Evalyn had said to him earlier about the crag she had seen in the shape of a knuckle, with a finger pointing to the sky.

Is it to tell me to pray? Save us, God. I know I'm not much of a one for prayer, but save the child at any rate.

It was a moment later that he saw the glimmer of light through the swirling snow, and wondered if he were hallucinating.

When Evalyn recovered consciousness she was on her father's knee in a strange cabin, where a strange woman bent over her. She registered the warmth of the place with pleasure and then, when she tried to move, the leaden numbness of her hands.

'She coming around,' the woman said, and instantly her father was holding her tighter.

'Evalyn, my darling! How do you feel?'

Evalyn wondered at the fuss. The strange woman brought snow and rubbed it into her hands. To Evalyn it felt like fire and she began to cry, and tried to snatch her hands away.

'What are you doing that for?' she sobbed.

'It's good for your fingers, love,' the woman said. 'Try to bear it.'

Evalyn looked around and saw she was in a neat room with curtains on the window, and with two oil lamps casting warm yellow light. It had a cast-iron stove. A man with whiskers stood before it and looked from her to her father with an expression of interest and compassion.

'I thought we were lost, Father,' Evalyn whispered. 'I thought you had lost the way!'

'Lost?' Tom said. 'Not a bit of it! I told you we'd be all right. Sure Mr and Mrs Grady here were waiting for us. Sure didn't I know where to find them!'

Mrs Grady directed a look at Tom that was part frown, part reluctant smile.

'You should tell the truth,' she said. 'The Lord directed you, make no mistake about it!'

She rubbed pungent bear grease into Evalyn's hands and bandaged them.

Tom said, 'Lucky for us He was on duty today, eh?' But his joke elicited only a grim head shake from his hostess. 'That's no way to talk about the Lord,' she said severely. 'He is always watching us.'

But, privately, Tom was chastened and severely shaken. It had been the nearest thing he had ever come to meeting the Grim Reaper, and he knew it. But just as hope had deserted him he had seen the glimmer of light, had had just enough strength left to turn the pony towards it, had stumbled against the strange cabin door and, when it was opened, had fallen, caked in snow and ice, across its threshold.

'My daughter, my daughter . . .' he had whispered, ashamed, even at this mortal juncture, of his failed strength, of the hand that would hardly point to the sled where his child lay unconscious under the frozen bearskin. Icicles had formed on his moustache and his mouth was stiff.

Mr Grady had carried the child indoors; his wife had wrapped her in blankets while her husband had gone back into the blizzard to shelter the pony. Tom could not walk, but he stumbled into the chair pushed towards him and sat by the fire, and when the returning circulation sent needles of torment pricking their way along his limbs he wanted to howl aloud with pain and with the joy of deliverance.

'What had you out on a night like this with a child?' the woman now asked him, and Tom whispered, suddenly longing to weep with shame and relief, that he had been a fool and should be shot.

'We could have stayed back up with Andy Richardson, but I was sure I'd make it!'

'To where did you think you would make it, mister?' his host demanded laconically, reminding him for a moment of Ted Lafferty. 'The next world? You should go right down on your two knees and thank God.'

Later, as the night deepened, Mrs Grady gave him blankets and a mattress to sleep on and retired with her husband to the adjoining room. But before she left, she banked down the fire and said, 'Now don't let that

155

child put her hands near the fire. We'll have to dress them again in the morning.'

Tom nodded. He knew the received wisdom about frostbite: it was essential that the afflicted flesh be brought back to body temperature very, very slowly, and he sent a heartfelt prayer to heaven for his daughter's hands, and gratitude for her and his own salvation.

He checked that Evalyn slept and lay near her on his mattress, listening to her breathing. But as he drifted into sleep, he heard the howling blizzard and shuddered at what they had escaped. Then his mind reverted to Carrie. She would be frantic. He vowed to make it up to her. The woman is a saint, he thought, to have put up with me all these years!

What happened might be a warning, he thought then. I should take it seriously! I should give up prospecting. Maybe Carrie is right when she says I have a crazy bee in my bonnet that will ruin us all!

But after a few moments he shook his head at this prospect. If I stop, what else can I do? Where else can I go? What can I give my family? And it's in the blood now. I'm a lumbering old ship; I can't change course. I was going to do great things for Father and Peggie and I failed them. But I won't fail Carrie and the children. It may end in the death of me, but I have to go on. If I can't, it will mean that I have lived in vain. And if I have, he added bitterly, so be it. At least I will have done my best.

But despite Tom's renewed determination, things went from bad to worse. Although both he and Evalyn had recovered from their near disaster, and although Carrie's distress at their failure to return home on the night of the blizzard had turned to joy and then to anger, Tom's finances were hitting a new low. Certain cheques he had drawn on his account would soon fall due for payment, and it was not clear how they were to be honoured. He thought of the smelter at Silverton, still operating despite the depression. There must be some good fluxing ore somewhere in the Imogene!

So many of his old friends had already been reduced to penury. Whenever he thought of Horace Tabor he felt ill. That the great Silver King, who had dressed his wife, Baby Doe, in diamonds and given her carriages and mansions, could have been made bankrupt! So many men he had known who had lived like princes were now facing a straitened future. Leadville, according to Maria's letters, was fast becoming a ghost town.

Tom had already covertly sold whatever personal effects might bring in some cash – his diamond shirt stud, the chased gold watch, the fine gold cufflinks. He wondered should he give in and sell his claims in the Imogene Basin. But he would get little for them.

His partner in the smelting business, David Wegg, had opted out and returned to the East. Tom eventually wrote him in despair.

156

I am utterly unable to go on with the leases I have on hand. I will give up soon. I have no money for myself or my family beyond our support. I feel that I recovered victory from defeat at Silverton, made what was a lost investment into something, but unfortunately the same cannot be said of Kokomo, which was ruined by the drop in silver. I don't know how we struggled along so well, but now I am disheartened and sad, tired of making rosy promises and giving blue results. I wish you were here to advise me for I am in need of calm advice now if I ever was. To add to my troubles my wife had to go to Denver three weeks ago because here she suffers continual headaches.

I am very poor. I have nothing to look forward to. My position is desperate and I must do something to protect my name.

As he signed the letter Tom thought bitterly of the money he had made in the past and should have had the sense to hold fast, instead of bringing his family to the edge of destitution by his investments in what were no more than possibilities. I have failed them, he berated himself. I was wrong and I failed them all! What can I do now?

Hold on, a small voice inside him said. *Hold on*.

Chapter Eleven

By 1896 Tom had mortgaged or sold the remains of his Denver real estate. But he held on to his claims around Ouray and the management of the smelter in Silverton, and he continued prospecting. At night he would stay up late, poring over maps and books, making notes. Carrie, often alarmed at his pallor, his fatigue, and the cough he brought back with him from the mountains, remonstrated.

'For God's sake, Tom, it's one thing to gamble your entire fortune; it's another to gamble your health. You have two young children, remember!'

'I know, Carrie, I know . . . Why do you think I'm doing this? I have studied those rock formations again. You see, Carrie, nature spilled out its treasures in the great movements that formed the mountains . . .'

'Every nook in those mountains has by now been gone over with a fine-tooth comb,' she cried.

Tom drew a configuration on a piece of paper. 'Look – here are the Rockies. I grant you the main trend of it has been scratched over, and parts of it have been well prospected, but there are innumerable spurs that have not been checked. It's only a matter of time Carrie before—'

'It's a matter of time, all right!' Carrie replied, regarding him through welling tears. 'The Grim Reaper will have you the way you're going!'

Tom took her in his arms. 'What's this? Is my Carrie giving way to doubts? We'll come through this. Remember, my darling, Fear is a poor counsellor.'

But however much Tom pooh-poohed her anxiety he needed no reminding how the hand of Fate hovered over the affairs of men.

In June Tom said he was going up into the Imogene Basin, in another attempt to locate fluxing ores. Vinson was in Denver with his grandmother. Evalyn was in the parlour, reading one of her mother's magazines. On the coffee table lay those to which her mother subscribed – *McCalls Magazine*, the *Ladies Home Journal* and *Harpers Bazaar*. It was the latter magazine that held the nine-year-old's attention. She was reading an article about an actress, gazing long and hard at the photograph of a pretty woman in an evening gown, who was half covered with what Evalyn assumed were real jewels. She heard the sudden busy humming and looked around, saw that a wasp had got through the open window. It flew straight towards her and alighted on the settee.

She screeched, jumped up, and ran to the kitchen where her parents were talking together in low voices.

'I just met a wapse face to face,' she informed them breathlessly.

Tom looked at Carrie and chuckled. 'Wasn't she lucky she didn't meet him end to end!' he said. 'But you should *always* look *wapses* in the eye,' he told his daughter with as much gravity as he could muster. 'It is the proper mode of conducting your interviews with them!'

Carrie laughed, a tinkle of surprised mirth that filled her face with life, and Evalyn forgot the wasp when she realised that her father was making preparations to go prospecting. His pack was sitting beside him on a chair, and Annie was making sandwiches. 'Can I go with you, Father?' she asked in a wheedling voice.

Tom glanced at Carrie, who shook her head.

'You don't learn, do you, young lady?'

'But that was in the *winter*, Mother. It's different now.'

Secretly Evalyn looked back on that near-fatal episode in her life, now that it was safely in the past, with a frightened delight. She was proud that it was *she* who had been with her father when he found himself at the edge of the abyss, at a moment when both their lives had hung by a thread. She suspected now that he *had* been lost, that he didn't know the people who had saved them, that he had chanced on them by accident.

She wondered darkly if, when he had realised the worst, he had been glad it was she who had been in the sled and not Vinson; that she was the one who would die.

I wouldn't blame you, Father, she thought sadly. Mother is right: Vinson is much nicer than I am.

'Well, winter or not,' Carrie was saying, 'there's that awful Canyon Creek Road. Only last month Peter Ashenfelter had a pair of his horses killed there by a fall of ice.'

'I know,' Tom said. 'But the ice is gone now.'

'Please let me go, Mother.'

Carrie looked at Tom. He murmured so that only she could hear, 'It would be good for her, I think . . . help her to forget the last time. I don't want her to grow up afraid of anything . . .'

Carrie turned to her daughter. 'If I say you can go, will you do everything your father tells you?'

Evalyn's eyes brightened. 'Of course I will, Mother.'

'Get your coat. It's chilly in the hills.'

★ ★ ★

Annie prepared a packed lunch for two. Carrie handed it to her husband with the injunction, 'Remember, you're not as young as you were! So don't overdo it, Tom, please.'

'I'm forty-six,' Tom said, looking at her a little lugubriously, 'Is that so old?'

'You're not a spring chicken; your colour is terrible. You're not well.'

Tom knew this better than anyone. What Carrie did not know was that he had recently been to see Dr Rowan, who had been uncompromising in his advice.

'You've got to stop, Tom. For years you've been killing yourself, up there where the air's too darn thin for mortals, subjecting yourself to every stress in the book. Right now you have jaundice; you need treatment, a proper rest cure!'

Tom now looked at Carrie and sighed inwardly at the anxiety in his wife's face.

'I'm well enough, Carrie. And I promise you faithfully there'll be no delays this time. We *will* be back for supper!'

It was a lovely summer day. Above the town glowed the Amphitheatre, its striations of burgundy rock vivid in the sunlight. Like the layers of a rich cake, Evalyn thought, and then she looked at the majesty of Mount Abrams and decided it looked like a breast, with a lop-sided nipple. She had seen Annie's breasts one morning when the maid was dressing. Recently she had started wondering what it must be like to have them – sticking out there in front of you like upside-down pudding bowls. It would happen to her too, one day. Already her nipples were expanding; she wondered what kind of a bosom she would have, small apples, or generous melons. She decided that in between would do her fine. She was going to be an actress. She wanted to be beautiful.

Mounted on Dewdrop, her pony, she followed obediently behind her father, who was riding Nig, and soon was on the narrow Canyon Creek Road above the town. Below them Ouray nestled among its mountain battlements. To their right was the sheer canyon wall; to their left was a ravine that plunged down hundreds of feet to Canyon Creek. Across the canyon the firs growing on top of the escarpments and out of crevices looked down on them like a sentinel army sizing up intruders.

There was a mountain breeze. Evalyn heard the clopping of the hoofs, and the song of the river in the ravine. When the horses dislodged small stones from the path, some of them skittered to the edge and fell into the canyon. She waited for the small, hard sound as they landed somewhere far below.

Her father turned to her in his saddle.

'Be especially careful on the next stretch. Keep Dewdrop walking slowly.'

'Yes, Father.'

She was happy to be with him, to have his confidence, to know that he trusted her.

'It looks different from the last time I was here with you, Father,' she said to break the silence when they had passed the most dangerous part of their route. 'Everything was covered in snow then . . .'

'I made a bad error of judgement that day, Evalyn,' he said in a serious tone after a moment. 'I am very sorry that I put you in such danger. But I will not repeat it,' he added grimly, 'and in time I hope you will forget it!'

'It doesn't bother me, Father,' Evalyn said, surprised and touched at being treated like a grown-up. 'It was an adventure. What are you looking for today?'

'Copper, iron . . .'

'Not gold?'

Tom smiled. 'I am always looking for gold! Every stone and outcrop, Evalyn. They say a man earns his gold mine if he ever gets one!'

'I wish silver was still valuable – like when we were rich.'

He shook his head. 'There's no money in it now. These mountains are full of silver mines that are now abandoned – like the Gertrude and the Una. I have acquired them and many undeveloped claims hereabouts. All the millions once spent in this region on erecting stamp mills and driving tunnels and sinking shafts have been wasted. But it is imperative I find some way to make my investment pay.'

'Are we poor, Father?'

Tom hesitated. 'At the moment, Evalyn, I'm afraid there is no other word for it!'

'Were you poor before, Father?'

'I was very poor once. But I was presumptuous enough to think I had left it behind me!'

They dismounted at a grassy spot, where the perilous trail opened on to a green, tree-lined sward, tied Nig and Dewdrop loosely to some trees, and sat on riverside boulders to eat their sandwiches. The air was cool and, up above them, patches of snow still clung to shaded parts of the mountains.

'When I grow up,' Evalyn announced suddenly, between mouthfuls, 'I will be very rich!'

Tom glanced at his small, plump daughter and laughed. 'Will you indeed?'

'I'm going to be a famous actress.'

Her father laughed heartily, but there was an edge to his mirth.

'Would you like to see me on the stage, Father?'

'No, Evalyn. Acting is a career even more uncertain than prospecting! I do not advise it; in fact I would be against it under all circumstances.'

Evalyn looked at her father in dismay. 'Even if it made me rich, Father,

161

so that I could wear all the jewels I liked, and was able to help you and Mother?'

'Yes. Even if it made you rich!'

A blue jay landed a few feet away and then cheekily hopped to devour a piece of sandwich that Evalyn had left on her lap.

'Shoo . . .'

'It's hungry,' Tom said. 'It's not much fun being a camp bird when the camps are gone!' He offered it a few morsels from his own lunch and watched it gobble them.

Evalyn, head thrown back, looking up at the top of the mountain basin, suddenly said, 'Look, Father, there is a rock shaped like a knuckle. I remember that from the last time I was here with you. And there,' she pointed at the abandoned workings by an old tunnel, 'is the abandoned mine we saw last time. We can actually see it now with the snow gone.'

'What a memory! You're quite right. That old mine is the Gertrude. I had Andy look at it, but he found nothing there except some zinc and silver.'

'I thought you liked to sample everything yourself?'

'Good comment, except that it's not possible to do all of it myself. But I *will* take some samples before we go, which is why we are lunching here, young lady.'

For Evalyn the rest of that day was bliss. She loved the sound of her father's pick at work, the clunking of the broken bits of rocks, their hard clatter as they were thrown into the saddlebags. When samples had been taken at the Gertrude they moved on to the old drift tunnel of the Una, and while her father delved and the sound of his pick echoed Evalyn played at being a famous actress. She stormed on to her fanciful stage, mouthed her home-made lines to the chipmunks and to Dewdrop, who cropped the grass and looked at her wonderingly from his sad, black eyes. In this private scenario she was beautiful, visible, admired, and clothed in gems.

A few days later Tom met Dr Rowan in the street. He had been pondering the assay results of his recent foray into the mountains. In the main the results were disappointing – no copper worth mentioning, although there was a little gold present in the few samples he had cursorily taken at the Gertrude on the day he took Evalyn with him. I must have another look there, he thought.

'You're looking mighty feverish to me,' the bewhiskered doctor informed him bluntly. 'Either you go for a complete rest and do as I say, or I won't be responsible. You must be the most stubborn critter I ever did come across! I knew a mule once who was a bit like you. No one could budge him. But he got caught in a rockfall and that was the end of him!'

Tom grinned. 'I take your point, Dr Rowan. I'll get myself a rest cure as soon as I can. Right now I'm kind of busy.'

'Graveyards are full of people who were always kind of busy! Get yourself down to Excelsior Springs, and stay there until you have recovered. And don't pussyfoot around if you want to be here this time next year. You'll do your family no favours if you end up in Cedar Hill Cemetery.'

Tom, unprepared for so much bluntness, started. 'You've a mighty persuasive way about you, Doc,' he said drily.

'I know I've put it to you straight, Tom,' the doctor added, 'but that's what doctors are for!'

But August was upon him before Tom was able to get away. Before he went he sent for Andy Richardson.

'Andy, while I'm away I want you to continue sampling the old tunnels, and don't forget the Gertrude . . . Give the samples to Munns. Charlie will wire me the results. We have a code . . .'

Evalyn overheard, but was uninterested. She was arranging her dolls into an appreciative audience.

Tom returned to Ouray after only a fortnight in Excelsior Springs.

Far from being recovered his pallor had now mutated into a yellow patina that affected even his eyes. He seemed strangely agitated, said he had to go back up the mountains. Carrie almost wept.

'I can't take any more, Tom. Why are you doing this? You're a very sick man.'

'Ah, I'll be over it in a few days, Carrie,' he said brusquely. 'I had a wire from Munns. I just need to check back on the Gertrude.'

Carrie was taken aback. 'But, Tom, it's September; we've just had our first snow. Conditions will be awful. Andy has already sampled that old mine and he found nothing worth talking about! And other people owned it before you and they must have checked it out!'

In fact the new assay results had shown zinc, silver and a little copper, but there had been an incidence of gold in the samples considerably higher than those Tom had taken himself in June; they ran at $30 per ton. This might be a freak, Tom knew, but he was not going to assume anything in this game ever again. He had begun to suspect that something lay deep under the surface at the Gertrude that was of considerable interest, but he wasn't going to speak of it to anyone just yet.

'I know, Carrie,' he said sternly. 'I just want to check it again for myself! I will return straight away. I'm not going any further than the Gertrude.'

'Tom,' Carrie replied after a moment, and her eyes filled, 'I didn't want to burden you with bad news right away. But I need to go to Denver. Mother is not well.'

'What is wrong?'

'They think it could be pneumonia.'

Tom tried to keep the concern from his eyes. But Carrie knew as well as he did that pneumonia for an old person was very bad news.

'I'm very sorry, darling. Give her my love. Stay for as long as she needs you. I'll see to the children.'

'Promise me you'll stay in bed!'

Tom sighed. 'I promise.'

As he gave his wife money for the journey he wondered if they were being targeted by some malign influence.

With Carrie gone the house assumed an almost soulless character. Tom spent the day of her departure in bed, as he had promised. He knew that he needed this rest. He consulted his map of the Imogene Basin and wished his fever at the bottom of Box Canyon.

Vinson wept that night. He hated being separated from his mother. Tom heard Annie's footsteps as she went to him in the night; heard her voice: 'She'll be home soon, my bonnie bairn. No need to get yourself into such a dither.'

Tom got up, went to Vinson's room and sent Annie back to bed. He told his son a story about a leprechaun who had his crock of gold stolen by the king of the fairies. Vinson went to sleep, his mouth opening slightly, his new front teeth still a bit askew. Tom listened to his breathing, remembered the first time he had seen him, the small fist that had gripped his finger. He touched his son's silken head and felt the love tighten around his heart. Somehow or other he *had* to build a future for this child of his, for his family, worthy of them. Somehow he had to escape the penury that, unless something extraordinary turned up, was now staring him in the face.

The following evening, when Annie brought him his supper, he said abruptly: 'I'm going into the mountains in the morning, Annie. I'll be gone for the day.'

Annie looked aghast. 'But Mrs Walsh said—'

Tom put up a hand to forestall her.

'Never mind what Mrs Walsh said. Will you be all right on your own with the children, just for the day?'

'Of course. But the snow came down thick last night.' She paused, adding in a rush, 'Those heights is doin' you no good, Mr Walsh! If you ask me it's not right for a sick man to be going up there.'

When he didn't reply, but regarded her sternly in a way she found daunting, she retreated and added, 'I'll pack a lunch for you . . .'

Tom nodded, but in fact he had hardly been listening. Since Carrie's departure he had been intensely preoccupied.

Evalyn woke when she heard the creak of the stairs, got out of bed and drew back the curtain. In the blue-grey light she saw her father, mounted on Nig, go out the gate and down Fifth Avenue, leaving hoofprints in the fresh snow. She went back to bed and snuggled under the blankets. There was still some time before she had to get up for school.

Her mind was racing. Why had Father left so early? Where was he going? To the mountains . . . in the snow?

She thought of the time when she had accompanied him in the sled and her heart missed a beat.

'Come home early, Father,' Evalyn whispered. She thought of her father's sick face, and the treacherous, slippery path before him. 'Dearest Father, just come home.'

Chapter Twelve

In later years Tom would remember everything – the snow that choked the old tunnel, the bitter cold, the dump of the abandoned mine, the lonely majesty of his surroundings high above Ouray where the mountains enclosed him and snow-laden firs were rooted into the mountain wall. He would remember the way his lungs hurt and the alerted racing of his heart. He was determined to take samples today that would represent something from deeper within the mountain. The old dump, detritus from former workings, was one obvious target. He also wanted to get as far as he could into the old tunnel and see what was inside.

The snow flurried as he brushed it from the mound. He used his pick carefully. The ice cracked as he released a sample from the dump. He was a cautious man, with half a lifetime's prospecting experience already behind him, but now he stared fixedly at the rock sample in his hand, saw its glistening golden pyrite – the so-called 'fool's gold' that he knew at a glance – saw the sparkle of mica, saw dowdy grey quartz with black spots.

This was what interested him. Caution insisted it was just a freak. He rubbed it, took his hand from his thick leather glove, wet his finger and rubbed again. The saliva froze on the stone, but it was clear that the black spots were indeed imbedded in the rock. Black threads, in fact, were spread through it, like some kind of petrified fungus. He knew from the study he had made over the years that gold presented itself in many forms. And gold dissolved in tellurium was black.

The mouth of the old tunnel was clogged with snow and ice. He took his shovel, cut into the snow. For hours he laboured, sweating and panting, until at last he had cleared an entrance large enough to admit him. Inside, he lit a candle. He heard the water dripping far back in the cavern and held up his candle to study the rock wall. He saw the modest zinc vein and then, on the opposite wall of the tunnel, the grey, unremarkable-looking quartz. He held the candle close and saw the same black threads imbedded in the rock.

He worked his pick again, the small exertion making him gasp. His lungs gulped the cold air filtered by the woollen muffler that Carrie had knitted for him and that covered his mouth and nose. Small icicles had formed on it. He brushed them off and loosened the scarf. It was warmer in the tunnel and the air did not burn his lungs.

He filled a gunny sack with pieces of rock and carried it outside. His boots crunched the snow. Nig, as though to remind him that nightfall was not far off, flared red nostrils and rattled the bit.

Tom restored his damp muffler over his mouth, re-examined the dump outside the tunnel and plied his pick again. The exertion was almost beyond him now; the sound of his heart reverberated in his ears. The thud of the shovel echoed from the mountain walls around him. He knew he could precipitate an avalanche, and that night was falling, but he would not leave until he had filled his saddlebags. By now he was absolutely certain that the former owners of this mine had simply thrown on to the dump material loaded with gold. They had not recognised it, and, for some reason, whatever assaying they had commissioned had not revealed it.

His instinct told him that what he had found was remarkable; every sample told the same story. It occurred to him that he was hallucinating; he was running a fever in freezing temperature at more than ten thousand feet, and it was a possibility that his eyes were playing tricks. The doctor had warned him, after all. What if he were more seriously ill than he knew? But Munns assay office would not hallucinate and would soon tell him the truth; he would ask them to test the samples as priority.

The rocks clinked as he packed them, buckled his saddlebags with stout leather straps, and mounted Nig. He let the horse find his way down the steep path, only half aware of the long shadows from the sentinel firs, and the call of a coyote to the approaching night. What if his suspicions about the Gertrude turned out to be true? He thought of Carrie, now in Denver with her ailing mother, thought of Evalyn and Vinson, waiting for him with Annie, in the warm clapboard house at the corner of Ouray's Fifth Avenue.

'Easy boy,' he muttered to Nig, as the horse slipped on ice, dislodging a stone that skittered over the edge of the path to fall with a sound that muffled itself in the ravine below. Tom glanced back. Behind him Mount Abrams thrust skywards; he saw the freezing mist searching down the mountainside as the light faded, bringing plunging temperatures and death.

A long way from Clonmel, he thought suddenly. And this thought brought with it the memory of the Comeraghs, the spring rain and his mother's grave. For a moment, because he was tired and hungry and overwrought by the prospects suddenly before him, the tears he had not shed for years filled his eyes and froze on his cheeks.

Tom emerged from his reverie when he reached the turn just above Ouray. Below him the town nestled – snow on the roofs, on the roads, clinging to the striations of the Amphitheatre, crowning Mount Hayden.

His thoughts dwelled on every aspect of what he had found in the Gertrude drift tunnel and dump. The cold was biting through his gloves, freezing his fingers to the bone. He thought longingly of the warm parlour waiting for him at home.

It was past nightfall when Dandy began barking. Evalyn, who had thought of her father all day, had done poorly at school, being reprimanded more than once for inattention. When she got home she had been sent early to bed by Annie. But she could not sleep, her imagination running riot. In her mind's eye, she saw her father picking his way through another blizzard, saw him droop in the saddle, felt the icy death searching through his clothes. Her tears soaked the pillow. She heard the avalanche that suddenly tore down the mountainside, enveloping him and Nig and taking them away for ever. They would only be found in six months' time when there was a thaw.

She was almost beside herself with imagined horrors when Dandy began barking and then she heard the slow clipclop entering the yard.

She jumped out of bed and raced to the window, clapping her hand over her mouth to stifle her relief. It was her father, riding a weary and heavily burdened Nig. She saw him glance at the house, at the upstairs windows, but she was peeking and he did not see her. From behind her curtain she saw him take Nig into his stable and she waited until, a little later, he came towards the house carrying two heavy saddlebags. He always brought his samples into the house, and generally kept them overnight under his bed.

She opened her door, heard his voice downstairs – warming the whole house it seemed to her – a tired, but normal voice, speaking to Annie, who was clanking dishes and evidently putting his dinner in front of him. But she did not sleep. After a while came his footsteps on the landing; she saw the approaching lamplight underneath her door. She heard him open Vinson's door. When he looked in on her she pretended to be asleep, so as to make no demands on him. He was home and that was all that mattered. But through her lashes she could see the weary tenderness in his face. The lamplight retreated. He left her door slightly ajar, and evidently his own also, for she could hear the creak of the big brass bed and his sigh and then his cough. Only then did she allow herself to sleep.

In the morning when she came downstairs he had already gone into town. She had expected this; he always went first thing to bring the samples for assay.

Tom returned from Munns, greeted his children, who were dressed and ready for school, answered their questions, joked at their fears for his safety the day before – 'It was a grand ride' – and said he was going back to bed.

When they returned from school he was still in bed, sleeping, Annie said, like the dead.

But the following morning he was up and dressed when the children came down for breakfast, and ready, he told them, to go to Munns.

Tom knew he was early, and because he did not want his impatience to be evident at the assay office he moderated his pace. In any case the sidewalks were treacherous, a mix of frozen snow and slush. The air was very cold, although the warm smells of horse manure rose now and then from fresh deposits on the street.

He looked around him at the town he had come to love, at the buildings set out so neatly, the shops and houses, so normal and civilised it was difficult to remember that this place was high in the Rocky Mountains, and had once been inhabited only by nomadic tribes of Ute Indians. He made his way to the Uncompahgre River and the Munns Bros. Sampling works.

The peculiar assay smell greeted Tom as he came into the Munns office – burned rock, molten metals, dust. This room was lined with shelves full of labelled canvas bags of ore samples, and had a built-in desk worktable. There was no one in the office so he walked through into the laboratory. Here was the assay furnace, its door open. Although the window sashes were up and the hood above the furnace drew out hot air, this room was stifling. The shelves were full of the crucibles, scorifiers, cupels and roasting dishes used in the assay process. On a table to the side were the delicate scales that decided finally whether the ratio of ore to rock made it worthwhile developing a claim. From the room beyond came the noise of the apprentice crushing samples on the 'bucking board'.

Charles Munn, his face red from the heat, was taking a crucible from the furnace muffle.

' 'Day to you, Charlie . . .'

Charlie nodded and carefully poured the contents of the crucible into 'button' moulds on the bench.

'Ah, Tom, you're early,' he said when he was finished what he was doing. 'But I have your results. We gave them priority, like you said.'

'And . . .?' Tom said as casually as he could.

In the ensuing few seconds every sound in the town seemed magnified: the muted sound of hoofs outside on the snowy street, the rattle of a cart, the crunch of footsteps on the icy sidewalk, the laughter of two women who went by the window. Tom heard the beating of his own heart, and tried to read the assayer's poker face. Could I have been wrong? he wondered. Am I getting old and fanciful?

Charlie, looking grave, glanced towards the room where the apprentice was grinding rock to powder.

'Come into the office . . .'

Tom followed him and Charlie shut the door.

169

'Please sit down.'

Tom obeyed. He felt like a patient awaiting a dreaded prognosis. Charlie was too placid, too deadpan to be harbouring outstanding news. Tom was suddenly tired as he had never been, tired in body and soul.

When Charlie Munn was seated behind his desk he said evenly, 'Well, Tom, not only did I assay the samples immediately like you asked, but I reran them, just in case there was a mistake.'

He drew a sheet of paper and a small box from a drawer. Suddenly he beamed, lighting up his whole face with conspiratorial glee.

'I'm not surprised you were in such a hurry! Here are the results, Tom. Make of them what you will; send samples to Leadville and Denver too if you like, but I'll stake my reputation on their accuracy.'

Tom took up the assay statement. It said:

> Munn Bros.
> Assay Office and Sampling Works
> Ouray, Colorado
> 12 September 1896
>
> The ore marked Walsh – 4 sacks – assayed for Mr Thomas F. Walsh yields Gold $3,000 coin value per ton of 2000 lb.
> Charles Munn

Tom stared at the figures. They seemed to dance before his eyes.

'And you say you reran the assay?' he asked in a very grave voice.

'I ran them three times to be honest, Tom. I couldn't believe them!'

Tom suddenly found that his hands were trembling, and that a huge well of emotion was rising from some inaccessible place within and threatening to overwhelm him. He concentrated on the noughts behind the figure three, counting them over and over as though he were five years old again and learning arithmetic under the strict eye of his old Master in Tipperary.

'It's all correct,' Charlie murmured, watching Tom's face, 'although I must admit I've never seen anything like it.'

'But, Charlie, most of it was stuff I took from a dump!'

Charlie opened the small cardboard box and emptied on to the table a number of assay 'buttons' – the end result of the assay process. The small round nuggets gleamed in the light from the dusty window.

'Well, someone didn't know gold when they had it,' Charlie said, indicating them, 'did they?'

Tom surveyed them, raised his head and looked at his assayer.

'But *why* didn't they know it, Charlie? They must have had their samples assayed like anyone else!'

'They were looking for silver, and they found it. In the first test button the gold would have been hidden in the silver. They evidently looked no further at that time. And God knows how they were dissuaded – snowslides, illness, lack of funds . . .? As per your instructions, *I* concentrated only on the gold. There's silver there too, of course, but as you were in such a hurry I didn't—'

'Charlie, you know I'm not interested in the silver,' Tom said, sweeping up the fat globules of pure gold and putting them in his pocket.

'With gold values of $3,000 per ton, I reckon congratulations are in order, Tom,' Charlie added with a grin. 'If there is a good lode it looks like you've really struck it!' He shook his head and compressed his smiling lips, then rose and came around to clap his client on the back. 'Looks like you've struck it mighty!'

Tom walked home in a daze. He found he was weak, sweating and feverish so that he had to go back to bed. But his mind was hectically going over the titles he owned in the Imogene Basin and the other properties that impinged on the claim – 'tax titles' that had been abandoned and might be purchased from the County Commissioners for relatively little. He realised he already owned most of the area around the Gertrude; these were the claims he had bought against all advice. The realisation began to dawn on him slowly of exactly what the morning's news portended. It was strange to lie in his bed and look at the crack in the ceiling and realise that his instinct had not betrayed him.

'Providing, of course,' he said aloud, 'that there is a decent lode up there and not just some kind of freak.'

He looked through the window at the morning sky above Mount Hayden. Now, God, he said silently, I hope you're not suffering from a warped sense of humour. I am a sick man. My wife is in Denver; there is no one here I dare share this with. If the fever gets worse and I die before she returns my family may be cheated of a great fortune.

He thought of making a map, and leaving it in an envelope for Carrie. But if he died, God alone knew who might open that envelope.

In the evening Evalyn brought him some soup on a tray.

'How are you feeling, Father?'

'I'm just a bit tired.' He put the soup on his nightstand, dislodging some pieces of rock, which he threw on to the bed.

'Shut the door, Evalyn. I want to talk to you.'

Evalyn obeyed. She sat on the side of his bed.

'Do you remember the last day we went on the Canyon Creek Road? In June?'

Evalyn nodded. It was a day she had thoroughly enjoyed. She remembered the audience of chipmunks she had held spellbound.

'Do you remember the place we stopped to eat our lunch?'

'Sure.'

'Do you remember the old workings?'

'I do, Father. You said it was the drift tunnel of an old mine, one that you had already bought, called the Gertrude. You took some samples.'

'Would you know it again?'

'Of course.'

'Good girl. Now, Evalyn, what I am going to tell you is a big secret and you must not breathe a word of it to anyone except your mother . . . if I am not here when she comes back!'

'Are you going away again, Father?'

He laughed. 'No, not for the moment. At least I hope not . . . Are you able to keep a secret?'

'Of course I am,' Evalyn said indignantly. 'I'm *ten*.'

Tom sighed. He looked at her consideringly for a moment.

'I'm relying on you, Evalyn. It's a very important secret and you must promise to say nothing about it to anyone, not to Vinson, not to Annie, not to anyone . . . except Mother, if I'm not here when she gets home!'

Evalyn's face became solemn. She put her hand on her heart. 'I promise.'

'Two days ago I took further samples from that tunnel. And these samples had something special. The assayers examined them; I saw Mr Munn this morning . . .' He stared at his daughter's expectant face, picked up a piece of rock from the bed, wet it with his finger and held it out to her. 'What do you see?'

'I see little shiny bits.'

'That's only the mica in the quartz. Look closely. Do you see the little black threads in the rock?'

'Yes.'

'Daughter,' Tom said, his voice low and husky, 'that is gold!'

Evalyn felt a strange shiver climb her spine. She wanted to whoop, but she clapped her hand to her mouth.

'If the ore in the mine continues as rich as the samples,' her father continued in the same subdued whisper, 'a very strange thing has happened. I was offered it once, and turned it down, but I knew it would give me one more chance.'

'What is it . . .?'

'The very strange thing that has happened, Daughter, is that we've struck it rich!'

Carrie came home. Her mother had recovered, but she herself was exausted and cold from the long journey.

Tom comforted her. He chafed her hands, sat her by the fire, saw to it that she had hot tea and the crumpets that she loved and that Annie made to perfection.

'I'm tired of these mountains,' she said. 'I never get headaches in Denver. Could we go and live there, Tom? Please. Mother has plenty of room and says she is leaving me her house. I don't want to live at these altitudes any more; I'm getting to be a tired sort of person!'

'You won't be so tired when you hear what I have to tell you, my dearest, patient, love.'

Tom had tried to keep the excitement from his voice, but Carrie heard it and shrank back apprehensively.

'What have you got to tell me, Tom?'

'Carrie, prepare yourself for a shock – but a pleasant shock, I hope. I took as representative a sample as I could from the Gertrude while you were away – no, don't scold; I know I should have stayed in bed. Charlie Munn gave me the assay results this morning!'

Carrie sat up a little straighter. 'And what were they?'

'Mighty, Carrie – to quote his own words, three thousand dollars per ton . . .'

Carrie laid her head back on the armchair and tears began to flow silently down her face. 'You know perfectly well that is not possible,' she whispered. 'Just what has been going on?'

'It could be just a small, lucky streak,' she said a few minutes later, when Tom had convinced her there was no mistake. 'The kind of strike you're thinking of happens only once or twice in a century! It could be just one small pocket.'

'I know,' Tom said. 'Bear with me, Carrie. I have to see this through. But I promise you this – if this lode lets me down I will quit prospecting and go to live in Denver or anywhere else you like. I'm getting the mining engineer David Reed to do a survey.'

David Reed's report estimated the lode as six miles long. Even the discarded detritus Evalyn had seen on her trip with her father contained a tidy fortune. No one, neither the original owners who had mined silver and zinc, nor the others who had passed this way and looked at the rock, had recognised gold in its tellurium mantle. But Tom Walsh had studied his subject well and had seen in the black veins running through the quartz the elusive stuff of his dreams.

By New Year Tom owned it all; adjoining abandoned claims, 'tax titles', had been purchased from the County Commissioners for sums in the region of $10,000. It was now his land; he had no partner. He owned nine hundred acres of rich ore-bearing mountain. The only people he had to placate for the moment were his bankers and they were as excited as he was: the initial results showed almost free milling gold.

In spring, the work of extracting the gold commenced. The telegraph office in the Beaumont Hotel buzzed with Tom Walsh's orders for plant.

Strange pieces of machinery, pumps and jacks, crates of dynamite, great timbers from the Ouray sawmill, were dragged by teams of Peter Ashenfelter's mules up the steep path to the mine. The town, the county, the state buzzed with the news that a large gold mine had been found near Ouray.

'Just pray that it lasts, Tom!' he was told by some enthusiasts. 'Gold just doesn't come out of the ground like that! This has to be a limited little freak of nature!'

But Tom had heard this before, years ago in Deadwood.

'Like the pot of gold at the end of the rainbow?' he joked, remembering the old superstition from his childhood, and recalling all the rainbow ends he had chased as a child, and all the rainbow ends he had pursued as an adult, only to find that they kept receding.

He remained cautious, maintained everything as usual, forbade Evalyn and Vinson to mention anything to do with the mine.

'If you open your mouth to brag about something the luck leaves it,' he said bluntly.

Carrie looked at him, surprised.

'You can take the man out of Old Ireland,' she said to him later with one of her old coy smiles, 'but I'm beginning to think you can't take Old Ireland out of the man!'

Tom laughed. 'That's very true, Carrie.'

'What are you going to call the mine?'

Tom was in high good humour. He had colour in his face; his vigour and energy were back. He turned to his daughter.

'Remember the jay who paid us a visit, Evalyn, the day we went up to the Gertrude?'

'Who pinched some of my lunch?'

'I'm going to name it after him. It will be called the Camp Bird Mine.'

Local papers – the *Solid Muldoon* and the *Silverite Plaindealer* – photographed the Walsh family at home and published accounts of the great new find above the town.

Camp Bird Mine was soon a feverish place. Out-of-work miners flocked there for employment; a manager, John Benson, whom Tom had known for years and trusted completely, and several foremen were appointed. Work commenced on the erection of a stamp mill, boarding house, barns and stabling, manager's house, shops and warehouses.

In the first months of 1897 the mine was already producing a substantial quantity of gold on a daily basis. The stamp mill at the US Depository Mill located a mile below Camp Bird was used initially to crush the rock; but soon a new twenty-ton stamp mill was well in the process of erection on the site of the new gold mine.

Camp Bird was on three levels; the lode continued high up into the basin behind the original tunnel, and the workings there were to be connected to the new mill by a vertical, two-mile aerial tramway, surveyed and built by David Reed. A new concentration plant was built that would amalgamate and concentrate the gold, capable of processing seventy tons of ore every single day.

The gold was extracted using mercury, which combined with the precious metal, was put through a refining process and then the pure gold was turned into ingots. Every day a coach with a strongbox full of gold ingots made the journey down the steep mountain road into Ouray, for shipment by rail to the Denver Mint. The driver was armed with a pistol and there was an armed guard sitting with the treasure.

The gold poured out – five thousand dollars worth at least, every single day.

Slowly, subtly, the Walshes' lives began to change. Their neighbours and friends, the bank manager and the shopkeepers, having read about them in the papers, knowing that they now possessed a rich private gold mine, assumed bemused demeanours, as though in the presence of minor deities, when Tom or Carrie was around. Both Tom and Carrie realised with shock that they had become famous and that life could never be the same for them again.

But we are the same, Tom thought, amused. We are exactly the same. It is others who perceive us differently.

'How do you feel about all this, Carrie?' he asked one evening.

'Frightened. I only hope . . .' She became silent, then blurted: 'It's too much good fortune to have fall into your lap without any price to pay.'

'There was a price, Carrie, I can assure you there was a price. It's called Unremitting Toil.'

But his Irish soul insisted on the balance of things and wondered if Carrie were right.

'Everyone,' Tom said, 'is going to share in this good fortune. My miners will be the best paid, have the best working conditions, lodge in the best accommodation! No one who works for me will shiver when his shift is done and eat rubbish off tin plates!'

The town buzzed with excitement and astonishment as a first-class hotel was erected in the Imogene Basin, and Ashenfelter's teams of horses and mules dragged the finest building materials, the finest fittings, the finest porcelain baths, high up into the Rockies. When the hotel was completed crowds came up to see it.

'It's a marvel,' Dr Rowan announced. 'The like of it has never been seen at ten thousand feet.'

There was a dining room with modern kitchens, bathrooms with the porcelain baths whose transit had caused so much comment, hot water, central steam-heating, electric light, a library stocked with the latest books and periodicals, a smoking room, a sitting room with a phonograph, nicely appointed bedrooms. In the basement was the miners' club room, with a bar and snooker tables.

'The shifts will be no more than eight hours,' Tom decreed. 'The dust must have time to settle from the preceding shift. There are already more than enough cases of miner's lung in these parts. The Sisters' Hospital in Ouray will not be filled with people who work for *me!*'

As the months went by returns exceeded even the highest expectations. It was apparent that Tom Walsh had made one of the great prospecting finds in American history.

But he continued to be cautious, ploughing the major part of his newfound wealth back into development of his mine.

Tom took his family to Denver. He wanted to see his brother, Michael.

Michael had aged beyond his years. Tall, gaunt and stooped, there was little left in him now of the fiery youth who had left Ireland thirty years before. Lame from a wound sustained in the Indian campaign, he lived a bachelor existence in lodgings. Only his eyes were as fierce as ever. He brought Tom and the children into his room. It was filled with mementoes from the past – US cavalry memorabilia, tomahawks, a bow, arrows beautifully fletched, an assortment of pistols and a rifle. All his talk was of days long gone. He smelled of bourbon.

'So you've struck it, Tom!'

'They say I did!'

'Maria used to say long ago that you had something queer in store for you. And if this isn't queer I don't know what is!' Then he added, 'I suppose you'll be looking for a good manager, someone you can trust.'

Tom thought of John Benson, whom he would trust with his life.

'I already have a manager.'

'Have you now . . .? So you haven't come to offer me a job?'

'No. It's hard, dangerous work, Michael.'

'And since when have I been a stranger to hard dangerous work?'

Tom sighed. 'I can't offer you a job – you know nothing of mining – but I can make your life very comfortable, if you will let me.'

In the subsequent silence he took a check from his pocket and put it down in front of his brother.

Michael took it up, read it.

'Twenty-five thousand dollars – you're a very rich man to be giving this sort of money away. But I don't want your largesse.'

He tore the check in two and glared at Tom, narrowing his eyes.

'I should have stayed in Ireland. We should all have stayed and looked after our country. What earthly use is all your wealth, Tom? Will it even be lucky for you? You're thousands of miles from where you belong. Parnell is dead and Home Rule is only a memory. And poor little Peggie is three years in the ground.'

Tom's sense of wellbeing deserted him. He felt for a moment as though a shadow moved over his grave.

Vinson, playing with Evalyn among the memorabilia of the Indian war, stood up and went to his uncle, took his hand.

'I wish I was like you,' he said.

The fierce face softened above its grey moustache.

'Do you now?'

'Yes. I want to ride with the army and fight like you . . . Will you tell me about your best battle?'

Tom glanced at Carrie as Michael took the child by the hand and proceeded to show him, item by item, the souvenirs of fights both great and small.

'I was with Custer, you know . . .'

The boy listened, his mouth open. 'I'd like to be a scout,' he said after a moment.

'Custer's best scout was a *woman!*' Evalyn interjected scornfully. 'She was the best scout he ever had. Isn't that right, Father?'

'She was certainly formidable,' Tom replied, with a smile for his little, rotund daughter, who was always so keen to maintain a feminine perspective.

'Where is she now, Uncle?'

'She's a married lady, and a mother. Her scouting days are over!'

'And your Colorado days are over too, Tom Walsh,' Carrie said softly, while Michael entertained the children. 'Please let's move East. Let's move to Washington!'

Tom demurred. 'Why do you want to move East,' he asked her quietly. 'We're happy here, aren't we?'

Carrie looked so disappointed that he was sorry he had spoken. It was time, he knew, to give her everything, and if everything included moving East, he could no longer rationalise remaining in Ouray. But all the same he wondered – why pick up stumps, why go to another world and leave the one we know and love? He was pensive for the rest of the evening.

When they left Denver Union Depot for the overnight trip back to Ouray, Tom thought of his days on the railroad. The train took them through Golden and he looked out at Castle Rock and thought of the man who had been cut in two by the winch and the Chinaman who had cast the *I Ching* for him and then turned hurriedly away. Had he seen something in the fall of the little ivory sticks? A slow *frisson* climbed his spine.

Lord God, how bizarre it had seemed at the time. All those years before he had been looking for a sign that he was following the right course for his life, and he ruefully conceded that he needed one now, to tell him whether he should stay put or accede to Carrie's request and go East, leave his beloved mountains. So tell me, he whispered silently, addressing the Presence he suspected was always nearby, what should I do?

He remembered suddenly how Maria had turned up in Golden with her trunk. He thought of Arthur Cramer and smiled grimly, wondered for a moment if he were still alive. If I was a vengeful man, he acknowledged, I would buy Cramer's bank and deal with him appropriately. But I am not a vengeful man.

A terrible squealing of brakes, a loud crashing noise and a violent jolting woke Tom. He was propelled from his berth into a darkness of breaking carriage windows, dust and screams. His first thoughts were for Carrie and his children.

'Carrie! Vinson! Evalyn!' he shouted. Carrie gasped somewhere beside him. He heard the children whimper in the darkness, dived through a mound of Pullman cushions and bedclothes, and found them.

'The train is on its side. We have to get out.'

One by one he pushed his children, then his wife, through the opening made in the broken window.

'Slide down to the ground and run away from the track.'

Sitting on the embankment with Vinson, Evalyn saw the railroad men with swinging lanterns, heard the moans of the injured, the cries of children. She saw her mother helping a groaning woman, but there was no sign of her father. He was still in the carriage. Far down along the train, long spears of flame were shooting from beneath the carriages.

'Where is Father?'

'He's helping others escape,' Vinson said.

A man crawled towards them along the ground. Evalyn went to him, aware, like all mining children, of the duty to help an injured person. She took his head into her lap, patted his cheek, said, 'It'll be all right . . . it'll be all right, mister . . .'

The man was saying something, but she could not understand him.

'It's all right, mister,' she said again.

But all attempt at speech deserted the man and with it all movement. She felt the slick wetness on her hand, seeping into her lap. When a gout of flame illuminated the embankment she saw that she was covered in his blood, but she did not cry out or attempt to remove herself. Instead, inspired by some sixth sense she hardly understood, she crooned to him softly an old Irish lullaby her father used to sing, and cradled his head.

By the same light she saw the people still exiting through the same broken window, assisted by her father. She saw him clearly, and then he disappeared from view. When the flames had reached the carriage she tried to stand up, screaming, 'Father, Father . . .' but the head in her lap had become very heavy and her legs had gone to sleep.

'Father's coming,' Vinson said after moment, and she heard in her brother the effort to keep his anxious voice from cracking.

She looked and saw her father, in his white nightgown, push himself out of the broken carriage just as flames approached him. He slid to the ground and raced away from the train.

'We're here, Father . . .'

Tom came to where his children sat shivering from cold and shock. He looked at the man whose head lay in Evalyn's lap, bent down and closed his eyes.

'It's all over for him, Evalyn.' He glanced at his little daughter and added, 'You are a good, brave girl.'

'You're bleeding, Father.'

'Just a few scratches.'

Tom was more shaken than he pretended. His heart was pounding, his palms slick with cold sweat. In his mind he heard the echo of his brother's voice: *Will it even be lucky for you?*

When they got back to Ouray Carrie was adamant. The suggestion she had made in Denver was now an obsession.

'There's no point in staying here any more. I can't take the altitude; it is certainly one of the most dangerous places in the country for the children, and it is killing you, Tom!'

'It's not killing me. I'm healthier than I've been for years . . .'

'You've got away with it for a long time,' she insisted, her eyes flashing, 'and you have made me many promises. But it *is* killing you and I want those promises honoured!' Her voice became rigid. 'I want them honoured *now!*'

A few days later, on the Canyon Creek Road, Carrie's words would return to haunt him. He was trotting Nig down the narrow trail from Camp Bird when suddenly the horse shied violently just where the drop to the canyon floor was most precipitous. From the corner of his eye Tom saw the flapping object that had frightened Nig, a coat a roadworker had left on a shovel. Nig backed against the verge of the precipice and his hind hoofs began to slip over the edge. It was only a matter of seconds before horse and rider would find themselves in a crumpled heap on the canyon floor.

Tom leaned forward, saying soothingly, 'Easy boy, easy . . .'

It was another moment when his life hung in the balance. Hesitation would mean death. He threw himself on to the horse's withers, dismounted on to the shaky edge of the trail, and flung himself towards firm ground, hurting his elbow and grazing his hands. Then he turned, and pulled Nig by the reins from his impending rendezvous with the bottom of the ravine.

Two narrow escapes in as many months, he said to himself, as he quieted Nig, stroking his nose and whispering to him, blowing into his nostrils. They come in threes. Next time perhaps . . .

Carrie, he decided, was right. In any case, it was the end of a chapter, and one of life's tasks was to recognise when a chapter was over. The next one would have to do with his family's future in the great, wide world.

'I've been thinking about it,' Tom said to his wife that evening, 'and we'll do what you want, Carrie. It's time we did!' He looked from one of his children to the other, pre-empting Evalyn who was about to protest. 'My mind is made up! I'm taking you away from Colorado. It's high time to attend to both your educations. We're going to live in Washington!'

'Where the President lives?' Evalyn demanded.

'Just so.'

'I would like to meet him.'

Her father burst out laughing. 'Evalyn, you may be a hoyden, but you have the spirit of a tiger.'

'Don't I also have a tiger spirit?' Vinson asked quietly.

Tom regarded his nine-year-old son. 'You have the heart of a lion,' he said, and then he added in a low and tender voice, 'and the soul of a gentleman!'

Evalyn looked nonplussed. 'That's something I don't need to have,' she announced confidently.

'No,' Vinson agreed sarcastically. 'You are supposed to be a lady!'

Evalyn snorted derisively. 'I don't want to be a lady. All they do is have airs and graces and look down their noses . . . I want to be an actress!'

'Evalyn, will you stop that nonsense!' Carrie said in a voice full of irritation.

'Very soon, children,' Tom continued,' when the new aerial trams are working and the mine is running like clockwork, we will pack our bags and I will take you and your mother far away to a place called Europe. And there we are going to visit a strange little country.'

'What country is that?' Evalyn demanded, scanning her extremely modest knowledge of geography without much success.

Vinson looked at his father's face, then turned to her scornfully. 'It's called Ireland,' he said softly. 'Isn't that right, Father?'

Tom studied his son. The years, the long effort, the toil, the failures, were as nothing. Suddenly he was a young man, with a sore heart, and the coast of Ireland was disappearing below the horizon.

He swallowed, walked to the window and looked out at the Amphitheatre.

'Your father,' he whispered, 'for a little while at least, is going home.'

By the Fall of 1898 a 9,000 foot tramway had been constructed at Camp Bird. It had 46 towers and stretched a distance of 1,350 feet between the tram house and the mill.

Nine months later, when the vessels hoisting the ore were incessantly clanking and grinding their way down the steel cables, and Camp Bird Mine, enlarged and running like clockwork, was churning out a fortune every single day, the millionaire Walshes set sail for Europe. They were making a grand tour of France, England, and Ireland. Tom wrote to John Healy, advising him of their advent and telling him he looked forward to meeting him and his children.

Two weeks later the White Star liner *Majestic* weighed anchor off Roches Point. Waiting on the first-class deck, bracing themselves against the sea wind, were a small group: a middle-aged man, two middle-aged women, a girl of twelve, and a young boy. All of them were elegantly and expensively dressed. All of them were looking around with interest. They saw the white lighthouse above them on the cliff, the bay before them with its waves and bobbing buoys, the sky massed with grey and white clouds through which the light played over distant Queenstown. They could see the tenders approaching to take the passengers ashore, making steady progress in the swell.

The youngsters were laughing, but two of the adults, the man and one of the women, stood rigidly, shoulder to shoulder, in silence.

'Well, Maria,' Tom whispered, 'what will you tell me now?'

It was thirty years and three months since they had left.

Book II

Evalyn

'There was no one like her, and no institution like her parties, and there probably never will be again.'

Judge Thurman Arnold, writing of his friend
Evalyn Walsh McLean after her death

Chapter Thirteen

Ireland, July 1899

Tom stepped on to the quay. He turned to give his hand to his wife and sister; they were quickly followed ashore by Evalyn and Vinson. Tom felt at one remove, as though the screeching of the gulls, the buffeting of the summer sea wind, the bump the tender made against the harbour wall, were happening somewhere else.

So it existed after all, this country, rooted so deep in him that not even thirty years could dim the power of its strange, poetic melancholy!

He affected control; he did not look at Maria. Above them, Queenstown stood in the shifting sunlight under a wild sky. Tom saw the play of light across the Victorian rooftops and the Catholic cathedral with its dominant spire. In an Ireland where Catholic worship had once been proscribed, it seemed a statement of a new order.

'They were only building it when we left,' Maria said, indicating it with a movement of her head. Her voice shook.

From somewhere along the quay came a piped lament. It seemed elemental, like the sea wind itself. Tom saw his sister clap a gloved hand to her mouth and her eyes fill. His own throat was stiff; he dared not speak but he took her arm and reached for Carrie's hand.

'Maria,' Carrie whispered, 'are you all right?'

Maria nodded, but the tears continued down her face in silence.

Other than the new cathedral, little had changed. The women of the town wore black shawls as formerly, or hooded cloaks; the shops still advertised last-minute purchases for travellers; private hotels and lodging houses had cards in their windows advertising vacancies. A crowd, similar to the one she had herself formed part of thirty years before, waited patiently in the harbour to board the returning tender, their first step on the way to the Promised Land.

A porter was procured, the heavy leather Walsh trunks were put ashore, and then they walked the short distance to the small, red brick station. The train waited for them as though no time had passed at all, as though it were the same train and had stood there for thirty years against their return.

Tom shepherded his family aboard and tipped the porter. The man regarded the wad of banknotes in his hand – a year's income suddenly materialising before his eyes.

'May God bless you, sir . . .'

The train hissed steam, coughed smoke, lurched into life, chugged through Rushbrooke, Carrigaloe, Fota, across the water to Glounthaune and Littleisland, on its way to Cork. Tom and Maria were silent; Carrie and the children, sensing intensity, took their cue from them. There was no sound in the compartment except the staccato beat of the wheels on the track and the bluster of the wind through the partly open window. All Tom could think of was a breezy April morning in 1869, and two young people on this selfsame railway. Where were they now?

He glanced at his sister. She was sitting opposite him, elegant in her new Paris afternoon gown and stylish hat; but he saw the salt-stung eyes, the care in her face, the grey at her temples, and the sudden clenching of her mouth as she stared out at the scudding clouds and the changing light over Littleisland. Carrie sat beside him, very straight, a little anxious, he guessed, in case the moment's taut emotion would overflow. Evalyn glanced at him from time to time, but today her chatter was conspicuous by its absence.

Vin was seated by the window, but was more absorbed in watching the grown-ups and in fidgeting with the water pistol he had bought at Cherbourg, than in noting the panorama outside.

Tom broke the tension with a rueful comment to his son: 'I hope that thing is empty!'

Vin grinned. 'It's full, Father. I have to guard the camp!'

For a second Tom felt as though he were back on the prairie, with the wagons circling for the approaching night and peril just over the horizon. But glancing around at his family in their elegant clothes, catching his own reflection in the glazed picture of the Killarney lakes behind the opposite seat, the groomed and well-dressed man in middle life, he knew fear of the future and the vagaries of Fortune would never trouble them again.

Vinson put down his water pistol and stared out the window, his nose against the glass, his breath misting the pane.

'What do you think of Ireland, Vin?' Tom asked after a moment, curious at the sudden intentness.

'I'm not sure, Father. It has a strange feeling . . . It feels wild,' Vin turned from the window and looked at his father with a frown, 'like when someone is very sad . . . and cannot find any comfort . . .'

Tom started. Is it blood that speaks? he wondered. Or acute sensibility?

'I know why,' Evalyn cried. 'It's because Vin is seeing the oul' sod for the first time!'

Tom laughed. The expression was absurd in her twelve-year-old mouth with its accent of the Rockies. 'That's what you used to call it, Father, "the oul sod"!' she added, delighted to have elicited the familiar paternal chuckle, 'when we used to go into the mountains and you talked about Ireland. Is this the same railroad you travelled on when you left?'

'It is!'

Listening to their exchange Maria remembered the close, humid compartment, the fogged windowpane, the fear of the future and the smell of the sea. She heard again her brother's words: '*It will be all right, Maria, I promise you.*'

She glanced at Tom, aware of how moved he was. His eyes darkened, as they had long ago.

They stayed that night in the Imperial Hotel in Cork city.

'Tomorrow,' Tom told them at dinner, 'we will go by train to a town called Clonmel, where I will hire a carriage to take us to a little house near the foot of a mountain . . .'

Carrie and the children looked at him in consternation when he put down his knife and fork and turned away his head.

The boreen wound from the main road. It passed the roofless ruins of the old Famine cottages, wound around by the cottage that had once housed Mrs Hegarty. Above it the land sloped gently, green and smoky blue in the sunshine.

'That is Sliabh na mBan,' Tom said in answer to Carrie's question. 'It means the Women's Mountain.'

The boreen culminated in the yard of a whitewashed thatched cottage where an unruly fuchsia took up the entire south-facing wall and where the hens wandered at will.

A startled face looked out at them over the half-door. A balding, wiry man of middle years, in a peaked cap and collarless shirt, came out to meet the strangers whose carriage had stopped in his yard. His eyes were sunken beneath grey, tangled eyebrows; he had the forward, stooping gait of a man used to walking on hills; he smelled of turf smoke.

'Are ye lost?' he asked with diffident courtesy. 'Can I help ye find where ye want to go?'

Tom did not immediately recognise his old school friend. But then he saw the familiar kind eyes and the tilt of the head.

'No, Seamie. I still know my way around here . . .'

Seamus Farrelly pushed back his greasy cap, then suddenly seized the stranger's hand in both of his.

'Holy God,' he said slowly in a low voice, while his face registered every emotion from disbelief to joy, 'are my two eyes deceiving me, Tommy Walsh, or can it be yourself that's in it?'

'It is, Seamie. This is my wife, Carrie; these are my children.' Tom gestured towards Maria, who was holding out her hand. 'Do you remember this lady?'

Seamus seized the outstretched hand, with obvious emotion. 'Ah, Maria,' he said sadly, 'sure I should have known you at once. You always had a look of Peggie! But come in, come in,' he cried, moving back from the door and motioning them to enter. 'Ye're welcome as the flowers of May.'

The kitchen was dim, lit only by the small window and the open turf fire that was mostly ash with glowing embers. Seated by the oilcloth-covered table, Carrie saw her husband's eyes move from the hearth, to the mantelshelf above with its picture of the Sacred Heart, to the smoke-stained walls, to the doors of the two rooms on either side of the kitchen, to the dresser with its dusty willow-pattern plates, to the rafters and the underside of the thatch. She saw him swallow, saw his eyes on Seamus as the latter bent into the fireplace to put sods on the embers and pull the sooty crane with its black kettle over the new flames.

There were footsteps outside. A cheery voice rang out at the open door. 'God save all here!'

A stout woman with a basket on her arm appeared, her face full of curiosity.

'Ah, Noirín, come in,' Seamus said with a twinkle, 'and meet the Quality.'

The newcomer glanced shyly from one of the Walshes to the other.

' 'Day to you, ma'am, sir . . .'

'Will you guess now who these people are, girl?' Seamus demanded with a laugh, pointing at Tom and Maria. 'They left us a long time ago and divil a hope any of us had that we'd set eyes on them again!'

'I remember *you*, Noirín Donnelly,' Maria said, rising and holding out her arms. 'I shared a bed with you more than once when I used to play down at your house!'

Noirín's mouth opened in astonishment. 'Maria Walsh!' she cried, adding, as she stared at Tom, 'And is this Tommy? Who used to pull my plaits? Well, you've changed! I'll say that for you! Whatever they've been feeding you it hasn't done you one bit of harm!'

Tom brought his family forward.

'This is my wife,' he said, 'and my children, Evalyn and Vinson.'

'Did you know my father when he was little?' Evalyn demanded as she shook hands with the stranger.

'Aye,' Noirín replied, with a mischievous glance at Tom. 'A right clever divil he was too! But he went away to the mill in Clonmel, and he barely twelve years old. We only saw him the odd time after that!'

Others neighbours came later, eager to meet the returned emigrants. The women bustled to prepare refreshments and men hurried off to find more chairs. In no time the table was covered with a white embroidered cloth, set with cups, saucers and plates, bread and butter and slices of fruitcake.

A glazed brown teapot was kept filled from the black kettle. The voices rose and fell, Tom and Maria, animated as Carrie had never seen them, wiped away tears of laughter.

'Are you Irish yourself, Mrs Walsh?' Noirín asked Carrie.

'I'm American. My people were originally English,' she said, 'but they came over to America to find a better life!'

'Poor Seamie's wife is dead this twelvemonth,' Noirín confided, with a gesture at the untidy kitchen, 'which is why the place is the way it is.'

'Has he children?'

'No.' Then she added softly, with a sidelong glance to see if the men were out of earshot, ' 'Twas sad, for she kept losing them. The *creatúir* was trying too hard! Seamie married late. He had a great notion of Tom's sister for many years, you know, but she married someone else! I think the reason he took over this place after the old man died was that he wanted to live in the house that had been her home.'

'You mean Peggie?'

Noirín nodded, dropped her voice still further, leaned towards Carrie confidingly. 'It was going down to live with the Cork people that was the ruination of her lungs. Sure there was never a sign of the consumption in that family before.'

It was as though even to speak of Peggie's fate carried some kind of stigma. It's all right, Carrie wanted to say, the unfortunate woman was unlucky enough to catch a disease; she didn't *invent* it.

Evalyn, her mouth full of fruitcake, cried, 'Mother, I'm going out to play.'

Through the small square window, Carrie saw her son sneaking up on the hens, who cocked amber eyes at him and hopped away with a squawk and a flutter of wings.

'Be careful,' she whispered to her daughter. 'Tell Vin not to scare the hens . . .'

But Evalyn was already gone.

'Your children are grand altogether, Mrs Walsh,' Noirín said.

Although she answered questions and asked a few of her own, Carrie felt increasingly on the edge of things, as though she were trying to look through a frosted glass at other lives. She did not follow much of what was said, what with the forays into Irish, the sudden acid quips, the turn of phrase that seemed a *mélange* of Elizabethan English and Irish idiom. She tried to imagine Tom and Maria in this very kitchen as children, tried to see their mother tending them. She glanced at Maria, who was at the other end of the table, absorbed in the personal history of this person and that whom she had evidently once known. The women turned to Carrie to include her in the conversation, asked coyly how she had come to meet Tom, questioned her about what it had been like to set up home in the Rockies. The fire was blazing now; the room uncomfortably warm, although the door was open.

Carrie looked to Tom, but the men had gravitated to a group of their own. They drank porter, pouring it from a brown earthenware jug. She hardly knew the Tom Walsh who sporadically joked in another tongue, who was completely absorbed in a conversation about politics.

Maria took up the burden of describing life in America and Carrie tried to hear what the men were saying.

'There's a new spirit abroad now, Tom,' she heard one of them explain. 'Did you know there's a Gaelic revival afoot . . . and plenty of people – aye, Dublin Jackeens too – rushing off to the Gaeltacht to learn the Irish. It's become a craze. Everyone is looking to the past, to what we had once . . . and if we got off our arses, that we might have again.'

Tom wiped a fleck of froth from his moustache.

'I suppose the present owner of Kilduncan House is keeping up family traditions?' he said drily.

'Aye, he lives in London; there'd be little reason for *him* to show his face here now. Och, we pay the rents all right, though some refused during the Land War and were evicted. But not one person would go in behind them and the farms sat there idle. 'Twas terrible queer to see the land with the hay rotting in the fields. There's a few have bought out their farms under the last Act, but the money's hard come by. The Government, God help them, thought if they let us buy our land back, we'd forget all about Home Rule!'

'Why should we *buy* it back? They didn't buy it from us!' one of the younger men muttered darkly.

Carrie was glad when the impromptu party was over. She saw Tom say goodbye to old friends, saw the delight with which he went covertly to his pocket and then discreetly to the pockets around him. But she also saw how reluctant the recipients were, and how quickly they vanished.

He's only alienating these people, she thought. They are ashamed of their need.

'It's come out of a mountain four thousand miles away,' he said to Seamus when the latter muttered that he was grand, that he needed nothing and had plenty of money, and tried, with some embarrassment, to decline his old friend's largesse.

'I might just as easily never have found it,' Tom went on, 'and you'd be a right *amadán*, Seamus, if you don't let me have the pleasure of sharing a morsel of it with you!'

'Can we go back to the hotel now?' Evalyn demanded when the gathering had dispersed.

'Soon,' Tom said. 'Maria and I have a walk we must take first. We have an appointment with one or two ghosts.'

Brother and sister put on the galoshes they had bought in Clonmel and went away together to the high field where the water still foamed around An Cailleach.

'Funny how it's smaller!' Maria said. 'I used to think it was such a torrent.'

'I used to think it was Niagara,' Tom replied. He lowered his voice. 'Do you remember the day . . . we were all up here . . .?'

Maria glanced at him. 'When Mother . . .? Of course I do. How could I forget?'

'Did you know at the time what happened to her was because of me?'

He said it matter-of-factly. Maria was instantly reminded of her own bereavement, and Paul's terrible guilt and distress. She realised now that her brother had carried a nameless weight for three decades and never said a word. She burst into tears, releasing the tensions of the day, of the year, of her young widowhood and broken hopes. She refused her brother's sympathetic arms and turned on him in fury.

'It was *not* because of you,' she said, raising her voice. 'Our darling mother died from hunger and hardship, from the terrible effort to pay an unjust rent for her own land, and live.' She straightened her arm, pointed into the valley below, where the tall chimneys of Kilduncan House could be seen through the trees, and cried: 'She died because of *that*!'

Tom grabbed the distraught woman, his sister as he had never seen her, and rocked her in his arms.

'It's all right, it's all right, *a chroí*.' When her sobs had subsided he added, indicating the white manor in the distance with a movement of his head, '*That* is a broken yoke, Maria.' He wiped his own eyes and shook his sister gently. 'Didn't you hear them talking earlier? It's only a matter of time before the system that destroyed this country crumbles!'

'Huh,' she replied, 'You were always one for dreams!'

Tom shook his head.

'No, Maria. Nothing is static. Arrogance loses its patina, falls from its pedestal. Only Justice endures!'

He released her, took out his handkerchief and wiped her tears.

'You said once you would like to buy Kilduncan House,' she said after a moment. 'Now you can.'

'I know, Maria. I have much to consider . . .' Maria straightened at the cryptic response, looking at him enquiringly, but Tom had turned back towards the house.

★　★　★

191

On the way back to Clonmel they bought a bunch of red roses from an old lady with a flower garden, stopped the coach by a small Catholic church and climbed the stone stile into the graveyard. Tom removed his hat.

The children, following their parents and aunt, fell silent. Evalyn looked around at the profusion of cowslips, nettles, buttercups, at the tombstones, new and weathered, at a stone angel pointing mournfully to Heaven.

Maria whispered: 'Where is her grave . . . Father's grave? I can't remember . . . they've changed the place . . . there are so many new plots. Oh, Tom, I can't remember where my mother's grave is . . .'

But Tom led the way unerringly to the fourth row below the stone wall, counting the plots without a word. He stopped and stood before the tallest Celtic cross in the cemetery. Then he bent and gently laid the roses on the mound.

Maria ran her hand along the lettering in the stone that was already covered with pale yellow lichen. Carrie glanced at her silent husband and sister-in-law, dropped her eyes and prayed to the God she fervently believed in to comfort the pain she felt in her spouse. Evalyn sensed the emotion as though it came through the soles of her feet.

'. . . *Faoi bhrat Dé go raibh a anamacha dílís*,' Tom whispered.

Vinson, ever aware of verbal nuances, glanced at his father. 'Was that Irish, Father?' he asked diffidently as they left the graveside. 'What you said?'

Tom nodded.

'But it's a dead language, isn't it?'

'No, my son, although they did their best to kill it.'

Carrie heard the bitterness. It was so unlike her husband that she wanted to interpose some word of her own to soften it, but could think of nothing.

'But what did it mean?' Vinson went on. In Tom's mind's eye was an anxious red-haired woman, rushing towards him across a stony field, a wiry man, prematurely aged, regarding her with anxiety and love.

' "May their kind souls," ' he said in a voice so low and unsteady that they had to strain to hear it, ' "be sheltered by the cloak of God." '

Tom walked slowly by the tombstones, registering the names of the dead – some of them people he had known, had played with, been at school with. He saw, near the church gate, the simple stone cross for Father Doyle, the priest who had toiled in this parish during the worst of the Famine, the priest who had comforted him long ago.

The door of the little church was open; the family followed Tom inside, heard their footsteps echo on the flags.

'This is where Maria and I were baptised,' he told Carrie and the children. 'Do you think the people would like a fine new church?' he added in a low voice, looking around.

'Why don't you ask the parish priest?' Carrie said with a smile.

As they returned to their coach, a middle-aged man in a black soutane watched them from one of the presbytery windows. He had already heard all about them.

Chapter Fourteen

Other than Father it's really only Aunty Maria who is interested in this part of the journey, Evalyn thought to herself.

It was two days later. They had driven all over the county, it seemed to her, to the towns of Cashel and Tipperary and the Glen of Aherlow, and even up to the lower slopes of the Comeraghs. They had also gone back to the little church where her father had been baptised. He had disappeared into the presbytery while the family had gone for a walk. Evalyn knew he had gone to offer the parish priest a new church, and she anticipated the latter's delight at her father's generosity. But when they got back to the coach he was already waiting, and he was strangely abrupt and taciturn.

'What is it, Father? Didn't the priest want a new church?'

'It seems not, Daughter.'

'Well, money then?'

'Not money either.'

Carrie was about to say something, but Maria frowned and shook her head.

In fact, Tom was smarting from his interview. The soutaned priest had invited him to sit; waited politely while he explained his business.

'You were christened in our little church, Mr Walsh, I believe?' he had asked when Tom had finished.

'I was. I was born and went to school in this parish. In fact – although I haven't talked this through with my family yet – I'm considering returning.'

'Indeed?'

'Yes. I'm making enquiries about Kilduncan House.'

There had been silence. Then the priest had said, 'You would then be the new landlord?'

Tom had laughed drily. 'Only briefly. It would be my pleasure to restore ownership of the land to where it belongs!'

After a stunned pause the priest had said softly, 'I hear you have not remained a Catholic, Mr Walsh?'

Tom had sighed. 'It is true that I do not practise, but—'

'And your wife is a Protestant, is she not?'

'She is, but I fail to see—'

'And you did not marry her in a Catholic church?'

'No . . . But we had a bless—' Tom had started to say in dismay, disliking the way he was being put on the defensive.

'Thank you, Mr Walsh. I'm sure your offer was well-intentioned. But however poor we may be, we cannot accept lavish gifts from apostates, especially those who are – if you will forgive me for the truth – openly living in mortal sin!'

Tom had stood up, picked his hat from the chair, his face red with astonishment and anger.

'And another thing,' the priest had continued, 'I understand from my flock that many of them have received money from you. I have already warned them from the pulpit – as is my pastoral duty – that accepting anything of the kind from you may prejudice their immortal souls.'

Remembering, Tom clenched his fist and told the coachman to drive on.

His heart was racing with shock and affront. He calmed himself by looking at the sky above Sliabh na mBan. The wild clouds danced above a splendid, civilised land, he thought, a thousand years before Ireland ever heard the ranting of bigotry. In truth, the country labours under not one, but *two* foreign yokes.

That afternoon their tour continued. Evalyn saw prehistoric Ogham stones with strange writing; she was struck by the lush greenness of everything, the hedgerows full of wild flowers, the thatched whitewashed houses. But she saw the beauty of the countryside with an impatient eye; there was nothing to do here except accompany her strangely silent father, and her increasingly fatigued mother. There was no great empty wilderness, such as she was used to. Instead, every piece of land had been lived on, cherished, farmed, hedged, for generations without number. When she compared it to America it was claustrophobic.

She saw how Vinson stuck close to his father, as though he understood the long parental silences. And she also saw how her father's hand would automatically caress the boy's dark head. Because she loved Vinson she refused the jealousy. Instead, to fend off a sense of invisibility, she tried to amuse everyone by performing cartwheels on the country road, or by putting on some of the strange accents and stranger colloquialisms they had met on their travels.

'Don't be making such an exhibition of yourself, Evalyn,' her mother said crossly. 'Behave like a lady, for Heaven's sake.'

'I don't want to be a lady, Mother,' she replied half under her breath. 'They have boring lives.'

Carrie, for her own part, saw the richness of the land, the poverty of the farms, and the contrasting grandeur of the landlords' great houses with astonishment. She began to understand the old sorrow in her husband, and she blamed it for making him so taciturn and withdrawn. They were staying in Hearns Hotel in Clonmel, and when it rained, all Tom wanted to do was stay indoors and read every issue of the local paper, the *Nationalist*, he could get his hands on. He seemed much affected by what he found in it. The editorials were trenchant, Carrie thought, casting an eye over some of them.

> The intense pressure experienced by the agricultural community of Ireland under foreign competition, excessive taxation and oppressive rents, emphasises more keenly than ever the old national claim – 'the land for the people'. The cruel rent screw is working as of old and the evictor is close behind the rack-renter.

On 19 August, the newspaper reported, the Union Jack that had fluttered proudly in the rear garden of the Bank of Ireland in Tipperary town had been pulled down and the police who had come to intervene had been fired on.

One evening after dinner, when Carrie was putting the children to bed, Tom showed selected newspaper articles to Maria.

'Funny that after all the country has been through, its spirit still won't lie down and die,' she observed when she had finished. 'I suppose they caught the fellows who fired on the police. But where is it all going?'

'It's coals under a kettle, Maria. When the heat is sufficient it will boil over!'

His sister observed him from troubled eyes. 'You've lost your joy in being home, Tom. And I know how much it meant to you, how you dreamed of it! It wouldn't have anything to do with that visit of yours to the parish priest?' she added in a low rueful voice. 'Or is it just the rain?'

'Oh, Maria,' Tom said with a disgusted snort, 'to tell you the truth, I *was* toying with the idea of coming home to stay – if Carrie could be persuaded – and raising the children in Ireland. But after the *inquisition* with that man . . . that litany of bigotry . . .! Can you *believe*, Maria, he has actually warned the people not to accept money from me?'

Maria looked at him with pity and love.

'Tom, think! A poor country priest finds that one of the richest men in the world has suddenly arrived on his doorstep. This is a man who has made his fortune despite having lapsed from his religion, one who is unlikely to accept any priestly authority in his life. But he is quite ready to pave the parish with gold, and is even thinking of settling there! He *had* to scare you off! Don't you see, Tom, he is afraid of you, and everything you represent?'

196

Tom was taken aback.

'You don't understand how things have changed!' his sister went on. 'People cannot help the way they see a man who has found the treasure at the end of the rainbow!'

Tom shook his head. 'The gold in my pocket came out of a mountain, Maria. The rainbow keeps its mysteries.'

Carrie came back from tucking the children into bed, registered the sudden silence as she came into the sitting room.

'You're both making me feel shut out!' she exclaimed. 'It's been like this for days. You're always talking together in whispers. I may as well not be here!'

'Carrie, my darling,' Tom said, 'it's just that Maria and I find things a . . . little strange, and can't help comparing old memories.'

'Memories!' Carrie exclaimed. 'If you ask me it's grief! I have never seen you like this! But you should talk about it. The children have a right to know where they have sprung from, and who their father is! How can you exorcise so much pain if you will not speak?'

The following evening Tom drove his family to the viewing point above the Glen of Aherlow and for the first time talked to them of the past. He told Vin and Evalyn about the wonderful civilisation that had once flourished in Ireland. He told them about foreign invasion, about Cromwell, the Penal Laws and the Famine that had decimated the population. Evalyn saw how her father's hands clenched and unclenched as he spoke.

'Are you very angry, Father?' she asked when he had finished.

Tom sighed. 'The past is out of reach, Daughter, and poisoning oneself with anger or hatred because of it is a great mistake. I learned in America the power of human co-operation. I put my faith in that!'

He smiled at Carrie and reached for her hand.

The following day Carrie had an attack of her old enemy, migraine, and opted to stay back from the latest excursion, lying in a darkened hotel room and accepting only tea for breakfast. Tom offered to stay with her but she said she needed to sleep.

'I think your mother is tiring of our expedition,' he said ruefully to Evalyn and Vinson.

'It's time we found Peggie's children,' Maria said. 'Did their father ever respond to your letter?'

'No. But we'll find him!'

They went to Boherbue, found the small two-storey house where John Healy had lived with Peggie and their children. The aproned woman who responded to the knock on the door seemed perplexed.

'Sure Sergeant Healy is gone. Wasn't he transferred to Tralee . . .? Ask them down in the barracks.'

The police barracks was a heavily fortified cut-stone building with narrow, barred windows. The heavy outer door was opened by a constable in a dark green uniform with a Webley at his waist. Through a narrow hatch in the hall, Tom saw a desk and a stack of papers, saw the sunlight pick out the dust in the floorboards, saw the rifles carefully stacked against the wall, and the incongruous tabby sleeping on the sunlit windowsill.

The constable was looking at him interrogatively. Tom said he was looking for Sergeant Healy.

'He's been transferred to Tralee, sir. He's been gone this twelvemonth.'

'And his children?'

'They're with his widowed sister . . . a Mrs Murphy, I believe, living in Monaghan.'

Tom was crestfallen. 'That's a distance away. I thought I would have plenty of time! But we're due in Queenstown on Tuesday for the journey back to the States.'

Secretly Tom was impatient to return. He had received a telegram from John Benson to say a cable on one of the hoists had snapped; one of the men – Hank Hoban – had lost his left hand. It made Tom shiver when he remembered the accident in Golden when he had been working on the railroad.

What was it about luck? Why had the Fates been kind to him, and not to others? Hank was a hard and honest worker, but his life as a miner was now over. He had a wife living in Ouray and two children.

We'll fix him up with a good pension, he thought.

But the accident depressed him; catastrophe at the mine into which he had invested so much in safety features felt almost like an accusation. He was tired and emotionally spent after his visit to Clonmel, and wondered if the old fever was coming on again.

'There's another grave we must visit, Maria,' he said when they left the police station.

She turned compassionate eyes on him. 'I know.'

The children followed them along the gravel path from the cemetery gate. Maria laid a bunch of white roses on the plot, plucked a few dandelions from the overgrown grave, traced with her fingers the words inscribed on the small limestone cross:

IN MEMORY OF MARGARET (PEGGIE) HEALY (née Walsh)
1856–1894
Requiescat in pace

Goodbye, Peggie, Tom thought. *Forgive me.*

Carrie had recovered, but she was tired and anxious to go home.

She said to Tom when he debated the merits of going to Monaghan: 'Your nephew and nieces, and the woman who is rearing them – how would they regard your sudden appearance in their lives – total strangers? Would it not be an ordeal for them? Not to mention how long it would take us, going and coming . . .'

Tom thought Carrie could be right. He did not have to meet Peggie's children to enhance their lives.

'There are lawyers in Cork,' Maria reminded him.

In Cork Tom reinstalled his family at the Metropole.

The following morning Maria took the children on a trip to Dunmore East, and Tom, acting on the hotel manager's advice, presented himself at Wheelan, Sorohan & Co., a firm of solicitors near the hotel. He was shown up polished linoleum stairs to an office overlooking the river where a balding middle-aged man in a pin-stripe suit sat behind a walnut desk.

The solicitor rose, then signalled to the secretary to shut the door.

'Alfred Wheelan,' he said, extending his hand. 'What can I do for you, Mr Walsh?'

'I'm on my way back to the States,' Tom said when he was seated, 'but I have nieces and a nephew in Ireland whom time prevents me from meeting. I would like to benefit them.'

'In what way?'

'I want to settle a lump sum that will provide for their education and maintenance, and for each one to take a share in the capital at age twenty-one.'

'Are these persons all minors?'

'Yes. But the eldest will be twenty-one in November.'

'Then you will need to set up a trust. A minor cannot give a valid receipt.'

'Can you deal with this quickly? We are leaving from Queenstown tomorrow.'

'It requires a deed to be prepared.'

'I'll double your fee, Mr Wheelan, for an expeditious service.'

The solicitor inclined his head politely. He put on his spectacles and poised his fountain pen above a sheet of paper.

Later that day Tom returned to Alfred Wheelan's office and signed the engrossed Deed of Trust. Two trustees had been required. Tom had nominated the children's father as one and, in the absence of any other possible candidate, had nominated the lawyer himself as the second. In this way he gave the sum of one hundred thousand dollars to John Healy and Alfred Wheelan on trust for three young people whom he had never seen. The deed was witnessed by a secretary who left her typing to come into her employer's room and watch Tom append his signature beside the red wax seal. As soon as she was gone Tom wrote out a check drawn on his bank in Denver. It was made out to John Healy and Alfred Wheelan. Mr Wheelan undertook to notify Sergeant Healy immediately of the trust fund. Tom thanked him and paid his fees in cash.

Alfred Wheelan stood up and extended his hand. 'I wish you a safe and pleasant journey home, Mr Walsh.'

When his latest client was gone, Alfred Wheelan put the cheque in a drawer of his desk and glanced at his appointments book. He had an appointment at five, the last one of the day – a farmer who had a dispute with his neighbour over a boundary. He sat for a while looking out at the river. He thought of his racing debts, which were presently making his life a misery. He leaned his head on his hand. There was a filly called Hunter's Slip in the Bettystown Hurdles, a real certainty . . .

He took out the cheque, looked at it in disbelief for a while before putting it away. He had never seen anything approaching that amount of money in his life.

It was in the evening, after his last appointment had left and the secretaries had gone home and he sat alone, tweaking the ends of his greying moustache, and considering his options, that he endorsed the cheque with his own signature and, with only a moment's hesitation, also endorsed the name of the other payee, John Healy.

The bank would not question it; the law did not require them to question endorsements. Now it was just a matter of getting it cleared. He could replace whatever he had used of it after the Bettystown Hurdles . . .

In his luxurious stateroom Tom lay and stared at the ornate ceiling and listened to the throb of the liner's great engines. Carrie was asleep. The long trip had exhausted her.

He was drained emotionally, but felt he had laid some old ghosts. He lingered on the worst moment of the visit – which had occurred in Queenstown on the return journey. A drunk woman had come begging along the platform just as the Walshes had alighted from the train. Tom had always detested the sight of drink on a woman, and when she had clutched at his arm he had drawn back coldly. She was the only person to whom he had refused largesse in Ireland.

'I see ye're too grand for the likes of me!' she screeched at him. And then her eyes had fallen on Evalyn, and she had added, stabbing her dirty finger at the child, 'I curse your fine daughter here. Before she dies she will know all about drink . . . aye, and worse . . . I curse her . . .'

Tom pushed past her, shepherded his family down the platform and left the virago behind. Carrie looked as though she would faint.

'An Irish curse!' she whispered in a stricken voice. 'Oh dear Lord, Tom . . .'

'Carrie!' he said into her ear. 'You'll frighten Evalyn. It's just the ranting of a drunk!'

But he wished the incident had not happened. It, and the interview with the parish priest, had soured the whole trip. But at least one important thing had come from it – he had settled enough money on Peggie's children to provide for them to the end of their days.

In the adjoining stateroom Evalyn woke up briefly, remembered where she was and turned over in her bed with delicious anticipation. She knew she was bound for a great new life – America and freedom and home.

Chapter Fifteen

It didn't take Evalyn long to decide that her country's capital wasn't a patch on her old home town. In Ouray she had known almost every passer-by, but in Washington, as she was quick to discover, she was merely a stranger.

She missed being at the centre of Ouray's excitement over the great gold mine her father had discovered. She even longed for her old school where she had been able to idle away her time in comparative peace. Her new school, the Mount Vernon Academy, was not so accommodating. And when the initial excitement over the Walshes' smart new abode began to fade, she longed for the clapboard house where she had been so happy. But most of all she missed Dewdrop: her thoughts before going to sleep conjured up his black eyes, his velvet nose, his kind, patient nature and she would long to bury her face in his mane. He was now being cared for in Mr Ashenfelter's stables, and she hoped the men were being kind to him.

Dewdrop, she thought, I haven't abandoned you; but they've made me live far away, where everything is horrible. I don't know anyone, the streets are full of people I've never seen before, they won't let me out unless Annie goes with me; there's no one I can call on . . . Why did we have to come to silly old Washington?

But everything had changed irrevocably, and however much Evalyn chafed, she knew that the change was immutable. Thomas Francis Walsh, her father, was America's newest mining millionaire.

Now that he no longer spent his days at high altitudes, and had a holiday and sea voyage behind him, Tom had recovered his health, and in the first week of their removal to the capital, he took his family on a tour of the city that was to become their home. Their carriage brought them down Pennsylvania Avenue, past the White House, and then to the Capitol.

The family climbed the white steps of their country's legislature and looked around at the urban landscape. Eleven-year-old Vinson pointed to the Washington Monument that soared like a great stone pencil.

'Where did that come from, Father?'

Tom put his hand on his son's head. 'It's a monument to George Washington.' He turned proudly to his wife. 'We have an enquiring mind here, Carrie!'

He glanced at Evalyn, who was shifting her feet. She was keenly aware that she was not expected to have an enquiring mind, so she compensated by looking bored.

'And what do you think, Daughter, of this fine city?' Tom asked.

Evalyn shrugged. 'Do we *have* to stay here, Father?' she said in a wheedling tone. 'It's full of stuck-up people. I want to go home to the mountains!'

'No one could ever accuse you, Evalyn, of suffering in silence!' he said with a chuckle.

But Carrie was not amused; she clicked her tongue.

'There are mountains here too, Evalyn,' she said, 'invisible ones. This is our nation's capital, one of the most elegant cities in the world! To be accepted by Washington society is to be accepted everywhere.'

'Oh, Mother,' Evalyn cried, 'who wants to be *accepted*? *I* don't!' She glanced at her father defiantly, ready for his rebuke.

But he merely said, 'Quite right! The judgement of others, after all, is only opinion informed by prejudice and limitation; it is not the judgement of God!'

Carrie looked chastened. 'I didn't mean that one should *seek* approval.'

'You shouldn't care a fig, Carrie, whether we are "accepted" or not,' Tom told his wife. 'It is beneath your dignity even to consider it.'

'All right,' Evalyn muttered to herself when the tour was completed, 'so Washington's got the White House and the Capitol and all the rest of it, and plenty of old brick houses, and streets with snooty, fashionable people! So what?'

Pondering her unrest she finally hit on the reason. Not only was her personal liberty circumscribed, but Washington itself did not *feel* like a place with freedom. It was not like Ouray, where you were surrounded by the wilderness.

I can't live like this, she informed herself with growing desperation. I'll have to think of something.

But life was not so easily excited. Each portion of her day was now accounted for – school, homework, confined her a good deal to the house.

Her mother was unyielding: 'No, Evalyn, you can't go wandering around on your own. I never heard such notions.'

'But in Ouray . . .'

'You may recall that even in Ouray there were certain streets you had to avoid.'

'Yes, Main Street because of the saloons, and Second Street because of the Bird Cage and the Bon Ton where the miners went . . . What did they go there for, Mother,' Evalyn continued, articulating a recent suspicion, 'when there were so many saloons on Main Street?'

Carrie looked aghast. 'Never mind, Evalyn. A lady doesn't know about such places.'

Huh, Evalyn thought. There is a mystery to be solved here. When I go back to Ouray I'll have a closer look.

As time passed the sense of confinement troubled her more and more. At night she thought of the sun on Mount Hayden, of the dangerous Sneffles Road, the Million Dollar Highway, the wilderness overlooked by Mount Abrams where once she and her father had nearly died. She would bury her face into her pillow when she thought of Dewdrop.

But the huge mining engine her father had built up at Camp Bird was churning out its riches at that very instant, and because of it their lives could never be the same. The mine had become something of a town in its own right, with its own post office and dairy and stores. She knew any traveller could dine in its restaurant and stay in its hotel free of charge – like at monasteries long ago in Ireland, her father said. He talked so much of his plans for it that she was sure he would go back to visit it soon. And when he did she would make sure he took her too.

The funny thing about money was that it wasn't as marvellous as people thought. It still left you with yourself, and, inside, you were just the same, with the same needs, uncertain about the same things. Sometimes she fantasised that she would wake some morning and find herself back in the old clapboard house, with her friends down the street and her beloved father setting out on one of his prospecting trips into the mountains. How would she feel, she wondered, if their present circumstances turned out to be temporary?

Their Washington home was in Le Roy Phelps Place, a house that her father had bought fully furnished.

When Evalyn woke each morning, her eye was immediately caught by the satin canopy over her bed. Sometimes she would not know where she was; then it would come to her with a powerful sense of unreality that she was in Washington, in an elegant three-storey, yellow brick house with a tiled roof, where the walls of her bedroom were covered with blue figured satin, and her closet was full of wonderful new dresses.

Needing to put her own stamp on things, she decided she didn't like blue walls; but she did love the dresses and her new silk drawers and chemises, reminding herself that once she had had to wear red flannel underwear. Her mother now had gowns from Worth, and furs from Gunthers, and Vinson had all the toys he had ever dreamed of.

It was strange to be suddenly surrounded by servants – a butler, two housemaids, a cook, a kitchenmaid, a gardener, and, of course, Annie, now housekeeper, but more a member of the family than anything else.

But why did she, Evalyn, have to keep convincing herself that all this meant something? Why, she wondered, did a strange unease seize her, a sudden tightening of her stomach that seemed to say: *This is not really what you want; it is not what you need for a happy life?*

And if this wasn't enough she felt she didn't know who she was any more. Her body had changed; small breasts had made their appearance; her hips had rounded, and recently she had had her first period. It was as though there was a force inside her that didn't care what she thought.

She looked at herself in the mirror on her French dressing table; but the mirror showed only a plump thirteen-year-old, with a neat plait of dark hair secured by a white satin bow.

Evalyn stuck her tongue out at her reflection.

'I hate you,' she said aloud. 'Why can't you be slim and beautiful, and *make* everyone love you?'

'Do you like your new room, Evalyn?' Tom asked his daughter one morning.

They were in the breakfast room that looked out on the garden. Through the open French window they could see the last of the roses, vivid reds and pinks against the greenery of the lawn. Esther, a black maid in white apron and cap, was serving breakfast; the room was redolent of coffee and fresh muffins and scents from the garden. Annie no longer served at table; as housekeeper, she took her duties seriously, and kept the staff on their toes with her ascerbic tongue.

'I would prefer the walls of my room to be pink!' Evalyn replied, her mouth full of scrambled egg. 'Or purple . . . or anything but blue.'

Tom smiled at her with whimsical eyes. 'Your mother has a decorator lined up,' he said. 'I'm sure she'll let you pick out your wallcoverings yourself . . . within reason,' he added hastily as he glanced at Carrie.

'This is an elegant house and I quite like your room the way it is, Evalyn,' Carrie said disapprovingly. 'Do you really want to change it, or is this just the caprice of the moment?'

'Blue walls give me a stomach ache, Mother,' Evalyn said, unable to articulate her need for some kind of mastery over her life.

Her mother looked exasperated. Vinson put down his fork and stifled a laugh. He was no longer the automatic champion of his sister's whims.

'How can a colour give you a pain?' he demanded scornfully.

'*You* needn't talk,' Evalyn retorted, feeling his defection as yet more evidence of the sea of changes with which she had to contend. 'Your room is stuffed with everything you fancy . . . a billion things . . .'

Vinson retreated, giving her one of his old winning smiles. 'It's not *stuffed* with them,' he said rather grandly. 'But it is adequately appointed . . .'

Tom raised his eyebrows and looked at Carrie, and Evalyn felt his pride.

Evalyn said crossly: 'You're always using big words.'

* * *

Annie said to her one morning: 'Will you stop moaning? If you woke up tomorrow and found it was all a mistake – that Camp Bird really belonged to someone else – how would you feel? Your parents would have to sell this lovely house; you'd get no more new dresses. You'd be back in Ouray, whining for the riches you had lost, and your poor father would be back up in those murderous mountains!

Evalyn knew this was true; it forced her to consider the contradictions in her own heart.

'The trouble with you, wee lassie,' Annie added, 'is that you want everything!'

For a while Evalyn began to worry that, as punishment for her ungrateful soul, their old precarious situation *would* return, and her beloved father would indeed be condemned to go again and again into the Imogene Basin, until the cold and altitude killed him. For a while she watched anxiously for any reversal in their fortunes. But of this there was no sign; her mother only had to mention something that she admired in her father's hearing – furs, or gowns, or *objets d'art* – and they arrived the next day.

'This is pure extravagance, Tom!' Evalyn overheard her say to him one morning, when the rustle of paper from the open door of their bedroom indicated that Carrie was opening yet another box from Gunthers. Evalyn had been about to leave the house for school, but had gone back upstairs to pick up the poetry book with which she had struggled the night before. The class had been told to learn one of Emily Dickinson's poems and she had worked hard to master the assignment, even as she reflected darkly on how poets were allowed to torture normal people with their blather.

But now, hearing her mother demur aloud about her father's latest gift, she paused in the landing, curious to hear his response.

'Carrie, my darling, do you think anything I can give you would put even the smallest dent into what the San Juan Mountains are giving *us*?'

'You shouldn't smile about it, Tom!'

Her father's reply was teasing. 'Is that superstition I hear from you, Carrie Walsh? I'm the one who's supposed to be Irish.'

'It's just that the change is so sudden,' Carrie went on, 'as though someone were playing a huge practical joke on us, and we're gullible enough to think it's real!'

Evalyn, astonished to hear her mother articulate the same kind of anxiety as she felt herself, moved closer to her parents' door.

'You must let me indulge my family, Carrie. I've dreamed about it for years. I was so afraid I had ruined everything for you all . . .'

Evalyn heard her father move across the carpet and she ducked into her own room. She found the hated poetry book and rushed downstairs, afraid of being late and having Miss Royce, the headmistress, greet her in the hall,

206

as she had recently, with a supercilious, 'Evalyn dear, this is a school, not some jamboree with ad hoc times of arrival.'

In the streetcar she thought of the day ahead of her. At least today she would know the poetry assignment by rote and if called upon to recite it, would not look foolish before the class. She hoped to avoid the contempt of Jessica Stanford, a classmate she half worshipped, half envied, for her poise and beauty, and around whom the other girls clustered like bees around their queen.

When Evalyn went through the door of the school cloakroom, Jessica was fixing her silken blonde hair before the mirror.

Evalyn, desperately trying to think of something smart or witty to say to her, heard the whisper her idol confided to one of her acolytes: 'Here comes Miss Mountain Piggy . . .' and she absorbed it, and the muffled shrieks of laughter it provoked, like a dagger to the heart.

Later, her English teacher, Miss Rannion, buxom and tightly laced, scanned the class over her spectacles.

'Are there any volunteers? Ah, Evalyn, it's good to see you put your hand up for a change.'

Evalyn stood, but found that the class had become a small sea of faces. Emily Dickinson vacated her brain, leaving her with just the first lines. Even as she said them, a shiver climbed her spine and nestled in the roots of her hair.

'Because I could not stop for Death –
He kindly stopped for me –'

She saw with strange, impersonal clarity, the sunlight shining on the desktops, the chalk dust on the blackboard, and Jessica's slanting blue eyes. Knowledge of something hidden in a time as yet unborn touched her for a moment and was gone.

She sat down heavily. 'I'm sorry, Miss Rannion. I have forgotten it . . .'

Her teacher sighed. There was a small *frisson* of amusement in the class. Someone else stood up and delivered the poem word-perfect.

In contrast to Evalyn's fortunes, Washington high society took a kindly view of the country's latest mining millionaire. Tom Walsh did not pretend to be other than a self-made man, but he came from a culture where people were not defined by money and he needed endorsement from no one.

Although she was now free of the headaches that for years had made her life a misery, Carrie's retiring nature shrank from the high-profile parties to which she found herself and her husband invited. But to the eyes of a jaded, rule-bound, Washington élite her diffidence had its own grace, as had her husband's blunt charm. There was nothing 'nouveau' about the Walshes. They remained as they had always been: decent, straightforward, delighting in wit and humour. Tom's natural presence, his generosity, drollness, his chivalrous nature and his wife's refinement, convinced an initially bemused and curious Washington society to adopt the unpretentious newcomers. Soon they were invited everywhere.

Tom was courted by politicians eager for party subscriptions. He would return home with senators and congressmen, with businessmen and builders, with geologists and metallurgists. The Walshes, in turn, began to throw lavish parties, to which Washington society came in droves.

Evalyn looked on. She was not allowed to attend these soirées, and her parents were so taken up in the busy round of their new life that she began to feel she didn't know them any more.

'I'm an invisible girl,' she told her sad, overweight reflection in the mirror. 'Nobody really sees me. I'm only Miss Mountain Piggy. I might as well be a ghost.'

John R. McLean came to dinner. One of the most powerful and richest men in America, owner of the *Cincinnati Enquirer* and intent on acquiring the *Washington Post*, John R. was inquisitive about this newest Croesus from Colorado. He was expecting, at best, a rough-hewn mining man; he found an urbane, witty, natural gentleman.

John R.'s wife, Emily, was sponsoring a dancing class for children, attended by their own son, Ned, and she pressed Carrie to send Evalyn. So Evalyn soon found herself dispatched every Saturday afternoon to the McLeans' cavernous Florentine-style villa in I Street where a dancing master, Monsieur Duambre, put a number of youngsters through their paces.

Evalyn hated it, not because of the dancing, but because of the secret, unspoken rules that everyone seemed to know automatically – except herself.

'I cannot understand what is the matter with you, Evalyn,' her mother burst out one day when Evalyn said she didn't want to go to the dancing lesson any more. 'It's a very good chance for you to learn how to dance and to meet other boys and girls of your own age.'

'I don't want to go! You can't dance with whom you want, or the way you want. You have to wait for a boy to ask you.'

'Ladies wait to be asked, Evalyn! That is one of the conventions of life.'

'Oh fiddle diddle, Mother.'

'Don't be impertinent, young lady. Off you go now. Annie will take you.'

'You're a wee scald,' Annie informed her when they were seated on the streetcar. 'Didn't you hear what I said to you before? Why can't you be grateful?'

'Of course I'm grateful. It's just that I'm not allowed to be *me* any more, and I don't know how to be anyone else!'

'There's many a one would change places with you, wee lassie, and welcome!'

But as Evalyn watched her parents being lionised, saw how her father was happy and expansive, how her reserved mother was learning to play high society hostess, she felt only a growing sense of loneliness and abandonment. Vinson seemed at a distance too; he had made new friends, was doing well at school, and was taking to Washington as though he had been born there.

One night, peering from behind her new bedroom drapes at her parents' departing guests, hearing their gaiety and laughter, Evalyn found herself wondering what they drank at these parties that made them all so happy. She heard her parents come up to bed; glanced at the carriage clock on her mantelpiece. It was 1 a.m. Because of the hour, the servants would not clear up until morning, so she decided to do some investigating. She gave her parents enough time to settle down and then she put on her dressing gown and tiptoed downstairs.

On the dining table she found empty glasses, some with brandy dregs, some containing the remains of liqueurs. She sniffed at them, tasting them with the tip of her tongue. The fiery flavours seemed worthy of further exploration and she tried the door of the liquor cabinet. It opened easily. The mysterious bottles were there before her. They seemed to whisper, *Take a little taste, Evalyn . . . What harm can it do?*

After a few exploratory sips she warmed to the task in hand. It was a bit like Goldilocks testing the beds, she thought with a giggle. Bourbon – was too 'hot' and she spat it out; sherry was too sweet; gin was disgusting; but the collection did possess one gem. It was as green as an emerald and was called crème de menthe.

After several appreciative sips she drank a small glassful. Three generous measures later she had begun to forget her woes, her tubbiness, her new school, her loneliness and homesickness for her darling Ouray. She went back to bed and slept heavily. She was thirsty when she woke and her tongue was coated with something unpleasant, but she scrubbed her teeth and helped herself at breakfast to plenty of grapefruit.

'Are you all right, Evalyn? You're looking a bit pale.'

Evalyn started. 'Oh yes, Mother . . .'

'What's happening to the crème de menthe?' her father asked quietly at luncheon one Saturday. Evalyn contained the quickening of her heart, turned innocent eyes on him, rounding them into deliberate, dramatic astonishment.

'It's either the servants,' he added, 'whom I do not suspect, or it's an 'alcoholic ghost, or,' and here he turned his penetrating blue eyes on his family, 'it's one of my children!'

'Maybe it's evaporating,' Evalyn suggested helpfully, reaching for some more mashed potato. But when she next glanced at her father, his shrewd eyes held hers and the innocence of her gaze faltered.

'Well, Evalyn,' he said quietly, 'have you something you would like to tell me? No lies now, remember.'

'I didn't do anything!' Evalyn began. But as her father's stare remained fixed, she dropped her eyes and added, 'I . . . just have . . . little drops of it . . . sometimes . . . Father . . .' Her voice trailed away and she studied the design in the damask tablecloth.

'Since when did two bottles constitute "little drops"?'

Evalyn looked at her mother, saw her shock, the thin disappointed line to her mouth that she dreaded.

'We'll lock the liquor cabinet from now on,' Tom said in a tight voice, 'which is a pity, as I would prefer not having to lock anything in this home of ours.'

Evalyn burst into tears. 'I'm sorry, Father.'

'I'm getting you a governess, young lady,' her mother said in a very even voice. 'Someone to keep an eye on you every moment that you are not in school! You're far too ready to give in to yourself.'

Evalyn dried her eyes and tried not to look mutinous. Privately she was thinking: Governess indeed! I'll soon get rid of *her*!

'Don't think you can wriggle out of this,' her father added severely. 'This person will be a fire-breathing dragon who'll soon put a halt to your gallop!'

Evalyn looked at her father from the corner of her eye. He looked back at her sternly, but as her woeful eyes met his she saw, with some satisfaction, that his lips twitched behind his moustache.

The really great thing about Father, she told herself, is that he is so hopeless at hiding his sense of humour.

That afternoon Evalyn went to her brother's room. He was practising tricks with a conjurer's set, one of his birthday presents, and looked up sympathetically at his sister.

'Look, Sis,' he said after listening to her tale of woe, 'just go along with it, and then you'll be able to convince them you can do without a governess!' He grinned and added curiously, as with a sleight of hand he produced four aces from a silk hat, 'But *why* did you guzzle the crème de menthe?'

'Because it's lovely – like peppermints on fire! You should try it!'

'No, thanks.'

'It's the first thing they've had to lock up because of their children!' Evalyn whispered, and her self-pity overflowed into tears. 'I wish I could be like you,' she added after a moment as she dried her eyes and surveyed her brother. 'They're so proud of you, Vin. You're doing well in school. You don't give trouble. I hate growing up and having to be a lady. I'm lonely here. I have no friends. I'm fat and everyone in school hates me.'

She was going to tell him about being Miss Mountain Piggy, but decided it might be dangerous. Vinson had a very good memory and she didn't want to give him any ammo.

'It can't be as bad as that!' Vinson said. 'It's just that you're taking time getting used to things. And I'm *not* perfect. I just keep remembering how sick and overworked Father used to be and I try to make him happy.'

'You do make him happy,' Evalyn said. 'The best I can do is make him laugh! And,' she added sadly, 'they're not the same thing!'

Carrie knocked and entered. She was elegant in a new pink tea gown. Evalyn had always been struck at the queenliness of her mother's carriage. She knew it was because she had had to wear a back-board and balance a glass of water on her head when she was a girl. Recently, with all the talk of turning *her* into a lady, she had begun to fear that she might expect her to do the same.

'Evalyn, so this is where you are! Annie is waiting for you. You'll be late for your dancing class at the McLeans'. Come along and change.'

Evalyn sighed, stood up and left the room. Her mother followed her to her room, took from her closet a yellow silk dress and helped her daughter into it, tied back her dark hair with white ribbon. Evalyn regarded herself in the mirror, saw a tubby young girl with a flounced hemline that reached to mid-calf, and a pair of dainty laced boots in soft black leather that covered the lower part of her legs.

'Now get your dancing shoes and your coat,' Carrie said, 'and off you go.'

Evalyn went downstairs slowly, dragging her feet on every step. Annie was in the hall, already in her hat and coat.

'Hurry up,' she said. 'We haven't got all day!'

'Will you get my dancing shoes?' Evalyn demanded in the imperious Little Rich Girl voice she sometimes tried on for size and that worked with the other servants.

'Get them yourself, you bossy little baggage,' Annie replied tartly, glancing into the French ormulu mirror near the staircase and adjusting her hat. 'I'm housekeeper here, not your personal slave.'

Evalyn found this deflating. Annie came to her and put a hand on her shoulder.

'You're always in a right dither, young lassie,' she said in her soft Scottish burr. 'What's wrong with you at all?'

'Oh, Annie, I don't want to go to the dancing class. I'd much rather go out for a ride on Dewdrop!'

'Dewdrop is in Ouray, Evalyn,' Annie replied in a serious voice, 'a thousand miles away. This is Washington and your life has changed. You have to understand that. And you *have* to learn how to dance. It is nice of the McLeans to invite you.' The timbre of her voice became conspiratorial. 'They're very big people, you know. They own a newspaper. They have an estate just outside the city, called Friendship. Isn't that a nice name?'

'It's a stupid name! And I don't care if they own the moon! I always have to dance with their son and he steps on my toes.'

Annie sighed. Evalyn put on her coat, fetched her dancing slippers, and trotted with her down the front steps to the streetcar which brought them to the 1 Street house of Mr and Mrs John R. McLean.

A knot of apprehension gathered in Evalyn's stomach as they were admitted by the butler. In the cloakroom Evalyn took off her velvet-trimmed coat, changed into her dancing slippers and went to stand by the ballroom door.

'Ah, Miss Walsh,' Monsieur Duambre said, approaching her, 'will you partner Mr McLean for ze next dance, pleeze?'

Ned McLean was a tall, dark-haired boy of fourteen, who looked as though he would rather be anywhere than on a dance floor. He brightened when he saw Evalyn, approached her and bowed with an exaggerated flourish.

'I'm glad you came,' he said into her ear when they were together on the dance floor.

'Why?' Evalyn demanded suspiciously.

'You don't make as much noise as the others when I stand on your feet!'

'Well, you'd better not stand on them today. I'm in a very bad mood!'

Ned grinned. 'What's eating you, Evalyn? You can tell me . . .'

Evalyn whispered into his ear, 'They found out I was drinking the crème de menthe.'

Ned gave a howl of laughter, lost the rhythm of the dance and his foot came down painfully on Evalyn's instep.

'I hate you, Ned McLean!' she screamed, hobbling for a chair, while Monsieur Duambre signalled to the pianist to stop playing and came forward to help her.

At that moment Ned's mother entered the room. She was wearing a grey dress that swept the floor. She looked majestic. Evalyn had met her before, and thought she was a bit frightening with her haughty carriage and her handsome face.

Her hostess now bent down and said to her, 'Evalyn, my dear, what has that bad boy done to you?'

'He broke my foot,' Evalyn cried, 'and now I'll never be able to walk on it again.'

Mrs McLean turned to her son. 'Ned, come here and apologise.'

212

'I'm sorry, Evalyn,' Ned said, approaching sulkily. 'But it's your own fault for making me laugh.'

'What was the joke?' his mother asked, eyebrows raised, an expectant smile on her lips.

Evalyn directed an imploring look at Ned.

'Ah, it wasn't anything, Mummie,' he said with a shrug. 'Evalyn is just funny. But I know what would make her better.' He turned to his guest. 'She'd like a drink! Wouldn't you, Evalyn?'

Evalyn's heart missed a beat and her face turned crimson.

'Iced lemonade is her favourite,' Ned went on slyly. 'I'll get it . . .'

Mrs McLean beamed. 'He's such a thoughtful boy,' she told Evalyn as her son made his way to the refreshment table.

Ned returned with a brimming glass. Evalyn, her momentary terror over, and pleased at being the centre of her hostess's attention, sipped her drink and rubbed her injury. Ned, in reluctant obedience to his mother, was soon piloting another girl on the dance floor.

Mrs McLean leaned over and said to Evalyn, 'Poor Ned hates being so awkward, you know. Has he really hurt your foot?'

Evalyn nodded. 'He's banjaxed it!' She stuck it out, wriggled it, then remembered to groan. 'I can barely move it!'

'I don't think you like dancing very much, do you, Evalyn?'

Evalyn looked at the formidable Mrs McLean, and detected sympathy. She relaxed a little.

'I never had dance lessons in Ouray,' she confided. 'But when Father took me into the mountains I used to dance among the trees and sing to the chipmunks.'

'But things have changed for your family,' Mrs McLean responded quietly, as though she didn't find Evalyn's confidence in the least risible. 'Your father is now one of the richest men in America, even in the world, Evalyn, and wealth brings responsibilities. And one of his daughter's responsibilities is to learn how to acquit herself in the society she will move in for the rest of her life. You will be married some day; you will be the wife of a prominent man, and a society hostess.' When her young guest only looked despondent at this prospect, Mrs McLean added, 'You would like to please your dear parents, wouldn't you?'

Evalyn nodded. 'Yes, But I'm always in trouble. Mother says I give in to myself; and it's true! I do silly things.'

'At thirteen, one does,' her hostess said. 'But one does not remain thirteen for very long. So cheer up! And when you dance, Evalyn, don't worry so much about the steps. Just listen to the music; the steps will follow.' Then Mrs McLean added conspiratorially: 'Someday soon, you must visit us at Friendship. There's a pony there who'd be delighted to meet you!'

Evalyn beamed. 'What is his name?'

'Fortune,' her hostess said.

The waltz ended; the boys and girls retreated to their respective sides of the room, looking back at each other uncertainly. Ned approached.

'Why not go back on the floor for the next dance, Evalyn?' his mother said to her young guest, 'and give the lesson another chance. Here's Ned, who needs a partner.'

Ned put out his hand and Evalyn reluctantly stood up.

'If you stand on me again,' she told him through her teeth when they reached the dance floor, 'I'm going to belt you one.'

Ned seemed to find this funny. The music commenced and they moved together fluidly.

'Very good,' Monsieur Duambre said. 'Excellent, Mr McLean . . . Miss Walsh . . . much improved . . .'

When the music stopped Ned whispered in her ear 'I shouldn't have laughed at you earlier – but if it's any consolation you're not the only one who gets at the liquor cabinet.'

Evalyn's eyes rounded, but she waited for the refreshments to be served before she asked Ned diffidently, looking over her shoulder in case anyone could overhear, 'Have you been drinking crème de menthe too?'

'Nah, that stuff is for women. Bourbon is a man's drink.'

'But what if you get caught?'

'Nothing,' Ned said airily, adding with unselfconscious arrogance something Evalyn would remember long years in the future: 'I'm a man, and men can do what they like!'

The following week Evalyn received an invitation to Friendship. Ned was having a birthday party and the young people from the dancing class had been asked.

Evalyn wore a white dress with a simple blue satin sash, and brought new white dancing slippers. She was collected by the McLean carriage.

Friendship was a huge mansion in the country just beyond Georgetown, set in several hundred acres. As the carriage swept through the gates and up the driveway Evalyn looked out at the carefully tended gardens and lawns. Her main concern was to meet Fortune, Ned's pony.

Ned seemed glad enough to leave his guests and take her down to the stables, where she was introduced to a black pony with a white blaze on his forehead and white socks. The horse smell, the coarse hairs that came away on her hands when she stroked the pony's neck, made Evalyn feel grounded again, in touch with a reality she had lost. She ran her palm down Fortune's nose, and let his rubbery lips caress her fingers.

Ned watched her. 'You're not afraid of horses, are you Evalyn?'

'No.'

'You're not afraid of anything!'

'I'm afraid of silly manners and having to be something I'm not!'

'So am I!'

They laughed together.

Ned took her to a summerhouse behind the stables that was half covered in ivy. He took a key from his pocket and unlocked the door. Inside there were cupboards and a bookcase, an armchair, a table on which rested a half-finished jigsaw. There were two chairs, and boxes and boxes of discarded toys and games.

'This is my place; no one bothers me here . . .'

'I wish I had a place like this,' Evalyn said. But, all the same, she was struck by the solitary nature of her young host's life.

'Have you been at the crème de menthe again?' Ned asked after a moment with a grin.

'No. Father has locked the liquor cabinet. Have you been at the bourbon?' she added, aware suddenly that in the clutter of Ned's private hideaway anything might be hidden.

'Ssh,' Ned said, and looked over his shoulder. 'I suppose we'd better get back,' he added with a sigh. 'My mother's guests will wondering where I've escaped to.'

'They're *your* guests,' Evalyn said. 'It's your birthday party!'

Ned turned to smile at her. 'But *I* didn't ask them. The only one I asked Mummie to invite was you!'

Evalyn enjoyed this party; she played charades with the best of them and forgot all about being tubby and a bumpkin. When the carriage came to take her home she said to her hostess: 'Thank you very much, Mrs McLean. I had a really fine time!'

'Why don't you call me Mummie, Evalyn?' Mrs McLean said. 'I feel as though we're old friends!'

Chapter Sixteen

Evalyn's new governess was Hortense Lion and she had been recommended by a reputable agency. Carrie, having interviewed her in the sunny drawing room, sent for her daughter and introduced her to her duenna. Evalyn looked at the dark-haired woman with the funny French accent with a sinking heart, but she held out her hand politely.

'How do you do?'

'*Enchantée, mademoiselle,*' the young woman said, taking the reluctant, outstretched hand delicately.

I bet she isn't really French at all, Evalyn thought darkly. I'll soon unmask her . . .

But Mamselle proved to have a command of the French language that could not have been acquired by proxy. In the mornings she would rouse her new charge by pulling off the bedclothes and announcing cheerfully, '*Alors, lève-toi, petite paresseuse,*' and in this manner Evalyn learned to rise for school with an alacrity hitherto unknown to her.

But in school there was still no end to her troubles. She felt keenly the catalogue of her imperfections. She was a poor student; she spoke with the accent of the mining towns of the West; compared to daughters of the city's patriarchs she felt herself utterly graceless. The lovely Jessica, who despised her, came to school each day in a carriage and sniffed so superciliously whenever her eyes alighted on Evalyn, that the latter now wanted to kick her shins. But the days when she could solve life's little problems with a well-directed thump were over, and alternatives had to be found.

One evening she went to her father's study, knocked, entered and stood uncertainly on the big blue and gold Aubusson rug. Her father's mahogany desk was ordered – papers in wire trays, family photographs in silver frames, including one of herself as an infant in a frilly white dress, lots of drawers she had once tried to investigate but had found locked, a big white blotter with inky hieroglyphs. Her father was dictating to Terry Wickerman, his secretary, and eyed his tubby daughter over his reading spectacles.

'Evalyn?'

'Father,' she said diffidently, 'can I ask you something?'

Tom leaned back in his chair. 'That will do for the moment,' he said to Terry. 'We'll finish it later.'

When Terry had gone to his own office through the adjoining door and had closed it behind him, Tom said, 'Is something wrong, my darling?'

'Father,' Evalyn said carefully, 'do you think you could afford a carriage for me, and a horse?'

Tom's expression wavered between hilarity and gravity.

'What do you want them for?'

Evalyn did not tell the whole truth. Instead she murmured with what she thought was the right note of yearning. 'I'd like to know what it feels like to go to school in a carriage! Other girls in my class do!'

'Girls in your class have their own private carriage?' Tom asked on a note of incredulity, raising tangled eyebrows above his amused eyes.

'Well, their family's carriage . . . But I'd like to have my own.' She shifted uncomfortably, turned her foot until her ankle almost rested on the floor.

She heard her mother's step in the hall outside and in a moment Carrie came into the room.

'Evalyn,' she said, 'I thought you were supposed to be practising your scales. I was just going to look in on you in the music room.'

Tom said with a straight face, 'Our daughter has just suggested that I provide her with a horse and carriage so she can turn up for school in style!'

Carrie looked aghast. 'Surely you're not thinking of—'

But Tom, surveying his child's eager face, remembered a time when there would have been no possibility of entertaining such a request and he could not bear to deny it.

'Sure why not, Carrie?' he said *sotto voce*. 'It's a small enough thing if she really wants it! I'll just hire it for a few terms.'

Two mornings later Evalyn, deliberately late, turned up for school sitting primly in a new blue victoria that was drawn by a pair of shining sorrel ponies. A black coachman, in silk hat and white gloves, handed her down from the carriage as though she were a duchess. In fact Evalyn had prepared for this arrival by practising hauteur before the mirror in her room, aping Mrs McLean in the tilt of her head and the proud expression on her face.

Jessica Stanford and friends saw her through the schoolroom window; Evalyn noted with secret delight how their mouths opened. Later, when she explained that she couldn't stay behind for an extracurricular class in deportment because 'her' carriage would be arriving to take her to the McLeans, she received another lesson in unearned respect. The girls flocked to look at the new victoria and Jessica Stanford was left standing alone. There were no whispers today about Miss Mountain Piggy.

That evening at supper her father said, 'Well, Evalyn, you're very quiet!

Aren't you going to tell us how it felt arriving for school in your own carriage?'

Evalyn looked around at their expectant faces: her father with his kind whimsicality; her mother, who looked concerned; Mamselle, who had already indicated it was '*très drôle*'; Vinson, who laughed and said it was a lark.

'It was very nice, Father,' she replied truthfully. 'Now the girls think I'm different. I made plenty of friends today!'

'And that made you happy?'

Evalyn sighed. 'Yes, except I can't help the feeling that if they didn't like me to begin with, they should not have liked me no matter how many carriages I had!'

'Fortune doesn't change the recipient of her bounty as much as it changes other people's attitude,' Tom said. 'All you can do is be yourself. And you will have to decide, Evalyn, if you really want to be delivered to school every morning in this rather conspicuous fashion.'

Evalyn put her elbows on the table. 'But I do! I like being "conspicuous". I wish I could dye my hair red and give them all a good fright.'

Her father laughed out loud in spite of himself. Evalyn experienced the surprised bursts of mirth she was able to elicit from him with great satisfaction. But her mother's face filled with horror.

'Over my dead body!' she exclaimed. 'If I catch you attempting anything of the kind, Evalyn, I'll give you a good hiding!'

Evalyn made a *moue*. 'I don't think you will, Mother,' she said with an artful tilt of her chin. 'It would go too much against the grain! I don't think you would give me a hiding even if I painted my face and walked to school on my hands!'

'Don't push me too far, young lady.'

'Anyway,' Evalyn said, 'I'm thirteen, too big now to be slapped – *even* by my mother.'

Tom felt the rising tension and interposed before Carrie boiled over.

'I've a bit of interesting news for you, Daughter, if you will allow me to get a word in. Next April, if you buckle down and learn French from Mamselle, I will bring you back to Europe. The President has just appointed me as a Commissioner to next year's Paris Exposition.'

Evalyn had heard of it; some of the girls in school were going with their parents to the great World Fair. She put down her dessert fork and clapped her hand to her mouth.

Vinson smiled at her from a face brimming with pride and said slowly, articulating each word, '*Our* father is going to represent the United States of America in Europe! And the Fair in Paris will be the biggest one ever . . . people and exhibits from all over the world.' He glanced at his father and added with a hint of triumph, 'And Father and I are going back to Ouray for a visit in March.'

Evalyn jumped from her chair, threw herself down on the carpet and tried to embrace her father's knees.

'Can I come? Oh, Papa, please let me come. I'll be good. I'll do anything you want. I don't mind about Paris but please bring me back to Ouray.'

'She has school!' Carrie said.

Evalyn burst into tears. 'I hate school. But if you let me come, Papa, I'll work *terribly* hard and make up the lessons and never give you and Mother any more trouble . . . for as long as I live! And I will learn French. I promise, I promise, I *promise* . . .'

Tom looked at Carrie and patted his daughter's hand in an embarrassed fashion. 'It's up to your mother.'

He turned to his son. 'I want Vinson to come because it's important for him to know something of Camp Bird. After all, unless I sell the mine, he'll have the overall management of it one day.'

Vinson's face was pink with pleasure. He looked at his sister and explained, 'Girls can't manage gold mines! They wouldn't know how.'

'Oh, Father,' Evalyn said, tears of vexation in her eyes. 'Let me come. I so love Ouray and the West.'

Tom turned to his wife. 'It would be like old times, all four of us together in Ouray. What do you say, Carrie?'

'*I* can't come, Tom,' Carrie said. 'I have two charity bazaars coming up, and I'll have to start the preparations for Paris soon. There will be a small mountain of trunks, and as for Evalyn . . .' She turned to look at her daughter consideringly.

Evalyn had resumed her seat and regarded her mother with imploring eyes.

'If I let you go to Ouray, promise me you will do your French lessons with Mamselle and behave yourself?'

'I will, Mother.'

'The reason I would even consider letting you go,' Carrie went on, 'is because I do realise how much Ouray means to you, and how infrequently you will have the chance of seeing it again. Because of that I am inclined to stretch a point!'

'Thank you, Mother.'

When supper was over Evalyn raced to find Annie, embraced her, crying aloud, 'Oh Annie, wonderful news! I'm going back to Ouray. I'm going home, I'm going *home*.'

Carrie, on her way upstairs, came upon the scene.

'Evalyn,' she said coldly, 'don't be making such an exhibition of yourself! Self-control in this life is never an option!'

Evalyn was immediately silent. Carrie proceeded to her room, aware that her child was simply waiting for her to be out of earshot before continuing her happy ebullience.

Maybe I am too hard on her, she thought as she let herself into her bedroom and closed the door. But I am so afraid for her, and of what will become of her. She thinks she can behave exactly as she did in Ouray. She doesn't understand what has happened to us. There is no going back to a normal life; we must stay in this new world, be part of it, shine in it, survive it. With wealth like ours there is no middle ground that is not too gross to think about!

She sighed. Rubbing shoulders with the rich had wrought in her a deep disquiet. It was not a disquiet based on any sense of inadequacy, for many of the people she met were neither as well read nor as educated as she was; it was one founded on a new fear. A certain *savoir-faire*, a certain panache, was all too often this new world's substitute for thought. She had expected in old money some kind of greatness. Instead, observing them at close quarters, she saw that many who possessed inherited wealth were two-dimensional, half formed, as though they inhabited a perpetual childhood. Temptation was surrounded everywhere by infinite ways of indulging it, and style was too often a substitute for morality.

And my poor child is wild and innocent and headstrong, and does not understand how she may be destroyed.

When she thought of Vinson her heart rose a little. He, at least, had some wisdom.

Chapter Seventeen

It was strange to be back in Ouray. Evalyn realised how impatient her father was to get to the mine when he bundled them straight out of the train and into the stagecoach with six horses that was waiting for them at the depot. This was one of the Camp Bird stages that regularly brought the gold ingots down from the mine to the railroad for shipping to the mint in Denver.

It was twilight and the misty Amphitheatre was surreal with 'alpenglow' and white with snow. There was no time for Evalyn to visit the town and see her friends.

The Canyon Creek Road had been freshly gritted, but it was still a narrow, dangerous route, and Evalyn, who had never travelled it by coach before, felt her stomach lurch with terror as she looked out at the precipitous drop beside her. So she concentrated on the horses labouring between the shafts, on the bouncing harness that left patterns in their sweat.

But soon the travellers' ears were filled with another sound, one Evalyn had often thought of in Washington: the voice of Camp Bird itself. As they approached it became louder and louder – the rhythmic pounding of the stamp mill, the clanking of the aerial tramway, and their echoes resounding from the canyon walls. Tom became immediately silent, his face serious, his eyes half closed, as though he were listening to every nuance of the cacophony that represented the rewards of his persistence, intuition, and long years of toil.

As they turned the last curve in the road the brilliance of a huge electric arc light, suspended more than one hundred and fifty feet above the ground, illuminated everything with its harsh, bluish light.

'There's the new mill,' Tom said, pointing to the huge structure with a long sloping roof.

'But there are so many new buildings, Father!' Vinson said.

'Yes, new storerooms, retort room, assay office, new houses for the manager and assistant manager . . .'

The three-storey miners' hotel stood out, its windows lit, its snow-covered roof brilliant in the blaze of the arc light.

'Why have you put up such a huge electric light over everything, Father?'

'Because this is a *gold* mine. The work of the mine and the mill never stops. And day and night, winter and summer, the place must be protected. The watchmen must be able to see who is entering and leaving Camp Bird.'

'Can we stay at our old house, Father?'

'No, Evalyn. There is a cottage waiting for us at the mine.'

'But I want to see my friends.'

'Of course you'll see them.'

In the morning Evalyn got up when the first light crept over her bedroom windowsill in the new cottage at Camp Bird. She donned a heavy woollen sweater and a pair of pants with suspenders she had found in a closet, rolled up the trouser legs and regarded her reflection with delight, sticking her hands in the trouser pockets and sauntering up and down in front of the mirror. Then she tiptoed into Mamselle's room to tell her that she was going down for breakfast and that there was no need for her to bother getting up just yet. She found her governess wrapped in her warm dressing gown, gazing from behind her curtains at the clapbord house opposite. Evalyn followed her glance and saw Mr Cahill, the assistant manager of the Camp Bird, shaving by his bathroom window.

'What are you spying on Mr Cahill for, Mamselle?'

Mamselle laughed. 'I am not spying, I am admiring. He is a handsome man, no?'

'I'll tell him you think so,' Evalyn said. 'He'll be joining us for breakfast.'

'Do not tell him zuch a thing . . .' The governess leaned back suddenly and stared at Evalyn. 'Where did you get zose awful clothes? Get out of them at once. You are a girl, not zome kind of working man!'

'Dresses are useless up here. I'm going up on the tram!'

'*Mon Dieu,*' her governess whispered, casting her gaze back through the window, this time to where the aerial tramlines crossed two miles of valley to the white rim of the mountain basin. It was from there the ore was shipped down in tram cars to the stamp mills that filled the canyon with their muffled thunder. Men could be seen riding the empty cars up to the top of the basin.

'You do not have to come with us, Mamselle.'

The governess looked relieved. 'But you might fall out! You would be killed! Have you asked your father?'

'Not yet,' Evalyn grinned. 'Vin and I are going to wait till he's busy!'

Downstairs, a few minutes later, both Jim Cahill and the manager of Camp Bird, John Benson, made their appearance in the stove-warmed dining room. Tom welcomed them to table. One of the chefs from the miners' hotel had come to cook breakfast. The air was full of the scents of cooking and coffee.

Evalyn loved the presence of the men at the breakfast table. She loved the sense of their strength and their confidence. Vinson sat at one end of the table and listened to what they were saying, almost as though he were a man himself. Her father was asking about some new workings, and the conversation was animated.

'It will connect with the upper hoist,' Jim Cahill said, 'just above the second level.'

'Father, what's a hoist?' Vinson asked.

'It's a lift, Vinson, inside the mountain. It carries the men down into the workings and back again. We had a problem last year with one of them. A poor man lost his hand!'

'Oh, Father, now he will not be able to work.'

'That is true, but I have looked after him. He and his family will want for nothing.'

When the door opened and Mamselle appeared the men stood up. Tom introduced her; she smiled flirtatiously at each of them in turn. She was smelling of cologne and wearing a woollen dress with a tight bodice. When she was seated, Evalyn noticed how Jim Cahill's eyes dwelled occasionally on her governess's bosom, while she looked at him through her lashes and gave him the merest hint of a smile.

After breakfast Evalyn and Vinson went with their father to his office. Tom sat down in his wooden swivel chair and was soon immersed in the matters that awaited his attention. The children looked through the windows at the small town that had taken shape outside, and particularly at the steel cables above them bringing the laden ore containers down to the mill.

'Father, can we go up on the tramway?' Vinson asked softly.

'*Please*, Father . . .' Evalyn echoed.

Tom had work to do, but he did recognise that the children, if only to keep them out of mischief, had to be entertained. He sent for John Benson.

'John, when you're going up top, will you take these two with you on the cable car?'

'Sure.'

Tom turned to his son and daughter. 'Now, wrap up in warm jackets, with those woollen helmets your mother packed, and gloves, so that not one inch of skin is exposed. And do *everything* Mr Benson tells you.'

John Benson took the children to the platform high up on the mill wall – the terminus of the cable trolley – and saw them safely into a tram car that had just disgorged its load of ore into the mill. He got in behind them, put an arm around each of them and told them to sit still and to grip the edge.

A minute or so later, the car swung out over the canyon.

Evalyn shut her eyes; her stomach felt as though it had been left behind and, for a moment, she was afraid she would be sick. But as the car clanked its way upwards, she opened her eyes and peeped over the rim of the container that swayed high above the canyon floor. The icy wind whistled, making her glad of the warm hat that covered her ears and the tight, high collar that protected her neck. Beside her, Vinson was gaping at the trams that passed them on the sister cables, bringing the grey quartz with its precious ore down to the mill.

When they got to the top of the mountain John Benson supervised his charges' disembarkation and brought them into the shelter of the loading dock, where the tram cars, as they arrived, were filled. The air was full of dust and the sound of rock clanking into the bins. But, as they moved into the shelter of the mountain, the bitter air became warmer, and they took off their hats and gloves and stuffed them into their pockets.

John signalled to a foreman. 'Look after the children, Mike. I'll be half an hour. This is Mr Jones,' he told the children. 'Stay with him and do whatever he tells you.'

Men, grimy and dust-covered, were coming up in a steel lift.

When John Benson was gone Vinson said to the foreman, 'Can we go down in the hoist?'

'I suppose so,' the grimy foreman said with a grin. 'But it's a long way to the bottom – more than a hundred feet.'

'We don't care,' Evalyn said stoutly.

They stepped into the small enclosure, and the hoist clanked and brought them quickly to the bowels of the mountain. They stepped out, and the lift was called away to the surface.

It was strange to be marooned down here, far from the sunlight. The tunnel had a narrow-gauge rail track intended for ore cars, and was lit by dim electric light. Around them was the plink-plonk of dripping water and the sounds of work in an adjoining level. Evalyn and Vinson walked a little distance on the rails, looked around them, and tried to work out exactly where they were inside the canyon wall.

'Have you seen enough?' Mike Jones asked. He walked back with them and raised his hand to pull the signal for the hoist.

'Don't bother about the lift,' Evalyn said. She indicated the vertical ladder running up the side of the lift shaft. It was bolted to the rock face and intended for emergencies.

'We can climb back up on this!' she added in a surge of bravado. She remembered Vinson's remarks about girls not being able to manage a gold mine and she wanted to show him, and this foreman for good measure, that girls were people to be reckoned with.

'No, you certainly can't.'

Evalyn turned on him with the icy hauteur she had been practising.

'But we *want* to climb up!' she said imperiously. 'And it's *our* mine!'

'Please, Mr Jones,' Vinson said, and smiled at the man.

The foreman was good at mining; but he was not good at dealing with spoiled kids. He was afraid that if he refused they would report unfavourably on him to their father, and he wanted to hold on to his job at Camp Bird. There was no other mine where recreational facilities were provided, and where you returned to a top-class hotel at the end of your shift. There was no other mine where shifts were only eight hours long, with a four-hour interval between them to allow the dust to settle and spare the lungs. So in a moment of weakness he decided to let the Walsh children have their way. He did not pause to consider whether the children would have the strength to maintain a grip on a vertical steel ladder.

Initially Evalyn and Vinson tackled the ladder with gusto. But as the ground receded below them, and the top of the ladder seemed further away than ever, it became clear to Evalyn that this particular escapade was definitely what her father would have called a 'second-best plan'. Vinson, climbing ahead of her, missed his footing, and clung for a heart-stopping moment to the rung above, before regaining the courage to go on.

She looked down and froze. The ground seemed miles away now. Immediately below her on the ladder was the foreman. She glimpsed his sweaty face, but did not know that he was cursing himself for a fool.

'Don't look down,' he commanded her in a strained voice. 'We'll be at the next level in a minute. Keep going.'

But the rungs of the ladder were cold and wet, and Evalyn found her hands too small for the work required of them. Vinson, ahead of her, was moving more and more slowly.

'I hate this ladder,' he whispered suddenly, his voice laden with desperation. Even as he spoke, the rung from which he had just removed his weight, parted company with the ladder and clanged to the bottom of the shaft, sending an echo that reverberated like a warning. Vinson held on, but he wept with fright. Evalyn ducked the falling rung, and clung more tightly to the one in her hands.

'I can't go on . . .' she said in a frightened voice, aware that her next handhold was gone.

'It's all right,' Mike Jones said in a deliberately calm voice. 'I'll push you and you reach for the rung above it. It's OK, Vinson,' he added. 'We're nearly there.'

Vinson moved up another rung and Mike Jones heaved himself up to lift Evalyn, and in this way she was able to access the next step.

'Good girl, good girl . . . Not many more now,' he added as cheerfully as he could, although he was half blinded by the cold sweat that covered his whole body, and made his palms slick. 'Hold on tight and you'll be fine!'

Evalyn, stifling her own fear, tried to pretend they were on the attic stairs in the old house in Ouray. But the dripping of water and the echoes in the shaft made such feats of the imagination impossible.

When they got to the service tunnel strong arms were waiting to lift the children to safety.

John Benson, his grey moustache bristling, yelled, 'You're fired, Jones. You should be shot!'

Vinson saw the foreman's expression. His sense of justice recoiled. He remembered only too keenly how he and his sister had cajoled this man into letting them climb the ladder; but as he was about to protest his father came rushing up. Tom was panting, his hair wild and his face white. He put his arms around his children and stared at his erstwhile employee with hot, resentful eyes.

'You nearly killed my children, Jones!' he told the foreman who, ashamed of his stupidity, was hanging his head. 'You will never work in this mine again, or any other mine either!'

Tom took Evalyn and Vin by the hand and led them away, brought them down in the tram car in silence and then to his office, one big hand on each of their shoulders. But once the office door was closed he hugged them fiercely to him, the force of his relief like a contained storm.

'Oh, thank God,' he whispered. 'Thank God you're all right!'

'We're fine, Father,' Evalyn whispered.

'You promised you would behave yourself,' he said sternly when he had regained his composure. 'And you have let me down. You knew better than to try to climb that ladder.'

'I'm very sorry, Father.'

'It was my fault,' Vinson said. 'Please don't fire Mr Jones, Father,' he added, and the tears that he had been ashamed to shed coursed down his cheeks. 'I begged him to let us do it. He didn't want to. I thought it would be a lark.'

Tom listened. His face softened and he put a hand on his son's head.

'It was me he was afraid of!' Evalyn said. 'I kept staring at him like this,' and she beetled her brows, and stared out crossly from beneath them, folding her arms.

'I think you're going to frighten a lot of people, Evalyn, before you've finished! But no matter what you said or did, Jones is a grown man and he knew the risks.'

Later, Vinson renewed his pleading. He hit on a strategy he was certain would make his father change his mind,

'His family will be *hungry*, Father.'

Tom's face changed subtly. 'All right,' he said eventually. 'Jones can stay, but neither of you is setting foot in this mine again.'

'But, Father—'

'No buts. From now on when we visit Ouray you will stay below in the town!'

The following day Mamselle brought Evalyn down to Ouray. Evalyn could not wait to see her old home, and hurried ahead of her governess along the wooden sidewalk of Fifth Avenue, on whose planks she had so often skipped, and every crack of which she knew like an old friend. The house looked just the same – gentle and unassuming, with its porch and two dormer windows, and picket fence, as though waiting for them to come home. She went to her old school, told Mamselle to wait in the hall, and walked right into her old class. Every face in the room turned to stare.

Mrs Hurlburt said, 'Well, how are you, Evalyn Walsh? Are you coming back to live with us after all?'

Evalyn enjoyed being the centre of attention. The class clamoured in asking questions. She told them about Washington and her new school and even about the blue victoria and the coachman. It was in the recounting of this that the atmosphere began to change; she did not know how it happened but by the time she had finished the story the class was silent and she was no longer one of them. She experienced this transformation as though bands of ice were being strapped around her heart.

She tried to reverse it; she joked about the house in Le Roy Phelps Place, the servants, but only made things worse.

'I'd better go,' she said lamely at last. 'My governess is waiting.'

There was a gasp from her former classmates.

When school was over she waylaid her old friend Faith Thompson. But Faith now looked at her carefully as though there was a mark upon her. The girl glanced sideways at Mamselle, smiled shyly at Evalyn and, saying that she had to help her father in the drug store, hurried away, looking back just once over her shoulder with an apologetic half-smile.

It was the same with all Evalyn's friends. They were polite, but newly diffident, as though they no longer spoke her language.

Why does no one want me any more? Evalyn thought. I haven't done anything terrible, and I love them all so much! She looked around at Mount Hayden, Mount Abrams, the red Amphitheatre, and told them silently and sadly, 'I should never have left you. But I won't be able to see much of you any more. I have to be a rich girl now.'

Only Dewdrop, when she went to see him in the Ashenfelter stables, treated her the same as always, and rubbed his velvet nose on her shoulder. Evalyn gave him the sugar lumps he loved. She wanted to go riding but, as Mamselle couldn't ride, Tom said she would have to wait until the next time she came back to Ouray. 'I don't want you riding alone, Evalyn!'

'But why not, Father? I know every road . . .'

'Be said by me, Evalyn,' he said sternly. 'I'm a busy man.'

227

Mamselle, who was excited at the prospect of going to Paris, talked incessantly of clothes. She discussed the fashions in French, pointing to various outfits in magazines, encouraging Evalyn to repeat some phrases after her.

'*Voilà une robe . . . et voilà des bijoux . . .*'

In the picture a wasp-waisted woman in a chiffon gown, tight sleeves and a flounce of lace above the wrist, jewels at her throat, diamond rings on her hand, reclined on a chaise longue.

'I like the bijoux,' Evalyn said.

'*J'aime les bijoux,*' Mamselle corrected. 'Say it in French. You promised your mother you would make an effort.'

Evalyn obeyed, but the Frenchwoman seemed unimpressed. On the other hand she seemed very receptive to the admiring glances she was receiving from Jim Cahill when she stood at the window and watched him cross the compound.

That night Evalyn heard Mamselle's door opening, heard the creak of the stairs, heard the back door close. She got out of bed and looked out of the window. Her governess was furtively crossing the small open space between the cottage and the assistant manager's house. The door of the latter opened mysteriously to admit her.

What's she visiting Mr Cahill for at this hour? she wondered. She stayed by the window, but the house next door remained in darkness and she went back to bed.

Vinson's scream, coming from the adjoining room, jolted her out of returning sleep.

'Mother! *Mother!*' he was calling in a voice filled with horror. Evalyn ran to his room but her father got there before her.

'It's all right, my son, it's only a dream . . .'

But Vinson, looking up at them from his pillows, kept shaking his head.

'Mamselle must be a deep sleeper!' Tom commented, when there was no sign of the governess.

'She isn't asleep. She's gone to visit Mr Cahill.'

Evalyn saw her father start, and look at her strangely. 'Is she indeed?'

'What did you dream about?' Evalyn demanded at breakfast.

'I can't remember. All I know is that it was about us.' He looked meaningfully at his sister. 'I mean you and me, Evalyn.'

When Mamselle still did not appear, Evalyn said she would go and wake her.

'Mamselle has left us,' her father said curtly.

The two children turned to stare at him.

'*Left* us, Father?'

228

'I met her early this morning,' Tom continued. 'She was returning from a . . . walk. She decided she would take the first train to Denver. Now come along, children. You'll have to amuse yourselves in my office for an hour or two, and you are not – and I repeat *not* – to move out of it without my permission. Is that perfectly clear?'

'Yes, Father.'

Tom looked at his two youngsters anxiously. High time, he thought, to take them home.

He rose from the table. There was something he wanted to set in train before his return to Washington. Ouray needed a library. There was an Indianapolis architect by the name of Keith who had been recommended to him. He would write and ask him to draw up plans and lay them before Mayor George Scott and Ouray City Council. It would be a fitting gift to the town he loved.

Chapter Eighteen

Paris was another world.

The Walshes had taken almost the whole of the second floor of the Elysée Palace Hotel on the Champs-Elysées. When they had slept away the fatigue of their long journey, Evalyn and Vinson ran from room to room, looking down at the cobbled boulevards with their rows of trees and smart carriages, glimpsing the white archway of the Arc de Triomphe from their parents' suite. They went out accompanied – with their parents for the first glimpse of the Exposition and with Annie to the gardens of the Louvre – chafing at the restrictions placed once more on their lives. Thousands of people, they were told, were converging on the city and they must not go out alone. In their parents' anxious voices were unspoken warnings.

'They're afraid someone will run away with you!' Annie told them. 'Ever hear of kidnapping?'

They laughed. 'No one would dare!' Evalyn exclaimed. 'I'd scratch their eyes out.'

Annie sighed. 'Aye, but they'd soon draw your little talons. You're only a wee lass.'

Vinson quickly made friends with an English boy called Jonathan Ainsworth, who was staying at the hotel with his parents. The family were removing to Le Touquet for the summer and invited Vin to join them.

'I'd much rather go with Jonathan than stay in Paris. We can go fishing and swimming and everything.'

Tom and Carrie made appropriate inquiries before giving their consent, and soon Evalyn found herself alone. She sensed the fever in the air, watched the fashionable throngs on the Champs-Elysées from the second-floor windows, regarded her lonely reflection in the mirror and munched chocolates to cheer herself up.

Paris was in exhibition fever. A whole *quartier* – the *Gros Caillou* – had been barred to traffic and made over to the *Exposition Universelle*. The area taken up by the Exposition included the Champs-Elysées, the Esplanade des Invalides, the Quais, the Trocadero and the Champs-de-Mars. Lavish new *palais*, purpose-built to house the exhibits from all over the world, adorned these locations with almost Babylonian splendour. They had great staircases and galleries, cupolas topped with fluttering pennants and national flags. On the Champs-de-Mars, in the shadow of the Eiffel Tower, from which the Tricolour fluttered proudly over Paris, was the *Palais des Mines et de la Métallurgie*. Among the exhibits here was one of a Colorado gold mine called Camp Bird.

The weather was glorious. Easter Sunday and Monday brought out the crowds with their picnic baskets. There had not been an exposition in Paris for eleven years, and the Parisians entered into the spirit of it with relish. They queued patiently at the entrances, found shady corners in which to eat, before riding with exclamations of delight on two of the exhibition's wonders – the moving pavement and the electric trolley that carried visitors from one location to another.

Tom and Carrie had a full schedule; a high profile position left them little time for private enjoyment. They gave dinner parties, *soirées musicales*, and banquets at the Ritz, entertaining politicians, Parisian society and distinguished visitors.

Annie was more than happy to accompany Evalyn to the Exposition, being as curious as the next to sample the delights of the spectacle on their doorstep. She took her young charge to *Le Vieux Paris* – a reconstruction of Medieval Paris built on the Seine by the Pont de l'Alma – with half-timbered houses and crenellated towers. It stretched as far as the new *passerelle* built as a temporary crossing of the Seine opposite the *palais* of the Land and Sea Armies.

'Do you realise that people lived in houses just like these, Annie, long before America had ever been heard of?'

'Of course I do, you silly bairn! Let's go and find the Camp Bird exhibit? I can't wait to see it!'

The Palace of Mines and Metallurgy was a sumptuous building with arcaded galleries, and cupolas with rows of pennants moving lazily in the breeze. Within a few minutes Evalyn and Annie found the exhibit they were looking for: 'Camp Bird Mine, Ouray, Colorado, USA.'

Evalyn felt the catch at her heart. Here in the middle of the great Paris Exposition was a working model of Camp Bird! But, among the crowd viewing it, only she and Annie knew the years of effort that had gone into its discovery, knew that Thomas F. Walsh, so respectfully referred to on the printed legend, had almost died in the attempt. She watched how the 'ore' was loaded into the mini stamp mill and pulverised, then passed through the amalgam process to extract the gold which was finally turned into ingots.

'Look,' Annie whispered with delight, 'there's the miners' hotel and the Ashenfelter stables and the dairy, and the manager's house – and even Mount Abrams. It's so true to life!'

Evalyn read the printed legend. 'The property of Mr Thomas F. Walsh, who discovered it in 1896, Camp Bird produces an average of $5,000 worth of gold each day.'

'Do you see that, Rawlinson?' someone behind Evalyn exclaimed in a languid voice. 'The eighth wonder of the world – a *private* gold mine! A daily fortune! What proportion would you say goes into Walsh's pocket?'

Evalyn, horrified to hear her father under discussion, strained to hear the response.

'At least sixty per cent of it, I would say!' a voice replied. 'After all, they estimate his annual income at $1.2 million – possibly the largest on earth!'

There was a low whistle. 'It's practically indecent!' The same voice then enquired with a subdued laugh, 'I say, he wouldn't have any unwed daughters, would he?'

Evalyn registered the voices as English and turned to stare at their owners. Both men wore grey silk cravats, top hats and sported neat moustaches with thin, waxed ends; one of them had a silver-handled cane.

She looked from one to the other with scorn and announced at the top of her voice, 'If you had risked *your* life every single day for twenty years you mightn't have so much to say about things you obviously know nothing about.'

Annie tugged at her arm. 'Evalyn, for God's sake!'

Evalyn allowed herself to be pulled away. She heard a whisper, 'Good Lord, isn't that the Walsh heiress?'

Annie pinched her arm and hissed in her ear, 'Don't be making an exhibition of yourself.'

'But it makes me mad to hear people say stupid things about Father,' Evalyn hissed back.

She looked over her shoulder as Annie dragged her off. The two elegant Englishmen were gazing after her in smiling bemusement. Suddenly, painfully, she felt like one of the exhibits herself; she had become someone she didn't know, someone people whispered about, someone who was known as The Walsh Heiress.

'Why can't we go for a nice long walk and see Paris? I mean the real Paris . . . where nobody knows us?' she said in Annie's ear. '*Outside* the Exposition.'

Annie was glad of any excuse to get Evalyn away from the possibility of further provocation.

'All right,' she said. 'But keep your big mouth shut!'

They slipped out of the building and in a few minutes had left the Exposition.

Evalyn's energy fed on the sights and sounds of the city. The Parisiennes were all in summer clothes with hems and trains sweeping the pavement, high-necked lace collars, flat hats with piles of tulle or feathers, balanced as if by magic on upswept coiffures; all of them wore gloves. The men sported silk hats, bowlers or straw boaters; they had narrow ties and wing collars; many carried canes. But the real romance for Evalyn was Paris itself: the high buildings with wrought-iron balconies; the carriages – glossy black, bright yellow, dark blue; the horse-drawn omnibuses, rattle of wheels and clop of hoofs; the smell of horse dung that reminded her of home. But, unlike Washington, Paris had an atmosphere that seemed to say, 'Pleasure is not an option. It is life's only purpose.'

Thoughts of Washington brought memories of the 1 Street house of the McLeans and the Saturday dance class, and Ned; of Friendship where he had shown her his favourite haunts while she had pitied him for his queer, lonely life.

I never imagined I'd miss Washington, she thought. Why do you only see things when you are away from them?

An old woman in a tattered black dress, propped against a wall, held out an enamelled tin cup in which she rattled a few coins. As Evalyn passed she saw that the cup was similiar to the one her father used to take with him on his trips into the mountains. She darted back and deposited into it all the money in her pocket. The woman's sunken eyes met hers in brief astonishment.

'How much did you give her?' Annie demanded.

Evalyn shrugged. 'I don't know. The money Papa gave me this morning! About five hundred francs.'

'He shouldn't give you money like that!'

'He thought it would last us for a while.'

'And what are we supposed to live on while we wander around this big foreign city?'

'We'll live on you, Annie. Father will give it back to you!'

'I've only four francs . . .'

Suddenly Annie gasped, clapped her hand to her mouth.

'What is it?'

The housekeeper was staring at a poster advertising some kind of music hall called the Moulin Rouge, in which dancing girls lifted their skirts and displayed their frilly underwear to a male audience.

'Don't look!' Annie cried. 'It's scandalous!'

But almost every *colonne Moris* they passed had the same poster, and Evalyn absorbed the image avidly.

It was already lunchtime when they passed the Place Pigalle; the pavement brasseries were filled with Parisiens and lunching tourists, and the warm air was redolent of soup, garlic and fresh bread.

'I'm starving,' Evalyn announced. 'Let's have lunch.'

'I haven't enough money! But at least we can sit down . . .'

But Evalyn was staring at the mock windmill sails that adorned the front of a building in the shape of a mill, and the legend that said 'Le Moulin Rouge'.

'Isn't that the place where the dancers show their knickers?' she whispered to Annie. 'Let's take a look inside?'

'Over my dead body!'

Two young women with rouged faces and bright red hair walked by, challenging men with their eyes. Every man at the pavement tables looked after them, some smiling, some calling out compliments, *'Alors, on y va?'*

'Stop staring!' Annie said. 'Those women are streetwalkers!'

'What do they do?'

Annie's face assumed a grim expression. 'Never mind what they do, missy. I'm getting us a cab.'

That night Evalyn thought about her day. She remembered the street-walkers and their wonderful life of strolling around, painting their faces, dying their hair, and being admired by everyone.

The following morning, just before she left the hotel with Annie, she licked the red covers of a Baedeker and put the colour on her cheeks.

'Dear God,' Annie whispered when she saw her thirteen-year-old charge on the street in broad daylight, 'what have you done to youself? You've got a face like a tart!'

But Evalyn was busy mimicking what she had seen the day before. A man approached along the pavement and she gave him the coy glance employed by yesterday's beautiful redheads. He stopped, turned his head, smirked and raised his black silk hat with a prurient familiarity that made Annie pale. Then he turned and began to walk towards them, still smiling, his hot eyes fixed on Evalyn.

'Scat!' Annie cried, raising her voice and waving her right arm at him, as though he were one of the toms that used to sneak into their yard in Ouray to pay their respects to the neighbouring cat.

She seized Evalyn by the arm and propelled her back to the hotel, muttering under her breath.

'I was only doing a bit of acting,' Evalyn protested, trying to pull away. But Annie had her in a death grip and wouldn't let go. She marched her straight up to her mother's room. Carrie was eating breakfast in a Second Empire bed, propped up with pillows under a white canopy, her plaited hair over her shoulder. She started and stared at her daughter.

'Evalyn, what on earth have you got on your face?'

'You should have seen her, Mrs Walsh!' Annie cried. 'She did that to her face when I wasn't watching, and when we were outside on the street she looked at a man with . . . just like . . .' She checked herself, glanced at

Evalyn and lowered her voice. 'I can't be responsible for her if she goes on like this! The truth is – she's just not safe!'

Carrie paled. She pushed away her tray.

'Wash that stuff off your face immediately, Evalyn,' she said in a cold, dangerous voice. 'And come back here when you're fit to be seen. I'm going to talk to your father!'

When Evalyn returned to her mother's room it was empty, but the connecting door to her father's dressing room was open. She heard his voice, low and soothing.

'She's just an unsuspecting child, Carrie! It was just silliness . . .'

'That kind of silliness is dangerous! It's time we put our foot down, Tom. This is *serious*. Do you realise what might have . . . if Annie hadn't been there? I dread to think of it.'

Evalyn crept away. What's all the fuss about? she thought. Anyone would think I'd robbed a bank!

She went to Annie, but found scant comfort.

'They'll punish you now, miss,' Annie said. 'But as I am chained to you by the ankle, they'll punish me too!'

Two days later Evalyn found herself with Annie in a carriage that was taking them across Paris. It was humid and overcast. The scents of the city came powerfully through the open carriage windows: horse dung and urine, coffee, and the perfume of blooms where *fleuristes* plied their wares on the pavements. Then the urban scenery changed; there were no longer elegantly dressed people, just tired-looking, badly dressed crowds. Evalyn wanted to tell the driver to stop so she could get out and look around, but the driver had his instructions and the carriage bowled along smartly. He was to deliver his passengers to the Couvent du Sacré-Coeur, in the rue de Picpus. And Evalyn had had such a talking-to from her mother that she was nervous about disobeying her.

'I'm sending you to a convent for a while, Evalyn, one recommended by a friend. Your father and I have no time to superintend you, and you will be safe with the nuns. And you will receive daily French lessons!'

'But I'm perfectly safe as it is, Mother!'

Carrie had turned stern eyes on her and said in a dangerous voice, 'You will obey me in this, Evalyn.'

The convent at 35 rue de Picpus was a sandstone building abutting directly on to the pavement, with barred ground-floor windows. But inside it was all parquet floors and tiles, and smelled of beeswax. In a niche by the stairs a statue of the Sacred Heart was surrounded by vases of deep blue irises. A young nun came to meet them; conducted them up a curved wooden staircase to a room at the back of the building. It overlooked a garden with gravel walks, and the barely glimpsed monuments of a graveyard. Except for a crucifix hung high on the wall, the floor and walls of the room were bare. There were two narrow beds with white coverlets. Laid out on each was a plain white dress with a short white veil.

A horrible suspicion dawned on Evalyn. She turned to the nun. 'What are those for?'

'*Ils sont pour vous,*' the soft-spoken sister said. '*Il faut vous habiller dans cette robe là,*' and she held up a dress and thrust it at Evalyn.

'I can't wear this!' Evalyn said with a nervous giggle when the nun was gone. 'Do you realise what it is, Annie? It's a religious habit!'

'Prison uniforms!' Annie said sourly. 'Call a spade a spade.' She looked around grimly at the spartan chamber where the two beds took up most of the wall space. 'I hope you don't mind sharing, miss,' she added, 'but it's been arranged the better to keep an eye on your highness!'

'I don't mind sharing with you, Annie,' Evalyn said hotly, 'but I don't understand why I have to be treated like a criminal. I haven't done anything wrong!'

Her voice trembled; Annie put her arms around her.

'Of course you haven't, you poor silly thing. But you can't go around aping every tart you see. Your mother is distracted over you. She's only thinking of your safety, and hoping you'll learn a wee bit of French.'

'No, she's not, Annie!' Evalyn replied in a low voice. 'She would much rather be rid of me.'

The days passed and the newcomers entered, after a fashion, into convent life. Annie retained her dour Scots perspective: the place was heathen, she said, a den of Popery. But Evalyn decided this experience was so strange that she might as well act the part.

'I will be a little nun!' she told Annie. 'It's better than being bored!'

Annie looked on askance as Evalyn, in her white habit, crept quietly along the polished corridors, dropped her eyes, curtsied to the Mother Superior, joined her hands and bowed her head under her white veil. In the chapel she looked up at the vaulted ceiling, at the pink, green and blues in the high stained-glass windows, at the flickering candles, at the white backs of the nuns, ghostlike in prayer. She heard the mellow sound of the Angelus that came from the bell above her head. She invented dramatic translations for the Latin inscription '*Fiat illud quod tam sitio*' that adorned one of the chapel walls.

She soon realised with some satisfaction that she was creating quite an impression. This newfound sense of visibility encouraged her to work at her French lessons, and she made progress.

When I came here, she thought, observing her new surroundings behind downcast eyes, they assumed I was some kind of delinquent. They didn't know they had a saint on their hands. When Mother gets my report she'll realise how much she has wronged me!

She waited avidly for reprieve, but two weeks passed and the short letters she received from her parents did not evince any great hurry to spring her. Instead she read, in the newspaper that Annie had bribed from a lay sister, of the private dinner party her father had given for distinguished guests. He had converted a steamer on the Seine into a floating palace, at an estimated cost of $40,000.

'For one dinner party!' Annie sniffed. 'Your father is mad!'

'He's doing it for the honour of America!' Evalyn said hotly. 'He is not showing off!'

But the knowledge that her parents were the talk of the French capital only increased her loneliness. With lives like theirs, it whispered, why should they even remember a wilful daughter?

'*Tu es une bonne fille*,' the Mother Superior told Evalyn one day in the garden, patting her hands. The old nun used a Bath chair, usually pushed, as now, by the same little sister who had shown Evalyn and Annie to their room on their first day.

'*Merci, ma mère*,' Evalyn replied, keeping her eyes on the gravel and the edge of the formal flowerbeds.

'You like it here?' the old nun said in English.

Evalyn shrugged. 'It's fine,' she replied, unwilling to be rude.

'This is an interesting place, Evalyn,' the nun went on, 'historic even. Have you seen the special graveyard?'

'No, *ma mère*.'

'Well, come along, child and I will show it to you.'

The graveyard was separated from the garden by a wall. Evalyn accompanied her guide, and the young nun opened the squeaking iron gate. As Evalyn tried to read the inscriptions on the tombs it dawned on her why this was no ordinary cemetery; all of the names were those of counts and princesses, duchesses and barons. Towards the back of the cemetery was a simple stone slab towards which the nun directed Evalyn's attention. She saw the inscription; the name leaped up at her. She turned excitedly to the Mother Superior.

'But he was important to America, *ma mère* . . . Lafayette! Is he really here?'

'Yes, Evalyn. The Marquis de La Fayette is buried here.'

Evalyn indicated another gate, behind which were simple grassy mounds.

'What is that place?'

'Do not ask my child. It will give you dreams!'

Evalyn said to Annie that evening, pointing out their window towards the cemetery. 'Lafayette is buried a few hundred yards away from us!'

'I know,' Annie said. 'I've seen the place while you were sucking up to the nuns. But I bet they didn't tell you that in the locked cemetery behind him is the mass grave of thirteen hundred headless corpses. While you were playing Little Saint Evalyn I was finding out about this dump from the porter. He speaks English almost as well as I do. We're surrounded by ghosts, my wee girl. All those bodies were brought from the guillotine – which was just down the road! Their heads were brought later in sacks and thrown in on top of the bodies! The streets around here must have been running with blood!'

That night Evalyn woke in terror, her heart pounding. The eyeless sockets of thirteen hundred skulls were staring at her.

She woke Annie, who said groggily: 'It's just a nightmare. Go back to sleep, for God's sake, and let the rest of us get a few winks!'

But Evalyn was out of bed, and already slipping in beside her companion.

'I have to get out of here,' she whispered, clutching at Annie's hand. 'I cannot live here any more. I'll tell Mother Superior in the morning. She will send a message to Mother.'

After breakfast Evalyn went to the Mother Superior's office.

'*Ma mère*,' she said, bobbing a courtesy, 'I would like to talk to you.'

'Is it a spiritual matter, *ma petite*?'

The voice was so gentle that Evalyn was certain she was on to a winner, so she inclined her head and murmured, 'Yes.'

The nun smiled. 'Sit down, child. Now, I think I know what you want to say to me. I have been observing you for some time. You are thinking of becoming a Catholic,' the old nun went on softly, 'like your father! Am I right?'

Evalyn was momentarily speechless. But she raised her head and stared the nun in the eye.

'But Father doesn't even go to church, *ma mère*,' she blurted.

'None the less, I have been watching you. You have natural piety, and you have fitted in here so well.'

'I . . . could become a Catholic,' Evalyn said slowly. The thought had a certain appeal and was obviously politic at this moment.

The old nun nodded approvingly and continued, 'And in due course, you might even wish to be accepted here as a postulant? *Le Bon Dieu* would be very pleased . . . Were you thinking along those lines, Evalyn?'

Evalyn was now filled with panic. It was as though she had walked into a trap, albeit one of her own making.

'Think about it, my dear child. I will arrange for you to have instruction.'

Annie laughed out loud when Evalyn reported back to her.

'She thinks God would be pleased!'

'He might be amused,' Annie said, 'but I think that's about as far as one could pitch it!'

'I'm sick of the way they assume He's poised on a puffy white cloud waiting to pounce. He's got more to do than spend His time watching what I get up to. It's a big world!'

'But it's apparently not big enough for you, miss,' Annie replied, 'which is why your parents dumped us here!'

'Annie, we have to get out. They're trying to turn me into a nun!'

'You should have thought of that before you behaved like a strumpet!'

Evalyn looked at the grinning face before her and said hotly: 'I didn't mean anything. I was only acting. But we have to get out of here before it's too late!'

'I've been thinking of an escape plan,' she confided to Annie in a whisper when she saw her at lunchtime. 'I have it all worked out . . .'

Annie mouthed at her to shut up. One of the nuns was reading from a book called *L'Histoire d'une Ame* and the others were eating their soup with downcast eyes.

Evalyn addressed an envelope that afternoon, and in the evening, just before Vespers, she and Annie approached a side door, and asked the novice who was seated beside it if they might go out to post the letter.

'It's to my mother,' Evalyn explained. The novice looked at her doubtfully. 'A private matter; it's very urgent!'

'Wait. I will see . . .'

As soon as the girl was gone Evalyn slid the heavy bolt, lifted the latch, opened the door, and she and Annie sped down the rue de Picpus. Annie stopped the first *voiture* they saw, an old victoria drawn by a white horse with broken knees.

'Elysée Palace Hotel, monsieur!' she cried at the driver, pushing Evalyn in ahead of her.

'*Vite! Vite!*' Evalyn urged breathlessly, looking back to the convent door where the novice's white face was now scanning the street.

Carrie was dressing for the banquet they were giving in honour of the French Minister for Industry and Commerce. The necklace that Tom had given his wife in Washington was around her neck, and she was putting on the ruby earrings he had only the day before bought for her in Cartier. She heard the knock on her dressing-room door.

'*Entrez*,' she said with a laugh. With Evalyn safe in a convent she had relaxed. She expected to see her husband, but the reflection in the mirror showed two nuns. She turned on a sharp intake of breath, before realising the identities of the bedraggled *soeurs*.

'What on earth are you doing here? You're supposed to be in the rue de Picpus,' she said, laughing despite herself at the sight of Evalyn and Annie in veils.

Evalyn registered the familiar scent of her mother's cologne. She was drained after the drive across the city, during which she had looked out of the back window of the *voiture* in case a carriage bearing the Mother Superior came thundering after them. Now, safe at last, she wanted to throw herself into her parents' arms, but she searched her mother's face in vain for signs of delight at the sight of her.

'They were cruel to me, Mother!' she cried.

'Tom,' Carrie called, her voice filled with half-suppressed hysteria. 'Come here and see who has arrived!'

Tom, fastening a white bow tie against his throat, came from his own dressing room, unprepared for the sight of Evalyn and Annie dressed like nuns. He gave a bellow of mirth.

'My God, Daughter,' he gasped when he was able to speak, 'but it's hard to keep up with you!'

'I don't like being locked up. I won't be locked up!' his daughter cried, stamping her foot and tearing off the white veil she had forgotten she was wearing until she saw her reflection in the mirror. 'Please don't send me back. It was like being buried alive! And you just left me there!' she added, bursting into tears. 'In a place where there are thousands of bodies that don't even have heads.'

Tom looked bewildered.

'Will you have sense, Evalyn?' Carrie said, knitting her brow. 'What are you talking about?'

'Victims of the guillotine,' Annie explained. 'They're buried in the convent cemetery!'

'All right, sweetheart,' Tom said, putting his arms around his sobbing daughter. 'We didn't know. No one is going to send you back. But how did you make your escape?'

As Evalyn explained, Carrie hid her face behind her hand to hide her smile. But in a moment she said seriously: 'But if you won't stay in the convent I'll have to find you a governess. I brought Annie here as my maid. She can't spend all her time with you.'

'Get a governess for me if you like, Mother. Anything will be better than the rue de Picpus!'

She wondered why she could no longer fling her arms around her mother. It came to her on a wave of loneliness that once ground was lost in a relationship it was no easy task to reclaim it.

Chapter Nineteen

A few days later Evalyn was summoned to her parents' sitting room. Seated on the sofa and talking to her mother was a young woman in a blue dress and black straw boater.

'This is Mademoiselle Raye,' Carrie said. 'She will accompany you on your outings and give you lessons in French.'

Mamselle rose, and Evalyn shook hands with her, taking in her grey eyes and gentle manner, and the faint but exquisite fragrance that filled the air around her. She liked her immediately.

'I am very pleased to meet you, Evalyn,' the new governess said in her accented English. 'Where would you like to go today?'

'Please stay within the grounds of the Exposition, Mamselle,' Carrie said, directing a warning glance at her daughter. 'Evalyn is not permitted to leave it!' She turned to her daughter. 'You can show Mamselle the Camp Bird exhibit.'

'Yes, Mother,' Evalyn said meekly.

After Evalyn had shown Mamselle the exhibit, they left the *palais*, walked down the Champ-de-Mars, then strolled to the *Château d'Eau*, where a cascade of water tumbled to a central pool which erupted with myriad fountains. The arcade behind it brought them to the *Palais de l'Electricité*, and the giant Ferris wheel.

Evalyn looked up at it. Its passengers were animated, pointing out various landmarks to each other with excited voices, and the wheel rotated slowly and sedately.

'Do you mind heights, Mamselle?'

'I do not like them,' she replied, 'but the ride is only two turns.'

Near the wheel was a souvenir stall with a striped canvas canopy. Evalyn looked at the goods on offer, selected a model of the tower built by Monsieur Eiffel, that dominated the Champ-de-Mars.

'Is it for someone special?' Mamselle asked.

'It's for a friend back home in America,' Evalyn replied. 'His name is Ned.'

Mamselle purchased two first-class tickets and Evalyn followed her on board one of the cars that swung from an axle on the Ferris wheel's outer rim. Soon the wheel was moving and Evalyn began taking in the unfolding vista of Paris: the roofs with their dormer windows, the turrets of the Conciergerie, the gilded dome of Les Invalides, and the whole panoply of the Exposition, with its flags and air of excitement.

'What do you think of the tower?' she asked Mamselle.

'One gets used to it. It's been here for eleven years now.'

'Father thinks it's wonderful. I climbed it on our first day here, and my legs were like jelly for two days afterwards! Mother thought I shouldn't, but it was worth it for the view!'

'Do you always do whatever you want?' her new governess enquired gently.

'I suppose so . . .'

'Is that because you are an heiress?'

Evalyn thought about this. 'I don't think of myself like that, Mamselle! I always did whatever I wanted – if I could – long before Father discovered Camp Bird. I always liked people to notice me.'

'Why is that, Evalyn?'

Evalyn shrugged. She could not tell her governess that half the time she felt invisible, felt that if she did not assert her existence she would fade like a ghost.

'You are probably one of the richest girls in the world,' Mademoiselle Raye continued, shaking her head, 'and so you cannot fail to be noticed.' She added softly, 'Do you think it's a good idea, having and doing *everything* you want?'

Evalyn looked at her with candour, eyebrows raised. 'But what's the point of having so much money if you can't?'

Mademoiselle Raye regarded her gravely. 'Things come at a price, *petite*,' she said softly. 'That seems to be the rule of life.'

'What you are saying,' Evalyn said in a sudden rush of horrified insight, 'is that it is not lucky to be so lucky!'

Even as she said it a shiver began in the small of her back. 'Oh, please don't talk about it, Mamselle. If you knew how hard Father worked and how he nearly died . . .'

Tears started in her eyes and she wiped them away hurriedly. 'Look,' she cried, desperate to change the subject, 'isn't that our hotel?'

They were at the zenith of its rotation when the Ferris wheel stopped and showed no inclination to start again. The breeze shook their car; they were high above the throng below, suspended in a small container. Mademoiselle Raye looked down at the upturned faces on the ground – where the women were holding on to their hats to gaze up with concern at the marooned passengers high up on the giant wheel.

'*Zut*,' she moaned, 'the wheel is broken.'

Evalyn realised that her governess was genuinely terrified. She suppressed her own sense of abandonment and tried to distract Mamselle.

'Nonsense,' she said cheerfully. 'It's just stopped. There's a great view up here. They'll get us going again in a moment!'

A workman climbed up the frame of the wheel, came to their car and explained in rapid French the cause of the problem. He handed them a basket and climbed down again.

'*Petite*, we will be here for hours,' Mamselle whispered.

Evalyn heard the fear in her voice. She investigated the basket, and found a picnic supper. 'Oh good,' she cried. 'Look, Mamselle, cheese and bread and fruit.'

'How can you think of food in such a crisis?'

Evalyn shrugged. 'The drop below us is nothing compared to ones in Colorado.'

But what she did not add was that she had never before been abandoned on the edge of a precipice, and that she was no more enamoured than her companion at being stuck in this swaying contraption. None the less, she picked at the governess's spurned portion of food with a show of bravura when she had eaten her own, and tried to keep Mamselle's spirits up, chattering about America, about Washington and Ouray, telling her of the time when she and her father had been lost in the blizzard, telling her how she had been with him when he had taken the first samples from the Gertrude; anything to distract the young Frenchwoman from gazing with such horror at the ground far below.

Evalyn was pleased to see how her companion began to relax as she became involved in the story. But the hours went by, the sun went down over the city, and suddenly it was dark, except for the lights glittering and winking across the metropolis. The Eiffel Tower was lit, and its pinnacle blazed with incandescence like a giant star; all the *palais* in the Champ-de-Mars were shining with brilliance. She could see the reflections in the Seine of the *Pavilions des Puissances Etrangers*, and the illuminated splendour of the Porte Monumentale by the Place de la Concorde.

Mamselle's distinctive fragrance wafted in the cool evening breeze.

'What is that scent you're wearing, Mamselle?'

'Muguet.'

'It's really lovely. Where can I buy it?'

'You can't. It comes from Caillan – my home in the south. My grand-mother, who is a *sorcière*, makes it from the small, white lilies of the wood.'

'What's a *sorcière*?' Evalyn asked after a moment.

'A witch!'

Evalyn's mouth opened and she stared cautiously at her companion who was silhouetted against the city lights.

'Well, *witch* is not a good word,' Mamselle continued with a small laugh, 'but she is a wise woman!'

After a moment's silence Evalyn asked tentatively, 'Mamselle, do you have an admirer . . . someone special?'

She was about to apologise for the question when Mamselle replied quietly, 'There is someone I care for; I think he cares for me. But he is married, and so it is *impossible* . . .' She hunched her shoulders and raised her hands.

In the ensuing silence Evalyn heard the wind rattle the cars on the wheel. She also heard, albeit subliminally, the sadness of her companion.

'I am sometimes attracted to . . . married men,' the young woman went on in a low voice. 'They seem so much wiser, kinder . . .'

Evalyn was a little shocked by this but her voice did not betray her as she asked: 'Is he in Paris?'

'No. He lives near Caillan. He has much land, a big house, horses – and five children! I have come to Paris to be away from him!' She laughed, shrugged. 'It is like a battle, *petite*, one I am waging with myself; one I have to win!'

Evalyn was silent for a while, aware that she had been made privy to a private struggle she would never have dreamed existed.

'It must be strange,' she said, 'to know that someone really cares! I wonder will it ever happen to me!'

Mamselle turned her head towards Evalyn and her voice was gentle. 'Why shouldn't it?'

'Because I am rich. And because I am . . . invisible.'

'What a thing to say! You are strong and beautiful, Evalyn!'

Touched and astonished Evalyn found herself surprised by tears. She brushed them away.

'Are you more relaxed now, Mamselle? In spite of being up here?' she eventually ventured shyly to break the silence.

The governess laughed. 'Thanks to you.' She looked up at the night sky. 'I feel as though I have my head in the stars!' She turned to Evalyn and added softly, 'Is it true that you are afraid of nothing, or is it just an impression you like to give?'

'It is an impression, Mamselle,' Evalyn replied in a low voice. 'I am afraid that if I do not keep it up something terrible will defeat me!'

The governess reached out silently and touched her hand. After a moment she said hesitantly, 'You will not . . . tell anyone my little secret?'

'Of course I won't!'

The governess smiled. 'It was foolish of me to mention it.'

* * *

When the wheel was finally restarted, and its beleaguered passengers brought safely back to earth, Evalyn and Mamselle took a *voiture* back to the hotel.

By now Tom and Carrie had contacted the police, cancelled their appointment for the opera, telephoned hospitals, scoured the grounds of the Exposition and searched the surrounding streets for their missing daughter and her governess. They were sure by now that she had been kidnapped and were awaiting a ransom message with frantic anxiety.

'I don't know how you do it, Evalyn,' Carrie said, weeping with relief. 'But no matter where you go, things happen to you!'

'The wheel broke down by itself!' Evalyn protested, adding crossly, 'Why do you always blame me, Mother? I didn't do anything!'

'You don't need to, *petite*,' Mademoiselle Raye murmured, *sotto voce*. She turned to her employer and said, 'But you should be proud of your daughter, madame. She kept so cool; she told me stories because she knew I was afraid of heights. She hid her own fear; she is the bravest and the kindest girl I have ever met.'

Evalyn was embarrassed; no one had ever spoken of her in such terms. But Carrie remained pale and subdued.

'Bravery or foolhardiness?' she asked a little caustically. 'With Evalyn the lines tend to get blurred.'

Later, in her room, Evalyn asked her governess, 'Mamselle, what did you mean when you said I didn't need to do anything for things to happen to me?'

The Frenchwoman was standing by the open window. Below her was the nighttime traffic in the Champs-Elysées – long lines of carriages with glowing lamps. She turned to smile at her charge.

'You will always attract drama, *ma chérie*, probably because you have need of it. But as time passes, as the years roll on, you will change. You will need peace!'

'I feel quiet when I am with you, Mamselle,' Evalyn confessed after a moment. 'And I *would* like to improve my French.'

The governess handed her a slip of paper, on which were written the lines of a poem.

'What's this?'

'It is an easy way to learn. It is a poem about you. We will talk about it tomorrow.'

Evalyn asked dubiously, 'Did you write it yourself?'

'I did! Good night now; I must sleep after our day's excitement. I will see you in the morning and we will talk about all the things you want from life. *Dors bien.*'

I want to be loved, Evalyn thought in a burst of private candour as the door closed behind Mamselle. It is the only thing worth living for.

She perused the poem without understanding it. But in the morning she was able to read it for Mamselle, although her accent owed more to Colorado than to Paris.

> 'Petite fille éclose
> Avec tes épines et tes roses
> Sur ta joue vagabonde
> Que le soleil inonde
> Une larme a jailli
> Venue de l'infini.'

Mamselle translated it:

> 'Young blooming girl
> With your thorns and your roses,
> On your sunkissed, wandering cheek
> A tear has fallen,
> Sprung from the infinite.'

Evalyn, bemused, said, 'But Mamselle, you said the poem was about me!'

'It is! Your life is only beginning. Remember that you cannot be defeated by anything, Evalyn . . . unless you let it defeat you.'

Evalyn digested this. The thought that she was in charge of her destiny gave her a sense of personal sovereignty that calmed her inner turmoil for days.

Georges Nagelmackers, the President of the Compagnie Internationale des Wagon-Lits, had become a friend.

'You must visit Belgium,' he said to Tom when he and his wife were dining with the Walshes at the Ritz. Carrie, tightly laced, was elegant in a cream silk gown by Jacques Doucet, with lace upper bodice and sleeves, ottoman broderie and mousseline de soie. She listened to the men's conversation while she examined the menu, deciding eventually on the melon frappé and the filets de Soles au Champagne. She liked dining at the Ritz. The food was superb; the legendary Escoffier was chef, and, even for elegant Paris, the dining room was breathtaking with its huge windows overlooking the gardens, its immense mirrors, its fauteuils covered in pink brocade.

'Someone there would like to meet you,' Georges was saying. 'It's only a short train journey. I'll put on a special, and you can bring the family . . .'

The waiter came to take their orders. The wine waiter hovered while Tom chose the wine – Meursault and Château Laffite 1875.

'Whom would you have me meet, Georges?' he demanded. 'You're very mysterious!'

Tom Walsh cabin   Road from Camp Bird mill to
Imogene Basin   Hidden Treasure Group

Camp Bird mill site, dump and offices

all photographs courtesy of Joseph Gregory

One of the workings inside Camp Bird

Camp Bird dining room

Tom in his office at Camp Bird

Drawing room of the 1 Street house

McLean summer residence at Bar Harbor, Maine

Thomas F. Walsh c. 1905

Walsh Mrs T. JPG c. 1900

Evalyn c. 1904

Evalyn c. 1910/11, wearing the Hope Diamond and the Star of the East

Georges dropped his voice. 'Someone who is fascinated by your achievements. He thinks you are Midas, and that you can repeat what you have done.'

Carrie turned and said with alacrity, 'Tom has done enough! I don't ever want to see him abusing his health again. Who is this person who thinks we've nothing better to do than traipse off to Belgium at a moment's notice?'

'His name is Leopold Saxe-Coburg, Mrs Walsh,' Georges said with a twinkle.

'And what is his line of business?'

'His line of business is quite specialised,' Mrs Nagelmacker said in a low voice, leaning across the central floral display with a gentle smile. 'He is a king.'

'What do you say?' Tom demanded of his family the following morning at breakfast. 'A short trip to Belgium to meet a very important man?'

Vinson, returned from Le Touquet, pricked up his ears.

'Why does he want to meet you, Father?'

'He is curious, my son – about Camp Bird and about me.'

Evalyn took a third croissant and spread it liberally with apricot jam.

'Can Mamselle and I come too?'

'Of course, Evalyn,' Tom said with a chuckle. 'Where would we be without you?'

'Who is he anyway?' she added. 'Some boring mining man?'

Her parents exchanged conspiratorial glances. They had decided not to reveal the identity of the person Georges was taking them to meet until the last moment.

'He's a mining man of sorts. His name is Leopold Saxe-Coburg,' Tom said, parroting Georges and enjoying the joke.

'Umph,' Evalyn said. 'Never heard of him.'

But Mamselle's face was a study. She interpreted the warning look she received from Carrie and put a hand to her mouth.

The Walshes travelled to Belgium in a train specially laid on for them by Georges Nagelmackers. They lunched in sumptuous style, then relaxed in a 'drawing room' with oriental rugs, window drapes, and paintings, while liveried servants served coffee. Evalyn sat with Mademoiselle Raye, and watched the flat countryside of the north of France flying by. She repeated phrases in French: '*J'aime la compagne . . . Je suis en route pour la Belgique . . .*' and then she tried to interest Mamselle in some card tricks that Vinson had shown her.

'You see,' she said triumphantly when she was able to identify the ace of hearts that Mamselle had selected, 'I have magic powers!'

247

'*Tu es une vraie magicienne,*' her governess said, laughing.

Carrie, observing the exchange between her daughter and the governess, said to herself: Evalyn is quietening. Perhaps she is beginning to grow up. This governess has a good effect on her.

And then she saw the glance Mamselle directed at Tom. He did not seem to notice it, absorbed as he was in conversation with Georges.

They alighted from the train at St Hubert, a small station hidden in the Ardennes. Two carriages were waiting for them, each with a liveried driver and two liveried footmen. After a formal greeting from the emissary sent to meet the party, their bags were placed on the roofs of the carriages and strapped down. Mamselle, who was standing behind Evalyn and holding her small valise, stumbled on a broken flagstone, turning her ankle and dropping her valise. Tom immediately stooped to pick it up, and issued directions for it to be placed with the rest of the baggage.

'Are you all right, Mamselle?' he asked gently, giving her his hand.

'*Mais oui.* Thank you.'

In a few minutes they were bowling through the forest, two footmen clinging stiffly to the back of each conveyance. Like in the storybook pictures of Cinderella, Evalyn thought. At the stroke of midnight, the footmen would turn into mice and the two coaches into pumpkins, and the Walshes would revert to plain people from Ouray.

'This is the Ardennes,' Tom told his family, 'Belgium's great forest.'

Evalyn was aware of the green world around her, the shafts of light through the trees, the undergrowth, the bluebells, the birdsong.

'I think a fairy godmother has put a spell on us,' she whispered to Mamselle.

'Oh, I think the magic is closer to home,' Mamselle replied in a voice so low that only Evalyn could hear. Looking at her, Evalyn saw that her governess's eyes were fixed on her father, and saw her mother's eyes move suddenly from appraisal of the forest to rest on her employee.

Then she saw the château, hidden in its green fastness, and the sense of fairy tale was heightened. The castle was covered with Virginia creeper, had turrets and white louvred shutters, and a steep, slated roof.

The coaches rattled over the drawbridge and into the forecourt where six huntsmen in green suits waited on either side of the stone steps to the castle entrance. Raising hunting horns, they sounded a welcome that put the birds to flight and echoed through the forest.

Evalyn's mouth opened. Then she saw a tall man with an enormous beard and a limp come down the castle steps.

'Is that the mining man?' she whispered, awed at the bearing of the stranger, the subservience of the huntsmen, and the beauty and mystery of the secret green realm she had penetrated.

'Yes indeed, Evalyn,' Carrie whispered. 'But you must be on your best behaviour now. That gentleman is not an ordinary mining man. He is Leopold II, the King of the Belgians.'

'A *real* king, Mother?' Evalyn breathed, aware of the sudden quickening of her heart. 'He doesn't look like one!'

'He's as real as they come!' Carrie replied, a little nervously.

At dinner Evalyn confided to her brother, 'I thought kings wore crowns!'

Vin followed her gaze to where their host sat at the head of his table. He had a big nose and a morose expression that was only broken when he smiled.

'You wouldn't expect him to wear a crown every day, Evalyn, would you?'

'In his shoes I would!' She glanced around the table, but saw no sign of anyone who might be the queen. 'I wonder, is he married?'

Vinson shrugged.

The king was gobbling his food and engaging Tom in conversation. Evalyn could hear her father tell the story of how he had found Camp Bird. Vinson was straining his ears; he never tired of the story.

'The old guy seems to have taken a real liking to Father,' Evalyn murmured, 'but no one seems to have told him he shouldn't talk with his mouth full!'

'He's a king!' Vinson said.

'But so is Father.'

'That's true,' Vinson said with a laugh. 'He is a king in Colorado – which is about six times the size of Belgium.'

'That makes *us* princes!' Evalyn said, and laughed.

The return trip to Paris three days later on the 'special' found Evalyn half surprised at the fields and farmhouses of the normal world again. Everyone was quiet. Her governess was reading, and Vinson was perusing an illustrated catalogue of the new-fangled invention that the young were crazy about. They had shining lamps, big wheels and steering devices and were called automobiles.

Carrie came to sit beside her daughter.

'Well, Evalyn, did you enjoy your visit?'

'Very much, Mother,' Evalyn replied, delighted with the unexpected maternal attention. 'I was thinking how strange it is that during all those years while Father was searching the mountains, King Leopold was living in castles and having everything he wanted. We hardly knew he existed, and never imagined we would be his guests!'

'Life, Evalyn, is always stranger than one expects!'

'Will it be strange for me too, Mother? There are so many things I would like to do!'

'Time will tell,' her mother replied with a smile. 'But remember, Evalyn, pleasure must always be tempered with discipline. Man can only propose; it is God who disposes!'

Evalyn wanted to ask if that applied to Woman too, but decided against it. Instead she asked after a moment: 'Will Father be going back to see the king?'

'I don't know. But *he* will be coming to Paris. The reason he invited us to his château is because he wanted to talk to your father about mining. He has his own gold mines, you know. They're in the Congo!'

Vinson looked up from his magazine. 'That's in Africa,' he offered with a sly grin, 'in case Sis has temporarily disremembered!'

Evalyn aimed a kick at her brother's shins, which he dodged. Mamselle raised her eyes from her book, looked at her in mild surprise. Evalyn resisted the temptation to try again, aware that, for reasons she could not identify, she wanted Mamselle's approval.

'And he is coming to Paris soon!' Carrie went on. 'He will be taking an apartment in our hotel.'

It's like a play, Evalyn thought – royalty and châteaux and special trains – or as though they were living inside the pages of a novel. But, unlike ordinary novels, she thought with an instant's anxiety, this was a story of which no one knew the end.

Chapter Twenty

King Leopold came to Paris and the Walshes gave a banquet in his honour. Evalyn thought as she watched the preparations: a few years ago we were living in Ouray. No one outside of Colorado had ever heard of us. Father was unwell and down on his luck. Now he gives banquets in Paris and has a king as a friend! Is this just about money?

It's more! she thought on a spurt of pride and love, remembering what Mamselle had said about his magic, and watching the way her father put people at their ease. He was joking with the Hawaiian guitar orchestra, who were tuning their instruments and settling themselves beneath the palms that touched the ceiling of the banquet hall. She saw him look up as her mother entered in her new gown of Irish lace over silk, saw him approach and touch the fine garment reverently.

She heard his whisper: 'It's beautiful. I knew someone else once who would have loved it.'

Evalyn saw the compassion with which her mother looked into her father's eyes and put a hand on his arm.

She said to Vin later, 'Father was very moved tonight. Sometimes little things touch him deeply, but I never know why.'

'Evalyn, did you know that your face lights up when you speak of him?'

'I love *you* just as much,' Evalyn said stoutly, embracing the twelve-year-old in a passionate hug, 'when you're not showing off how many new words you've learned.'

The King stayed in Paris for a week, and then, saying that he would visit the Walshes in America the following year, he returned to Belgium.

But the summer had ended. All along the Parisian boulevards the trees were shedding their leaves. The Exposition closed on 10 November amid expressions of delight at its success and melancholy at its closing. More than forty-three million tickets had been sold. Some people talked jokingly of the future, of the Exposition that might be mounted in one hundred years time by their great-grandchildren to mark the turn of the millennium.

But such considerations seemed too far off to dwell on. The world their great-grandchildren would inherit was bound to be extraordinary, with electricity providing power, and automobiles almost certainly in everyday use, at least by the rich.

France honoured Tom by awarding him the Légion d'Honneur. The honour was conferred in the Elysée Palace itself by the President of the Republic.

The Walshes said goodbye to the dusty streets of a city they had come to love, in which the last of the fallen leaves lay in the gutter. Their trunks were fastened and sent to the Gare St-Lazare for shipment to Cherbourg. They took their farewells of Mademoiselle Raye, into whose hands Tom pressed a fat envelope. The governess thanked him with quiet dignity and put the envelope unopened into her pocket.

'We owe you a debt, Mamselle,' Tom said. 'You have helped Evalyn, and made her stay in Paris very happy. Thank you.'

'You are kind, Monsieur,' she said, reddening, her eyes lingering on Tom's face. 'I will always remember it.'

Evalyn embraced her governess in her room.

'I'll write,' she whispered, dazed at her sense of loss. 'And someday you will visit us in America, or I will see you again in Paris.'

'Of course you will, *ma chèrie*.'

'I don't know what I will do without you, Mamselle,' Evalyn continued, borne along by the moment's emotion. 'After I left Ouray my life felt like a load of stones until I met you. And now I have to go back to Washington and pretend to be someone I'm not; my real feelings are all wrong for the new life I have to live.'

'But, *petite*, your feelings are your truth; it is right that you should search them for who you are. You will never be able to have an ordinary life and you have need of all the strength you can find.'

This sounded to Evalyn like a forecast of doom.

'But I want an ordinary life; I'm just an ordinary girl.'

'Not any more, Evalyn. You are now the Walsh Heiress and your life belongs in the spotlight! Isn't that what you wanted?'

Evalyn shook her head. 'No. The spotlight is only on what people think I have; it is not on me!'

They sailed from Cherbourg for New York on the steamship *St Paul*. Tom was taciturn and withdrawn, keeping a good deal to his and Carrie's stateroom, pondering matters he did not share. Evalyn saw that he often had his lower lip stuck out beyond his moustache, as he stood on deck looking into the sea.

It's Camp Bird, she thought. He's anxious to go back, and she began rehearsing her plea to be allowed to go too.

But when she asked her father if he was worrying about the mine she got a surprise.

'I'm just thinking,' he said, chucking her under the chin, 'that the house we have in Washington is hardly big enough or grand enough to entertain a king!'

'Who cares? I don't like that old king! But I don't mind if you want to buy a bigger house, Father, one where I can have my own suite, and a private bathroom with gold faucets! We could use some of the left-over gold from the mine . . . for the faucets and stuff.'

Evalyn was joking, and was gratified that her father laughed out loud.

'For heaven's sake, Evalyn,' her mother interjected, 'don't be absurd. No one has gold faucets!'

'I want my walls lined with pink silk,' Evalyn said petulantly, keeping one eye on her father and thinking of further outrageous requirements to provoke his laugher. 'Mother won't let me have it done in Le Roy Phelps Place!'

'I think the budget can stretch to pink walls,' Tom said, 'and as for gold taps—'

'Don't be absurd, Evalyn,' Carrie said with some irritation.

Evalyn pouted and glanced at her father.

'The Government has decided the matter,' he said with a chuckle and a glance at his wife. 'And as for "left over gold", Evalyn, where did you come by such a notion?'

'She's just being silly,' Vin interjected. 'How much will you spend on our new house, Father?'

'Oh, about a million dollars, maybe,' Tom confided, patting his son's head. 'Do you think that will be enough? And another couple of million to furnish it to your mother's satisfaction . . .'

That night, Evalyn and Vin spoke in low voices of the new house their father intended building.

'He's going to spend millions on it,' Vin said in a troubled voice. 'When you think that lots of people live on less than a hundred dollars a year . . .'

'What if the money runs out?' Evalyn said dubiously.

'It won't run out,' Vin replied. 'But I wouldn't mind if we had a lot less, provided Father was well. I hated it when he was worried and sick and always going into the mountains.' After a moment's silence he added softly, 'You see, Sis, I *really would* like to have an automobile of my own, and if we stop being rich I won't be able to have one!'

When they arrived in New York Tom put his family up at the Waldorf and took his wife shopping for new winter furs. Evalyn wanted to go too; she wanted to be with her parents, but she saw immediately that her mother wanted to be alone with her father.

I wish she loved me as much . . . she thought hungrily . . . as much as she loves Father and Vinson. This prompted a darker thought and she added crossly aloud, 'I wish she loved me at all.'

That afternoon she wrote to Mamselle.

> I miss you. I was a much nicer me when I had you than I ever am on my own. Thank you for being so patient with me, and for listening and teaching me French and other things.

When they got home to Washington the bulk of their luggage had arrived before them. Annie, who had not stayed in New York, had already done Evalyn's unpacking, and had left on her dressing table something she had found tucked into the pocket of her trunk. It was a small bottle with a glass stopper. Even closed it emitted a wonderful scent, and immediately Evalyn felt as though Mamselle were in the room. Wrapped around the gift was a small sheet of blue paper. Evalyn undid the ribbon. The missive said:

> 'Petite magicienne, rappelle-toi – la vie est le sublime courage de ceux qui ne veulent pas être vaincus.'

She dabbed on some of the glorious Muguet, brought the note to her writing table, found her school French dictionary and eventually translated into English: 'Little magician, remember that life is the sublime courage of those who will not be defeated.'

That evening she said at table, 'I found a present from Mamselle in my trunk. Some of her beautiful perfume and a note.'

'We'll have to find you another governess, Evalyn, and I hope you get on as well with her,' Carrie said.

'You could ask Mademoiselle Raye to come to America! I don't want anyone else . . .'

'It's a pity you didn't think of this while we were still in Paris,' Tom said. 'But I don't see any reason not to write and ask her if it's what you would—'

Carrie's frown silenced him.

'Do you think she'd want to come?' Vinson asked. 'A long sea journey on her own . . .'

'She wouldn't mind that,' Evalyn whispered. 'She's grown up!'

Carrie's face was thoughtful. 'I'll talk to you about it later,' she said.

When the meal was over Tom went to meet his architect Henry Andersen at the building lot he had bought at the southeast corner of Massachusetts Avenue Northwest, and Twenty-First Street. It was situated near a string of mansions owned by the super rich in this newly fashionable district.

Alone with her mother, Evalyn brought up the topic of Mademoiselle Raye again.

'You're very keen on the French girl, Evalyn, but it seems a bit outlandish to ask her to come this distance. There are plenty of good governesses to be found here in Washington.'

'Like Mademoiselle Lion?' Evalyn said slyly, aware in hindsight of possible interpretations of that lady's nocturnal call on Mr Cahill.

'No, Evalyn. She was a mistake.'

'But I *want* Mademoiselle Raye!'

'Why?'

'Because she is my friend. She makes me feel *real*!'

Carrie frowned. 'What sort of nonsense is this? You know perfectly well that you are real. You need no governess to tell you! And quite honestly, Evalyn, I don't want her here . . . making sheep's eyes at your father!'

Evalyn's jaw dropped. 'But, Mother, she never, *ever*—'

'That's final, Evalyn.'

Evalyn got up and fled the room. She threw herself down on her bed and wept, pummelling the pillows. When she dried her tears she reread the note from her friend.

'Mamselle is right!' she muttered aloud. She drenched herself in Muguet and added sullenly, 'I won't be beaten!'

Chapter Twenty-One

Evalyn decided that not only was she not going to become a lady, but she would wear her hair frizzed and parted in the middle and brought down over her ears, like the actress Edna May. This new coiffure was recreated for her by Jules, hairdresser to the avant-garde elements in Washington society, and heavily lacquered to keep it in place. The girls in school stared at her, but this determined Evalyn all the more not to disturb it, and she left it that way for days on end while her ears turned yellow from the lacquer, and her headmistress wrote to Carrie to complain.

Miss Royce's letter precipitated Carrie coming into Evalyn's room one morning with a hairbrush and a determined expression, but Evalyn evaded her mother's ministrations. She had decided that no one would be allowed to touch her coiffure.

'No, Mother. I'm old enough to wear my hair the way I want it!'

Her mother's lips were white with anger. 'Why do you give so much trouble, Evalyn. Why can't you be like your brother?'

'Because I can't, Mother. Because I'm *me*. Can't you see?'

Carrie angrily left the room and Evalyn looked at herself in the mirror, sprayed more lacquer on her hairstyle and pretended she still liked it.

Carrie went to Tom.

'She's driving me crazy,' she told him. 'She'll have mice living in that hairdo if this goes on much longer!'

Tom, hating the tension in the house, and out of his depth with feminine problems, went to see his daughter in a conciliatory mood.

'Now, Evalyn,' he said, 'is there anything I can do to make you change your mind about that hairstyle?'

'Anything you can *do*, Father?' she echoed flippantly, adding in as reasonable voice as she could muster: 'I suppose you could buy me a diamond ring.'

Evalyn expected her father to laugh and scold her. But Tom just lowered his voice.

'Well, if you wear your hair to please your mother, and back off your ears like nice girls do, I'll give you a diamond that will make your friends whistle!'

Evalyn was silent. She had longed for jewels for years, knew that she was still too young for them. But now she felt that she was getting her own way too easily, that a diamond ring acquired in this manner was strangely valueless. She knew that Vinson would have been met with stern paternal remonstrance and be forced to toe the line. In some corner of her being she longed for the same absolute parameters, and for the personal respect that went with them.

But all she said was, 'You've got a deal, Papa mine.'

'We won't mention it to your mother,' Tom said, with a conspiratorial twinkle, amused at this new endearment. He added almost diffidently: 'And, Daughter, you should try to get along with her better.'

'I know,' Evalyn conceded, 'but things just seem to go wrong. Maybe if we went back to Ouray for a while . . .'

Tom laughed. 'We'll go back, the whole family, in summer, for two months, Evalyn. The new library is due to be completed in July and we will have a party to celebrate. Will that do?'

'And invite everyone?'

'Of course. And I will put on a special train to bring our friends from Denver.'

When her father was gone Evalyn considered what he had said about her relationship with her mother.

I suppose it *is* my fault, she conceded, thinking of the recurring friction with her mother. Why do I keep provoking her? And then she whispered, acknowledging the truth, 'I want her to *see* me. If she really loved me I wouldn't be bothered doing these things.'

She felt very uneasy at having penetrated into hidden causality, as though she had discovered that at some level she was a stranger to herself.

Carrie found out about the diamond, of course. When the small box was delivered from Tiffany she was in the hall, and saw it before it was relayed to Tom's office. Coming from Tiffany it was clearly a jewel; she assumed it was yet another gift for herself. But when no more was heard of it she became suspicious and asked Evalyn straight out if her father had given her any jewellery.

Evalyn had now abandoned her coiffure, and her dark hair was worn back in the customary way, and tied with a ribbon.

Evalyn hated lies; she told the truth.

'Yes, Mother. Father bought me a diamond ring!'

Carrie stormed out of her daughter's room and down to Tom's office.

'You promised me you would let me deal with Evalyn, Tom. And now I hear you bribed her to get rid of that hairdo by giving her a diamond! I can

257

hardly believe you could do something so preposterous! You promised me you would not cut across me in her upbringing.'

Tom sighed. 'I'm sorry, darling, but I hated to see things becoming so stressful between you; I thought it might help your relationship if I got her to shampoo that haystack . . . and a little diamond seemed a small enough price.'

'Tom, you're losing your sense of proportion! You have given a *diamond* to a girl who is not yet fifteen as a bribe to wash her hair! You would not take so lax a stance if it were Vinson who was giving trouble!'

'That's true enough, Carrie! But Vinson will be a man one day. And a man has much more expected from him.'

'No he does not! Women's lives are very hard; they need every bit of backbone they can find.'

'Oh, Evalyn doesn't lack for backbone,' Tom said. 'She was always as courageous as any man. But we were faced with the problem of how to get her to undo her hairstyle without using unnecessary discipline.' He added teasingly, 'And she is a young lady now and a bit old for you to take a cane to her, Carrie.'

'There are some *fathers* who would discipline their daughters,' his wife said darkly.

'You don't mean that, Carrie. And if you do, I can only tell you I would not lay a finger on my daughter to save my life!'

Evalyn wore the glittering diamond on her right hand and enjoyed the stares she got in school.

'You're showing off, but what do you expect from a parvenue?' Jessica Stanford said when she saw the diamond on Evalyn's finger.

Emma Clarendon, one of Jessica's friends, added, 'People whose ancestors came over on the Mayflower should not be expected to mix with someone with an Irish peasant background.'

Evalyn thought she would blow every fuse in her brain. Into her mind came the face of her gallant, kindly father.

She said in a penetrating voice, 'No, it's far too good for them. Ireland's civilisation was the only light in Europe when your ancestors were illiterate savages!'

Jessica glared at her with resentful eyes. 'You should mind your tongue, Evalyn Walsh. Just because your daddy was lucky enough to strike gold you think you can do and say what you like!'

'Oh, I've always done that,' Evalyn retorted, 'and I'm not about to change now, Miss Fat Head!'

But, unknown to Evalyn, Miss Royce had come on the scene and observed the exchange between her pupils. She summoned both girls to her study.

'Jessica Stanford,' she said, 'I'm ashamed of you. Good manners don't just disappear at the first provocation.' She turned to Evalyn. 'And as for you, Evalyn, you should know better than to wear diamonds to school! We will have our work cut out for us if we are ever to turn you into a lady!'

'But I don't want to be a lady!'

The headmistress observed her with cold, considering eyes. 'It is becoming more and more evident, Evalyn, that you will succeed in that ambition! But I would remind you that if you are determined on this course there is no place for you in this establishment.'

The Saturday dancing lessons at the McLeans' were a thing of the past, and Evalyn had not seen Ned to give him the small souvenir she had bought for him in Paris. But Carrie had arranged new lessons for her daughter in a recommended dancing school called the Select Dancing Academy, and Saturday afternoons were occupied as before. Evalyn had come to like dancing, and was good at it, something she privately ascribed to following Mrs McLean's advice.

She noted with delight, as she saw herself in the mirrors set at intervals along the walls, that she was much slimmer of late, and that she even looked graceful as she floated by in her partner's arms in her white dress and satin cinch. She had grown a good deal in the last year, and the girl who had gone to Paris was now almost a young woman, with dark ringlets down her back.

She often thought of Ned. He was rather like herself, an odd man out. She found herself missing the entente between them, as though both of them understood the other in a way the rest of the world did not.

I wonder when I will see him again, she mused. I'm bound to bump into him sometime.

In fact Ned turned up at the Select Dancing Academy before many weeks of the new spring session had elapsed, and stared at Evalyn as though seeing a ghost.

When the music stopped he made straight for her.

'You've changed, Evalyn,' he said awkwardly. 'You used to be such a fat kid!'

'Thanks very much.'

'Did you like Paris?'

'I had a chequered history there,' she replied demurely, using one of Vinson's new words. 'They put me into a convent for a while.'

Ned gave a peal of laughter. 'Well, I'm sure it was for good reason. But it must have done something for you. You're quite a stunner now.'

The pleasure of this compliment warmed Evalyn.

'I brought you a souvenir,' she whispered. 'But I didn't expect to see you today.'

'May I call for it?'

He came to Le Roy Phelps Place the next day; was shown into the drawing room. Through the open window he watched the maid going into the garden where Evalyn was seated on a white wrought-iron chair in the shade of a weeping willow. She was wearing a pale pink dress, and her hair was falling untidily down her back.

She seemed to be writing a letter; she had a pad of paper on her knee. When the maid spoke to her she sprang up and hurried to the drawing room.

'Ned . . .' she said a little breathlessly, 'I didn't think you'd come!'

'But you said you had a souvenir for me.'

'It's in my room. I'll get it.'

She rushed off. When she returned Ned noticed that there was a wonderful scent in the air and that her ringlets had been restored.

'Did you put a ribbon on – fix your hair – just for me?'

Evalyn looked annoyed. 'Don't be silly, Ned. It's Sunday. Mother gets annoyed if I'm not spruced up for dinner.'

'I never thought that would worry *you*! What's the perfume?'

'It's called Muguet! My French governess used to wear it. In fact I was just writing to her.'

Evalyn handed him the little model of the Eiffel Tower, still wrapped in its striped paper. Ned undid the wrapping and held the dainty model in the palm of his hand.

'What's it for? Is it a paperweight?'

'It doesn't have to be for anything. It's a tower in Paris.'

'I know that. Father was talking recently about the fuss they made about it when it went up! But thanks very much for remembering me,' he added awkwardly. 'I'll put it on my mantelpiece and think of you!'

When he was gone Annie came into the drawing room with a bowl of hyacinths. She put them down on the table by the window and regarded Evalyn slyly.

'So you've got yourself a beau?'

'Don't be silly, Annie!'

'Och, will you look at her, and she all delighted with herself.'

Evalyn looked at herself in the mirror, pulled the ribbon from her hair and stuck her tongue out at Annie.

'If you're going to be rude,' the housekeeper said, lowering her voice, 'I'll change my mind about the free advice I was going to give you!'

'What advice?' Evalyn demanded with a laugh.

'About men! You have to keep them guessing. Never tell a man you love him, my wee girl; never ask him if he loves you!'

Oh Annie, Evalyn said to herself, what would you know about it?

But from then on the Saturday class saw Evalyn Walsh and Ned McLean dancing together at every opportunity, until their teacher gently suggested that it was a good idea to change partners as much as possible in order to get accustomed to dancing with different people.

Ned's father gave him a present of a new motor car.

'It's a DeDion-Bouton,' Ned told Evalyn, 'a French car. I saw it in a magazine and Father had it imported specially for my birthday. It's amazing to drive.'

When Evalyn mentioned it at home Vinson's face filled with envy.

'The lucky dog!' he exclaimed in an uncharacteristic outburst. 'I'd give anything to be in his shoes!'

Carrie looked up from the catalogue she was perusing. 'But you're still just a young boy!' Her voice was full of teasing raillery; she smiled across the drawing room at her son with eyes full of love.

'It does help for the driver to be able to reach the steering wheel,' Evalyn added helpfully.

Vinson, shouting, 'I'm *not* a baby! I'm twelve!' jumped up and looked at her furiously.

'Children, children . . .' Carrie remonstrated.

'Ned is far too young for a motor of his own,' their father said decisively. 'John R. spoils him.'

'Oh, Father, don't be so stuffy,' Evalyn cried, flopping, laughing, into a chair and regarding her brother with suspicious alertness. 'I'd like one sometime too . . .' she added, 'when I'm older.'

'Girls can't drive motors,' Vinson said.

'Oh yes they can.'

'They wouldn't be able to crank the engine.'

'I'll show you how well we can crank!' Evalyn cried, springing from her chair and rushing at her brother. Vin fled – through the open French windows into the garden. She ran after him and when he turned to face her she saw that his face was set and angry.

He said hotly, 'You all think I'm just a soft kid! But one of these days I'll show you.'

'Oh, Vin, don't be so childish. I didn't mean—'

But Vin was gone.

The following Saturday, as she danced with Ned, he whispered into her ear, 'Let's sneak out for a ride in my new motor.'

Evalyn thought about it for only an instant. Her mother would disapprove but what mothers didn't know wouldn't hurt them.

'OK, I'll meet you in the hall.'

She slipped out of the room, changed out of her dancing shoes, put on her white straw boater, secured it with hatpins and ran outside to where

Ned had parked his automobile. It was beautiful, a deep grass green, roofless, with buttoned leather upholstery, and brass lamps. There was room for two in the high, carriagelike seat. Ned handed Evalyn in, took off his boater and cranked the engine. It spluttered into life and in a moment they were off, chugging through the Washington traffic, Ned squeezing the horn as seemed necessary, impervious to the carriage horses flattening their ears and showing the terrified whites of their eyes.

When they came to the countryside Ned opened the throttle and let the car fly along at a breath-taking thirty miles per hour. Evalyn held on to her hat; she felt the rushing summer breeze, brushed at the small insects that arrived in clusters on her face and looked behind at the trail of dust they left in their wake. Not even when riding had she experienced such exhilaration. Ned looked fully *au fait* with the controls, and took corners with so much panache that once or twice Evalyn was afraid the car would turn over.

They stopped at a farmhouse offering strawberries and cream. Evalyn was laughing and breathless. Her hat was askew and her hair tangled. She removed the boater, and tried to comb her long tresses with her fingers.

'You need something in front to stop the wind,' she said. 'And I should have had a veil as big as a tent, for I've swallowed half the State's midges! But it was great!'

Ned watched her for a moment as she worked on her hair. Then he suddenly leaned forward and said in her ear: 'You're a real sport, Evalyn Walsh. I think we should get married!'

Evalyn felt his warm breath against her ear like a caress. It was a very strange feeling to be caressed at any level and she did not reply. Although he could only be joking, the moment possessed an intimacy that was entirely new and that made her heart beat faster. But, when she turned to look at him, she saw the uncertain expression on his face, as though he was intimidated by his own temerity, and laughed.

'Is that all you have to say?' Ned demanded.

'What do you expect me to say? You're not serious!'

'I am serious,' he replied sulkily.

'But you're still only sixteen and I'm not yet fifteen. I won't even be putting up my hair for ages yet!'

'That doesn't mean we can't get engaged. No one else need know!'

Evalyn put a hand against his cheek, but his lips hungrily sought hers and she tasted them, moist and intimate. She pulled away.

'You're beautiful,' he said huskily.

Evalyn felt like a queen, the centre of the cosmos, powerful with life. The sense of possessing beauty was novel but, however delicious it was to be courted, she knew that Ned's proposal was only the caprice of the moment.

'I don't want to get engaged to anyone just yet Ned,' she said after a moment, 'if I ever do. And you don't either! Not really!'

His face darkened. 'Go on,' he replied, 'tell me I'll have to wait till you're forty.'

Then he smiled and they laughed like children as they seated themselves in the shady farmhouse garden and placed their orders.

They took their time over the fat strawberries, eating them with relish, pouring the cool white cream liberally and touching hands shyly across the table.

Across the garden another young couple regarded them whimsically. The young woman was wearing an engagement ring and Evalyn thought for a moment how wonderful it must be to have someone who would adore you for the rest of your life. She covertly examined Ned for the role, before telling herself not to be stupid. He was just the boy from dancing lessons who used to stand on her toes.

When she got home she expected to find herself in trouble for being late, but her mother was out and her father was in his study. She went up to her room, mulling over her afternoon escapade with private delight. When she had taken off her hat, washed her face and brushed her hair, she knocked on Vinson's door. She was bursting to share her secret with him, and when there was no answer she turned the porcelain door knob and found the room empty. On her brother's bureau was a short note. It took her a moment to realise that it was addressed to her.

Dear Sis,
I have gone away to find adventure.
   All my love, Vin

Evalyn stared at the note for a few seconds before its full ramifications sank in. She looked around his room: everything was in place. She opened a few of his drawers, but all was neat. He can't have gone far, she thought. Is he serious?

But her heart began to pound as though it already knew the answer. She grabbed the note and ran downstairs, meeting Annie as she crossed the hall.

'Annie, have you seen Vinson?'

The housekeeper shook her head. 'Isn't he in his room?' She stared at Evalyn's face. 'Is something wrong?'

Evalyn waved the note in front of her. 'He's run away . . .'

She tried to check the frightened tears, but by the time she reached her father's door they were coursing down her face.

Tom was poring over the drawings for the new house when Evalyn burst into his study. One glance at her convinced him that something

263

serious was afoot and not just another impasse with her mother. He put aside Henry Anderson's plans and elevation, took the note from her hand, read it quickly and rose to put his arms around her.

'Vinson will be back, my darling,' he said calmly. 'Now dry your tears and we'll search the house.'

He called Terry, and soon the servants were alerted and the house was searched from attic to cellar, and the garden too. Evalyn checked every cupboard and closet, but of her brother there was no trace.

When she returned to her father's study he was telephoning the police. Evalyn heard the front door open and shut, but it was her mother's step that entered the hall. She glanced at her father when he put the mouthpiece back, saw that he was looking stern and worried.

'Have you heard something, Father? Have the police?'

'No. But he's taken one of my six-shooters, Evalyn – a hog leg – and six bullets!'

Evalyn clapped a hand to her mouth.

'Don't upset your mother now. Don't mention the gun.'

'Oh my God!' Carrie cried a few moments later as she read the note. 'What will he do? Out there, in this big city, God knows where, on his own!'

'He'll come back very soon. It's summer; he won't die of cold. He has many friends. Every child runs away at some point.'

'I didn't, Father.'

Tom turned to his daughter. 'This kind of caper would be a much more dangerous exercise for a girl!'

Evalyn sighed under her breath.

The night seemed interminable. No one slept. The police, contacted at intervals, had nothing to report. At six in the morning, while Tom was sitting in his office with his head in his hands, he heard the front door open softly and shut with a muted click. Vin came creeping into the house, and nearly jumped out of his skin when his father materialised before him in the hall.

Tom turned on the lights in silence and surveyed his young son. The first thing he looked for was any signs of injury; but he saw only guilty fatigue. Then he looked for the hog leg and ammunition, held out his hand for them without a word. Vinson yielded up the weapon, and his father counted the bullets with relief.

And then Tom did something unusual for him. He propelled his twelve-year-old sternly to his study, shut the door, held the boy across his knee and gave him a hiding with a leather slipper.

'That's not for running away,' he said through his teeth. 'It's for taking the gun and the bullets. Just what did you think you were playing at?'

Vin did not cry out. In a way he almost welcomed the parental ire.

But when he was vertical again he said angrily to his father through the sobs he was no longer able to check, 'Everyone thinks I'm the little goody around here, the one who never gives trouble, the soft kid of the house. Well, I'm not! I wanted to do something on my own, I wanted to have an adventure before it's too late! You've had so many, Father . . . and, because we're rich, I'll probably never have a single one.'

Tom's ire dissolved; he was filled with sorrow and regret.

'My son,' he said, 'life will give you adventures you never dreamed of. But do not ever inflict this kind of anxiety on your family again.'

Vinson sulked for two days, but as the school holidays loomed, and with it the prospect of going back to Colorado, he forgot his humiliation and said no more, for the moment at least, about his lust for adventure. In a queer kind of way he felt he had made his point.

'Would you like to find another mine, Father?' Evalyn demanded a few weeks later as they sat on the train that was bringing them West.

'Sure.'

'Why? Do you need more money? Is building the new house more expensive than you thought?'

Tom laughed. 'We have more money than we can ever spend, Evalyn, even if all of you did your worst! No, my interest in prospecting is now purely for the thrill of pitting my wits against nature and winning!'

He was in an expansive mood and patted his son's head as he spoke in a mute gesture of apology.

'Would *you* like to discover a gold mine, Brother?' Evalyn asked Vinson.

'No,' the boy said with a half-glance at his father. 'What would really give *me* a thrill is an automobile of my own.'

A chill began at Evalyn's hairline and ran down her spine. Vin looked at his father and Tom chuckled. 'So you'd like a motor of your own? Well, you're a bit young yet, but later on—'

'Don't give it to him, Father!' Evalyn said the words before she had consciously formulated them. They came as much of a surprise to her as to her family. Both her father and brother stared at her, the former with arrested attention, the latter with resentment. Her mother, about to speak, bit her lip and frowned.

'Don't be such a spoilsport, Evalyn,' Vin said reproachfully. 'Just because Mount Vernon has asked Father to find another school for you doesn't mean that you have to ruin things for everyone else!'

Evalyn could find no answer to this. She was ashamed of her scholastic history, but she was relieved to be free of the school. She also wished that she had spared her parents the worry she had caused them.

Tom's face closed. He regarded his son with narrowed eyes.

'You're far too young to be thinking of automobiles,' he muttered. After a moment he gestured to the sweeping prairie beyond the window and commented on the number of homesteads.

'When I crossed the plains thirty years ago they were almost empty.'

'You never thought then, did you, Father,' Vin asked, 'that someday you would make the same journey on a train, returning to visit your own gold mine and to dedicate to your adopted town a new library?'

'No, my son, I did not!'

'Will you and Mother be giving a party for the dedication?' Evalyn asked, fired by the prospect of gaiety in which she might be included.

Carrie laughed and glanced at Tom.

'Of course!' Tom said with a chuckle. 'Of course we'll throw a party!'

'And I can come . . . and Vin too?' Evalyn added with a half-apologetic glance at her brother.

'I see no reason why not,' Carrie said. 'At least for the dinner . . . providing of course that you behave yourself!'

Evalyn took a deep breath, looked out the flat fields of Kansas and longed for the first sight of the Rockies.

Chapter Twenty-Two

Carrie said that staying at the cottage up at Camp Bird gave her headaches.

'It's not just the extra altitude, Tom. It's the noise of the stamp mills and the tramway! It never ends!'

'It's music, Carrie!' Tom said with a twinkle. 'But we can take a floor of the Beaumont, if you like.'

'No. Let's go back to Fifth Avenue, like old times!' Evalyn begged. 'It will be great . . .'

Next day, the Walshes moved back into the old clapboard house that had once been home.

Evalyn was up early the following morning, delighted at being back in her old room. Her father was already gone up to Camp Bird, but the rest of the household was still sleeping. The morning was fresh, the light bright on Mount Hayden.

Her first call was to see the new library, which was almost next door to the Sisters' Hospital. Built of brick in a Palladian style, it had a white pillared loggia, and a square clock tower surmounted by a cupola with a brass bell. Her heart swelled with pride.

It's lovely, she thought. And with the rare books Father has bought for it, it will have the most valuable collection in the West.

But most of all she thrilled to the prospect of the forthcoming party, mulled it over as she went on to the Ashenfelter stables to see Dewdrop. He whinnied and came forward to rub his nose on her shoulder, looked at her from melancholy eyes in which there was not the slightest sign of reproach.

'I knew *you* wouldn't forget me!' she whispered, offering him one sugar lump after the other on the palm of her hand while he gobbled them with a deft twitch of his lips and a quick grinding of molars. Evalyn ran her hands along his flanks, noting that he seemed to be in good condition, scratched between his ears and kissed him.

'You're the nicest horse in the whole world,' she informed him. 'You have no idea how much I've missed you! And tomorrow we are going for a lovely long ride!'

Next morning brother and sister halooed with joy as their mounts kicked up the dust of the canyon floor. Alone in the cool mountain air, with only the tinkle of the streams and the distant rumble of the stamp mills, they were far from Washington and the strictures that in the space of a few years had tightened around their lives. Evalyn rode astride, wearing a black riding habit with a long divided skirt, delighting in the scent of the wind and the warmth of Dewdrop's withers against her thighs. She wore no gloves, preferring to feel the worn reins and Dewdrop's coarse brown mane against her fingers. The wilderness didn't care if you were rich or poor, she thought, turning in the saddle to survey the glories around her; it gave everyone the same – the mountains, the shadows of the canyons, the tang of the firs.

Maria, who was living in a house Tom had bought for her in Denver, arrived for the opening of the new library. She had put on weight and had lost the haunted look that had come with her bereavement and which had never left her throughout their time in Europe.

Paul came with her. Now twenty, he was already part-owner of a livery stables in Denver, a business that he and his partner were building up together.

Tom, who had not seen him for several years, clapped him on the back.

'How are you, Paul?'

'Very well, Uncle.'

'How is the business?'

Paul indicated that it was thriving. He looked around at Ouray as they made their way to the Beaumont, where Tom had reserved rooms for them, squinting against the sunlight as he surveyed the mountains.

'I had forgotten how beautiful this town is.'

'There's nowhere like it!' Tom replied ruefully. 'Come up to the house as soon as you're ready,' he told his guests when he parted from them at the hotel. 'Carrie can't wait to see you . . .'

Evalyn would remember that afternoon for the rest of her life.

Lunch was over. She wanted to go riding, but her mother told her to stay back and help.

'*You* wanted us to stay here, Evalyn, where there are no servants – except Annie, who is run off her feet! You seem to forget that we are expecting guests!'

Evalyn sighed privately, but she stayed to help Annie freshen the parlour.

'I haven't seen Paul for four years,' she told the housekeeper. 'Last time we visited Aunty Maria he was out of town. And he didn't come with us to Ireland.'

'He's grown up!' Annie said. 'He has his business to think of!'

'Do you remember how he ran away when his father died . . . hid in our barn? He became so quiet after that. I sure hope he has more to say for himself these days.'

'Some people have a lot to say for themselves and other people don't,' Annie retorted with more than her usual asperity. 'But that doesn't mean they don't *think*! And that boy has had plenty to think about.'

Evalyn sensed mystery. She glanced at Annie but could not read her face.

'What do you mean, Annie?'

Through the open window came the sound of the gate creaking, voices, footsteps on the path. Evalyn glanced out, saw her Aunt Maria approaching the door. Behind her was a young man. He was tall and lean, was dressed in a grey suit with shirt and necktie.

'It's *them*!' she cried, heading for the front door and opening it with a flourish.

'Aunt Maria, it's wonderful to see you!'

She looked up at Paul, took his outstretched hand. She registered that his palms were calloused and that his hand was strong.

'Do you remember me?' he asked quizzically, leaning back on his heels to look at her. 'I haven't seen you for a long time!'

'Of course I remember you, Paul Lafferty!'

His eyes were grey, deeper-set than she remembered. His chin had squared, and he had a moustache of sorts on his upper lip. Only his smile reminded her of the boy he had been.

Carrie brought her guests into the parlour and Evalyn lingered for a moment in the hall, wondering why her mouth was dry and why her heart had quickened as though she had been running.

Maria exclaimed with pleasure at the gowns Carrie had brought her from Paris. Later they went to Ashenfelter's to meet the black mare Tom had bought for her as a gift.

'A lady's horse,' he said. 'Her name is Rebecca. I'm told she's gentle as a kitten!'

Maria put her nose to the finely tooled side-saddle that smelled so powerfully of new leather.

'Always brings me back, Tom . . .'

She mounted Rebecca, and Evalyn coached her in side-saddle riding while Paul looked on.

'Keep your left foot firmly in the stirrup, Aunt Maria, and your right leg around that pommel. They're your only anchors!'

'My God, Evalyn, are there any more hobbles they'll get us to use? I have no control at all over this animal and my back is already aching!'

'Oh, just ride her astride, Aunt, and don't be bothered with all this stuff,' Evalyn cried after a moment as she watched her aunt wince as she twisted

269

her body to sit square in the saddle. 'Use an ordinary saddle and set a new fashion in Denver! I always ride astride when I can!'

She turned to her tall cousin who was looking on, caught his amusement.

'Well, what do you think, Paul? Do you want a mother with a spine like a corkscrew?'

Paul chuckled. 'She's right, Mother. Set a new fashion in Denver!'

'I think I'll use Rebecca to pull my new landau and forget about becoming a noted horsewoman!' his mother replied.

'We're expecting some more visitors,' Carrie announced next day, 'a Mr Edwin Hartland and his son.' Evalyn had never heard of him before.

'Why is he coming here?'

'He's a mining man. He's coming from London to see Camp Bird. And he'll stay for the dedication of the library.'

Alarm bells rang in Evalyn's brain. She cornered her father when he came down from the mine that evening, and asked him straight out, 'Father, has this Mr Hartland who's coming to see us some idea that you will sell him Camp Bird?'

Carrie came in, heard the question and looked at her husband aghast.

'You wouldn't Tom, would you?'

Tom sighed. 'He represents a London syndicate which wants to buy the mine, Carrie. I've no intention of selling, but that doesn't mean we can't extend him common courtesy.'

Carrie was shaking her head. 'You'd be a fool to listen to him, Tom Walsh. God gave you something special. Don't throw it back.'

'Oh, Carrie . . .' Tom murmured, 'there's no need to fret. Whatever happens to the mine will not be done without a great deal of thought!'

Edwin Hartland and his son, Jack, arrived at the end of the week. Tom went down to the depot to meet them, and brought them back to the house in Ouray for the evening meal.

Edwin Hartland was charming to Carrie and anecdotal about London, well able to mimic the Cockney accent and make everyone laugh. Jack was the same age as Vin, and the two boys were soon inseparable. Jack would come down from Camp Bird in the mornings on one of the supply wagons, spend the day with his new friend in Ouray, or Vinson would go up to the mine to be with him. Tom had relaxed his stricture about his children's presence in Camp Bird. They were no longer children, he reasoned, and their guest had to be entertained.

So Vin was able to take Jack up on the aerial tramway, and down into the mine workings, using the hoists. In Ouray they explored Box Canyon where the Canyon Creek River decanted itself into a deep gorge, and inspected the acre of goldfish in the warm thermal pond in Chipeta Park, one of Ouray's main tourist attractions.

When she tried to join the boys in their activities, Evalyn quickly discovered that her presence was surplus to requirements.

'We don't want any *girls*,' she heard Jack Hartland whisper to Vinson, 'do we?'

'No,' Vin agreed, a little shame-faced.

Evalyn felt the exchange like a sword thrust. Vinson had betrayed her, siding automatically with the closed, secretive world of men.

'I can go riding on my own,' she muttered rebelliously. 'Who needs boys anyway?'

Paul, who had just come from the Beaumont with his mother, offered himself as a substitute. He glanced at Carrie as he said this, and she nodded, eager to talk with Maria.

Evalyn donned her riding habit and the two cousins set off for Ashenfelter's where Evalyn introduced Paul to Dewdrop. Soon they were both mounted and heading out of town for the wilderness, Paul on a grey gelding called Bachelor, named after a local mine, and Evalyn astride her pony. She led the way, glad to show her cousin the world she loved.

'You should have come with us to Ireland,' she said a little later as the horses plodded side by side with the small clinking sounds of iron on stone. 'It was weird visiting the little house where Father and your mother used to live. An old school friend of his has it now. It's got a thatched roof and only three rooms. We never met our Irish cousins, though.'

'I couldn't leave the business. But I'll go some day. I'd sure like to see Ireland, and meet our relatives.'

Evalyn was keenly aware of him. He sat on a horse as though the animal had been designed for him. He was grown up, she realised; his demeanour was of someone poised and focused, someone who knew where he was going and who didn't mind the price.

Like Father, she thought, pleased with her analysis. So different from the rich boys she danced with at the Select Academy, whose questions were so often covertly geared towards sussing out the extent of her father's wealth. So different from Ned McLean, who smelled too often of bourbon. There was a gravity about Paul, an ease and safety in his company, but also an excitement that put butterflies in her stomach. She wondered why this was so. They had not been there when she had met him as a child.

This made her think of the night she had found him in their barn in Ouray, and his glazed, unfocused eyes. His father had been killed and he had run from the horror of it. Now he did not look like a young man who would run from anything.

'Evalyn, is something bugging you?'

271

She turned to meet his intent grey eyes; but she did not want to remind him of that dreadful night.

'Oh, Paul, I'm . . . just afraid Father is going to sell the mine. I'm sure Mr Hartland is trying to persuade him.'

'Why don't you ask Hartland straight out?' Paul said after a moment. 'Then you'll know the truth!' He considered his cousin for a moment and added gently, 'Is that all that's bothering you, Evalyn, or is there something more?'

'What gave you that notion?'

'You seem preoccupied. But so far as your father is concerned, you needn't be afraid he'll lose his fortune. If he does sell the mine it will be for a great price!'

Evalyn nodded. 'I know. He is already one of the world's richest men!'

She shrugged as she spoke to convey that she was not overwhelmed by this truth. But she was covertly watching her cousin. How did *he* feel about her father's wealth? Her comment elicited in him no sign either of envy or greed, and this pleased her.

'A bit like shouldering planet Earth, isn't it?' Paul suggested after a moment. 'But your father is like Atlas; he has broad shoulders!'

'You like him, Paul?'

'I like and respect him very much indeed. You are lucky to have such a man for your father – with or without a fortune!'

'You give the impression, Paul Lafferty,' Evalyn said after a moment, 'of being wise, or something.'

'Don't ever think that of me,' he replied. 'Once I made a terrible mistake.'

Evalyn thought suddenly of what Annie had said on the day of his arrival – *'That boy has had plenty to think about.'*

'What mistake was that, Paul?' She saw how the tension knotted in his face.

'I don't speak of it.'

They moved on. Evalyn began to talk of Europe, of Paris and the marvels of the *Exposition Universelle*, and of the wonderful governess she had had there. She also told him about the convent in the rue de Picpus.

'I bet you don't know where Lafayette is buried!' she said with a sudden laugh.

'No,' Paul agreed, looking at her whimsically. He was still laughing at her account of the escape from the convent. 'But I think I am about to find out!'

'In a cemetery behind the Couvent du Sacré-Coeur, with heaps of other aristos!'

'What did you do, Evalyn, when you were not reliving the Revolution or escaping from convents?' he asked after a moment.

'I went to stay with a king.'

She described the trip to Belgium on a train that had its own drawing room, the château in the forest, and the king with his long beard. In the recounting she found all of these events even more extraordinary than when she had actually lived through them.

'. . . And Father and Mother were hosting balls and dinners and meeting people with titles.'

'And it didn't knock a feather out of them?' Paul suggested.

'Well, I think it was tiring. But Father is not impressed by things other people would sell their souls for. He likes being rich, of course, but the only thing that really impresses him is strength – any kind of strength!'

After a few minutes Paul said, gesturing towards Camp Bird, the rumble of whose stamp mills could be heard more clearly now, 'Perhaps I shouldn't ask this – but have you ever felt, Evalyn, that it is all . . . too much?'

They were by the Canyon Creek. Evalyn let Dewdrop drink. The leathers creaked as she stood in the stirrups; the breeze loosened her hair. She did not look at her cousin. Her erstwhile enthusiasm seemed to have deserted her.

'On the contrary,' she replied dully. 'In a queer kind of way it's not *enough*! That is the trouble with money. It takes up all the space . . . makes new rules. It wants your *life*!'

'I didn't know you were such a philosopher,' Paul said in a voice tinged with a surprised respect. 'So, if it were up to you, would you be content to live simply with just enough for your needs?'

'Heavens!' Evalyn exclaimed with a laugh, suddenly beset by the prospect of only having *enough* for the rest of her life. 'Of course I couldn't. Think of all the things I can have now and would never be able to have otherwise . . . like travelling to Europe whenever I want, and having beautiful dresses . . . and especially – when I'm a bit older – heaps of jewels, and houses and servants – things I'd never dreamed I'd be able to have.' She shrugged imperiously as her prospects warmed her. 'In fact *anything* I want *for ever*.'

Paul was silent. Evalyn glanced at him and saw him watching her without expression.

'Would you like to dismount?' he asked. 'Stretch our legs for a bit?'

When she nodded he threw a leg over Bachelor's head and leaped to the ground, held out a hand to help her dismount. She slipped from Dewdrop's back and they walked on, side by side, the horses huffing and flicking their tails. Paul bent down to pick a piece of quartz from the canyon floor.

273

'I suppose you think I'm just spoiled and greedy?' Evalyn said in a subdued voice after a moment. 'I suppose you're thinking of the horrible divide that exists between the rich and the poor . . . But to tell you the truth, Paul, I'm glad I'm on the right side of that divide. The other side – when Father was down on his luck – was terrifying.'

'And do you think the one you're on is any less frightening?' When she didn't reply to this he added, 'Evalyn, the real divide in the world is not between the rich and the poor.'

'Isn't it?'

Paul looked at her as though daring her to laugh. 'It is between those who are able to love and those who are not!'

'What are you saying, Paul?' she asked stiffly, stroking her pony's neck. 'That I do not know how to love?'

Her colour rose. To be here in the canyon talking to Paul Lafferty about *love* . . .

'On the contrary,' Paul said in a full voice, 'I never met anyone like you in my life, Evalyn Walsh.' He flushed scarlet, reached out a sunbrowned hand and gently touched her face. 'You are the most wonderful girl I have ever met.'

Evalyn felt his fingers on her cheek. She turned in confusion, muttering about getting back, but her heart was beating a strange, new tattoo against her ribcage.

That evening, when everyone was seated around the dinner table, Evalyn caught Paul's eye, but was distracted by Edwin Hartland saying: 'I believe you know Lord Rawlinson, Miss Walsh? I believe you met at the Great Exhibition?'

Evalyn took a moment to realise to whom he was referring, then knew immediately that Mr Hartland was fully *au fait* with the scene she had created in the Palace of Mines and Metallurgy. Her face crimsoned.

I might have known *that* man would be involved in this syndicate, she thought, willing her face to stop blushing, but it stubbornly burned the brighter. The family looked at her curiously, her mother with a puzzled frown. But Evalyn felt Paul's encouraging eyes and soldiered on.

'Yes. I met Lord Rawlinson at the Camp Bird exhibit in the Palace of Mines. He was wondering aloud how much of the income from the mine went into Father's own pocket.'

There was an embarrassed silence. Edwin Hartland looked at Tom, but the latter only laughed.

'Everyone speculates about that,' he said.

'But, Father—'

Behind her, Evalyn felt Annie, who was serving vegetables, dig sharp fingers into her shoulder blades.

'What were you about,' the housekeeper said when the meal was over, 'embarrassing everyone like that? Keep your trap shut!'

The guests had gone to the Beaumont, and her parents and Vin had accompanied them. Evalyn was alone with the housekeeper.

'Something is definitely going on, Annie. Rawlinson and his associates are trying to get their hands on Camp Bird! Hartland is their front man, and he will charm and wheedle until he gets what he wants.'

'Do you think your father is a fool?'

But despite various self-assurances Evalyn could not sleep that night. At 1 a.m. she slipped out of bed, went to Vin's room, opened his door and closed it behind her. Her brother was asleep.

'Vin!' She shook him. 'Vin, I want to talk to you. It's important!'

'Whaa . . .? For God's sake, Evalyn . . . What are you doing here?'

She sat on the edge of his bed. 'Shh. Keep your voice down! Look, Vin, I smell a rat! I think Hartland is in cahoots with that Lord Rawlinson who was in Paris. They want to get their hands on Camp Bird by hook or by crook!'

Vin sat up. 'Father won't sell,' he said groggily, 'so what are you worried about? He'd never sell Camp Bird.'

'Wouldn't he? Even if pressure was put on him and a great price dangled?'

Vin was silent.

'We'll have to think of something to send Hartland packing,' Evalyn went on.

'Don't get up to any of your tricks, Evalyn. I like him being here. I like Jack!'

'Do you want to grow up to be the owner of Camp Bird or don't you?' Evalyn demanded. She stood up and flounced out of the room.

In the morning Jack presented himself after breakfast and he and Vin announced they were going up to the mine.

'Are you going too, Evalyn?' her mother asked.

'She'd only be squeaking all the way,' Jack muttered. Evalyn overheard, watched Vin for his reaction, was furious when he laughed.

'No, Mother!' she replied proudly. 'Not this morning. Paul and I are going riding!'

Evalyn watched the boys leave to catch the stage in a state of impotent fury. She donned her riding habit and set out for Ashenfelter's, where she had arranged to meet Paul. Although she was early he was already waiting, and soon they were mounted and had left the town behind them.

'Paul, do you think that I squeak?'

He looked at her, threw back his head and laughed. 'Evalyn, what are you talking about?'

'Oh, just something that stupid Jack said.'

'And *you* take heed of that little worm?'

Evalyn relaxed. The angst, the invisibility was gone. Whenever I am with him, she thought in wonder, smiling at him as they leaned forward into the canter, it is as though everything in the whole world is in its rightful place . . . and I am at its centre.

On 24 July Tom dedicated the new library to the people of Ouray. He put on a special train to bring eighteen friends from Denver and Colorado Springs, among them the Governors, the mayors of both cities, the postmasters and their wives, and entertained one hundred and thirty guests in the banquet room of the Beaumont Hotel to a five-course dinner. The room was decorated with valley roses intertwined with green from the Ouray hills and sparkling with twinkling lights.

One speaker after another expressed their heartfelt thanks for the priceless gift their host had given the town. Then Tom spoke of the obligation of man to his brother, and of the pleasure it gave him and Carrie to make this gift.

Evalyn, Vin, Jack and Paul sat together and when the orchestra started up Paul rose to his feet.

'Would you care to dance, Miss Walsh?' he asked with a grin and a courtly bow.

Evalyn, delighted, jumped up. They were the first couple on the floor. She saw the Governor lead her mother to open the dance, and when she caught her eye she knew she would be in trouble again.

'Paul,' she whispered in his ear, 'I forgot. I'm not supposed to dance. Mother is very strict.'

'Even with your cousin?'

She blushed, acutely aware of the magic he represented, the sense of belonging. She glanced at him from sparkling eyes. 'Even with my cousin!'

Carrie was beside them as soon as the music stopped.

'I think it's time you went to bed, darling,' she murmured to Evalyn. She turned to her nephew and added in a tone of mild reproof, 'She's not quite fifteen you know, Paul . . . and we are in public. The idea was that she would simply *watch* the dancing – for a while!'

For once Paul looked abashed.

'Your father will escort you home now, Evalyn,' Carrie went on. 'Go and get your wrap.'

As her mother moved away to tell Vinson it was time to go home, Evalyn glanced back and indicated with a tiny movement of her head for Paul to follow her.

He casually left the banquet room and found Evalyn waiting in the corridor.

'As you're going back to Denver tomorrow,' she whispered, shyly taking his hand, 'I just wanted to say good night, and to thank you for making this stay in Ouray so happy.'

Afterwards Paul could not remember precisely how it had happened that he had his fourteen-year-old cousin in his arms and was telling her he loved her.

Chapter Twenty-Three

'Well, it's as much my world as anyone's! Just who does the little jerk think he is?' Evalyn muttered to herself when she thought of the snubs handed out by young Jack Hartland. 'I can go to Camp Bird when I like!'

She was missing Paul. Half the night she had relived the kiss in the Beaumont corridor, and each time it had thrilled her more. His words – '*I love you, Evalyn Walsh. I will love you always . . .*' were still echoing in her brain. The call of something deep in her being, something she hardly understood, asserted itself and made demands. On the one hand, she wanted to be back in Paul's arms; on the other she wanted to be 'one of the boys' again, safe in childhood. But I will see him again soon, she thought. We'll be spending a night in Denver on the way back East.

Vin and Jack went to the mine without her and she followed defiantly on her own, riding Dewdrop at a leisurely pace up the Canyon Creek Road. As she dismounted at the Camp Bird stables her father approached with Mr Hartland, and greeted Evalyn with a kiss, and a stern whisper: 'I hope you were careful on that road, Daughter?'

'Of course I was, Father.'

Tom turned to a groom and asked him to saddle two horses.

'May I come with you and Mr Hartland, Father?' Evalyn whispered eagerly. 'I'll be very quiet.'

Tom looked at his guest interrogatively. Edwin Hartland said with a smile that he would be delighted if she would come.

'Maybe the boys would care to join us too,' Tom said. 'We're just going up the Sneffles Road: Mr Hartland would like to see some of the old claims.'

'I'll ask the boys,' Evalyn said. 'Where are they?'

'In the retort room.'

Evalyn soon found her brother and his friend. They were not so much involved in learning the finer points of how gold was turned into ingots as in sniggering over a photograph that Jack hurriedly stuffed into his pocket. They were patently displeased to see her.

'What's that photograph?' she demanded.

'It's not for girls!'

Evalyn detected her brother's rising colour and the note of panic in his voice, glanced at Jack and saw that he was smirking.

She wanted to prise the photograph from his pocket but, as this was not an option, she suppressed her irritation and asked: 'Do you want to come riding? Father and Mr Hartland are going up the Sneffles Road.'

Vin's face betrayed instant enthusiasm; he glanced at his friend.

'Will you come, Jack? There's heaps of old tunnels and abandoned cabins. And it's wonderful above the timber line – beautiful and empty except for eagles and marmots.'

'The stables have a nice quiet pony that will suit you,' Evalyn said sweetly. But Jack demurred.

'I don't like riding much,' he said, adding by way of explanation when he saw the effect this had on Vin, 'I had a fall last year.'

'The only way to deal with falls is to get up and ride again!' Evalyn declared stoutly, determined in that instance that if this worm did ride with her she would show him a trick or two that would cure him of some of his assumptions about girls. We'll soon see who'll be doing the squeaking, she thought.

Vinson and Jack accompanied her to the stables, but Tom was no longer there; Mr Hartland said he had been called away by John Benson, and had suggested they go on without him, that he would catch up.

'Your father said you knew the road, Vin – and Evalyn too, of course,' he added hastily when he caught her eye.

He looked at his son, asked him if he now understood the gold extraction process; but there was something proprietorial in the question that made Vin and Evalyn glance at each other.

'Of course I know the road,' Evalyn declared. 'I've been on it winter and summer, Mr Hartland, and even in a blizzard!'

'If I remember correctly,' Vin interjected, 'you were *not* on it in that blizzard, which was why you, and Father, almost did not return.'

Evalyn directed a venomous glance at her brother, who looked instantly contrite. He did not want to fall out with his sister, but he was having a wonderful time being the centre of his new friend's attention.

'You're quite an intrepid young lady,' Edwin Hartland said.

Uggh, Evalyn said to herself.

'I wonder if Mr Hartland can ride,' she whispered to Vin after a few moments, when their two guests were out of earshot, 'or if *both* of them are softies.'

Vin looked uneasy. But he understood what she was saying. If they could show Mr Hartland up as a weakling, they reckoned his chances of influencing their father would be undermined.

'Let's put it to the test,' Evalyn added. 'Let's go for a gallop while Jack is making up his mind about whether or not he'll trust his precious ass to the back of a horse!'

'Ah no, Evalyn . . .'

'You've gone soft too,' she said scornfully. 'You're being sweet-talked into losing your inheritance!'

Vinson was naturally sociable and he could not bear to think ill of either of his guests. He loved his sister, and felt guilty about abandoning her. It occurred to him that she might be right. Perhaps he really *was* a softie and a pushover, and everyone was aware of it except him. Suddenly it did not seem such a bad idea after all to show off his riding prowess to his new friend.

'All right!' he said quietly. 'Count me in.'

They ducked into the stables where the saddled horses were waiting, mounted their own, and had almost gained the Canyon Creek Road before the Hartlands knew what was happening.

'I say,' Edwin Hartland shouted after them. 'Come back here, you two.'

But Evalyn wasn't listening. She galloped on to the Canyon Creek Road with Vin behind her. She whooped as she balanced into Dewdrop's stride, urging him to greater effort, ignoring the clots of foam that formed on his coat, ignoring the canyon below them. The surge of energy was not just a deliberate prank to show Jack Hartland and his father what girls were made of; it was a release of the tensions and confusion of the past week, and an exorcism of everything that had descended on her life and robbed her of freedom.

Hoofbeats thundered behind them. Glancing back through the cloud of dust, they saw Mr Hartland galloping after them and calling on them to stop, but this only spurred Evalyn and Vin to ride all the harder. They had almost reached Ouray before they pulled up. It was then that Evalyn heard Dewdrop's hoarse, tortured breathing and, horrified and guilt-stricken, she immediately slipped from his back.

'Dewdrop!' she cried. 'My darling Dewdrop . . .'

But Dewdrop just hung his head low and pushed his muzzle into the dust of the road. He stayed like that for a few moments, while Evalyn stroked his neck, and then as it became clear that he could not raise his head, she burst into a storm of tears, caressing her beloved pony, telling him between wrenching sobs, 'I'm sorry, Dewdrop. I didn't think . . . I didn't know . . .'

But Dewdrop could not be cajoled. He was an old horse who had given his all to the gallop. He sank to his knees and rolled over in the dust. Evalyn threw herself on him and hugged him, uncaring that her face and arms streaked with foam and dirt.

Tom was not far behind his children. He came upon a poignant scene:

280

Evalyn embracing the dead Dewdrop, his son looking on in tears, Edwin Hartland, still mounted, obviously at a loss.

Tom dismounted and approached. He was breathing heavily and his face was closed and angry.

Evalyn cried out in anguish, 'Oh, Father, poor Dewdrop... Oh, *Father*...'

But there was only scorn in her father's eyes.

'How many times have I told you, Evalyn, to be kind to animals, but all you have been able to think about is your own selfish excitement. Dewdrop was old and spent. He could not possibly have sustained that gallop without killing himself.'

Evalyn bent her head and cried as though her heart would break. But her father's tone did not soften.

'If you had thought about him for two seconds you would have realised that, Daughter!' he went on. 'But of course you had no regard either for the fright you were giving Mr Hartland or me, or the scapegrace antics in which you involved your brother. I expected to see you both in bits below on the canyon floor!' He turned to his guest. 'It was good of you to ride after them, Edwin. You don't know the road and you took a considerable risk!'

Vinson turned and looked at his sister, but she did not meet his eyes. She was still hugging her dead horse.

'I'm sorry, Father!' she whimpered, her voice incoherent with sobs. 'I'm so sorry!'

'You have to learn responsibility!' Tom said in the same cold voice, turning from one of his children to the other. 'What these mountains have given us should not blind you to that. You are responsible for your actions. It is the business and the price of being human!'

When they returned to the mine, he brought both his children into his office and told them in a tired voice, 'How can I possibly hold on to Camp Bird when every time you come here all I can think of is the necessity of getting rid of it before one of you is killed?'

'I think it's called being hoist with one's own petard,' Vin confided later to his sister. 'I shouldn't have listened to you.'

'Oh, just buzz off and look at your dirty picture,' Evalyn cried.

'It wasn't a dirty picture,' Vin said, reddening. 'It was just a picture of—'

'Bottoms!' Evalyn finished for him. 'Big, horrible bottoms!'

She felt defeated and couldn't help wondering if perhaps she was the kind of person who never got away with anything. For several nights she cried herself to sleep over Dewdrop. But there was one thing for which she was grateful: Paul had not been on hand to witness his death. At least he could not despise her on that account. When she thought of their time together, returning always to the kiss the night before his departure,

281

his whisper – '*I love you, Evalyn Walsh. I will love you always . . .*' – she felt as though her bones had turned to jelly.

She knew her life was changing. In a couple of years she would be able to put up her hair and become a different species – a young woman. She could hardly wait for it now. She had something special to look forward to.

I love you too, Paul, she thought. You make me so happy.

The Walshes returned to Washington at the end of August. Evalyn came back subdued. Their stop-off at Denver had been a disappointment. Paul had not been in town. He had had to go to Boulder – on business, Aunt Maria had explained; he would be so sorry to have missed them.

Evalyn was now enrolled in a new school – the small, select Holten Seminary – and comforted herself that she would see Paul the following year.

'I was really glad you came to Ouray,' she wrote to him. 'Now I'm stuck back at school and I keep thinking of our rides. But I'll be really grown up the next time I see you.'

That winter she had plenty of opportunity to consider the advantages of the adult state. At a party thrown by her mother for Alice Roosevelt, the White House débutante, Evalyn hid in Carrie's closet and peeped out from behind the velvets, furs and satins at the President's daughter, watched her tidy her hair at the dressing table and powder her face. She gasped when she saw her offer a cigarette to the beautiful Countess Cassini, the Russian Ambassador's daughter. Half choked and afraid to breathe, she watched the two young débutantes smoke and laugh together.

She longed to be like these fine and exotic young women, but she knew their daring did not extend beyond the four walls of the room. Once they left it they would revert to being 'ladies'. She was learning the ropes of the high society into which her family had been so readily accepted, was becoming sensitive to its nuances and its excitement.

She longed for a letter from Paul, but though his mother wrote at Christmas, there was only a short message from him, wishing all the family well.

But he *kissed* me, she thought. He told me he *loved* me . . . Yet he doesn't even send me a line.

She refused the anger, but the old sense of being invisible began to tug at her again.

Her scholastic performance at her new school was mediocre. Subjects such as English and Math showed her wanting. Her spoken French was good, but her knowledge of grammar was so poor that her teacher threw up her hands.

'Evalyn, how can you speak the language at all if you know no grammar?'

282

Evalyn tried to study. But it was boring compared to thoughts of Ouray and last summer and Paul. I wish I could write to him, she mused, but what if he doesn't write back? I'll feel such a mug!

'She's very smart,' the headmistress told Evalyn's parents. 'But she lacks confidence. A pity really...'

'How can she lack confidence?' Evalyn overheard her mother ask her father. 'She's always been the most buoyant and outgoing girl!'

But her new academy's tolerance was soon stretched. At a class in etiquette, Evalyn, reprimanded for her clumsiness at curtsying, and scolded for daydreaming while the teacher was running through the appropriate manner to mount and descend stairs in male company, was unable to contain her exasperation.

'Miss Carson,' she said, 'etiquette is based on silly assumptions. Why should we always get ourselves knotted over what men think? Why not ask a man to dance, for example, if we want to dance with him?'

There was a sharp intake of breath, but Evalyn had the bit between her teeth.

'Why should we not tell a man we would like to see him again, or even propose marriage to him if we love him? Why should we have to live our lives eternally waiting, while what we long for slips out of our reach?'

There was a gasp from the class, then giggles.

'Really, Evalyn,' Miss Carson said, 'this is too disgraceful!'

'Miss Carson, I am a girl from the mining towns in the West where women have more freedom than the richest ladies in Washington! If you have to wait for men to make sense of your life, you will either wait in vain or have a very short season! And as for curtsying,' she added, 'it is simple servility.'

That evening Carrie took her daughter aside and showed her the note that had been delivered from the headmistress.

'I can't understand, Evalyn, why you are always so provocative. How *could* you say such things?'

'But, Mother, I simply told the truth.'

'You must apologise tomorrow!'

'No,' Evalyn muttered darkly. 'I won't!'

She went to her father's study. He would soon be apprised of her misconduct and she wanted him to hear it from her. He listened attentively.

'Did I do wrong, Father?' she asked, reddening.

Tom sighed. 'There are conventions, Daughter, and you know this perfectly well. Whether these conventions are always sensible, or just, bears examination, but society has a way of punishing those who transgress them. The questions you asked about the enforced dependency of women gave offence, probably because it rubbed your teacher's nose into an unpalatable truth. You should apologise for that. And as for curtsying – I have always found it questionable. *My* daughter need bend her knee to nothing and no one – except God!'

Next day Evalyn said to Miss Carson, 'I apologise for offending you. But I spoke the truth! And I will never curtsy again!'

The teacher shook her head. 'I make the rules here, Evalyn,' she said quietly. 'Not my pupils! If you cannot understand that, you would be better off at another academy.'

Before the end of September a bulky missive came from London. It was a formal offer for Camp Bird from the London clients of Edwin Hartland.

Carrie was aghast.

'Don't sell it, Tom,' she pleaded. 'Don't even think of it. You've let that Edwin Hartland hypnotise you!'

Tom sighed. 'Look, it's true I've been considering his suggestion. Tell me why I shouldn't sell, Carrie. Mining is not an easy business. There are so many dangers; for example every time the children are at the mine we rub shoulders with catastrophe. I want to invest in other, safer, things!'

'For God's sake, Tom, you own land with a six-mile vein of gold running through it! What could you put your money into that would be a safer investment than that? You can always keep the children away from Camp Bird if it's them you're worried about.'

'No, Carrie. Every time I went back to Ouray they would clamour to come, and I would not be able to deny them! If I sold I could hazard some new ventures. I could invest in stocks, real estate, more manageable assets. And Carrie, face facts, I won't last for ever!'

Carrie paled. 'None of us will! But I have a feeling that to sell would not be lucky. When you think of what you went through to find it, the number of times you almost lost your life . . . it's like giving away part of your soul. It's like—'

'That's all very well,' Tom said, 'but, Carrie, if anything happened to me, how would you cope with a thousand miners and a huge gold mining operation?'

Carrie looked angry. 'You think I'm a nincompoop?'

'I'm not putting you down, my darling,' Tom went on. 'I'm thinking of your welfare. And, besides, *I* can't live a life of ease and leisure. I *need* a challenge! And if I sold the mine it would free up capital for something else I'm thinking of.'

Evalyn and Vinson had entered the room midway through this conversation and now Evalyn cried: 'I know what you're thinking of!'

'Do you indeed, Daughter?' Tom said mildly, but his eyes were steely.

Evalyn was unabashed. 'It's that old king, isn't it? He's got you interested in his schemes out there in Africa!'

Tom looked annoyed.

'Since you're so perceptive, Daughter, yes. There's gold, copper, zinc, and God knows what else in the Congo, just waiting to be dug out of the ground! I've seen the engineers' reports. Camp Bird is as nothing compared to what would flow from investing in Africa!'

Carrie gave a groan of horror. 'Don't, Tom. I'm telling you. I just *know*. Don't sell the mine and don't join that king in partnership.'

'Please don't, Father,' Evalyn echoed.

Tom's face clouded. 'Well, at least I know where my womenfolk stand,' he said in a deadpan voice. He turned to Vinson: 'What about you, Vin? What do you counsel?'

'I'm only thirteen, Father,' the boy said in his newly broken voice, 'but I think you should do whatever you want!' He looked askance for a moment at his sister and continued in grave solidarity, 'It's your mine and it's your money, and no one has the right to tell you what you can do with it!'

Carrie shook her head in disbelief and left the room.

'You little rat,' Evalyn hissed on the verge of tears. 'I'll never speak to you again!'

She followed her mother, her mind churning with the thought of Camp Bird being in other hands, of permanently saying goodbye to Ouray. But more than this was the feeling in the pit of her stomach, as though something were terribly wrong and she could not name it.

She found her mother lying on her bed. She had opened the top buttons of her dress and was lying back on her pillows dabbing at her forehead with some cotton wool soaked in eau-de-Cologne.

'Are you all right, Mother?'

'Oh, Evalyn,' Carrie said in voice tight with misery, 'what do you think of all this?'

Evalyn sat down on the edge of the bed, pleased at the maternal confidence.

'I feel like you do, Mother, as though it's wrong! And not just because of not seeing Ouray any more.'

'Your father is not a greedy man, Evalyn. You know yourself how kind and generous he is. But he needs challenge in his life, and he thinks he can repeat what he has done on an even grander scale.' Carrie looked at her daughter from eyes filled with anxiety. 'But Camp Bird will never be repeated, even if he lived to be a thousand. It was something special given to him . . . because he was worthy of it! You don't throw back gifts like that.'

'I know, Mother,' Evalyn agreed darkly.

But Tom made a deal with Hartland. The contract was drawn up by his attorneys, Guggenheimer, Untermyr and Marshall, of 30 Bond Street, New York City, and he went there in the New Year to sign it. The contract stipulated that he would receive cash, ore and stock, would be wealthy beyond his wildest dreams even if he never worked again.

He was almost fifty-two.

After signing he went for a walk, craning his neck at all the new developments, the Park Row Building, the new skyscraper underway in Fifth Avenue, marvelling at the city's change, and comparing his present circumstances with those of his nineteen-year-old self when he had first set his feet on this continent. But in his heart he felt as though an umbilical cord were being cut, as though he had, once again, to make his way in the world. He had pooh-poohed his womenfolk's reservations; it made sense to sell for a variety of reasons, but he privately acknowledged that for himself and the family, it was the end of an era.

But change *is* necessary, he thought, as he mulled things over. It opens up the future. And I have to move on.

The deal went ahead. On 1 May 1902, Tom was paid $3,100,000 in his lawyer's offices. In addition the purchasers contracted to pay him one-fourth of the net proceeds of the mine until he had received another $2,000,000, and he also received $100,000 worth of stock. And he already had millions invested in stocks and real estate that were giving him a huge income.

He was in his suite at the Waldorf, preparing to dine with his former smelting partner, David Wegg, when a telegram was delivered by a bellboy. Tom tore open the wire. But as soon as he glanced at it his throat closed and he reached unsteadily for the nearest chair.

VERY SORRY TO TELL YOU STOP MARIA KILLED IN ACCIDENT TODAY STOP CARRIE

Tom sat for a while. He heard the sounds of New York, clopping hoofs, turning carriage wheels, call of a newspaper boy, muted hotel noises. They seemed to come from far away. Much more real to him was a young woman in a royal blue cloak straining for a last glimpse of her father and sister on a distant stony road. For years she had been almost as much a part of his life as the air he breathed. He sent a message to David Wegg asking to be excused and spent the evening alone, his mind full of the past.

Next morning he took the first train to Denver. On arrival he learned the details of the accident. Maria had been driving in her new landau, drawn by the new mare, Rebecca. The coachman had reined the horse and got down to deal with snagged traces, passing the reins to Maria. She stood up to take them, but at that very moment something had frightened the animal. Rebecca had bolted, pulling the landau behind her at speed. Maria, the reins jolted out of her hands and no means of controlling the runaway horse, had acted quickly and jumped from the moving vehicle. But she tangled her feet in her long skirts, fell backwards on to the street and shattered her skull.

In his funeral oration Tom spoke with a full voice of their childhood together and of the great adventure they had undertaken in coming to America: 'No man was more blessed to have had such a woman for a sister and a friend.'

His family had joined him in Denver for the funeral, and Evalyn and Vin listened in tears. The former was acutely aware of Paul in the pew in front of her, in a new black suit. He was staring at the casket containing his mother's body with rigid fixity. Her heart was breaking for him; on impulse, she reached out into the pew in front and grasped his hand. His own was warm, the skin calloused, as she remembered. He started, but he returned the pressure.

'That damned mare . . .' he said to her tonelessly afterwards. 'If only we had realised . . . But she showed no sign in the stables that she was frisky.'

'You're not blaming Father?' Evalyn whispered.

Paul shook his head. 'Of course not! It could have happened with an ordinary hack!'

But it didn't! Evalyn thought. It happened with the fine lady's horse my father bought Aunt Maria, which was supposed to be as gentle as a kitten! And on the very day that Father signed the deed for the sale of Camp Bird.

But she shied away from such thoughts.

'Will you show me your livery stables?' she asked him. 'Your mother was so proud that you and your partner were building it up yourselves.'

In the stables she inhaled the scents she loved – of horses and hay and dubbin and leather.

'I would like to see you a lot more, Paul,' Evalyn ventured shyly, while she stroked the nose of a chesnut mare. 'I loved being with you in Ouray, riding out together,' she added, flushing, 'dancing with you and . . . everything . . .' She stumbled over the words. She was unable to mention the harsh, thrilling contact with his lips, or his words on that last night.

Paul leaned down, lifted the mare's hoof and inspected her shoe. His body language was awkward and embarrassed.

'Really?' he whispered.

'It made me feel so real. You are the second person in my life who made me feel real,' she went on in a low voice.

Paul straightened. 'Who was the other one?'

'A governess I had in Paris!'

Paul's sudden laughter made the mare flatten her ears.

'You sure know how to make a fellow feel special!'

'I didn't mean . . .' she said in some confusion, flushing brighter. 'What I want to say is, will you come to Washington to visit us? You can stay for as long as you like.'

Paul looked at her eager face, sighed and took her hand.

'Young cousin,' he said gently, 'would that be wise?'

'Oh yes, it would. Of course it would.'

'We both like each other very much.'

'So?' Evalyn said.

'You know as well as I do where that could lead. We are from different worlds, you and I. And your mother and father . . . have other plans for you!'

Evalyn cursed the heat in her face. She felt about five years old.

'Has someone been talking to you?'

Paul stood in silence for a moment. Then he looked into her face. 'No, Evalyn. At least not lately . . . although after our last stay in Ouray, Mother did point out how different our worlds are, and how ambitious your parents must be for you.'

'So what? They don't own me! If we wanted to get married they would have to listen. I'm nearly *sixteen* now.'

He smiled at her sadly, pressing something into her hand.

'Sixteen is very young. You will forget me.'

'No . . .'

She looked at her hand; saw he had given her a piece of quartz.

'I took it from the Canyon,' he whispered in her ear, 'that last day . . .'

'Paul is taking it as well as could be expected,' Carrie said when the Walsh family were on train home. 'But it will be worse for him in a few days' time. That's when the emptiness comes.'

She lapsed back into silence. Evalyn was turning over in her pocket the stone Paul had given her. She felt that if she did not talk about him she would burst.

'He's different,' she said tentatively. 'There's something about him.'

'He's a very fine young man!' Tom said. 'His father's son!'

'Poor Maria's death could be an omen,' Carrie said suddenly in a voice that was just audible above the beating of the wheels on the rail. 'I think you should find some reason to renege on that agreement!'

'Oh yes,' Evalyn echoed in a whisper.

'Carrie,' Tom said irritably, 'please leave the superstition to me! The deal is done!'

Carrie retreated into silence and Evalyn eyed her father nervously.

Tom took Maria's photograph from his wallet. Taken years before in Leadville, it showed a young woman, hair upswept, classically beautiful.

Goodbye, Maria, he thought. Nothing will ever make me forget you. And, even if I live to be a hundred, nothing will ever be the same again!

* * *

When a letter arrived from Tom's attorneys a few weeks later, enclosing copy inquiry from the purchaser's lawyers which suggested that a mistake had been made in the conveyance of Camp Bird, Carrie said it was a sign from Heaven. Twenty miles of water pipeline crucial to the mine had been omitted from the deed of sale.

'It's your chance to change your mind, Tom,' she said, steeling herself again to this subject. 'Without the pipeline they'll be only too glad to sell Camp Bird back to you.'

'But I meant to include it, Carrie,' he said tersely, 'and you know perfectly well that my word is my bond.'

He instructed his lawyers to prepare a supplementary deed and, when everything was finalised, made some gifts to his friends, among them David Wegg, to whom he sent $100,000, and made liberal disbursements to charity.

And then, almost as though he could not bear to be in America any longer now that Camp Bird was no longer exclusively his, he announced to his family that he was taking them to Europe for the summer.

'Can we visit the new house before we go, Father?' Evalyn asked. 'I know it's not ready yet, but I would like to see inside it.'

The new house was already referred to as 'Twenty Twenty', being the street number it would have on completion, and Carrie was already spending a good deal of her time planning the décor. She was determined it would be a Belle Epoque marvel, a beaux-arts palace.

It had sixty rooms and five storeys. Its Art Nouveau mahogany staircase was like the one in the liner *Majestic* that she had admired so much. It swept up to a musicians' gallery and then divided in a dual approach to the first landing. This landing in turn was galleried, with fluted mahogany Ionic columns that supported the second landing above. A great canopy of stained glass presided over the entire stairwell, but above its level was a further floor with a great skylight. Here, at the top of the house, the ballroom was situated, alongside the bedrooms for the women servants, and a small theatre intended for Vinson. Above it again, accessed by narrow stairs, was the roof garden, where the city of Washington could be viewed from a private prominence.

The house would be served by two main entrances, one on Massachusetts Avenue, which opened directly into the great hallway. The other entrance, which had a glass *porte-cochère* intended for carriages, was on 21st Street. It would have its own hallway with a white marble French fireplace. The service entrance, in turn, was at the back of the building.

There was a library, an enormous drawing room, a sunny conservatory. Behind the drawing room – through folding doors – was the music room, where a baroque organ was already installed. This room led to the dining room, which had been modelled on King Leopold's. There was a serving room just off the dining room, and from it ran a narrow staircase to a hidden room, sandwiched between two floors, whose only other means of access was directly from Tom's office on the floor above. It was in this concealed room that Tom was installing his massive safe.

The ground floor contained the kitchen and pantries, staff sitting rooms and the menservants' bedrooms. Behind the house the stables and quarters for the grooms were being erected.

'When do you think the work will be completed, Tom?'

'End of the year, darling. And then you will have your hands full furnishing it. But, meanwhile, do let's go back to Europe.'

He wants to see that king, Evalyn thought, dismayed at a gut level by the prospect that her father might go into business with a man she had disliked on sight.

Chapter Twenty-Four

The Walshes returned to Washington in the fall of 1903, and soon after left the house at Le Roy Phelps Place to move into their newly completed house at 2020 Massachusetts Avenue, where everything was of the best and most expensive. The electric Otis elevator alone had cost $5,000. Panelled in dark, polished mahogany, it moved with smooth swiftness from floor to floor. The Otis company had also installed an electric dumb waiter that connected kitchen and dining room. Most of the bedrooms had marble-tiled bathrooms ensuite. On the third floor there was an apartment fit for a king, designed with King Leopold in mind.

Evalyn loved the new house, the entrance doorways with their pink marble columns, the reception hall that soared three storeys to the stained-glass canopy, the gilded panelling, the sweeping staircase in the shape of a Y. She loved the Louis XIV drawing room with its walls covered in pink damask, its ceiling covered in cherub frescos and, through its folding doors, the music room with its organ. The celebrated interior decorator Mrs Anna Jennesse Miller had been retained by Carrie to help her furnish and decorate the mansion, and had been run off her feet.

There had been decorators, art dealers, rug merchants and furniture makers to be dealt with. Carpets had come from Persia, pictures from dealers in the Boulevard Poissonnière in Paris and from the Avenue Louise in Brussels. Flemish tapestries had appeared on the walls. The library had been filled with rare and beautiful books.

But the most impressive thing of all to Evalyn was her own quarters. She walked into a suite of rooms that were all her own – walls lined, like the drawing room, with pink silk damask, a spacious sitting room, bedroom and bathroom. The door pulls were gold-plated, as were the bathroom fittings.

She was just seventeen. But she found it strange that her perceptions of luxury had altered in a matter of a few years. The delight in her new home did not have the same edge as it would have had three years earlier. It was as though something in her had become hardened. There had begun in her a kind of weariness in having everything she wanted, almost as she wanted

291

it. The toilet things on her dressing table had solid gold tops or gold handles, but this did not enthral her any more. Nothing in all the splendour around her compared, in Evalyn's mind, to the photographs on her mantelpiece in simple silver frames, of her father, mother and Vin, or to the old riding boots she kept in her trunk with Dewdrop's smell still on them, or the piece of rugged quartz from Ouray that Paul had pressed into her hand and that she now kept in her small jewel box.

But when her father twinkled at her, 'Are your quarters to your liking, Daughter? We even used some of that "left over" gold you once mentioned to keep you happy,' she laughed and embraced him.

'You are the kindest father in the world.'

She felt very close to her father these days. On their trip to Europe, the two of them had gone together to meet King Leopold again, travelling south to the spa town of Bagnères-de-Luchon in the Pyrenees where the king was taking the waters. It had necessitated a fifteen-hour journey.

Evalyn had loved Luchon because it reminded her of Ouray. The blue and purple mountains descended almost into the town, and the town itself was beautiful – full of lovely houses with wrought-iron balconies. They had been the king's guests for dinner and she had met his mistress – a girl of nineteen called Baronne Vaughan. She had listened in fascination while the king addressed the Baronne as *Très Jeune*, while she called him *Très Vieux*.

And it had been in Luchon that her father had told the king that he would not be joining him mining in Africa after all.

'From what I hear they handle things very badly down there in the Congo, Evalyn,' he had confided on the return journey. 'I've had inquiries made and I'll keep my money where I can see it, not squander it on a venture that is steeped in slavery and brutality.'

Evalyn had wanted to cheer. Her mother too had been delighted at this decision, and even Vinson had evinced relief.

Vinson was now fifteen. His room in 2020 was filled with everything he had asked for – a gun case, a bookcase filled with books, a sterling silver ship, a stuffed alligator, two sets of armour and a shield, a silver man on horseback, a bronze horse, an ivory elephant. Beside his bed he kept a picture of his hero, the racing automobilist Camille Jenatzki – called the Red Devil because of the colour of his beard – who had won the Gordon Bennett road race in a Mercedes on 2 July. The race, which had taken place in Ireland, had been won at astonishing speeds of over a mile a minute.

'I wish I had a motor car,' Vin confided to his sister. 'If I hint about it to Father I hope you won't put the dampener on it again!'

'You're too young, Vin!'

'Don't be such a bore!'

The boy's most treasured possessions were in the top of the house, in the little theatre near the ballroom. Here, some weeks after they moved into the new house, Vinson put on the first of his magical shows, and disappeared like Houdini from various restraints, pulled wriggling rabbits out of hats, and did card tricks with amazing sleights of ingenuity. All the young crowd had been invited – his and Evalyn's friends. Among the latter was Katherine Elkins, and Flora Wilson, who had a fine singing voice.

Tom sat at the back of the theatre in the half-dark and looked around him. His mansion was built and splendidly appointed; his wife was relaxed and laughing; his clever, gentle son, whom he loved more with every passing day, was delighting his audience; his daughter, so thorny, so capricious and so headstrong, seemed to be happy. School had never suited her, and now that they had agreed it was not for her she was blooming. His fat little duckling was growing into a swan.

Evalyn spent a good deal of time at the white piano in the ballroom, picking out tunes, perhaps finding in music, Tom mused, the challenges she thought she had left behind in the West. She had even asked Dr James Wheaton Howard of St Aloysius Church, the organist Tom had on retainer to play for their guests, to teach her the organ; and her practice sessions made the whole house resound. She had made friends in Washington and was right now clapping enthusiastically beside young Florrie Wilson, who was exclaiming loudly, 'Bravo, Vin . . .'

The young magician's friends took up the cry and stamped their feet until the whole house seemed to resonate.

Tom's heart filled with love and pride. He beamed at his children's guests as the lights came up and he saw all the glowing young faces around him. Now is the blessed harvest time he thought, the reaping of what has been sown.

The youngsters asked Florrie to sing. She looked questioningly at Carrie, who nodded encouragement.

Evalyn conferred with Flora, went to the piano and struck the keys. Flora cleared her throat and in a moment an old song filled the top floor of the great new mansion in Massachusetts Avenue.

'Believe me, if all those endearing young charms
Which I gaze on so fondly today
Were to change by tomorrow, and fleet in my arms,
Like fairy gifts fading away!

'Thou wouldst still be adored
As this moment thou art
Let thy loveliness fade as it will,
And around the dear ruin each wish of my heart
Would entwine itself fervently still.

'For the heart that has truly loved never forgets
But as truly loves on to the close . . .'

Tom felt his throat tighten. He remembered the night in Leadville all those
years ago – the same song . . . and the lovely young woman who had sung
and played. He caught Carrie's eye; she has not changed, he thought. He
put a discreet finger to his lips and sent her a silent kiss. But, even as he
watched his daughter's fingers ripple the keys, from the halls of memory
came Peggie's lilting voice, and for a moment he was back in Carraig Mór,
the half-door was open to the evening and, outside, the wind was soughing
down Slievenamon.

The new Walsh residence was soon the scene of some of the capital's most
lavish entertainments. On 8 December 1903, the *Evening Star* newspaper
described the first major dinner party there, to which had been invited a
number of Senators and their wives, the Belgian Minister and numerous
other powerful and influential friends.
  '*Mr and Mrs Walsh entertained at a dinner last night in their new home
on Massachusetts Avenue, which in every detail was one of the most sumptuous
affairs ever given in the Capital. The dinner table was adorned with yellow
orchids of a very beautiful variety, their coloring being the keynote to the
superb decoration of the board, where a service of gold made from glittering
nuggets taken from the Camp Bird Mine, was used for the first time.*'
  Evalyn, reading the newspaper account in her mother's sitting room,
observed, 'We are never out of the papers these days.'
  Carrie looked up from the catalogue she was perusing.
  'That is true, Evalyn. During our lives we probably never will be
again.'
  'But isn't it weird that afterwards everyone will forget us! After all this
fuss, in a miserable hundred years or less, no one will know that we ever
lived.'
  Carrie shrugged. 'Does it matter, darling? After all we will be safe in the
hands of God.'
  'That's a nice way of looking at things, Mother. Do you think God will
throw parties?'
  Carrie laughed a little reprovingly.
  'I suppose His parties will be even better than ours,' Evalyn pressed on.
'But I'd rather not wait that long. I'd really love to attend the ball you are
throwing for Alice Roosevelt.' She waited with bated breath.
  'You're too young! You must wait for another year!'
  'Oh, Mother . . .'
  'I know best, Evalyn.'
  Evalyn recognised the tightness around her mother's mouth and knew

she could not be moved. She bit her tongue, aware that she had already strained maternal patience to breaking point.

But I'm seventeen, she fumed in silence.

On the appointed day she watched the preparations for the ball. Hot-house flowers arrived in boxloads. The maids polished the parquet in the Louis XIV salon, and in the yellow-brocaded top-floor ballroom. The pink marble walls of the first-floor hallway, the gilded plaster cornicing, the gilded mouldings on the walls, the gold-plated door handles – all glowed in the light of the five-branched, gilded bronze flambeau sconces affixed to the walls.

Before the first guests arrived a violin quintet took their seats on the orchestra landing at the point where the stairs forked. Evalyn waited her chance and insinuated herself here behind the parlour palms.

'Don't mind me,' she told the violinsts. 'I just want to watch. I'll be very quiet!'

From this vantage point she watched the couples going up and downstairs, so close that she could have put out her hand from behind the potted greenery and touched the men in white gloves and tails and the bejewelled women wearing gowns that rustled like mountains of tissue paper. Each of the guests, she knew, would leave that evening with a 'favour' – a small present: lace fans with tortoiseshell handles for the ladies and solid gold pencils for the gentlemen. These were now in baskets in the library.

When everyone was upstairs she slipped down to that room, which smelled of old books and leather bindings, helped herself to a fan, and then hurried to the elevator to find her own suite on the second floor.

As the strains of Johann Strauss wafted through the house, she took her small inlaid jewel box from her dressing table. The first thing her fingers closed on when she opened it was Paul's piece of quartz. She held it to her lips, then threw it on the bed.

What good are you? she asked it angrily. You just fill me with sadness. *And* you're only an old piece of rock!

But she knew she could not throw it away. She put it back in the box, decked herself before her mirror, donning the diamond ring, the turquoise and pearl necklace her father had given her when she went with him to Luchon, and the discreet pearl earrings her mother had presented her with for her birthday. She put rouge on her cheeks and lips, fanned herself before the mirror, pretending she was a sophisticate in a satin gown, and then danced around the room. Next year she thought. Oh, roll on next year. I'll be grown up and I'll be free. The world, the whole world will be mine!

But the mood did not last. She put down the fan, fingered its Brussels lace for a moment, and wondered why its beauty was of little consequence to her. She could remember a time when she would have regarded it as the loveliest thing she had ever seen. What if money and possessions were like drugs, that you always needed more and more to get the same thrill? The old loneliness was there again, as though, even in the midst of the gaiety echoing through the house, a dark shadow had reached out and touched her. She undressed, had a bath and got into bed, but she kept her bedside light on, and deposited on her nightstand the diamond ring and the turquoise and pearl necklace. They gleamed at her coldly, a bloodless substitute for love and life.

She was almost asleep when she heard the discreet knock at her door, dragged herself into a sitting position and called, 'Come in.'

It was Vinson, in his quilted dressing gown. The dance music followed him into the room, was muted again when the door was closed.

He sat on the end of her bed.

'I couldn't sleep. I wonder how many guests there are in the house.'

Evalyn shrugged. 'Three hundred and twenty-five. I heard the butler talking earlier. It sounds like thousands – dancing and drinking as though the stuff were about to be banned.'

'And,' Vin said drily, 'they owe it all to Father's luck!' He paused, looked at her seriously and continued, 'I worry about Luck, Sis. What bugs me is this: that it can give one person something like the Camp Bird Mine, while many people wonder where the next meal is coming from.'

He picked the turquoise collar from her nightstand, rubbed his fingers along its length.

'Father's luck didn't come from the roll of a dice,' Evalyn replied, recalling the nights in Ouray when he had stumbled home exhausted in sub-zero temperatures. 'I remember it better than you do – all the terrible work, study and determination. It wasn't luck at all!'

Vinson brightened.

'And another thing,' Evalyn said with a grin, 'it's Camp Bird that will fund the acquisition of that motor car you want so much!'

Vinson won her with his rueful smile. In the conversational lull they noticed that the revelry in the house had abated.

'I think the pests are going home,' Vin said. 'About time too.'

The rattle of carriage wheels and the echo of iron-shod hoofs came from the street below, and then the sound of raised, cheery voices.

Vin laughed. 'It's a skill,' he said, 'isn't it? Enjoying yourself!' He regarded his sister sardonically. 'One *you've* always had!'

It's not true, Evalyn thought.

'When I own this house,' Vin went on rather grandly, 'I might let you come to my parties.'

Evalyn threw a pillow after him as he left the room. But when he was gone she found she could not sleep. The house became silent at last. The clock said four thirty. She got up, put on a warm dressing gown, and went out on to the gallery landing. The house seemed even bigger in the darkness. She took the elevator to the top of the house to survey the ballroom, bent down to pick up something from the floor. It was one of the 'favours', a gold pencil. She put it in her pocket, wandered restlessly out of the ballroom and up the narrow stairs to the roof garden. Here, at the edge of the flat roof, she could look over the nighttime city. She saw the dim bulk of Washington Cathedral in the distance. She turned towards the west. Away over there, a thousand miles away, was Denver and Paul!

Chapter Twenty-Five

Summer returned to stifle Washington. Tom was asked by the President to go to Colorado and use his influence there to help stabilise a fraught situation. Miners were striking; there was unrest throughout the state.

Evalyn was delighted when her grandmother, Arabella Reed, asked the family to stay with her in Denver. The old lady was frail now, getting around with the help of a stick. She had refused Tom's offer of a larger house, and lived quietly with a servant companion, a woman called Rose.

But after the great rooms of 2020 Massachusetts Avenue, Evalyn found her grandmother's clapboard house suffocating. She missed her father – he was away most of the time, travelling throughout the State – and her mother was preoccupied with anxiety about Vin, who had stayed back East. He was getting treatment for a skin rash that had begun in spring and still seemed to defy the doctors.

They would not be going to Ouray and the only light on Evalyn's horizon was the prospect of Paul's visit. She had written to tell him they would be in Denver, a deliberately light-hearted letter full of Washington gossip.

She wished her Aunt Maria were still alive. Quite apart from the delight in seeing *her*, she would have run into Paul virtually immediately. But Paul has sold his mother's house and used the money to expand his business. He now lived in bachelor accommodation. Or so her father had told her.

Delighted to hear you are in town. Will call Sunday 3 p.m. if convenient. Paul

The note was in her grandmother's mailbox one morning with the rest of the post.

Evalyn prepared herself carefully for his visit. She was no longer wearing young girls' dresses and realised that this would be the first time Paul would see her in a full-length frock. She chose a figured muslin daydress, with a high lace neck, soft sleeves that were gathered at the wrist, and a flounced hem that swept the floor.

'Can I put my hair up, Mother? Please? After all, I will be eighteen in a fortnight!'

'Do you want to put your hair up just because your cousin is coming?'

'Oh, let her,' Arabella said. 'The child is simply longing for it.'

When Paul appeared at the door it was opened by a young lady he hardly knew. Elegant, expensively dressed, tightly laced, hair coiffed around her head, pearls in her ears, a diamond on her right hand, his cousin Evalyn seemed for a moment a creature from a fashion magazine, as remote from the girl he had ridden with in the Ouray Canyon as any Washington socialite.

She saw the eager expression on his face, the sudden dilation of the pupils, the instant retraction, felt the brotherly kiss on her cheek, heard the cousinly raillery.

'Evalyn, is it really you? I didn't recognise you!'

But he was the one who had changed, she thought; he was no longer a youth, but a young man in charge of his life. He wore a light grey flannel suit; his blue silk tie was carefully knotted under his high collar. Evalyn realised that he had dressed for this meeting as carefully as she had, and as Rose served a supper of cold roast beef and pickles, Evalyn studied him covertly. He glanced at her occasionally, a smile, half conspiratorial like two years before, half reserved as though she were a stranger. His certainty lent him charisma; he charmed Grandma Reed.

'You're looking very well, Paul, very prosperous!' Carrie said.

He seemed pleased. 'We've expanded, Aunt Carrie. We – my partner Martin Moore and I – secured some important new accounts recently. We've bought the adjoining building so we've plenty of space. We aim to become the biggest livery stables in the city.'

'Bravo!' Evalyn cried.

He turned to her, seeming abashed by the general interest.

'But that's enough about me! Tell me what *you've* been doing.'

Evalyn did not know if Paul were really interested or not. His eyes were too deep set to read easily, but his demeanour was one of complete attention. Because she wanted to impress him she rattled on, told him about the new house in Massachusetts Avenue.

'There's sixty rooms, Paul, so there's plenty of space for guests if you would like to visit. We have twenty-three servants . . . there's an elevator . . . King Leopold is going to visit . . . if you would like to meet him.'

The attention in Paul's face began to falter; his eyes began to glaze. Evalyn felt as though she had been given a chance at something terribly important and had somehow muffed it.

'You must call again,' Grandma Reed said as he was leaving. 'It's dull for Evalyn here, and, of course, your Aunt Carrie and I would be glad to see you too . . . so nice to be with young people.'

'Thank you, ma'am . . .'

As he left his eyes moved to Evalyn, dwelled on her. Something sad and hungry flickered in them and was gone.

'Well, Evalyn!' her grandmother said when the door was shut, 'there's one young man who thinks you are the moon and the stars!'

'Don't put such notions into her head, Mother!' Carrie cried.

'How do you know, Grandma,' Evalyn whispered when her mother was out of earshot, 'that he thinks so well of me? I thought he hardly noticed me!'

Arabella Reed smiled. Her hair, Evalyn thought, was the same colour as the silver on the top of her cane.

Arabella gave her tinkling laugh. 'My dear child, there are two things that cannot be hidden. One is a cough, and the other is love!' She patted her granddaughter's hand. 'But you'll have so *many* beaux at your feet, my dear, before you're done. You don't want to be bowled over by the first.'

I don't want beaux at my feet, Evalyn thought. I only want him.

Days went by but Paul did not call again. Evalyn's pride was piqued. The mirror told her she was a prize fit for a prince; her heart yearned for the mutuality she had had with him in Ouray, and with guilty longing she ached for his lips on hers again. 'I love you!' he had once said. And now he behaved as though there had never been anything to remember.

'Mother, I would like to go shopping,' Evalyn announced one morning.

'Well, we can go this afternoon!' Carrie said. 'What is it you want to buy?'

'Oh I don't know . . . I just want to look around the stores. It's a long time since we shopped in Denver!'

They ordered the carriage for two o'clock. The day was sunny, but not stifling, perfect for a walk, Evalyn said, persuading her mother to alight in Sherman Street. They told their driver to collect them later at the Capitol building.

But Carrie was quick to notice that their itinerary quickly brought them to the door of a livery stables known as Lafferty and Moore.

'Oh, look, Mother . . . Paul's stables. Let's go in and see him.'

'Evalyn!' Carrie exclaimed in irritation. 'So that's why you wanted . . . You are simply making an exhibition of yourself!'

Paul was seated in a swivel chair in his office. He rose as his aunt and cousin were shown in, held chairs for them.

'It's just that we were passing,' Evalyn explained. 'And I haven't seen this place for two years, and Mother was curious.'

'Would you really like to see the stables, Aunt Carrie?'

Carrie thought of horse manure and straw and the hem of her gown.

'Actually, I feel a little tired.'

'But I'll go!' Evalyn exclaimed, jumping to her feet. 'I'd like to see what changes you've made.'

'We've made quite a few since you were here last.'

Evalyn heard the pride in his voice as she followed him from the room. As they crossed the threshold into the stable yard a young woman came in from the street. She was delicately holding up the hem of her dress. She brightened when she saw Paul and looked curiously at Evalyn.

'This is Miss Moore,' Paul said, 'my partner's sister.' He turned to the newcomer. 'Amelia, may I present my cousin, Miss Walsh.'

They shook hands. Miss Moore was thin, with fine brown eyes and dark hair under a stylish hat.

'Martin's not back from lunch yet,' Paul told her. 'He said he'd be late.'

The girl left and the two cousins proceeded on their way.

Evalyn was wearing buttoned patent-leather bootees, and she picked her way carefully over the cobbles of the stable yard. Paul offered his arm and she held it for a moment with half-closed eyes, suffused in bliss.

'Paul,' she said desperately as they neared the end of the tour, 'the last time I was here you gave me something as a keepsake. I've kept it and I haven't forgotten . . . And I'm old enough now – aren't I? I'm not a child any more.'

They were alone in a tack room. Around them were racks of bridles, stands of saddles, horse collars on pegs, rows of stirrups and martingales, shelves of horse blankets. Against the opposite wall was a cabinet of medicines and beside it an iron pot-bellied stove. The air was full of the old familiar smells of dubbin and leather.

Paul looked at her for a moment. Then he lifted her chin, took her face between his hands and kissed her hungrily. When he felt for her hand his finger rested on the diamond ring her father had given her.

'Father gave it to me . . .'

He raised her palm to his lips. His silent intensity seemed answer enough to her question. But his voice was careful when he spoke.

'Dearest Evalyn, I've been thinking about us . . .'

Evalyn waited. Her heart quickened; she could hardly breathe. Would he ask her now?

'You can marry anyone,' he went on. 'I wouldn't be surprised if you ended up as a duchess. But if I married a rich woman, lived on her wealth, I would be – I don't know how to put this – I would be dispossessed of myself!'

'But we *love* each other,' Evalyn cried, tears starting in her eyes. 'What are you talking about?'

'I just wish to God,' Paul said, 'that there was a way.'

'So you're going to let a girl you love walk out of your life . . . when she loves you and hasn't done anything wrong . . . just because her father is rich?'

Paul's face became set. 'I wish . . . Oh God, Evalyn, how I wish . . .'

'Well then, do something.'

He said darkly: 'I learned at an early age, Evalyn, that impulse can be mortal! And,' he added, 'if the truth be told, I can see how wealth is already changing you. You are becoming someone else.'

'No I'm not! I am the very same! Tell me how I'm different and I'll change it.' She reached up and touched his face. 'I don't *have* to be rich, Paul.'

'Don't you?'

She tightened her grip on his hand. 'But *why* couldn't we be rich together? What's wrong with it?'

'Nothing!' he said with a short laugh. 'But not on *your* money!'

'Are you telling me I have a choice?' Evalyn whispered. 'That I must give up my prospects of inheriting a fortune if I am to be your wife?'

'I could not ask that of you, Evalyn! Think of how, one day, you would hate me for it. Oh, my wonderful Evalyn, you love it all, and who can blame you? Enjoy it; be happy. And,' he added huskily, 'I'll always be there for you. I will never forget you!'

'I hate you, Paul Lafferty!' she cried, biting back the tears that threatened to overwhelm her. 'You can forget me as soon as you like!'

Well, who cares anyway? she told herself for days afterwards. Who does he think he is? There are plenty more fish in the sea! I am an heiress, after all, and I can have *anyone*! Imagine expecting me to give up *millions* . . . And I humiliated myself.

'If Paul visits us again,' she told her mother, 'will you tell him I'm not in?'

'Of course, darling. I do understand and I think you are being very wise. It would be very foolish to . . .'

But Evalyn did see Paul once more before the Walshes left Denver. She watched him from her window as he walked slowly away. He had called, and Rose, as instructed, had told him Evalyn was not at home. It was seven in the evening and the light seemed to gild him. She was on the point of rushing downstairs; she wanted to knock at the window; she wanted to bring him back somehow. But her pride was too strong for her. She watched from behind the lace curtain as he retreated.

When she went down to dinner Carrie asked her if she had been crying.

'I was reading a sad book, Mother.'

Oh Paul, Paul . . .

For days after that Evalyn behaved strangely, so much so that when Tom returned from his travels Carrie told him that his daughter had spent days demanding constant diversions, card parties, outings.

'She's young!' Tom said. 'Denver can't be much fun for her when all her friends are in Washington!'

Arabella introduced Carrie to the Christian Science religion.

'There's nothing like prayer, Carrie,' she told her daughter when the latter spoke to her of Vin's persistent skin rash. 'It is always answered.'

When the family was reunited in Washington, Carrie insisted on bringing Vin to the Christian Science Temple for a laying-on of hands. Within the week the rash had almost gone, except for a few reddish blotches that still clung stubbornly to his chin.

Evalyn was aware that he had grown while they were apart; he was now a slim, handsome boy, a curious mixture, his sister thought – mischievous but reserved, gentle but often steely. They were close friends. She made him laugh a good deal, distracted herself in doing so and dreaded his return to boarding school when she would have nothing to do but think of how Paul had rejected her.

Carrie, meanwhile, had become a faithful follower of her new religion. Reading the Bible took up an increasing amount of her time.

'Come with me to the Temple if you like, Evalyn,' she said one day when her daughter complained of being bored. 'After all, God is the really important person in one's life.'

'If I were to change religions, Mother, I think I'd prefer to become a Catholic than a Christian Scientist! Catholicism goes about things with style!'

Carrie clicked her tongue. 'How can you be so irreverent? You'd need a better reason than that for joining a religion! And I thought your experience in the convent had—'

'Put me off? Not necessarily!'

Oh, hell's bells, Evalyn thought to herself, why am I always annoying my mother?

On the night before Vin was due to return to school, Tom threw a dinner party for his political friends. Among his guests were Secretary of War William Howard Taft, and Archibold Butt, the White House military aide. Evalyn watched the preparations.

'Will there be musicians tonight?' she asked her father.

'Not tonight, Daughter. As your mother will be out it will be a gentlemen's dinner.'

This gave Evalyn an idea.

'There's a bunch of stiffs coming to dine with Father,' she told Vinson, 'all loaded down with importance. What do you say we interfere with their little complacencies?'

Vin looked at her suspiciously, then laughed.

'What do you have in mind?'

'You know the musicians' landing at the fork of the stairs?'

Vin nodded.

'And you know the painted canvas screen between it and the dining room?'

'Sure.'

'Well, I thought we'd give them a little music of our own.'

Later that evening a corpulent Secretary of War Taft had his consumption of champagne temporarily interrupted by a pea that hit the left side of his nose. And, the next moment, handsome Archibold Butt, sitting up as straight as a pole in military dress uniform, felt a sudden stinging to his upper lip. The projectile landed on the table and he picked it up. It was a hard, wizened pea.

'It came from there!' Archie exclaimed, pointing to the wall of the dining room above the doorway, where a painting depicted nymphs and shepherds in a peaceful Arcadia. His keen eyes detected the small hole in the canvas and the peashooter that was sticking through it. He jumped to his feet.

'Gentlemen, I fear we are under attack!'

There was momentary consternation, then laughter rippled around the table.

Tom raced into the hall, just in time to see his two teenage children fleeing to the escalator, pea shooters in hand.

'Come back here, you two.' He motioned them sternly into the library and shut the door.

'Oh, Father,' Evalyn said, laughing, 'please don't scold us. We just wanted to liven things up for you.'

'We only put a *little* hole in the screen,' Vin said, 'and you must admit they do all look so stuffy.'

Evalyn saw the familiar twitch of her father's moustache.

'You two take the biscuit,' he said. 'I'll deal with you tomorrow.'

Major Butt, with a cursory knock, entered the room.

'I see you have apprehended the culprits, Tom!' he said, and turned in mock severity to the two young people. 'Which of you have I to thank for my smarting lip?'

'I'm sorry, Major,' Evalyn said, looking at him demurely from under lowered lashes. 'But you must admit my aim was good!'

Willie Taft came into the room behind him.

'Someone has put my nose out of joint,' he boomed.

'I'm very sorry, sir,' Vinson said with a grin.

Taft reached out his hand. 'How about a truce now, young sir? Can we go back and eat our dinner?'

But next day Tom was much graver about the incident.

'To think that my children – who are respectively eighteen and sixteen – should have so little sense. I'm particularly surprised at you, Daughter. I had hoped you were growing up.'

'We're very penitent, Father,' Evalyn said, hanging her head. 'It was too bad of us – and just as poor, famished Mr Taft was really tucking in too.'

She was gratified by the reluctant peal of parental mirth.

'Don't do it again!' Tom said. 'However much you like to play with absurdity, it's a considerable embarrassment to your father.'

Later Evalyn said to Vin, 'We got away scot-free.'

'That's true. But I think Father's right. We *should* grow up. I'm going to buckle down at school and grow into a strong man who will be able to help him!'

He glanced at Evalyn tentatively as though he expected her to scoff, but she just said quietly: 'Good for you! It *was* a silly joke and one of us should do something to make him really proud!'

Vinson was as good as his word. A pupil at the Hill School at Pottstown, he had got himself on to the staff of the *Dial*, the school paper, and delighted in his role of editor and reporter. He had taken, with all the gravity of newfound responsibility, to reminding his sister that she had to get an education before it was too late.

'You can't go through life, Sis,' he told her when he came home on a weekend break, 'with as much information as a savage. You're supposed to be a young lady!'

'I've left school!' Evalyn replied. 'And I've been saying for years that I don't want to be a lady – old or young.'

Vin looked exasperated. 'So what do you intend doing?'

'I'd like to be Calamity Jane – you remember Father's stories about her in Leadville when he first came out West? She did what she wanted and she said what she wanted and no one messed around with her and she had a fine time.'

Vin regarded his sister with some irritation. 'You can't be Calamity Jane. You're an heiress and you live in Washington. Look, why don't you make an effort to please the parents – acquire accomplishments, stretch yourself a bit, see what you can do?'

'Oh, Vin, you know I'm not much use . . .'

When she was alone she told herself: I can't go on obsessing myself with someone who doesn't care enough for me to make me happy. If I could only escape on my own – maybe to Europe . . .' She sighed, put her fists to her head. 'Or anywhere I could have a wild time and get away from myself.'

Evalyn's brainwave came when she was talking to her friend Flora. Flora's lovely voice was now partially trained, but she said that she needed more lessons if she was ever to be really good.

'I wish I could go to Paris. They have the best teachers there.'

Evalyn thought of the French capital, of the Exposition and its excitement, of Mamselle and the Ferris wheel. She had kept a few drops of the precious Muguet and although she no longer wore it, the supply being nearly exhausted, she liked to take it out and put her nose to its fragrance. She often wondered where her governess was now. She had once requested her father to find out, but whenever she asked him if there was any news he said that he was still awaiting the result of his inquiries.

'She can't have disappeared off the face of planet Earth, Father,' she had cried on the last occasion Mamselle had come up in conversation, 'so you must be able to find her!'

'I know that Evalyn, but there are certain difficulties . . .'

Something in the way he had said this made her suspect he knew more than he was telling her.

I'll find you, Mamselle, she had thought. One of these days I'll solve the mystery and find you myself. Even if you're down on your luck. I've plenty of money and I'll fix things for you.

Now she thought that the best way of solving the puzzle was to go back to France.

'You *can* go to Paris!' Evalyn told Flora. 'I think I know a way. How would you like the two of us to go together?'

'On our own? Are you serious?'

'Just leave it to me!'

Later that evening Evalyn said casually that she was bored doing nothing and would love to study French and music. Tom and Carrie looked at her carefully.

'Are you serious, Daughter?' Tom demanded. 'I had formed the opinion that you and study of any kind were mutually antipathetic!'

'I *am* serious. It's true I hated school, but I'd like to study French and music on a freelance basis. My French isn't too bad, but it's a long way from being perfect.'

Carrie could hardly believe her ears.

'My French accent is really poor,' Evalyn went on, 'and there's only one way to perfect it.'

'You mean go to France?'

'Yes, Mother. If I went to Paris I could combine both French and music.'

'I'd have to go with her,' Carrie said, looking at Tom. 'She can't possibly go on her own!'

'No you wouldn't, Mother. Flora would like to go – you know what a wonderful voice she has – and she needs singing lessons. We could stay together in some little apartment.'

Tom chuckled, and Carrie smiled a little grimly.

'Alone on your own in an apartment? In Paris? Two young girls? That would not be possible, Evalyn. You know that!'

But Tom and Carrie both approved of Flora and knew she was perfectly serious about her singing. They suggested that she go to Paris with Evalyn, at their expense, but strictly on the understanding that both of them stay with someone they knew in the French capital.

When Flora leaped at this prospect Carrie began to make the necessary arrangements for the lodging and chaperoning of the girls while they were abroad. Mrs Fanny Raven, a former socialite whom she had met in Paris during the Great Exposition, and who was something of a *grande dame*, was approached. She sent Carrie a wire to say she would be delighted to have both girls for the summer.

'In Paris you must do everything Mrs Raven tells you to do,' Carrie told her daughter. 'And that means *everything*! If you cannot promise me this, I cannot let you go. You are a young girl, and no matter what you *think* you know about life, you know virtually nothing at all.'

Evalyn gave her word. Everyone knew it was her bond and so the matter was settled. It was also settled that Annie would go with her.

So in September 1904 Evalyn and Flora embarked with Annie on the SS *Deutschland*, bound for Cherbourg. Tom had given Evalyn a $10,000 letter of credit to fund her expenses in Paris. When the two young women went to their stateroom they found it bedecked with flowers, with a loving note from both sets of parents wishing them a safe voyage and a productive time in Paris. Evalyn wrote to thank her parents in an effusive letter, her love underscored and repeated. 'Darlings, darlings, you are so wonderful and I am so happy!'

It was the first time she had been away from home in any kind of self-regulatory mode, and she intended to make the most of it. She and Flora soon spent most of the time in the first-class smoking room, talking to the male passengers while the ship rolled and pitched. Most of the other women had disappeared to their cabins, so there was no one of their own sex around to disapprove. Annie didn't bother them because she was seasick. They met William Gibbs McAdoo, and also his brother, Henry, who had completed the first tunnel under the Hudson River.

'It must have been fun to dig under the river!'

The McAdoos were bemused.

'I suppose it was, Miss Walsh, though we didn't think of it in that way at the time!'

'Pity you can't tunnel under the Atlantic as well, and save us all this inconvenient mode of travel!'

The engineers laughed. 'That would be a horse of another colour altogether! And you might not care for such a long journey in the bowels of the earth.'

William took a cheroot from his pocket, asked the two young women if they minded if he smoked.

'Not a bit,' Evalyn said. 'I'd like to try one myself.'

In a moment, to Flora's dismay, she had a lighted cigar in her hand, but her first puff disabused her of any notions about taking up smoking. She coughed until the tears came.

'Second-best plan,' she conceded, echoing her father's phraseology. 'Men must have iron plating on their lungs . . . or is it just engineers?'

Her new friends laughed and assured her it was just a matter of persevering, but Evalyn had already foresworn cigars for ever.

'I never mind sailing,' she confided to Flora later, 'but smoking makes me feel sick!'

'Cheroots are too strong,' Flora said. 'I tried a cigarette once and I didn't mind it!'

Next evening Evalyn decided to have a cigarette. She held it daintily in a long holder. She felt grown up and, for the first time in what seemed an age, very happy.

The McAdoo brothers accompanied the two young ladies and Annie on the train from Cherbourg to Paris.

'Will you call on us sometime?' Evalyn asked as they parted. 'We're staying at 187 rue de la Pompe.'

'Of course,' the two gentlemen said, raising their hats as a porter took the young women's luggage to a waiting victoria.

Evalyn, Flora and Annie were soon at Mrs Raven's apartment. A maid opened the door and Evalyn and Flora were kindly received by an elderly woman with a mass of carefully arranged white hair, who brought both her young guests into her exquisite *salon*.

'How wonderful to see you, Evalyn. You were just a little girl the last time I set eyes on you!'

'When was that, Mrs Raven?'

'Oh, four years ago, when you were here with your parents! I was able to recommend a certain convent for you, but I gather your stay there was truncated.'

Evalyn was at a loss. So this was the person she had to thank for her incarceration.

'You may call me Aunt Fanny,' Mrs Raven continued kindly, looking from one of her new charges to the other. She signalled to a maid. 'Mimi will show you to your rooms, and then you must join me for some tea. We dine at eight thirty.'

Evalyn and Flora followed the maid along the shining parquet, and were shown to two small bedrooms that overlooked the interior courtyard. Evalyn could think only of the rue de Picpus, and a sense of suffocation began to tug at her.

'We'll be stifled if we stay here,' she whispered to Flora. 'We need a place of our own!'

'Well, you tell her, Evalyn,' Flora said with a sideways roll of her eyes. 'Not me!'

Later, sipping tea from small china cups, Evalyn responded to Aunt Fanny's question as to whether their rooms were to their liking.

'They're great. But the only thing is, Aunt Fanny . . . when I am studying I need a lot of space to pace the floor!'

Aunt Fanny looked at her carefully. 'I had no idea, my dear, that you were so assiduous a student. I must congratulate you.'

'So I . . . Flora and I . . . really need somewhere bigger. We were thinking of renting an apartment.'

Aunt Fanny digested this in silence.

'Well, as you must be chaperoned, the only apartment you could conveniently rent would be in this building. And, as it happens, there *is* one such apartment vacant, the one under the roof. It would be rather warm, perhaps—'

'Oh no. I'm sure it would do us very well.'

'If I allow you to do this, it is on two conditions, and I need your word that you agree to them!'

'Of course, Aunt Fanny.'

'You must keep me strictly informed of your visitors and you must never go out without being accompanied by either myself or Annie.'

Evalyn sighed. Dear God, she thought, it isn't fair! Will I ever manage to get a life? She looked at Flora, saw the excitement in her face at the prospect of even this provisional freedom.

But they agreed to Aunt Fanny's conditions and were installed in a matter of days. The apartment had a *salon* and two bedrooms, a *chambre de bonne*, a quaint bathroom and kitchen. They announced to Aunt Fanny that their first guests would be the McAdoo brothers. They had asked them to dinner on Saturday; they had already sent an invitation to their hotel.

'That is very nice, my dears. But as you cannot entertain gentlemen unchaperoned, I shall be there too!'

The following week, when Evalyn hired an electric brougham and informed Aunt Fanny that she was going to take Mr Henry McAdoo for a ride in the Bois de Boulogne, she was told: 'That would be very nice, Evalyn, provided you take Annie also!'

Evalyn reluctantly obeyed. She did not want to run foul of her duenna, break her word to her parents or compromise her reputation. Privately, however much she chafed, she accepted that the world had its secrets and conventions, and that to challenge them *was* perilous.

'I wish we could really be free!' she exclaimed to Flora. 'You know, like the men.'

'Well, you're not a man!' Flora replied. 'And this is the best time of your life, make no mistake about that! As soon as you get married everything changes – and not always for the better!'

Evalyn laughed. 'What a cynic you are, Flora Wilson! I'm determined to have a wonderful life! But there is something I have to do first. I must find Mamselle Raye.'

'Why is she so important to you?'

'She was my friend when I needed one.'

Every time she looked at the Eiffel Tower Evalyn remembered their time on the Ferris wheel, and the sense Mamselle had always given her that she was someone who mattered, not because she was rich, but because she was in some way unique and precious.

She confided to Henry McAdoo that she wanted to trace a certain Frenchwoman. He took down the details and said he would contact a private detective.

But the report that came within three weeks turned Evalyn's world upside down.

'Mademoiselle Jeanne Marie Raye,' the detective's missive said, 'died in childbirth on 6 September 1902, leaving a son who is living with her grandmother. She was unmarried.'

'Oh God,' Evalyn whispered to her pillow at night, 'oh God, why did you let that happen? Mamselle was so good, so pure . . .'

She thought about it for days on end. Who was the father and why hadn't he married her? It must have been that man she mentioned, the one with the horses.

Mamselle's words came back to her again: *Things come at a price, petite. That seems to be the rule of life . . .*

Horrible, horrible, horrible, she wept into her pillow. Why should she have paid such a price? She was young and struggling and she only wanted to live! It seemed to Evalyn, in that moment, that it wasn't so much a question of 'price', as one of some secret force, an underground current that waited for you in the darkness.

The grief plunged her into a new turmoil that displaced all thoughts of Paul. She had always thought that she would meet Mamselle again, surprise her by her command of French, please her with the success she was making of her life. Now she realised that she would never be able to do so, and was filled with a panic that resonated with her private fears. Life was fragile and unforgiving. You had to grab it before the ice cracked under your feet, do all the things you ever wanted before it was all too late.

Evalyn gave Aunt Fanny the slip one morning when she was with Flora at the singing master's, saying she was going out for a few moments. She went straight to a hairdressers – Georges – who looked at her dark brown hair and refused point-blank to change it to red without written instructions from her father.

'Eet ees more than my life is worth, Mamselle. Without ze Papa's agreement I cannot . . .' and he made a throat-cutting gesture to underline the seriousness of the situation.

Evalyn said to herself that men were cowards, and decided to take matters into her own hands. When she left Georges, she went straight into a *pharmacie* and bought a bottle of chemical hair dye that guaranteed results. It was her life's dream to be a redhead like her father had been, and she no longer saw any reason why she should not become one, now that the only person whose good opinion she craved was dead. She applied the dye that night, adding a bit more than the quantity indicated.

'Better to be sure than sorry!' she told herself. When she woke up the next morning her hair was unlike anything she had ever seen – it was red in places, green and yellow in others. She shrieked.

Flora came running and put her hand to her mouth.

'My God, Evalyn,' she breathed, 'you've really done it this time!'

Annie bustled in. 'What's all the commotion?' But she stopped short when she saw her young mistress's reflection in the mirror. 'If your father could see you now,' she said, 'he'd lock you up. And locked up you should be, for you're as mad as anything that ever went into Bedlam!'

Evalyn burst into tears. 'Don't be so unkind to me, Annie,' she sobbed. 'It wasn't meant to turn out like this!'

'What's to be done?' Flora demanded. 'She's not fit to be seen!'

'I'll just have to go back to Georges,' Evalyn said.

'Georges?'

'The hairdresser. It's all his fault. If he had done it for me yesterday, I'd never have bought the bottle of dye! But he's the only one who can save me now!'

They wrapped Evalyn in veils and marched her off to Georges, from whose establishment she later emerged as a coppery redhead. She was excited, glancing at herself in the mirror. She looked completely different, glamorous certainly, but with a new patina of artificiality that sat oddly with her youth.

Flora and Annie had gone shopping and returned to collect her. They gasped.

'Let's go to Worth's!' Evalyn exclaimed excitedly when they left the hairdresser's. 'I have to buy something that goes with my hair!'

She bought pretty dresses, one of them yellow velvet with lace and inset diamonds.

'You take the biscuit,' Flora said dubiously. 'What's wrong with you that you've started behaving so strangely? You're like someone who is running away from something. Why don't you just relax? You don't have to prove anything; you don't have to *have* everything. You don't need to be a redhead and have yellow velvet dresses. You were perfectly lovely as you were!'

'Oh, don't be so stuffy!' Evalyn cried, and bought some black lace underwear.

Fanny Raven was angry when she saw what Evalyn had done to herself.

'If you had consulted me first, Evalyn . . .' she said reprovingly.

Evalyn, suddenly terrified that Aunt Fanny would write to her parents of her latest escapade, turned on all her charm.

'I know, darling Aunt Fanny, I should never have done it,' she said hastily. 'That's why I didn't ask you. But do you think you could bear to go to the Opera tonight? I have this lovely new gown I want to try out.'

Aunt Fanny said nothing when Evalyn appeared that evening in yellow velvet, with lace and inset diamond stars.

'I've bought a new Fiat,' she confided to her duenna, 'yellow to go with my dress. 'I'm sure you'll like it. Will you let me drive you?'

Aunt Fanny looked like a woman who didn't know whether to laugh or cry.

'Is something wrong, Evalyn?' she asked gently.

'Why should something be wrong just because I bought a few little things with the money Papa gave me to enjoy myself? I haven't done anything improper!'

'But if you go on like this, Evalyn, you'll run through all your father's money!'

'Oh, no I won't. I'm afraid there's so much of that – it's quite impossible!'

Flora shook her head. 'But she sure means to try!' she said with a giggle.

Aunt Fanny suddenly laughed, a melodious chuckle that reverberated off the chandelier and rang in the room.

'I don't know what the young women of my generation would think of you, Evalyn,' she said, 'but they might envy your courage and the way you insist on freedom!'

Courage, Evalyn thought to herself in a burst of bitter, private candour that evening, as she fingered a certain piece of quartz, has only let me down. And freedom is something I have already lost.

Evalyn met any number of Americans in Paris and eventually the word got back to Tom and Carrie in Washington that their daughter was seen all over Paris in her yellow Fiat, chasing pleasure as though there were no tomorrow.

Tom sent a cablegram to tell her to come home immediately. Evalyn replied by cablegram that she was studying so hard she needed to stay until spring; then she went out and bought more dresses, a sable coat, shoes and gloves. Her father cabled back that he was stopping her credit and that he was sending Mrs Wickerman, Terry's wife, to bring her home.

This lady duly arrived, took Evalyn in charge, and sailed with her on board the SS *Deutschland* for New York. The crossing was rough and the ship arrived at Quarantine sheathed in ice.

Evalyn had been warned by her father to declare everything she had bought, but she was not too diligent about this. She had eight trunks of clothes, furs and accessories; it was a boring job itemising everything, and besides, as she told herself, there was so much to declare that she hadn't enough time.

Tom and Carrie had come to New York to meet their daughter, and had put up, as usual, at the Waldorf. Evalyn greeted them with tears and multiple embraces. But it was only when she was back in their suite at the hotel, and had removed her veil and hat, that Tom and Carrie saw how changed was their daughter.

'Your hair,' Carrie gasped, and put a hand to her throat as though she were being strangled. 'What have you *done* to your hair? I thought Paris would refine you, and instead . . .'

The telephone shrilled. It was the US Customs, looking for Mr Walsh. Tom glanced at Evalyn with one eyebrow raised as he listened to the voice of officialdom. She shrugged and tried to grin.

'Yes . . .' he said into the receiver. 'I see . . . It was probably a misunderstanding. I'll go down to the customs house right away!'

He replaced the receiver and turned to his daughter.

'Well, young lady, looks like you forgot to mention a few items when you made your customs declaration! But your trunks have been inspected and the deficiencies in your statement have come to light. You'll now be thrown into a cell and the key disposed of!'

Evalyn looked so glum her father started to laugh.

'All right,' he said. 'I'll go and pay the fine. It's about fifteen hundred dollars! I'll tell them your wits are scrambled.' He added severely, 'And to tell you the truth, Daughter, sometimes I think they are!'

When the trunks came home to Washington Carrie confiscated all the Paris dresses.

'But, Mother . . .'

'No buts, Evalyn. These gowns are far too old for you. When are you going to get some sense?'

The roots of Evalyn's dark hair were now visible, but Carrie would not let her get them touched up.

'You're going back to being a brunette, my girl, as God and nature intended. Meanwhile, don't be seen anywhere without a hat and pray that your hair grows back in time for your coming out.'

'It's so unfair,' Evalyn told herself, as she cried with vexation. 'I really

313

liked those dresses! And my hair will never be grown back in time for my dance at the end of January.'

But she began her list of guests. Carrie checked it.

'Do you think I should ask Paul, Mother?' she whispered miserably.

'Oh, Evalyn, he'd hardly come all the way from Denver!'

My world is already thinning, Evalyn thought. Once I had Paul, and once I had a wonderful friend; but *he* walked away from me and *she* died.

Reminded, she cornered her father and demanded: 'Father, did you not know that Mamselle had died?'

Tom sighed and did not meet her eyes.

'Why didn't you tell me?' Evalyn cried.

'I didn't want to upset you. And she died in such circumstances that—'

'That a nicely brought-up girl shouldn't know anything about? But I don't live in a bandbox, Father, and I do know about it, and I hate the man responsible. I'd like to hang him up by his balls.'

Her father looked so shocked and embarrassed that she turned and left the room.

Vinson was at last the proud possessor of a motor, a Pope-Toledo, his father's gift, which he drove with panache. He was possessed of a confident gravitas and seemed displeased with his sister. Evalyn noted that when he was at home his mother's adoring eyes followed him around.

'Why couldn't you behave yourself while you were in Paris?' he demanded when he and Evalyn were alone together for the first time after her return.

'I didn't do anything wrong!' she replied hotly. 'Who said that I did?'

'Oh, no one said you did! But we heard how you were always at the opera, always enjoying yourself as though you were living only for the moment! Father and Mother were so looking forward to your settling down to some serious study and coming back refined. And instead . . .' He gestured at her hair.

'Don't get so stuffy on me, Vin. They wouldn't know who I was if I turned all sophisticated! And as for living for the moment . . .' she glanced at her brother, and her voice became perfectly serious, 'sometimes I feel that is true. I feel that the time I have available for happiness is running out!'

'I wish you wouldn't talk like that,' her brother said. 'You're young and have a your life ahead of you! Are you afraid of getting married?' he added slyly. 'Is that it?'

'Now you sound like Flora Wilson. I've decided I will never marry anyone, so you needn't waste your breath talking about it.'

Vinson laughed and said in a conciliatory tone, 'Well, I'm sure glad you're back, Sis.' He dropped his voice and added with a twinkle, 'I guess things will liven up here now!'

'I guess they will,' Evalyn replied, relaxing a little. 'What about a drive in your new car?'

Vin proudly drove his sister to visit some friends in Maryland.

'You're a good driver,' she told him. 'Father is proud of your skill.'

'I'm better than Ned McLean!' Vin said. 'We race each other sometimes and I generally win!'

'Mother doesn't like him much!' Evalyn said. 'She says he's spoiled!'

'We're *all* spoiled!'

Vin opened the throttle. The keeper of the tollgate at Sligo, Maryland, raised his hands in horror when the vehicle containing the two young people went through the village at thirty miles per hour, twenty-four miles above the speed limit.

'The speed limit through a village is six miles per hour,' Evalyn informed her brother, 'in case it's of any interest to you. And he wanted you to stop to pay the toll.'

'No point in stopping to pay sixty cents, Sis. We'd only have got an earful.' Vin grinned at her. 'He'll write for the toll fees!'

As the car roared through the countryside Evalyn thought how dashing her brother looked, how much she loved him and how good a driver he was. So why did a small, nagging fear begin to tug at the edges of her mind?

Ned McLean came to call. He was no longer the gangly youth who had taken Evalyn for a ride in his motor car. During the months of her absence he had, like Paul, aquired a new *savoir-faire*. He was shown into the conservatory where Evalyn was enjoying a late breakfast in the sunshine that streamed through the stained glass.

'Here's a sight for sore eyes!' Evalyn exclaimed when she saw him. 'You and Vin are turning into such handsome devils.'

Ned bowed with exaggerated politeness, but straightened quickly and stared at her.

'What on earth did you do to your hair, Evalyn?'

'Don't you like it?' she asked with affected indifference, lifting her head and patting her coiffure. 'I just thought it might be amusing to change the colour.'

He laughed. 'I think it's . . . topping.'

'You were always a dear thing, Ned!' she said, borne up suddenly by the sense that Ned was a real friend, almost the only real friend she had these days. He never judged her; he never found fault.

Ned seemed suitably pleased at the compliment. 'Was I really?'

'Yes. You don't care two cents for what people think.'

'Can't stand people,' Ned said. 'Never could . . . except you, of course, Evalyn.'

315

She leaned up and kissed his cheek, noting with some chagrin, as she did so, the scent of bourbon on his breath.

Ned's eyes were suddenly bright. He raised Evalyn's chin, and would have hungrily reciprocated, had footsteps not been heard crossing the drawing room.

'That's my mother!' Evalyn said, pulling back, half ashamed of her relief.

Carrie took in the scene before her with a glance.

'Ah, Ned,' she said politely, extending her hand, 'how are you?'

Ned took her hand. 'I'm well, thank you, Mrs Walsh,' he replied. 'I trust you are well also.'

Heigh-ho, Evalyn thought, watching these two people disguise their unease in each other's company. Ned's urbanity seemed to have deserted him and her mother was stiff. When will I convince her, she wondered, that Ned and I are just friends?

'As well as can be expected,' she heard her mother reply. 'We've just had some sad news. My husband's brother has died in Denver!'

'Uncle Michael!' Evalyn exclaimed. 'We haven't seen him for years! What did he die of?'

Carrie made a noncommittal noise.

Ned's face dropped. 'I am very sorry, but does this mean you will be in mourning?'

'Indeed,' Carrie said. 'He is a near relative . . .'

Ned left after a few further polite exchanges and muttered condolences.

'I hope you didn't give him the wrong impression, dear,' Carrie said when he'd gone. 'You have to be so careful with men.'

Chapter Twenty-Six

Tom travelled to Denver to arrange Michael's funeral, mourned for the brother he once had, for the fierce sixteen-year-old who had stood by the fire in Carraig Mór and declaimed on the state of Ireland. He had not seen him since 1897. They had rarely met during all their years in America. Michael had long since lost the dynamism that had characterised him as a youth. His years in the army had hardened him; his injuries had resulted in his demobilisation; disillusionment had turned him to alcohol, and he had died of dropsy of the liver. But his death made Tom think of a lost time, when life was fresh and its mysteries ahead. He was surprised by the strength of his grief. He knew it was not just for Michael, but for what he saw as his own neglect of him, and for what might have been. He wore black, and insisted the family did likewise, but he could see that Carrie cavilled at the whole family being plunged into mourning for someone they hardly knew.

It was Christmas before Evalyn met Ned again. Their two families greeted each other after church on Christmas Day; the McLeans offered polite condolences. Ned's mother, after chatting for a few minutes with Carrie, turned to Evalyn and put an arm around her.

'How's my girl?'

'I'm fine, thank you, Mummie.'

'When are you coming to see us in Friendship again?'

'I suppose when we're out of mourning!'

'Such a pity you'll be missing your ball! I was so looking forward to your coming out and so was Ned.'

Evalyn sighed. She was bitterly disappointed that her father had insisted all plans of a joyous nature must be cancelled. From the corner of her eye she saw him and Vin talking to John R., who was full of hearty Christmas greetings.

When Mrs McLean turned to talk to Carrie, Ned leaned over and whispered: 'The whole Season is just too boring without you!'

'How do you think *I* feel? I'm bored witless! And I hardly *knew* my uncle.'

'We'll make up for it,' Ned said conspiratorially, dropping his voice. 'What do you say we—' He was about to suggest a drive in his motor, this time to Baltimore, but fell silent when he realised that both mothers were listening.

'How are you intending to make up for it, Ned?' Carrie asked with a smile, and Ned evaded the question, saying it was a shame to be dull at New Year, that he had been looking forward to dancing with his old classmate, and that it really was too bad that she had to miss all the fun. 'Evalyn dances the waltz like no one else.'

Vin, approaching, overheard.

'That's very nice,' he said with a grin. 'I remember a time when Annie had to drag her to the dancing lessons in your house!'

'Oh, shut up, Vin. I was a kid then!' Evalyn cried, and stamped her feet from the cold.

The chauffeurs had the cars waiting, and after repeated good wishes the two families piled into their respective vehicles and went home.

'What do you think of Ned McLean?' Carrie asked Vinson later that day when she got him alone.

'Ned is a great man to have by your side in a crisis, Mother. If he didn't drink like a fish he'd be the best in the world!'

'What kind of *crisis* have you ever been in, Vinson,' Carrie cried, 'that you needed Ned McLean?'

'Not me, Mother,' Vin lied uncomfortably, remembering a car race in Virginia when he had ended up in the ditch.

That night, alone in their bedroom, Carrie discussed the McLeans with Tom, and anxiously reviewed their hopes for their young daughter's future.

'I know they are big newspaper people,' she said, 'but that is not going to guarantee happiness. That boy is too spoiled to make anyone a good husband. He has been brought up to think his wishes are the centre of the universe.'

'Maybe,' Tom replied. 'But Evalyn is headstrong enough to give anyone headaches!'

'A woman's life is different, Tom. Evalyn doesn't realise yet how different. Once there are children everything changes. She'll hardly have time to think of herself; they'll be her whole existence. And Ned drinks. Vinson told me.'

'Many young men drink,' Tom said, 'but many of them grow out of it. All *we* can do,' he added after a moment, 'is make sure she has plenty of chances to meet other young eligibles.'

'She was very sweet on her cousin Paul – for a while,' Carrie said tentatively after a moment.

Tom looked at her in evident surprise. 'A fine young man! But I suppose it was puppy love? There was nothing in it, was there, Carrie?'

Carrie hesitated, then shook her head.

Because they would not be entertaining that winter, the big Washington house was gloomy and there was little for the twenty-three servants to do. Evalyn moped. She went up to the ballroom and imagined it full of guests for her dance, heard the plink-plink of the violins as they were tuned, saw the silks and satins of the ladies, the white gloves of the gentlemen; but then reality swamped everything and the empty ballroom echoed as she thought of her own gown of white moire still wrapped in its tissue paper.

'I wish people wouldn't die,' she said to herself irritably. 'It's very selfish when you think about it.'

She held out her hands to an imaginary partner and began to dance.

Carrie, who had come looking for her, stood at the half-open door of the ballroom and watched as her daughter, eyes closed, twirled to some private accompaniment. She felt moved and sad for her.

The elevator connected on the landing and then a young housemaid came forward and said, 'Oh, ma'am, Mr McLean is downstairs. He's called to see Miss Evalyn. I showed him into the library.'

'Evalyn!' Carrie called. 'You have a visitor!'

Her daughter emerged from her private ballet.

'Mother . . . I didn't know you were there . . .'

'Ned is downstairs!'

'Oh, great! Now I'll get all the news.' And she rushed past her mother and out of the room.

'It's hard on Evalyn,' Carrie said to Tom after dinner that evening. 'She was so keyed up at her coming-out and all her plans are dashed. She has to look on at the gaiety. And Ned McLean makes it worse when he calls by telling her all about it.'

'What do you say we take her to Europe?' Tom said 'Vin will be going back to school shortly, but I see no reason why we can't spirit her away for a few months. In Europe she could enjoy herself! And,' he added a little ruefully, 'this time she will be under *parental* supervision.'

'She'll be away from Ned McLean's ambit, anyway!' Carrie said, adding half to herself, 'As far as I'm concerned almost anything would be better than that!'

Vin went back to his boarding school and on 7 January 1905 Mr and Mrs Walsh and their daughter left on the SS *Deutschland* for Italy. The weather in Rome, when they arrived, was mild, and Evalyn did a great deal of sightseeing, usually with her parents, sometimes with Annie. She particu-

319

larly liked the Pincio terrace where she could look out over the city. She loved the city's warm ochre walls that held the sunshine, the twisting blue of the Tiber, the ancient monuments of the Forum and the Colosseum, and the stately cypresses in the distance. She absorbed the foreign atmosphere, the accents, the sight of so many ragged beggars for whom she consistently emptied her purse, the strutting officers in polished high boots and plumed hats, who eyed her as she passed, the scurrying priests in black cassocks with black hats, women with heavy baskets of laundry or fruit on their heads, the laden donkeys, and the smells – of coffee, spices, leather, and poor drains.

Friends came to call on them at the hotel, and introduced the Walshes to various Italian friends of theirs. Evalyn again heard herself being spoken of as 'the Walsh heiress' and noted the servility of the various *maîtres d'hôtel* with annoyance. She had come to dislike being pandered to.

A ball was held in the hotel where the Walshes were staying, and Evalyn prepared for it under the watchful eye of her mother. She donned a simple gown of pale blue tulle, and wore as ornaments only the pearl earrings her mother had given her.

'No, you can't wear that turquoise dog collar, Evalyn,' Carrie exclaimed with some irritation, 'or the diamond ring either! You are a young woman, not a Christmas tree!'

Her mother allowed Annie to dab a little powder on her daughter's nose, but drew the line on the application of rouge. 'You are a young American lady, not a music-hall attraction!'

'Fiddlededee,' Evalyn said to herself. 'I'm always being told what I'm not . . .'

When her mother's attention was elsewhere, Evalyn fell back on her old mainstay, the red cover of the Baedeker, and the result provided as much colour as she wanted for lips and cheeks. Annie, by now equal to every trick, came with a wet flannel and wiped it off without a word, and then, with hands on hips, supervised her charge's descent downstairs behind her parents.

Evalyn sat down at one end of the ballroom with her mother, tapping her toe to the music while her father drifted off to talk to people he knew. He came back with a sleek young man.

'This is Prince Paolo Coronna,' her father said. 'Prince, may I present my wife, Mrs Walsh, and my daughter, Evalyn?'

The prince kissed the ladies' hands.

'Would you care to dance, Miss Walsh?' he said courteously in perfect English, inclining his head.

Saying, 'Why, thank you, Prince,' Evalyn rose to her feet and was swept into the waltz. The 'Blue Danube' filled the ballroom from the ensemble of twelve violins, a harp and two cellos positioned between parlour palms that touched the ceiling. Evalyn looked over her partner's shoulders at the rest of the dancers – men in white gloves and tails, women in varying degrees of décolletage, most of them wearing jewels – and thought with some frustration how nicely her turquoise and pearl collar would have gone with her dress.

But as she whirled to the music in her partner's arms she forgot these considerations, concentrating instead on the joy of the dance.

I'm so glad we came to Europe, she thought. Instead of being bored silly in Washington I'm here in Rome, dancing with a prince! This is the best fun I've had for years.

When the music stopped she was flushed and breathless.

'What do you think of Rome, Miss Walsh?' Prince Paolo asked, and his black eyes dwelled on her appreciatively. 'Is it what you expected?'

'I think it exceeds my expectations, Prince. It has an atmosphere I did not anticipate.'

Evalyn thought she acquitted herself well by this. The prince smiled, as though he had been personally complimented, but his smile became fixed as he looked at the young man approaching behind her. Evalyn turned as they were joined by a tall, blond and very handsome man who bowed to her and to the prince and who addressed himself immediately to the latter in Italian.

'Mi piacerebbe molto fare la conoscenza di questa bellissima donna.'

Prince Paolo's face tightened, but he made the requested introduction.

'Miss Walsh, this is Prince Alberto Galtieri. Prince, this is Miss Evalyn Walsh.'

Evalyn extended her hand, which Prince Alberto immediately raised to his lips.

'You would like to dance?' he asked in a heavy Italian accent, and Evalyn found herself swept away into another waltz in the arms of the second prince of the evening. She smiled over his shoulder at Prince Paolo Coronna, who was biting his lip.

'Your friend didn't care for the interruption one bit!' she ventured, but her new partner merely shrugged. She made a few more comments and the prince raised his shoulders apologetically.

'You should learn to speak English, Prince Alberto,' Evalyn said severely when he took her into supper.

The prince inclined his head in agreement, and then asked softly, 'And you – Italian? No?'

Evalyn laughed. 'Touché,' she said. 'It's true I'm a bit of an ignoramus.'

She glanced at her companion, saw that he did not understand.

'I'm only half educated,' she explained. 'I kept . . . leaving school . . .'

Her mother, who was approaching, overheard this comment, and looked anything but pleased. But the prince seemed amused by the young American's peccadilloes.

'Ah, *school*!' he intoned, shaking his head and raising his hands. 'For one so *bellissima* in Italy there would be no school! You would have governess only.' He shook his head again.

Evalyn wanted to laugh. But she controlled herself, and eventually, when she left with her mother to retire for the night, she heard Prince Alberto Galtieri ask her father 'Would you object eef I called upon your daughter tomorrow?' and had the satisfaction of seeing, from the corner of her eye, the person of Prince Paolo glowering from the sidelines.

'For heaven's sakes, Evalyn,' her mother said, as they came upstairs, 'do not go around telling all the eligible young men you meet that you're only half educated.'

'Why not? It's more or less the truth!'

Carrie sighed. 'It makes you look wild, dear. And wild girls do not attract nice men!'

'I think they do!' Evalyn said. 'Men are like women: they can't stand stiffs!'

Annie was waiting in her suite when Evalyn went upstairs.

'How did it go?' she whispered as Evalyn threw herself on to the bed with a groan of exhaustion.

'It was *fabuloso*!' Evalyn said, hugging her knees. 'Not one but *two* princes were fighting over me!'

Annie drew her breath in sharply, and dug Evalyn in the ribs as she sought the hooks on her gown.

'Fighting? Over *you*?'

'Well . . . contending in their own little way.' She turned and added, 'Annie, did you know I am *bellissima*? Did you know I am so . . .' and here, with much giggling, she mimicked the accent of her erstwhile evening's partner, '*loffly*?'

Annie pursed her lips, and muttered in her dourest Scottish brogue: 'Hold still; I'm trying to get this gown off in one piece! You'll have it in tatters!' Then she added: 'Don't let a few silly compliments go to your head! They're after your money, my girl! That's all!'

Evalyn thought with wonder as she went to sleep that night: something very strange has happened. I am no longer invisible!

In the morning she opened a big box, whose fragrance announced its contents before the lid was even removed. It was filled with white and yellow roses. The card said simply, 'Prince Alberto Galtieri presents his compliments.'

'Can you believe this?' she cried to Annie when the lid came off. 'Flowers! For *me*!'

After that, every morning began with a box of flowers. Prince Alberto

322

would call about eleven, conduct a halting conversation. He had taken her advice and was evidently working on his English.

'You're coming along,' she said with approval when he delivered himself of a few perfect sentences. With his handsome bearing and his blond good looks she thought he looked very much like a prince, more so than Prince Paolo Coronna.

One morning he said he would like Evalyn and Mrs Walsh to meet his mother.

'Perhaps she would join us here for luncheon?' Carrie offered.

The prince's mother arrived for lunch three days later, dressed all in black with real black lace and no jewels at all. She was a slender, haughty woman, with pale skin, and silvering hair.

'You see, Evalyn,' Carrie said to her daughter afterwards, 'a real lady does not display her jewels as though she belonged to a troupe of travelling players. They are only worn on the right occasion!'

Evalyn sniffed. 'She probably has no jewels, Mother, worth talking about!'

But when the principessa invited the Walshes to dinner in the Galtieri Palace, Evalyn saw how mistaken she had been. Reposing on the principessa's bosom was a necklace of diamonds such as she had never seen.

Ooh, I'd like those, Evalyn thought. The sheer size of them! I think they would suit me very well.

She said as much to her mother later, and Carrie replied with a coy laugh, 'Well, Evalyn, they are Galtieri heirlooms. If you really want them there is only one way to get them.'

'Mother!' Evalyn exclaimed. 'I think you want to turn me into a princess!'

'Oh no, dear,' Carrie responded with the same coy laugh, 'but I think Prince Alberto does! And we *have* been invited to their fancy dress ball.'

'Carrie,' Tom said reprovingly, 'don't be filling Evalyn's head with nonsense. We are due to see the Pope tomorrow and I want her becomingly demure, not half daft with silly speculation about young lads with titles as long as your arm and not a penny to speak of!'

Evalyn did look demure for the papal audience the following day. She and Carrie wore the regulation black from chin to toe, with black gloves and black lace mantillas. They were admitted to the Vatican by two Swiss Guards in medieval costume of blue and yellow stripes, with burnished helmets.

'I wonder what I'd look like in one of those costumes,' Evalyn whispered. 'I mean for the Galtieris' fancy dress party,' she added hurriedly when she caught the look her mother directed at her.

323

'You will not be going as a Swiss Guard, Evalyn,' Carrie said quietly, 'of that I can assure you.'

They were met by Cardinal Merry de Val. Dressed in crimson robes, with a chain of gold around his neck supporting a cross studded with gems, he had a formidable presence – power overlaid with studied urbanity. An usher in a suit of black satin appeared and conducted them down a long corridor to a modest room, and there they met a man dressed all in white, with a small gold cross on a chain around his neck and a white skullcap. Evalyn knew she was looking at no other person than Pope Pius X, Pontifex Maximus, head of the largest Christian denomination on earth.

Tom dropped to his knees to kiss the Fisherman's ring. Evalyn and Carrie followed suit, but the ring evaded their lips. It dawned on Evalyn that only members of the faithful would be permitted to kiss that particular piece of jewellery. Her father was a Catholic, albeit a lapsed one, but she and her mother were not.

The Pope conversed politely through an interpreter: he hoped they were enjoying their stay in the Eternal City.

Tom spoke of the Catacombs and the Forum and the Colosseum. He seemed touched in a way his family had never seen him, as though he were a small boy confronting an extraordinary adventure.

Afterwards he talked about it for days.

'Meeting his Holiness – it was the most extraordinary thing I've ever done! What would they have said at home in Ireland long ago if they'd known some day I'd kiss his ring?'

Eventually Evalyn could keep quiet no longer.

'Kiss his silly old ring? He should be kissing yours. *You're* the one who's had real adventures, Father, done real things that required courage and endurance! What has that old pope ever really done, except stuck around in his palace boring everyone to death? What would *he* do if he found himself in a blizzard at twenty below, or trapped in a den of rattlers. He'd be dead as a plank.'

Tom laughed heartily. 'Well, Daughter,' he said as he wiped his eyes, 'you've a knack of cutting things down to size. Come and give your old father a kiss.'

Evalyn obliged. Then she whispered, 'Father, the fancy-dress ball next week in the Galtieris' palazzo . . . I would make a lovely Swiss Guard.'

'Second-best plan, Evalyn! You heard your mother. Proper young ladies do not wear male attire, even to fancy-dress balls.'

'Don't be so stuffy, Father. I used to wear breeches in Colorado.'

Tom sighed. 'This is Rome and you know the old saying – when in Rome do as the Romans do!'

'In that case,' Evalyn muttered after a moment, 'I will beat them at their own game!'

Evalyn went to the ball in a classical white costume as a Roman lady of the ancient world. She looked stunningly elegant; her green eyes and brown hair, her lovely skin, her superb figure, all excited admiration. But most attractive of all was her uncertainty, the freshness of her innocence, and of this she was completely oblivious.

Again, Carrie had overseen her preparations and Annie had been on hand to ensure she did not go out with artificially reddened cheeks and lips. But Evalyn didn't need any aids to beauty. The excitement of hearing her name linked to Prince Alberto Galtieri made her glow. 'Princess Evalyn Galtieri,' she said to herself, trying on the title for size. It sounded so much better than being Mrs Someone or Other.

The prince showed Evalyn and her mother around his ancestral home. The palace had a massive stone staircase that swept through five storeys to the loggia at the top of the house. Here Evalyn and Carrie stood between the Corinthian columns that supported the roof and looked across the city haze to the dome of St Peter's. Next they were shown the reception rooms – full of Renaissance paintings, portraits and statuary, carved oak chests, massive tables, tapestries where nymphs and fauns cavorted in pastoral landscapes. They descended to the shady garden, where Nepture spouted water into a stone basin and the terrace had cast-iron vases overflowing with fiery geraniums. The music spilled on to the gravel walks. Evalyn absorbed the effortless elegance. She saw how the guests glanced at her and at the prince. By the time the ball was over she had made up her mind to accept him.

But that night, too tired to sleep, thoughts intruded from recesses deep within. She had turned off the light and lay in the gloom with only the soft slats of dimness from the shutters. She moved her legs, felt the crisp coolness of the sheets, and wondered what it would be like to share a bed with this prince. She thought of his face when she had said good night. He had bent over her hand with a smile, but his eyes had been as cold as stones.

What would it be like to have him lying beside her, to hear him breathing, to make love with him, have his children, to live far from home with him in this foreign land? These were the realities she had to examine, for these things would be her life. How often would she get to Ouray then? How often to America? And then the inevitable thought came from the sidelines: would she ever see Paul again? She was no longer angry when she thought of him; she was just sad.

The sense of vulnerability, the knowledge that everyone she loved would be half a world away, made her feel almost ill. Marriage, any marriage, seemed suddenly a dangerous and capricious gamble.

In the morning Carrie woke her, obviously excited.

'We had such a wonderful evening, didn't we, darling? Did you ever see anything as splendid as that palace?'

There was an underlying unspoken question to which Evalyn longed to give the answer her mother wanted to hear. Her thoughts of the night before seemed trite and foolish in the face of her parent's enthusiasm and expectation, which seemed to say – what girl in her right mind would refuse a prince? This is the next chapter in your life's story!

It was Waldo Story, the American sculptor who lived in Rome, who echoed her misgivings and in so doing validated them. He had been present at the Galtieri fancy-dress ball and had invited Carrie and Evalyn to his studio. They visited it two days later. When her mother was discussing a marble bust with another of his guests, he took Evalyn to one side.

'And how is the principessa this fine Roman morning?'

'Oh, Mr Story, don't call me that. I feel as though things are somer-saulting out of my control.'

Waldo glanced at Carrie, saw she was immersed and said quickly: '*Waldo*, Evalyn! You make me feel about a hundred and ten. All I want to say to you is this – will a magnificent palazzo warm your heart when you are alone in your section of it and your husband is in bed with his mistress?'

Evalyn looked shocked, but he continued, 'You're a nice American girl and this glamour bunch, with all their fine titles, are shallow as an oil slick. You'll be miserable if you marry that dago! I'm telling you now for what it's worth!'

Evalyn said little in response to this, but she set about studying the American women they met who had married into the Italian aristocracy, and what she sensed behind the smiles and the glamour appalled her. She saw the way their eyes swivelled to their husbands as though they were no longer creatures possessed of their own autonomy, but just clothes horses, jewellers' models, owned, coralled, even frightened. *Products*, not *persons*, she thought, echoing an old complaint to her father.

What if Galtieri was always telling me what to do and watching me and disliking my American ways? she asked herself.

You could run away, the old Evalyn said.

But a new and reluctant maturity thought otherwise: You cannot run away from anything any more. Whatever you do from now on you have to stick with.

I would be his prisoner, the answer came. That is the truth of the matter! He would have a fortune because of me and I would be his prisoner!

She began to feel nauseous at the prospect of what she might have got herself into.

The next time she visited Waldo's studio he looked at her quizzically.

'Well, has the heiress lost her head or is she just playing her cards like a sensible girl? Better buy a car than a prince, that's my advice. The car won't answer back!'

'Actually, Waldo, I did see a lovely red Mercedes the other day.'

Waldo gave a hoot of laughter.

That evening Evalyn, alone with her father in her parents' sitting room, took him into her confidence.

'Look, Father, can I talk to you?'

Tom, in a brown study, was standing by the window, his eyes fixed on the Tiber and the crowded streets of Rome. He turned to her with a start and regarded her with concern.

'Is it about that prince?'

'Yes, Father.'

'Are you thinking of accepting him?' he asked in a low voice, adding hastily as though he feared the answer, 'because I'm not sure he'd make you happy, Evalyn. I think you're far too young. And he's got dollar signs in both eyes – although he hasn't asked me for any money yet. Your brother's written to say you shouldn't even consider it, while your mother seems to think . . . But it's your life, Daughter, so what do *you* say?'

'I don't intend to marry him, Father,' Evalyn said quietly. 'I'd much rather have a new red Mercedes!'

Tom's belly laugh resonated through the high-ceilinged room until even the frescos and plaster cornices seemed to join in the mirth.

'Well, that's fairly easy to arrange,' he gasped. 'I'll telegraph Livy Beeckman in Paris and he'll arrange shipment.'

'Can we go to Venice as soon as the car arrives?'

'Sure!' Tom said. 'Venice it is!'

He patted her hand. 'I like a girl who knows how to make up her mind!'

They engaged a chauffeur, motored to Venice, booked into their hotel on the Grand Canal, went sightseeing to San Marco and the Ducal Palace. But when they returned there was a card waiting for them; Prince Alberto Galtieri had called to present his compliments and would call again in the morning.

'I might have known he'd follow us! I don't want to be pestered by him,' Evalyn cried, and told her mother to tell the prince she was ill.

But next day, after the prince had called and left, and when she thought the coast was clear and went out with Annie, the person of Prince Alberto materialised from one of the cobbled side streets as though out of the stones.

'Miss Walsh,' he said with a bow. 'I am so glad to see that you are better!'

'We'll have to leave Venice if I can't go out without him waylaying me!' Evalyn told her parents that evening. 'It's spoiling everything. I don't want to be rude to his face, but what can he expect if he won't leave me alone?'

Two days later they left Venice for Monte Carlo, Carrie complaining that poor Annie had no sooner unpacked than she had had to pack all over again.

In Monte Carlo they stayed at the Metropole Hotel. Nearby was the famous Casino, surrounded by its luxuriant gardens.

'It's like a North African coastline,' Carrie exclaimed with a gesture which took in the palm trees and the burning blue of the sea.

'From what I hear they dress differently in North Africa, Mother. And they don't gamble. But do you think we might try our luck?'

'Certainly not. Casinos are no places for young ladies!'

Carrie glanced at her daughter's disappointed face and indicated the sloping ridge of mountain that looked down on the town.

'Why not go for a drive on the Corniche instead?'

'With me at the wheel? Would you trust me, Mother, on those bends?'

'Of course! I am proud of my automobilist daughter!'

Delighted with this maternal confidence, Evalyn ordered the car, dismissed the chauffeur and soon the two women were purring along the winding Corniche in a vehicle that made even the citizens of Europe's richest principality stand and stare. They wore motoring coats, and hats swathed in fine muslin that covered their faces. When they pulled in to examine the view, they saw below them the long sweep of the bay and the rocky isthmus jutting into the sea. Evalyn got out the map. As soon as she opened it the wind snatched it and flattened it against the windscreen. Her mother retrieved it and held it on her knee.

'That's the old town of Monaco,' Carrie said pointing, 'out there on the isthmus, and the crenellated towers must belong to the royal palace!' She let her eyes wander down the length of the bay. 'And if Italy is just over there, this place is tiny!'

'It's only a pimple on the French coast, Mother! Father was saying this morning that the whole of Monaco is only about one and a half square miles! If you compare it to what we own in Colorado . . .'

'Would you swop?' Carrie asked smiling.

Evalyn shook her head. 'Not for the world. But sometimes . . . I wish we had been able to stay there, Mother.'

Carrie regarded her daughter's suddenly pensive face in silence.

'You're thinking of Ouray?' she asked eventually.

'Yes . . . and Denver . . .'

'Paul, you mean?' Carrie asked gently.

Evalyn bowed her head. 'He didn't want me, Mother, because I'm rich.'

Carrie gave a snort of exasperation. 'He could hardly have expected you to give it all up to become the wife of a livery stables owner. It would never have done.' She added in the same soft voice, 'Now would it . . . when you think of who you are and the glittering chances ahead of you?'

'But he was his own person, Mother, like a rock. I need a man like that.' She glanced at her parent. 'Oh, you don't understand . . .'

'I understand more than you think, my dear child. Of course you should marry a strong man, but let it be a man who is *someone*.'

Evalyn sighed.

'There's a bit of news your father's had from Denver,' Carrie continued in a gentle voice. 'I didn't know how to tell you. It's why I wanted to come out on this drive . . . so I could talk to you on our own.'

'What news? Tell me, Mother.'

'Your cousin Paul is married!' Carrie put a sympathetic hand on her daughter's shoulder. 'He married his partner's sister last Thursday. Her name is Amelia Moore.'

The sense of loss hit Evalyn in the stomach. Tears stung her eyes and she angrily dashed them away. She thought of the slender, brown-eyed Miss Moore daintily picking up her hem as she stepped into the stable yard.

'I wish I had never wasted time on him,' she whispered. 'I'm such a fool. He was probably courting her all the time.'

Carrie took out her handkerchief and silently dabbed at her daughter's tears.

'Don't cry, my poor dear. Your heart is young and will mend! I wonder if that assiduous Prince Alberto will follow you here too?' she added after a moment in a coy, half-joking tone.

'Who knows? Who cares? Oh, how I wish they'd all go home to their palaces and leave me in peace!'

But it was Prince Paolo Coronna, as though alerted that his rival was out of the way, who appeared in a matter of days and said he had taken a suite at the nearby Hôtel de Paris.

Chaperoned by her mother or Annie, Evalyn allowed him to escort her on her drives. Flowers began to arrive again, hot-house orchids this time, or red roses, delivered every morning.

'Well, Evalyn, what do you think of *this* prince?'

'He speaks English well, Mother, so I have the advantage of knowing what he is saying.'

Carrie invited the prince to lunch. Two American ladies whom she had met in Monte Carlo, Mrs Fulton and Mrs Proctor, were also her guests.

Evalyn, seated beside Prince Paolo on the terrace, looked down with pleasure on the sunlit water, and the rows of palm trees with their fronds moving lazily in the sea wind. Yachts with furled sails waited in the harbour, and behind it in the distance, rose the rock of Monaco and the towers of the princely palace. The wisteria, planted in tubs along the terrace and clinging to the stone balusters, was in bloom. The drooping clusters of mauve flowers turned to purple in the shade and sent out a sweet, powerful fragrance, attracting fat black bumble bees with dark blue wings.

Evalyn turned to find the *maître d'hôtel* showing a fair-haired young gentleman to an adjoining table and realised with a start that it was Prince Alberto Galtieri. He bowed to her and her parents.

'Why Prince Alberto,' Carrie cried, 'you must join our table!' And in a few moments Evalyn's erstwhile suitor had kissed all the ladies' hands, had bowed to Tom and Prince Paolo, and was seated directly opposite Evalyn.

The luncheon progressed with rising tension. Mrs Proctor opined that it was just so *awesome* to sit at table with not one but two princes, and added in a cheery, teasing voice that she expected both of them were in love with Evalyn.

Evalyn cringed privately and tried to avoid Galtieri's smiles, directed at her from across the table.

'Certainly,' he said, 'who could resist a woman with ze eyes of a Madonna?'

Evalyn longed for the meal to end. She heard Prince Paolo reply laconically that no one could help being bowled over by so beautiful a young lady, but that, of course, no one could deserve her who did not speak English fit to be understood.

Prince Alberto rose to his feet, picked up his glass of red wine and threw it over his rival. Then he bowed to his hostess and left. Coronna quietly mopped the drops from his face and dabbed at the stains on his white linen suit, but Evalyn could feel his anger simmering behind his urbane exterior. His eyes were hot with murder.

'You provoked him, Prince,' she said quietly, turning to him, 'and I do not want to see either of you again!'

'That was quite an exhibition on the part of your two swains,' her father said with a rueful chuckle afterwards. 'And I thought we were going to have such a nice cheerful lunch!'

'It's like two prospectors staking a claim, Father,' Evalyn said. 'Galtieri reckons I'm his by right of effort, and the other one thinks he got there first! But I've done with both of them now.'

Prince Alberto, however, turned up the following day and when Annie, by then exasperated beyond endurance, said, 'Shoo . . .' he lost his temper and jumped on her corns.

'I've had enough of princes to last me my entire life!' Evalyn said to her parents that evening. 'I would just like to go home!'

That night she thought of Paul, of their rides together in Ouray, the sense of belonging that filled her whole being at the mere sight of his face. She thought of him standing before an altar with another woman, heard his quietly spoken vow: '*I will!*', saw him take Amelia's hand and slip a gold band on her finger.

I don't care, she told herself angrily. He can have his Miss Moore and I'll have anyone I like . . .

Chapter Twenty-Seven

Evalyn returned to the States on the best of terms with both parents. She felt she had matured in Italy. She had not been dazzled by the prospect of marrying a prince; she had become weary of incessant travel and novelty. Washington might not have the history or colour of Rome, but she loved its atmosphere, the simplicity of its Georgetown brick, and basked in the pleasure of being surrounded by the people and voices she knew. The White House seemed as gracious in its simple architecture as anything she had seen in Italy.

'There's something very fine about America!' she announced to her family.

'Are you only finding that out now?' Vin exclaimed. 'America, Sis, is the best place on earth!'

He had come home from his boarding school eager to see his family. When he saw his sister he embraced her, lifted her into the air, before holding her at arm's length critically.

'You've changed. You've lost that innocent gaucherie . . .'

'Really, Vin!' Carrie exclaimed, looking horrified.

'I'm talking about the gaucheness, Mother, not the innocence!'

Evalyn affected a mock swipe at him, but he laughed and dodged it.

'You're the one who's changed!'

She was struck by it. It wasn't a physical change; it was deeper than that. His innate elegance now informed everything he did. He was droll and articulate; he was sensitive to others and he knew how to charm; and to cap it all had received his best school report to date. His father beamed with pride, and Evalyn saw the long, approving glances he gave his son when the latter was not aware he was under scrutiny.

'It's such a comfort to an old miner,' he said to Vin, 'to know that his son is growing up into such a fine young man.'

'Father! *You're* not old!' Evalyn cried. 'You're only fifty-five, almost a spring chicken!'

Her father's infectious laugh filled the room. 'It's the first time anyone's remarked on that particular resemblance, Evalyn, even before my grey hairs . . .'

'A touch of grey only makes you look distinguished, Tom Walsh,' Carrie cried. 'You're still a young man!'

Summer was with them; the heat was increasing by the day; even in spacious 2020 the air was heavy and close. It was time to leave for their first season at Newport, Rhode Island, the queen of American resorts, where the élite congregated for the summer. Tom had rented a house from Cornelius Vanderbilt II for the season. Vin had already met the latter's son, Reggie, a passionate automobilist like himself, who had described in glowing terms the motoring he had done at Newport and the number of pedestrians he had knocked down.

'He always got off,' Vin said.

'He just threw money at the problem,' Tom said, 'which is not an ideal way to conduct one's life!'

With them on holiday went Evalyn's pride and joy – the red Mercedes that had been shipped from Europe. Emile, their imported chauffeur, drove it.

The first thing Evalyn noticed about Newport was the taste of salt in the breeze and the smell of the sea.

'It's so good,' Carrie said with a relieved sigh as she pressed yet another handkerchief soaked in eau-de-Cologne to the nape of her neck, 'to have escaped the humidity of Washington.' She looked around at her children. 'And good that you'll both be surrounded by fashionable young people for the summer.'

'Oh, Mother,' Vin groaned. 'Who cares about fashionable people? I just want to do some driving!'

The house in Newport was called Beaulieu. Situated at number 614 Bellevue Avenue, a leafy boulevard lined with the summer palaces of the world's richest Brahmins, Beaulieu had a gate house and a driveway that wound to the mansarded red-brick and brownstone mansion set amongst smooth green lawns overlooking the Atlantic. It was almost 'next door' to Mrs K. Vanderbilt's extraordinary palace, the Greek revival Marble House.

On the first morning of their holiday, brother and sister stood in the sunshine on the edge of the lawn. Below them was Cliff Walk, the Gull Rocks, and the murmuring sea that pelted the rocks with foam. The water was crystal clear, turquoise near the shore, shading to amethyst further out.

'I've been longing to ask you about Italy!' Vin said to his sister with a conspiratorial grin. 'I hear you were a considerable source of frustration to a couple of poor, passionate suitors.'

'I opted for a car, Vin, if that's what you mean!'

Vin burst out laughing. 'For which much thanks. Otherwise I would not have the prospect of driving a forty-horsepower job for the summer. And I knew you wouldn't be such a sap as to marry one of those fellows, Sis! What on earth would we have done with you thousands of miles away? Marry an American. That's my advice!'

'Looks like I'll have to,' Evalyn conceded ruefully. 'Mother has us in Newport with a view to my matrimonial prospects. We could have gone to Bar Harbor and been cooler.'

'But she knows the McLeans are there. She doesn't want you getting too pally with Ned.'

She said crossly: 'Ned and I are just friends.'

'If Mother has her way you'll make plenty of new ones here.' Vin gestured to the mansions along the coastline with their perfect lawns sweeping down to the rocks. 'But, as Newport is the snob capital of the universe,' he added with a grin, 'prepare to be snubbed by anyone whose money is three years older than ours!'

'I don't give two cents for such nonsense,' Evalyn declared. 'Old Vanderbilt started out with a loan of $100. His family may be the richest people in the world right now, but they began the same way Father did.'

'Reggie didn't let it go entirely to his head,' Vin said. He pointed across Sheep Point Cove to The Breakers, the great house owned by Cornelius Vanderbilt II, and the largest mansion in Newport.

'The library fireplace there came from a château in France and has some legend on it that you should laugh at wealth, as nothing but wisdom matters in the end!'

Evalyn turned to her brother with a grin. 'Yeah . . . one of the few things you cannot buy!'

Vin replied with one of his wry smiles. 'But, Sis, we are too young for wisdom!'

Evalyn saw beyond the angle of her brother's chin the glittering sea dash itself on the rocks, heard the scream of the wheeling seabirds. For a moment her brother seemed like a shadow in the sun.

'Can't we just have a good time, for a while at least?' he went on. His voice was full of teasing vitality.

'There is no reason,' she replied, 'why we should not have a good time for ever!'

Despite Vin's sardonic warnings, Newport society accepted the Walshes. Even though she knew this was her real entrée into American life as a marriageable young woman, Evalyn fully intended to have as much fun this summer as she could. She needed a break, she told herself, a last frivolous flurry before the serious business of finding a partner for life. Carrie, cheated of the prince she had once envisaged as husband to her daughter, had already begun to plan the ball she would give that winter in Washington to present Evalyn formally to their friends.

Meanwhile, Evalyn and Vin soon found themselves popular with the Newport young set and were invited to coming-out receptions and dinners given for the season's débutantes. They spent their days in a social whirl of luncheon and tennis parties, and drove together in Evalyn's Mercedes. But there was one stricture imposed on them by their father: he did not want them driving the new car on their own.

'Let Emile bring you wherever you want to go!' he said. 'That's what I employ him for. You youngsters can enjoy yourselves, have a glass of champagne if you want it, and leave the driving to someone else.'

They obeyed. Life had never been fuller. Sister and brother were happy to be together after their long separation. They reminisced about Ouray and promised each other that, even though their father no longer controlled the mine, they would return there together some day. They spoke of their trip to Ireland, how strange it had been to have visited their father's homeland, and the different perspective it had given them of him.

'We'll go back again sometime!' Vin said. Evalyn agreed. And when she thought of Paul she put him deliberately from her mind.

'Our children are more like twins than just ordinary siblings,' Carrie said to Tom as she observed her offspring. 'They've never been so close!'

Tom nodded. 'It's good to know they will always have each other, Carrie . . . after we're gone and so on.'

'Oh, Tom!' Carrie cried. 'Such a lovely summer and you can talk like this!'

She looked at him sharply. Something had been troubling her of late – dreams that made her wake up frightened, but that vanished as soon as she woke. It occurred to her that perhaps Tom had been touched in the same way and wondered if he had been bothered by intimations of mortality.

Well, there can't be anything wrong with *him*, she mused as she regarded her happy, smiling husband. He's good for another twenty years at least!

One morning Vinson asked Emile to get out the Mercedes.

'I want you to drive me to Thames Street,' he told the chauffeur. 'I have a luncheon appointment with Reggie Vanderbilt.'

Emile obeyed and they set off shortly after midday. But before they got to Thames street Vin told the chauffeur to pull over.

'Here, Emile,' he said, handing him a wad of dollars, 'get yourself luncheon somewhere and wait for me at Memorial Boulevard – at the junction with Bellevue – at four.'

'But Master Vinson—'

'I know, I know . . . Look, Emile, I shouldn't make up excuses, but I want to drive this monster myself. If Father had his way I'd never get a chance.'

Emile ate an anxious, solitary lunch, privately cursing the fact that he had been drawn into subterfuge. He made sure he was at the junction of Bellevue Avenue and Memorial Boulevard on the dot of four, but an hour passed and there was no sign of Vinson. After a further thirty minutes he walked back to Beaulieu, where he was met by his seething employer.

'Vinson was arrested!' Tom told him angrily. 'He was speeding. Police Chief Crowley is bringing him home! *You* were supposed to drive him.'

Emile hunched his shoulders and gestured with his hands. 'I know that, sir, but what can I do when he will not let me?'

Later, Tom reprimanded his son.

'I don't know what you think you're playing at, young man. You were breaking the law!'

'I'm sorry, Father. I just wanted to put that car through some of its paces. I'm a good driver.'

'I know you are, but Newport is not the place to prove it! You got yourself arrested. Because you were my son you were not charged – at least not this time. But if it happens again that Mercedes will have to go.'

'Yes Father,' Vinson said, ashamed of having been caught. But even as he spoke he knew he did not mean it.

Saturday, 19 August 1905 began as another lovely day in that enchanted summer. Evalyn got up late, rang for coffee and fresh orange juice, and had a leisurely bath before Annie came to lace her.

'Where are you off to today, young lass?'

'The Clambake. Mrs Clement Moore has invited us to luncheon.'

Evalyn donned a lawn blouse and a fashionable skirt with the hint of a train. The blouse was elegant with trimmings of fluted muslin, and tight sleeves that extended beyond her wrists to cover half her hand.

'You look lovely,' Annie said, when she had fixed Evalyn's hair and surveyed her handiwork. 'Make sure you don't get the sun, or you'll look like the gargoyle you used to resemble when you used that red stuff on your face.'

Evalyn giggled. 'Oh, Annie, I was a terrible scald. Thank you for putting up with me.' She dropped a kiss on Annie's forehead, noting for the first time that Annie had grey at her temples.

There was a knock on the door and then Vin's impatient voice: 'Hurry up, Sis. We'll be late.'

Evalyn put on her wide-brimmed straw hat, secured it with hatpins, threw a light veil over it that she tied beneath her chin, gathered up her skirt, blew Annie another kiss and rushed downstairs. From the forecourt she could hear the putt-putt-putt of the waiting Mercedes, and the voices of Vin and Emile. She put her head around the library door. The windows were open and the room was full of sunlight and shade, and scents from the garden.

Her father was alone, reading the newspaper. He looked up at her over his spectacles; he was the picture of serenity and relaxation.

'Vin and I are off now, Father, to the Clambake . . . Mrs Moore's luncheon.'

'Vin told me. Enjoy yourselves.'

When he heard the revving of the engine and the crunch of gravel, Tom rose from his chair and went to the window. He watched as the red car moved along the dappled driveway and turned right on to Bellevue Avenue. The uniformed chauffeur was sitting up straight, his pleasure in his work patent. Vin was saying something to his sister; he heard the faint resonance of his teasing voice. The veil and the brim of her hat hid Evalyn's face. She put her hand to it as the car turned at the gate.

Yesterday, Tom thought, they were little children. Today, they are the bastions of the future.

The Clambake Club at Easton's Point had a panoramic view of coastline and ocean. Brother and sister were greeted by their hostess and were quickly engaged in conversation by their new friends, among them the young widow Eloise Kerohan, who had already thrown a tea party for Evalyn.

There was champagne throughout lunch. The bubbles were still effervescing in Evalyn's veins when they left the Clambake at four o'clock. They had agreed to take Eloise Kerohan and two other friends, James Oelrich and Herbert Pell, with them for the ride back.

Eloise turned her fine eyes on Vinson and said coyly: 'Reggie Vanderbilt says that you're the best driver in Newport, Vin – after him, of course!'

Vin glowed. Emile was about to hand the ladies into the car when Vin said to him urgently: 'Hey, Emile, I'll take the wheel.'

Emile stiffened. 'You know how your father feels about that, Mr Vinson,' he said in a low voice. 'Last time—'

'Heck, man, it's just a short ride. Look, I won't drive this thing again while we're in Newport! But just for today . . . And you can take the wheel back before we get to Bellevue.'

'Good idea,' someone said. 'Let's see Vin put this beast through its paces.'

The friends piled in. Emile reluctantly cranked the engine and took his place on the outside seat. Vinson, his face full of delight, drove off with a loud backfire that made everyone jump. Soon he was overtaking the other motors on the road. He opened up the throttle on the rise behind the beach and raced down Tuckerman's Avenue.

It had rained while they'd been at lunch. The road was wet; the air was very fresh. Evalyn, holding on to her hat and relishing the sense of life and

337

happiness in every pore, registered with sudden alarm that they were going far too fast. Foreboding swooped on her, like an eclipse suddenly blotting out the day; it was followed in a moment by a sound like gunfire. The car slewed wildly. Emile was thrown into the ditch. Someone screamed. Evalyn used her elbow to wedge herself firmly against the door; her hat, its veil and hatpins unseated, came adrift and blew away down the road into the dust.

'Tire's blown!' Vinson said, his voice sounding uncertain and very young. 'Goddamn!'

Evalyn saw her brother's knuckles whiten on the steering wheel but, despite all his attempts at control, the red Mercedes was swaying this way and that, skidding headlong. They came upon the bridge across the creek, which ran from Easton's Pond into the bay, at frightening speed.

Evalyn heard the splintering of wood as though it were happening far away and had nothing whatever to do with her and Vin or any of their happy, youthful party on a summer's day. Then darkness dragged her to oblivion.

When she woke her face was pressed into mud and water, and she was riding high waves of pain that rose and ebbed as she tried to move. She realised she was under the car – for how long she did not know – and that it was wedged half into the river. A voice came from somewhere.

'Don't move, ma'am.'

'I'm all right,' she called back through chattering teeth. 'I think my leg is broken; but otherwise I'm fine.'

And then the vehicle was being slowly levered up and she was pulled to safety.

Someone tried to get her to drink something.

'I'm a doctor,' he said when she attempted to push the glass away. 'This will help your pain.'

But Evalyn, bleeding, covered in mud and shivering violently, looked around wildly. She saw the small crowd that had gathered, saw among them white-faced people she knew – Alfred G. Vanderbilt and Fifi Potter Stillman, who took off her exquisite coat of Irish lace and put it over her. She saw Mrs Oelrich, James's mother, help her muddied, limping son into a car. But there was no sign of Vinson.

'Vin!' Evalyn cried. She turned to the doctor. 'Where is my brother?'

'He's . . . all right . . .'

But Evalyn knew that if Vinson were all right nothing would keep him from her side.

'Please let me see him. Oh, please let me see him . . .'

'He's been . . . hurt. They're dressing his wounds.'

Evalyn heard the hesitation in the doctor's voice. Oh God, she prayed, as the tears trickled down her face and into her mouth, please let this be a bad dream.

'Vin!' she called, and her voice sounded reedy and thin in her ears.

Two policemen put her on a stretcher, carried her past the crashed Mercedes. As she looked at her car she saw that the front wheels had been wrenched loose and that, sticking through the vehicle from one end to the other, like some ancient weapon of impalement, was a heavy wooden railing from the bridge.

'Brother,' she whispered. 'Vin. Oh, Vin . . .'

The stretcher-bearers moved quickly so that she did not see the blood that stained the driver's seat and puddled on the floor.

And then she saw her father. He approached her in calm concern. Relief flooded her, momentarily blotting out the agony.

But he was terribly pale. His lips had a bluish cast; the pupils of his eyes were dilated; there was an expression on his face she had never seen, the look of someone in mortal pain. But he took her hand and she felt his strength flow into her, calming her. He kissed her forehead.

'How are you, my poor darling?'

'I'm fine, I'm fine . . . Where is Vin?'

'Your brother has been taken to hospital,' he replied levelly, putting a warm rug over her. Then he turned to help a blood-stained Eloise Kerohan tenderly into a trap. Eloise was shocked and weeping, her hair in disarray and her dress torn.

The ambulance came, the horses sweating from their race along Memorial Boulevard.

'Take me home, Father. Make them take me home.'

A week later the *Newport Journal and Weekly News* reported:

Newport had its first fatal automobile accident Saturday afternoon in which Vinson F. Walsh, son of Mr and Mr Thomas F. Walsh of Washington, was killed. Their daughter, Miss Evalyn Walsh, suffered a broken leg and Mrs James L. Kerohan, Mr James Oelrich, Mr Herbert Pell and the chauffeur were slightly injured. The accident, which was caused by the high rate of speed at which the automobile was being driven and the bursting of a pneumatic tire, took place at the eastern end of the road back of Easton's Beach at the wooden bridge which crosses the little creek into the ocean.

Young Walsh was evidently dying of a concussion of the brain when he was picked up. Death occurred almost immediately after arrival at the hospital. On Saturday night the remains were taken from the hospital to Beaulieu. The funeral service was held there on Monday at 10 a.m. in the room in which Miss Julia Dent Grant was married to Prince Cantacuzene of Russia six years ago next Friday.

Vinson Walsh was known throughout the city as a daring driver.

Evalyn, lying in pain in her room, did not know that her brother's corpse, surrounded by wreaths and messages of sympathy, was in the room beneath hers, and that his funeral service was already in progress. The house was hushed; she heard little except soft footsteps and quiet voices, but she attributed this to her own dire straits. The doctor had left; the nurses made her as comfortable as they could. Her parents came to her in ordinary clothes and spoke to her with apparent cheerfulness. She accepted that Vin was in hospital and that she had to be brave.

'When can I go to see him?' she asked. 'I really need to see him . . .'

'Not yet. But we must go away for a couple of days.'

'To be with Vin?'

'Yes.'

They bent their heads. She saw the tears that crept in silence down her mother's face.

'I will be all right, Mother,' Evalyn said. 'I promise.'

Tom and Carrie gave back the Newport house to Cornelius Vanderbilt and took their injured daughter to Garden City Hotel in Long Island in a deep basket. They stayed by her bedside until her broken leg was set in plaster from thigh to ankle and she was completely out of danger. And then her parents came to her like two old people, to tell her that her brother was dead.

'And I did not even have the chance to say goodbye,' she wept. 'Oh, where is he, Father? Where is his grave?'

'In Washington,' Tom whispered. 'In Rock Creek Cemetery.'

Evalyn thought of that quiet place with its patrician monuments and its trees. For Vin who had been so bursting with life?

'Take me home,' she whispered. Her mouth was full of mucus and salt; her eyes were sore and red, but her mind insisted there was some terrible mistake, that this could not be happening, that they were all locked into a nightmare.

'Back to 2020, darling? Are you sure?'

'Oh no. All his things are there!'

She could not return as yet to the house that was filled with Vinson, his memory, his belongings.

Evalyn struggled, but she could not keep her head above the seas of grief and pain that engulfed her. The distress in the broken limb did not abate. She was fed morphine, but notwithstanding this, the agony was unendurable; the nights were long and she could not sleep. More and more morphine was prescribed until she was getting ten grains per day, but even then the pain found chinks in her being that had not been sedated. Grief for Vinson was ever present; a wild animal that howled inside her night and day.

Not to have even said goodbye . . . oh, Vin . . . oh, my darling brother . . .

The long days and longer nights crawled by. Letters of sympathy and encouragement came in bushels, including one from Paul.

Dear Aunt Carrie, Uncle Tom and Evalyn,
Nothing I could possibly say would express the depth of my sympathy for your dreadful loss. The terrible news reached us Tuesday.

I remember Vin with great fondness. The happy times we all had together in Ouray on that wonderful summer of 1901 will always be with me. He loved life and other people, and most of all his family. He is a loss to society, for he was destined to become a significant figure in American life. Our hearts go out to you.

Amelia joins me in sending heartfelt wishes for Evalyn's speedy recovery.

Affectionately,
Paul

'We,' Evalyn said to herself as she studied the letter. '*Ours! Amelia joins me . . . The happy times we all had together in Ouray! . . . Affectionately!*'

She traced her finger over the signature, the long upright of the letter P.

Well, Amelia, you have him and the decent thing is to hope you will both be happy. It was just a silly crush. And I am nearly over it.

The pain leaped up at her as though it knew she lied.

'I need more morphine,' she cried, and the nurse came hurrying.

The time came, some two months later, when she tried to stand again. Supported by the nurses, Evalyn stood on her left leg and saw with horror that her right leg was inches short and did not meet the floor. When she leaned to put her weight on it, the pain sprang up at her so that she sceamed. She knew, without being told, that the two broken ends of her thigh had not knit together; the setting had been botched.

She was put back to bed. Her only comfort was her gramophone which she played almost incessantly, day and night. Friends came to call. Ned McLean, sporting a reluctant moustache, brought all the latest gramophone records and did everything he could to cheer her up.

The doctors examined her, performed X-rays, frowned in private professional speculation, and left the room to confer with her parents.

She heard some of their discussion outside her door, her mother sobbing, her father saying Evalyn would have to make the decision herself.

'What decision do I have to make?' she asked them when they came back.

Her father replied slowly, his voice almost toneless, 'They are telling us you have a very stark choice, Evalyn . . .' His voice petered out. He bowed his head. She saw how grey he had become, how haggard and ashen.

She asked gently, 'You mean I might die, Father?'

He nodded in silence. Her mother sat on the edge of the bed and took her hands.

'What is the other alternative, Mother? Being lame?'

'You might have to . . . lose the leg!'

Evalyn lay back on her pillows and stared at the ceiling. Only a few months before she had been waltzing in Rome, walking in Venice, laughing in Monte Carlo at two assiduous princes who wanted her for a wife. Only a little while ago she had set out for the Clambake Club with the debonair brother she so loved. What had happened to the girl with her world intact and her brilliant life ahead of her? Now her beloved brother was dead, her parents were ageing before her eyes and she herself was in mortal danger, at the very least a one-legged freak, crippled for life. She dared not even think of the frightful destiny that loomed before her.

'What happened?' she whispered. 'Why did it all go wrong?'

Her father's groan echoed through the room.

'If the mountains had only told me . . .' he cried. 'If they had said, "We will bargain. We will trade our gold for your children" . . .' He stared around as though he were dazed.

The nurses looked at him with compassion, tears starting in their eyes.

He punched his fist into his palm.

'*Why?*' he repeated on a high note of pain, then abruptly left the room.

When Ned McLean came to call that afternoon Evalyn told him the terrible choice ahead of her. Her voice was dazed and quiet. From her morphine-sedated world it all seemed far off.

'I'm either going to have my leg amputated, Ned, or I'm going to . . . die!'

Ned looked horrified. 'I never heard such nonsense! You're nineteen years old! I'm going straight off to talk about this to my father!'

'What can he do about it?'

'If anyone knows who can fix you up, Pop does! He's not a newspaper giant for nothing! He didn't buy the *Washington Post* without knowing what's what!'

John R. came with Ned to visit Evalyn on the following day. His presence filled the room; his toughness, his robust assurance were a tonic in themselves. But he was the soul of gentleness as he sat beside the invalid's bed and took her hand.

'So what's all this, Evalyn? Are you game for a bit of real surgery by the best man in the business? I know someone who'll have you up and about in no time.'

'Surgery to cure me, to mend my leg? So that I won't have to lose it?'

John R. nodded, his tough, calculating face, oddly tender and filled with pity.

'Of course I'm game,' Evalyn whispered. 'I would do anything . . .'

Her eyes filled, but her heart had begun to beat faster, suddenly buoyed by this man's belief that life would always yield to his will. 'I don't mind any surgery; they can cut me open from head to foot if it will save my leg!'

John R. directed at his son a look that said: 'Now, didn't I tell you that Pop would fix it?'

He signalled Tom and Carrie to follow him out of the room.

The doctor's name was John Millar Turpin Finney, and he was a physician without parallel. He was attached to John Hopkins Hospital in Washington, and when he had examined Evalyn he did not try to play down the seriousness of her situation.

'You need surgery urgently. Your leg will never heal without it.'

He took a notepad from his pocket and a fountain pen. 'Look,' he said, drawing on the pad. 'This is the break. It has been left for so long that part of the bone is dead, so I will have to cut the dead parts away and insert silver rivets to bring the two ends of broken joint together. It will be a very long and dangerous operation.'

'Will I be lame?'

The doctor looked her in the eye. 'I cannot guarantee that you will not. I will try to make up for the present deficiency when the necrotised bone is removed.'

Evalyn looked at him for a moment and then asked in a low, even voice: 'What are my chances of surviving the operation?'

The room filled with silence. The nurses looked at their hands. Tom and Carrie stared at the doctor. The latter rubbed his lower lip with his thumb, and regarded his incisive young patient with respect.

'An even chance,' he said gently. 'That's as high as I can put it, Evalyn. You must know the truth.'

Evalyn heard the silence; it had a substance and presence of its own. Why, she wondered with strange detachment, do people always think they have problems when they have none? *I* have a real problem. I am against the wall. Being the Walsh Heiress will not save me now.

She glanced at her stricken father. 'It's up to me, Father, isn't it? No one else can decide?'

He nodded. His voice was very low. 'Only you can say.'

Evalyn turned to Dr Finney, saw his grave professionalism, his sacerdotal air, the cool clean lines of his hands.

'What would you do, Doctor, if I was your daughter?'

'I would tell her the facts as I have told you! But I would not operate on my own child!'

Evalyn fought the fear. *'Always face your fences . . .'* her father had often counselled. She saw his face now, pale and haggard and tense with dread; but the lines around his mouth were as strong as ever.

I will not be cowed by anything Fate has to throw at me, she thought on a private surge of anger and pride. I am Tom Walsh's daughter.

'All right,' she said, forcing cheerfulness into her voice. 'Go ahead. Do the operation. But I want it done at home!'

'In that case you must go home at once,' the surgeon said crisply. 'There is no time to be lost.' He checked a small black diary he took from his pocket. 'I will operate on Friday.'

As he was leaving he picked up the small phial which contained the morphine.

'How much of this is she getting?' he asked her doctor *sotto voce*.

'She is in great pain . . . About ten grains . . . sometimes more . . .'

Dr Finney's face registered shock. 'This may yet prove the bigger problem!' he muttered under his breath.

Annie stayed in Evalyn's room in 2020 on the night before the operation. Evalyn talked feverishly through the hours of darkness, as though, with Death waiting to salute her in the morning, she wanted to squeeze life out of every second that remained. She reminisced about the early days, about Ouray, and when she lapsed into silence she let her mind dwell on the summer of 1901, the ride with Paul in the canyon, the voyage into love.

I have forgotten him, she assured herself. It's over . . .

But all the same she said to Annie, 'Annie, there is something I want you to do in case I die.'

'Don't talk such nonsense. You're going to come through this.'

'I know. But just in case . . .?'

'Of course, I'll do anything you want!' Annie said, wiping her silent tears with the sheet.

'In my jewel box there is a small piece of quartz. If the worst happens, I want you to send it to Paul.'

Annie nodded. She did not seem surprised.

The early morning sun touched the pink damask walls of her room.

'I feel like a condemned prisoner,' Evalyn whispered. 'This may be my last sunrise! Oh, Annie, I am so frightened!'

The housekeeper, who felt as though her eyes were burning a hole in her head, said in her warm burr: 'You were never a bairn for sunrises, anyway!' She held her close and whispered, 'Remember what your father used to say about courage?'

Evalyn nodded. *'It carries all before it.'*

The medical team arrived and began their preparations in Evalyn's pink and gold bathroom, and soon the smell of disinfectant filled her suite like the scent of an arcane peril. She limped into the improvised surgical theatre on crutches. An operating table had been set up in the middle of the bathroom, and above it had been hung a huge electric lamp. Beside it was a table on which, neatly laid out, was a range of surgical instruments.

'I want to see every knife and every saw!' she told Dr Finney. 'You're not going to work on me unless I know what you're going to use!'

Dr Finney was unused to demands of this order from his patients and was a little rocked by the intrepid nineteen-year-old, but he showed her the lancets and scalpels, the surgical saws.

'Are you ready now, Evalyn?' he asked gently when she had seen everything. 'If you are, we are.'

When Evalyn woke it was late evening. She was flat on her back in bed and in terrible pain. Her injured leg, encased in a plaster cast, was held up by pulleys and counterweights. Dr Finney and her parents were at her bedside, but in strange multiples. They seemed insubstantial beings, duplicated according to some vagary of the light. But her mother's face as it bent over her, although it was in duplicate, had never looked so sweet.

'She's coming out of it!' Carrie whispered.

'There are two of you all,' Evalyn whispered. 'Which one is real?'

'That is an optical illusion from the anaesthetic,' Dr Finney said in a reassuring voice. 'It will pass. The operation went well, Evalyn. How are you feeling?'

'Terrible. The pain is . . . *terrible.*' She gasped as it crashed over her, pushing her back into the dark world from which she had just emerged. 'You must give me morphine . . .' She closed her eyes.

The doctor looked grimly at her parents.

'For now,' he said, 'we will.'

Evalyn's leg took five months to heal. Lying flat on her back, her leg in pulleys, tormented with pain and discomfort of every kind, driven half mad by the inaccessible itching of the wound as it healed, Evalyn saw that the world was a very strange place, and her own tenure in it fragile. She saw that the important things in life were the people one loved. She had always accepted this as received wisdom, but she had never fully realised the potency of its truth.

Her new philosophical turn of mind might have hastened her recovery, were it not for a fact that was now increasingly apparent to everyone: Evalyn was addicted to morphine. As she began to recover the doctor restricted it, a little less every day. But the power of her hunger for it drove her on more than one occasion to attempt throwing herself out of bed, with the intention of crawling downstairs and outside to the nearest drug store, where she fantasised she would hold the owner at gunpoint. The nurses held her back; Annie came running, screaming at her that she would destroy the work Dr Finney had done.

'Please, Annie . . . get them to give me more morphine. I cannot bear it . . .'

But the doctors were adamant: it was time to break this addiction and break it they would.

Her father came and sat with her, and she saw how old he had become, so much older than his fifty-five years.

'I do not want to live,' Evalyn said in a flat voice. 'The price is too high!'

There was silence for a moment, and her comment, its pathos and despair, hung in the air. Tom bowed his head.

'Evalyn, I would spare you any suffering. If I could have Vinson back, and you well again, what do you think I would not do? I'll tell you . . .' he said on a strained note of anguish, something Evalyn had never heard from him and which frightened her almost as much as her own dire straits, 'I would find every ounce of that gold and put it right back into that mountain! I would dedicate to it my remaining years . . .' His voice broke; he put his head in his hands.

Evalyn saw his grey head bowed before her and a determination was born in her to break her addiction, no matter what it cost her. I will do it or bust! she told him silently. I will do it for you, my dearest Father.

After that she bore the agonies of withdrawal with dogged, determined patience, taking the decreasing relief she was allowed, thanking God as the hunger gradually abated. But at the back of her mind was a niggle of anxiety. Was she cured? Or was her addiction merely in abeyance, waiting for her to weaken, waiting for another day?

On 18 March 1906 Evalyn's cast was removed. She found she could move her leg in any direction without any discomfort. Dr Finney measured both limbs; the right leg was still marginally shorter than the left. He did not labour this point, but congratulated her on her recovery. 'You will be able to walk again,' he said.

Evalyn studied his face and asked softly: 'Will I be lame?'

He sighed. 'A little, perhaps. Just a little. You can build up your shoe. It will not be noticeable.'

I am not yet twenty, Evalyn thought, and I will spend the rest of my life 'a little lame'. Mademoiselle Raye was right. *Things come at a price.* But why such a high one? Why such a price for Vin, for Father and Mother, for me?

★   ★   ★

Two weeks later Evalyn was carried to her sitting room where Dr Finney and her parents were waiting for her. This was the moment she had anticipated with hope and dread.

'Now,' he said, 'we will put it all to the test. Are you game, Evalyn?'

She nodded, was helped to stand on her 'good' leg. She was so weak from months of inactivity that she was afraid the nurses would let her go and that she would crash to the floor. But their strong arms were reassuringly around her. When she had found her balance on her left leg, the command came from Dr Finney, reminding her, for a moment, of a story from the New Testament.

'Take a step, Evalyn. Walk!'

While the nurses held her, she moved her right leg forward and put it on the floor, then rested her weight on it. With a feeling of wonder and gratitude she found it bore her weight without complaint. She took another step. She was able to move, as freely as her weakened condition allowed. The surge of euphoria made her want to dance. She knew the leg was marginally shorter than it should have been, but she could walk, was free of pain.

She looked at Dr Finney and her eyes filled with tears.

'Thank you,' she said simply.

He smiled at her, his own expression full.

'*You* did it! Evalyn. Never doubt it. And if you could pull through this, break from morphine, fight the pain, endure what you endured, what iron have you not got inside you? You are a formidable person, and you must never believe otherwise. It has been my privilege to have treated you!'

Tom and Carrie smiled through their tears.

'Well, darling,' Tom said gruffly, 'what would you like to do to help you convalesce?'

'Can we go back to Colorado?' Evalyn whispered. 'I have been in a sick room for so long that I have a terrible longing to breathe the air of the Rockies.' She glanced at her parents and added softly, 'We were lucky there, weren't we? Maybe our luck will come back to us again.'

She put her hand to the back of her head, which was almost bald from seven months on the flat of her back.

'And it will give me time to get myself fit to be seen!' she added with a half-smile through sudden tears. 'I am afraid to look in the mirror.'

'We'll buy a place in Colorado,' Tom said. 'Would you like that?'

'Oh yes, if we can afford it, Father.'

'We can, Evalyn,' her father said drily. 'We can afford it all right.'

Tom bought an estate called Wolhurst in Douglas County about twenty miles from Denver. It had nearly five hundred acres, a fine house, stables and gardens.

The house, modelled on a typical English manor house, had been built by Senator Edward Wolcott in 1890. The ceilings of its great reception rooms had oak beams and baronical fireplaces. It had a sixty-foot-long library, a billiards room, coach house and caretaker's cottage, and over-looked an artificial lake with swans. The entrance avenue was lined with ash and pine trees.

Tom was glad to go back to Colorado. Anything was better than staying on at 2020 and pretending that everything might go on as before. The anniversary of Vin's death was looming, and with it renewed grief, so fresh that the catastrophe might have happened the day before. But at least in the new surroundings there were no constant reminders of the son he had lost.

On 19 August 1906, the first anniversary of Vinson's death, Tom got up at daybreak and picked his way around the lake, sat for a while among the trees, so sick at heart that he did not notice the susurration of the water, the wind of dawn, or the first exploratory cheeps of the birds.

My son, my Vinson . . . When you were a little boy and hurt yourself I would hold you, tell you it was all right. And when I saw your body, lying so still in that hospital, I wanted to hold you, comfort you, say it would be all right . . .

Tom looked up through the summer leaves at the brightening sky. The sobs that wrenched themselves from him made strangled sounds of despair that carried along the shore.

'It is not something a father should see,' he cried suddenly, pounding the earth with his fists, 'the corpse of his only son! You have broken me, great God in Heaven. You have destroyed me . . .'

Evalyn had been unable to sleep. When she had heard the footsteps on the gravel below her window she had got out of bed to see who was astir, and decided to accompany her father. But by the time she was dressed he was nowhere to be seen, so she let herself out through a back door, limped slowly along the dirt lane that was lined with cottonwood trees and dusted with white cottonseed fluffs. She directed her steps towards the lake. The sounds torn from her father's heart carried along the water, stunning her with their ferocious grief.

She sank out of sight against a tree, convulsed with sorrow. Only one little year ago she had woken with joyful expectation of another wonderful, idle, carefree day. One little year!

She thought of Paul, but the ache was muted. She did not want to see him any more, nor his wife, whom she had heard was now expecting a child.

Her leg began to ache. The pain carried to the hip joint and down to her ankle, danced up and down as though it played a dirge on her bones. She saw Vin's face as it had been that morning, the lick of silken dark hair, the grin, his seventeen years, half boy, half man, so anxious to prove himself, so funny and deep, so concentrated when he drove. If that tire had not blown . . . or if it had blown half a mile back . . . or if she had never pestered her father for a Mercedes and had married a prince instead and stayed in Europe . . .

She brought her knees up, wrapped her arms around them and buried her face in her skirt, rocking herself, wiping her tears in silence. She longed for her father's arms, for comfort, any comfort that would ease the agony. But she would not intrude on him when he was like this, and would wait out his anguish, keeping vigil with him. He need not know.

After a while she heard his steps. He was coming in her direction and she flattened herself against the trunk of the oak, but he saw her suddenly, came towards her through the dappling shadows, turned her face up to him, wiped away her tears and put a hand on her head. Then he helped her rise, drew her arm through his and they came back to the house in silence.

Carrie met them in the hall. She looked white and strained.

'I was wondering where you had gone.'

She took in their hollow faces, the marks of weeping; her own face crumpled and her tears flowed in silence. Tom and Evalyn wrapped her in their arms and they stood like that for a while, sheltered by each other.

In the following days, Evalyn felt the quietness that came to dwell in her parents' hearts. They were like marionettes, still moving to an ordained choreography, although the curtain had fallen and the lights gone out.

It's up to me now, she thought, to make them live again!

Chapter Twenty-Eight

The New Year of 1907 saw the Walshes back in Washington. Life had returned to a semblance of normality. The sole of Evalyn's right shoe had been built up and, unless she was very tired, it was not particularly noticeable that she was lame. She became adept at hiding her disability while in public, but in private she still relied a good deal on crutches. She went to parties and threw her own, but the coming-out ball to which she had once looked forward never took place.

With her recovery the sense of invisibility returned to taunt her. Bereavement, she thought, was more than loneliness; it shook the foundations of one's understanding, the way an earthquake made you question your faith in the earth. Vin, no matter how much he had found fault with her, had known who she was. No one could replace him. And her mother, despite Evalyn's secret hopes that she would now turn to her, mourned for her lost son in secret passions of her own, in which her daughter had once or twice surprised her. For her mother, it seemed, the pain of bereavement was a private matter between herself and God.

One thing had helped lift the pall a little. The Republicans invited her father to become their nominee for the Senate.

'You'd make a fine Senator, Papa!' Evalyn said. She thought of how proud Vin would have been, but she did not mention his name.

Tom agreed; but he used the situation to let his views on accumulated wealth be known. The *Denver Post* carried his words on the front page:

Accumulated and concentrated wealth, both corporate and individual, is crushing from the masses the life of individual ownership, individual independence and almost individual existence . . . We should establish a new basis for compensating the masses.

His opponent, Simon Guggenheim, the smelter king, defeated him in a close contest. But Tom did not seem very disappointed.

*   *   *

As the year wore on Evalyn saw more and more of Ned McLean. They met socially; he called to see her; he was her friend and confidant. Sometimes he suggested, half seriously, half joking that they get married and she just as flippantly said maybe they should; but the following day they would be sure to have a fight. Alcohol made Ned possessive and Evalyn could not stand his woozy ownership, the way he could turn in an instant from a sensitive friend to a boor.

'I can't marry a goddamn drunk!'

'I'm not a drunk.'

'No? You were so smashed at last night's party you had to knot a scarf around your shoulder to support your elbow.'

Ned stormed off. He was used to being indulged, to his every caprice having the force of law. He had never known discipline, never had to defer the pleasure of the moment, never been forced to work for his princely allowance. But sometimes he radiated a vulnerability that resonated with Evalyn. She recognised that between them there was a bond, reinforced when she had been facing a terrible choice and he had anchored her to life and hope. But even this bond could not withstand his persistent abuse of alcohol.

I'm fed up with Ned, Evalyn told herself. He follows me around, gets drunk and behaves obnoxiously. I'll show him he's not the only pebble on the beach. There are other men who are interested in me, and there are other things to think about!

So when Ned came to put his arm around her at a party and asked in a slurred voice if the prettiest girl in Washington would care to dance, she turned on him and hissed: 'Leave me alone, Ned McLean. You're drunk again! I don't want anything to do with you any more!'

Ned looked stunned; he walked unsteadily away.

'I've broken with Ned,' she told her mother. Even as she registered the maternal relief, she wondered at the void that yawned in her heart as the days passed and Ned did not call.

Can't do with him, and can't do without him, she thought ruefully. Why is everything, and everyone, in life so addictive? But I won't telephone him and I won't see him. If he cares about me he'll stop drinking.

She filled her days with outings, drives, seeing her friends and catching up on events in their lives. One of them, Katherine Elkins, was the subject of excited press speculation. She had been escorted for some weeks by the Duke of Abruzzi, a member of the Italian Royal Family, who had arrived in America in command of a visiting Italian warship squadron. Katherine's father, Senator Elkins, owned railroads and coal mines in West Virginia. Evalyn thought of her own brush with Italian princes, but conceded that the Duke of Abruzzi was not cut of the same cloth. He was a man in every fibre and it was obvious that he and Katherine were deeply in love.

351

'Are you going to marry him, Katherine?' she asked one day, unable to contain her curiosity. 'He's simply divine!'

Katherine's eyes darkened.

'Oh, Evalyn, I wish life were not so complicated. The problem is – as he's in line to a throne and I am not, it would have to be a morganatic marriage.'

'What's that?'

'I would have to forego royal status for myself and my children! And I couldn't do that, Evalyn,' Katherine added with a proud tilt to her chin. 'I could not become a second-class citizen within my own marriage.'

Mrs McLean telephoned Evalyn one afternoon and asked conspiratorially, woman-to-woman, if she would let her know when Katherine announced her engagement. It was the first contact Evalyn had had with the McLeans since her rupture with Ned, and his mother's kind, familiar voice reopened the wound.

'It would be a scoop for the *Post*, my dear, to be the first with the announcement that an American girl is marrying into the Italian royal family.'

'She won't marry him with what she calls the left hand, Mummie. She's too proud for that!'

'The girl is a fool if she passes up such a glittering chance,' Mrs McLean replied. Then she added gently, 'Ned is pining for you, Evalyn. You know how much he cares . . . how much he needs your friendship . . .' Her voice became coaxing. 'Won't you be friends again?'

'Of course we're still friends,' Evalyn said politely. She did not want to talk of Ned, and especially not to his mother, so she changed the subject and joked about her own skirmish with Italian princes. '. . . But it was different in my case, of course. Katherine is really in love . . .'

'You sound a bit wistful, my dear child. Have you any regrets?'

'None at all, except that if I had accepted one of them . . . I would have stayed in Italy . . .' Her voice faltered, 'and the accident in Newport would never have happened . . . and,' she added, biting back the grief that still waited on a daily basis to ambush her, '. . . Vin would still be alive.'

'My poor dear girl, I didn't mean to upset you!'

'Oh, Mummie,' Evalyn cried, 'I cannot, ever, get away from it for long.'

'Come for a visit and we can have a good long talk! There's nothing like sharing grief to ease it.'

But Evalyn demurred. If she went to see Mrs McLean she would be bound to meet Ned.

'Thanks, but at the moment I'm up to my ears. We'll be going to Colorado soon for the summer.'

A few weeks later Evalyn was back among her beloved mountains. A party of friends had followed the Walshes to Wolhurst, and every day was filled with activities. Evalyn threw a picnic on Pike's Peak for the Duc de Chambrun, one of their guests. For a while romance seemed a possibility between them. But when she pondered becoming the next chatelaine of the Chambrun château, it felt like a rerun of her Italian experience. She knew a brilliant marriage would please her mother, but the prospect of living away from America seemed, once again, intolerable. She was not really in love with the duke and was finding the marriage market something of a minefield, wearisome and perilous.

'The real divide in the world,' Paul had said, '. . . is between those who are able to love and those who are not.'

He was a father now; he and Amelia had a son. He made no attempt to see Evalyn, although her father sometimes called on them when he was in Denver and brought back news of a business that continued to thrive, having branched into automobiles. But her thoughts still turned to him with a sense of bewildered loss: Am I never to see you again, Paul? Have you really forgotten me?

Evalyn celebrated her twenty-first birthday at Wolhurst, listened to the champagne toasts, saw how the fireworks set the birds to flight. When the guests had gone to bed she walked alone in the garden on which her father had spent $10,000 on rose trees and $1,000 on bird seed, and wondered where she was going with her life.

By the New Year of 1908 Evalyn still met Ned socially from time to time, but hardly spoke to him, although there was always an ache in her heart when she saw him look at her wistfully and turn away. She kept hearing the echo of his mother's words: '. . . he needs your friendship . . .'

Uncomfortable new promptings were surfacing from deep within. These were whispering that she would be twenty-two on her next birthday, and that, no matter how she tried to forget it, she was maimed. In spite of her father's wealth she was no longer quite the prize she had been.

'I will accept the next American who proposes to me!' she told herself when fears of ending up on the shelf rose to taunt her. 'Providing he is decent and really cares about me.'

So, in the spring, at a party in Washington's Williard Hotel, Evalyn encouraged handsome Billy Hitt's advances. Billy courted her over the winter season, coming to lunch and taking her to the races, and she ended up inviting him to Wolhurst when the family were due to go West again for the summer. But she knew there was no real rapport between them.

Does it matter? she wondered. She was choosing her wardrobe for the vacation, sliding outfit after outfit along the rails of her closets, feeling bored and listless as one elegant silk and linen ensemble succeeded another. Does it matter whether there is any genuine empathy between me and the man I marry? Billy's kind and he's decent and Ned, like Paul, seems to have forgotten me. Of course, I'm a freak now, so why shouldn't he?

When the telephone rang; she picked up the gilded handpiece thoughtlessly.

'Hello?'

'Evalyn, what's this I hear about you inviting Hitt to Colorado?'

It was Ned.

Hearing his voice after such a long time had a strange effect on Evalyn. It was like finding a missing piece of the jigsaw that was her life. But her pleasure was short-lived. Ned sounded very cross, but also, she conceded, perfectly sober.

'Stop treating me as though I were property in which you had shares,' Evalyn cried. 'It's none of your business, Ned, whom I invite to Wolhurst!'

'What do you see in him? If you're going to encourage *him* I want my letters back!'

'I'll tell you what I see in him – I see sobriety, and dependableness. And if you want your letters back you can come and collect them! I'm not going to send them!'

Ned rang off abruptly. When he did not contact her the following day, or the day after, she found herself worrying if she had offended him beyond recall; this filled her with a renewed sense of desolation. She recognised reluctantly that the bond between them still lived on; that, despite everything, it contained an effortless empathy she could not bear to forfeit. To lose *that* again would be to court emotional bankruptcy.

And he needs me, she reminded herself. Unlike Paul, he *needs* me . . .

By the end of the week her turmoil was driving her half mad, but she tried to please her mother by attending the dinner she was giving for the Red Cross. Although Billy Hitt could not be present, Evalyn dressed for the occasion in a Worth gown of emerald green. It was a particularly becoming dress, accentuating the colour of her eyes, and the rich darkness of hair. She smoothed the silk bodice, turned to regard her slim self in the mirror and smiled when she remembered how she had once used every ploy at her command to cover her face in rouge, and how Annie had always lain in wait with a soapy flannel. I was such a child, she told her reflection. But I am not a child any more. Soon, I will be twenty-two.

It seemed a great age – only life's major choices and responsibilities ahead. So many of my friends are already married, she thought. I like Billy, but . . .

'Oh, Ned,' she whispered aloud in a burst of despairing candour, 'I've known you for ever and I do want to marry a friend. If only . . .'

When the dinner was over, and the company was withdrawing, the butler came discreetly to Evalyn and whispered in her ear, 'Are you at home to Mr Edward McLean, miss?'

Evalyn excused herself and followed him from the room.

Ned was waiting in the hall that served the *porte-cochère*. He was looking glum, staring at his own reflection in the gilt-framed mirror that took up almost the entire wall. Although Evalyn's heart skipped with delight at the sight of him, she feigned nonchalance and greeted her visitor as though they had never spoken a word in acrimony.

'How are you, Ned?'

'I'm very well, Evalyn. How are you? You are looking extremely well,' he added stiffly, but Evalyn saw the admiration in his eyes, and also noted that although it was half-past nine in the evening he was sober as a judge.

'As you see. Quite well,' she replied with a smile. Then she added, for Ned was patently ill at ease, and the servants who moved between the kitchen stairs and the drawing room were not blind, 'Would you like to come into the library? We can talk there.'

Ned nodded and they stepped into this sanctum, her father's favourite room. As soon as the door was shut he turned to her plaintively.

'You can't keep this up, treating me as though I'm some kind of pariah, Evalyn. I've always loved you and you've always loved me. Please say you'll marry me. We were meant for each other.' He paused and added sadly, 'Oh, Evalyn, have you a heart of stone? I've given up drinking, and I've even taken to work. I couldn't bear to lose you.'

Evalyn steeled herself against the rush of tenderness.

'They're trying me out – as a cub reporter for the *Post*,' he went on. He pulled out a notebook and some pencils from his pocket. 'See – I even have the paraphernalia! But I'm so tired of trying to live without you!' He looked at her in silence, went on his knees and reached for her hand. 'Please marry me. I am desperately in earnest.'

Evalyn thrilled to this proposal. It had none of the flippancy of earlier ones. It smacked of a new maturity.

'I promise you, Evalyn, that if you accept me I will pull my life together and cement our marriage. I'm sure you'll help me . . . There is no end to what we could do together.'

Evalyn saw herself instilling in this pampered scion of a great American family some of the iron of Colorado.

She left her hand in his and said gently: 'If you really want to marry me, Ned, you'll have to talk to Father!'

She knew the prospect of facing her formidable parent would test Ned's ardour more than anything else. He got up from his knees and drew a deep breath.

'All right. I'll come and see him tomorrow. But before I go looking for his blessing, my darling, I need to hear something from you.' He grasped both her hands, pulling them to rest against his heart. 'If your father consents, will you marry me, Evalyn Walsh? Will you be my wife?'

Evalyn looked into his anxious eyes, saw his love and earnest resolve. With a curious sense of detachment she heard the butler's footsteps in the hall and the noise of traffic from the street. She knew she was now facing a crossroads in her life; if she rejected Ned now he would probably go away for ever. She was borne up by a sense of her own power; and with it came a surge of love, and of faith and hope in the future.

'Yes,' she said simply. 'If Father consents I will marry you.'

When Ned was gone Evalyn wondered if his resolve would crack. He was shy where her parents were concerned, knew perfectly well that neither Tom nor Carrie was overboard at the prospect of him for a son-in-law.

'If he's got the guts for it,' Evalyn said to herself, 'to go to Father and speak to him, then he's got enough character to do what he has promised – give up drink, become a good husband and, in due course, . . . a good father. After all,' she added to herself, 'I'm getting on. I can't go fooling around much longer. And he can be so lovable when he wants, and such fun and a wonderful friend . . . And Mother will be pleased when she sees how well it all turns out.'

In the morning Evalyn went to confide in her father. Knowing that he always rose at dawn she got up early to catch him before the household was astir.

Tom, wearing a plain dressing gown, was seated in his favourite armchair by the open window of his second-floor study. The dawn chorus had started outside; the freshness of morning filled the room and the stained glass of the bay window sent small pools of vermilion and blue on to his desk.

He looked up from his papers when his daughter, in her pink crepe-de-Chine wrap, came in, and carefully closed the door behind her.

'Father . . .'

Tom heard the breathlessness in her voice. He had noticed her limp as she crossed the floor, and he let the pain of it into the wound that lived inside him and had never healed.

'What is it, my darling? Why don't you sit down?'

Evalyn sat on the leather-covered armchair, leaned forward and announced, 'Ned came over yesterday evening. He asked me to marry him!'

Tom took off his reading glasses. He had been perusing a report about the miraculous new element called radium, and was about to set up a trust for research into it in memory of his dead son.

Evalyn's confidence did not surprise him. Ned had asked her to marry him so often it was almost a family joke. He sighed. 'This must be Ned's proposal number fifty-two!'

'It's not quite that many, Father!'

'Did you accept him . . . again?'

'Provisionally. I told him he'd have to talk to you!'

The indulgent smile vanished from Tom's face. He looked sharply at his daughter.

'You sound as though it's serious this time.'

'It is. He's coming to see you today.'

Her father looked troubled. Evalyn saw how he picked up his fountain pen and put it down again. She saw a heading across the sheet of paper on which he had been taking notes, deciphered it upside down. It said 'The Vinson Walsh Memorial Fund'.

Oh, Papa, she thought, I have come at a bad moment.

But her father seemed completely focused on the subject in hand. He said almost sternly, 'And what do you want me to say, Evalyn, because what I will say depends on you. Do you mean to have him or not? I know the boy has his faults, but there must be something right about him or you would have forgotten him long ago! You could have anyone, you know.'

Evalyn took a deep breath. 'I mean to have him, Father. He has promised to make good and I think he will! He's not drinking any more, and he's even taken a job with the *Post*.' She drew a deep breath, 'And, Father,' she added, 'I have to face the facts. I *cannot* have anyone. I'm lame.'

Her father's face crumpled. He looked down at his desk.

'I'm not sad about it any more,' Evalyn went on gently. 'But I do have to face it. And I know Ned so well and for so long. And he knows I'm hurt and he doesn't mind . . .'

When her father glanced at her again his eyes glistened with tears.

'How the years fly!' he whispered. 'One minute my baby is a toddler, the next considering marriage. I must be getting very old!'

Evalyn went round to his side of the desk and dropped a kiss on the top of his head where the grey hair was thinning. 'You're as young as ever, Father,' she whispered, adding on a welling of compassion for this mellowed, saddened, iron-willed patriarch, 'And I so love you!'

Ned arrived at the front door at a quarter to two. Evalyn saw at once how nervous he was, but she did not spare him.

'You've done it now!' she informed him cheerfully as she walked beside him down the hall to the elevator. 'Your goose is cooked and there's no turning back. I told Father and he is expecting you!'

Ned groaned. 'I'd rather do anything than face the lion in his den and demand his daughter! I'd cross Niagara first . . . but I'll do it for you, Evalyn. If it's not a proof of my feelings for you, I don't know what is!'

When the elevator door shut, Evalyn stood on tiptoe to kiss him. 'Good luck! He won't shoot you!'

Ned straightened his tie, took a deep breath and knocked at the door of the study where Tom was waiting for him. Evalyn hung around outside, straining to make sense of the murmured voices within and pretending when the housemaids passed that she was merely examining the contents of a glass case filled with mineral samples from Colorado, including the great gold nugget souvenir from Camp Bird.

She saw the butler cross the hall below and take the elevator to the study in response to her father's ring; then she watched him go to her parents' sitting room and return behind her white-faced mother who glanced at Evalyn and whispered, 'Wait upstairs, darling. We'll come to your sitting room.'

Her mother had been pale and taciturn since Evalyn had broken the news to her at breakfast, but she had uttered not one syllable to indicate her state of mind.

About fifteen minutes later her mother came to find her.

'Well, Mother?'

'Your father and Ned are talking . . . on good terms,' Carrie said. She smiled at her daughter a little wanly. 'Oh, Evalyn, are you really sure this is what you want?'

'I am, Mother. We will be able to do so much together, Ned and I. He's really a very good sort. And he's changed and grown up so much. He's becoming a reporter for the *Post* . . . and he's not drinking any more . . . and we're such friends.'

Carrie nodded without much conviction.

Ned seemed elated when Evalyn saw him ten minutes later. He followed her father into the sitting room and gave her a covert thumbs-up sign.

'Well, it's all fixed,' Tom said. 'The boy has undertaken to make you happy.' He grinned. 'He knows he'll have to answer to me if he doesn't! So we'll announce your engagement and you can name the day!'

Evalyn embraced her father and mother.

Then Ned took his fiancée's hands and smiled into her eyes. 'I can't wait to tell my parents. They always hoped it would be you, Evalyn, you know!'

He turned to Tom and Carrie. 'Mummie always had a soft spot for Evalyn since the old dancing days in One Street when she told her I had broken her foot!'

Carrie glanced at her daughter with an uncertain smile. 'Broken your foot, Evalyn? What nonsense was that?'

'Just a dodge, Mother! You may remember how insistent you were that I went to the classes and how I had other ideas.'

Ned kissed Carrie's hand with a flamboyant gesture. 'If I have you to thank, ma'am, for making her go to One Street, I am greatly in your debt.'

Carrie's smile died. But she joined with Tom in congratulating the two young people, and then they left them alone.

When the door was closed Ned took a small morocco box from his pocket, opened it, took from it a magnificent diamond ring and slipped it on Evalyn's ring finger.

'It's lovely, Ned . . . my second diamond!' she added mischievously.

Ned was taken aback. He glowered. 'Who gave you the first?'

'My father, silly.'

Ned grabbed her and held her down on the sofa for a long, wild kiss.

That evening, the Walshes were invited to Friendship and in the great drawing room there a toast was offered by both sets of parents to the two young people.

'To Evalyn and Ned. God bless them both and give them every happiness!'

'Amen!' John R. added.

The glasses were raised and the champagne drunk. Then the talk was all about the young couple's future – where they might like to live; when they would be married. Carrie favoured Washington as the obvious place; Evalyn suggested Ouray, but this met with little enthusiasm.

'You couldn't expect guests to travel that distance, darling.'

Evalyn and Ned looked at each other and after a few moments left their elders and slipped away into the garden. They walked to their old childhood haunts, to the stables, to Ned's playhouse, and he reminisced about the first day he had brought the twelve-year-old to see it.

'I knew you were a good sport then!' he said.

'I'm not a "sport". I'm your fiancée!'

Ned embraced her hungrily, turned her face up and sought her lips. His hand strayed to her breast, caressing it.

'I can't wait for us to be married!' he said in her ear.

Evalyn felt the sensuality of his touch, and closed her eyes. It seemed to her in that moment that life had regained some of its bearings. Not only was the world before her again, but also the mysterious kingdom of the senses, the domain of love. The pressure of Ned's hand moved towards her nipple. She started as he squeezed it.

He kissed her again, fervently, and whispered, 'So the Holy Ghost does not, after all, reside in the bottom of a bourbon bottle!'

Evalyn pulled away from him. Her cheeks were flushed, but she laughed shakily as she regarded Ned's eager face. She knew that he had drunk nothing but water for days now, that his ardour was real and owed nothing to the contents of a liquor bottle.

She pushed back a tendril of hair, looked at him shyly and asked, 'Are you coming with us to Colorado for the summer?'

'Just try to stop me!'

Tom had been appointed a Colorado delegate to the Republican Convention in Chicago. He was supporting the candidacy of William Howard Taft for the Presidency, and Chicago was the first port of call on their journey to the West. There were endless parties to attend there, but Ned and Evalyn still found time to themselves. Ned had not gone back to drinking, and Evalyn was pleased and proud of him.

They went on to Wolhurst. Evalyn loved this place and knew her father did too. As the car turned into the gateway Evalyn saw the notice he had had affixed to the gatepost:

> Don't shoot the birds on these premises.
> Thomas F. Walsh, Wolhurst Estate

So like Father! she thought with a lump in her throat.

The caretaker, Mr Cousins, had prepared the house for their arrival as usual, and was there to greet them.

On 4 July 1908, Evalyn and Ned's engagement was announced in the *Denver Republican*, and Ned, to his delight, was referred to as a '*Washington Post* editor'.

'Seems I've been promoted,' he quipped, waving the paper at Evalyn.

'It's the least I'd expect,' she replied. 'I need a real newspaperman for my husband!'

To mark his arrival in the West, Ned dressed himself up in a cowboy suit, with high-heeled boots, chaps, a brass-studded belt, a holster and forty-four, and a blood-red bandanna.

'You look like Billy the Kid,' Evalyn said, and ran to find her camera.

The champagne corks popped and the firecrackers sparkled that evening, but the young pair drank only water and orange juice; they were happy, holding hands, whispering together in the warm night, longing to be alone.

'This wedding will be the biggest society event of the year!' Ned's mother wrote from Maine. 'Why not have it here at Bar Harbor? Wouldn't that be a good idea?'

Evalyn read the letter aloud but when she turned to Ned for his opinion she found him taciturn and almost irritable.

'Oh Lord, Evalyn – do we really have to go through all that society wedding stuff? It's more than I can bear!'

Evalyn was dismayed. She *wanted* a large wedding, was excited at the prospect of being the star of her own big day, the centrepiece of an event that would be reported in every newspaper in the country, and in most of the European papers too.

'You're the nicest exhibitionist I know!' Alice Roosevelt had once said to her. This had only shocked her for a moment. It was true, and her wedding was going to prove it.

Now she looked at Ned ruefully.

'Oh, Ned, please let us have a decent wedding. I'm so looking forward to it, and Mother is busy planning, and my wedding gown is being designed

– lashings of lace and a train a mile long. It will be wonderful, the best day of our lives . . . and we'll have masses of flowers and organ music and all our friends . . .'

'A thousand bores,' Ned muttered, 'boring us to death!'

Every morning there was a stack of congratulatory mail for the newly affianced pair, including a note from Paul and Amelia Lafferty to wish them every happiness. Evalyn put it on display with all the others. She imagined Paul at her wedding, sitting there with his wife, while she and Ned took their vows . . . or maybe he wouldn't even come!

A sick sense of things being out of joint tugged at her for a moment and she shrugged it away. But she reverted to happiness at the sight of the drawing room at Wolhurst, where the mantelpiece and every table in that baronial space was festooned with expressions of goodwill.

The more messages arrived, however, the quieter Ned became.

On 22 July, Ned and Evalyn set off for a drive, with her mother's secretary, Maggie Buggy, as chaperone, and Platt, who had replaced Emile as chauffeur. As they approached Denver, Ned turned to Evalyn abruptly and said: 'Let's get married!'

'You've already asked me!' Evalyn replied, looking at him with a laugh. 'Have you forgotten?'

'You know what I'm talking about. Let's do it *now*!'

'Now this minute?'

'Why not? Be a sport! If you love me, save me from a society wedding, from all those gushing guests. Marry me right now this minute, Evalyn Walsh!'

Evalyn's initial response was to laugh. But she quickly realised that Ned was perfectly serious and that the idea had a certain charm in its suddenness and daring.

Maggie looked aghast. 'What would your mother say?' she demanded. 'Evalyn, you can't possibly be considering this.'

'Why can't I?'

Even Platt, usually phlegmatic, registered shock. His jaw dropped when Ned suddenly ordered him as they passed a store: 'Pull over here. I'm going to find a telephone and arrange a licence!'

Ned turned to look at Evalyn with his eyebrows raised, as much as if to say, 'Well, are you on for it or not?'

She laughed, thrilled by his audacity.

'You take the biscuit, Ned McLean! But, all right!' she added, when she saw how bright and happy his eyes were. 'Let's do it if you're so mad keen on it! I'm even halfway dressed for the occasion!'

She was wearing a white broadcloth dress and a hat with white ostrich plumes. 'And,' she added, getting out of the car and opening her arms as though she would fly, 'the wonderful thing is that I will be married right here in my own wonderful Colorado!'

Maggie looked at the chauffeur, who grinned and shrugged.

A few hours later Evalyn and Ned were married in St Mark's Episcopal Church. The bride clutched the posy of violets her groom had bought for her. She looked very young and grave; she was filled with love and determination. She would make this marriage work, she told herself. If she had done nothing else right in her life she would make a success of this. She was marrying a man who didn't give two hoots whether or not she was an heiress, and this made her the luckiest girl alive. She was marrying him here, at home, in her magnificent Colorado, within sight of her beloved mountains that had once opened their riches to her father.

When the ceremony was over the few close friends who had arrived in response to Ned's invitation, hugged and kissed them both. Then they all went back to Wolhurst.

Carrie heard the laughter and saw the car returning along the dappled driveway. She had to sit down with relief. She had waited luncheon for Evalyn and Ned's return, but it was already past two o'clock and there was no sign of them and no word either. It had been difficult to hide her agitation from her house guests.

Since Vin's death she had fallen prey to a host of fears. She was grateful for the succour she found in Christian Science, for the solace of prayer. But her fervour had not removed her secret dread that a motor accident would take her daughter from her too. Today Tom was away in Kansas City and she had been wrestling with strange premonitions since early morning. When Evalyn and Ned had not returned for lunch, these premonitions became first apprehension and then terror.

The car came to a standstill. The engine noise died and Platt, looking suspiciously deadpan, jumped down. Ned was already out of the vehicle and handing Evalyn out; their faces were full of coy conspiracy. Carrie looked at Maggie Buggy and registered immediately that her secretary was regarding her uncertainly as though she would spare her whatever news they had to impart. She saw now how flushed and excited her daughter was, and steeled herself.

'What happened?' she asked. 'Did you have an accident?'

'Of a sort, Mother,' Evalyn said breathlessly. 'Ned and I got married!'

Carrie gasped. For a moment she thought Evalyn was joking and then she saw the shining gold band on the hand her child held out to her. For a moment shock displaced every emotion except a desire to weep. All the plans, all the excitement, gone in an instant! And not even to have *attended* her only daughter's wedding! What would Tom say, she wondered. Would he be hurt, furious? But how could their child have been so thoughtless?

362

Evalyn, watching her mother's face, looked suddenly stricken, as though it had only now occurred to her that she should have thought a bit longer before rushing headlong into Ned's scheme; that there were other people with a personal stake in the biggest venture of her life.

'I'm sorry . . .' she said lamely, and the light died in her eyes. 'I didn't think . . . Oh, please don't be upset, Mother. We're happy. It was just that Ned couldn't bear the thought of a big wedding . . . We're going to Colorado Springs tonight to begin our honeymoon. We've sent a wire to Bar Harbor to tell Ned's parents.'

Carrie remembered her earlier state of anxiety in case something terrible had happened to her remaining offspring. At least nothing of that sort had occurred, and the young couple did look radiant, so the best must be made of it. She forced herself to smile and she embraced the newly wedded pair with tears in her eyes.

'Congratulations to you both!' she cried. 'I hope you will be as happy as Tom and I have been.' She dabbed at her eyes, rang the bell. 'Now, we must have a wedding luncheon!'

Evalyn went in search of Annie and broke the news to her, but to her consternation the little housekeeper burst into tears.

'Och, why couldn't you have waited like a Christian? And your father away, and all the preparations that are being made . . .'

'This is my wedding day,' Evalyn said sadly after a moment, 'and everyone is in tears!'

'What did you expect?' Annie replied, wiping her eyes before convulsively embracing the new bride. 'But the deed is done, wee lassie, so long life and happiness to the pair of ye!'

Soon friends and house guests were toasting the newlyweds and eating a gourmet lunch. Ned and Evalyn drank water and looked at each other with full eyes. After lunch Platt drove them to the station to catch the train to Colorado Springs.

It was late when they got to the Antlers Hotel where their suite had been reserved. The restaurant was closed, but they strolled arm in arm to an all-night diner where they had a wedding supper of lamb chops and ginger ale.

'Well, Mrs McLean!' Ned said, as he raised his glass to her. 'Here's to you and to us and the future!'

Evalyn clinked her glass against his.

'Here's to life,' she whispered shyly.

And Ned, glass raised, hungry eyes on his bride, echoed softly, 'Oh yes, my darling, to life.'

When they returned to their hotel Evalyn went into the bathroom, and quietly locked the door. She undressed, bathed and regarded herself critically in the mirror. The hated scar was long and white, a thin ribbon on her thigh to show where it had been split open. Thinking of Ned touching her, seeing her body, her mouth was suddenly dry.

She reached for one of the modest lawn nightdresses with the long sleeves and the pintucks that Annie had packed for her. When she came into the bedroom Ned was already under the covers. She crossed the room self-consciously and got in beside him. He cradled her for a moment and then leaned over and put out the light.

The warm darkness gave her the scent of his body, of his breath, the dull thud of his heart. She felt the hands that gently pulled up her nightdress, that found and lingered gently on her scar, kissing it, before moving over her whole body with a kind of homage. How did he know to do these things, she wondered, gasping at the intimacy and the surges of pleasure, but after a while she allowed herself to be borne away on a tide the existence of which she had hardly dreamed. When she cried out Ned covered her face with kisses.

'It's all right, my darling,' he whispered. 'It's all right. Sleep well now . . .'

Chapter Twenty-Nine

Tom did not by word or gesture betray his shock that he would never walk up the aisle with his daughter. That she should have given herself away was so like Evalyn that he would have smiled, were it not for the acute sense of disappointment that he had not been at her side on the biggest occasion of her life. The sense of isolation that had plagued him since Vinson's death – such as he had never known even in the most remote reaches of the Rockies – returned to pull at his soul. He knew that wealth had taken away far more than it had given: his son, his peace, his hopes for the future. It had also turned an always wayward Evalyn into a capricious young woman. He acknowledged his own part in this; he had wanted, he still wanted, to give her everything. The overwhelming pride he felt in being able to do so had, he admitted privately on occasion, stifled his better judgement. What, he wondered, would the discipline of life in Colorado have done for her had he never found Camp Bird? Would she have been tired at thirty, old at forty? Or would her natural qualities have made her into a woman of character and prudence?

He would have liked to have talked to Carrie about this, if only for reassurance. But Carrie was so taken up with her charitable pursuits these days, and her religious devotions, that she had no time for him. And you could not ask for it, the time of those you loved.

The McLeans came to Wolhurst as soon as they were apprised of the marriage. When the newlyweds returned from Colorado Springs, they set off with both sets of parents for a few weeks together at the McLeans' summer residence at Bar Harbor. But Evalyn and Ned were longing to be alone and to embark together on some kind of adventure that would mark the beginning of their married life.

'We need a *proper* honeymoon!' Ned said. 'This holidaying with the parents is all very well, but we're man and wife now!'

'Woman and husband, you mean,' Evalyn said with a sudden giggle. 'You've got a little problem with your priorities!'

They were in their bedroom in the McLean summer residence at Bar

Harbor. Ned laughed and tumbled Evalyn on to the bed.

'I do love you, Evalyn. You're fun! I'm so glad you had me.'

'For a whole month I've done very little but *have* you!'

Ned grinned. 'Where would you like to go on a real honeymoon?'

'Completely on our own?'

'Well, except for a chauffeur who can double as my valet; and you'll need a maid. Heaven forbid that we should have to look after ourselves!'

'*I've* looked after myself and Vinson too . . . long ago . . . when we had nothing.'

Ned kissed away the frown, and the tears that sprang to her eyes as she mentioned her dead brother's name.

'But ever since Father found the gold,' she whispered, 'I've been so spoiled. I must be the most indulged daughter on the face of the planet.'

'Nonsense. You've had more than your share of troubles for someone who is just twenty-two.' He rubbed the palm of his hand gently along her injured leg, and bent to kiss it. 'I'm the one who's spoiled!'

'Oh, I know that!' Evalyn whispered, although she was touched to the quick by his gesture and his avowal. 'I've always known that! When did your parents ever deny you anything? At least Mother always stood up to *me*!'

'So where will this spoiled boy take you?' Ned asked after a moment with feigned truculence. 'Europe, Egypt, Turkey, Timbuktu?'

Evalyn sat up straight and turned to him.

'I've been to Europe, but I'd simply love to go to Egypt . . . and Turkey,' she laughed excitedly. 'We could go to Europe first, and then motor on to the other places!'

'Let's take our time,' Ned said. 'Six months or something. Let's make it a grand tour!'

Their parents seemed to understand. 'You'll need some money,' Tom said to his daughter, reaching into his desk. 'I don't want you running short.'

Even Evalyn, inured to wealth for so many years, gasped when she read the draft and saw the size of the gift.

'A hundred thousand dollars is a great deal of money, Father!'

'Is it?' He looked at her quizzically. 'Well, I haven't given you a wedding present yet. I want you to be able to buy something that takes your fancy!'

That night Ned showed her another draft.

'Father wasn't going to be outdone by Tom Walsh!' he said with a laugh. 'He had to see him dollar for dollar! But he made it clear it was intended to set us up!'

'How much is it for?'

'A hundred thousand, of course!'

'Let's be very thrifty,' Evalyn said, 'and show them we *can* be sensible!'

'If I thought you were serious, Evalyn, I'd sue for divorce.'

It was a joke. But Evalyn glanced at him, and saw with unease the sudden restlessness at the corners of his mouth.

'I'm not famous for being sensible,' she said. 'You above all people should know that!'

'I do know, darling,' Ned said with a laugh. He pounced on her, kissing her wildly. 'What on earth could a man do with a woman who had sense?'

On the day of their departure their Packard, a yellow roadster with red striping, was hoisted carefully into the ship's hold. Evalyn and Ned stood on the quayside and watched for a moment. Maggie Buggy, who was to attend Evalyn on the journey, was already on the ship, and Platt was seeing their luggage safely stowed.

Ned and Evalyn embraced their parents, walked up the gangway, stopping every few paces to wave back. They found their state room. It was mahogany-panelled, its ceilings adorned with frescos, and it was filled with flowers and messages wishing them bon voyage.

As the ship moved through Long Island Sound Evalyn looked back at the Statue of Liberty and it suddenly seemed to her that life was like the tide, ebbing and flowing, and each high watermark brought new flotsam and jetsam and each ebb took something away.

I'm *married*! she thought, glancing at Ned. I am to stay with this man for the rest of my life . . .

A reluctant insecurity intruded: will we be different when we come back from Europe? Will travelling together change us? Will Ned be tired of me and I of him? For an instant she experienced a sense of suffocation.

Maybe it wouldn't have been any different with Paul! I don't care! I am going to enjoy my life; that is what it is there for. And, above all, I am going to enjoy my honeymoon.

Platt said to her a few days later: 'I wonder will you be comfortable in the Packard, madam – having to share it with me and Maggie? We will be motoring great distances and there's the luggage to carry as well. The rumble will be full to overflowing!'

They were standing on deck. Evalyn, grasping the rail and watching the watery horizon that went on day after day, longed to get out and push this great iron leviathan that seemed to move so slowly. The salty wind was chill, but she was wrapped in a cashmere coat and scarf, and a hat with a muslin veil protected her face. Platt was wearing his fur-lined coat. His voice was careful.

'What are you trying to tell me, Platt? That the car is not big enough? That we need another one?'

'The Packard would be all right for *two* people, madam, and the luggage overflow could be easily accommodated in the back seat . . .'

Evalyn laughed. 'What you're really suggesting is that we should get another car and travel in convoy?'

'I think you would definitely find that more comfortable, madam. Mr McLean could drive one car and I could drive the other!'

Over dinner Evalyn said to her husband, 'I was talking to Platt earlier today. He seems to think that, with the luggage, the Packard will be quite a squeeze for four people.

'If we get a bigger car what will we do with the Packard? Leave it on the quayside?'

'No. Why not have two cars? I'd love another Mercedes! I was so mad about the one I had . . . until . . .' Her eyes clouded.

'Buy another car? Oh, Evalyn,' Ned laughed, shaking his head, 'you're worse than I am!'

'But it makes a certain amount of sense. With two cars you can never be stranded; there will always be one to fall back on! Remember, we will be motoring over very long distances.' She dropped her voice and her eyes were haunted as she whispered: 'And if there were ever an accident, the other car would be there to help.'

Ned went to see the ship's radio officer and the order was sent off to Paris, with instructions to have the Mercedes delivered to Amsterdam where they were due to disembark in a couple of days. 'But tell them not a red one!' Ned instructed. 'Yellow! Make sure it's yellow!'

An enormous two-seater Mercedes was waiting for them on the quay in Amsterdam. Evalyn had not anticipated its size: she looked at its great hooded engine, its huge headlamps, and thought she had never seen a car so big, bigger even that the red one that had taken Vinson's life. It was a shining, bright yellow.

'You'll never be able to drive it!' she told Ned when they had taken possession of the keys. 'It's more like a locomotive than a car.'

'Won't I?'

Ned saw Evalyn comfortably installed, tucked a rug around her, and got into the driver's seat. Platt handed him a pair of goggles, then cranked the engine; it fired almost immediately with a staccato, throaty purr and a cloud of exhaust.

'Hold on to your hat, Evalyn. Next stop Berlin!' Ned cried above the noise of the engine as he engaged gear. Evalyn found herself flung backwards as the powerful car lurched forward. She looked behind and saw Platt preparing to follow them, an anxious-looking Maggie beside him.

'Go slowly,' she said, 'wait for Platt.'

'He won't get lost,' Ned snapped. 'The man has a map.'

The days passed. Cities came and went – Dresden, Leipzig, Cologne. In each one the newlyweds went on a shopping spree. Ned bought his bride a gold travelling case as a wedding gift, an exact copy of one owned by the Crown Princess of Germany. Evalyn bought a chinchilla fur coat. In Leipzig they decided that the Packard didn't look good alongside the Mercedes, so they bought another Mercedes, and disposed of the Packard.

Evalyn closed her ears to the occasional internal prompting of wild extravagance. I'm on honeymoon; if I can't have a good time on honeymoon, when can I have a good time? What did Papa give me all that money for if it wasn't to enjoy myself?

They visited Vienna, and then went on to Constantinople. This, for Evalyn, was the most exciting part of her journey so far, arriving at the Golden Horn and seeing the minarets and domes of the Ottoman Empire's capital. But there was a tense atmosphere here; a group of rebellious dissidents who called themselves the Young Turks were trying to unseat the Sultan.

'I would like to meet the Sultan!' Evalyn announced to the American Ambassador, John Leishmann, a friend of her father's for many years. 'Do you think there is any chance that I might?'

He laughed. 'You're as direct as your father.'

'I would also love to see the inside of his harem.'

The ambassador laughed louder, and asked her whimsically if she wasn't afraid the old boy might keep her there.

'Oh no. If he tried he'd soon be paying Ned to take me back!'

'That's true,' Ned said. 'The Young Turks could all go home. Evalyn doesn't put up with too many restrictions. She would do the job for them!'

A few days later, Evalyn and Ned had coffee in the Royal Palace. Her host was a stooping, ugly old man, with a hennaed beard, wearing a fez that sported a huge emerald. This man was Abd-ul-Hamid, sultan of an empire that in its heyday had stretched from Persia to the gates of Vienna. The coffee came in small cups ornamented with diamonds, and the sultan was surrounded by armed bodyguards in silken robes. Evalyn stared at the her exotic surroundings until she thought her eyes would pop out. Later, she was ushered to the royal harem by a eunuch, while Ned, looking extremely uneasy, was forced to wait for her.

Here, in a whole section of the palace removed from the eyes of every male except the eunuchs and the sultan himself, a collection of fat women sat around on divans. Some of them were old, some young; all looked bored and unhappy. In this sad and dispiriting place Evalyn drank more thick, dark coffee, and allowed the ladies to examine her clothes and question her eagerly through an interpreter. One of the women was wearing a big blue gem set in gold around her neck. It is a sapphire? Evalyn wondered. I've never seen one that size. Or that extraordinary colour.

Looking back on it years later Evalyn would find it remarkable that not one single *frisson* of premonition had touched her when she saw that stone.

'It's not right,' she told Ned that evening. 'The harem is nothing but a luxurious prison! Poor things – their souls are being crushed to facilitate that fat creature and his self-indugent system. They definitely need a revolution here, but it's the women who should do the revolting!'

'My, my,' Ned said with a chuckle. 'I can see I'd better get you out of Turkey before you get us arrested!'

'Where are we going next?'

'Egypt! Are you game?'

It was all thrilling and exhausting, this extraordinary honeymoon. They donned the loose garb of the desert and saw the pyramids from the backs of camels, attended by a retinue of similarly mounted servants. Then they went on to Jordan, rode in convoy in two victorias, each drawn by four horses, with an armed escort of nine Arab horsemen, whom they paid lavishly. They met desert tribesmen, who treated them with curiosity and eyed Evalyn as though she were a piece of exotica that had dropped from the sky. They went swimming in the Jordan to the delight of the male Arab audience, many of whom had hardly ever seen a woman's face, much less a female body in a bathing suit. But Evalyn, who couldn't swim, was gripped by the current and nearly drowned. Ned had to pull her out of the river by her hair to cries of encouragement and delighted clapping from the on-lookers.

When Evalyn was finally safe and Maggie had wrapped her in thick towels, Ned produced a bottle of whiskey, and Evalyn only then realised that he had a case of it in the rumble all the time. She wanted to cry.

'Oh, Ned, please don't tell me you're drinking again.'

'Of course I'm not. I only brought some along for medicinal purposes.' He poured her a measure. 'Here, drink up. You need it. *I* need it!' And to Evalyn consternation he immediately swallowed a measure of the spirit.

The Arabs were aghast. Their religion proscribed alcohol; their censure was heavy in the air. The atmosphere subtly changed. Evalyn refused the whiskey; she felt miserable, cold to her bones, cold in her soul. It struck her suddenly that as long as one excitement, one distraction, followed another, she was happy. When the distractions stopped, or when they soured, she was left to confront herself. And the self she encountered was lonely and half desperate. Marriage had changed nothing; at heart she was just the same little girl from the Rockies afraid of dissolution.

Vin knew who I was and he died, she thought. Paul knew who I was and he married someone else. Ned does not really know who anyone is. How did I get myself married to him? What can I do now?

'I want to go home!' she whispered miserably to Maggie, glancing around her nervously.

Ned overheard. He sighed loudly, and swallowed another tot.

'The next ship is leaving Jaffa tomorrow. We'll never make it!'

'Yes we will, if we hire a special train!' She looked around at the growing crowd of on-lookers, all men. They seemed to be getting closer, circling the travellers with a curiosity that seemed menacing, commenting among themselves and eyeing Evalyn with a bright-eyed prurience. 'I have to get out of here! Please, Ned!'

Sensing matrimonial disharmony, the audience came closer still, grinning and offering suggestions in Arabic until Ned seemed to swell on the tide of male solidarity.

'Oh, all right,' he said eventually, raising his eyes to heaven in a theatrical gesture of a man patient under provocation. Evalyn realised that he was playing to the gallery and that, in that moment, she was less important to him than the crowd of male strangers. It was an unpleasant feeling of alienation and betrayal, reminding her briefly of Vin's defection to Jack Hartland all those years ago.

Why do they bother with us at all, she thought angrily, if all they really want to do is congratulate each other? But Vin was only a boy, she reminded herself, a boy who never lived to be a man.

They hired their own train and set off on the long journey to Paris, the two automobiles carried behind their carriage in eight wagons. When they arrived in France they were broke, but they put up at the Bristol Hotel in the Place Vendôme, and Evalyn promptly wired home for more money. Her leg was aching; she had neuralgia and wondered if she could possibly have inherited a tendency to it. Maggie was exhausted and Evalyn let her rest. Ned slept like the dead.

Tom sent her a fresh credit immediately. John R.'s wire, on the other hand, indicated only horror at his son's extravagance and told him to come home at once.

'No fear!' Ned said. 'Not until he cools down!'

After a couple of days' rest Evalyn felt her energy return. The city was beckoning and she asked Ned to drive her around Paris.

'Platt will drive you.'

'But I don't want Platt to drive me,' she said coyly. 'I want you to do it. I like being driven by my husband!'

She wrapped up well in the new chinchilla coat and hat, and Ned chauffered her through the city she remembered so well, with its elegant buildings and lovely balconies. They drove alongside the Seine, by Notre-Dame, the Place de la Concorde, the Champs-Elysées. She was nostalgic for a time when she had come here as a schoolgirl, when Camp Bird had still been the private preserve of her father, when Vinson had been alive, and the world was opening to the newly wealthy Walshes. And for the time she had spent here with Flora, her only period of semi-autonomy.

Gazing up at the Eiffel Tower Evalyn was reminded of seeing it once from a Ferris wheel, and then, like the ringing of a far-off bell, she heard again Mademoiselle Raye's voice: *'Things come at a price, petite. That seems to be the rule of life.'*

Although she was cocooned in rugs, she shivered. A twinge of pain began at her thigh and travelled to her ankle.

Oh, Vinson . . . Vinson! She tried to slough off the depression that had dogged her since the near-drowning incident in the Jordan. She glanced at Ned. She had been on honeymoon with him now for months on end, close quarters every day. They were friends, but he seemed incapable of giving her the passion for which she hungered; he seemed incapable of accessing her real self. Sometimes there was silence between them, one she felt would have gone on indefinitely if she did not rush to fill it with some outrageous comment, with anything that would make him laugh.

Half the time I am behaving like a child, just to amuse him, she thought.

She began to feel like a genie, visible only through her own conjuring tricks, but otherwise nonexistent. Is it because Ned and I are too alike? she wondered. Or too much in each other's company? Is that it? Why can't he see me? I would let my real self out of the bottle if he could see who I really am. He could give me peace. And I know it exists, she added a little sadly, remembering a brief, far-off, rapture.

She turned to him, but saw at once that his thoughts were far away.

'I haven't bought my wedding present yet!' she announced, searching for something to enliven the moment. 'Father said I was to get something I liked.'

'But you've already spent the money!' Ned said crossly. 'And I've spent my money! And now we're poor as sparrows!'

'We're not.'

'I don't know what you would do if you had to live on an ordinary income!'

'You should talk, Ned McLean!' she said crossly. 'You're every bit as bad as I am. Anyway, what's money for if we can't spend it?'

Ned sighed. 'So what do you want to buy?'

'I don't know. Let's go to Cartier!'

They were driving along the Quai d'Orsay. Evalyn gave directions to number 13 rue de la Paix, an address she recalled very well.

She was remembered in Cartier and greeted effusively.

'Madame, congratulations on your marriage. We read about it . . .'

'This is my husband, Mr McLean.'

Ned extended his hand.

'Enchanté, monsieur!'

They were conducted to a private room. 'What can we do for you today, madame?'

Evalyn began to explain a little breathlessly, 'Well, we're going home soon, and we haven't got much ready cash, but Papa said I was to buy myself a wedding present.'

'Of course, madame. What would you like?'

'I don't know. Maybe a necklace . . .'

Ned caught the jeweller's eye.

'Don't be tempting her with anything extravagant,' he said. 'We've just returned from Constantinople, where her eyes were out on stalks. I had to prise her out of the seraglio.'

Evalyn ignored Ned's attempt to draw Monsieur Cartier into a man-to-man exchange.

'I was allowed to visit the sultan's harem,' she told the latter, 'but I can assure you I needed no inducement to leave. Even though they were wearing some fabulous gems – one of them had a particularly marvellous sapphire – the ladies looked sad and fat and down on their luck.'

'But unlucky things are lucky for Evalyn,' Ned persisted. 'Isn't that right?' he demanded, turning to his wife. 'You get out of scrapes that would finish other mortals.'

Evalyn could not help tacit assent. It suited her self-image.

Cartier invited Evalyn and Ned to sit by the window where the winter light was at its best and in a few minutes he had put before Evalyn a necklace the like of which even she had never seen. Nestling against black velvet was a row of diamonds set in platinum, supporting a huge pearl, from which hung a great emerald. Below the emerald hung an enormous diamond that flashed fire to the bright winter sunlight. Evalyn gasped. The splendour of the thing took her breath away. She had often wondered why she liked jewels so much. After all, they were only stones prised from the earth; when cut and polished why did they have the power to so enthral her? Now, looking at this wonderful necklace, she felt she knew: it was not only that jewels captured the essence of colour and the secret of light, but that they were ultimately dependable; they would outlast everything.

'The diamond is called the Star of the East, madame. It is a great jewel, one of the world's finest! It weighs 92½ carats . . . The emerald is 34½ carats . . .'

'May I try it on?'

'Mais certainement.'

Evalyn's fingers trembled as she put it around her neck.

'The pearl is very fine too, madame – 32½ grains . . .'

Evalyn saw herself in the mirror, saw the pulse beating in her throat above the Star of the East. The jewels shimmered, sparking fire.

373

I am mortal, Evalyn thought, but this magnificence is not. Unlike love, she realised a little bitterly, it will endure for ever.

She turned to Ned. 'I must have it. I can't walk away from it.'

Ned said caustically: 'Why don't you ask the price? It might help to cool your ardour!'

She looked at Monsieur Cartier.

'Six hundred thousand francs, madame,' he said calmly, as though discussing the price of a hat.

'That's only one hundred and twenty thousand dollars, Evalyn!' Ned said conversationally. 'But don't let that put you off!'

There was silence. Evalyn paled and hesitated. She thought of her father and all the money he had already given them. But as she looked at the necklace her determination increased. After all, jewels like this were really an investment. They would hold their value no matter what. And, as it was 15 December it would double as both a wedding and a Christmas present.

'It'll be my Christmas present as well,' she said to Ned *sotto voce*. 'With a name like that it's almost an omen.'

'What are you talking about, Evalyn?'

'The Star of the East. It guided the Three Wise Men to Bethlehem!'

Ned suppressed a groan. He raised his hands. 'The Star *in* the East, you mean, Evalyn! Where this one should be too, and not here as a source of temptation!'

Evalyn ignored him. She turned back to Cartier.

'All right,' she whispered. 'I'll take it . . . But at the moment I haven't got any money.'

'Oh, that's perfectly all right, madame,' Pierre Cartier said smoothly. 'If you and Mr McLean will sign a receipt, that will do very well. You can buy it on the instalment plan, you know.'

Ned and Evalyn signed and the assistant blotted the paper.

'You have made a great investment,' the famous jeweller told them as the necklace was boxed and wrapped and handed over. 'If you are interested in further remarkable acquisitions I might make . . .'

'Not for a while, anyway,' Evalyn said a little nervously.

Pierre Cartier bowed and the two young people escaped into the darkening streets of Paris, carrying with them, in a box lined with velvet, a stupendous necklace bearing the fabled diamond known as the Star of the East.

'You shouldn't have bought that thing!' Ned said at dinner when she wore it around her neck. 'It's staring at me like an accusation! We're in no position to pay the customs duty on it when we get home.'

'I'll just smuggle it in!' Evalyn said. 'It'll be easy.'

'If you do that you'll never be able to wear it in public again, at least not in the States!'

'If you loved me at all,' Evalyn said sadly, 'you wouldn't talk like that. *You* always do precisely what you want.'

They spent Christmas in Paris, a lonely Christmas for Evalyn, despite cabled messages of love and goodwill from home. But, to her relief, Ned hardly drank over the festive week, and seemed intent on practising urbanity on all his parents' friends whom they called on in Paris. When they set sail early in the New Year, Evalyn found that their cabin had been lined, both walls and ceiling, with orchids.

She gasped with delight and her heart lifted. The depression of the last few weeks seemed unworthy of her. Ned really *did* care after all.

'Oh, thank you, darling!' she said, and embraced him. 'They're absolutely wonderful!'

'Don't ever think that I don't love you, Evalyn!' he said in teasing voice. 'This represents the last of my cash!'

She kissed him, but in a few minutes he was restless, saying he had to go on deck for a few minutes.

'Promise me you won't go to the bar!' she whispered.

'Hey, Evalyn, would you lock me up? I want to meet some people!'

'Well, promise me you won't drink!'

Ned promised with ill-suppressed irritation. But when he returned some hours later he was smelling of spirits. Evalyn, who had been waiting for him in her orchid-clad stateroom, longing for an interlude of love and intimacy, was unable for the disappointment and burst into tears.

'I stayed off the juice over Christmas specially to please you!' her husband said with a slurred voice. 'And I damn well won't be nagged and pestered by anyone, not even by my wife.'

Evalyn thought: he promised me, and he has broken his promise. I cannot trust him; I will never be able to trust him. He will always be mercurial. He said what I wanted to hear to get me, and now he feels invulnerable because he has me! He has acquired me, and I am stuck with him for ever!

But the next day Ned was looking for forgiveness.

'I mean to give it up, Evalyn, I really do. Dash it all, it's just that it's New Year and we're going home. Can't a man celebrate a little?'

He put his arms round her and kissed her, and Evalyn kissed him back. She felt ashamed. Maybe she *was* overreacting she told herself.

It was a rough crossing and Evalyn was glad to get back to Washington and the safety and familiarity of the great house at 2020 Massachusetts Avenue.

It was good to be embraced again by her loving parents, to have them ply her and Ned with questions about their travels, to hear their laughter, to detect not one single note of reproach for the amount of money she and Ned had spent.

They went for a celebratory dinner to the McLeans' 1 Street house, and as they were being served in the cavernous dining room where the walls were lined with Gobelin tapestries, Tom leaned over and asked his daughter, 'Did you buy yourself a little wedding present, Evalyn?'

'I did, Father. We signed a receipt for it. It's very wonderful, but it's a wedding and Christmas present combined!' she added hastily. 'I have it here. Close your eyes and I'll put it on.'

She had the necklace in her velvet evening purse and she stooped to take it out and put it on as her father obligingly closed his eyes and the rest of the table watched. When he opened them he whistled.

'The diamond is called the Star of the East,' Evalyn said, looking around the table for approval.

'Tell me, Evalyn,' her father demanded drily, 'did you pay the duty on that thing, or am I asking a silly question?'

'I smuggled it in!' Evalyn said.

Only then did she notice the looks of horror on the faces of her in-laws.

'This could ruin us!' John R. said. He looked around the table. 'Can't you just see the headlines in rival papers – "Newspaper tycoon's daughter-in-law smuggles gem!" '

'I'll go down and pay the duty in the morning,' Tom said soothingly. 'There'll be no problems. I'm glad to buy it for my Evalyn. I'll get my lawyer to explain that she is a little . . . excitable,' he tapped his head and directed a look at Evalyn that was half reproof and half apology, 'and that she forgot to declare it.'

Carrie and Mrs McLean were silent, the former frowning, the latter staring into her glass.

'Don't you like it?' Evalyn asked them diffidently, hurt by her father's inference, albeit jocose, that she was not in full possession of her faculties.

'To see a thing like that on the bosom of a child makes me feel quite ill!' her mother-in-law hissed in an uncharacteristic outburst. 'You should return it at once.'

'Oh, Evalyn,' Carrie said to her later when she got her daughter to herself, 'you won't find happiness in things outside yourself. Putting all of your substance into them will never make you content. You'll have to start looking within! Aren't you happy with Ned?'

Evalyn remembered how much her mother had been against this marriage and now lied. 'Of course I am.' To herself she added the horrible, reluctant truth – I don't know yet. Strangely enough, it's too soon to say.

Suddenly weary, she wanted to cry. Life did not behave as it was meant to behave, and happiness did not come when it was supposed to come and nothing was as it ought to be.

'I'm very tired, Mother. If you don't mind, I really need to turn in . . .'

She went to her room, sat before her mirror. The blazing diamond, the emerald, the great pearl, shone back at her above her lace-covered breast. She removed the necklace, stood up to ring for Esther to help her undress, picked up the swirling satin skirt of her gown, and went to her jewel case. Her eyes fell on the piece of quartz she had placed there, incongruous beside its beautiful cousins. She opened it, clasped her fingers over the rough stone and closed her eyes. She saw the carefree girl, her hair down her back, and the young man with the tender eyes, riding among the Ouray hills.

You can comment all you like, she told the quartz as she shut the box with a clap, but I won't send the necklace back. Why should I lose something I really like? Everyone else at the table tonight has what they want out of life!

Ned came to bed late. She woke when he caressed her, but he was quite drunk and quickly fell asleep.

Chapter Thirty

'I'm pregnant!'

Evalyn announced this with as much sang-froid as she could summon. But, inwardly, she was as excited as if no one in the history of mankind had ever before expected a baby. It was May 1909. The cherry trees were in bloom and Washington and the world seemed celebratory, as though rejoicing in her own personal miracle.

Ned's face was a picture of delighted astonishment, like a man who had found in his partner some strange power he had hardly dared to consider.

'My God, Evalyn. Are you *really* able to do that?' He embraced her and then held her tenderly at arm's length. 'I forgot . . . We have to be very, very mindful of you now!'

As his breath touched her face, the taint of last night's bourbon was a reminder of her greatest rival, the demon that had been his first mistress and that held him still.

'The best way to be careful of me,' she said, putting a hand to her stomach, 'of both of us, is to stop drinking.'

Ned sighed. 'I will. I will. But so must you, Evalyn. You were fairly lowering the champagne last night!'

'I solemnly swear that not a single drop will pass my lips until this child is born! I will do exactly as the doctor says – take exercise, rest, drink water . . .' She laughed. 'You are looking at a reformed character. Oh Ned, isn't it wonderful?'

Ned seemed stuck for words. He looked down at her stomach.

'Are you sure about this, Evalyn?' he whispered. 'There isn't even a sign.'

'Oh, I'm sure, you silly boy. But there's another seven months to go. I'll be like a whale before this is over and you won't be able to lift me up even if you want to.'

'Let's tell the parents!'

Carrie's eyes filled with tears. 'That is wonderful . . . the best news . . . Oh, Evalyn, you must look after yourself now. You owe it to your unborn child. No more late nights! He comes first!'

'I know that. He *is* first! Aren't you, darling?' she whispered looking down at her perfectly flat stomach.

They were having tea in the conservatory at 2020. Outside the sunlight was shifting across the garden to the pergola, with its vines and flowers and its brick wall and ornamental columns.

'How do you know it's going to be a boy?' Tom said with a quizzical smile, putting down his cup. There was colour in his cheeks, something his daughter had not seen for some time.

'I just know, Papa. It's a feeling.'

'Have you thought about a name?' Carrie asked.

'Evalyn's the boss on this one!' Ned said with a smile when she turned to him.

'You should call him after Ned's father,' Tom interposed. 'That'd please John R.'

'I'd much rather name him after you, Father!' Evalyn replied. 'But I have already decided on a name, and I'm sure you'll all understand!' She looked from her husband to her parents. 'I'm calling him Vinson,' she said in a low voice.

Tom turned abruptly to gaze into the garden, then reached out and put a hand on his daughter's head. Carrie moved to embrace Evalyn.

'How strange it all is,' she whispered, 'life going on . . . after all that has happened. But we trusted in God . . .'

'Of course we did, Mother! You don't mind naming him for Vinson, do you, darling?' she said, turning to Ned.

'Of course not,' Ned replied, and broke the emotional tension with a laugh. 'Vinson was the best driver I ever knew. If our son is anything like him . . .'

Evalyn saw that the colour had left her father's face.

'Are you all right, Father? You've been very pale lately.'

'I'm fine,' Tom replied. He smiled at his family. 'Congratulations to you both. You've made us very happy.'

He stood up and indicated to Ned to follow him to his study.

Evalyn knew, as Ned followed her father, that he would receive yet another check from him. His allowance from John R. was a thousand dollars per month, not nearly enough to fund his lifestyle. Gifts of ten thousand dollars in the month from Tom were not uncommon. Once Evalyn had even taxed her father on it.

'Father, Ned is even more extravagant that I am. You shouldn't encourage him!'

'What is the money for?' Tom had replied. 'Camp Bird is exceeding all expectations; the stock I retained is paying substantial dividends – this year, in fact,' he added, gently tweaking her chin, 'more than half a million!'

'So much, from the mine alone?'

'There is more than enough money for anything that you and Ned can think of to make you happy.'

Evalyn didn't tell her father that her happiness and Ned's were not necessarily compatible. She saw his eyes watching her, as though weighing the truth about her life. She would die before she told him that Ned was often out all night, and she hadn't a notion where he went.

Later, her father came to her sitting room, knocked on the open door, glanced around swiftly as though to ascertain that she were alone.

'Come in, Father.'

Tom shut the door behind him, perched on a chair and regarded his daughter.

'I just wanted to know if there is anything you and Ned would like? That both of you would enjoy together?'

'Well,' said Evalyn, thinking of an estate in Colorado that she and Ned had seen the previous year and thinking how nice it would be to have a summer place of their own, 'if the Sears Estate were to come up for sale . . .'

Her father grinned. 'Say no more, Evalyn!' Then he added, 'By the way, Daughter, I'm thinking of renaming Wolhurst!'

Evalyn looked at him. 'But why? What's wrong with the name?'

'Nothing. But I can think of another name that would suit it, and me, better!'

Evalyn heard the wistfulness in his voice. 'What name might that be?'

'Clonmel!' Tom said, and suddenly there was in his eyes that faraway look again, as though he had absented himself through time and distance to another world. 'It's from the Irish, you know,' he added, and she heard the half-suppressed nostalgia, the words rolling from his tongue as though he caressed them – *Cluain Meala*: the Meadow of Honey . . .'

He glanced at her, sighed and went on: 'I'm getting old, and like all old creatures I can't help thinking of home! We're going to Wolhurst – or Clonmel, as it will be known – for the month of August. Willie Taft is coming to stay! In fact he will rename the place.'

Evalyn liked William Howard Taft who was now President of the United States. She remembered with mixed emotions how Vinson's aim with his peashooter had once met its target.

'Oh, Papa, I want to be there too when the President comes!'

He looked at her gently. 'Would that be wise, Evalyn, in your circumstances? That long journey . . . and then the journey back?'

She was about to say she didn't give two cents about the journey and that her baby should be born at home in Colorado anyway and that she would stay on there for the birth. But then she thought of the vulnerable and precious cargo growing inside her, and the exhausting journey.

'You're right, Papa. I'll stay here. My child comes first!'

Ned's parents were as excited as children over the news.

'I knew you were a clever girl,' John R. told Evalyn. He beamed at his son, as much as if to say that he was obviously made of good stuff after all and knew how to get something right.

Mrs McLean took Evalyn to her sitting room and advised her to follow a routine, a brisk walk every day, a nap in the afternoon, early nights. 'And later on,' she confided, 'when you are nearer your time, it is in the baby's interest that you do not allow Ned any . . . relations with you. I hope you will forgive me for mentioning this!'

Evalyn blushed scarlet. It was something she had been wondering about herself. How did people make love when one of them was fat as a porpoise? Her own mother would never have mentioned such a thing.

'Have you decided which doctor will attend you for the birth, Evalyn?'

'It's long way away, Mummie,' Evalyn muttered lamely. 'I haven't thought about it yet.'

'None the less . . .'

Evalyn felt for a moment that her mother-in-law knew something she did not. What was birth like? Women who had been through it always dropped their voices when they referred to it, and never discussed it in front of women who had not experienced it.

'Do you mind if I suggest Dr Whitridge Williams?' Mrs McLean pressed on. 'He's the dean of John Hopkins.'

'But it's a natural process,' Evalyn said crossly, suddenly crowded at the propect of a doctor attending her at all. 'So why do people make such a fuss? Most women in the world manage it without doctors!'

'Nevertheless—'

Before Mrs McLean could continue Ned came into the room with his father, took his wife to one side and handed her a small square box. Inside, wedged into white satin, was a simple eternity ring, a circle of perfect, shining diamonds set in platinum.

'It's a family heirloom,' he said. 'Father and Mother want you to have it.'

But even as Evalyn exclaimed at this gift she heard the whispered exchange between her parents-in-law, John R. saying, 'I hope you haven't been frightening her,' and his wife's reply: 'That child doesn't know what's ahead of her, especially after that accident four years ago. It's bound to—'

'Bound to do what, Mummie?' Evalyn asked out loud, crossing the room and standing in front of Mrs McLean. 'What's the accident bound to do?'

'Nothing in itself, Evalyn,' Mrs McLean said smoothly, 'except that you were very tired after the operation. It took a great deal out of you. You should have the best medical help available. It is always wise!'

Evalyn replied simply, 'I'll do whatever I should for the baby's sake, so don't worry about it any more. And,' she added, 'you don't seem to realise that I'm nearly twenty-three years old and strong as a horse!'

She barely registered the compassion in the older woman's eyes.

It was a long summer. Evalyn and Ned spent most of it in Friendship, during which time Evalyn coped with morning sickness, and watched her body blossoming around her. One August night she woke, lay motionless and enthralled for a while, and then put her hand gently on her belly.

Ned was snoring beside her, but something extraordinary was happening. Inside her there was a stirring, like a small bird fluttering its wings.

'Ned,' she whispered, afraid to move in case she scared the tiny creature who lived inside her, 'Ned, our baby is moving!'

'Could be indigestion,' he muttered helpfully in a jerky voice from the land of Nod. 'That pudding at supper . . . enough to scupper anyone.'

Evalyn said silently to her baby, 'You'll have to excuse your papa. He is very sleepy right now. But I know it is you, my darling, and I love you!'

In September Evalyn avidly devoured the newspaper reports of the President's trip to Colorado. There were photographs of him and her smiling father, with Vice President Fairbanks and the watchful face of the secret service bodyguard.

Something gnawed at Evalyn's heart as she examined the press photographs of the renaming of Wolhurst. Her mother looked well, if a little plump, in her white gown and plumed hat. But there was an otherworldly aura about her father that gave Evalyn pause.

'Father is not looking well,' she whispered. 'He looks drawn!'

'He's fine,' Ned said, glancing over her shoulder. 'Losing a bit of weight, but there's no harm in that! It can't be very relaxing, entertaining Taft. Just look at all that bulk and that energy!'

Evalyn smiled. The white-moustached, merry President was obviously enjoying himself, his head thrown back in laughter, his corpulence evident despite the elegance of his morning dress. Behind him was her father. The smile died on Evalyn's lips as she studied him again. By constrast with the portly, ebullient Taft, he seemed haggard; his eyes had a haunted look, and his drooping, grey moustache seemed to drag at his features, as though it were too heavy for them.

On the day of her parents' return to Washington, Evalyn went to 2020, waited in all afternoon, longing for the sight of them. Through the open windows of her sitting room she heard the sound of car doors opening under the glazed carriage porch, voices, the butler directing the footmen about the luggage. She dropped the magazine about babies, hurried to the elevator and arrived in the hall as her parents crossed the threshold, saw their eyes light up. She embraced her mother, but her father held back, looking at her almost as though he had seen her for the first time.

'I've rounded out a bit since you saw me last, Father,' she said with a laugh, and put her arms around him. But the man in her arms was not the man who had left Washington. He had failed; the massive strength was gone from his arms; she could feel his bones; his skin was parchment. Fear, like ice, filled her heart.

'Are you quite well, Father?'

'Never better, my darling. Just a little tired, but it's good to be home, and to see you blooming. How are you, and Ned?'

'Ned is well. He's gone to Baltimore; he'll be back tomorrow.'

She laughed as she saw her father glance at her belly, took his hand and put it gently against her stomach.

'Your grandchild is very active, Father. He can hear you, you know, and he has a notion that you've lost a great deal of weight.'

'Pooh,' Tom said. 'Just a pound or two.'

Evalyn looked at her mother. But Carrie did not seem unduly concerned.

'Of course your father has lost weight. He is worn out! It was nonstop . . .'

'With a few days' rest I'll be good as new,' Tom said a little testily, as though weary of the topic. He turned to his wife and added almost wistfully: 'But it was glorious, wasn't it, Carrie?'

They took the elevator while Carrie described the high points of their sojourn.

'We invited half of Denver and Littleton to meet the President, put on a special train to bring them out to Wolhurst. He did the renaming with style. There's a plaque on the wall by the front door now, and we had a great party with fireworks.'

December came. Everything was ready for the baby's birth. King Leopold sent a gift of a solid gold cradle. Carrie and Mrs Mclean prepared the layette.

'You'll use the McLean christening robe?' the latter asked and Evalyn said she certainly would.

She was in good health. Ned drank only occasionally these days, and looked after her tenderly; they spent a good deal of time together in their suite, discussing the child.

'This time next year we'll be preparing to celebrate his first birthday!' Ned reminded her, when she expressed nervousness at the ordeal ahead of her. 'Isn't that something to look forward to?'

Evalyn thought of her baby, laughing up at her, and her heart overflowed. 'I can't wait to see him. I wonder who he'll look like. I wonder,' she added, half to herself, 'if he'll look like Vin . . .'

On 14 December Evalyn woke before dawn, dragged from fitful sleep by a sharp pain that speared from the small of her back. She caught her breath, and waited; but the pain abated. Half an hour later it came again, sharper than before, and then returned again after another short respite.

I've definitely started! she thought with a mixture of fear and elation. But there's nothing to be afraid of! A few sharp pains, after all, shouldn't be beyond Evalyn Walsh McLean!

The pain returned again and when the first light of day crept into the room she elbowed Ned.

'Whaaa?' he asked sleepily.

'The baby's coming!'

Ned jerked as though he were attached to wires. He got up at once, turning on the bedside light.

'Are you sure? I'll get the doctor . . .'

Evalyn drew her breath in sharply as another pain came thrusting through her insides like a red-hot knife. Ned looked at her aghast.

'Just tell my mother,' she gasped. 'She'll know what to do.'

Her mother came; Dr Williams from John Hopkins came. As the day wore on Evalyn found she inhabited a strange demonic world which was ruled by a goblin called Pain. All of her wits, all of her cunning, tried to devise means of escaping him; she panted and grasped the bedhead, lifted her body up as the contractions came, but every effort was futile. The torment crashed over her like the sea, something elemental and merciless that she had no means of controlling. She heard terrible groans and cries, and hardly registered that they belonged to herself. She registered low voices: 'I daren't give her morphine at this stage; the child is at risk!'

Outside it was snowing and the world was hushed.

Someone sponged her forehead, held her hands. Her mother's voice came through a fog. The fog cleared for a moment and she saw her parent's face, the anxiety, the greying hair, but then the goblin took her away again, brought her to a higher place in his kingdom.

The days passed; the torment intensified. All of her body shook, every muscle trembled from exhaustion. And still the baby did not come.

'Push, Evalyn!' her mother said, her voice low and strained. 'Can you push a bit more?'

It was the fourth day.

She pushed with the last ounce of her strength. She felt her body tear and the hot blood rush between her legs. But still the baby did not come.

'Her muscle tone never recovered,' she heard the doctor say, his voice far away. 'It will have to be a high forceps otherwise the child will be lost.'

Evalyn swirled in and out of consciousness. She barely felt the pad of chloroformed cotton over her face just before the doctor cut into the birth canal and then with his forceps eventually drew out her son.

There was a small cry from the baby. Evalyn lay as though dead. Carrie held back the tears as she regarded her tiny grandchild, wet and waxen and covered in blood. His head was shaped strangely, high and narrow and dented.

'His head!' she exclaimed.

'We'll get Dr Cushing to come,' the doctor said.

'The brain surgeon?' Ned asked, sounding sick.

'Yes . . . just to be on the safe side.'

It was 18 December 1909. Outside the world was under several feet of snow.

Ned put on a special train to bring Dr Cushing from Baltimore. Tom came to look at his grandson. He had seemed to recover after his exhausting summer, but he was still thin. As he looked into the cradle he was seized by a paroxym of coughing and had to move away.

Carrie looked at him anxiously. The doctor frowned.

'That chest, Mr Walsh . . .'

Tom gave the physician an almost imperceptible shake of his head that motioned him to silence.

'It's all right,' he said. 'It's just a touch of bronchitis. The cold weather . . .'

Tom had already seen a specialist, and he knew he should not spend the winter at home.

When it became clear that not only would Evalyn recover, but the baby, who had seemed so near death, would obstinately cling to life, Tom and Carrie informed Evalyn that they were going south to Palm Beach.

'For a few weeks, darling,' Tom said, taking her hand. 'Doctor says I should do it for the old chest. We'll be back at the end of February.'

But he sat beside her and held her hand for a long time.

Evalyn was very weak. 'I'll miss you,' she said. 'I wish I was going too.'

Tom seemed disinclined to leave her side. He touched the satin sheet, fingered the lace edging of her pillow, and his eyes were far away.

'God bless you, my darling,' he said eventually, and rose to take his leave. But he still seemed reluctant to go and stood looking into the gold cradle at his grandson, reached out and touched his tiny hand. At the door he turned. Evalyn saw how his eyes lingered on her, how they moved from her to the cradle and back to her again, as though he would imprint the tableau on his memory. Then he smiled and was gone.

Chapter Thirty-One

Evalyn often woke in the darkness and listened. By straining her ears she could hear the sounds she loved, the tiny breaths of her baby who slept in his gold cradle beside her bed. Reassured, she would go back to sleep. She would wake again an hour later and repeat the same procedure, wait to hear him breathe. Whenever the baby cried she rang for the nurse, who changed him and handed him to her in her big bed, waiting while she fed him. She insisted on this, although they told her that she was not strong enough and that it would wreck her figure. They also told her she should only feed him at three-hourly intervals.

'It will ruin his stomach, madam,' her maternity nurse informed her, 'if you do not stick to a strict routine!'

'Fiddle-nonsense!' Evalyn replied. 'In that case the whole human race should be extinct. What did all the generations before us care for such notions? I will feed my baby when he cries, as nature intended!'

'But, madam, you are still very weak!'

'I'm weak but I'm not dead!'

The baby began to thrive. His head assumed the normal shape of a newborn. Soft, dark down covered the fontanelle, which pulsed almost imperceptibly with his life. He slept between feeds, his small hands thrown out on either side of his face. When Evalyn put a finger in his tiny fist he gripped it as though it were a lifeline from another world. Sometimes he started in his sleep, throwing back his arms as though preparing to fend off attack. His mouth was like a rosebud, his face angelic, his fingers wrinkled, his nails perfectly manicured. Whenever she kissed him she got her nose in his eye.

Evalyn would croon to him, old songs she had heard her father singing, songs from Ireland. Sometimes his mouth crinkled in a smile.

'Look,' Evalyn told the nurse, 'he's smiling!'

'That's only wind, madam! He's too young to smile!'

'He's smiling!' Evalyn said firmly. 'Do you think I don't know my own baby?'

Friends and relatives came with gifts and congratulations, the President being one of the first. Among the messages was a polite card from Denver: 'Heartiest congratulations. Amelia and Paul.'

The newspapers referred to the little newcomer as the 'hundred-million-dollar baby.' This made Evalyn laugh.

'You'll be very rich,' she told him, 'but maybe not quite that rich. And certainly not if your father continues the way he is going!'

Ned was out most nights, as though making up for lost time, returning in the small hours and sleeping in his smoking room. But, during the day, he was very solicitous of his wife, sitting by her bed for an hour at a time, telling her all the Washington gossip and rocking the cradle.

'It's a variant on the silver spoon, eh, Evalyn?' he said with a laugh. 'A cradle in solid gold!'

'Much the baby cares! He just wants to be warm and loved and safe.'

Letters from Evalyn's parents spoke of the warm Florida sunlight, and looked forward to their homecoming. But, without warning, the letters from Florida stopped and although Evalyn waited and wrote there was no reply. When she contacted their hotel by telephone she was informed that they had left.

'Why doesn't Father or Mother contact us?' she asked Ned. 'Something is wrong.'

Ned had never been good at hiding his feelings. Evalyn read his face, saw the chagrin, the compassion in it, and the inability to share the reason.

'What is it, Ned?' she cried. 'You're keeping something from me!'

When he didn't reply she sat up in bed. 'Tell me'

The baby woke and began to cry. Evalyn put her hand out and gently rocked the cradle until his sobs subsided.

'Now,' she whispered to her husband, 'I want the truth.'

Ned sat beside her. 'I didn't know how to tell you, Evalyn. Your father is not well . . .'

'Not well! What does that mean? Stop looking at me like that, Ned, and spit it out!'

'It means . . . he has had a haemhorrage of the lungs!'

Evalyn fell back on her pillows, her heart sinking slowly and sickeningly. Into her head came the memory of the rasping cough her father had brought back from prospecting trips when they lived in Ouray. Oh darling Father, she thought. The mountains ruined your lungs long ago.

'Is he staying in Florida or coming home?' she whispered. 'The best doctors are here!'

'Your mother has taken him to Texas, to San Antonio!'

'Why?'

'She wants him to see some Christian Scientist or other, some damn quack, Evalyn, with a cure for everything! Your mother would believe the moon is made of light if some religious nut assured her of it strongly enough!'

'She just doesn't know what to do! Quick, Ned, we have to get down to San Antonio.'

'Evalyn, you must be mad! You're not well enough!'

But Evalyn was already out of bed and ringing for the nurse, and for Esther to help her dress, giving instructions as she did so.

'I want a telegram every hour about the baby,' she told the nurse. 'Every hour without fail!'

The nurse looked alarmed. 'Yes, madam.'

When they got to San Antonio Evalyn found that her parents had taken a small cottage and that the care of the sick man was in the hands of a woman with no medical credentials whatsoever. She was a Christian Scientist who had promised Carrie that she would perform a faith healing. Tom was in a small bedroom, and Carrie had the air about her of someone in a trance.

It was plain to Evalyn at a glance that her father was in agony, and that he was enduring it with the dogged perseverance he had always brought to adversity. It broke her heart to see him so wasted, so weak, the last of his strength channelled into mastering his body's response to overwhelming pain.

She turned and hissed at the woman by his bedside, 'Get out, you murdering cow. If you're not out of Texas by tomorrow morning I'll have you prosecuted for practising medicine without a licence!'

The terrified woman scuttled away. Evalyn embraced her father. Tom managed a rueful grin, although the sweat streamed down his face and he gasped as he spoke.

'I knew you wouldn't be too long, Evalyn. I'm afraid my number's up, darling . . .'

Ned found the best doctor in San Antonio; he came and injected the dying man with morphine. Evalyn felt the grip of the journey's fatigue, and her own overwrought state, as her father settled at last into a peaceful sleep. But she refused her tiredness, sending off telegrams to find the best doctor in America for treating the dying, and a week later Dr Lewellys Barker came from Baltimore.

Only then did they bring Tom home to 2020 Massachusetts Avenue – by special train that pulled their own carriage and some baggage cars for extra weight.

There they took him to his room in 2020 while Evalyn rushed to the nursery to see her baby.

Baby Vinson was looking very well – smiling, dribbling and waving his hands at the rows of small coloured balls strung over his cot. The nurse got out her records and recounted his weight gain. But he did not seem to recognise his mother and this was like a knife thrust.

'He's only four months old,' Carrie said. 'You've been away from him for several weeks. They don't remember at that age.'

Evalyn picked him up, carried him to her father.

'This is your grandfather, Vinson,' she said into her son's ear. 'If you become half the man he is, you will make your mother very proud!'

'Such nonsense, Evalyn,' Tom murmured, but he took the baby in his arms and his face lit up.

'Well, well,' he told his grandson, 'you've put on weight since I saw you last.' He touched the baby's small, fat hand.

The baby grabbed his grandfather's finger. Evalyn bent her head over both of them. Vinson looked up at her and suddenly crowed.

He does remember me, she thought with a lifting of her heart. Of course he does.

Tom said into her ear as she took the baby from him, 'I'll be gone soon, sweetheart! But I see I am leaving you in the best of hands!'

'Oh, Father,' Evalyn said, 'I would give everything we have to make you better . . .'

'Sssh, my darling.' He put a wasted hand on hers. 'Make it a simple funeral – no flowers, no music . . . just family and friends.'

'Yes, Father . . .'

When Carrie came into the room, he added in a voice so low only Evalyn could hear it, '. . . And look after your mother.'

Tom felt himself slipping into a place where pain was banished and effort would never be required again. So this is what it is like, he thought, the final, powerless leave-taking! This is where we finally surrender our will.

He could no longer speak, but he heard the whispers of his wife and daughter, and then other voices, once loved, came softly. He knew them well.

Except to see her baby, Evalyn never left her father's side. She thought of his life, his fairness, his sternness and gentleness, the way he had prospected year in, year out until his health was compromised. She thought of his generosity once he had found Camp Bird. She thought of the friends he had made, from kings and presidents to chance acquaintances whom he had charmed with his kindness. She thought of the contribution he had made to mining techniques, to irrigation of arid Western lands, to science, and of the lovely houses and estates he had bought. She wept in silence when she remembered Vinson's death, the single great affliction which she suspected he felt was punishment for his indulgence; she pondered the destruction of his lungs, the price he had paid for challenging the Rockies.

Was there ever such a man! What would that emigrant lad have said, she wondered, if it had all been shown to him as he stood on the quayside in Queenstown that far-off day in 1869? Or that night, long ago, in the blizzard, when Death had reached out to both of them with icy hands?

A few days later, on 8 April 1910, at 11.25 p.m. Thomas Francis Walsh died. He was four days short of his sixtieth birthday. Evalyn, holding his hand in hers, felt the moment when his pulse stopped. She bent over and kissed his brow, laid her cheek against his leathery one, trying to take into her his last breath.

'Goodbye, my love,' Carrie whispered as she kissed her dead husband's lips.

'Never say goodbye,' Evalyn whispered fiercely through the river of her tears. 'Just say – "Until we meet again" . . .'

The following day a front-page headline on the *Washington Post* announced: 'THOMAS F. WALSH DEAD'. The nation's newspapers carried his obituary.

The house was almost instantly flooded with telegrams and messages of condolences. Evalyn lingered over a Denver wire from Governor John F. Shafroth:

ALL COLORADO MOURNS WITH YOU
YOUR LOSS IS A PERSONAL ONE TO THE ENTIRE WEST
OUR HEARTS GO OUT TO YOU AND YOURS IN DEEPEST
    SYMPATHY

She looked for another cable and eventually found it. It said:

DEEPEST SYMPATHY PAUL

Carrie went to her room, pulled down the blinds and refused to see anyone except her daughter.

'I cannot attend your father's funeral,' she told Evalyn. 'I could not bear to see them lowering the casket . . . Please stay with me.'

Evalyn remembered her dying father's injunction and said she would stay.

The following day a service was held at 3 p.m. in the drawing room. Evalyn looked at the mourners – President Taft, Admiral Dewey, John R. McLean, David Wegg . . . It was a sad and almost silent farewell, without music or flowers. The prayers were said and then they took Tom away to the Walsh mausoleum in Rock Creek Cemetery, to lay him to rest beside his only son.

Evalyn went up to the roof garden and listened for the sounds of her father's casket being carried through the *porte-cochère* on 21st Street to the waiting hearse. She heard the hearse door shut on her father's remains, and then the sound of the automobiles as they slid down the short driveway. Her heart felt as though it would burst.

When the funeral cortège was gone, she went quietly down to her father's second-floor office, sat in his chair and looked around her. The blinds were drawn, the dust motes visible in the desultory light. Small pools of colour touched the shades from the stained-glass panes. She looked at the button-back chair where she had sat that morning she had divulged Ned's proposal.

She saw the two photographs her father always kept on his desk of herself and her mother in their simple silver frames, including the old one of her as a toddler in a white frilly dress.

What happened to the ones of Vinson he used to have as well? she wondered.

She opened a drawer; it was full of papers. She opened another and found, smiling up at her, Vinson's face. It was taken that last summer in Newport. Vinson was wearing his sardonic grin, elegant in young manhood, his whole life ahead of him. She wiped the tears that fell on to the glass.

She rummaged further. Underneath the photograph was an envelope that was soft to the touch. She took it out and emptied its contents on to the desk, considered them with some puzzlement. They were only a few pieces of faded velvet ribbon.

Evalyn restored everything to the drawer and closed it. The tears came in hot streams again; she tasted them in her mouth.

Until we meet again, Father, she told him silently.

Chapter Thirty-Two

'Your mother can't go on like this!' Ned said to Evalyn a few months later. 'Keeping to her room, the blinds drawn . . .'

'She's grieving! She and Father were together for thirty-one years. She blames herself for his death and says she is waiting to follow him!'

Ned grimaced. 'It's ghoulish, if you ask me! Can't you do something to jolt her out of it?'

'She isn't interested in anything except the baby. I tried to talk to her about Father's estate, but she just looks blank and says that money never interested her.'

'It would interest her quickly enough if there wasn't any,' Ned muttered sourly. 'But *there's* your answer – the baby! Put her in charge of little Vinson. They can spend the summer at Bar Harbor while I take you away for a while, for a rest and a change. We must have *some* time together.'

Evalyn looked at her husband's eager face. He had been so loving since the baby's birth, and a tower of strength when her father had died. And she *was* weary in body and spirit, run down and anaemic – or so the doctor said – and should benefit from a sea voyage, from a change of scene. But to leave the baby?

'Where do you want to take me?'

'France, Evalyn. I'd like to take you back to Paris. You were always happy there. When you think about it, you've had almost a whole year of hell!'

'But I can't leave the baby!'

'Is your husband not important, Evalyn?' he asked testily. 'Your marriage? Your health? Where do I fit in all of this? Vinson is a big bouncing boy now and your mother will emerge from that decline of hers if you leave him in her charge. Or do you want her to follow your father?'

Evalyn knew when she was beaten. She went to see her mother.

Carrie was in a darkened room, lying in bed and staring at the ceiling. She had lost weight, and her face was as white as her bed linen.

392

'Have you a headache, Mother?' Evalyn said, sitting beside her and taking her hand.

'No, dear. I was just remembering . . . all those lovely days and years. I feel so amputated. Every day it's worse, knowing that I will never see his face again . . . Thinking about how young and happy we were in Leadville and knowing that I must grow old without him . . .'

'In that case you won't be up to looking after the baby. Ned and I are thinking of having a holiday. He wants to take me back to Europe!'

'But, Evalyn, little Vinson is only seven months old.'

'All the more reason. We can't go away if you don't agree to mind him, Mother. I wouldn't leave him with anyone else, and both Ned and I badly need a break! We didn't have one last summer.'

'I know, you poor darlings,' Carrie cried. 'You must be quite worn down! Your pregnancy, the birth, and then your father's death before you had recovered! Ned was so wonderful through the whole thing. I don't know what we would have done without him.'

Ned *had* been wonderful, Evalyn conceded privately. During one of the most terrible times of her life there had been no sign of the hard-drinking, selfish young man she knew; someone else had emerged, the man she adored, a thoughtful and competent partner. She was in love with him again and was looking forward to some time away with just the two of them.

Why isn't he always like this? she wondered. But it hardly mattered now; she was sure he had turned a corner. Fatherhood, as she had anticipated, had conferred maturity on him.

'So will you look after the baby, Mother? I don't think it's a good idea to take him all the way with us to France!'

Carrie came to life at that.

'All the way to France! Across that awful ocean? I should hope not! Poor little mite . . .'

Carrie was out of her room by the end of the day and walking the baby in the garden. Ned and Evalyn saw her and Vinson safe in Bar Harbor before they left for Europe.

In Paris they stayed at their old haunt, the Bristol Hotel. It was strange, Evalyn thought, as she woke on their first morning, to be back in this city which had been the focal point of so many pivotal events in her life – her first trip to Europe, her 'foreign education', her honeymoon. But it was only now, when she was a young matron, married for two years, that she felt relaxed about the physical side of marriage. Ned had made love to her half the night. There was a hunger in him that startled and excited her, although in the midst of it a doubt had intruded as to whether his ardour was really for *her* or the body in his arms.

Ned pulled the sheet to the floor and looked down at his naked wife, stretched diagonally across the big bed, her plait undone and her hair in dark waves on the pillows. Even in the shuttered light he could see how graceful her body was, recovered already from pregnancy and childbirth, and he also saw the long, white scar on her right thigh. Evalyn caught the glance, reached out and pulled back the sheet.

'You are lovely,' Ned said in a grave voice, 'and a continuing source of temptation . . . but right now I feel that if I do not get breakfast I will die!'

He bent down to kiss her and she wrapped her arms around his neck and said, 'You do *love* me, Ned, don't you?'

He pulled back to look into her face, gave a harsh laugh.

'What a silly question, Evalyn! How can you possibly ask it . . . after last night, especially?'

It was the wrong question, she knew. She remembered Annie's words: *'Never tell a man you love him; never ask him if he loves you!'*

Was that where I went wrong? she thought, suddenly and ashamedly besieged by the memory of Paul.

She slid out of bed, grabbing her silk and lace dressing gown. While Ned rang for breakfast, she crossed the bedroom, pulled back the ivory brocade curtains and peered through the slats of the shutters. Ned followed, opening the French windows. The noise of the capital came in on the warm morning air, with smells of coffee and fresh bread.

'Paris is waiting for you, Madame McLean . . .'

Evalyn laughed, feeling suddenly like she was eighteen again.

After breakfast she had her bath and chose one of her Paul Poiret outfits, a vivid green dress with a softly draped skirt that narrowed so much at the hem that only tiny steps could be taken. Many women wore a hobble garter with the new fashion, to prevent them taking normal strides and so splitting their seams.

'I don't think this damn fool fashion is going to last,' she muttered as the maid did her up at the back. 'They have us mincing along in the very year when suffragettes are demonstrating.'

She completed her ensemble with a large hat, the crown of which was upswept at one side, and adorned with plumes of different shades, varying from coolest lime to bottle green. Ned regarded her critically in the mirror.

'You don't look a day over twenty.'

His compliment conjured painful memories. She had turned twenty at Wolhurst, with the first anniversary of Vinson's death looming and her father's grief. Now she had the raw memory of his own recent passing.

'Let's go shopping, Ned . . .'

She bought gowns by Jacques Doucet and dresses in wild silk by Paul Poiret. In the evening she wore the Star of the East arranged in a platinum bandeau around her head when they went down to dinner. Every eye in

394

the restaurant was fixed on the young woman whose jewelled headdress sparked green and white fire, reminding her of the sensation she had caused years ago at the opera when she had arrived in a yellow velvet dress with diamond insets.

Ned bought a racing Fiat and engaged a chauffeur, but Evalyn found she couldn't access the excitement that drives through Paris had once held for her.

It was inexplicable, she admitted eventually to herself, but none of it was the same. She was seeking excitment where once she had found it but, while the former sources of her pleasure were there for the taking, she had somehow moved on. She found the warm days unbearably humid; the cobbles, pavements and buildings soaked up the summer heat and radiated it back.

I'm wilting, Evalyn thought.

Was it the same for Ned? Was he too chasing fun eternally only because he did not know what else to do with life? But there *was* something else to live for now.

Whenever she mentioned the baby, though, he played down her anxiety.

'For God's sake, Evalyn, there has to be life after parenthood! Are you with me or not? What has happened to the impetuous girl I married?'

They telegraphed Bar Harbor daily, and Carrie's replies assured them little Vinson was thriving.

'See, he's fine. Nothing to worry about. So stop being so banal in your preoccupations and let's just enjoy ourselves, Evalyn. After the year we've just been through, let's have some fun for a change!'

It would have been easy once. She tried to please Ned, but her heart was no longer in the game. She went with him for a few days to the spa town of Vichy, took the waters, won hugely at the Casino, but still he was restless.

'What is it you want?' she demanded one evening at dinner. 'Every day it's the same. . . . It's as though you are looking for the leprechaun's pot of gold my father used to tell us stories about!'

'Don't get all Irish on me, Evalyn Walsh,' he replied, looking at her with an unsteady grin. 'I've already got the pot of gold. What I'm looking for is the wild girl I once knew.'

'The wild girl became a woman! What *you*'re looking for is the Alchemist!' Evalyn was taken aback by her own pronouncement, which seemed to have a meaning beyond any she had intended.

But Ned only laughed. He ordered two brandies and swallowed both of them. Then he extended his hand to her with a determined smile, led her upstairs to their suite and began to undress her. As her gown fell to the floor and she found herself propelled on to the bed, Evalyn experienced a powerful sense of her space being invaded. She knew she existed for Ned as a woman in that moment, but as a person she was equally certain that she did not exist at all.

She pushed him away. 'I'm very tired, Ned. And we did make love yesterday, you know.'

'I didn't realise it was rationed.'

He stared at her with angry eyes, went to the mirror where he restored his bow tie, and then he moved to the door.

'Sleep well, my dear. I'm going out.'

The following morning Evalyn received a letter from her mother.

> Vinson is doing well and is putting up another tooth. He's the happiest of babies and you have nothing to worry about on his account. We spend the day in the garden and he generally sleeps all night.

Evalyn mulled this over, wondering why she felt so uneasy. She thought of her son, of his small cherubic face, the fat legs he churned like windmills, the small, plump fists, and she felt bereft. He's three thousand miles away, she told herself, even if he is in best hands in the world. The distance seemed unbearable. She longed to hold him, to hear him breathing, see him clench and unclench his toes as he fed. His absense was a void, a growing anxiety.

Trying to distract herself from thoughts of the baby, she put the letter down and turned to Ned, who was sipping coffee and toying with his breakfast. Over the last couple of days the thoughtful husband she had known had disappeared. Right now he was in his dressing gown and yesterday's beard was still on his face. His breath was volatile, and his eyes bloodshot; he had been out half the night.

She said, for want of something to say: 'Ned, will you come shopping with me this morning?'

'Christ, Evalyn, haven't you been to enough shops? Where do you want to go?'

'To a milliner's I've heard about . . . a woman by the name of Chanel.'

The phone rang. Evalyn reached to pick up the mouthpiece.

'Yes?'

'There is a gentleman here to see you, madame.'

'Who is he?'

The receptionist lowered her voice discreetly. 'Monsier Cartier, madame.'

'Ask him to come up.'

Ned looked interrogatively at his wife over his coffee cup.

'Who's bothering us at this hour?'

'It's eleven thirty, Ned,' Evalyn said irritably, 'and I could do with some diversion!'

Pierre Cartier was dressed in morning coat with oyster-coloured spats and held his tall black silk hat in his right hand. He stood on the pink and blue Persian carpet and bowed with a quiet flourish.

Ned groaned almost audibly, but the jeweller did not appear to notice.

'I trust I find you well, madame . . . monsieur? He directed a shrewd glance at Ned, who was glowering into his moustache, and added smoothly, 'But perhaps the time is inconvenient? I will call again.'

'No, Monsieur Cartier,' Evalyn said. 'Please sit down. Would you like some coffee?'

'No, thank you, madame.'

Ned got up. He said, 'Excuse me,' and went to the bedroom, closing the door smartly behind him.

Evalyn looked at her visitor.

'You must excuse my husband. He is not himself this morning. He had a . . . late night.'

Cartier's smile said that he understood perfectly.

'I was very sorry to hear of your father's death, madame,' he said gently. 'May I offer my condolences?'

'Thank you.'

Evalyn wondered what had brought Cartier to her. It could not be just a call of condolence. She watched as he reached inside his coat and extracted a package wrapped in paper and sealed with wax seals.

'What have you got there, monsieur?' she asked with a laugh. 'I hope you're not trying to tempt me with some extravagance.'

'No indeed, madame, but I will tell you a story.' He looked keenly at Evalyn before he continued. 'I think you told me on the occasion of our last meeting that you had been to Turkey and had been favoured with a visit to the late sultan's seraglio?'

'Yes. It was full of fatties.'

'Indeed, madame. I think you also mentioned that you had seen there a great blue jewel around the neck of one of the ladies?'

Evalyn thought for a moment. Into her mind came the memory of a plump and pretty dark-haired girl, with a big blue gem around her neck.

'I did. What of it?'

Cartier smiled a little mysteriously. 'As you know, the Ottoman Empire is now no more. The lady on whose throat you saw that jewel was stabbed to death!'

Evalyn's eyes widened.

'The gem she was wearing was almost certainly the Hope Diamond,' Cartier went on. 'It is a blue diamond, one of the rarest of the earth's gems.'

Confident now of his listener's complete attention Cartier proceeded to give Evalyn a short history of the Hope Diamond. He told her how it had been brought back to France from India in the reign of Louis XIV, how it had been among the crown jewels of France, how after the Revolution it had come into the possession of an Englishman called Lord Francis Hope and how it had been sold to a Turkish collector in the early years of the nineteenth century.

'Am I to understand that you have brought this priceless gem with you, Monsier Cartier?' Evalyn enquired in a low voice with a glance at the bedroom door. 'That, in fact, you have it in that package in your hands?'

'Indeed I have, madame.'

'And you would like me to see it?'

'If madame pleases. It is worth seeing.'

Pierre Cartier undid the seals on the package and in a moment held up before Evalyn's eyes a great blue gem set in gold, suspended on a diamond necklace.

'Is this the jewel you saw in the sultan's harem, madame?' he asked softly.

Evalyn stared. The blueness of the thing was incredible; it was, she thought, the kind of blue you could expect in a cave under a tropical sea.

'I suppose so,' she whispered. 'I can't remember. How did you come by it?'

'I bought it from a man called Rosenau. He acquired many jewels that until recently belonged to the late Turkish sultan . . .'

Ned, now shaved and dressed, came back into the room. He looked from his wife to the famous jeweller to the shining diamond. He approached, eyebrows raised, a sardonic half-smile on his face.

'Let me see this thing against Evalyn's throat!' he exclaimed. 'Will you try it on, Evalyn?'

'Please, monsieur,' Pierre Cartier said quickly, putting out his hand to forestall him, 'do not touch it. It is reputed to be unlucky. Some even say it is cursed.'

Ned stopped in mid-stride, looked at the jeweller and then laughed. 'You can't possibly be serious! I never heard such humbug!'

Cartier raised his shoulders a fraction. Then he said, 'Maybe so, but it seems that everyone who has ever owned it was subsequently touched by tragedy.'

Evalyn felt the fine pricking sensation at the nape of her neck that she recognised from long ago. Fear flooded her and, for or a moment, she could not speak.

'In that case why did you bring it here?' Ned demanded testily. 'Are you trying to murder us with some kind of spell . . . with *blue* magic?' he added, gesturing to the stone before him. 'Ha, ha . . .'

'Don't be so tedious, Ned!' Evalyn said.

Cartier smiled at the two young people. 'Nothing of the kind, monsieur,

I assure you. But I remember madame telling me once that unlucky things were lucky for her!'

'That's true,' Evalyn said as robustly as she could, 'But only because I don't believe in superstition! Well . . . mostly I don't!'

'My wife is half Irish and as superstitious as they come!' Ned said. 'But if you think you will whet my interest in this thing by scaremongering you can think again!' He reached out his hand and picked up the jewel. He turned it over, examining it, holding it to the morning light and, for a moment, his face was touched by cerulean fire. He turned back to Cartier. 'It's certainly very fine! What exactly is its provenance?'

'It is said that once it was the eye of a Hindu idol.'

A shiver moved along Evalyn's spine.

'How much?'

Cartier seemed taken aback at Ned's directness, but before he could respond Evalyn interjected smoothly.

'Monsier Cartier, thank you for showing this to us. But I am not interested in acquiring it.'

She saw the light from the idol's eye burn blue on Ned's hands, tried to rationalise the feeling that she should distance herself as far as possible from the necklace before her. 'I do not like the setting.'

Cartier rose from his seat and bowed. He did not evince the slightest disappointment. He restored the necklace to its case, delivered himself a few urbane comments, and in a moment was gone.

'No interest at all?' Ned said when the door closed. 'Did I hear correctly? No interest in one of the great gems of the world? Can this be you, Evalyn? Or are you sickening for something?' He put his hand on her forehead, let it slip to her neck and then to her bosom. 'Yes . . . I definitely detect a certain feverishness!'

'Now, now, Ned!'

Ned removed his hand. He stood sulkily.

'I have other things on my mind right now!' Evalyn said in a conciliatory tone. 'And the main one is a little fellow called Vinson. Mother's letter this morning says he has cut another tooth.' She shook her head; her voice quivered. 'I miss him so terribly, Ned! I've had enough of Paris. Can't we go home?'

Ned sighed. He looked at his white face in the mirror.

'You're right, Evalyn!' he said after a moment. 'Home and Vinson! Don't worry about me! Get our stuff packed and we'll sail as soon as possible!'

He suddenly turned, went to the window and looked down on the Place Vendôme.

Evalyn heard him mutter half under his breath, 'I wish to God life wasn't so interminably boring!'

* * *

By the time they were back in Washington, Paris already seemed to Evalyn like a dream. As soon as the car stopped in the *porte-cochère* of 2020 Massachusetts Avenue she hurried to the elevator and up to the nursery, cursing the new fashion that prevented her from running. The nurse came to greet her but Evalyn pushed past her to where Vinson, bigger and stronger than when she had left, was crawling in his playpen. She picked him up and covered him with kisses, ecstatic at the touch of his velvet cheek and the scent she always associated with him of milk and soap. The child looked at her with wide, curious eyes, before turning to his grandmother, who had followed Evalyn upstairs, and putting out his arms to her.

Evalyn felt as though her heart had turned to ice. He doesn't know me, she thought. He has completely forgotten me.

'It's like last time,' she whispered to her mother. 'But this time he has forgotten me completely!'

'Give him a little while,' Carrie replied soothingly, taking the weeping child on her lap. 'It'll be all right. Just sit here for a while and let him come to you.'

Evalyn obeyed. Vinson, now quiet, observed his mother from Carrie's arms. When Carrie put him on the floor he sat and watched his mother with a perplexed expression, as though she reminded him of someone he just couldn't place. After a few minutes, as she talked to her mother and feigned disinterest in him, he suddenly crawled across the floor and seized her knees with a loud cry. Evalyn held back the tears as she took him up and cuddled him.

Ned came up later. He was more subtle, making no overt overtures, but he made the baby laugh by jumping in and out from behind the nursery door.

'He really is a topping little fellow, Evalyn!' he exclaimed later. 'I didn't realise babies could be so much fun!'

She laughed. 'Oh, Ned, you are his father. And he needs you very much.'

'Do you really think so?' he said, looking pleased. He added after a moment in a thoughtful voice: 'I suppose I should be a proper dad and dump the booze for him . . .'

'It all depends on your priorities,' Evalyn said gently, 'and I think *he* is worth being first!'

Ned, Evalyn conceded privately as the days passed, had become a wonderful father. He would dandle the baby on his knee and sing funny songs about an Indian rajah and a frog that went a-wooing. Vinson would laugh, his chirrup irresistible. Carrie would laugh too; she called the baby her 'moppet'.

She had undergone rejuvenation in caring for him, and Evalyn rejoiced at the change in her; she had put on weight; she looked ten years younger. But, deep in Evalyn's own heart there was a tiny *frisson* of terror at the thought that Vinson might never have turned to her, his mother, again. Another week perhaps and it would have been too late to re-establish the intense contact of mother and child that had once pulled both of them from under the shadow of death.

'Don't be absurd,' Carrie told her when Evalyn voiced her fears aloud. 'You were only away for a few months!'

But looking at Vinson, Evalyn said, 'How could you know that, my darling child? You must have thought I had abandoned you.'

Ned was scarcely drinking. Most days he spent time with the baby, crawling around on the nursery floor.

'We boys have to stick together!' he whispered to the small person, who waved fat fists at him and laughed at his antics. He pointed to the nurse, to Evalyn. 'You see the Deadly Duo? Don't let them bully you, my lad. You have to show them who's wearing the trousers.'

The nurse, who had a good sense of humour, doubled over in laughter. 'He's wearing *diapers*, Mr McLean! And will be wearing them for quite some time!'

Why is Ned a man of so many contrasts? Evalyn asked herself as she watched her husband. Why is he capable of loving sensitivity, and unbearable testiness? Why can't I rely on him, drop my guard, stop trying to be tough? He wants all of me; but how can I give the whole of myself to a man who can turn in an instant and become someone I don't know?

Sometimes she wondered would her life have been happier if her father had never found Camp Bird, if he had never emigrated, if she herself had been born in Ireland. She imagined herself in a thatched cottage, with the valley stretched out below and the bulk of Slievenamon, the Women's Mountain, against the sky.

I have cousins in Ireland, she thought. One of them is around my own age. Father was always interested in what happened there.

'Do you know what's going on in Ireland?' she asked her father-in-law when she saw him that evening.

'A certain amount of noise!' John R. said in evident surprise. 'I didn't know you were interested in politics!'

'What kind of noise?'

'Well, they're looking for Home Rule. But the House of Lords in London – which has a veto – won't have it. However, *its* teeth may be drawn shortly,' he added with a chuckle. 'The thing about power is that, if you use it, you eventually lose it.'

*   *   *

401

In November Ned received a letter from Cartier of Fifth Avenue, New York, to say that Monsieur Pierre Cartier would shortly arrive from Europe on board the *Lusitania* and hoped to be honoured with an appointment.

He showed the letter to Evalyn as they were getting ready for a dinner with Reggie Vanderbilt, dropping it on to her dressing table while Esther was arranging her hair. She picked it up and read it; signalled to the maid that she could go.

'I knew that guy wouldn't leave it at that!' Ned said when the door had closed.

'What do you mean?'

Ned's eyes met hers in the mirror. 'He wants to see *you*, of course. Where else will he find someone rich enough and frivolous enough to buy that trinket? Who else would take it with its history?'

'But, Ned, I don't want it! I told him as much!'

'Not now you don't. But if I know you, Evalyn McLean, you will! And you will want it for precisely the same reason that you once stopped off on a motor car ride to marry me – you will see it as a dare! You will thumb your nose at the suggestion that it might be the worst move of your life!'

She looked at him, sudden tears starting in her eyes.

'You don't mean that, Ned! I married you because I loved you. I love you still!'

'Do you?'

She considered the lines of renewed frustration in her husband's face. Maybe there is something he needs that I *cannot* give him, she thought, and maybe what I crave is something that he cannot give me.

'You're not going to turn on the waterworks, are you, Evalyn?'

But when her eyes filled Ned's face softened. He put his arms around his wife and pressed her face to his midriff.

'Hey,' he murmured, 'come on now . . .'

He held her for a moment, patted her back. Then his embrace became tighter. He tilted up her head, but as his mouth sought hers and his tongue began exploring, Evalyn pulled away.

'Not now, Ned. We have to finish dressing or we'll be late! Wait until we come home.'

She gave a small evasive laugh, brushing at the flecks of powder on his starched shirt front. Ned glowered.

'There's always an excuse these days, Evalyn, isn't there? If it's not Vinson, it's something else – anything else in fact. What did you think marriage was all about? *Playing* housie? *Pretending* to be grown up?'

Evalyn refused to be drawn into confrontation. She made a *moue* at him in the mirror.

'Don't be so cross. You know perfectly well that we have all the time in the world to be grown up. There's tonight . . . and tomorrow night . . .'

She laughed a little flirtatiously. But Ned turned away and she did not see how his face had darkened. She felt the sense of something slipping, as though a landslide was beginning under her feet.

Chapter Thirty-Three

'Madame,' Pierre Cartier said, 'I have never seen you looking so well.'

They were sitting in the Louis XIV drawing room in 2020 Massachusetts Avenue. Evalyn saw her visitor taking in his surroundings with a connoisseur's eye.

'It's motherhood,' she replied with a smile. 'Last time you saw me in Paris I was pining for my baby! Now I am with him all the time and I have never been happier!'

Cartier inclined his head.

'If you have brought the Hope Diamond to me again, Monsieur Cartier,' Evalyn said gently, 'I'm afraid that you are wasting your time.'

'Indeed, madame, I do not wish to waste either your time or mine!' the jeweller said. 'However, it is true that I have it with me.'

He took a small parcel from his inside pocket and laid it on his knee. 'I have changed the setting.' He glanced at the package and at her, his fingers poised to open it. 'With your permission, madame?'

'By all means let me see it,' Evalyn said, 'but my mind is made up.'

Cartier removed the leather box from its wrappings.

'If you recall,' he said, 'last time the setting was of gold. Now it is somewhat different.'

He opened the box to disclose a necklace of diamonds, from which was suspended the huge blue stone that Evalyn had seen in Paris. But it was now set in platinum and framed by white diamonds. In the winter light of the drawing room its strange colour was like crystallised summer midnight, or like the blue of certain eyes that changed according to the light. Then she remembered it was an idol's eye, torn from its pagan setting, supposedly carrying a curse from a time beyond recall. Such nonsense, she thought.

'Do you like the setting better now, madame? It has sixteen white pearshaped and cushion-cut diamonds. The necklace itself has forty-five diamonds. The stone has forty-five carats . . .'

The 'stone' stared back at her, hypnotic in its cynicism and cold perfection.

'It is nicer,' Evalyn conceded, contending with a sense of unease and struggling for urbanity. 'The white diamonds set off the blue . . . But that does not mean that I—'

'Oh, I appreciate that, madame. I know your interest in gems and I brought it merely for you to see. I fully expect to find a purchaser for so unique a piece among American collectors or connoisseurs.'

He paused, looked around him, then lowered his voice. 'But perhaps I might ask a favour of you?'

'What is that, Monsieur Cartier?'

'I do not like to leave the necklace in my hotel or walk around Washington with it in my possession. And I do not like it to be handled by anyone susceptible to its . . . dark side.' He paused, glanced at her as he closed the box. 'As I know you are not troubled in that way, I was wondering if – just over the weekend, you understand – I might ask you to . . .'

He paused, glanced at her and Evalyn said, 'Take care of it? Is that what you mean?'

'Yes . . . But perhaps I am being presumptuous?'

Evalyn felt flattered, but her gut reaction was to refuse. She challenged this. Why should she not take custody of the necklace during the weekend and accommodate the urbane and charming Monsieur Cartier? Why should she allow herself to be ruled by superstition?

'Not at all,' she said smoothly. 'The necklace will be safe here, monsieur. We have fifteen private detectives on our staff and several bodyguards . . . because of our son,' she hastened to add when she saw the expression on her visitor's face.

When Pierre Cartier was gone Evalyn went to her suite. She met Esther on the gallery, carrying a pile of fresh linen. Helping her was Sharon, the maid's ten-year-old niece, who had been allowed by Carrie to share her aunt's bedroom while her own mother was ill. The child was a quadroon, very beautiful, with slanting black eyes.

'Good morning, ma'am.'

Evalyn smiled at them, opened her door to a newly turned-out sitting room, fresh with white and yellow hot-house roses.

She went through to her bedroom, took the necklace from its box, stared at it and, with a sense of personal bravado, fastened it around her neck. The stone was splendid, she conceded, as she regarded herself in the mirror, as wonderful as the Star of the East, but its light was far more mysterious. How would one describe a shade that played so with the light? Not Prussian Blue, not Peking Blue, not Sapphire Blue nor Sea Blue. And for a *diamond* to possess it!

In the street outside a motor car suddenly backfired with a sound like gunfire. Evalyn, wrenched from her reverie, jumped. When she looked at her reflection again it seemed that the stone was watching her, that a dark

405

pupil at its core widened with impersonal venom. Her heart missed a beat.

I will not tolerate such nonsense in myself, she thought.

In the nursery next door Vinson woke from his nap and began to fret. Evalyn, responding as she always did to his slightest sound, rushed to the nursery and found the nurse, trim in her starched white uniform, bending over the child's cot.

'Poor little guy . . .' the latter murmured, picking up a flushed and tearful Vinson. 'We're having nasty teething pains . . .'

The 'poor little guy' saw his mother and stretched out his arms to her. Evalyn took him and cuddled him. His sobs subsided. He stared round-eyed at the jewel on her bosom and tried to grab it.

Evalyn caught his hand. For a moment she felt only horror. Everything Pierre Cartier had intimated about this jewel, everything her own imagination had prompted, flooded into her head. The nurse looked at Evalyn and laughed.

'If he had his way he'd cut his teeth on something mighty fine there, Mrs McLean!'

'Take him,' she told the nurse on a note of rising agitation. 'I don't want him to touch it!'

Vinson wailed.

'You don't want to damage your mother's lovely necklace,' the nurse crooned, 'now do you?'

Evalyn took off the necklace and stuck it into her pocket. She took her son back, throwing him a few inches into the air and catching him until he laughed. An unmistakable aroma filled the air and she wrinkled her nose.

'I think someone could do with a fresh diaper,' she told the nurse, who immediately took Vinson away to change him.

Evalyn looked after them, wondering why she had allowed herself to be bullied by superstition? But no matter how she reasoned with herself she still did not want him to touch the blue diamond in her pocket.

Soon her precious darling would be one year old. It would be one year since she had writhed for four days in a labour that had seemed without end. And only eight months since her beloved father had died. Oh, Father, she whispered, as the pain of his loss returned to tear at her heart, I will never get over you.

She returned to her room, restored the necklace to its box, then glanced at her father's photograph that stood on her dressing table, warmed at how distinguished and elegant he looked, and at the twist of humour at the corners of his mouth. Then she stared into her own haunted eyes in the mirror and wondered at the loneliness that nothing seemed to assuage.

Over dinner that evening she told Ned about her visitor and what he had brought with him.

'What did I tell you, Evalyn? Are you going to buy the thing?'

'Of course I'm not going to buy it! I told Monsieur Cartier as much. But I did agree to mind it for him over the weekend!'

Evalyn suddenly saw how Ned would interpret this – that she was a weak and foolish woman who was clay in the hands of a wily Frenchman.

He laughed out loud. 'Mind it over the weekend? *Mind* it? My God, that guy has a nerve!'

'Why do you say that?'

'It's obvious! It's his way of getting you to change your mind!'

Evalyn stiffened, but did not respond. A row was the last thing she wanted. Tonight, for reasons she was not able to unravel, she *needed* reassurance, human warmth, a husband's arms around her, the shelter of his love.

'I've no reason to change my mind,' she said with a hint of coquetry. 'After all, I have everything I want . . .' She glanced into Ned's eyes and added, 'Not only do I have a wonderful baby but I have a wonderful husband too.'

She wanted to say, 'I feel insecure, Ned. Someone is walking on my grave. Take me in your arms; love me and make me safe.'

She had deliberately worn a gown he liked, one that she had bought in Paris at Caillot Soeurs; it was empire line, made of black satin and lace, with a discreetly low neckline. She had arranged her hair the way he preferred it, curled about her forehead. For jewellery she wore only a single string of pearls. Sitting opposite him she tried to read his face for signs of desire, but Ned seemed preoccupied.

The butler approached with the cheese board. Ned waved it away, pushed back his chair and rose to his feet.

'I must be off. Don't wait up . . .'

Evalyn felt the free fall of her spirits.

'Couldn't you stay in this evening . . . with *me*?' She said this softly, almost pleading, but Ned hardly seemed to hear.

'I have an appointment, Evalyn. Can't let people down now, can I?'

'With whom is your appointment? Maybe you could cancel it . . . just this once?'

Ned's face registered impatience. 'You know perfectly well I can't go around cancelling arrangements.'

Ned left. Evalyn sipped a solitary coffee. She thought of spending the evening with her mother and then remembered that Carrie was with the Red Cross people and would not be back until late. She went to the nursery to look in on Vinson. She had put him to bed before dinner, had hummed him a lullaby, watched while his eyes had glazed and then closed, but because he would wake and stare at her accusingly when she tried to tiptoe out, she had ignored the mellow summons of the dinner gong until she was certain he was really asleep.

Ned had been irritated at her coming late to table. It was, she reckoned, part of the reason why he had insisted on keeping his appointment. He had often complained that she thought of nothing except the baby.

Now the nursery fire threw a soft glimmer over the room. The nurse was reading by the light of a solitary lamp.

'He hasn't woken since you left, madam,' she whispered as Evalyn stood looking down at her rosy-cheeked son. She longed to clutch him to her, to cover him with kisses, to wake him up and play with him. Instead she contented herself with gently placing her hand on the crown of his head, loving the feel of his silken baby hair.

The prospect of an evening alone panicked her. It seemed to stretch ahead of her interminably. She thought of telephoning any one of a myriad friends, but this prospect did not please her either. Her leg was hurting, as it often did when she was tired. She limped to her bedroom and lay on the bed, took the Hope Diamond from its box on her nightstand and examined it again. Its colour was restrained in the subdued light, but it seemed to her that she felt its power against her fingers, startlingly cold, almost alive. It had been in the hands of kings and emperors, around the necks of concubines, and once it had looked out from the head of an idol on a pagan world. She put it away with rueful self-reproof. Monsieur Cartier would call for it on Monday morning and her imagination need never be exercised about it again.

Her mind reverted to other matters, things she did not know how to handle – to do with her father's estate. Her mother had no head for business affairs, and had consulted her. Evalyn had intended to ask Ned, although she knew perfectly well that any advice he would give would be filtered through his father, but her mother need never know the source of the advice. She wondered where Ned had gone in such a hurry. Out drinking again? If so, he would be like a bear in the morning.

Ned came home when dawn was breaking. Evalyn surfaced long enough to ask him where he had been, but he was evasive. He seemed tipsy, but not unusually so. He did not appear for breakfast and towards midday Evalyn went to see if he would be coming down for luncheon. He got out of bed, but as he crossed to his dressing room Evalyn saw in the mirror a dull red mark at his neck.

'What is that, Ned, that mark?'

'What are you talking about?'

Evalyn followed him into the dressing room.

'That mark!' she cried. 'Either you're sickening for some disease or someone has bitten you!' Ned put down the cut-throat razor, lifted his wife up and put her down outside the door. Then he closed it in her face. She tried the handle.

408

'Unlock this door, Ned McLean. I want to know why you come back here with love bites on your neck . . .'

Ned unlocked the door, put his head around it and hissed, 'I come back with love bites, as you call them, because I went looking for some excitement. There isn't any at home, after all.' Then he shut the door again.

'Is she a whore?' Evalyn cried through the door.

'No!' he answered angrily after a moment's silence.

'Who is she?'

Ned did not reply for a moment. Then his voice came brutally, 'She is an eminently desirable woman.'

Evalyn stood for what seemed a long time in the same place. Tears filled her eyes and dripped silently on to the carpet.

When she turned round the first thing she saw was the box with Pierre Cartier's necklace. She took it out and fastened it defiantly around her neck.

If I cannot have love, she thought, I will have the best and most outrageous of everything else. She looked at her reflection in the mirror, the flashing jewel on her bosom, the chain of diamonds sparkling. I will have this thing and wear it and it can do its worst! What do I care for its ridiculous magic? If I cannot have a life worth living, every single thing the world can offer me is valueless. But I will smile and pretend until I die.

She turned her head and saw her father regarding her from his photograph. Grief welled in her. Father, Father, why did you have to die? You spent your whole life slaving. You found your El Dorado. Now *I* have the worry of it, but why, *why*, can't it buy just a little bit of happiness?

The need for comfort, even for oblivion, was imperative. She lay back on the rumpled satin sheets and closed her eyes. When Ned came out of his dressing room he walked past her out the bedroom door. She heard his footsteps receding down the landing.

Morphine – the thought came suddenly. It is the only thing that will help me bear the pain of being alive. But she immediately recoiled from this thought, frightened that it had even presented itself, remembering what it had cost her to break from it. She cast around desperately for something to take her mind away from it, and from the aching void within. The Hope Diamond moved against her neck like a caress.

When Pierre Cartier called for the necklace on Monday Evalyn told him she would buy it. He did not seem overly surprised and quietly told her the price was $154,000.

'But there is just one thing – I would like to know more of its story, monsieur, before I sign for it. What happened, for example, to the first person who owned it?'

'The first European, you mean, madame? He was a man by the name of Tavernier. Some say he stole the diamond, in 1668, I believe—'

'Yes, yes, from a Hindu idol. What happened to him?'

'He was eaten by wild dogs, madame.'

Evalyn gulped. 'And after him?'

'It was bought by Louis XIV; it became part of the French Crown Jewels.'

'And the king?'

'He died of gangrene; all his children predeceased him.'

Evalyn stared at the jeweller. 'But such things could happen anyway . . .'

'Indeed, madame! After the king's death the diamond remained with the Crown Jewels until the Revolution.'

'You're not going to tell me the French Revolution was caused by a diamond?'

'Certainly not, madame. It was caused by the misgovernment of a nation over a long period. I am just relating what has been rather foolishly attributed to it, as you asked!'

'I apologise, monsieur. Please go on.'

Cartier inclined his head. 'It was stolen from the Louvre during the Revolution and brought to London, divided into two parts that were wonderously cut and polished. The larger diamond was purchased by a merchant banking family called Hope – hence its name.'

'What happened to the other part?'

'I do not know, madame.'

'And I suppose every single death in the Hope family was blamed on the stone?'

'I hardly think so, madame, but they had their share of tragedies. Eventually Sir Francis Hope, an unfortunate gentleman, madame, forced its sale some years ago to a dealer who in turn sold it to the Turkish sultan.'

'And we all know what happened to *him* and to his empire!' Evalyn interjected, remembering the coffee she had taken with the same sultan, and her visit to his women's prison called a harem. 'All thanks to a diamond! Nothing to do with the intrinsic malignancy of his regime or the march of progress!'

Cartier chuckled. 'I can see you are not persuaded that the stone is evil, madame! I was always struck by . . . your blunt good sense, if you will pardon me for saying so!'

'You must be the first person who ever noticed it!' Evalyn said with a slightly hysterical laugh. 'I will buy your diamond and thumb my nose at its nonsense. Now, if I bought it on the instalment plan . . .'

Before Pierre Cartier left Evalyn asked him one more question.

'Remind me again which idol the stone was supposedly stolen from, monsieur?'

Cartier paused. 'It is only a story, madame . . .'

'None the less . . .'

'A goddess of the Vedic myths – Sita. One of her eyes, I believe.'

Evalyn thought testily: I didn't think it was her nose, unless, of course, she was related to Ned. Though his is not quite blue yet.

This made her laugh privately. She rang to have Monsieur Cartier shown out.

Emily McLean was horrified when she heard that her daughter-in-law had purchased the Hope Diamond. She came to call on Tuesday morning and Evalyn decided to tell her the news before she could hear it from her son. She had the necklace beside her in its box and she opened it to show Mrs McLean.

'You are squandering your fortune buying such things!' her mother-in-law exclaimed. She picked up the jewel appraisingly. 'However beautiful it is, it's something you cannot even wear, with its taint of endless tragedy. How many lives has it touched or blighted?'

'It's only a stone, Mummie, although some say you shouldn't touch it! As far as I am concerned it can no more blight a life than any other stone. And of course I intend to wear it!'

'I've been told it came from some Eastern idol. And that it was owned by people like Marie Antoinette . . .' Mrs McLean restored the necklace to its box. 'We all know what happened to her!'

'The French Revolution had nothing to do with any particular diamond, Mummie,' Evalyn replied, remembering her conversation with Pierre Cartier. 'From what I heard it was long overdue!'

Evalyn closed the box with a snap. But her mother-in-law had the bit between her teeth.

'There were so many other people whose lives were destroyed by it—'

'Everyone goes through tragedy, Mummie. It's the common human lot.'

Mrs McLean started as though she found the comment out of character.

'Is something troubling you, Evalyn?' she asked gently after a moment's silence. 'You are looking peaky, not yourself . . .'

Evalyn shrugged.

'Is it Ned?' her mother-in-law continued in a low voice.

Evalyn let her silence speak for her.

'Is he drinking much?'

'He's out every night,' Evalyn whispered. 'He's seeing someone.'

'He's basically a good boy,' his mother said after a moment. She dropped her voice, 'And you are a woman, and a woman knows how to hold a man!'

But I don't want to know how to hold a man, Evalyn thought fiercely. I don't want to keep him by guile, or pretence, or by exploiting his sensuality.

I want to hold him because he loves me, because he wants to find me, because I inspire his fidelity, because there are things to be discovered together about ourselves and the world . . .

But the matter was too delicate and she did not reply.

'You must return the jewel, Evalyn. Send it back to that Frenchman at once!'

Evalyn's spirit was at a low ebb. She shrugged. 'If it bothers you so much, Mummie, all right. I'll make sure he gets it today!'

She sent it back to Cartier that afternoon. The next day he returned it to her, with a polite note to the effect that the diamond now belonged to *her*, and that at this particular juncture he had no wish to reacquire it.

Evalyn took it out of its wrappings and looked at it half aghast. What have I done? What have I *done*? Even the jeweller doesn't want it back, although he might have negotiated on the price. Have I bought something with a malevolent power that will watch me always?

But common sense reasserted itself. I'm the one who's alive, she thought, so I'm the one with the power. And I can stare down any old diamond any day!

The press got hold of the story and letters began to pour in from people who heard Mrs Evalyn Walsh McLean had become the new owner of the Hope Diamond. They warned her of its curse. One of her correspondents was the actress Mary Yohe, the former wife of Lord Francis Hope who had forced his family to sell the jewel in 1902.

'Get rid of it,' she advised. 'You don't know what you're dealing with. It destroyed my life. Don't let it wreck yours!'

Evalyn looked at the warnings with dismay. She reached for bravado. Are people mad? Do they really expect me to to bow to hysteria?

'It's all blather,' she told her secretary, Nancy, who seemed intimidated by the whole business. 'Just burn the stupid letters. Don't let them bother you . . . What's *this* one?' she demanded with a mirthless laugh, as Nancy put out a hand to cover a sheet of white paper.

The message was in capitals, written in green ink with fine brush strokes. The letters were startling in size, foreign in execution, with a small lip at the end of each word as though the brush had been whipped from the paper.

RAVANA WAITS

The drawing below the message was vibrant in execution. The two women stared at it. It seemed to dance. Alien and male, ten heads and as many limbs, it was hideously alive.

'It's some sort of idol,' Nancy whispered. 'If you ask me, Mrs McLean, he looks like a mutant spider . . .' she turned to look at Evalyn and added, 'waiting to spring.'

That night Evalyn dreamed of him, the man spider. She woke with a cry, put out her hand for Ned. But Ned slept in his smoking room nowadays. She sat up and put on the light. Over there, she knew, glancing at her jewel case, was Sita's missing eye.

Her mind raced over the warnings, lingered on the horrible drawing of the day before, the mutant spider. *Ravana*? It was a name she had never heard.

You'd go mad if you listened to all the nonsense there is in this world, she told herself.

In the morning Maggie Buggy said to her as she passed her in the hall, 'Someone didn't get much sleep last night!'

'I had a nightmare.'

'It's that thing,' Maggie confided, lowering her voice and glancing over her shoulder. 'Get it blessed, for the love of God. That's the only way to knock the divil out of it.'

'What are you talking about, Maggie?'

Maggie tightened her lips. 'You know what I'm talking about – your latest bauble.'

'Oh, Maggie . . .'

'Monsignor Russell will do it. He's a wonderful man!'

A few days later, Evalyn and Maggie had the stone blessed by Monsignor Russell in the ice-cold sacristy of his church. Evalyn put it on a velvet cushion and the priest donned his robes. When he was ready Evalyn noticed that the light from the window had dimmed; she glanced out and saw that the sky had darkened.

The priest began the prayer, raising priestly hands. The light grew dimmer still. Then a growl of thunder reverberated through the church, followed by a flash of lightning that flooded the room with brilliance. From outside came a sudden, ear-splitting sound.

Maggie went white and clutched at Evalyn.

'What's that, in the name of God?'

But the priest appeared unmoved and continued the Latin intonation that called on the power of the Almighty. Evalyn stood stock-still, shocked by the sudden storm, half hypnotised by the Latin.

'If it's not been sanctified now,' she whispered nervously to Maggie when the prayer was over, 'there's no Hope for it!'

Maggie's pupils were dilating and Evalyn realised her pun had fallen on deaf ears.

She opened her long sable coat, fastened the stone around her neck and covered it with her collar.

'Thank you, Monsignor,' she said, pressing a discreet envelope into his hands. 'Thank you very much.'

He showed them out. The day was bright again. But across the road was the smouldering remains of a tree that had been split in two by lightning.

'Oh Lord above,' Maggie whispered, 'do you see that?'

'Of course I see it! It's the result of a storm. We have them all the time!'

'No we don't!' Maggie muttered.

No we don't, Evalyn echoed privately. Oh God, can there really be something here I do not understand?

As the chauffeur drove them home Evalyn said hardly a word, although Maggie was blabbing on about the strange experience they had just had.

'Don't say a word to Mother about this, Maggie,' Evalyn warned eventually. 'She'll just get into a state.'

'I won't open my mouth! The less I have to think about that thing the better I like it.'

'But it's been blessed now.'

Maggie nodded. 'Good thing too.'

Evalyn saw the chauffeur's curious eyes regard them in the mirror.

'You needn't bother with the carriage porch,' she told him. 'We'll get out in the yard.'

As they came in through the service entrance, Maggie clutched her arm.

'What is it, Maggie?'

'Evalyn, don't you notice . . . the ground is *dry*?'

I don't believe this, Evalyn thought. Aloud she said, 'It must have been a very localised storm. It does happen.'

But once she alighted, the sight of the house and the carriage yard seemed so cheerful and normal that her spirits lifted. She ran up the kitchen stairs, eager to share the morning's adventure with her husband. She longed to bridge the stand-off between them. She blamed herself for his unfaith-fulness. She had neglected him. He was repentant, she knew. She could bring herself to forgive him, and they could start afresh. She would make more time for him, spend a little less with Vinson . . .

'Is Mr McLean in?' she asked the butler.

'No, madam. Mr McLean went out about an hour ago.'

'And Master Vinson? Is he in the nursery?'

'Mrs Walsh is walking him in the garden.'

Evalyn ran across the drawing room and let herself out through the conservatory. Her mother was pushing the squeaking perambulator among the shrubs and young trees of the garden.

'Hello, Mother,' she said cheefully.

'You startled me, darling. Vinson and I are just getting some air.'

Sitting up and looking out at his world with round, curious eyes, a dribble on his chin, was a well-wrapped baby.

'Ma-ma,' he cried loudly as soon as he saw her and waved his mittened hands. She bent to kiss him and felt the pull of the now warm necklace as it fell against her clothes inside her coat.

'It's your birthday next week, young man,' she said. 'And we will have a baby party.'

'What does a child of that age want a party for?' Carrie demanded with a half-laugh.

'Mother, he needs to see other babies sometimes! Otherwise he'll think he's grown up!'

'I was wondering where you were!' Carrie said after a moment.

'Maggie and I went for a little drive!'

She was already wondering if it was a silly superstition to have had the diamond blessed. Her mother had joined Mrs McLean in telling her to get rid of the jewel and she dreaded to think of her reaction if informed of the morning's happenings. There's an explanation, she told herself. There has to be! In this country there are all kinds of odd, localised weather patterns.

'Would you like tea, Mother?' she said before her mother could ask her where she and Maggie had gone. 'We could have it in my sitting room.'

'No, thank you, darling, not at the moment.'

Evalyn made an excuse and went indoors. Her shoes rang off the parquet. The house seemed to echo. God alone knew where Ned was, or when he would be home.

She went to the elevator, pressed the button. In her sitting room she shrugged off her coat and sat at her dressing table for a moment, regarding the diamond in the mirror.

You've been tamed now, anyway! she told it with a certain grim satisfaction. You can do your worst! Like it or lump it, the spite has been knocked out of you!

She rang the bell.

In a few moments came a knock on the door. It was Esther's niece, Sharon.

'They told me I could answer the bell, ma'am.'

'I would like some tea, Sharon.'

'Yes, madam.'

Evalyn saw how the girl's black slanting eyes were riveted on the necklace.

'Diamonds!' she told her. 'My new necklace. What do you think of it?'

The girl gazed wonderingly at the gem and grinned with delight. 'It's so beautiful,' she whispered shyly, approaching across the floor to get a better view, and before Evalyn could react, she suddenly reached out and touched it.

'Don't!' Evalyn cried.

'I'm sorry, ma'am!' Sharon exclaimed, drawing back.

'That's all right. I'm just being silly. You can't damage it.'

415

When the door was closed, Evalyn picked up the portrait of her father. You wouldn't have begrudged it to me, Father, and yet you would not have approved! Oh God, how I miss you . . .

She kicked off her shoes, felt the ache in her injured leg as she put her weight on it, caught her reflection in the cheval glass, a young woman ludicrously adorned who limped like an old woman.

Why are they so long about the tea? she wondered after a while. It must be twenty minutes. Surely Sharon was able to convey a simple request to the kitchen.

She rang again.

This time it was Annie who appeared, carrying a small silver tray with a silver tea pot, cream jug, and a cup and saucer.

'You could die of thirst in this house!' Evalyn said irritably. 'It must be half an hour since I asked Sharon.'

The housekeeper was unusually silent. Evalyn looked up at her and registered her pallor.

'What is it, Annie?' she whispered. 'Has something happened?'

'It's the little girl, Sharon,' Annie said, frowning. 'We've sent for the doctor. I'd better get back downstairs.'

No! Evalyn thought, hurrying after her. It can't have anything to do with . . . I will not accept such a preposterous notion for one moment.

'When did it happen?' she demanded as she and Annie went down in the elevator.

'Fifteen minutes ago. She wanted to bring up your tea, but she dropped the tray and started shaking.'

Esther was by her little niece. The child was on a sofa in the servants' sitting room, breathing but unconscious.

When the doctor came, Evalyn left the room and went to her own. When the telephone tinkled she picked it up with relief, sure it would be word that Sharon was all right. But it was Ned.

'I'm at the *Post*. I'll be home late, Evalyn, so don't wait dinner.'

'Oh, Ned, we've had some trouble here. Little Sharon, Esther's niece . . .'

'What about her?'

'She's had convulsions!'

Ned's silence indicated perplexity that she should trouble him with this intelligence.

'Children are always doing that! She'll be all right! And she's only a servant, Evalyn,' he added into the distraught silence. 'What are you getting yourself worked up for?'

'I'm not.'

'Oh, by the way, I met a cousin of yours today,' he added cheerfully. 'Chap I never saw before.'

'Who?'

'A Mr Lafferty. Someone's guest at lunch . . . in Washington on business . . . automobiles . . . He was asking after you.'

Evalyn's heart seemed to stop.

'I hope you asked him to call.'

'He was going back West, Evalyn . . . night train . . .'

Evalyn put the mouthpiece down. She tried to understand the depths of the despair that came to devour her. It was a wild presence against which she was powerless.

She went to a corner of the room and lifted the carpet. Underneath was a small packet of powder she had recently bribed from a druggist, getting him to send it to her in the post. She mixed this with some bourbon from the cabinet in Ned's dressing room, swallowed it, then lay back on her bed.

Help at last! she thought, as the spirits and morphine coursed through her system and every cell in her body relaxed into drugged peace.

Chapter Thirty-Four

After Sharon died the days became a blur. At Vinson's birthday party friends commented on his mother's serenity. Christmas came and went. Evalyn ate little. There was the usual round of festivities and she drank champagne. She wore the Hope Diamond around her neck or in her hair. Sometimes she wore it and the Star of the East together. On her wrists she wore diamond bracelets. She favoured the latest 'Empire line' Paris dresses in crisp, vivid silks that came to just above the ankle, wore them without a corset, as was the latest trend for the very slim. Her laughter was too loud. She did not remonstrate any more when Ned stayed out all night. Sometimes she was nauseous; sometimes she fell asleep at odd hours, on a settee or armchair, and would wake to find one of the servants had covered her with rugs.

Her mother looked at her anxiously. 'You're burning the candle at both ends, Evalyn. You can't keep this up!'

'Nonsense, Mother. When was I happier?'

Baby Vinson was restive in her company, and although she danced around the room to amuse him, he looked at her with doubtful eyes.

Spring arrived and with it the thaw. Carrie had gone to Palm Beach but she wrote and telephoned regularly. For Evalyn some days were better than others, more focused than others, more assured of personal mastery.

It's doing me good; I'll break from it when I want . . .

But despite her self-assurances she knew, in incisive moments of painful introspection between fixes, that the grand solution had become a monster. Every day she needed a little more morphine. It was relatively easy to get if one were cunning, if not morphine then laudanum, if not laudanum then chloral. She forged prescriptions; she paid druggists whatever they wanted. The dazed peace brought her relief from turmoil, and from every anxiety except the one that became the most pervasive – how would she obtain the next supply, and the deeper, more desperate one that surfaced unbidden and that questioned what she was doing to her life.

Ned looked at her strangely, but she didn't need him any more. The absence of any criticism from her, overt or implied, seemed to unsettle him. When he came to her bed one night and reached for her urgently, she turned away from him.

'Have it your own way, Evalyn!' he said angrily. 'But don't blame it on me if we're washed up!'

And as the habit grew, and the dose escalated, she began to withdraw. Sometimes she was nauseous and vomiting, would tell the servants that she was not at home to visitors and spend the day in her suite with the drapes drawn, barely picking at the meals the servants brought. Ned was out most of the day, in his office at the *Post* – or so he told her.

Carrie returned from Florida in April, and although Evalyn had instructed the servants to tell her mother she had a headache and did not want to be disturbed, Carrie insisted on coming straight up to her daughter's room.

'Evalyn, what's this I hear about you hiding yourself away? If you are having bad headaches you must see someone . . .' She pulled back the curtains, turned to the bed and put her hand to her mouth.

'Oh my God, you're ill!'

'I'm not ill, Mother!'

'You've lost so much weight, and you're white as a sheet! And your eyes . . . they look strange . . . Evalyn, what have you done to yourself? I'll get the doctor immediately!'

'No, Mother! Please leave me alone! I assure you I'm fine . . . just tired . . . Let me sleep now and I'll see you at dinner this evening. I had a very late night . . .'

When her mother had left the room Evalyn, dreading the afternoon and evening ahead of her, ordered her car brought to the carriage porch, wrapped herself in a warm woollen 'duster', donned a hat with a veil and slipped downstairs in the lift.

She dismissed the chauffeur and drove alone down Massachusetts Avenue. She drove in a dream. She had no plan, she did not have a destination. She ignored the tooting horns, the vehicles that swerved out of her path. A woman shrieked at her – something unpleasant that she didn't bother to register.

I'll go to Friendship, she thought after a while when the sense of torpor became too much and she no longer could be sure which side of the road she was on; Mummie will be there. She was always a rock.

There was a sudden squeal of brakes, a thump and a crunching sound. Her head hit the steering wheel and there was darkness.

'Are you all right, ma'am?'

The voice was Irish, the moustache red, the eyes blue. But the uniform banished the hazy notion that her father was near. Evalyn nodded, only half aware that a crowd was forming. She raised her head, glanced at the vehicle with which she had collided, a tin lizzie. A man, evidently its owner, was sitting, dazed, on the sidewalk and the car was being pushed to the kerb.

She said to the policeman, 'I hope nobody is—'

'Nothing too serious, ma'am. An ambulance is on its way. But there's a bit of damage to property.'

'I'll pay. But I don't need an ambulance.'

'What is your name and address please, ma'am?'

'I'm Mrs Edward McLean. My address is . . .' But for a mind-numbing moment it escaped her, and she had to search for it in the labyrinths of a brain that no longer wanted to think. 'My address is 2020 Massachusetts Avenue, Northwest. Please send for my husband.'

The policeman wrote something down. His buddy came along.

'Would that be the McLeans who own the *Post*?' he asked.

Evalyn nodded. Her head felt as though it would split; there was a vivid pain behind her eyes.

She half heard the two policemen discussing her and then one of them said, 'Don't worry, ma'am. We're sending a message to your husband.'

Ned arrived just as the wailing siren heralded the arrival of the ambulance. He was the same Ned who had appeared after her father's death – calm, pragmatic, soothing ruffled sensibilities. The owner of the damaged Ford was compensated on the spot; a wad of notes was pressed into his hands. The policemen became like silk.

'My wife hasn't been too well lately,' Ned told them. 'She's under doctor's care and should not have been out.'

He took Evalyn from her car, brought her into his, shut the doors and drove away.

'The first question is this, Evalyn,' he said calmly, 'do you need hospital or home?'

'Home!'

He brought her back to 2020, half carried her to the elevator and up into her sitting room.

'Now,' he said, depositing her on to the settee, 'what is all this? By all accounts you were driving like someone out of bedlam! You're just lucky you weren't killed or didn't kill someone else!'

Evalyn began to weep. She leaned her head back against the cushions and let the tears come. They came in torrents. She wept for her disappointed life, for her departed childhood, for her dead father and lost love, for the brother who had never lived to be a man, for the recent death in the house that was tainted somehow with her guilt. She wept for her lameness, for the marriage that did not nourish her, for the destruction she was wreaking on herself, when she should be the wife and mother she longed to be.

Ned looked on, but evinced only exasperation.

'What is the matter with you, Evalyn? I don't know who you are any more.'

'I'm taking morphine,' she whispered. 'Oh, Ned, I just thought I'd take a little, but it's got me again!'

Ned's face darkened. He did not respond immediately, but he sat down beside her on the settee and after a few moments took her hands.

'You're freezing,' he said. Then he added gently, 'Why have you done this, Evalyn? You broke from it after the accident . . . You were so brave then! Why have you let it claim you again?'

'I don't know . . . I've been miserable! Ever since you told me you that you—'

Ned started. 'Don't pin it on me, Evalyn!' he said sternly, pulling back from her. 'You are making a terrible choice, but it is still your choice! You know what will happen if you go on. It's slavery, maybe death. You'll have to stop. Think of Vinson.'

'I do think of him. Oh Ned, I will stop. I promise I will.'

'When? Right away?'

'Of course. But I must go to bed now. My head is killing me.'

Ned helped her into her room. 'Are you sure you don't want a doctor?'

'I just need to sleep. If I don't feel better when I wake I'll send for him. And please don't upset Mother with all this . . . Will you unhook me?'

He complied.

'I've a good mind,' he said suddenly, 'to get rid of that blue diamond of yours. For all you know, all of our troubles could be due to it.'

'No, Ned! I really do think it's lucky for *me*. I had it with me when I had the accident and no one was hurt. And you were contactable, and the police didn't get officious. Wait and see – it will help me through this.'

'You had it *with* you? In the middle of the afternoon?'

'Yes. I always have it with me! I won't be bullied by a silly diamond or a stupid piece of superstition!' She raised her voice, 'I won't!'

Ned left. Evalyn took off her dress and got into bed. The sleep that came was fitful and troubled by strange dreams in which various animals came to look at her and discussed her among themselves. When she woke the day was advanced and her whole body was crying out for what it craved. She remembered her promise to Ned. 'Tomorrow,' she whispered. 'I'll give it up tomorrow.' She went to one of her secret hiding places, found her powder and mixed it quickly, swallowed it greedily, and waited eagerly for the ecstasy of relief.

But with relief came self-disgust and fear. She knew perfectly well where this road would lead her, knew it unequivocally. As soon as she was herself again, courtesy of the drug that gave her transient normality, she saw the future clearly – a figure that was herself, feeble and wizened, eyes vacant, slobbering. Oh God, don't let me become that awful thing, the woman destroyed. Break me of this.

Only you can break it, Evalyn, a cold interior voice answered her. It is a harsh and terrible journey, but it is all up to you.

She phoned her doctor. He came within the hour.

'I've been in an accident!' Evalyn told him. Dr Hardin took her blood pressure, felt her pulse, listened to her heart, examined her eyes and evinced alarm.

'You should be in hospital.'

'No. No hospital.' She reached out a hand and touched her doctor's sleeve. 'I need your help. I have a confession to make and you must not judge me. I am addicted to morphine.'

The doctor looked at her with shock and concern.

'I became addicted to it six years ago when I was smashed up in that accident I told you about,' she went on. 'I broke from it, but it has me again. And this time I cannot destroy its hold on my own.' She added humbly, 'Will you help me?'

'The trick is to get you off it gradually,' the doctor said after a moment. 'How much are you taking?'

Evalyn told him and saw his eyes widen.

Before the doctor left he put a bottle by her bedside.

'When you desperately need it, take a teaspoonful of this . . . and no more than a teaspoon.'

'Is it morphine?'

'No. A substitute. Now, where is your cache? I presume you have one?'

Evalyn whispered locations around the room to him in the tone of a penitent divulging her sins. He went from one place to the next, from the underside of the carpet to a secret drawer in her bureau, and found her entire illicit store.

'That's all of it. I have no more. Destroy it!'

The doctor went away saying he would call in the morning. But when he did come back the following day he found Evalyn in a coma. The green bottle he had left with her was empty.

It was ten days before Evalyn came back to the world of the living. Two strange women in nurses' uniforms were sitting in the room near her bed. The doctor was talking to Ned by the door, saying something about a sanatorium.

'No! If she has to be locked up we'll have a sanatorium here. The top floor can be used for it. If she were to come out of this dependency into some goddamn madhouse her mind would flip!'

'I won't be locked up!' Evalyn whispered. 'Just don't try to lock me up!'

Instantly they were at her bedside.

422

'How are you feeling, Evalyn?' It was Ned's voice. She opened her eyes, focused them for a moment and closed them with the pain.

'Awful.'

'What do you want to do?'

'I want to fight it and I want to win.'

The days passed. The time of trial was upon her. She walked the house with a nurse at either elbow all night long. When she tried to sleep, nightmarish creatures crept from under her bed and clawed at her. She heard them, saw them, smelled them.

The nurses said, 'Now, Mrs McLean, you're imagining things. There is nothing there.'

'They *are* there!' Evalyn cried. 'Look!'

But the nurses only looked at each other.

The days were easier; she began to catch a little untroubled sleep.

When the doctor came one morning she said to him, 'I am ready for any regime you advise. I am ready for any test. If you leave some morphine tablets here on the table by my bed I won't touch them!'

The doctor looked at Ned, at Evalyn's mother, who hovered anxiously, at the nurses.

'I won't touch them,' Evalyn repeated. 'I need this test. If I can do this, I will be cured!'

Ned nodded at the doctor who left a small bottle of white pills on the nightstand.

All day long Evalyn resisted the lure of the small tablets. She tried to read, but the words danced before her eyes. Her mother tried to make conversation; Evalyn's replies were terse and rambling.

'How is my baby?' she kept asking. 'How is my Vinson?'

'He's very well, Evalyn.'

'I want to see him.'

Carrie brought the baby into his mother's room. Evalyn reached out her arms to him, and Carrie put the child into them. Evalyn held him so tightly and looked at him so fiercely that the boy began to cry. Carrie's own eyes were moist as she took the howling baby back.

'You have everything to get better for. He needs you, Evalyn! Do you want him growing up without you?' She glanced at the nightstand and the glass bottle full of tablets. 'Let me throw these away.'

'No!' Evalyn cried. 'They stay! They are my test and my torment!'

Carrie took Vinson away, settled him, rocked him until he slept, and then went to her own room. The fear that had dogged her since the discovery of Camp Bird had become terror. She had already lost the two people she most loved. And now it seemed that Evalyn was bent on self-destruction.

She kneeled by her bed and prayed.

Night came. For Evalyn there was no sleep. The world had condensed into a small glass bottle filled with white pills. She lay on her side and looked at them. Forces she hardly recognised tried to override her will. Just one, they whispered; just one little pill. It won't matter and you can continue your fight. Dr Hardin did say that you should *ease* yourself out of it . . .

Then she heard the echo of her mother's voice, '*Do you want him growing up without you?*'

'No!' Evalyn cried aloud and she dashed the bottle of pills to the floor. The night nurses were instantly by her bedside.

'What is it?' they asked of their sweat-drenched patient. They looked at the small glass bottle lying overturned on the carpet, and looked at Evalyn.

'I want to go for a walk,' Evalyn said, climbing out of bed. How slick the sweat was; how it covered her like oil, between her breasts, down her back, its scent pungent!

'I need a bath,' she whispered as she crossed and recrossed the landing outside Vinson's door. 'I will not see my child again until I am broken of this! I do not deserve to see him until I am broken of this. I am a human being and not an animal!'

In the morning the doctor said, 'Well done. But you must remember – not a drink, not a cigarette. You must take none of those things until you are fully cured! If you do you will be hooked again!'

Evalyn nodded. She was exhausted. The glass bottle was reinstated on her nightstand. She cared less about it today. She needed real sleep.

After what seemed an eternity the day came when she woke from a sweet sleep to a world she had forgotten, a world that was wholesome, where it was good just to draw breath. She felt washed out, like a rag that someone had put through a mangle. And for a welcome change, neither her bedlinen nor her nightdress was soaked in sweat.

'Would you ask my husband to come up?' she said to the nurse when she had been sponged and scented and her hair brushed.

The nurse came back a little later to say that Mr Mclean was not at home.

'Where is Ned?' Evalyn asked her mother when she came in with a breakfast tray. 'Is he at the *Post*?'

'I don't know, Evalyn,' her mother replied. 'I'm sure he'll be home soon.'

Evalyn ate her breakfast, tasted the wonder of the fresh orange juice, the deliciousness of the coffee, as though for the first time.

But Ned did not come to see her until the afternoon, and then he stood at the bottom of the bed and regarded her stonily.

'I'm cured!' she told him.

'Is that so?' he replied wearily.

'You of all people have no right to the moral high ground, Ned McLean!' Evalyn cried. 'You must be the worst husband in Washington! From what I gather, you didn't come home last night again.'

Ned's face darkened. He made to leave the room.

'Don't go . . . Look . . .'

She took the bottle from the nightstand, unstoppered it and looked inside.

'See . . . I don't need them . . . I don't need them any more!'

'Of course you don't!'

Ned took the tablets from her, put a few into his mouth and chewed.

'What are you doing?' Evalyn screamed.

'They're not morphine!' Ned said. 'They're just placebos! Did you really think the doctor would leave morphine by *your* bed?'

Ned left, saying he was going back to the *Post*. But he did not come home that evening and Evalyn eventually phoned him at the office.

'Ned, aren't you coming home?'

'No. Not tonight!'

'But I need you tonight!'

'Tough, but as I'm the worst husband in Washington, you hardly expect to see me.'

Evalyn felt the old sense of abandonment.

'If you don't come home, Ned, I'm going to . . . drink a double bourbon on the rocks.'

There was an intake of breath at the other end and then Ned's voice said tightly: 'If you do that you know what it will mean! But I won't be blackmailed by you any more, Evalyn Walsh! Drink if you must. The funeral is all yours . . . and Vinson's too, of course. But I'm not coming home!'

He hung up. Evalyn, desperate for comfort, phoned the doctor, who had left a number where he could be contacted at a hotel in Baltimore.

'I've just told Ned I'm going to take a drink. He won't come home.'

There was a bare second's silence before the doctor said: 'Evalyn, get dressed and come over here. At once!'

She complied. His command gave her a sense of direction. Any action was a salve and a distraction. She told her secretary to reserve a suite for her in Baltimore, then ordered her car and took the nurses with her.

When she got to the hotel in Baltimore Dr Hardin was waiting for her.

'So Ned won't come home and you're going to drink?' he enquired gravely.

'That's right.'

'Is that adult?'

'I thought I might find some sympathy from you!'

'You have better things to do with your life, Evalyn, than drink and look for pity!'

Evalyn ordered a tray of cocktails to be brought up. A waiter came and deposited them on a table. She put ten dollars into his hand. He thanked her and left.

When the door had closed Evalyn half expected the doctor to seize the cocktails and throw them away. But he sat still on the other side of the fireplace and regarded her wearily. When she stood up to help herself to a drink he did not move.

As her hand touched the glass, Evalyn felt his contempt. She saw herself suddenly as a spoiled and selfish woman, who had been given too much for too long, and who thought only of herself. For some reason she remembered some words of her father's from long ago. *'Cultivate courage, Daughter. Cultivate endurance! People without endurance are chaff in the wind!'*

She did not drink the cocktails. She moved back, seeing herself with the doctor's jaundiced eye and wondered at the power of the impulse that would have destroyed her. For the first time it occurred to her that maybe disappointment was normal, and that the difficulties life presented were something from which no one was immune.

She sat down again. Tiny bubbles winked on the cocktail glasses, like encouragements to thumb her nose at Fate. But the unblinking eyes of the watchful doctor, who in the last several weeks had worked so hard to pull her through detoxification, reminded her of the price. She thought of the power of narcotics and the power of alcohol and the pain and loneliness of being alive. And, after a little while, she shamefacedly picked the cocktails up, one by one, and poured them into the parlour palm by the window.

She turned to the doctor as she pulled on her gloves.

'Thank you. I have, as you say, better things to do.'

'Where are you going, Evalyn? It's the middle of the night!'

'I have a child and responsibilities. I'm going home!'

Chapter Thirty-Five

When the spring came, Evalyn went back to Paris. She was accompanied by Maggie Buggy.

'I just need some new gowns,' she told Ned, demurring when he offered to come with her. But the real purpose of the trip was an attempt to recapture a sense of her own wholeness. On her own in Paris, she reckoned, she might rediscover the *joie de vivre* she had experienced on that last carefree summer of her youth when she had gone there with Flora Wilson.

'It was the best time of my life,' she remarked to Maggie as they watched the flat French coast grow larger on the horizon. 'Flora was right . . . The last time I was there with Ned—'

'You're not dead yet, my dear girl! You're twenty-five . . . not quite in your dotage!'

They were sitting on the first-class deck, their hats swathed in muslin to defeat the sea wind. A couple leaned on the rail nearby; their low, conspiratorial voices carried back on the wind. On the woman's ungloved hand was a sapphire set in diamonds.

Maggie stared and added in a whisper: 'But you could have left *It* behind, Evalyn.'

'*It*? Maggie?'

'You know what I'm talking about . . .'

'Please!' Evalyn said, clicking her tongue. 'Don't you start!'

'I know . . . I know . . . But I was *with* you that day . . . when Monsignor Russell . . .' Maggie continued, lowering her chin. 'And I remember what I saw and what I heard. If you take my advice you won't wear that necklace again.'

'Will you please allow me to be mistress of my own life?' Evalyn said sharply. 'I was able to dump morphine, and no piece of jumped-up carbon is going to dictate to me now. Which is precisely why I *will* wear it!'

Maggie dragged a sibilant breath through her teeth.

'Anything else,' Evalyn went on dangerously, turning to look at her

427

companion, 'is unthinkable. And we had it blessed, remember. So quit bugging me.'

In the ensuing silence a steward came by, offering them rugs. They covered their knees.

'That grand new ship we're to return on sounds a wonder,' Maggie offered after a moment. 'They're saying it's the length of four blocks.'

Evalyn laughed. Maggie, she thought, was entirely predictable.

'I think you like high living even more than I do, Maggie. We'll have to get our butts back to Cherbourg for April the tenth. Half the people we know will be on board that ship.'

'They say its like for luxury has never sailed the seas,' Maggie replied.

'It should be just up your alley!'

Maggie did not disguise her pleasure. She thought of the descriptions of the vessel – the Aubusson tapestries, the Axminster carpets, the elegant reading room for ladies with a big bow window and a fire, and she sent up a prayer of thanksgiving to the Almighty that she was lucky enough to be employed by millionaires.

'But didn't they give it a queer old name?' she mused. '*Titanic* has a powerful ring to it . . .'

In Paris Evalyn and Maggie stayed at the Bristol. Along the Parisian boulevards the chestnut trees were in new leaf. The cobbled streets, the pavement cafés, breathed the atmosphere of old civilisation and gaiety that Evalyn so loved. Soon she had visited most of the couture houses. In Maison Jane she bought some evening gowns in chiffon and mousseline. She visited Worth and Paul Poiret and Jacques Doucet. She really loved the way the latter used silk. She also liked the new vee neck, although it had been denounced from more than one pulpit, and had doctors warning of pneumonia.

At a soirée in the Ritz, dressed in an oriental-style blue satin gown, with the Hope Diamond as a head ornament, she delighted in finding herself the object of universal attention.

A whimsical voice said in her ear: 'I trust you have no peashooter on your person this evening?'

She turned and looked into a laughing, handsome face she had not seen for a long time. It belonged to President Taft's right-hand man, Major Archibold Butt, whom she had once assaulted through her peashooter.

'Dear Archie, you made me jump! But you'll be relieved to know that you're looking at a reformed character!'

'That is very reassuring, Evalyn. When a fellow sees you he gets a little nervous. But it seems an age since I saw you.'

'Not since Father died. I was out of circulation last year. I was ill.'

He looked at her closely, saw the lines of strain around her eyes and mouth, glanced at the blue stone in the bandeau around her head.

'I hope you're better now. May I compliment you on the fine jewel you have there,' he added, gesturing to her head ornament. 'Is it the famous diamond?'

'It is! And I'm glad you didn't use the word "infamous". It sets my teeth on edge when people act like idiots! But what has you in Paris?'

'Business and pleasure. I've just come from Rome. Met his Holiness. I'm to report back to the President.'

'Is that why you're looking so pleased with yourself?' Evalyn lowered her voice and added coyly, 'Dare I ask, Archie – is there another reason? I heard a rumour.'

Archie smiled, leaned towards her and confided: 'I'm engaged, Evalyn, to the most wonderful, lovable girl. We haven't made it public yet,' he went on, 'but I know I can trust you to keep it under your hat. It's Miss Williams.'

'Colonel Williams's daughter?'

He nodded. 'We'll be announcing it in two months' time; we hope to marry in the spring. Can't wait to see her,' he added. 'I'm heading back home on the tenth.'

'Don't tell me . . . *you're* returning on the *Titanic* too?'

She wondered why all the lights in the room began to fade, why all the voices became a receding rumble, why her own voice sounded tinny in her own ears, as though it came down a long distance line. She registered Archie's voice, its rising note of consternation.

'Are you all right, Evalyn?'

The guests around her gasped when she swayed and dropped her glass. Archie caught her. He helped her to a sofa, kneeling beside her.

'It's only a faint. Keep your head down. Here, let me hold that thing,' he added, taking charge of the bandeau, which had slipped over her forehead. 'Don't worry about your headress. Just relax and I'll whistle up your driver.'

'So what had you fainting last night?' Maggie demanded next morning.

'Don't know, Maggie!'

Evalyn was sitting up in bed, a breakfast tray beside her. Her gown of the evening before was thrown across a chair and the bandeau she had worn was sitting on top of it, winking in the morning sunlight.

'I had only two glasses of champagne,' she went on. 'I came back here sober as a judge!'

'I hope Major Butt didn't think you were . . .'

Evalyn sipped coffee and shook her head.

'Of course he didn't. Look, Maggie . . .' she added hesitantly, 'I've decided to cancel our reservations on the *Titanic*. It's leaving us too little time for what we want to do.'

Maggie's face fell. 'After all the fuss I made to ensure you got one of the best staterooms . . .'

'We can reserve on the *Silver Star* instead. It sails the following week. But it gives me that extra few days in Paris.'

'Are you up to something? You didn't meet—'

'Love's young dream in the Ritz? I'll thank you to remember, Maggie,' Evalyn replied primly, 'that I'm a married woman. Speaking of which – you'd better send Ned a wire and let him know about the change in plan.'

When Maggie had gone she thought of it – love's young dream. Was it a mirage or reality? Would it have been any different with Paul? Would there ever be another chance? And then she thought of little Vinson. 'You, my darling,' she said with a sigh, 'will always come first.'

Less than four weeks later, Evalyn, too shocked for tears, came home to a country bewildered and in mourning. Ned seemed happy to see her and embraced her lovingly.

'I'm so damn glad you cancelled. Wasn't it terrible about poor Butt. The President is in an awful way over it. You heard how the poor guy stayed on the ship when he might have escaped?'

'I know. Archie gave his life to save women and children.'

'And Astor died like a gentleman too,' Ned said, 'and poor old Strauss . . . his wife wouldn't leave him, Evalyn. Did you know that?'

'She loved him, Ned, and he loved her!'

Ned, looking a little maudlin, suddenly crushed her against him. 'Would you have done that for me?'

Evalyn did not know how to respond.

'*I* would . . . for you!' he said.

Evalyn knew that this was true. In a major crisis Ned would be a hero, and this knowledge was part of the glue that bound her to him. A lump formed in her throat.

'Oh Ned . . . hopefully we'll never be in that position.'

Little Vinson, after regarding his mother suspiciously for a short while, put out his arms and cried, 'Mamma!'

She picked him up and covered him with kisses, listened to her mother recount with grandmotherly chagrin his latest achievement – the word 'No'.

'He *shouted* it out when I was trying to feed him stewed prunes, Evalyn.'

'I'm glad he's learned it, Mother. It's the most important word in any language!'

She went to bed early. She needed sleep; a part of her was still throbbing to the great engines of the liner. Another part was still shaking at the immensity of the tragedy that had overtaken people she had known, and at her own narrow escape. Glancing around her room she saw that her trunks were already unpacked – all save her jewel case which Esther would not touch.

When Ned returned from his night life at four in the morning he went to her room. She woke and watched him cautiously as he sat down on the edge of her bed.

'I didn't tell you how much I've missed you, old girl!' he told her woozily. 'And to think that you might have been on board that . . . It just wouldn't be the same without you!'

'Wouldn't it?' Evalyn said. She reached out and pulled from his sleeve a long blonde hair.

Ned regarded it with annoyance.

'People lose hairs all the time, Evalyn, without it meaning anything,' he said defensively.

'I wish I could believe you!'

'Of course you can believe me. I've been thinking only of you all the time you were away! I know I haven't been a perfect husband; I want things to change. I'll go easy on the juice from now on . . . So what do you say we put the past behind us – concentrate on the future?'

This was so much in line with her own longing that Evalyn could not help the rise of her heart. She looked at her husband's eager face and scanned his black evening dress for another blonde hair. But all was relatively pristine.

'Where would you like us to spend the summer?' Ned went on. 'Colorado? Bar Harbor? Newport? Personally I favour the latter. It's the most fun!'

Newport? Evalyn thought. Like Vinson I could scream *No*. I could say I never want to see that place again! But it would not be true. Newport is burned into me, for better or worse. If there is a beloved ghost there, flying along Tuckerman's Avenue, or in the soft breeze from Easton Bay, I will be glad to find him!

'At least Alfie Vanderbilt wasn't on board the *Titanic* after all,' Ned added suddenly. 'Wasn't it a good thing he stayed behind in London? Early reports said he had been lost.'

Evalyn remembered Alfie's white face on Easton Bridge seven years before, and she burst into tears.

'There now,' Ned said uncomfortably, patting her hand. 'I shouldn't have disturbed you. Sleep well and we'll decide in the morning.'

They went to Newport.

Evalyn visited every part of the summer idyll where she and Vin had spent time together. On 19 August she went out alone, retraced the route from the Clambake Club down Tuckerman Avenue to Easton Bridge, got out of her car and looked into the creek that flowed innocently from Easton's Pond into the bay.

How to turn the clock back, rewrite history? If only *something* had occurred that would have prevented that fatal journey. Vin would be alive today, one of the country's most eligible bachelors, with every socialite mother in Newport angling to have him at her luncheons and soirées.

When she got home Evalyn took out the last photographs of him, the jaunty seventeen-year-old so full of life, and put her finger over the sardonic smile she had known so well. The eyes looking at her from the past were full of youth and expectancy.

Vin, my darling brother, I never said goodbye. And I never will, because the word is nonsense. But, if I am to go forward, I have to bid you farewell . . . until we meet again . . .

Evalyn immersed herself in the social round. She threw a party for two thousand people. The dining tables were 75 feet long and there were 100 people at each table The guests were regaled by Paul Whiteman's thirty-piece jazz band. For dancing there was Meyer Davis's band.

She gave a dinner party for Ned's Aunt Mamie and Uncle George. It was to be a small, select affair, only forty-eight guests.

What can I do to make it really special? she wondered, and hit on a novel idea. At each table there were wire umbrellas, each covered with growing orchids, a fountain, and changing lights. The dinner cost $48,000.

But the summer's pleasure was about to end. A telegram for Ned came from Bar Harbor. It arrived on a particularly lovely day when Aunt Mamie had just called to discuss her own forthcoming garden party. 'MUMMIE HAS BAD COLD COME AT ONCE'.

Mamie immediately cancelled the party and set out for Maine with her nephew and his wife.

Mrs McLean was lying propped up against pillows in her shingled summer residence at Bar Harbor. She greeted her family in a wheezing voice and tried to smile. But she looked waxen, and was having trouble breathing. John R. sat by her bedside. The Bar Harbor house was silent except for the servants' careful footsteps and the murmur of the sea through the open windows.

They sent for Dr Barker, Mrs McLean's physician, but he was in North Carolina and the journey of thirteen hundred miles could not be accomplished in a day. The sick woman's condition disimproved during the night.

A fatigued Dr Barker arrived at Bar Harbor on 8 September, and was conducted immediately to the sick woman's room. The family waited downstairs in the drawing room and regarded each other in a virtual silence.

Evalyn was acutely aware of Ned, who stood by the open French window; of John R., who paced the floor; of Aunt Mamie, who sat beside her and nervously cleared her throat. She was aware of how the lace curtains stirred, how the sunlight was muted by the striped awnings, how the clock on the mantelpiece ticked out threats in monotone.

Her heart was in her shoes. She loved and respected the woman who was fighting for her life in the room above their heads, remembering all too well how she had helped her reconcile herself to life in Washington.

The ceiling creaked; they heard a door close softly in the landing and the doctor's step descending the stairs.

The family rose to their feet.

Dr Barker entered the room, looked at John R. gravely and shook his head.

'Pneumonia . . .'

Ned drew Evalyn through the French windows to the lawn.

'Did Mummie ever touch that damn diamond?' he demanded. 'The one you said was so lucky for *you*?'

Evalyn smelled the bourbon on his breath. She saw the sunlight sparkle on the ocean beyond the lawn. She remembered how Mummie had come to see her after she had bought the diamond from Pierre Cartier.

'Once maybe . . . around the time I bought it . . . But—'

'She was all right until it came along!' Ned cried. 'She was strong as an ox! You should put it out with the trash! In fact, if you don't I will.'

Evalyn did not respond. It was neither the time nor the place for a row. She had determined she would not be influenced about the diamond, and although this crisis had nothing to do with it, an undermining shiver crept along her spine.

'I hope you have never let Vinson touch it!' Ned added with fierce sibilance.

Evalyn, very pale now, shook her head. She was remembering with sudden, unaccountable terror the time Vinson had reached out for the stone and she had stopped him.

'No, he never has . . . and I never will allow it . . .' She glanced at Ned who was breathing heavily. 'I promise you, Ned, over my dead body!'

'Or his,' Ned replied brutally. 'That's what I'm afraid of . . . *his!*'

Evalyn fought the irrational fear that lurked just out of reach.

Hadn't the jewel been with her in Paris, and hadn't she cancelled her reservation on the one ship where she might have died? But poor Archie had had it in his hands, she remembered with a sick sensation. Poor dear Archie and his poor bereaved Miss Williams . . .

As the hours passed the family waited around Mrs McLean's bed. The minister came and prayed. John R., his powerful, shrewd face ashen, spoke to his wife in a low voice full of love. Eventually he signalled to the doctor who approached and took his patient's pulse. He turned with grave compassion to John R.

'I am very sorry, Mr McLean . . .'

John R. kissed his wife's lips, whispered something to her no one else could hear, and closed her eyes.

Ned burst into a passion of tears and threw himself on his mother's body.

'Mummie, Mummie, oh, *Mummie* . . .'

It was, Evalyn thought, tasting the salt in her own mouth, like the wail of the damned.

When their year of mourning was up Ned, with ill-concealed exasperation, watched his wife prepare again for dinner parties. He watched her dance with other men and he could not hide his jealousy; he suspected everyone of having designs on her. He frequently refused to accompany her and went out alone, declining the following morning to confirm where he had gone.

'Never mind, Evalyn. If you must insist on going to those ridiculous parties you should remember that I don't have to endure them as well.'

If we had less money, Evalyn thought, I wonder would we have the kind of trust that belongs to people who only have enough. Whoever said that possessions possess you was right.

So why not get rid of them? came the prompt, reminding her for a moment of Paul Lafferty, and his focused, enquiring eyes.

She answered honestly.

Because without them, at this stage, I would not know how to live!

'But it's up to you to try bringing him round,' Alice Longworth, née Roosevelt, said to Evalyn that evening when the subject of Ned's absence came up. 'Most of the men are secretly wild as tomcats! If they were given their heads they'd spend all their time in the Little White House!'

'The *what*?'

Alice looked at her questioningly, and then laughed.

'Haven't you heard about it? Your own father-in-law started it. It's behind the offices of the *Post*. A nice little house, with a well-stocked bar, pink bedrooms and plenty of pink young women!'

'You mean a brothel?' Evalyn cried.

'Keep your voice down, for heaven's sake. There's hardly a man here who hasn't been there, and you can see for yourself how urbane they appear. But the girls from the Little White House could tell you another story! One of them had her skull broken recently when she got in the way of a champagne bottle that was thrown across the room, but it was all hushed up.'

'You mean . . . she *died*?'

Alice nodded.

'Money again,' Evalyn said. 'Throw enough of it at anything and you never have to face the consequences of what you do!'

'You're not in any position to complain about money!' Alice said. 'Look at you, dressed to kill, wearing the most infamous jewel in the world!'

Evalyn shrugged. She looked at the men in evening dress, trying to imagine them transformed by licence and lust.

'*La nuit, tous les chats sont gris,*' she muttered.

'What did you say?'

'It's a French proverb,' Evalyn said. ' "At night all cats are grey"!'

'True!' Alice replied, laughing heartily. She lowered her voice. 'If you want to keep your particular tom on the straight and narrow you should insist on accompanying him when he goes out! That's the only way of keeping him on a leash!'

'I don't particularly want to be a tomcat trainer,' Evalyn said, 'or to walk around with him hissing and scratching on a leash. He's bigger and stronger than I am!'

Even though both women dissolved in laughter Evalyn was determined to stick to her resolve. She would make one last attempt to make something of her relationship with Ned. But she conceded that if he were really visiting the revolting Litte White House, she could not endure it.

When she mentioned it to him in passing the following day, he said he had never heard of it.

'Tell me, Ned,' she asked him then, relieved at this intelligence, 'what would make you really happy?'

Her husband looked at her in surprise.

'Happiness is not something that can be had to order, Evalyn! If we've learned anything we must have learned that!'

'I know. But if, for example, we were to buy a farm and live there for part of the year – you would like that?'

'Would you do that for me? Give up Washington?'

She nodded.

'You're very kind to me, Evalyn,' he said in a low voice. 'I'm not a great husband, but I do care about you . . . a great deal . . .'

Evalyn swallowed. 'I saw an advertisement the other day,' she went on. 'Black Point Farm near Newport is on the market. What would you say if—'

'Wonderful idea! It's next door to Alfie and Reggie Vanderbilt!'

Oh please, God, Evalyn prayed, let this be the turning point. I don't expect anything again to match the happiness I had in Ouray, the bliss of being with Paul against which I have made the mistake of measuring everything. But I will play my part, I will be the best wife in the world, if You will only let Ned and me have a new beginning.

435

Chapter Thirty-Six

Evalyn stayed close to her husband as much as possible. She followed his country pursuits and ignored the social ones she had come to love; she learned how to drive horses; she went with him to Quebec for the fishing and shooting, and quantities of salmon and caribou paid for her decision. The Ned she knew on these expeditions was different to the Ned she knew in Washington – boyish in his enthusiasms, kind and amusing in private. She was almost in love with him again, but cautiously so.

Black Point Farm was a haven. With a staff of thirty Evalyn felt herself cocooned. The war that closed over Europe was hardly a murmur here, a rumble from a great distance.

On 4 July, Reggie Vanderbilt came to Black Point on a visit and suggested to his hosts that they go to the casino at Narragansett Pier to celebrate Independence.

Evalyn demurred. She did not want to leave Vinson, who always looked at her wistfully when she told him she was going out for the evening. She didn't want Ned to go either.

'You needn't come if you don't want,' Ned said, 'but you can't spend your entire life mollycoddling that child.'

No, Evalyn thought in a burst of private candour, it's *you* I have to mollycoddle. But she said nothing of her apprehension that he would gamble until dawn, and she put Vinson to bed with kisses and promises of coming in to look at him when she returned. Then she climbed into their new Isotta-Fraschini beside Ned, carrying a small sack of diamonds with which to adorn herself later. They hired a ferry, crossed choppy Narragansett Bay, found the hotel and dressed for dinner.

Ned and Reggie met up with several of their cronies in the casino and in no time the cocktails were flowing. After dinner Evalyn refused everything except black coffee and when they went to roulette she was the only member of the party who was sober. Ned was at a different table. Evalyn played lightly and lost. All of her antennae were alert to what her husband was doing nearby, but she could not see him because a small group had clustered around his table. She excused herself and went to find him, stood for a moment behind the croupier, saw he was watching Ned intently from behind his green eyeshade. Over Ned's table hung an air of tense expectancy, like one that might attend a man crossing a cataract on a tightrope.

When Evalyn saw him her heart dropped. He presented a strange sight. His eyes were glazed, his mouth hung open; he was drooling and seemed half dead to the world. In front of him was a mountain of chips in disarray. He barely seemed aware of them, fumbling when he moved.

'What's going on?' she demanded sharply. She had never seen Ned like this, not even when drunk to the point of saturation.

'What does it look like, lady? This gentleman owes the house fifty-five thousand dollars.'

'Does he indeed?' Evalyn raised her voice until everyone in the room could hear. 'He's obviously incapable of playing roulette or anything else! He's my husband and I'm taking him home.'

She put a hand on Ned's shoulder and shook him gently. 'Come on, Ned. Time to go.'

Ned stirred and rose to obey. The casino owner, alerted by the croupier, came swiftly with pen and paper.

'You must sign this, sir,' he said to Ned, putting the paper on the table. 'You owe the house . . .'

'He'll sign nothing,' Evalyn cried. 'It's your own fault. You should not have let him play. It wouldn't surprise me if you have poisoned him!'

'If he won't sign now he stays here until he does!'

Evalyn looked at the soft, greedy face before her and rage came in murderous waves.

'Oh no,' she said softly, 'he does nothing of the sort. What makes bullies like you think you can get away with any kind of crap you dish out?' She put an arm around Ned. I wish I had a gun, she thought. I could kill the whole army of leeches.

She called out, 'Reggie!'

Reginald Vanderbilt left his table to find Evalyn in the middle of a small and fascinated crowd.

'I've a very loud and penetrating scream, Mr Whoever-you-are,' she said in a dangerous voice to the flabby casino owner, 'and the police will be here in no time. If that's what you want it's fine by me.'

Reggie helped Ned to the door. The crowd made way.

'You haven't heard the end of this,' the manager hissed at Evalyn.

She was shaking with fury at the way the bloodsuckers waited perennially in the woodwork, at the setback this represented in her relationship with Ned after all her work of nurturing it, and at the certainty that if she had not been there to stop him, he would have signed anything.

'He needs a doctor,' she said to Reggie when they were back in the hotel. 'Even when he's been drinking all day I've never seen him in this state. He's more like a doped horse than a man!'

Two days later the blood sample results confirmed that Ned's drink had been spiked.

'You're a target,' Evalyn told him. 'You could ruin us. Is that what you want . . . to run through Vinson's inheritance? Why do you put yourself in a position where crooks can do what they like with you? I thought you had put all that behind you.'

Ned was defensive.

'You're not such a saint yourself—'

'I'm not! But I'm not a liability either. And that's what you're becoming Ned, a liability!'

'Makes a change, doesn't it?' he sneered. 'Only two years ago *you* were in the rats.'

'But I dumped it, Ned. I dumped morphine. Please do the same with drink and I'll join you as a teetotaller.'

Ned's laugh rang hollow.

'Look, we're going to Marble House tomorrow evening,' she went on in a cajoling voice. 'Will you, just for that one evening, drink water? And I will too.'

The occasion at Marble House was a 'Chinese ball' which Mrs Alva Vanderbilt Belmont was holding in her Chinese pagoda, erected at the end of the garden, and directly overlooking the Cliff Walk and the sea. It felt strange to be so near Beaulieu, the last house Vinson had ever known.

The ball was a luminous affair. As darkness fell, the lawn and the red pagoda were lit with lanterns; the marble of the mansion glowed, and the talk and laughter of the guests rose and fell above the swish of the sea. Alva's daughter, Consuelo, was present. She was married to the ninth Duke of Marlborough, and was the mother of two sons.

'I will be returning to England next week,' she informed Evalyn. 'But everything is so uncertain since the war broke out that I'm sick with worry about the voyage. The German navy is rumoured to have a considerable presence in the Atlantic.'

'Surely they wouldn't bother a transatlantic liner!'

'Perhaps not, but one cannot help being anxious.'

The talk turned to the question of female suffrage, something dear to the heart of Consuelo and even dearer to her mother, who was already a leader of the American women's suffrage movement.

'. . . We must shelve it for the duration of the war,' Consuelo said. 'But afterwards . . .' She lowered her voice and added, 'Mother will not rest,

438

you know, until justice for women is achieved! Did you see her new tea service with "Votes for Women" written on every cup and saucer?'

Evalyn laughed and said she had not. But privately she was thinking, as she watched her remarkable hostess move among her guests: *that* woman has a passion. She knew that, forty years earlier, when Alva Smith had married into the newly wealthy Vanderbilts, she had forced New York society to accept them. Later she had thumbed her nose at the same society to divorce her husband, and had remarried another wealthy man, Oliver Belmont. Now she was the mistress of two great houses and of retinues of servants. And still she put her vast energies into something that for her could yield nothing in worldly terms, and would heap abuse on her.

What is it that drives such women? Evalyn wondered. Maybe it is something that I need too – passion and vision . . . for something more than saving my marriage to Ned.

She looked down at the blue diamond that hung around her neck. It seemed to say, 'But I am your obsession.'

Oh no you're not, Evalyn thought grimly. I've put you in your place!

Her reverie was broken by a cry from across the room.

'How dare you?'

Mrs Vincent Astor was staring haughtily at Ned. She was scarlet. Ned was grinning, looked dishevelled, and was obviously drunk.

Oh God, what has he done this time? Evalyn wondered. She crossed the room; put a hand on his arm.

'Come on, Ned, time to go home.'

'No!' he shouted, pulling back from her. 'I suppose you want to be rid of me, Evalyn, so you can have it off with these fancy boys.'

He gestured at the male guests. 'All these randy bucks . . . Do you think I don't know what goes on? Ha, ha . . . Do you think I don't know what they're like? And what you're like?'

Evalyn was too mortified to reply. Standing beside her was Harold Vanderbilt, who had escorted her into dinner, and his sister, the Duchess of Marlborough. They glanced at her pityingly and pretended not to have heard.

'I'm going home,' she told him. 'You can stay if you want.'

'It's disgusting, if you ask me,' Ned shouted after her. 'Opening your legs to every man jack of them . . .'

Afterwards, Ned avoided any confrontation with his wife. He left Newport the following morning. Evalyn went in person to her hostess to apologise for her husband's behaviour.

'Don't worry, Evalyn,' Alva Belmont said sympathetically. 'We all know it's not your fault. Look, I'm giving a small party for Consuelo tomorrow and I would love you to come . . . on your *own*!'

Evalyn refused the invitation. She knew she was being pitied. She did not know where Ned was, but she was sure he was too ashamed to look her in the eye.

I would be better off on my own, she thought. No matter how hard I try, my whole existence is mortgaged to his whims!

Ned had gone to Bar Harbor. When he telephoned to say how sorry he was and how much he really loved her, Evalyn told him she never wanted to see sign nor light of him again.

He began to send telegrams full of longing. Evalyn ignored them, but as the days went by and the telegrams continued to flow, sometimes in a private code they had devised in their early days, her heart began to lift again.

Maybe he does really love me, she thought. Perhaps our marriage can be saved. After all, nothing is as important as love. Like faith, it can move mountains. And like faith it can reform an alcoholic, and make him once more a man . . . It *has* been done before; it *can* be done again.

Her friends remarked on the change in her.

'You're looking so much better, Evalyn,' Alice Longworth told her. 'Dare I ask if Ned has anything to do with it?'

'He's contrite. He wants us back together.'

'Well, don't relent overnight. Men never appreciate anything they can have for nothing. In fact,' she added, looking sideways at her friend, 'you should consider carefully whether you should relent at all!'

'I've thought of that, Alice. But I must know that I have tried everything . . . for little Vinson's sake . . . And for mine too.'

The next telegram from Ned said: 'URGENT PAPERS TO BE SIGNED STOP ABSOLUTELY NEED TO SEE YOU'.

Was this a ruse or was there genuinely business that required her signature? Vinson watched Evalyn anxiously at the breakfast table as she read the wire.

'Is it from Papa?' he asked in a small voice.

'Yes, darling.'

'Is he coming home soon?' he asked wistfully.

Evalyn looked into her son's innocent, longing eyes. The sense of his fragility and loneliness struck deep.

'We'll be joining him soon,' she said. 'Are you pleased?'

Her son's radiance was answer enough. She sent Ned a telegram to say she was coming on the night train and fantasised for a while about the sort of life they could lead in an atmosphere of love and reconciliation. My God, she whispered as her heart rose before the prospect of a sober and reliable Ned, life could be paradise.

But an hour before she was due to leave she received another cabled message: 'NO NEED FOR YOU TO COME UNLESS YOU WANT TO'.

Evalyn went to her room, ordered her maid to unpack her luggage. She sat in silence.

He's ill, she thought. It's not an ordinary illness, it's something to do with his mind! He was failed and damaged in some way long before I met him. Did they know – the McLeans? At some level were they aware of how seriously he was impaired? Did they dump him into my lap and sigh with relief that he had someone to mind him for ever?

He could have been a wonderful man, her pride insisted.

Oh yes, she answered, but instead he has become a player of silly games, delighting in his power to hurt. Can he be cured? How much more of my life should I pour into sustaining him? Is not the sensible thing, for all our sakes, Vinson's too, to walk away for good?

She closed up Black Point Farm and took a first-floor wing of The Breakers, the great house at Palm Beach, a namesake for the famous mansion at Newport. But she was worried about Vinson; his gravity was becoming more and more pronounced. He spoke repeatedly of his father.

'I thought we were going to be with Papa. I don't like Palm Beach. Mother, I thought that we would join Papa. When are we going . . .?'

'I don't know just yet, darling.'

'Well, when is *he* coming to fetch us?' he persisted quietly.

My boy is such a man compared to his father, Evalyn thought. He is in pain, but he has a capacity for endurance. He does not even have a child's life. He spends so much time with adults that he hardly talks like a child any more. Someday perhaps, *he* will hold the torch of this family high again!

She decided to take him away from Palm Beach. She bought a cottage in Hot Springs in Virginia. There, she thought, away from prying eyes, she would make her separation from Ned a finality, begin a new life and somehow salve the sore heart of her little boy.

But Ned was again sending telegrams: 'WILD ABOUT YOU MY DARLING STOP DONT LEAVE ME'.

Evalyn found she was on an emotional roller-coaster ride. Don't be a mug, she told herself.

She stuck to her plan, took the train to Hot Springs.

Ned, alerted by his secretary as to his wife's movements, boarded the train at Jacksonville and surprised his family.

Vinson gave a whoop of delight when he saw his father. He turned to his mother and said fervently, 'Thank you, Mama.'

Ned looked wonderful – handsome, dashing, elegant; and perfectly sober. It was hard to believe he was the same person as the woozy, foul-mouthed individual who had insulted her in public.

Love is like a desert plant, she thought. You might think aridity has killed it, but the first few drops of water has it blooming again. Tears started in her eyes.

Ned took her into his arms.

'I so love you, Evalyn,' he whispered into her ear. 'I know I don't deserve you. I've been worse than a pig. I've let you down! Can't we try again? And this time I *promise* it will be all right! I never want to see another drink as long as I live. I couldn't bear it . . . to lose my best friend and my only child . . .'

It was easy to love him again in that moment. And as Vinson leaned against his father with adoring eyes, hope rose unbidden for a new chapter.

What should I do now? Evalyn wondered. Hold out for a divorce or try just one last time?

Father never gave up, she thought after a while. *He* stuck with what he had committed to. I must do the same! I must rescue Ned somehow. He is too important a person in Vinson's life to allow him to be destroyed!

Perhaps if we went back to country living . . . she mused. But not at Black Point. It's too near Newport. There's Belmont, the stud farm at Leesburgh, Virginia that Ned bought with money he inherited from Mummie.

'If we try again, Ned, would you like to live in Belmont?'

He looked delighted.

'But what about your friends, Evalyn? You're a city mouse after all.'

'I was a country girl long before I ever met you, Ned McLean. I'll still see my friends when I want. But I know how much you *need* your horses, dogs and your guns!'

The parental reconciliation calmed Vinson, who relaxed into childhood, delighting in the new toys his father had brought for him and in the sight of his parents together again. Ned was as good as his word: he stayed on the dry; he was fun to be with. He was absorbed in his country pursuits. Life was quiet and full. Vinson had a governess and he showed a keen scholastic aptitude that made both parents proud.

Ned rode every day. He was teaching Vinson, and the boy was making good progress.

'Can I have a brother . . . or a sister?' he asked his mother one day at lunch.

'I've been meaning to mention it myself,' Ned said slyly. 'Vinson and I could do with an addition to the family!'

'Please!' Vinson said, looking from one of his parents to the other, perplexed at the sudden mirth. 'Where do you get babies from, anyway?'

'The fairies,' Ned said. 'Isn't that right, Evalyn? The most beautiful lady fairy in the world.'

Evalyn replied with happy laughter, 'Do you think you are up to it?'

It will be fine, she thought. It will be fine. Life is back on course and everything will be all right.

442

Chapter Thirty-Seven

Evalyn's second son was born on 31 January 1916 after a labour that was neither as long nor as perilous as the first. They called him John after Ned's father. She wondered as she held him tenderly to her breast if he and Vinson would, in due course, take over the publishing empire of their grandfather.

'Two brothers,' she said to an ecstatic Ned. 'A perfect business partnership!'

'Two brothers?' Ned teased her. 'Only *two*?'

'You shouldn't suggest to a woman who has just given birth to go through it again!' Evalyn cried. 'Or if you do, you needn't complain about the black eye.'

Ned laughed and dodged out of range.

'It is true we have only two newspapers,' he said musingly after a while, seating himself by her bed, 'but who knows, there may be more. I have some plans . . .'

Evalyn's heart was full. The thought of a sober and industrious Ned taking up the reins of power, forging an even greater empire to leave his sons, was satisfying in the extreme. He had honoured the promise made more than a year ago – or almost honoured it. When he did drink he did it in moderation. These days she never saw him drunk.

I am proud of you, Ned McLean, she told him silently as she cradled her new baby, now two days old and peering at her with half-opened milky-blue eyes. So proud of my whole family, she added, looking at her darling Vinson as he bent over his new sibling with an expression of wonder and delight, and at her mother who stood behind him, beaming and cooing at her new grandson.

John R. was announced. He breezed into the room, filling it as usual with his vitality, kissed Evalyn's forehead and looked at the latest McLean, who was soundly asleep.

'Well done, Evalyn. I always knew you were a good girl!'

'That's what you said the last time, Pop,' Evalyn said drily. 'You make it sound like I'm rendering *you* a personal service!'

443

'You are. I need grandsons, future steering for the *Post* and the *Enquirer* – isn't that right, Carrie?'

Carrie nodded absently. She was bending down to hear something Vinson was whispering and, in a moment, both of them had left the room.

John R. looked at Ned, who was lounging by the bedside, long legs crossed.

'*You're* looking mighty pleased with yourself!'

'What's wrong with that?' Ned replied laconically. 'I've plenty to be pleased about!'

'He thinks I should go into production again as soon as possible, in case you buy another paper!' Evalyn said.

John R. laughed and then scowled at his son.

'The pity is that I have to rely on my grandsons. *You* couldn't manage a paper to save your life!'

'I might surprise you yet, Pop,' Ned replied with an edge to his voice. 'Evalyn and I might buy our *own* paper.'

'Throw your money away on something more sensible, Evalyn, that's my advice. Buy yourself another diamond to match that blue one of yours . . . I presume you still have it?' he added. 'I never actually saw you wear it.'

'Mummie didn't like it, so I never wore it in 1 Street or Friendship. But Ned will take it out if you want to see it.'

'Gems will always hold their value,' John R. went on when Ned produced the leather case and handed it to his wife.

'That's what I always say,' Evalyn replied with a laugh. 'I keep telling Ned—'

'Provided you keep them insured,' Ned said. 'And you don't.'

John R. whistled when he saw the Hope Diamond lying in its open box.

'Some stone, Evalyn! You should keep it in a vault!'

'Nonsense!' she replied. 'I don't know what it's been up to before I bought it, but it's *my* lucky charm. I had it here with me when I gave birth, and you see how lucky I've been. You were lucky also . . . another grandson. So don't be complaining about this diamond! Anyway, no one touches it, except me.'

'Extraordinary colour . . .' her father-in-law said. 'I bought my Emily sapphires, but the blue doesn't compare. I don't wonder you're so fond of it. Pity about its reputation.'

'You're not superstitious, are you, Pop?'

He turned his astute and wily gaze on her and gave a curt, dismissive laugh.

'I wouldn't be a bit surprised if that Frenchman had made it all up just to get you interested. But one thing I *do* know – luck is made by using your head, and lost by not using it. Your little Irish soul is looking for reasons outside of yourself.'

Before Evalyn could stop him he had picked up the necklace and admiringly held it to the light.

'And, speaking of Ireland,' he went on when he had restored the jewel to its box, 'it's beginning to look as though the tension in your father's old country is going to burst one of these days.'

'Why do you say that?'

'As things stand, an amateur army they call the Volunteers have been out on Dublin streets – in full uniforms with fixed bayonets, carrying out various exercises! And the British Government just sticks its head in the sand. It thinks it will all go away!' He added with a harsh chuckle, 'I so enjoy watching the arrogant digging themselves a pit!'

'You are such a cynic, John R.! I must ask Nancy to cut out the articles on Ireland from the *Post* . . .'

Carrie came back into the room, Vinson behind her. He was holding something behind his back.

'Oh, Mother, let me see,' he cried, making a beeline for the blazing necklace. Evalyn put out her hand to fend off his, and closed the box.

'No, darling.'

Vinson's face darkened. 'But I only wanted to *see* it.'

Carrie touched him on the shoulder. 'Never mind about the necklace. Show your mother the card.'

'It's for the baby,' the boy said, holding out a folded piece of stiff cream paper. Evalyn took it, opened it and saw the drawing, in a painstaking childish hand, of a fat female figure looking down at a stick-like baby in what appeared to be a cradle. The woman was coloured pink and the baby blue. The legend underneath said: 'WELCOME TO MY NEW BROTHER'.

'Did you do this yourself, Vinson?'

The boy nodded proudly and tried to show his handiwork to his new sibling.

'The baby can't read yet,' Evalyn said gently, 'but he loves you,' she hugged him to her, 'as we all do!'

'Can I look at the necklace now?' Vinson asked, turning his innocent gaze on his mother. 'I promise not to scratch it!'

'Not at the moment, darling,' Evalyn said, alarmed at the sudden, sneaking panic in her heart.

John R. stood to take his leave.

'As soon as you feel up to it, Evalyn,' he said expansively, 'I'd like you to hostess a dinner party in the 1 Street house. It'd be like old times, eh? What do you say?'

Evalyn thought of the echoing rooms of her father-in-law's Washington home where once she had learned how to dance, and where a clumsy boy had stood on her instep.

'I remember the first time I went there,' she said. 'Mummie was so sweet. It was she who made me like dancing.'

She saw the immediate introspection, the loneliness, in John R.'s eyes at the mention of his wife, and could have bitten her tongue.

'It's damned queer getting old,' John R. said, suddenly gloomy. 'It's not something you become; it's something that's *foisted* on you . . .'

We are never prepared for age, Evalyn thought as she watched her father-in-law's brooding face, which *is* odd, because we see it around us all the days of our lives.

'You know I'd love to hostess your dinner party!' she said aloud. 'So tell me, Pop, whom will you be entertaining this time? Have you a new political protégé?'

John R.'s moustache twitched; his shrewd eyes narrowed.

'A senator from Ohio – Warren Harding. He came to see me the other day, one publisher to another!' He laughed. 'His little paper is like a postage stamp, of course, compared to the *Post* and the *Enquirer*. But I like him,' he added, 'and I'm going to back him!'

He kissed Evalyn's forehead and took his leave.

Winter eased into spring. On Easter Monday, Evalyn and Carrie sat in the garden at 2020. Evalyn was rocking the cradle of the baby they now called Jock with one hand and sipping iced lemonade with the other. Vinson, his imagination fired by the war in Europe, was building an 'army base' in the shrubbery with his toy soldiers. Carrie was reading. Ned, looking bored, came from the house, and collapsed into a deck chair.

'Well, ladies, where to this summer?'

'Bar Harbor,' Evalyn said. 'Best for the children.'

'Virginia,' Ned said. 'Best for Ned!'

Carrie looked up from her book and said: 'Aren't we fortunate that all we have to worry about is whether we go to Maine or to Virginia? When you think of what is going on in Europe . . .'

'Damn stupid war!' Ned replied. 'All at each other's throats over nothing! They'll drag us into it yet, if they can!' He turned back to his wife. 'Even that little dot of yours off the European coast has just jumped on the bandwagon.'

'Do you mean Ireland?'

Ned nodded.

'What's happened? Why is Ireland in the news?'

'They have it at the *Post* that there's been a Rising in Dublin!'

Evalyn sat up in her chair.

'When?'

'Today! Nothing very serious it seems . . . Some insurgents have occupied the General Post Office and a few other prominent buildings. The

446

British Government is expected to rush in troops and heavy artillery to crush the upstarts!'

'If you ask yourself whose country it is it might help you identify the upstarts,' Evalyn said with an edge to her voice.

I wonder what will happen? she mused, thinking of her father and his avid interest in anything to do with Ireland. The rebels can't win against an Empire.

Despite their summer plans the McLeans stayed in Washington. Carrie was organising her friends and acquaintances for war relief work – making garments to clothe refugees in the winter ahead. Ned was involving himself more and more with the *Washington Post*, as though determined to give real effect to the life changes he had promised his wife, and to prove his father wrong.

John R., on the other hand, began to absent himself from the paper.

'I'm fine, I'm fine,' he told Ned irritably when he telephoned to ask after him, 'I've been having a spot of indigestion lately, that's all. Stop bothering me!'

When his father failed to show up at the paper for more than a week, Ned went to see him at the 1 Street house and returned to 2020 to report that his father was acting strangely.

'He wouldn't talk to me. He just kept hiccupping all the time!'

Meggett, his father's valet, telephoned the next day. Evalyn took the call.

'Mr McLean is throwing bonds out of the window, millions of dollars worth.'

Evalyn alerted Ned and he sent Dr Adolph Meyer, Professor of Psychiatry in John Hopkins University, to see the old man. The latter certified him insane, but John R. escaped to Friendship with his private detectives and refused to come out.

'I'm not coming out and I'll shoot anyone who comes in. Especially my son,' the old man added. 'My son is my enemy!'

The doctor persuaded John R. to go to hospital. Later he told Ned and Evalyn that the old man had not long to live.

'You can see for yourselves how jaundiced he is. I'm sorry to tell you it looks like liver cancer.'

Ned started. 'How could he get that all of a sudden?'

'Cancer is an odd disease. It can lie dormant for years and then be suddenly activated. I suppose your father didn't suffer a shock or trauma of some kind in the last while?'

Ned stared at his wife.

'It strikes again!' he hissed. 'A few months ago Pop had It in his hands. It's like a serpent, gliding its evil into the heart of this family. Someday It will kill us all.'

The doctor looked perplexed. 'I'm sorry, Mr McLean . . .?'

447

'He's talking about the Hope diamond!' Evalyn said, trying to hide her agitation. 'He blames a piece of jewellery. And men say *women* are hysterical!'

That evening Ned brought home flowers for his wife.

'I'm always giving you a bad time about that necklace, Evalyn,' he said contritely. 'We're rational people, after all, and you should keep it if you like it. I suppose,' he added, 'that paying all this attention to it is itself unChristian!'

'Monsignor Russell would agree with you there!'

'What does he know about it?'

Evalyn shrugged. She was not going to tell Ned *now* that once she had had the diamond exorcised.

'I'm just supposing a Catholic perspective,' she said hurriedly.

When he returned from the hospital that night, Ned threw himself into a chair, looked at his wife with consternation and bewilderment and shook his head.

'They say Pop has a *week*, Evalyn. I can't get it through my brain! John R. McLean, publishing mogul, the richest, the most feared man in Washington . . . my father . . . has a *week* to live.'

He hit his forehead with the palm of his hand. 'He has to die, Evalyn. He *has* to leave this world, whether he likes it or not!'

'So do we all, darling . . . eventually.'

When he was gone she went in search of her blue diamond. She put it in a small inlaid box she had had since her teens, turned the little brass key, then secreted the box in her bureau.

I'm putting you away, she told it. I don't care what anyone says, I'm banishing you! No one will ever persuade me to let them handle you again!

She put the key into the drawer of her dressing table, pausing to look at the portraits in their silver frames. Tom Walsh looked out at her with his old whimsy; a debonair Ned was young and dashing; Carrie, nowadays so absorbed in her charity war work, was holding her first grandchild. There was Vinson in half-profile, grave and adorable, and little Jock gazed up in wide-eyed curiosity at his world.

Then she looked at the photographs of Mummie, already gone, and John R., who was now facing his last journey.

Ned and I should have another child, she thought, as though needing to assert the triumph of life over death. It would be good for Jock to have a companion near his own age. That was the mistake we made with Vinson. I will tell Pop tomorrow that there will be more McLeans. I will build a formidable family. And I will not worry any more. After all, she added, remembering Paul's words of long ago: *The real divide . . . is between those who are able to love and those who are not.*

448

She remembered their ride through the canyon – the joy and bravado of youth, the expectation of the future where there would be clothes and jewels and endless happiness . . .

That night she cried out in her sleep. Ned, dragged to the waking world, reached out to her. She woke, shaking and sobbing.

'It's all right, Evalyn; it's only a dream.'

'Thank God,' she whispered. 'I'm . . . so glad you're here, Ned.'

She sat up at once, put her feet out of the bed.

'Where are you going?'

'To check on the children.'

'They're fine. Look, I'll go.'

'No!' Evalyn cried. 'I *need* to see them. In the dream there was something . . . watching them.'

'What?'

'I don't know. It was like a shadow. It was in the corner of the nursery.'

She shuddered. The dream was fading, but taste of the evil was still in her mouth.

In the nursery all was quiet; the night light showed Vinson and the baby fast asleep.

'You must have drunk too much wine last night,' Ned observed when she came back to bed

'I wish we could go back to Friendship,' Evalyn whispered.

'Wait until Pop is gone!' Ned replied. He pulled her against his shoulder. 'I haven't been much of a son, have I? Or a husband? But I'll make you proud of me when I take over the *Post* and the *Enquirer*. Wait and see, Evalyn . . .'

Evalyn heard the grief in Ned's voice. She knew he would not sleep again. She stayed awake beside him, held him in her arms, returned his kisses.

'I'll go with you to the hospital in the morning!' she whispered.

'No. We'll take it in turns. It's vigil time now.'

Ned was right. Ten days later, on 8 June 1916, John R. died.

Chapter Thirty-Eight

On 28 July 1918 Evalyn gave birth to another healthy boy whom they named Edward after his father. She would have liked to have had the baby in Friendship; it was the place in the world she felt safest, both for herself and the children. But it had been turned into a convalescent home for wounded soldiers, the lucky ones who had survived the global carnage.

Her room in 2020 was filled with flowers. Messages of congratulation and goodwill crowded beside the family photographs. She wondered whenever she glanced at Vin and her father if they could see what was happening in her life. Here I am, the mother of three sons, she told them, as she cuddled her newborn. Three children whom I shall mind like their own shadow. She kissed the crown of the baby's head; he twitched in her arms. The sense of the miraculous, the victory of Life, made her feel euphoric. It was such a pity John R. had not lived to see this latest addition to the family.

But *out there*, she knew, the real world was off its bearings and was spinning out of control. Terrible things were happening and no one, not the richest nor the mightiest, was immune. The Romanoff dynasty, a line of absolute monarchs, had been wiped out of existence in a few seconds.

They probably took things for granted once, she thought. How I wish we were back in Friendship. Will this war ever be over?

The months slid by: Evalyn exercised to regain her figure.

'This baby business is all very well, but it murders one's muscles,' she muttered. 'However, I will die before I revert to being the tub I used to be, Miss Mountain Piggy.'

This made her laugh. She watched with pleasure as her slimness returned and her elegant gowns slid on effortlessly. She was now looking forward to October, when King Albert of the Belgians, and his consort, Queen Elizabeth, would pay a state visit to America. She and Ned were sure to be invited to meet them at the White House.

However, when October came, President Wilson was ill, and the White House could not be used for entertaining the royal couple, so Vice President

Marshall accepted Carrie's invitation to use 2020 as a substitute. The guests were many and splendid. Evalyn wore a dinner gown in pale green crêpe de Chine with the new dropped waistline and mid-calf-length skirt. On her head, worn as a bandeau, was the Star of the East. An ermine stole completed her ensemble.

'I knew your uncle, King Leopold, sir,' she told King Albert during the course of the evening. 'He took me on an outing once, in the Pyrenees. And he promised to visit us here, but he never did!'

'I am delighted to have rectified that oversight, madame!' the king replied with a smile. 'And my wife wishes to honour your mother.'

Later that evening the queen presented Carrie with the 'Order of Elizabeth, Queen of the Belgians' for her Belgian relief work during the war. Carrie glowed, looked younger than she had for years. Why is it that purpose is such a rejuvenating elixir? Evalyn wondered. Sitting on your butt just makes you go to seed. But I have my purpose, my children . . . and Ned.

She took a glass of champagne.

Shouldn't drink this stuff, she thought suddenly. It'll only give me more of those dreams.

When the guests had left Evalyn went to the nursery. Everything was quiet. The nurse had not yet turned in; she was reading by the soft dim light beside the fire. She smiled at Evalyn as she entered, and put down her book.

'Don't disturb yourself,' Evalyn whispered. 'I'm too keyed up to sleep. This time of night always makes me feel that someone is walking on my grave. It's as though there's something I must stand guard against.'

'Maybe that's why it's called the witching hour, madam.'

Evalyn shivered. She wished Ned were at home, but he had left with one of the guests, promising he would return 'in an hour or two'. Her mother had retired. The servants had been dismissed for the night.

Evalyn wandered down the landing gallery, looking over the carved balustrade at the hall below.

Father would come up those stairs two at a time, she thought fondly, thinking of the time when they had first moved into this beaux-arts mansion. He was still a young man not long out of Ouray! How safe I should feel now if he were still with us.

She crept down the stairs, remembering the early balls this house had known and the gay young throng that had traipsed up and down this selfsame staircase.

She opened the door to the library, turned on the light. This was the room where Ned had proposed. She could almost see his earnest young face, promising what he could not fulfil.

But he's not so bad now, she reminded herself as she looked around the

451

room. So long as I am with him, he keeps on the straight and narrow. And I am with him as much as I can be.

The tomes that her father had bought with so much delight lined the shelves, morocco-bound, leather-bound, many old first editions, many of more recent vintage. Her eye fell on the encyclopaedia whose volumes took up half a shelf.

I never thought of the encyclopaedia, she thought to herself, when I was wondering about Sita, and all the nonsense about the diamond. There must be something here about her, if it is genuine mythology.

She located the appropriate volume and put it on the table. And within a minute or two she had found the story of Sita, who had married the Hindu god Rama.

She pulled over a chair. The room, with its painted panels, its endless rows of books, suddenly seemed claustrophobic. She sat, eyes glued to the text, heart freezing. On the page in front of her was a drawing she had seen before – the hideous man spider. She read the text eagerly. She felt that the words on the page had been printed just for her.

Ravana had loved Sita, had taken her away to his kingdom. But *he* had been no ordinary potentate. The multiple-limbed monster with ten heads was none other than the Hindu King of the Demons. Evalyn uttered a cry and shut the book with a clap.

Oh God . . . oh God . . . Upstairs in a box I have . . . her eye . . .

The room seemed to observe her, the wisdom of centuries powerless on the shelves. Somewhere, nearby, silent and invisible, *he* was waiting. She heard the front door open and shut, heard footsteps cross the hall.

Someone was standing at the door.

Evalyn could not turn her head.

'I saw the light. What are you doing up at this hour?'

It was Ned's voice, a little querulous.

'I want the children watched day and night,' Evalyn cried, 'by armed men!' She burst into tears.

'Oh, Evalyn – what's all this? You know perfectly well that our security is already formidable! Come on now,' he added gently, putting a hand on her shoulder, 'it's been a long night!'

The war was finally grinding to a halt. The Armistice was signed in November, and when the last of the convalescent soldiers left Friendship it was restored to the McLeans a little the worse for wear. Evalyn, anxious to get her children back inside the walls of the securest place she knew, sent the decorators in immediately.

The family moved back to Friendship in February, returning in convoy. The baby was in a bassinet and Ned carried him into the house; little Jock toddled beside the nurse; footmen carried trunks into the house. Megget, whom Ned had taken on as his own secretary after his father's death, carried boxes of files. Vinson delighted in helping, bringing his teddy bears to the nursery. When he reappeared, Evalyn gave him a hatbox to carry upstairs.

'Let him help!' she told Carrie. 'It's not good for him to be waited on hand and foot.'

When the boy returned, Evalyn was giving instructions to Esther. From the corner of her eye she saw her son reach for something in her car; turning, she saw it was the inlaid box in which she had locked the Hope Diamond.

'No, darling . . . I'll take that!'

'What's in it, Mother?'

'One of my necklaces.'

'May I see it?'

'Not at the moment, darling. The box is locked.'

'Is it the one with the blue jewel? You *never* let me see it,' Vinson said petulantly, and his eyes followed the movement of the small brass key into his mother's pocket.

The children were soon installed in the sprawling nursery with its newly papered yellow walls. Their mother made sure that burly men with automatic pistols concealed under their arms watched them all day and stood guard over the nursery door at night.

The days passed; the children bloomed; Evalyn rationalised her fear. It was predicated on a fertile imagination. In daylight Ravana was a silly ghoul, a demon from a pagan myth, unworthy of her energy. The diamond had originally come from the earth, like all gems, like Camp Bird gold. She began to sleep again.

In May, Ned said to his wife, 'Come with me to the Kentucky Derby at Churchill Down.'

Evalyn longed to refuse. She thought of her three small sons, now nine, three and ten months. But then she thought of Ned. Dare she let him go to Kentucky on his own? She remembered only too well the night at the Narragansett Casino, when only her intervention had prevented him from signing anything the owner wanted.

'For heaven's sake, Evalyn,' he said, 'your mother will mind the children. She loves Friendship and you cannot leave them in better hands!'

Evalyn knew this was true. She also knew that the anarchic and mercurial element in her husband's character might reassert itself at any time. It was curbed now by the disciplines of domestic life. But, away from it, among his cronies and old friends, she did not trust him not to drink. It would be disastrous if the new horizons opening for him, now that Senator Warren Harding was likely to obtain the Republican nomination to the

White House, were damaged. Ned had backed his father's old protégé with the *Washington Post* and the *Cincinnati Enquirer*, and was now steering a course towards influence and power. If anything would finally save him from himself, she reckoned, prestige would do it, and nothing should be allowed to get in the way of that. If she went with him to Virginia he would drink less, gamble less, and cut a fair figure before the world.

'All right,' she said. 'I'll go with you. But I want two more armed guards posted at Friendship.'

'What a fuss you are, Evalyn,' he said irritably. 'The children will be perfectly safe! Look, I'll tell Megget to supervise them personally.'

She knew the children were so well protected that nothing short of a full-scale commando raid could access them. And yet, on the day of her departure, the malaise came again. Her luggage had been taken down and she was choosing her jewellery, selecting a couple of diamond bracelets and a matching necklace. For a moment she thought of taking the Hope Diamond. Some of her friends had asked why she didn't wear it any more, suggesting she was scared of it. She took out the inlaid jewel case, but could not locate the key.

'I'm sure I had it in this drawer,' she muttered, emptying the lawn handkerchiefs on to the carpet. 'Where is it? Maybe Esther knows.'

She rang, but Esther denied all knowledge. Foreboding mustered in the pit of Evalyn's stomach. She put the box back, regarded her reflection in the cheval glass – a young woman, pale and preoccupied, in a fashionable cream silk and linen costume with a dropped waistline, and a hat whose wide drooping brim hid most of her face. Ned called from downstairs. She went to the nursery and kissed and hugged her babies.

'Remember you're the man of the family while we're away,' she told Vinson. 'You must look after Grandmother and do what she tells you.' The boy looked at her with solemn eyes.

'Will you come home soon, Mother?'

'Very soon. I promise.'

When she was in the car she looked back and saw the small, grave face pressed against the nursery window. Vinson watched until the vehicle disappeared around a bend in the driveway; he waved a slow farewell. It was a picture that would recur to Evalyn for the rest of her life.

By the time they reached Louisville, Kentucky, Evalyn was so racked by a pervasive sense of menace that she was almost physically ill. Ned commented on her pallor, but she dared not share her disquiet. No matter how she examined the situation she could see no real danger to her children, and yet she could not rid herself of the ominous dread that wrapped itself around her heart.

Eventually she decided that the reason for the foreboding that became more powerful with every passing minute was that she herself was going to die. Given that the children were well and completely protected, it was the only thing that could explain the certainty of impending doom. When she told herself she was healthy she reminded herself that Death could come out of nowhere and strike like a Colorado rattler. Where would it come from, she wondered, the fatal stroke? She was certain it was very close. What tormented her was the thought of parting from her children, particularly from Vinson with whom her bond was so powerful. But so long as it's me, she told herself, and not one of them . . .

The Kentucky Derby went by her as though it were happening somewhere else. The celebrations that followed it she endured. She was a woman listening for a sound just beyond earshot.

The following morning, a Sunday, the phone shrilled in their suite. Ned took it. He sounded peevish, annoyed at being disturbed. His tone changed almost immediately. He lowered his voice, spoke carefully.

'When did this happen? . . . I see . . .' He replaced the mouthpiece, looked at Evalyn and reached for her hand.

'That was Dr Mitchell,' he said slowly. 'Vinson . . .' and here his voice changed and hesitated, 'has a touch of . . . influenza. I said we would go back immediately.'

Evalyn's breath caught in her throat. She sat up.

'He's had it before and shrugged it off. Is it bad this time?'

'No. There's nothing to be alarmed about. But knowing you as I do, Evalyn, I think we should take the next train out.'

Evalyn dressed hurriedly and went with Ned to the station. But there she saw something that made her heart stand still. Their private car was being hooked to an engine with only one other carriage for ballast. She knew with numbing certainty why she had been so tormented with premonition. There could only be one reason a 'special' had been laid on to draw their Pullman car: they were facing crisis. Ned, so quiet this morning, so kind to her, knew something he had not told her.

Oh, Vinson, she thought, oh, my darling child. I understand everything now. It is already too late.

Vinson's body was laid out in his bed. He looked as though he were asleep. A distraught Meggett, his face white, told what had happened.

'We were walking in the grounds and Vinson asked to go outside the gates. I could not see any reason why we should not go; everything was quiet, the sun was shining, the road deserted. So we went, walked a few yards and suddenly saw across the road a man pushing a cart.

' "It's Jeff," Vinson cried.'

Meggett looked at Evalyn. 'He was a gardener at Friendship once, ma'am. As soon as Vinson saw him he darted across the road after him. But a tin lizzie came right around the bend and he ran straight into its path. The driver braked. He was not travelling fast, but he wasn't able to stop in time and he hit Vinson. It wasn't much of a collison; the motor just pushed him to the ground and he bumped his head. I picked him up. He seemed all right, looked at the dust on his clothes and said his grandmother would be annoyed. So we brushed him down and he walked back through the gates with me, holding my hand.'

Meggett wiped his eyes.

'Mrs Walsh sent for the doctor. He examined him, said no bones were broken, but that he couldn't say if there were any internal . . .' Meggett's voice became a whisper and he dabbed at his eyes again. 'I'm so sorry, ma'am . . . I'm so sorry . . .'

Evalyn looked at the weeping man, at her mother's hollow eyes and was silent.

Why can't I weep? she thought. Why can't I speak?

Carrie blew her nose and whispered, 'His last words, Evalyn, were to say that he loved you more than God.'

Vinson's small white coffin was laid to rest a few days later beside his grandfather and his uncle.

'I am old now,' Evalyn whispered to her mother as they walked from the cemetery that contained so much of her heart. 'I will never be young again.'

Chapter Thirty-Nine

Evalyn struggled with her loss. Sometimes her pain was so intense that she wondered how she could possibly survive it. Her child's toys, his books, the jigsaw he had left half finished, the latest 'army base' he had built with toy soldiers on the morning of the day he died and told everyone to leave so that Mother might see it, the pervasive sense of his presence, burned her with loss. She blamed herself for having left him, created scenarios where she had refused to go to Kentucky, saw herself at the bend in the drive where she had looked back for a final glimpse of Vinson's small face at the nursery window, ordering the chauffeur to stop, telling Ned he could go without her.

When she was alone she would clutch Vinson's toys to her heart. She stroked the worn pile of his favourite teddy bear, soaked it with tears. *If only I had stayed at home . . . my darling child would be still alive . . .*

For the other children's sake she hid the desperation of her grief, and suppressed the bitter resentment she felt against Ned who had cajoled her into coming with him. She wore deepest mourning, as did her mother and Ned. She tried to comfort the former, but she would not be comforted. She tried to explain to her little Jock that his big brother had gone away to God.

'God is bad!' the child said, tears starting in his eyes. 'I hate God!'

'No no, God is good . . .'

She tried to mean it. She tried to understand, to accept. But all she felt was the pit of emptiness echoing with loneliness and loss.

'He loved Vinson so much that He wanted to have him to Himself, you see . . .'

But you *are* a monster, God, she told Him privately. And I will never forgive you!

Condolences flooded in. Friends came to call; they were cautious and uneasy, not knowing what to say. Evalyn could not mention her dead child's name. Monsignor Russell spoke of Heaven and the high place of children in God's kingdom. Evalyn didn't want to hear.

A letter came marked 'Private'. Nancy left it aside for her employer, but Evalyn barely glanced at it.

'You deal with it . . .' she told her secretary.

Nancy took it up; examined the postmark.

'It's from Denver, Mrs McLean . . .'

Evalyn glanced at the writing and put it into her pocket.

That night as she prepared for bed she took it out. She knew who it was from. She reached for a nail file and slit the letter open.

My dearest Evalyn,
I heard the terrible news and I wish with all my soul I could do something. Please tell me if there is anything within my power to do to help you at this dreadful time. Poor little cousin, my heart goes out to you.
Paul.

She traced his signature with her finger, heard his voice: *'I'll always be there for you . . .'*

Except for Jock, no one spoke of Vinson. Ned said as little as possible in an attempt to spare his wife. He seemed able to compartmentalise his loss, put it into a place where it did not torture his every waking moment.

Evalyn tried to forgive him, but was unable to talk to him of Vinson; every time his name was mentioned she was ravaged by a grief as fresh as the day he had died.

When she was alone she dulled her anguish with spirits – gin or vodka – rinsing out her mouth afterwards with a peppermint wash to disguise her breath. She remembered morphine, but slid away from that temptation. Other, even darker, enticements beckoned her now. I wish I could die, she thought; I would gladly go anywhere to get out of this world! She thought of sleeping tablets, and the quiet exit they might bring her in the night. But then she thought of Jock and baby Edward, so anxious and fretting, who needed her.

Everyone needs me, Evalyn thought. But what *I* need is nowhere within reach. What would I not give just to be a thoughtless girl again in Colorado!

She thought of the blue diamond in the inlaid box in her bureau. 'I really should stick it in a vault, or throw it into the Potomac,' she muttered. 'But I still don't know what I did with that damn key.'

Evalyn returned to her room one morning while Esther was supposed to be changing the sheets, and found her maid at her dressing table in the act of slipping something into a drawer.

The maid started when she saw her, quickly shut the drawer and went to the bed, where she began vigorously pulling off the sheets.

'What did you put into the drawer, Esther?' Evalyn asked, startled by the maid's furtive body language.

'Just some handkerchiefs, ma'am.'

Evalyn strode to her dressing table, removed the drawer and emptied it on to the carpet. Some folded lace-trimmed handkerchiefs fell out. But, as they did so, something small and hard hit the foot of the bed. She picked the object up and stared at it, glanced at Esther. The black woman's eyes were staring, the pupils wide with fear.

'Now,' Evalyn said in a low, dangerous voice, 'we both know this key was missing! So tell me the truth, Esther. Did *you* return it just now to the drawer?' Her voice rose. 'Did *you* have it all the time? Did you *ever* take that necklace out when I was not here?' Her voice was shrill now, and her body began to tremble. 'Did you *ever* let Vinson play with it?'

'No, ma'am.'

Carrie, alerted by the commotion, was suddenly in the doorway. She shut the door behind her.

'Evalyn, you can be heard in the kitchen!'

'Go away, Mother. This is important.'

Evalyn reached out and grabbed Esther by the hair. 'Tell me the truth before I kill you.'

The maid was sobbing, shielding her face with her arm.

'I didn't take it,' she cried. 'I *found* it.'

'*Where* did you find it?' Evalyn demanded murderously.

'Oh, ma'am, I was scared. I couldn't tell you . . . I found it . . . in the *nursery.*'

Evalyn, with shaking hands took the jewel box from her bureau, inserted the key and turned the lock. The leather box inside opened easily and the Hope Diamond shone out innocently at her from its satin bed. She picked it up and flung it across the room. Esther fled. Carrie waited. Her impassive stance quietened her daughter, who sank on to the bed, putting her head in her hands.

Oh Mother . . . I wish I were dead!

Carrie sat beside her daughter, stroked her hands. Evalyn felt the strength in her, the faith, and the acceptance. She turned and took her grey-haired mother in her arms.

'Dearest Mother . . . you were always the bravest. You loved Vinson as much as I did.'

'Ask God for help, Evalyn!'

Evalyn drew back. 'No, Mother. He has had too much of what is mine already!'

She rose, picked up the diamond that lay in a glittering coil in the corner. 'What will I do with this?'

'Whatever you do with it, don't imagine it was responsible, Evalyn!

That's idolatory, a superstition hinging on a Sanskrit poem!'

Diamonds and idols and poems and death, Evalyn thought. I have lost the feel of the real world, the wholesome world, the world God made for the living.

'Evalyn,' Carrie continued quietly, 'do you think it would help if, for a week or so, you went back to visit Ouray?'

That night Evalyn picked up the old piece of quartz, felt its weight in her hand. She wrote to Paul Lafferty:

I cannot tell you how glad I was to hear from you. I am going to Ouray, Paul. Is there any chance you might join me for a day or two? I need to talk to you before I go insane.

The reply came by wire: 'LET ME KNOW WHEN YOU ARE TO TRAVEL STOP I WILL PUT UP AT THE BEAUMONT'.

She rang for Esther.

'I owe you an apology,' she said. 'I was beside myself. I am sorry.'

'That's all right, ma'am,' Esther replied nervously. 'Terrible things have been happening.'

'Esther, I have a favour to ask of you!'

'A favour, ma'am?'

'Would you lend me some clothes?'

A few days later Ned came home to find a message from Evalyn waiting for him in a small white envelope.

Dear Ned,

I have gone to Colorado for a few days. I won't be staying at our estate; I will be in Ouray. If you need to contact me wire me at the Beaumont Hotel. I will be travelling under the name of Lawson.

The train slid into the depot at Ouray and Evalyn alighted, gazed around. Although it was August the air was pure and fresh. Serenity still reigned in this town that was safe as ever behind its mountain bulwark. The depot had grown: there were new sheds; railway cars were being shunted into new sidings; a wagon bore the legend *Camp Bird Mine*. A stagecoach bore the same name on the door. She provoked few curious glances, a woman in nondescript black clothes, clutching a carpetbag, and wearing a wide-brimmed hat that half covered her face. She took the waiting surrey to the Beaumont, and was pleased that the hotel was still elegant, still the prettiest in the West, and that the glass cases continued to line the lobby with specimens of ore from the local mines. Among them,

460

proudly displayed, were samples from Camp Bird.

Lone women checking into the Beaumont were something of a novelty, and the clerk stared at Evalyn dubiously for a moment, wondering if he should consult the manager. The ladies' entrance was at the side of the building, but this dame had come straight in the front door.

Evalyn saw that he had a look of the Carlssons with whom she had been at school. Did I know him when he was in diapers? she wondered.

'Six dollars a night, ma'am!'

Evalyn did not miss the condescension. 'I can manage that!'

'Will your husband be joining you, ma'am?'

'No,' Evalyn replied a little dangerously. 'I don't need my hand held whenever I check into a hotel.'

The clerk seemed a bit taken aback. She must be a teacher, he thought. But she doesn't really look like one . . . and she's not a tart either.

Evalyn removed her gloves to sign the register. The clerk's sudden start made her glance at him. He was staring at her hands, at the rings that sparked fire.

'I'll be staying two days,' she said. 'My cousin, a Mr Lafferty, will be checking in this evening. We have family business to discuss.'

The lobby was filling with men. The Manager of the Miners' and Merchants' Bank that occupied the corner of the hotel by Seventh Avenue emerged, locked the bank's door, made straight for the dining room. The clink of plates and cutlery, the scent of food filled the air. Father often lunched here, Evalyn thought. She could see him, leaning forward, absorbed in mining talk, could almost hear his voice.

The clerk thumped the bell. The bellboy appeared, reached for her bag and she followed him up the grand central staircase that she had last trod at the age of fifteen. The walls were still lined with pictures of local scenery; a Navajo blanket hung from the landing rail. She walked by the banquet hall, passing the spot where once, years before, a young man had taken her face in his hands and kissed her. The bellboy unlocked her door, deposited her bag, handed her the key. She tipped him; he stared at the five-dollar bill.

'Why, thank you, ma'am . . .'

When he was gone she locked the door, went to the toilet stand, poured some water, slipped off her rings, washed her hands and face. The double bed was inviting; she was tired from the journey. But she would rest later.

As the day wore on Evalyn took pleasure in being incognito. She walked around the town, lingered before the Walsh Library, looked up at the brass bell. There was a party once, she said to herself, when the prince of this town fêted his friends and dedicated this library to his town. I was there! I danced with someone who loved me . . .

She went down Fifth Avenue, stood for a moment outside the clapboard house that had once been her home. She leaned on the picket fence, glanced up at the window from where she had spied on her father as he departed on a momentous prospecting trip one snowy September morning. A young face appeared and looked down at her curiously. My room! she thought, moving away. And a girl the age I was then! It's almost as though it's me, looking out at the fool come back to reclaim her childhood!

The town bustled with wagons and surreys and mounted miners down from the hills. Tourists strolled down Main Street. There were new shops, new grocery stores, a new drug store. People barely glanced at her, although the occasional man tipped his hat to her in passing. Nobody knows me! she thought with involuntary elation and a queer, sick, disappointment.

She returned to the Beaumont, entered by the front door, glanced at the bar where some men were sitting, longed suddenly for a double bourbon on the rocks, followed by another and then another, until kind oblivion came to rescue her. But she passed up the stairs, sat by her window and looked down on Main Street, watched the people moving on the opposite sidewalk under the shop awnings, speculated as to the owners of the hurrying pairs of feet.

She glanced at her watch. She had time for a nap, and then she would go to the depot to meet Paul on the evening train. How many years was it now since she had seen him – fifteen? And it might have been yesterday.

That evening she waited by the track. She heard the sonorous call of the approaching train, saw the smoke against the fading sky and with grinding of brakes and hiss of steam, the iron monster slid into the depot. She scanned the people alighting – a family, a young couple, a woman with a child, an old lady and her daughter, a group of miners, some middle-aged men who might be engineers, some tourists. Porters hurried to help; bags were handed down from the carriages. She waited. No one else got off. The train was empty.

He didn't come! she thought with a sinking heart. He didn't come . . .

It was then that she noticed the burly man with the Gladstone bag who stood before her, regarding her quizzically. She registered the heavy greying moustache, greying temples, the deep-set eyes that looked out at her from behind crow's-feet with a once-familiar focus.

Her arms reached out to him at the same moment as his were opened to her.

'Dearest Evalyn,' he said against her forehead, 'it is so wonderful to see you!'

Evalyn closed her eyes. He was real! She felt his clothes, his warmth, heard the beating of his heart.

'Was it terrible of me to have asked you to come?'

He looked down on her with a laugh.

'You know perfectly well I would have come to the ends of the earth.'

She did not ask the question that presented itself – *Does Amelia know that you have come this distance just to be with me?*

'But you shouldn't have come to the depot,' he said, 'waiting here on your own. You should have stayed at the hotel.'

'No one has recognised me. Paul, how long can you stay?'

'Until tomorrow. I must take the night train.'

'So soon?'

'There's my family,' he said gently. 'And my business will not run itself.'

'Of course,' Evalyn replied. 'You must think me selfish. But I am desperate. I need my roots, Paul. I seem to have lost them. I don't know what is happening; I don't know who I am any more . . .'

'Are you very pale, or is it just the light?' He tucked her arm under his. 'And you're trembling. When did you eat last? Let's find the Beaumont, get a bite. Then you can tell me everything.'

That night Evalyn lay awake. Just a few doors away was a man she had loved, could love again, a man she had dreamed of down what seemed an infinity of years. They had had dinner together; she had poured out her heart. He had touched her hand, his fingers against hers, his eyes, compassionate, loving, never leaving her face. When they came upstairs together they had paused at the spot where they had kissed so many years before.

'Do you remember, Paul . . .?'

'Oh, Evalyn, do you think I could forget?' He laughed and his fingers touched hers fleetingly as though by accident.

He loves me still. It isn't dead between us . . .

She lay in the dimness; there was a rod of brightness under her door from the landing; the streetlights threw shadows at her window. Her silk and lace nightdress felt like gossamer in comparison to the starched sheets and the eiderdown quilt. Her body was bathed and scented, her hair brushed. Would he come? The minutes ticked by. The mahogany wardrobe, the dressing table on its Victorian legs, the oval mirror with its nocturnal mysteries, the toilet table with its white basin and ewer, seemed co-conspirators.

Just one night in his arms!

Someone was running a bath. The voices and laughter from the bar faded. She heard the front door being shut downstairs, a bolt thrown. Footsteps paused outside her door. She caught her breath. They proceeded down the landing.

She waited for a few more minutes, got out of bed, pulled on her dressing gown. He wasn't so far away; he might be waiting.

A dog howled suddenly a few doors away, a frightened yowl like a dirge. She went to the window, pulled back the heavy drapes.

Afterwards she wondered at the silence. It was in perfect silence that she saw the lone rider coming down the darkened street. He was slouched in the saddle; behind him his gunny sacks lay across the horse's rump; his pick and shovel were strapped to his pack. His hat hid his face, but she could see his wiry moustache, and the strong, tired hands that held the reins.

It's past midnight! she thought. It's 1919! Who prospects these hills nowadays? She watched him until he had plodded soundlessly out of sight, then she dropped the curtain, crept back to bed and lay still beneath the covers. The world seemed itself again, full of ordinary noises. There was revelry in Second Street, and coughing in the room beside hers.

Maybe nothing has been lost, she thought after a while. Maybe everything *is* still there, somewhere just out of reach . . . Father and Vin and Vinson . . .?

Her eyes reverted to the glimmer of light from under the door.

I know you will not come to me, Paul, she thought after a few moments. And I will not go to you. The time for it is over.

In the morning Paul looked as though he had not slept. But he ate a good breakfast and asked her: 'Will you ride out with me, Evalyn, like we did before?'

'It was eighteen years ago,' she replied. 'And I have done little riding since.' She added with a grin, 'But I brought my old riding habit all the same.'

'We can hire the horses at Ashenfelter's . . . But your legs will know all about it tomorrow!'

An hour later they were picking their way to Camp Bird, passing a few riderless horses that had been hired by miners and sent back when they had reached their destination, the reins tied over the pommels.

As they approached the mine she heard, louder and louder, the stamp mills fill the canyon with their thunder, saw from a vantage point on the road the sprawl of the great mine, a town in its own right.

They were challenged at the gate.

'We're tourists,' Paul said.

'This is a gold mine, mister. Ain't no tours here!'

As they moved away Evalyn said in a sardonic aside, 'I still have a sizeable holding of stock in Camp Bird, and I own hundreds of acres of the land around here.'

'Well, let's go back and tell them you're a major stockholder. They'll roll out the red carpet.'

She sniffed and he laughed.

They returned along the Canyon Creek Road. Ouray could be seen far below, nestling in its quarter-mile of valley floor. In the blue distance Mount Abrams surveyed its world.

464

'The snow will come in six weeks,' Evalyn said. 'The whole gorge will be filled; the mountains covered; the firs will be like snowmen. In the evenings you will hear the howling of the coyotes.'

Paul heard the ache in her voice.

'Are you tired, Evalyn?'

She shook her head. Her eyes were blinded by tears.

As they neared Ouray they left the road.

'I want to find the place where we watered the horses when we last rode out here together . . . from where you took this . . .' She reached into her pocket, held out a piece of quartz.

Paul took it from her, weighed it in his palm, returned it.

'I wanted to give you everything,' he said after a moment in a low voice, 'but you already had it all! That was so much of what happened . . . knowing I could never measure up.'

Evalyn sighed. They proceeded in silence. He helped her dismount and they stood side by side while the horses drank from the creek. Evalyn felt her feet on this beloved earth, as though her soles had sprouted roots, as though somehow the past had unravelled and wrapped her around.

'Father used to think it was the most dangerous place in the world for us!' she whispered. 'But we were safe here, Vinson and I.'

Paul moved suddenly and pulled her head against his shoulder.

'Oh, Evalyn, I cannot bear the pain in you. When I think of the young girl, blooming, laughing, teasing . . . who stirred my heart . . .'

Evalyn shrugged. She let the tears flow. After a moment she began to shake, broke from Paul, and screamed her torment into the canyon.

'My son is dead . . .'

Paul's jaw clenched; but he did not try to stop her. The echo came back, as the rocks joined in her grief. 'My son is dead,' they moaned, echo on bitter echo. 'My son is dead . . .'

She sank on to the stony ground. Paul sat beside her and took her in his arms.

'You are cold,' he said.

'And you are so warm,' she said after a moment, wiping her eyes with her sleeve and taking his hand. 'You always were. I used to dream about what our life would be like.'

'I had to respect your choice, Evalyn. I was so full of the pompous nonsense of the young. You must not blame me too much.'

'But you never even came, never visited. You were in Washington sometimes – Ned met you once – and you didn't call . . .'

'But not a day has gone by that I haven't thought of you. I walked by 2020 on a few occasions. But I could not call. I felt you had been turned to glass! I could not endure the unreality of the world you had embraced!'

'You sound so stern, like Father.'

'Not like *him*!' he replied with a short laugh. 'Your father was a giant, one of the breed who pushed back the frontiers, who built this nation! If he had been born a generation later, had stayed in Ireland, don't you think he would now be part of the movement that is shaking the British Empire, that may yet loosen its grip on the world? I will go to Ireland before I die, if only to honour him and my mother! I will find our silent cousins, see what they have done with life!'

Evalyn turned red eyes on him.

'And as for you and me,' he added gently, 'what do you think of us now?'

'We are not the same people,' she said sadly. 'The years have shuffled us into different coats. But I wish I was like Father and had a frontier to conquer.' She added with a shaky laugh, 'I think I could manage a frontier!'

'You have more than a frontier Evalyn,' he said after a moment. 'You are in a position to take on the whole horizon! All three hundred and sixty degrees.' He pressed his lips against her forehead, kissed her hands. 'And you don't need that bit of rock you carry around.'

Evalyn took the piece of quartz from her pocket. She looked at it for a moment before letting it slip from her fingers.

'You're right!' she said. It rattled on the canyon floor and was lost among the stones.

Paul left on the night train. She stood and watched as it puffed its way down the line. He was going back to his family, his future, his business. Tomorrow she would return to Washington to continue her life as one of the richest women in the world.

I will dedicate my life to people! she thought. They're the only real currency.

There was still the future. Surely out of all that determination and effort, shrewdness and success, mistakes and dissipation and suffering, lessons had been learned? A strength comparable to one she had known might yet steel rising generations.

In her heart she heard Mamselle's words of years ago: '*Remember that life is the sublime courage of those who will not be defeated.*'

She turned to look at the Amphitheatre, imagined she heard the clink of iron-shod hoofs on a stony road, saw, for a moment, an exhausted man on a stumbling Nig.

'I'm strong, Father. I will go on . . .'

Epilogue

Within the Irish side of your family, Tom, you are clothed in legend. I did not know what was true and what not, but I did know that to write your story I had to find you for myself.

So in September 1998, accompanied by my brother and cousin, I finally flew out from Dublin, destination Denver, Colorado. From there we drove to Ouray.

It was evening when we found your old neighbourhood at last, hidden there in that exquisite valley in the Rockies, at almost eight thousand feet. We could have been driving into Shangri-la; the town emerged from the mountain folds, incandescent in the evening sunlight, astonishing in its beauty. We drove uncertainly down Main Street, turned left, parked the car. We had no idea where to find you, but when we got out we found ourselves across the street from a red-brick building with a small white cupola. It was not the elegance of the building that riveted us; it was the legend in bold black letters just under the roof: 'WALSH LIBRARY'. Our childhood had been full of your extraordinary story. And here we had found you, instantly, after a journey of four thousand miles, accomplished in a manner even you could not have commanded.

A few doors from the Walsh Library was the Ouray County Museum, located in the building that had once been the Sisters' Hospital. We entered, approached the desk and said who we were. Tom Walsh! they exclaimed. You are related to *him*? You might have died only yesterday! The museum director, Ann Connell Hoffman, brought us to the 'Walsh Room', furnished as per your parlour at the time of your great discovery. And there, on a tailor's dummy, was the elegant evening dress you wore in 1906 when you were one of the richest men on earth. I put my hand on your sleeve.

A little later, we drove up the dangerous Canyon Creek Road into the Imogene Basin, two miles above the town, to see Camp Bird. We could not wait to see it – the private gold mine of our great-granduncle, Tom Walsh from Clonmel.

The mine is gone now; it was closed in 1995. All that is left is the tailings pond, a small mountain of finely mulched rock and thousands of pieces of broken quartz. The great aerial tramway that once dominated the whole canyon is no more; of the first-class hotel you built for your miners nothing remains. But the atmosphere in that abandoned place whispers of your strength. Did you hear me when I whispered, 'We are Margaret's great-grandchildren come from Ireland. A hundred years have passed!'?

I have spent three years novelising your, and Evalyn's story. It was a considerable challenge, Tom, not only because of the difficulty in marrying fact and fiction, but because the more I explored your saga, the more extraordinary it became. I have had to leave aside so much that was fascinating, while creating and honing scenarios to carry the narrative.

There are few stories like yours in the world. Far from ravaged Ireland, you pitted yourself against mighty Nature until you won.

But Evalyn discovered the malevolent force attendant on limitless wealth, and she lost, Tom – how badly you never knew.

Forgive the inventions; they were necessary to make a novel. I wish you happiness and peace in the Great Unknown beyond the mountains.